THE
BLACK MANTLE;
OR, THE
MURDER AT THE OLD FERRY.

CHAPTER I.

**THE MURDER OF THE YOUNG MOTHER.—
THE BLACK MANTLE AND THE BABE.**

A SHRIEK! such a shriek as may be supposed to awaken all within the sphere of its
influence—such a shriek as might arise from
some condemned soul at the instant it hears,
from the judgment-seat of Heaven, the
irrevocable sentence which speaks of eternal
despair—such a shriek as might come from
the half palsied lips of some wretch who has
clung to life with wild tenacity, but who, at
length, with his heart's blood, is rendering
up his being—a shriek that awakened every
echo for miles—that appalled dumb creatures

whose senses it came over like a blasting curse, a shriek that made people spring from their beds, and say aloud—

"What—what was that?"

Such a shriek broke over the ears of the slumbering inhabitants of Westminster, some fifty years ago, on a night which otherwise was so calm and still, that not the least sound had shaken its torpid air for hours previously, which rose higher than the usual confused murmur which pervades the air of a densely populated district.

It is no exaggeration to say that a thousand people were awakened by that shriek; and then before the boldest of them could recover sufficiently to reason calmly upon it, or to inquire from whence it had proceeded, it came again with the same fearful, terrible intensity as before.

Dogs howled as the loud dreadful sound aroused them from their kennels. Watchmen stood aghast and irresolute; and some windows were cautiously opened by adventurous people, who looked out seemingly with a vague idea that as something so extraordinary had been heard, surely something out of the common way was to be seen likewise.

And then it came a third time. Perhaps the sound was more lengthened and wailing when it so came, more full of the agony of some mind distracted from its own iniquity, or the criminality of others. But be that as it may, it was a dreadful sound to hear.

In some houses everybody got up, for some said it was high up in the air that the shriek came from, while others considered it as a warning of some fearful calamity about to occur, and that it behoved them to be up and dressed, and prepared for the worst.

They waited, but it came no more—all was still again. A light small rain was falling. A vast stillness reigned in the private, stately streets of Westminster. The shriek was over. Its faintest echoes no longer reached every ear. Those who believed it human sought their beds again with a shudder—those who thought it supernatural sat up trembling till the morning's light came, and produced, as it always does, such a remarkable alteration of opinion upon such subjects.

*   *   *   *   *

Let us change the scene. It wants a whole hour of the midnight at which so fearful a sound had disturbed the good folks of Westminster in their repose. We are out of the city—a quiet sylvan spot meets the eye. There are tall and stately trees gently waving in the light breeze, to whose impulse they yield so readily. The sound of a murmuring water-course may be heard, and glistening among sweet foliage, winding past banks of violets, which are throwing out their sweet perfume along the stream.

The same species of rain is falling as we noticed in the streets of Westminster—a soft, quiet, summer rain, which makes no sound—sweeps not on in eddies—does not perseveringly endeavour to insinuate itself into out-of-the-way places, as some bad dispositioned rains do; but it was one of those rains which continue so gently, that it would scarcely seem more than some condensed vapour about us, which was settling rather than falling upon every object.

By its being a rain of so much the same character as that which was falling in town, the supposition may well be, that the quiet, pleasant, sylvan spot to which we have conducted our readers is near at hand, and so it is, comparatively speaking—one hour's walk from town reaches it. Its precise locality we will point out in another place. At present we have to do with events we shudder to record, and which, in all their intense horror, could borrow no new pain from time or place.

Close to the stream, which was about sixty feet in width, was a huge, dim-looking, black object, mingling with the darkness of the sky and the trees in such a manner as to be scarcely discernible in its outlines, but which, if steadily looked at, would be found to be a long, low, rambling-looking house, principally built of weather-boarding, and the roof of which contained thousands of red tiles, while here and there large pieces had fallen completely in; and, from the dilapidated condition of the chimney tops, it would seem as if a long time must have elapsed since any human being inhabited that place.

The house was very close to the water's edge. Indeed, when the spring rains set in, and the water rose, the lower apartments would often become flooded, as they had been very lately, a circumstance which contributed very much to the decay of the house, but which, during the period when it was a human abode, no doubt was in some way provided against.

The doors hung loosely upon their hinges; the glass of the windows had long disappeared; and, take the place altogether, it had that most melancholy and dilapidated look which an old time-worn building assumes if completely deserted. Close to the door of it were several large posts, with strong staples set into them, and to one hung a piece of chain. Near these objects was one of the flat-bottomed, awkward-looking boats which are used for ferrying passengers across narrow streams. When it had last been used appeared involved in the obscurity of years gone by. It lay rotting in the water. A small stagnant pool of blackened liquid had collected in its interior from rains, and it looked more like some half-decomposed coffin than a boat.

But still there was abundant evidence that the house had at one time been thought something of. Curious lattice-work, which must have cost money in its day, was about it in its odd corners, and about the door there was some carving not badly or coarsely executed. It had evidently been a ferry-house, for, directly opposite to it, on the other bank of the little stream, were some more strong posts, and staples in them, which clearly proclaimed that between them the lazy, half rotten-looking punt to which we have alluded had been enabled to convey living cargoes for some small charge from side to side.

There must have been some great alteration of roads, or some striking circumstance connected with the place, which had caused it to be so entirely deserted as it now was, and had evidently been for some time.

But is it so utterly deserted? Is it quite destitute of human inhabitants? No. There is a dark, sombre figure. It looks like that of a man. It is closely enveloped in a large black cloak, and it stands like a statue by the door of the ferry-house, heedless of the rain, and gazing across the stream.

For all the movement this figure made, it might have been a statue. Not a muscle seemed to stir. There it stood, like the real spirit of that place, black and stern, and, to all outward show, as dead and profitless as any stagnant weed that had fallen to decay on the banks of the stream.

Down came the rain, and slight as it appeared, it was not so in reality, for soon it showed itself upon the black mantle of the stranger, to which it imparted a dull, glistening, lead-like colour; but the figure stirred not—spoke not—and thus passed away some minutes.

So ominous and strange a state of things was, however, not doomed to last long. Suddenly he spoke, and it was in a strange, sharp, cracked voice, that he said—

"She comes."

Instantly, then, as if reproaching himself for the tone in which he had spoken, he said—

"Hush—hush—hush!" and then in a low, deep whisper, he added—"She comes—she comes!"

On the opposite side of the stream the ground sloped downwards, not to a very great extent, but still sufficient to produce a hill, which, although a small one, was steep. The pathway which conducted from the neighbouring country to the ferry wound over the brow of this hill, and any person approaching was hidden completely until they reached a certain elevation on the other side, and then a curious effect was always produced by the individual apparently rising out of the hill.

First the head would appear to them, by slow degrees the whole body, and as the lower part of the person came in sight the last, it seemed as if by some mechanical means they were thus slowly elevated.

But upon that dim, misty night, he who made the sudden exclamation of "She comes!" must have had his attention fixed with painful intensity upon the object before him to be able, through the misty atmosphere, to see any form approaching. But he did see it, nor was he mistaken, for some one had just began to make an appearance above the brow of the hill.

"She comes—she comes!" he still repeated —"she comes!"

Through the mist the figure looked large, and he recoiled a step or two before he thought of what was the cause of the phenomenon. Then he at once advanced to his old position, and again, in a half choking tone, he said—

"'Tis she—'tis she! By Heaven, I did not think that she would come!"

Now the form which was advancing had reached the top of the eminence, and stood in clearer relief against the sky, which in that direction was rather lighter than in the other. Then she paused, and any one who had been sufficiently near to have an accurate observation, would have seen that the form which had sought that spot at so strange an hour, and in so inclement a night, was both young and beautiful.

Scarcely past girlhood, indeed, she seemed. Her figure was delicate in the extreme, but exquisitely proportioned; and but that the face was thin, and had upon it

"The pale cast of thought,"

it would have been radiantly beautiful.

As it was, no one could have disputed its claims to great beauty—that beauty of expression and intellect which is so superior to that of mere form and feature. Her hair hung, saturated with the rain, in long locks upon her neck and shoulders. Her garments seemed soaked with moisture. It might have been the rain, or it might have been tears which were rolling down her cheeks— at least, until one deep, tearful sob burst from her heart, a casual observer would have been at a loss to decide which it was; but after that there could be no mistake whatever.

She was weeping—weeping in that short, convulsive manner which proclaims that the agony of grief has lasted long; and yet there was upon her countenance, as she reached the brow of the hill, a look of hope and expectation, which mingled strangely with her tears.

Who could she be, and what could be the causes of her journey to that dreary spot at such an hour? Had she an appointment with that dreary-looking figure in the black mantle? Could she, so young, so fair, have anything to say to him, or to hear from him?

It would seem so; for now with one hand she strives to brush away the tears that had collected in her long silken eyelashes, and to pierce the dim obscurity beyond the stream, as if she were anxious to see if any one was there awaiting her coming.

But she could see nothing. She looked from a height down into a valley, and there, partly from exhalations arising from the damp ground and the contiguity of the stream, and partly from the rain which still fell like a cloud, she could see nothing, and the first words she uttered were—

"It is a mockery—it is a mockery. He will not come. God help me! He will not come."

The strange man, too, stood with his back towards the house, the dingy materials of which harmonised too well with the colour of the cloak he wore to enable him to be seen.

And now suddenly a strange wailing sound came upon the night air. It is the cry of an infant. Yes; she, that young and beautiful girl, carries, wrapped up in an old faded shawl, and pressed close to her bosom, a young child, and it is a wailing cry from it which has broken the death-like stillness that reigned about that spot after she had spoken the few words of agonised feeling which had come from her lips, at supposing that he who had come to meet her there had broken the appointment he had made.

"Hush—hush, darling, hush," she said, as she leant over the child. "Hush—hush —hush; I am with you. Be still, darling, be still."

She pressed the infant closer to her breast, and her tears fell like rain upon its cherub face.

"He will not come," she sobbed, "he will not come, and it is mockery after all."

She fancied then she heard some sound coming from the neighbourhood of the ferry-house, and a faint cry of hope burst from her heart as she eagerly stooped forward to listen. But all was still again, and, with a feeling of deep disappointment, she said—

"No—no; he will not come. It is but the rushing of the swollen water that I hear. There, again, it dashes against the old house. He will not come. My heart now tells me that he will not come. All is despair. Oh, my child—my beautiful, innocent child—would we were both in that dear home beyond the skies, where sorrow is unknown, and there are no tears—where joy is eternal, and the smile of God makes the sunshine of every heart. My child—my beautiful child!"

She removed the old tattered shawl from before the face of the infant, and, as if it had heard its mother's words, and knowing their import, sought to give her such consolation as it might in her deep affliction, it smiled in her face with such a look of heavenly happiness, that, for the moment, she forgot all griefs, all pains, all sorrows, all the harrowing circumstances that had blighted her young heart's joy—everything, but the joy —the pure happiness of that moment; and the babe's smile was reflected as if in a glass upon its tender mother's face.

"Bless you, my babe," she cried, "bless you! At once are you my care and my solace. Now may Heaven shower blessings upon thee, my beautiful child—my beautiful child!"

Her dream of joy was of short duration. Those circumstances which she had forgotten, were soon, too soon, brought back to her recollection. The object which had brought her at such a time, and such an hour, to that spot, was not for another moment to be banished from her memory. Even while the sweet smile yet lingered on the face of the babe—while she was pouring a world of kisses upon one of its little hands, she heard a noise from the other side of the stream, which at once awakened her from her dream of joy.

It was a voice she knew too well—by far too well for joy—by far too well for peace. It spoke in hoarse, cold accents. It pronounced but a name, but that name was hers, and well she knew from whose lips the familiar sound had come.

"Margaret—Margaret!" said the deep tones of the man who had kept the lonely watch by the deserted ferry-house.

She gasped for utterance before she could say to herself, in a tone of far more agony than that in which she had deplored the apparent non-appearance of that man—

"'Tis he—'tis he! He has—come!"

"Margaret! Margaret!"

"God save me now! I am here!"

He did not hear the faint reply; a sudden gust of wind had carried it in another direction, and louder still he shouted—

"Margaret!"

"Here—here—here!" she said, as loudly as she could. "I am here—I am here!"

He heard her then, and stepping carefully to the water's edge, he began unmooring the ferry-boat.

It was chained to one of the heavy posts that were sunk close to the water's edge; but the chain had got so thin, and was so weakened by being eaten through with rust, that one blow from a not very large stone broke several of the links, and the boat was free. Then it began to drift round with the stream; but the mysterious stranger leaped into it, heedless of the stagnant pool of black-looking water that lay at the bottom of it, and with a rude stake, which, from its appearance, had been recently torn from one of the surrounding trees, he commenced guiding it across the stream.

When once he had emerged from the deep shadow of the house, the young girl who was on the opposite bank saw him, and with tottering steps she began to descend the hill side. This was a task of no small difficulty, for the rain had made the place extremely slippery, and bad to walk upon; but by dint of great care and perseverance she did in safety reach the banks of the stream.

There she stood, tremblingly awaiting the coming of the man whose whole attention appeared to be engaged in guiding the ferry-boat across the swollen stream.

"Charles," she said, "Charles! Oh, let me hear your voice. It will be something to hear your voice speak to me. Oh, speak to me—Charles—Charles, for your dear child's sake, speak to me."

A hissing sort of noise came from his lips, as if he had intended to say something, and then repented of his purpose, swallowing the words even at the moment of utterance.

Again in imploring accents she besought him to speak to her, if it were but one word. Perchance she thought if she heard his voice she would be able to guess what humour he was in, and whether she had most to dread or to hope from the approaching interview.

"Charles—Charles, say but a word; speak to me—oh, speak to me. I ask but to hear your voice."

Still he made to her no reply, but having brought the boat close to the bank on which she stood, he pointed to the middle of the boat, as if he would have said—

"Enter—enter."

"Not a word—not a word, Charles?" she said, as she yet lingered on the shore. "Not one word?"

He made an impatient gesture, and she shrunk back involuntarily.

"Speak to me once, if it be in unkindness—speak to me before I set one foot in the boat. But a word—but a word!"

"What would you have me say?"

These few words he spoke in a tone from which but little was to be gathered. It had about it a studious forced calmness which might be really intended to smother passion from an honest resolve to do so, or only put on at the moment, in order to blind her to the real state of his feelings—which of these conditions of mind produced the apparently calm tone she could not say. He had, however, spoken as she had implored him; and however unsatisfactory to her the speech was, she had now no fair excuse for not stepping into the ferry-boat.

"I am coming," she said, and she entered the boat, heedless even as he had been of the quantity of water which was in it. Her thoughts were actively employed on very different subjects. Moreover, she had suffered quite sufficiently from the weather to prevent the state of the ferry-boat from much affecting her.

She sat down on one of the cross planks that served as seats, for she found herself unable to stand in the boat, as the rapid current of the now greatly swollen stream rocked it to and fro. She never moved her eyes, for a moment, from the face of the man, and yet she had not seen it, for his hat was slouched down close to his eyes, and the lower part of his countenance was effectually concealed by some wrapper which was tied around it.

"You asked me, Charles, what I would have you say," she remarked in a low, sweet voice; "did you not?"

He made no reply, and, after a painful pause, she added—

"I would have you speak one word of kindness to your child."

"No!" he shouted in a hoarse, cracked voice. "No, by God—no! By hell and all its fiends—no! My child—my child. Ha, ha, ha!—my child—ha, ha!"

The young mother screamed, and would have sprung to the shore again, but he pushed off the boat at the moment, and then she knew that she was at his mercy.

Her heart sunk within her—she covered up the face of the child, as if so doing would preserve it from injury, and in a louder voice than she had used before, she said—

"You wrong me, Charles; I am innocent We have not now met for one whole year, and better had we never met, than I had come to you to hear such words as those. I am innocent. I swear it—by the Heaven above us, I am innocent."

The boat had now swung out into the middle of the stream, and when it reached there, he succeeded, by forcing the large piece of wood he used as a paddle into the mud at the bottom, to moor it there, so that it remained tolerably stationary.

"Why pause we here?" she said; "why pause we here?"

"Here our conference must take place," he said; "here, or nowhere. Margaret, I have some questions to propose."

"Propose them. They shall all—all be fully answered."

"'Tis well. You see how calm I am. I have been a year abroad."

"Yes—yes, Charles."

"And, upon returning, I heard of that—that brat."

"Peace, peace. Call not the little angel innocent by such an epithet. He who died for all, said that of such was the kingdom of Heaven. For shame, Charles, for shame!"

"I do not come here to hear you preach, Margaret, or rave; I have had enough of that abroad. They placed me in a madhouse."

"A madhouse!"

"Yes. Did you never yet hear of a sane person being placed in a madhouse before?"

"Yes, yes; but, but——"

"You doubt if that were my case. Well, be it so. I was perhaps mad; but who drove me mad? Who drove me mad, I say? D——n! answer me that question."

"I will, Charles, answer it; but not according to your belief, I dare say. It was your own unbridled passions that drove you mad."

"Indeed?"

"Your own wild, ungovernable jealousy, made you the tool of every bold bad man who chose to play upon a feeling that drove you mad."

"Well said, well said! Ha, ha, ha! You fight it out bravely. Well said! I feel like the spectator of some mimic scene, and could applaud the actress who so well sustains her part."

"Is it for this you bid me meet you here?"

"No—no."

"What for, then? You asked me to come. I do not forget, although you could, the sacred obligation I was under to obey your commands. I am you wife, and am here as such. I am here because you sent for me, Charles; but if your sending was but for the purpose of rending my heart with such unavailing and God knows how undeserved reproaches, better had you left me to starve or beg rather than have sought me out again."

"I did not choose to do so. The child—"

"What of the child, Charles? Is your heart touched now that you are a father? Oh, pray to God it may be!"

"No—no. My heart is marble Its name is all I wish to know."

"Its name?"

"Yes; what do you call it?"

"What do I call your child?"

"No, by Heaven! not mine."

"Yes, by Heaven, Charles! I swear it by the eternal throne of God!"

"Now, woman, had you been honest, and named the child after the accomplished *roue* to whom it belongs——"

"I cannot hear this—I will not hear it."

"You shall. Had you done that, you should have escaped. Come, now, tell me what name you have bestowed upon the child?"

"The name of its father. Your name. The name of my husband."

"D—n you!"

"I have named the child Margaret Bertram."

"Oh, it's a girl?"

"Yes. Will you look upon its face?"

"No. Will you?"

"Will I! What mean you by so strange a question?"

"Because it will be your last look in this world. You stand now upon the grave's brink. Dying are you, though you feel no pain. You are drawing the few latest breaths you will draw in this world. Your hours—nay, your very minutes are numbered."

A kind of stupor seemed to come over the heart of that young creature as she heard these dreadful words. The certainty of her fate stared her mockingly in the face. Twice she tried to speak ere she could command the power of utterance, and then she cried—

"No—no—no! It is a dream!"

"Fancy it such, if you will. I have made a solemn vow that you or the child shall die!"

"Or the child—or the child? Then you will save the child? You—you will not dye your hands with its innocent blood? You have some touch of mercy yet? You do not intend—No—no. You never did intend to kill the child, Charles? Bless you, at least, for that mercy!"

"Indeed! You thank me for that?"

"From my heart—from my heart, I do!"

"'Tis well; but yet you did not entirely comprehend me. I do not want two victims."

"I understand you well, Charles—perfectly I understand you. I am innocent, and yet I bless you."

"Indeed!"

"Oh, yes. I am very wretched. You do not know what an amount of profound misery I have seen. What is life to me? All that made life pleasant has gone from me. This dear little one is the sole tie now left between me and the world."

"Still you do not comprehend me—I see that still you do not comprehend me. Look at this cloak."

"That cloak—that cloak!"

"Yes. Did you ever see it before?"

"It is the garment—the funeral garment which you superstitiously have preserved, because it has been worn at the funeral of any of your family whose remains you chose to follow to the grave."

"It is the same, Margaret. It is the cloak in which I was enveloped when I watched you enter the hotel where he whose name I will not pronounce was staying. It is the same in which I was enveloped when I attempted my own life, in the agony of my despair at finding you faithless. It is the black mantle of my family—I wear it now on this solemn occasion of death."

"As you please, Charles; and yet I am going to die."

"Ah!" you shrink."

"I am human. Would you have me look upon death with that stoical indifference which would argue want of human feeling rather than abundance of philosophy?"

"No. I would have death bitter to you, because you have made me suffer far more torture than a thousand deaths could inflict upon me."

"Accuse yourself for all that suffering."

"Rather accuse your faithlessness."

"No, I am faithful; I have been too faithful and too yielding. There is not, there never was, sufficient of that antagonistic feeling in my composition which would have enabled me from the first to exercise over you a more powerful moral control."

"Indeed! You speak bravely."

"The innocent should always speak bravely."

"But, do you forget——"

"Forget what?"

"The fixed purpose which has brought me here? You are to die—you are to die."

"You have said so."

"There is no help near, Margaret. You were beautiful, and I loved you; but yet must you die. You may scream, and the hoarse raven will alone return the cry. There is no help. You are doomed—you or the child. Do you understand me?"

"I understand," she said, as she burst into a flood of tears; "I understand that you will spare the child."

"His child!"

"Yours—yours, Charles. Yours, as I have a hope of Heaven's mercy."

"Could I bring my mind to look upon it, well I know it would have his damning features stamped upon its face."

"No—no—no!"

"It would; and I would not trust myself to look upon its face, lest all humanity should leave my heart, and in the moment of my frenzied hate——"

"No—no: speak not so—speak not so, Charles. Do not look upon the babe if you cannot look in kindness."

There was a little brightening of the sky, and she looked around her imploringly, as if she would have asked for aid from the inanimate objects around her; but aid there was none. Alas! there was no spot for hope to rest upon. The dove of expectation might fly from the mind's ark, but there was no place on which to rest its foot.

"Prepare for death!" whispered the man, whose name was Charles Bertram. "Prepare for death!"

"I—I—have no preparation to make," she sobbed. "One kiss on my child's lips—one prayer for joy to it, for mercy to you, and—and—I am ready. Oh, God! 'tis hard to die thus so young, and by the hand of one whom I have loved too fondly—too, too well!"

"Woman," said Bertram, in a hissing whisper, "there is still a hope left for you to cling to."

"What hope? Name it; speak to me of it; what—what hope?"

"'Tis very strange; you have not yet appeared to understand the purport of my words."

"Not understand them! Alas! they are too dreadfully explicit; I understand them too well."

"You do not—you do not."

"Gracious God! you have threatened me with death."

"I have; but you seem never to have comprehended the alternative I offered to you, an alternative by which you may save yourself, if you will."

"Save myself?"

"Yes, most truly."

"I heard it not, I heard no alternative. You said you would spare the child—I heard that; and I hope that such a consciousness will give me strength to bear my own fate with—with at least some resignation. These tears will come—I cannot help them. It is always hard and sad to die; and so soon, too—so very soon. Oh, God! oh, God! look down upon me now in mercy! Spare me, spare me."

"The bitterness of death is creeping on you."

"It is, it is."

"I knew it would."

"Are you human, or some fiend in likeness of him I once loved so well and truly?"

"You have but to sacrifice the child, and you shall live yourself. You have but to embrace that alternative, and not a hair of your head shall be injured by me."

"My child?—the babe?"

"Yes; I knew you did not understand what a chance of life I gave you. As you say, 'tis hard to die, but you need not embrace the hardship. Save yourself, at the cost of the child's life. Hand the babe to me, and say, 'Charles Bertram, cast it in the stream,' and you shall be free; I will love you again, and you may without fear of me, now or ever, go wherever your fancy may lead you."

"Horror! horror!" exclaimed Margaret Bertram.

"What say you?"

"Now, can this be real?"

"It is, I swear it."

"Gracious Heaven! Can I have sunk so low in any mortal estimation, that so much wickedness should be expected from me? I did not understand you. My ears heard the sound of your words, but my heart refused to take in such a proposal of shame and wickedness. Oh, Charles, Charles, put me to a thousand deaths, if you have the heart to be so cruel, but retract those words, and tell me even you, in your utmost hate, never believed that I could dream of life upon such terms."

"You cannot be mad enough to reject my offer. Surely, surely you cannot think of doing so?"

"Reject!"

"Yes, you have heard me."

"What would you have me say?"

"Accept of life; it is dear to you, but useless to this babe. You know what life is; you are loth to bid the world adieu. This breathing, but nearly senseless mass, knows no sensations but pain or pleasure. Let the babe perish, and save yourself."

"Now by the glorious hosts of Heaven, with whom my dearest hope is soon to be in sweet communion, if I thought that one wavering thought tended towards so much weakness, so much wickedness, I would not linger for a death at your hands."

"You would not?"

"No, by Heaven."

"Then die you shall. Have you no prayer? No last words?"

"My last words are,—I am innocent. My last prayer is compounded of a blessing and a prayer for mercy. Farewell, my child. My beautiful—my—my—"

Sobs choked her utterance as she convulsively kissed the child.

"Are you ready?" said Charles Bertram.

"The child——"

"Shall be taken care of."

"Then I am ready to save you from the sin of murder, by taking on myself a deed which I hope will find mercy with my God."

On the moment she plunged into the turgid stream. She had placed the child by her side, but a portion of the shawl clung to her, and, far contrary to her intentions, the little innocent was likewise hurried into the stream.

*   *   *   *   *

A shriek burst from Charles Bertram, and, exclaiming,—

"I meant it not—I meant it not!" he fell backwards in the ferry boat in a swoon.

CHAPTER II.

THE OLD RAM'S HEAD INN AT TOTTENHAM.—THE MERRY PARTY.—THE COLD GHOST OF THE FERRY HOUSE.

A MERRIER, harder drinking, more gossiping, credulous, stupid, generally speaking, party, than was assembled that same night at an old inn, lying considerably off the high road, near to Tottenham, could not well be imagined, and certainly could not have been matched in the vicinity.

What had been the subject of conversation, Heaven only knows ; but at the moment that the clock struck eleven, at least half-a-dozen voices were calling out,—

"Tell it—tell it. There's many here as hasn't *heerd* it."

"It happened a long while ago," said a man, as he knocked the ashes out of his pipe.

"But that ain't no detriment," said another. "Everybody asks about the old ferry as comes into these parts, and why shouldn't you let 'em know how it was that it came to pass as it got into such a state ; why, I recollect, when I was a boy, there was as reg'lar a path over the hill as ever could be, high or low."

"Always high. I should say that path was old, Tobias, wasn't it ?" said one who had not spoken, but who thought himself an amazingly clever fellow.

"Indeed, sir," said the one who had been called upon as the narrator ; "perhaps you can see half a mile further into a millstone than anybody else."

Upon this the amazingly clever fellow was put down by general consent, and, after a little further pressing, the gentleman who knew the story, generously said,—

"Then, here you have it. My grandfather used to tell it, and he always called the tale

THE COLD GHOST OF THE OLD FERRY.

And a cold ghost it was, too, as you shall presently hear. The old ferry stood by the river's brink ; the land was above the banks of the river, though it was tolerably high, yet in flood time it used to be under water, and even the flooring of the house was not free from it.

There was a ditch, too, that ran round the house, and caused a stream of water always to flow through it ; and willows were planted, and here and there were boardings and plankings to keep the edge of the banks up. Taken altogether, it was a specimen of its soil. There was, too, at the corner of the garden, a tall tree, that could be seen a long way off, and was known as soon as seen.

There were two trees growing on either side of the stream, and to these were attached a rope right across the river, and a landing-place upon either side of it. A post stood near the house, to which the flat-bottomed boat was attached, by means of a chain that was fastened to the boat, and then flung round the post. In ordinary weather the passengers used to be ferried over by the old man that used to live there, by means of the boat. There was a high hill on the other side, from the top of which there was a very beautiful view, and some very tall trees waved their heads to the morning breeze.

It was, altogether, a pretty spot, for, as you sat beneath the trees, you could see the distant hills crowned with wood, the winding of the river among the willow trees that studded its banks, and here and there a house, besides the ferry-house, which had, by some fancy, been painted at one time, the Lord knows when, blue. The green fields glancing sunbeams on the river's rippling bosom, like streams of liquid gold, added to the beauty of the scene.

But how changed is the same place in winter. It is the difference between youth and age—daylight and dark. One winter it had been very severe weather, for a long time past, and it was getting worse ; the wind blew from the north-east, and howled among the old trees by which the house was surrounded, and with a gloomy and ominous sound. Old Trappy, the ferryman, was within, warming his toes by the fire, and occasionally uttering a blessing when any stray twinge of the rheumatics alighted on any tender place.

"Cold night, gals," said the old man, carefully picking up a piece of half-burned wood, and thrusting it in the bars, first with his fingers, and then giving it the finishing stroke with his toe.

The wind yet howled louder than before, the chimney roared and bellowed, and the rushing sound of the wind through the trees increased to an alarming extent ; such a storm had not been felt for many years.

"I think," said Trappy, "that some of the trees will find their way into the river."

"Very likely," said his daughter ; "very likely. I don't recollect such a storm as this."

"No," said the old man, "nor I."

"It is getting very cold."

"So it is," said Trappy, giving a refractory piece of wood that stood out of the bars a kick that sent it in, but disturbing some of the white ashes thereby.

Having performed this feat, he arose and went towards the front door, and looked out upon the night. It was very windy, and the water rose and fell in heavy waves, and with a great swell. The clouds were heavy, and hid the moon's rays. It was bitterly cold, and, to add to these disagreeables, the snow had begun to fall very heavily, and the whole face of nature, as far as the eye could reach, was changed, and a white mantle was spread over the whole scene.

Where all had been green, and a pleasing relief, even in winter, to the eye, was now become suddenly and entirely blanched by the fall of frozen particles. Old Trappy shut the door, and put up the chain ; then entering the kitchen, he sat down again by the fire, saying, after he had been there some five or six minutes,—

"It snows."

"Does it?"

"Yes, and will, I dare say, for some time, though it comes down very hard."

"It may be warmer afterwards," said his daughter, "for it is cold enough now."

"Maybe; but I don't think so."

"Why, father?"

"Because I don't."

This was a clencher by way of argument, and no more was said at that time. Still the same roaring and rushing of the wind continued, with intervals of repose, as is usually the case with snow storms: the shrill clatter of the heron, as he flew by at the bottom of the hill, was distinctly heard more than once, as he felt that the frost had driven his prey beyond his reach, and disappointment, with a hungry maw, had been his portion for the night. The girls went to the window that looked out upon the fields. They could see nothing but the white flakes of snow that kept falling in a dizzy whirl, and lying in deep masses upon the earth, changing its very nature.

"The storm abates, I think," said one.

"Does it?" said old Trappy.

"Yes, it certainly does: there is scarcely a flake falling now."

"Then, you may depend upon it, it ain't done yet: ther'es more to come.'

This might be very true, and, therefore, there was no denying it; and, after some seeming doubts in the old man's mind as to the propriety of the step, he rose and went to the door again, and this time went out.

It was a bitter night; the wind was very high, and piercingly keen; the cold was in-

tense, and it would seem that the rigour of the climate had much increased. Old Trappy walked round the house, looked up and down the river, and then, having secured all the doors, he again sought the shelter of his own fireside.

"Is it any warmer?" inquired one of his daughters. "The snow has ceased falling."

"Yes, gal," said he, "the snow has ceased falling, and it's getting colder. Frost and wind will do what the frost couldn't."

"Then we sha'n't be much disturbed by visitors to-night, I should say."

"No, indeed; you need have no fear of that. If there be any here, I'll eat my hat, and that's not easy of digestion. If there's anybody alongside the water to-night, they may have all they have caught, for they must want 'em bad.'

"I think it's getting colder and colder, father," said the girl.

"And so do I," said her sister.

The old man got up, and taking a candle, went into the kitchen, where he chopped some logs, and brought them.

"There," he said, "put some of them on, and make up the fire."

They did so, and prepared to make their supper, which, as the cold was so intense, they had hot. The wind seemed to be getting up, and howled and roared in the chimney, while it whistled round the gable-ends of the tavern: there was not a hole or nook that it did not make its way into: whistling and screaming, it seemed as though the demon of the north had been let loose, and an icy climate had suddenly become created at the old ferry.

Supper was put upon the table, and Trappy's wife couldn't remember such a time, nor could they tell when it was the soup had cooled so quickly—there was no understanding it. Suddenly there was a voice borne on the wind, that caused old

Trappy to suspend the morsel he was conveying to his mouth.

"Was that 'boat?'" said Trappy.

"I only heard the howling of the wind."

"I thought I heard some one calling."

"Not such a night as this. It is not very likely,"

"Let them call again," said Trappy, putting the destined morsel in its proper place. "They won't be long in doing so, if there's anybody there."

"Boat!" cried a voice from the hill side of the river. "Boat, I say, boat!"

"There, I said it was," said Trappy.

"Well, who would have thought it?" said his wife, lifting up her hands.

"They have come over the hill," said his daughter, in astonishment.

"Of course they have," said Trappy. "They wouldn't stop outside without knocking, I am sure, such a night as this. They must be fond of an evening walk, anyhow, else they had not come here such a night as this."

With that the old man put on his hat, buttoned up his coat, and went out. He could scarcely bring to the door, so great was the cold and the force of the wind.

"Boat, boat!" shouted the strange voice.

"I'm coming," said Trappy. "I wonder who it can be?"

"Boat, boat!"

"Bawl away—I can't make yer hear. I shall be there as quick as I can; but Lord, how cold it is."

The truth was, the wind pierced through every stitch of clothing, and found out the most vulnerable places with the greatest facility, and it was surprising how keen the wind was, and how strong the stream was. When Trappy had got half way across, he looked about him, but there was nothing but snow—everything was white, and the hill looked like an immense sheet hung up before his eyes. The rope felt like an icicle, and the old man felt as if he were handling a bar of ice. When he got within speaking distance, he said to the stranger, who stood waiting, shivering with the cold, and rubbing his hands—

"Hope you haven't been waiting long, sir? Can't hear very well, the wind is so loud."

"It's very cold," said the stranger.

"Yes, 'tis 'nation cold. I don't know when I ever felt it so, as I have done to-night."

"No," said the stranger, "'tis very cold."

"Be careful how you step in, sir. The snow overhangs the bank, and if you tread there, it would give way, and you'd go in."

"It would be very cold."

"'Ecod," said Trappy, "I know them as'd bathe in any weather, and sleep with windows and doors open. I should like 'em to do so to-night, and then they'd deserve to be free of the North Pole."

"'Tis very cold."

"Sit down in the boat, sir; the wind blows up, and the stream runs down, so what between the one and the other, I shall have the tail of the boat up the stream. Hilloa, what's that?" said Trappy.

This exclamation was caused by something coming with great violence against the boat, so much so, as to very nearly capsize Trappy into the stream.

"Ah, there's somebody's timber loose, or piles brought down—there'll be some damage afore morning, I'm thinking."

"'Tis very cold," said the stranger again, as he rubbed his hands together very hard.

"Well, it is cold, as you say, very cold. I feel it much more so than I did at first. I can't think the reason of it, but as I draw my breath, it seems to go down half frozen."

"Ah, it's very cold."

"I know that as well as you do," muttered Trappy, getting displeased; "there's no secret about it, anyhow, as I can see. Nobody wants to keep it all to themselves."

By this time he had got to the landing-place, and had twisted the chain round the post, and thrown the staple into the boat.

"Now, sir, you can get out, if you please; it ain't pleasant staying here."

"It's very cold."

The stranger uttered these words in a shivering voice, and looked at the old man in the face very hard.

"Well, I know it's cold, uncommon cold, so you've said, and so I've said, and so you've said again and again. As you seem so very cold, will you walk into the house, and warm yourself by the fire?"

"Yes, thank you, it's very cold."

"It is; and I think, somehow or other, something very strange has happened to the weather, for it has come on so suddenly so much worse."

He somehow or other associated the idea of the accession of frigidity and the stranger so strangely together, that he could not help thinking there was something marvellously strange and unnatural. He looked, he thought, most unnaturally white; but then that might be caused by the extreme cold, and a good warming at the fire would make him quite the reverse of white.

"What's the matter, Trappy?" exclaimed his wife, as she heard him lift the latch.

"Matter?—nothing the matter that I know of. Why?"

"Because your bringing the cold in with you—it is dreadful."

"It is cold," said the stranger, as he closed the door after him.

"Goodness gracious!" exclaimed the daughters. "Here's a frozen cloud a-coming, and it's melting, and covering over everything. What is the matter?"

"Oh, it is so cold," said the stranger, as he followed his conductor into the apartment.

This was not a very large one, partly boarded, and partly paved with brick. A dresser ran under one window, and a desk under another, a smaller one, of a solitary pane. Then there was another table in the room, a round one, of suspicious security.

Mrs. Trappy and her two daughters gazed at the stranger with mingled sentiments of awe and disgust, on account of the dreadful chill that pervaded the apartment as he entered. They all shuddered, through a strange sensation they could not at all describe. They felt as though the very natural power of utterance had been frozen within them, and they couldn't speak till something should happen to thaw it.

"Sit down by the fire," said Trappy. "Here, the fire's almost out; put on some more wood."

Trappy executed his own command, and put the wood on himself; the women didn't know what to do.

"Hang the fire, I can't tell what's the matter with it. Now it will do, surely. How very cold it has become."

"'Tis very cold," said the stranger, in the same clear, monotonous tone, that savoured of something very unearthly.

The stranger was not very tall, though above the common height; broad, but very thin; his features were sharp-set, his eyes a light grey, and his hair iron grey. Altogether he was a most singular individual, and there appeared to be a kind of atmosphere that was peculiar to him—everything appeared intensely cold, and the kitchen seemed to be the very seat of the frost—the home of congelation.

Poor Mrs. Trappy was about to put half a glass of beer to her mouth, but it would not flow; it was frozen, and she might have turned the glass upside down, but it would not let out a drop of the liquid.

"Well," said Trappy, "this beats all I ever heard, and all I know; I never knew such a night as this before, I didn't."

"No," said the stranger, "'tis very cold—very cold."

"It is cold."

With that the stranger put his hands between the bars of the grate to warm them. Trappy watched this with some interest, but when he saw the fire was likely to go out, he arose, and, stirring it, put on more fuel.

"Have you been long here?" said the stranger, in the same cold, calm voice.

"Yes, many years."

"Ah, this is a very old house," said the stranger; "a very old house it is."

"Yes, my grandfather used to say it was very old when he was a boy."

"He was right. I recollect it longer than he," said the stranger, looking about him.

"Longer than my grandfather? Why, he's been dead these thirty years."

"That may be the truth; and yet I knew it long before his time. It must have been firmly built, or these boards would have given way long before this time."

"They would."

When the stranger last spoke, his breath came across to old Trappy, who was nearly suffocated; it was so intensely cold that it produced a strange and horrible sensation of choking. The females felt it, too, and soon removed further off.

"It is very cold."

"Ecod! it is, and, somehow or other, you don't seem very warm," said Trappy, looking at his visitor in something more than amazement.

"No; it is very cold."

Trappy was muttering something uncivil between his teeth, when the stranger got up and stamped upon the flooring, as if he were trying their solidity, and the firmness of the house.

"Ah, that's all good," said Trappy.

"Yes, yes," said the stranger. "I recollect this spot long before there was anything put here; it was covered with trees."

"Ye?"

"Yes; it would never have withstood the many floods if the whole place had not been well bound together by roots of trees that have long since been felled and burned."

Trappy sat and gazed at his visitor in a cold sweat. He was not an old man, and did not appear more than half his own age, and yet he spoke of things that must have happened at least eight or nine generations ago, a thing he thought impossible. The stranger's form was of a most ghastly paleness, and his eye was almost leaden, and very disagreeable in its expression.

The stranger here took the candle in his hand and looked at it a few moments, and then held his fingers in the flame one after another, each for some seconds.

Trappy looked very hard, and was amusing himself with the hope that he would soon be tired of that kind of amusement; but no, he appeared rather to like it than otherwise.

"You don't burn very large candles," said the stranger, looking at the flame, which he held in his mouth for a short time, and taking it out, he continued,— "About five-and-twenty to the pound, I suppose, is the run?"

"No; we consider them enough. We use them for lights, and not for furnaces."

"Very good; but it's very cold."

"Oh, bother the man! what's the use of complaining? Here am I frozen, and can't get up hardly. You've brought it with you."

"Oh, dear, no; it's very cold in these parts. I can't get anything to warm me."

"I should think not ; but there may be a place warm enough for you some day," muttered Trappy.

The stranger sat looking at the fire for a long time. Trappy was seated by the fire, but some distance from the stranger, of whom he stood in great awe and dread; he was altogether an unearthly being, of whom he could make nothing.

They sat some time thus, nobody breaking the disagreeable silence, and nobody having the power or inclination apparently to do so.

The wind blew a perfect hurricane, and the cold was no less intense than it had been. The noise in the chimney was as great and as fierce as ever it was; the wind whistled through the keyhole and the cracks beneath the door; the shutter shook, and the doors shook too; indeed, the whole place was in a terrible state that night.

The stranger put up his foot by the fire, between the bars, on the side he was sitting, and kept it there till it was going out, then he moved on the other side and put the other foot up till that side was nearly out.

"'Tis very cold," said the stranger, after a long pause; "can't you put no more wood on?"

Trappy arose and tottered about after some wood, which he brought and threw on the fire, for he was horribly cold himself, and almost incapable of motion. The fire burned up, and the wood crackled merrily, while the stranger looked at the blazing pieces of wood, and sighed,— "It is so cold."

This was dreadfully aggravating to Mrs. Trappy; she could not endure it, that she could not; yet, strange to say, she either dared not or could not speak; and what was as bad as could be was, that, notwithstanding all the fuel heaped upon the fire, it did not seem to give any warmth, and the place would, under any other circumstances, and at any other time, have been much more than warm—absolutely hot. But now all was as frigid as the North Pole—everything was deceptive; and the bright glare of the fire and the crackling of the flames was a mere illusion —a deception.

Presently the stranger took off a thick, round lump of wood that had become heated to a red heat, and gently rubbed it between his two hands, as though he would have warmed them by these means.

Trappy watched this manœuvre for some time, fully expecting to see that it was effective; but no, it was nothing to him. The red heat gradually cooled down, and in a few minutes the wood was a mere bit of charcoal, which he threw down, muttering,—

"It is so cold—so cold."

"Well," thought Trappy, "this is the rummest start I ever heard of. He's not of this world, that's certain. What he wants I don't know, and can't think. Surely it isn't the end of the world come, is it ? If so, we are all to suffer death by cold."

"It is so cold," said the stranger.

"Good God! it is cold. When will he be gone?" thought Mrs. Trappy. "We shall perish. We may as well go and sit in the boat."

Trappy looked at the stranger—he was each moment becoming more and more alarmed—he could not believe that he had a human being with him; it must be the spirit of the arctic regions broke loose, and rode hither upon the wings of the north wind to freeze the very heart in the body. The stranger huddled closer and closer to the fire, which, by degrees grew dimmer and dimmer, as if it were unable to support heat enough to burn, and that the vicinity of such intense frigidity was sufficient to destroy combustion. When the fire was quite out, the stranger looked at it sorrowfully, heaved a deep sigh, and turning to Trappy, said,—

"Well, it is out."

"I see it is."

"'Tis a pity—'tis so very cold."

Nobody spoke, when the stranger arose, and said, in the same voice,—

"I must go, but it's very cold."

This was happy news to Trappy and his family, and he arose to let the unwelcome guest out, when he said,—

"I must go over again."

"Very well, sir," said Trappy, who was getting drowsy from cold.

"Don't go—don't go," said Trappy's wife and daughter, but they were too late; he followed the stranger out, and then he shut the door.

Old Trappy did not come in any more that night; they could not tell what had become of him, and to look after him they could not—they durst not—they feared the icy stranger. They sat in that miserable condition for the whole of the remainder of the night, and when daylight came they saw old Trappy sitting upon his own door step quite dead. He was examined, but there were no marks of violence or apparent cause of death.

After that the house had an ill-name, and was deserted, but some time after it was again opened, and inhabited by a man, but he could do no good, the place was so cold, and they could never get the fire to burn there, and if they did, it would not be of any use, as nothing could be cooked, so it was again deserted, and has never since been inhabited by any human being.

I have often heard my grandfather say it was the coolest thing he ever heard talked of, and I know he wouldn't have said so if it wasn't.

The cold ghost was never heard of after that time, but it was a very severe winter.

CHAPTER III.

THE UNEXPECTED VISITORS.—THE CONSTERNATION AT THE INN.—THE DEAD BODIES.

SCARCELY had the last words of this somewhat singular narrative escaped the lips of its narrator, than such a shout from outside the inn met the ears of the assembled guests, that, involuntarily, they all started to their feet, excepting one, and surprise had a contrary effect upon him, for he fell into a corner upon the most extended basis of his animal economy. Before, then, any one could pronounce the popular exclamation of Jack Robinson, which people are supposed to be continually endeavouring to say against time, the shout was renewed, and this time, almost before

its echoes had subsided, accompanied by a loud voice, crying—

"House, house, house! Open doors—house, here—house!"

"W—w—what can it be?"

"It sounds like somebody wanting to come in," said another.

"It does, indeed," added a third wiseacre. "It does, indeed."

"Or like a dozen people wanting to come," suggested another.

They heard a great bustle at the door and in the passage. They heard the voice of the landlord, as he said—

"This way—this way! The kitchen is the warmest place. This way, if you please—right into the kitchen."

"What can it be?" said half-a-dozen of the petrified guests in the parlour; "what can it all be about?"

Strange to say, although they kept on asking each other this question in every variety of intonation, no one thought of going out to see, or if they did think of such an expedient, he was by far too much of a coward to make the least attempt to carry it into effect. The noise was very much decreased in intensity, although still there was a great scuffling of feet, and suddenly a voice cried—

"Good God! why can't you put them into a warm bed at once?"

"A warm bed?" said the landlord. "Oh, you said a warmed bed?"

"Of course, I did."

"A bed warmed?"

"I did. Yes, and get plenty of hot water. They must have plenty of hot water."

"Goodness gracious! what can it be?"

There was now a great scuffling of feet for some minutes, and then, suddenly, there came such a loud crash in the passage, that it seemed as if heaven and earth were coming together, and one of them had turned out of a very brittle and sonorous nature. The noise was perfectly deafening and tremendous, and it seemed never to be going to be done, for it went on rumbling and tumbling about, as if the house were coming to pieces. Here a loud voice cried out—

"Never mind—never mind. Try it again!"

"Oh, good God! what are they at?" said a little man, who had turned as white as paper with fear; "what are they at?"

"I—I can't say," remarked the man next him, as he, in his agitation, strove to smoke an empty pipe, and wondered it wouldn't draw, but rather was inclined to believe that its not doing so was a part of the series of frightful phenomena that were taking place.

"Why don't some of you thin, active fellows," said a fat man, who was perspiring in every pore with fear, "go out and see what it is?"

This was a question too troublesome to answer, so nobody attempted, and then they listened to another strange, unearthly sort of thumping and bumping, during which several voices were heard.

"Take care," said some. "Mind what you are at," cried others. "That'll do; now a little this way. There you are. Now for it," and then one added the diabolical words of,—"Do you think they are dead yet?"

The guests in the parlour looked at each other with horror depicted in their countenances.

"Lor! somebody's being murdered!" said the man who was making such vigorous efforts to smoke the empty pipe.

"They is—they is," said another.

The fat man gave a huge groan, which seemed to "shatter all his bulk," and looked as if, with a very little more provocation, he could find it in his heart to tumble bang off his seat on to the floor in a plethoric sort of swoon.

Suddenly, then, when wonder and fear had reached a painful climax, the door was opened, and the landlord made his appearance, rubbing his head with a napkin, and looking very hot.

"I don't think they are dead, upon my soul," he said.

"Good God! what do you mean?"

"Why, both of 'em, to be sure. We have done the best we could."

"Some animals, I suppose?"

"Not at all. A young woman and a baby."

"Why, you horrid brute!"

"Brute?"

"Yes."

"What for?"

"Don't you say you've done the best you could to kill a woman and a baby? Now, on your word, which was it, the woman or the baby that came down in the passage such a lump, and seemed all made of tin?"

"Made of tin?"

"Yes, tin, or iron, or something."

"Why, bless you, that was the bath!"

"The what?"

"The water bath. There's been a woman and a child fished out of the river, and they've brought 'em both here to try and resusticate them!"

The guests in the parlour drew a long breath.

"And," added the landlord, "we were carrying the bath up stairs to put 'em in, when that fool, Joe, as he always does, let go of it at his end, and it slipped over and came down in the passage with quite a little noise."

"A little noise?"

"Yes, there was a clatter."

"And who are they, landlord?"

"Ah, now that's just what I can't tell you; but there's a doctor there, and he says he'll have a good try and bring them to life again, if he can. You see, he don't know how long they've been in the water, so he can't tell."

"Lor! a woman and a child?"

"Yes, and quite a young woman. There's my missus up to her ears in it, a-doing all sorts of things, like a brick!"

"If she were a hot brick," said one, "and were to lie down on the pit of the stomach of one of them, she might do some good."

"Ah, very likely. I must be off, though, now, and see what's wanted. Doctor Bailey is there, and a very violent man he is, to be sure, as ever stepped. If you don't give him, in a moment, just what he wants, he swears more like a parson than a doctor, and if you leave him a moment, he lays hold of the bell and gives it such a tremendous——There he goes—there he goes! That's him, for a thousand pounds. I'd know his ring, I would, among a hundred and twenty-three, any day."

Away bustled the landlord to attend upon the irascible Dr. Bailey, who kept up the ring always till he got what he wanted; so it was good policy, for the sake of peace and quietness, to serve him always as quickly as possible.

"I tell you what it is," said the fat man who had recovered a great portion of his equanimity, and waved the stem of his pipe in the air oratorically; "I tell you what it is, my friends, it's no joke restoring a drowned person."

Several shook their heads gravely, and added, that they rather supposed it was the very reverse of a joke.

"But what I want to know," added the fat man, "is, where the souls of the people go to while they are drowned."

One present hinted his opinion that some of them went to blazes, but he was put down by general consent; and then, before the argument could assume any shape or consistency, the door was flung open again, and the landlord, who seemed to consider himself as enacting the old character of Rumour in some ancient comedy of the Elizabethan school, rushed in and said—

"They haven't recovered 'em yet, gentlemen; they've emptied the boiler, and are now getting as much hot water as they can in saucepans."

"Indeed!"

"Yes; and they are rubbing them with hot flannels, and blowing wind into them through a pair of bellows."

"Goodness gracious!"

Away flew the landlord again, for he dreaded another peal at the bell from the impatient Mr. Bailey.

The guests began to get into a state of intense excitement, and they agreed among themselves that, although twelve o'clock had come, they would not turn out of the house, but, in defiance of all authority, and all legal enactments to the contrary made and provided, they would stay to see the end of it.

One of them, of a more ingenious temperament than the rest, proposed to put the clock back an hour, and, in so doing—for the project met with general concurrence—he stopped it altogether.

"There's a go!" he remarked; "don't tell the landlord."

"Implicit secrecy," as they say in the advertisements offering to purchase government situations, was promised, and the next time the landlord came in, he said—

"Really, gentlemen, I must, you know, clear the house, you know—Oh—what—bless me, only half-past eleven! Oh!"

"You go by your own clock, I suppose," said the fat man, "such as it is?"

This implied reproach was, of course, sufficient to induce any man to bristle up in defence of his clock, and, as the landlord was human, he did so immediately, and said to the fat man—

"Sir, the clock has been in my family for a matter of five-and-twenty years, sir; and, after that, I should like to see the man who will say I am not to rely upon that clock, sir."

"Very good."

"It is very good, sir; and when, sir,—you, sir,—show, sir,—a little clock, sir—why, then, sir, d——e, sir——"

"Don't be excited," said one.

"I am excited, sir. Ah! kick me, sir, but don't abuse my clock, sir. Ah!"

"Ain't the works weak?"

"No, sir, you are mistaking the works of the clock for your own works. They are weak, dreadfully weak; but the clock's works are not. Coming—coming—coming!"

The vociferous bell again claimed the attention of the worthy landlord, and off he rushed, like a maniac in a white apron.

The guests could not refrain from a roar of laughter when he had gone from the room, and one put the clock on just five minutes, after which they resumed their conversation, which went on for about half an hour, when in bounced the landlord with a—

"Now, gentlemen, if you please, I shall have an information against me if you don't get——Hilloa! what, five-and-twenty minutes to twelve yet? Why—why—what's the meaning of this?"

"The clock's wrong," said one.

"No—no, not the clock."

"Very good, it's right, then."

"Of course, it is. Well, I'm very glad; she ain't recovered yet, but the baby is. Yes, the baby is; poor little, dear thing; it is sound asleep now, and the doctor says it won't be any the worse."

They were common, uneducated, and, in many respects, vulgar men who were in that room; but they were far from being destitute of those better feelings of humanity which, we are forced to say, are nowhere to be found more strongly developed than in our own country.

When they considered that the mother and the child were dead, their sympathies had not been strongly excited; but now the short, simple statement that the child had been restored, and was soundly sleeping, while its poor mother might be in the arms of death, had a very different effect upon them, and they all looked serious directly.

"Thank God," said one.

"Oh! thank God, for the poor child's sake," said another; "and, let us hope, friends, that the mother will live, too. What sort of people do they seem, landlord?"

"Poor—very poor."

There was a general expression of sympathy, and one said, in a voice of genuine emotion that exhibited the real state of his heart—

"Who knows, gentlemen, now, what may have driven this poor creature to despair, and what unkindness may have made her commit such a dreadful act? After all, perhaps, she is far less guilty than some wretch who may have been the real cause of it."

"Hear, hear," cried everybody, and the fat man shook his head from side to side, continuing the motion so long that the period when he would leave it off appeared to be very distant and doubtful indeed.

"She's quite a young thing," said the landlord; "and, if she wasn't so pale, poor creature, you'd go a long way before you saw a face like hers."

"Of course she's the mother?"

"Lord, bless you! yes. They're as like each other as two peas."

"It's dreadful to think of—it's dreadful!"

"It must be dreadful; for now there's Mr. Bailey—you know what a devil of a fellow he is for swearing?"

"Yes—yes."

"Well; he has been crying, and pretending to have a cold in his head."

"Has he?"

"Yes; but I know'd what for. As soon as ever he seed the child open its little blue eyes, and look up in his face, I seed as he was then a ready to bust, he was."

"To bust!—what about?"

"Feelins—feelins—don't you understand? Feelins—he's got his feelins as well as other people, I supposes."

"Ah! ah! now I understand. Oh! yes."

"What did he do?" asked the fat man, who seemed ready to laugh or to cry as things might turn up. "What did he do?"

"Do? why all of a sudden, when he saw that he gave a sort of gasp, and made an odd sort of noise in his throat, I could see the tears running over the bridge of his nose, and he looks at me then for about half a minute, and he says, says he, ' a violent cold in my head,' says he."

"And it wasn't?"

"Wasn't? No; to be sure not. It was all feelings, I tell you; and, if so be as he brings to life the mother, I don't know what he won't do. That's my idea, you know, about it."

"What, have you got an idea?" said the man who, on several occasions, had thought proper to be sarcastic.

"Yes," said the landlord; "ain't you envious?"

The man said no more, for the laugh was decidedly against him, and he had not quite enough of that ready small change of wit to make an immediate reply to the landlord.

While all this was going on in the parlour, the medical man, whom our readers, we are sure, will not think the worse of on account of what has been related of his "feelins" by the landlord, was continuing his indefatigable exertions for the recovery of the mother of the child he had already been so happy as to preserve.

Much emboldened, and rendered doubly hopeful by the success he had already had, he persevered in his efforts, and for the time being led the attendants who were about him such a life, that, as one remarked,—

"A slave in the Inges must be nothing to it, and lead a life of complete idleness, and not know how to amuse himself." But, be this as it may, immense exertion was necessary in order to present even a chance of safety. It was only by the most unrelaxing energy that the dormant vitality of the child had been called into activity, and, if anything effectual was to be done towards the restoration of the mother, it must be by similar means. The infant was very young, and it was very beautiful; its scanty apparel was carefully mended, in a variety of directions, and it seemed, when new, to have been rather of a costly quality. It is a fact beyond all dispute, that there are vulgar, low-looking children, as well as superior-looking ones. Take, at a month old only, the infant of intellectual and well-bred parents, and place it beside that of some of the lowest inhabitants of the new swept away rookery of St. Giles's, and the difference in the breed will soon be apparent.

This is a theory which don't suit those persons who pretend that all at birth have the same capacity of cultivation; but, nevertheless, it is one founded upon practice, and, as in the case of the lower, but frequently the more estimable and respectable order of animals, local circumstances, the education and habits of the parents, and a variety of other considerations, have a great effect upon human beings, and produce almost as great varieties as are to be found in the dog.

It would be as impossible to take some infants from the birth and make them gentleman, as it would be to take a greyhound pup, and strive by education to convert him into a bull-dog.

But to return from this digression.

The child had upon its countenance that undefinable look which proclaimed it to belong to no low person; and, although by far too young to allow of the features and expression developing themselves, yet, to an accurate observer, there they were in their first undeniable traces as plain as possible.

"Poverty and misery," said the surgeon, "have not been the natural elements of the existence of these people. Misfortune has pulled them down, I am certain, from some much higher condition than they now appear to be in."

When he thought nobody was watching him, he imprinted a kiss on the face of the babe, and then giving it a very small quantity of diluted wine and water, he had it placed in the warm bed, where it fell fast asleep—a repose, during which it recovered completely from the submersion it had undergone.

He could not but notice what a look of deep depression there was on the face of the mother, even during that mimic death which had for a time chained all her faculties. Well could he guess what in happiness and serenity she might have been. There was the beautifully chiselled mouth, the ample brow, the small rounded chin, the long silken hair, and, lastly, to draw an accurate judgment from her hands, which were so small and child-like, and had that shape of the nail, which is as rare as it is beautiful.

"Poor thing—poor thing!" he said, "she has fallen from some very different state to what she is in now. I would give something to know what induced her to throw herself into the river—but, hold! how do I know she threw herself into the river? She may have fallen in, of course. How do I know? or—or she may have been thrown in. No—no, not that. There are brutes in the world, but, surely, none capable of so diabolical an act. I have not the highest opinion of human nature, but I don't want to wrong it in any way."

He thought he saw a change taking

place upon the face of the sufferer, and then, animated by new hope, he continued his great exertions to restore her to animation.

Meanwhile, the rain had ceased, and yet the guests waited in the parlour of the public-house, and the landlord went on praising his clock, at the same time that he was dreadfully puzzled by the peculiarities of its mode of doing that which had been done for so long with such an amount of credit to itself, and great satisfaction to its owners.

"Well," he exclaimed, when he came into the room about one o'clock and found that it still wanted a quarter to twelve,—"well, I never, certainly, felt an evening go so slowly as this has done. I'll be hanged if it don't puzzle me atogether. It seems to me now—would you believe it? —as if it ought to have been twelve a good hour ago."

Everybody said they could not believe it, for it appeared to them quite rationally and naturally to be a quarter to twelve.

"Well, I know it is, of course," said the landlord.

"Yes; but the clock may be wrong."

"I tell you what. If the clock's found to be wrong, I'll send in a bowl of punch that shall make you wink again."

"Now, are you sure," said one, "that you have got in the house all the materials for punch making?"

"Oh, never fear. I've got 'em, but they won't be wanted."

"I don't know that."

"Perhaps you mean to order it?"

"Oh, no; but you do."

"Very good. We shall see now—we shall see. The moment I can get an opportunity, I'll ask Mr. Bailey what's o' clock. His watch is never wrong any more than my clock; and he always compares 'em together when he comes this way."

At this moment, and before any one could make any remark further upon the subject, in rushed no less a person than Mr. Bailey, and executing some wild kind of dance, he exclaimed,—

"All's right—all's right! She's all right at last—hurrah!"

"What, sir, is she alive?"

"Yes, of course, she is. Quite alive, and will do well, too. Of course, she is alive, and all right. She's in bed now, and asleep along with her child, as she ought to be, poor thing—poor thing. Landlord!"

"Yes, sir."

"Something to drink here, quickly. I am as tired as I can be; but where's the odds of that, as she is alive, and the babe, too? I never expected to save the infant."

"Didn't you, sir?"

"No. But they both of them must have been in the water only a very short time, indeed; it is but seldom that so really short a time is fatal. Who got them out? I should like to see the man who got them out, for it must be a great satisfaction to him to know that they are saved."

"Why, sir, he went away."

"Went away?"

"Yes, sir. He told me that he was riding along the narrow bridal road, by the south bank of the stream, when he heard a scream, and in another moment there came round the turn of the river something white."

"Yes, yes."

"It was the mother and her child. He plunged in, and got them out; but he left them at the door here; and who he is, or what he is, I don't know."

"Well, that's singular enough; but, I daresay, he'll call again."

"He may, sir. By-the-by, what's the time by you?"

The surgeon produced his watch, and said—

"Twenty minutes past eleven."

"Past eleven only?'

"Oh, dear, no; I forgot. I stopped my watch when I commenced resuscitating the bodies, to see how long it took me. What are you? Oh, there's something very wrong here, for I am quite sure I have been up stairs somewhere about two hours."

"So you have, sir," said a man, producing a large, old-fashioned silver watch. "It's now ten minutes past one o'clock."

CHAPTER IV.

THE MARRIAGE.—THE PREDICTION.—THE BLACK MANTLE.

BUT two years before the occurrences recorded in the preceding portion of our story, the bells in St. George's church, one "merry morn in May," were pealing forth their most joyous notes. Carriages were dashing about in that reckless manner which always, on particular occasions, characterises the proceedings of coachmen, and an idle collection of people had assembled around the door of the sacred edifice.

Of course, all these indications could mean but one thing, and that was a wedding. Yes—a wedding! High or low, gentle or simple, married or unmarried, somehow or another, everybody is wonderfully attracted by a wedding.

There are some particular subjects of which human nature don't seem to tire readily in taking an interest in, and one of those certainly is a wedding.

A good funeral is very well in its way; an execution is not amiss; a trial has its charms; and there are some besotted people who can see something even in that most dull, stupid, and troublesome of all ceremonies—a christening! But there is no mistake about the wedding. That is sure to be attractive, under all and every set of circumstances.

Some one has said that mankind might be divided into two great classes, namely, the hanged, and the unhanged; and, by a similar vein of reasoning, numberless equally opposite and philosophical divisions of the great human community might be made, and most certainly mankind may be with much more propriety divided into the two great classes of the married and the unmarried. To both of these classes a marriage is an interesting exhibition, and fraught with food for deep consideration.

To the unmarried, of course, the affair is deeply interesting, because there is no unmarried man who does not occasionally, in some moment of delirium, think of matrimony. To the married it is also deeply interesting, for they regard the spectacle with the same eyes that some ruined gamester regards a novice who comes, even as he came once, fresh, joyous, and hopeful, to the hazard table.

He knows all about it. He has found out how often matrimony becomes the grave of hope and sentiment, swamping completely, in the course of a few short years, every joyous feeling of romance, —and roughly, rudely awakening the mind to some of the coldest realities of existence.

We do not mean to say that all marriages are such deep disappointments, but we do mean to say that all, to a certain extent, are disappointments, and that some are hideous ones.

We have seen many a middle-aged man, whose face has sufficiently told us—ay, as sufficiently as if he had held us by the button and told us so—that he has been buffetted very tolerably in the world, and all the sentiment and romance knocked out of him long ago,—we have seen such an one loitering near a church where a marriage has been taking place, and the post-chariot has been waiting, with its four horses and its postilions, with their gay favours, to whirl the happy pair away for a month; we have seen him watch them coming out, and what a chuckle he has given—what an expressive chuckle! as if he would say to them,—

"Poor devils! what a delusion! The fool's paradise will soon be on the wane."

But this marriage which was about to take place at the church of St. George's surely promised better things.

The parties were well enough matched; both were young enough, and one was rich enough. That was the husband—as it should be. That is to say, without being rich he was in comfortable circumstances, and could afford to make a good show upon such an occasion as that, at all events.

He held a lucrative government appointment. The match was one of love; those most unhappy of matches. Love! Alas! what a slender, slippery capital to trade on. How perishable a commodity! How fleeting! how transitory! Yes! it was a love-match, and the bride was beautiful.

The bride was more than beautiful, for she was virtuous, true, noble-hearted, generous, and confiding. These should have been qualities to secure happiness, but, alas! they were to be weighed in the mental scales of another. They were to be seen through the medium of another's prejudices and feelings; and then of what avail are they?

Margaret Harrison—that was the name of the bride. She was an orphan girl; she was penniless; she was, indeed, by family bereavements, thrown upon the wide world alone and friendless.

Mr. Charles Bertram, the bridegroom, knew sufficient of her to know, or to fancy he knew, her virtues, and he proposed to her and married her. That was the wedding to which we are drawing the attention of our readers.

Poverty has few friends, and, therefore, was it that Margaret invited no one to her wedding. Not a soul who could claim kindred with her was among the well-dressed throng that came to grace the nuptials. She stood alone—the observed of all observers, the admired of all admirers.

And he to whom she was about to plight her vows, looked proudly on his beautiful bride; too proudly—for it would seem as if he prized her the more for that strange gift of beauty, than for aught else, and a more dangerous ground of matrimony to proceed on could not be.

But that was nothing at present. All was sunshine—all *couleur de rose.* There did not seem one cloud in the sunny sky of the joy of those two well matched persons, if we except in their fortunes. And surely, what nobler—what better use can a man make of his wealth than in bestowing it upon one who in return will give him such a heart as Margaret Harrison brought to Charles Bertram?

Gratitude towards him was mingled in her mind with an affection that was devotion itself. Alas! that was bad, too. Cold worldly wisdom tells us that not of such materials is domestic peace made, to say nothing at all of happiness. We cannot help being of the opinion of the man in the play, namely, that a decent share of indifference is the best of all feelings, if we wish, while we give up some of the joys of existence, certainly to escape some of its bitterest distresses, and greatest mental shocks.

The bells ceased their exhilarating jingle during seven minutes and a half, and then they burst forth anew. Margaret Harrison was Mrs. Bertram. She had spoken words which at once had altered the whole tenour of her existence—she had breathed a vow which was to blight her heart, and to inflict upon her, in its consequences, the direst pangs.

Oh, how elate and joyful Charles Bertram looked as he gazed on his beautiful bride! How full of pride was he that he could call one so truly lovely his own. With what a glance of satisfaction he gazed around him on the thronging friends who pressed forward to congratulate him.

Margaret was hanging upon his arm. Tears were in her eyes, but they were tears of gratitude and joy. She, so poor—so entirely destitute—so friendless, had been chosen by one who might have mated where fortune would have been freely tendered to him; but he must love her very truly to have abandoned all the advantages he might have gained. So thought Margaret, and she forgot to set a value upon the priceless jewel she brought him—a pure and an uncorrupted heart.

Congratulations and good wishes poured in upon the happy pair on every side; and, smiling and bowing from side to side, like some gracious monarch willing to be condescending to his people, came Charles Bertram towards the door of the church.

The travelling chariot which was to convey them to Worthing drew up close to the curbstone. The waiting multitude pressed eagerly forward to see the bride. There was interest and animation on every countenance.

The church door was gained, and Charles Bertram withdrew the beautiful girl from beneath his arm, in order to take her hand to place her in the carriage as quickly as possible, for he knew how she shrank from the publicity of the affair by the trembling of her arm in his.

At that moment, when murmurs of admiration at the beauty of the bride broke from every lip (for, in her hurry, she had doubled the veil she wore in such a manner, that she could not get it wholly over her face), a female of an aged aspect and generally repulsive appearance sprang forward, and, with a common table knife, which she held in her right hand, she made a sudden thrust at the breast of Charles Bertram, exclaiming, as she did so, in a loud, hoarse, screaming, half-demoniac sort of voice,—

"Death! death to you—death to you! Even in the hour of your fancied triumph of joy, death to you!"

Mechanically, rather than from any real presence of mind, he had suddenly thrown up his arm, and so warded off the blow. He was not touched by the knife, but he turned of a death-like paleness, and cried out aloud,—

"The woman's mad—the woman's mad! Let her go—let her go, I say! The woman's mad!"

Margaret screamed. The mob made a sudden rush to seize the woman, who had dropped the knife, and she was firmly held by half-a-dozen arms in a moment, before she could have the least chance of escape.

But escape she did not seem to meditate, although, when she found she had not succeeded in her object, rage seemed almost to be choking her.

"I am unhurt—I am unhurt, Margaret," exclaimed Charles Bertram. "I am not touched, dearest."

"Charles, Charles—my husband!"

She threw herself upon his breast in a passion of tears.

"To the carriage—to the carriage!" he cried.

But suddenly the woman, who would have taken his life, by a sudden exertion, freed herself from the hold of those about her, and, flinging herself at his feet, she clung round them so that he could not move, and then, while terror made him tremble and blanced the cheek of Margaret, she poured forth, in the course of about two minutes, a denunciation against him which it was awful to hear, and which filled every spectator with amazement.

"Betrayer! villain!" she cried; "your triumph is to continue. It is at present the will of Heaven that you are not to be punished for the evil that you have done. I see in the defeat of my purpose the finger of Providence, and I can say, what you dare not, Heaven's will be done. But, Charles Bertram, may the curse, the bitterest curse of a broken heart cling to you—of two broken hearts, for mine, as well as hers whom I need not name to you, is breaking. May the vengeance of God overtake you most fearfully, and may you, in some moment of your greatest confidence and gladness, be dragged down to that hell which is waiting you, and such as you. Twelve months—short of twelve months—I give you, Charles Bertram; and before this day next year you shall know what it is to suffer. I shall not see to-morrow's sunrise. I speak with the voice of prophecy. Take the curse to your heart! Let it haunt you—let it haunt you, sleeping or waking, in the most frightful shape it can assume!"

She raised her withered arms towards Heaven, and, although released, he could not move, but stood as if spell-bound to the spot; and while her voice grew harsh, hoarse, and almost inarticulate, she screamed—

"Great God! may the curse of the bereaved mother cling to this man and blight his existence!"

"No—no—no!" cried Margaret, who was nearly distracted by the dreadful scene. "No—no—no! God of Heaven! Charles, what means this?"

"To the carriage!" he cried, "to the carriage—clear the way—a mad woman—a mad woman!"

His face was as pale as ashes, and already, to look at him, any one would say that he was, indeed, as one accursed by Heaven, for his mental agony was intense. The drops of perspiration stood out in bold relief upon his brow; they fell like pattering rain upon the cold stones at his feet, as again he shouted, in accents of still greater excitement than before—

"Clear the way—clear the way! A mad woman, I tell you all! Good God! will no one take her from my path?"

It was easy enough now to remove her, for she had become insensible, and lay at his feet perfectly still and motionless. Several persons raised her, and she slightly recovered. Her lips moved, and those who were nearest to her, heard her say, in low accents—

"The *Black Mantle*—the *Black Mantle*! He dare not part with that. Ha! ha! ha! 'Tis part of the curse." Then she fell back into the arms of the bystanders, completely insensible.

By a tremendous effort, Charles Bertram cleared a way through the throng, and placed his nearly fainting bride in the travelling carriage. He sprang in after her, and said aloud to the postilions—

"Drive on—drive on!"

"Stop—stop," said a constable, who had been sent for. "I grieve to detain you, sir, but you must stay to give charge of the woman."

"Postilious," shouted Charles Bertram, "drive on! A guinea a piece for you to make the first stage under the time. On—on—on!"

The whips cracked, and off rattled the carriage, despite the remonstrances of the officer, at a good ten miles an hour.

CHAPTER V.

NEWSPAPER REPORTS.—THE DEATH OF THE MAD WOMAN.—CHARLES BERTRAM'S LETTER TO THE CORONER.

WHAT a rich treat to the newspapers was the singular circumstances which had occurred at Charles Bertram's wedding. If they had but confined themselves a little to the truth in their statements concerning it, all might have been well; or if, indeed, they had been a little careful in getting the proper names.

One morning paper, far more remarkable for its insolent rascality and unblushing effrontery than any that ever existed, of course we mean the *Times*, named him Burton instead of Bertram, and the church St. Giles's instead of St. George's, and said it was at a funeral that the affair happened, and, of course, the affair itself was dreadfully mutilated. But still the paragraph went the round, creating much gossip, and preparing a great fund of trouble and uneasiness for the newly-wedded couple, when they should return from their month's banishment.

In a day or two, however, at the utmost, there occurred proceedings which forced the matter in a more correct light into the public prints, and the following paragraph in one of them met the eyes of Charles Bertram himself:—

"THE LATE MYSTERIOUS AFFAIR IN ST. GEORGE'S CHURCH.—We are informed, upon competent authority, that the woman who made so diabolical an attack upon Mr. and Mrs. Bertram, at St. George's Church, has never spoken or rallied since that period. She was removed to the infirmary of the New Prison upon a temporary remand, and, notwithstanding the utmost exertions of the medical officers, she expired yesterday evening, so that the affair remains enveloped in the same cloud of impenetrable mystery which from the first has enveloped it. We expect that at the inquest, which will take place to-morrow, at twelve o'clock, some light will be thrown on the affair."

It was with a feeling of immense satisfaction that Charles Bertram read this communication through the newspapers. The death of the woman put an end to a world of trouble, and saved him from the necessity of explanations of the most painfull character; for however it might be convenient for him, situated as he was, to say that the woman was mad, yet well he knew that there was a cause for her madness.

As regarded his young wife, he had easily succeeded in quieting her scruples, if she had any. She had been too much alarmed by the whole proceeding to know well what the woman had said, and Charles's assurance that he had never seen her before, and that she was really some maniac, quieted her completely, and she only wept for the danger he had encountered—a danger which, had it proved fatal, would at so strange a moment have made her a widow.

Had Margaret been a little more versed in the ways of the world, she might well have considered that the attack upon Charles was of much too premeditated a character to be really the result of that species of insanity which prompts its unhappy victim to commit desperate crimes. But she did not reason in such a way; and who could expect a young bride, in the first week of her marriage, to entertain injurious suspicions of him whom she had just sworn to love and honour? Therefore, as regarded his wife, Charles was under no apprehension; but up to the moment at which he read the most welcome news of the death of the mad woman, as he persited in calling her, he was in hourly dread of some communication from London, which would make his presence there quite of a compulsory nature. Now, however, he breathed again. Not only was the woman dead, but she had been so obliging as to die without making the elaborate communication which she might have made, and which it marred all the happiness of his present situation to think she might each moment be actually making.

Simultaneously with the receipt of the newspaper containing the welcome news of the death of the woman, he received a note summoning him to attend the inquest of the body, which, for a few minutes, filled him again with alarms; but soon he reasoned himself out of them by saying—

" Why should I be dragged all the way from Worthing to London to attend a coroner's inquest? I can say nothing about the cause of the woman's death, which I apprehend is the legitimate ground of inquiry. I know nothing of how she came to die. How preposterous to send for me."

Animated with these feelings, he made up his mind that he would not go, and he wrote a note to the coroner explaining that he could give no evidence with regard to the cause of the death of the person named to him in the summons which had been sent him. The name of the woman had been ascertained from some papers she had with her.

And now Charles thought he had settled the matter; but the coroner was not so easily set aside, and though he met the jury at the inquest, he made so long and stultified a speech about the coroner's court being treated with contempt, and all that sort of thing, that the inquisition was adjourned, in order that some proceedings or other might be taken, of which the jurors only had a very shadowy notion, but which they were assured were of an extremely dignified nature, and calculated, of course, (they knew that), to make a great row, and produce a great amount of newspaper controversy.

But then the coroner was one of those happy souls who, salamander-like, live best in a fire, and he gloried in being up to his ears—they were pretty long ones—in contentions, and botherations, and explanations, and that kind of thing, which, to a great man, is torment of the most tormenting character.

Charles Bertram daily heard of the adjournment of the inquiries, and expecting how he was about to be tormented, he made up his mind to a move, which, for the remainder of his month's stay from the metropolis, promised him peace, and an immunity from the importunities of the coroner. He resolved to proceed at once to Boulogne, which he did, having received the ready assent of his wife to the step; for what was it to her where he went, so long as she was pleased, and she was with him?

Along with this resolution, he adopted a rather wise one, which was not to take up an English Newspaper until he came back to London, and by such means he considered he had got the better of the officious coroner for Middlesex, and preserved the peace and security of his own honeymoon. It would certainly have been rather hard for a man to be tormented at such a time, because an official personage found a pleasure in being in a perpetual fidget.

To two or three of his friends in town he wrote, merely desiring that no more letters should be addressed to him at Worthing, for he was taking a short tour; and there the matter rested, for he had the prudence not to mention where he was going to any one who was at all likely to feel the least interest in it.

In order, however, to get at once rid of a matter which we must clear away to make room for far more important ones, we may as well at once state that, at the adjourned inquest, the coroner, finding that Charles Bertram did not come, made a ferocious speech, in which he embraced every political topic which had agitated the public mind for a long time past. He wished for another adjournment, but the jury was tired at being so bothered about an old woman, so they would not have it, but, in accordance with the medical testimony, returned a verdict of " died from natural causes."

It was satisfactorily proved by the surgeon that congestive apoplexy was the cause of death, so there ought to have been no difficulty in the matter, and clearly Charles Bertram was not wanted; but there are coroners who seem to have got hold of the crotchet in some way, that they have some judicial existence, and that their province is not merely and solely, as it really is, to inquire into the cause or causes of the death of any particular person.

Had Charles Bertram read the English papers, he would have found out all this; but still it was wise of him not to do so, for the jury might not have been so obstinate, in which case the coroner would have continued to keep the game alive for months, and would have been down upon Charles the moment he arrived, with the most ruthless amount of troublesomeness in the world.

Margaret scarcely ever again referred to the subject after the first day; she was perfectly satisfied that it all arose from one of those accidental hallucinations of a lunatic, which frequently induces them to pitch upon some person whom they have never seen before as their most ruthless enemy. She only considered it dreadful that Charles should have been placed in such dangerous circumstances, and trembled at the thought of his narrow escape from a violent death before her very face. And Charles, how he blessed his stars that he had united himself to one so innocent and guileless herself, that she suspected no wrong in others! How deeply he congratulated himself upon the confiding simplicity of his wife, and contrasted her conduct with what it might have been had she been of a scheming, suspicious nature.

"I shall be very happy with Margaret," he said to himself, "and it is far better that this affair should be over as it is, for now I am far from apprehensive regarding a circumstance which might sooner or later have made itself known and embittered my domestic happiness considerably."

All things, therefore, showed now to Charles Bertram their sunniest aspect; and the curse which had been so remorselessly hurled at his head by the infuriated woman on the threshold of the church, seemed to have been converted into a blessing.

CHAPTER VI.

THE RETURN TO LONDON.—THE MYSTERIOUS BOX AT CHARLES BERTRAM'S HOUSE.

To a resident in London probably nothing is more delightful than a temporary rustication—unless we except the return to the metropolis, after one has been absent from it some time, and become thoroughly ennuied with everything and everywhere else. So thought Charles Bertram, when, at the expiration of the month of seclusion, which tyrannical custom prescribes to a newly married couple, he found himself with his beautiful young wife *en route* for the metropolis.

It must not be said—for that would be decidedly unfair, because decidedly untrue—that Charles Bertram had begun to tire of the society of Margaret; on the contrary, the more he came to know her intimately, the more he found ample reason to admire new traits in her character, and to felicitate himself upon the possession of such a prize in the matrimonial lottery. Each day some new virtue seemed to spring up spontaneously in her mind, and not one ungenerous or unworthy thought seemed capable of entering her mind even for a moment. She was of that nature that she had no comprehension of chicanery or vice; she could not comprehend how people could make themselves so unhappy as not to strive to make others happy. Her pure heart and intellect rejected all selfishness; she knew nothing but what was good and great—she would know nothing else, and Charles Bertram had quite sufficient sense to see the character of his young bride, and to admire it. Whether he was a man fully to appreciate such a disposition, and to make the proper allowances which were sure to be called for in consequence of some of the mistakes which so purely natural and unsuspicious a character was almost sure to make, remains to be seen. It might be so, or it might not; but there was certainly a vein in the character of Mr. Bertram which only wanted a little working on to induce him to view with a jaundiced eye all those features in his wife's disposition which he at present looked upon as so many excellences.

But we must not anticipate. What we have to do with at present is the return to London of the newly-married couple, and a singular and most unexpectedly troublesome circumstance which occurred immediately upon their arrival, and which was enough to excite suspicion and observation even from Margaret.

The journey and partly voyage from Boulogne to London was performed with all convenient celerity, and towards the afternoon of a sultry day in June, the same travelling chariot which had conveyed Mr. and Mrs. Bertram from the door of St. George's church a month before with so much celerity, drove up to his own house, which was situated in a pleasant spot not a hundred miles from Hyde Park Corner.

Of course, he had taken measures to let his household know of his return to town, and the servants were all on the alert to give a proper reception to their new mistress. The servants of bachelors have, of course, a great objection to the aforesaid bachelors ever marrying, for such an event is very sure to make a serious change for the worse to them. But the mischief is not so great when the bride is young and amiable, for then she is disposed to be as agreeable as possible to all, and rather to bind together with firmer ties the household of him with whom she has united her fate, than to dismember it. But when, as will occasionally happen, the bride is of the managing order of women, who are never so delighted as when they can succeed in setting everybody by the ears, and, figuratively speaking, turning the house out of window, sad is the change indeed.

If, however, any one was likely to be a welcome addition to the house of Mr. Bertram, instead of a torment to it, that one was Margaret; for she had not only one of the best tempers, but a gentle and kindly consideration for all persons, be their rank in life what it might.

The first glance at her was sufficient to assure the servants they had no harsh or uncfeeling task-mistress to fear, and when she spoke in her mild, gentle way, they knew that all was right, and told each other that it was very prudent of "master," after all, and they didn't blame him a bit, although they had done nothing for a whole month but eat, and drink, and sleep, and blame him.

But it won't do to be too curious in looking for consistency in human nature; if we do we shall lose our pains, and the best way is to take whatever good comes, at the time it comes, thankfully, without tormenting ourselves or others with the question of why it came not before, or it if be consistent or not with something not so good that has gone before.

Margaret had never been to this house. She had always met Bertram at the house of a lady of the name of Ogden, who was a mutual friend, and who resided not far off. Now, therefore, her first step into Bertram's house was as its mistress, and she could not but admire the extremely tasteful manner in which it was furnished and decorated. And when she was shown a room which she was told to consider her own exclusively, and found it crammed with all sorts of little feminine luxuries and prettinesses, her eyes filled with tears of gratitude and pleasure, and turning to Charles, she said—

"And so you have thought of all this for me, dear Charles? Oh, how can I ever sufficiently thank you?"

"By taking immediate possession, Margaret," he said, gaily, "of all you see, for all is your own,"

There were such sweet vases crammed with rare flowers; such elegant and sparkling bijouterie; such pictures; such a desk of pearl, inlaid with silver—a work-box of the same material and workmanship; and such numberless other items, that with delighted ecstasy Margaret exclaimed—

"Oh, I shall be a whole year in finding out everything and knowing everything well; I'm sure I shall."

"And long before that time," said Charles, "I hope you will think of a hundred other things which will help to adore this apartment."

"It wants nothing, I'm sure, Charles. What else can possibly be placed in it? It is full of beauties—a most charming room; I shall keep it sacred from all common intrusion. Yourself only, dear Charles, and a very chosen few, indeed, shall ever penetrate to this apartment."

Charles smiled, and pressed a kiss on the lips of his beautiful wife, as he said—

"Be it so, dearest; as you please. You are the autocrat of this room, remember, and may do with it what you please."

"You are too good to me, Charles."

"That is impossible."

"You will spoil me, and make me like some too much fondled child—pettish, and a trouble to you."

"I have no fear of that, Margaret."

"I will be careful if I can, that it shall not be so; but it is your own fault if it be, Charles, you know, so you will not blame me."

"Certainly not, dear."

"Then I will be happy—so happy."

"And in being so, you make me happy. Now, dear Margaret, I am not a rich man, but yet I have enough for every comfort, as well as something to spare for prudence and for luxuries. My government appointment forms the basis of my income, and what I have beyond only consists of the interest of some money, which I have—notwithstanding a character my friends gave me for a little extravagance—managed to save. Besides, this house is my own. I tell you these things, dear, that you may feel yourself at ease as to your mode of living; and if you fancy any little elegancy, do not restrain yourself from its possession."

"I will have nothing, Charles, but what borrows an additional value from the fact of having been given to me by you."

"Nay, dearest, do not say so; I wish you to feel yourself, to as great an extent as possible, a free agent, and to have the consciousness that you have power of your own to indulge a few whims."

Charles smiled as he spoke, and Margaret knew that he attached no unkind meaning to the word whims."

"I shall not have any whims," she said. "You know, Charles, from necessity, I have been brought up frugally."

"Yes; and so will you enjoy the more what it is my greatest satisfaction to be able to place within your reach."

"Mine is, indeed, a happy, happy fate, Charles. How merrily and pleasantly will the term of our lives pass away. Surely, we shall know but few cares. All the essential elements of happiness appear to belong to us. Do you remember, Charles, the words of the mad woman?"

Bertram started and turned pale as he said—

"Why, Margaret, ever allude to so painful a subject?"

"Painful, Charles?"

"Yes—yes; I, of course, sympathise."

"Oh, yes; you are full of generous sympathies; but I only mentioned her because our state of happiness gave so strong a contradiction to the curse which her insanity gave utterance to."

"Yes—yes," said Charles, abstractedly, "yes."

"She said we should not know happiness for one year. I cannot but smile, Charles, at the idle prophecy. What is there to disturb our happiness?"

"What, indeed?"

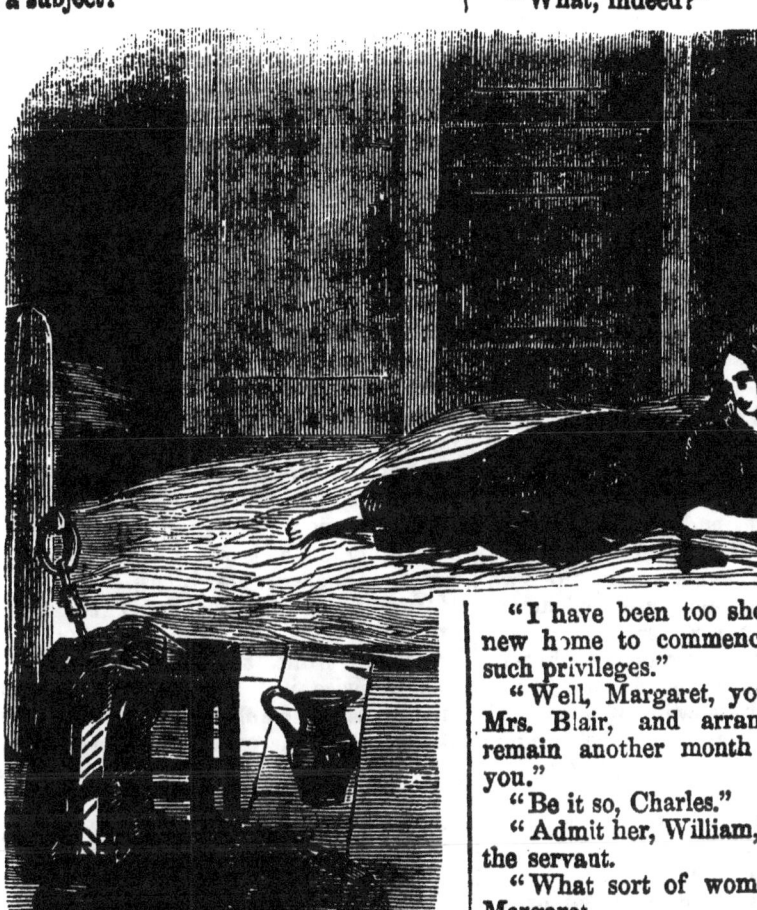

"Mrs. Blair," announced a servant at this juncture.

"Mrs. who?" said Margaret.

"Mrs. Blair, madam."

"Only my housekeeper—only my housekeeper," said Bertram. "A worthy soul—a very worthy soul. I gave her notice when I arrived that she must consider she was holding her situation, subject to your approval, and no doubt, worthy soul, she is fidgety to see you."

"Oh, Charles, I much regret you have done this."

"Why regret, dear?"

"I have been too short a time in my new home to commence the exercise of such privileges."

"Well, Margaret, you had better see Mrs. Blair, and arrange with her to remain another month on approval by you."

"Be it so, Charles."

"Admit her, William," said Bertram to the servant.

"What sort of woman is she?" said Margaret.

"Why, I consider her a very good sort of woman; but the only thing I do a little dislike is, too much religion."

"We will not blame her for that, Charles."

"Not blame her, but it is troublesome rather; but I believe she is perfectly sincere. You can judge for yourself. Here she comes."

CHAPTER VII.

THE HOUSEKEEPER.—A WOMAN OF SUPERIOR VIRTUE.—THE INTERVIEW.

Mrs Blair availed herself of the permission awarded and entered the room, and as she happens to be in our story rather an important personage, we think at once we had better place before our readers a full-length portrait of her.

She was rather above the ordinary height of women; her age was somewhere about forty; she was attired in black, a colour she always affected, and which, somehow or another, is considered quite the thing among evangelical people, who, of course, are all going to Heaven if no one else reaches there; therefore, it is quite surprising how gloomy they try to make themselves over a prospect which, if they really entertain it, ought to be one of the most delightful character.

Mrs. Blair was thin; she had no lips at all; there was a slit in her face which did for a mouth. There was about her eyes a constant quivering motion, as if she felt there was so much wickedness in the world that she was compelled to keep continually winking, so that she might not see it all. The expression of her face denoted wariness and close attention; some people would insist upon calling it cunning, but if she had claws, she, cat-like, knew how to hide them.

She always walked with a slow, gliding step, although she looked strong enough to step out like a grenadier, and no doubt she could, too, upon occasion. Her voice was low and gentle, and she assumed rather an air of timidity at times; whether that was a piece of hypocrisy or not, we shall have an ample opportunity of determining, as well as our readers.

When she entered the room she had in her hand something wrapped carefully in paper, and after the lowest of all possible curtsies to Margaret, she began quivering her eyelids according to custom, and said,—

"Madam, I put my trust in the Lord that he will grant you happiness."

"Thank you," said Margaret.

"If I might be so bold, madam, as to presume to present you with this small testimony of respect."

As she spoke, she took from the paper she had in her hand an elegantly-bound book of Common Prayer, which she placed before Margaret, who replied,—

"I accept your present with thanks."

Mrs. Blair turned up her eyes as if she had the capacity of seeing right through the ceiling, and so on up to Heaven without any difficulty, and said,—

"Madam, I am a poor sinner—a weak vessel, seeking divine grace, as best may; and I humbly hope I shall be able to do you good service, madam."

This was something of a feeler to know whether she was to remain or not, and Margaret understood it as such fully, as she replied at once, with the candour which formed so eminent a part of her disposition and habits of intercourse with every one,—

"Mr. Bertram has mentioned you to me Mrs. Blair, and I have but to echo your hope, uttered just now. Will you be so good as to remain with me one month from now, to see how we get on together?"

"Most certainly, madam; with the greatest pleasure. I hope the Lord will be merciful to us all."

To this pious observation Margaret did not think it at all necessary to reply; for, however much she esteemed her religion, she had that well grounded aversion, which every correct thinking person has, to having it and its cant phrases pulled in upon all occasions, and upon all subjects.

Charles Bertram glanced at his wife, as much as to say, "I told you so; she will worry you about religion," while Mrs. Blair bent her keen eyes upon the face of her new mistress, in order, if possible, to gather from her looks what sort of an impression she had succeeded in making upon her mind.

That, however, puzzled even the acute Mrs. Blair, for all she could see was a look of some confusion, arising, no doubt, from the conflicting feelings which at that moment found a home in her breast. Of course, Margaret was just the person to have as great reverence for religion as anybody breathing, while, at the same time, she was likewise just the one to have the greatest possible abhorrence of cant. The look of bewilderment, therefore, which she wore, and which really puzzled Mrs. Blair, was, in this case, from the difficulty she experienced in coming to a correct conclusion with regard to that personage.

It was not that Margaret suspected her of hypocrisy. No, she gave people always by far too much credit for their professions. but, as a downright matter of taste, she doubted if she could endure about her one who seemed to have a taste for conversing in Scripture phraseology, and to be so wedded to the terms only of religion.

Mrs. Blair never suspected for a moment that this was the subject of her young mistress's thoughts; she concluded immediately that her sincerity was doubted, and these two very different trains of thought into which she and Maagaret fell, was a striking illustration of the difference in their modes of thought and disposition generally.

"Well, Mrs. Blair," said Charles, who

saw there was an awkward pause, "we will consider that settled, if you please."

"Thank you, sir The grace of God be with you both There is one subject of arrangement, madam, which I cannot too soon mention to you. It lies near— very near to my heart."

"What is it?" said Margaret.

"Just to be allowed to attend an evening service on Wednesdays, as well as the morning service on Sundays."

"I daresay that can be arranged," said Margaret. "Of course, I am new to the economy of the household, and cannot tell so well, as I hope I shall soon be able, what can be done conveniently and consistently, and what cannot."

"Certainly not, madam; but I have known such grief in my day, madam, and now my only consolation will be in doing my duty by you, and preparing myself for another world."

"Exactly," said Charles, as he walked to the window.

Margaret did not know what to say.

"Those, madam," added Mrs. Blair, "will be my only two considerations— my earthly tie, and my heavenly tie."

"Yes," said Margaret, and she turned over the leaves of a book.

"I have now the honour, madam, of bidding you good-day."

"Good-day."

"The blessings of Providence be upon you, madam."

"Thank you."

Mrs. Blair bowed herself out, and when she was gone, Charles said,—

"You see, my dear, that Mrs. Blair, though an extremely useful woman in the house, is dreadfully evangelical."

"Do not say dreadfully, Charles."

"Well, but she is."

"She seems a very religious woman; but if she has, as she says, and, therefore, no doubt she has, seen a great deal of misfortune, we cannot wonder at her seeking consolation where alone it is to be found by persons so unhappily situated."

"Well, if you like her ——"

"If I like her, Charles? Nay, I cannot discharge a woman because she is religious. That would be most uncharitable."

"It would look so."

"And would be so, Charles, as well as looking so. Mrs. Blair will, no doubt, soon find out that I am averse to the use of such phrases and expressions, and then, when talking to me, she will discontinue them."

"Very likely."

"So we shall get on very well together."

Margaret was not aware that Mrs. Blair had already made the discovery that the style of conversation she had commenced was unpalatable. The moment she got fairly outside the door a remarkable change came over her countenance, and between her clenched teeth she muttered—

"And this is what I have been toiling for, is it? To be told I may stay a month upon liking. She does not like the religious gag. That won't do with her. I cannot drop it all at once; but I can, and will, gradually. It will go hard with me, indeed, if I cannot find out some weak point in her character. Adulation is sure to have some effect upon all."

So saying, the politic Mrs. Blair, who, it will be seen, had some rather stupendous designs of her own to accomplish, walked off to her own room; but on the road she met one of the servants, a mere girl, and to her she spoke in a tone of voice more like that of a boatswain of a man-of-war, than the humble, devout Christian she had appeared to be so short a time before.

"What are you about?" she cried.

"I've been to dust the dining-room," was the reply.

"And how dare you go sneaking about the house without my orders?"

"Sneaking, ma'am?"

"Yes, sneaking. I say, how dare you? But I know your motive. You want to meet your new mistress, and curry favour with her."

"Lor, Mrs. Blair. I——"

"Peace! Don't answer me. Go away with you to the kitchen, and do your work directly."

The terrified girl obeyed her, and slunk away, after which Mrs. Blair retired to her own room, and drew the bolt in the inside of her door, a precaution she always adopted. Scarcely had Charles and his wife had time to make the few remarks they had to each other, when they were doomed to another interruption, and a servant, after obtaining admission into the room, said—

"Beg pardon, sir; but it's my fault."

"What do you mean?"

"About the great box, sir."

"The what?"

"The chest, sir. I've had it moved into the library now, sir. It was left a fortnight and more ago by your orders, sir. It was to be put in the library, and nobody was to dare to touch it, sir. It's there, and quite safe. I forgot to mention it to you, sir, before. Beg pardon, sir."

"Why, this is inexplicable to me. I sent no box. I know nothing of any box. What on earth, man, are you talking about? You must be dreaming. I sent no box to the house at all, of any sort, large or small."

CHAPTER VIII.

THE CONTENTS OF THE BOX.—A MYSTERY. THE SOLUTION OF IT BY BERTRAM.

BERTRAM and his wife looked at each other with surprise depicted on their countenances, for neither of them had the least idea of what the servant was alluding to, when he mentioned a great chest as having been left at the house.

"A chest !" said Bertram.

"A chest !" echoed his wife.

"Yes, sir ; it's below. I assure you, sir, nobody has touched it. No one would presume to do so."

"But I know nothing whatever about it," he said. "What on earth can I want with a great chest? It's some mistake altogether, I am positive."

"No, sir. It is properly addressed to you, and there can, therefore, be no mistake."

"Charles," said Mrs. Bertram, "perhaps it may contain some present from a friend on account of your marriage, you know."

"I do not think so. Presents on such occasion do not usually require a large chest to hold them. But we are like people who receive a letter in a handwriting which is unknown to them, and waste time in wondering from whom it has come, when to open it would at once solve the seeming mystery."

"True ; and, therefore, let us go now and open the chest, which has come here so mysteriously."

A strange feeling of apprehension, he knew not why or wherefore, crept over Mr. Bertram as he went to the room in which was placed the chest. It seemed to him as if something very sad and serious were about to happen. An undefinable terror was slowly but yet surely creeping over him, and by the time he got to the apartment, he was pale and anxious, and much wished that he had not been so ready to propose the opening of the mysterious box, but had adopted some mode of postponing that operation until he was alone.

"You look ill, Charles," said his wife.

"Ill—ill !"

"Yes ; you are pale, and you tremble."

"Why should I ? This is all your own imagination, I assure you. I—I never was better in all my life. You are much deceived, if you fancy I am ill."

"And so glad to be deceived," said Mrs. Bertram, as she hung upon his arm, and looked fondly in his face. "So very glad, Charles, to be deceived on such a point, that I hope whenever such an idea crosses my mind, you will be always able truthfully to tell me how very wrong I am in my conjecture."

"You should not mark," said Bertram, "little trifling alterations of apearances. They may arise in the most healthy people. But I was thinking, Margaret——"

"Thinking what, Charles?"

"That, after all, as this chest most likely is left here by some strange mistake, and is not at all intended for me, that—that it would be as well to leave it alone."

"Not to open it?"

"Exactly. Not to open it."

"But, then, it may be intended for you; and how foolish it will appear to have a chest in the house, properly addressed to you, but the contents of which you know not. These contents, too, may be extremely interesting."

"Yes, but ——"

"Nay, now, Charles, I am not curious —although it is by you men imputed to us as a fault of our sex—but I own I should like to know what is in the chest."

"Of course, but——"

"Now, do not argue against it. Who knows but some letter of thanks to a kind riend for some very handsome present may be due?—and could you bear that any one should think you wanting in common courtesy?"

"What if there were danger in opening the box?"

"Danger?"

"Yes ; I have heard of such things as explosive mixtures being placed in boxes, so that the moment they were opened, by some diabolical means, the mixture would explode and kill, or perhaps at all events seriously injure the parties who were near at hand.'

"Oh, I will myself chance it, and open the chest."

"Well—well, if you must open it you must ; but I think it would be as well to leave it alone."

"Do not say so. I could not sleep a wink for thinking of it, it so unsolved a mystery were in the house,— not that I am curious at all, only I do like, Charles, to know everything if I possibly can."

They were in the room where the mysterious chest had been placed. It was large, although of a coarse, common style of manufacture. It was clasped at the corners with iron, and seemed to possess considerable strength. On the lid was a card, nailed firmly down, upon which was written, in a clear and unmistakable hand, the name and address of Charles Bertram.

"Yes, I see, but we shall have to break it open."

"What matters? It is locked, certainly, but, from the appearance of the lock, I should say but a small amount of force was sufficient to break it."

Still Charles hesitated, but his wife's curiosity was fairly aroused, and she insisted upon the chest being broken open. A chisel was procured, and with a hand that slightly trembled, Charles Bertram proceeded to break open the mysterious chest which had been brought to his house. What it could contain, he had not the remotest idea, and yet that it was something calculated to give him uneasiness, he felt assured, although why he so felt assured, was as mysterious a matter as the chest itself.

There are, however, some things which, although we have no direct evidence of them, come across the mind with the most marvellous distinctness notwithstanding, and we are able to say positively of what complexion a circumstance is likely to be, while we are in ignorance of what it is likely actually to consist of.

So it was with Charles Bertram; he had a notion—a kind of presentiment, or fore-knowledge—that the contents of that box would not be pleasant to him, although what they were, he had no more idea of than his wife. Besides, too, there was one state of things which probably helped most materially to infuse uneasy sensations into Charles Bertram's mind. He was unhappily, both for himself and all dependent on him, one of those

"Whose conscience with injustice is corrupted;"

he had not a clean breast. He knew he had done foul wrong, and, therefore, he had become a victim to that mental cowardice which besets all men who have the curse of such a consciousness.

Hence, then, might he well tremble at the solution of any mystery, for he could not know but it might have reference to a dark page in the past history of his actions which he never could obliterate from his memory. How different were the feelings of his wife as regarded the mysterious box. In her mind dwelt no sentiments off self-reproach. Her life had been blameless, and, therefore, curiosity was the only feeling she had as regarded the af-

fair. As she had said, it took but very little time or trouble to force that lock open. It was one of the commonest, and when the leverage power of the chisel was applied to it, it gave way almost on the instant.

"You see, Charles, there is no explosion," said his wife.

"No—no—no explosion."

"Come, raise the lid. How tantalising you are. Why don't you raise the lid?"

"I am raising it, Margaret, as quickly as I can. One screw holds it yet. There, it is free."

Mrs. Bertram herself assisted in raising the lid of the box, and their curiosity was not much gratified, for all that appeared immediately within was a quantity of straw and hay packed down very close.

"Oh, it is a hoax altogether," said Charles, in a tone of great relief; "it is some foolish jest of an acquaintance, who probably thought the occasion of my marriage a good one to get up a laugh against me."

"Do you think so?"

"Yes, indeed. Now, see what a litter you are making, Margaret, by pulling out all that hay. Surely there is no occasion to scatter it."

"There is something beneath it."

"Something beneath it!" said Charles, with a look of dismay. "What—what, Margaret, is beneath it?"

"Good Heavens! what is this?" said Mrs. Bertram, as she took from the hollow of the chest some black crape tied up curiously, "what is this?"

"That!" said Charles, who was as much surprised as she could be; "I really have no idea."

"Why, Charles, it is the sort of thing that is put on people's hats at a funeral. And here, too, here is a black cloak, likewise a funeral garment. How cruel of any one to send such appendages as these now to us."

"A—a black cloak?"

"Yes, look. A long *black mantle*, such as is only worn by the mourners at a funeral. Here, too, are black gloves. There is nothing wanting. Oh, Charles, Charles, what can be the meaning of all this?"

"I know no more than you do yourself, Margaret."

"But surely, dear Charles, there must be some special cause why these things are sent to you."

"I know not. Some people are fond of doing such things, and have no other reason than what can be found in their own mad caprice."

"Ah! A letter."

"A letter?"

"Yes. At the bottom of the box, and addressed to you. Now, Charles, we shall know all about it. Well, I am glad whoever has sent these dismal insignia of the tomb has likewise condescended to send an explanation."

"A—a letter?"

"Yes, Charles; you stand as if stupified. What has come over you, Charles? A letter, you perceive, and addressed to yourself. Shall I open it?"

"No—no—no."

This proposal seemed at once to have restored Charles to a consciousness of his situation, and he eagerly possessed himself of the letter.

"I should not," said his wife, "open a letter of yours, without leave, Charles, you may be assured."

She spoke in a slight tone of reproach, for he had rudely snatched the letter from her hands.

"I—I know you would not, Margaret," he said. "Excuse my seeming abruptness; but I was so lost in thought to know what all this could mean, that I knew not at the moment what I did. You will excuse me?"

"Excuse you, Charles? Ah, do not humiliate me by asking me so to do. Can I be angry with you?"

"No—no—no. I will read to you the letter. This room is rather dark."

Under pretence of getting more light, Charles Bertram moved to the window and opened the letter. The moment his eye fell upon the writing, he changed colour, and trembled so excessively that he could scarcely hold the epistle.

"What is it, Charles?"

He muttered something, and then, in a louder tone, he said—

"Nothing—nothing. I will read it to you, Margaret. See if there is anything else in the box, and I will read the letter to you."

"Nothing else, Charles."

"Now, invention assist me," he said, in a low tone. to himself, and then he began—

"HONOURED SIR,—As my poor master, Mr. Augustus Beam, is no more, and as he expressed an earnest, though odd wish, on his death-bed, that some one as your representative should follow him to the grave, I got a gentleman to do so. In my master's will it was ordered that each guest should be purchased a suit of mourning habiliments, consisting of a black mantle, hat-band, gloves, &c., and

as these have been paid for, as for you, I herewith forward them, considering that by so doing I am in the best manner fulfilling my poor deceased master's wishes. Permit me to subscribe myself, sir—"Your most obedient and humble servant,

"JOHN STOKES."

"There," said Charles Bertram, "now it is accounted for, you see, my dear, satisfactorily."

"Satisfactorily," repeated Mrs. Bertram, abstractedly.

"Yes, at least clearly, if not satisfactorily. My old acquaintance, Beam, was always an eccentric man. The idea, now, of sending me these things."

"It was foolish of the servant. He writes a tolerable letter, though."

Mrs. Bertram naturally held out her hand for the epistle as she spoke, which now having been read to her could be no secret; but Charles crumpled it up into his hand, and then thrust it into his pocket, saying—

"Let the matter drop. Let it drop, Margaret. It is not deserving of your consideration. Pray, say no more about it."

"And these things?"

"Throw them into the box again, and let it be put in some spare room, or closet, out of the way. As they are gifts from my old friend, Beam, I will keep them. Imagination only can invest them with disagreeables, for, after all, they consist but of crape and some few yards of black cloth."

"They are gloomy things to have in the house."

"But they need never meet our eyes. I know that there is a spare room, if not two, above stairs; let them be stowed away there, box and all, and we will banish the affair from our memories altogether, Margaret, and think of happier things."

"I wish they had not been sent."

"And so do I. But having been sent, we will not be so foolish as to allow them to have any effect upon us."

"No. And yet, how odd, Charles, that our marriage should be visited by two circumstances of a strange, and almost, what many people would think, an ominous nature."

"Indeed! Two circumstances?"

"Yes. There was that dreadful curse which was launched at your head on the church steps."

"Oh!" cried Charles with a forced laugh. "By the mad woman, you mean. I—I had really forgotten her, Margaret, quite. To be sure, there is the mad woman's curse."

"Could you foget it?"

"At least, when I say forget, I mean that it had quite ceased to make any impression upon me."

"But still, Charles, it was an incident full of discomfort to me. I could not for days banish it for a moment from my mind. And now, to add to uncomfortable recollections, here comes a suit of funeral clothing to the house."

"Disagreeable little coincidences, certainly," said Charles Bertram; "but only capable of borrowing importance from our superstitions or our fears. If we defy, as well as we may, such matters, they are at once conquered. What is there to make us unhappy? We are both young—we have means sufficient for all the comforts of life, and for very many of its luxuries —we love each other; and what, then, dear Margaret, can make us possibly unhappy?"

"Oh! Charles," said Margaret, as she threw herself into his arms; "the last item in your list of advantages and aids to happiness, is the only one I value."

"It is the most valuable."

"It is that, without which all others would be as nothing. True love is an impenetrable shield against all the shafts of fate. With truth and love towards each other, we may defy all and every evil that can assail us."

"I think we may, Margaret; so we will think no more of the box, and the black mantle which it contains; and now, as the London season is getting advanced, we had better at once set about leaving our cards at the houses of those with whom we intend to be on friendly terms."

"Yes, Charles, we will not have a host of visitors, not one in twenty of whom cares for us, or we for them. Let us try to get together a select few whom we can really esteem."

"Very good, Margaret. I am no advocate for crowds in one's house."

"Nor I; and the mock civility which entertains people whom we either are indifferent to, or positively dislike, shall find no home with us; we will not descend to such hypocrisy."

"I am glad to hear you are so much of my opinion, Margaret; if there be any one thing more than another which a man is entitled to do, without question it is to invite who he pleases, and to exclude who he pleases from his house."

"Unquestionably. We may despise the caprice which makes one man the favourite of a day, and then another; but consistent exclusion, and consistent invitation, is one of the things which is in every way and shape thoroughly correct and defensible."

"And now, my dear, that we understand each other upon this point," said Charles, "I am going to ask a favour of you."

"A favour of me?"

"Yes, Margaret; I want you to choose something for me to-day or to-morrow."

"What, Charles?"

"A carriage."

"Oh! what a favour, Charles! 'Tis I am favoured. Oh! how can I ever hope —how can I ever expect to be able to repay you for all the advantages you have given me? I, who was poor, friendless, and unhappy, to be lifted up to your state—to have so much bestowed upon me by you?"

"You repay it now at once," said Charles, "by professing this sense of it. All I wish of you, Margaret, is, to appreciate your new condition—to enjoy it—to feel all its advantages, and to present to me ever a cheerful face."

"And that I shall ever do, because it will be a true and faithful index of the mind."

*   *   *   *

"Indeed, indeed," muttered Mrs. Blair, the housekeeper, as she glided from the door where she had been listening. "Indeed—a-hem! we shall see—we shall see what will happen in due time—cheerful indeed!"

CHAPTER IX.

THE REAL LETTER OF THE MYSTERIOUS BOX.—THE VISITOR.—THE PROJECTED ENTERTAINMENT.

It was rather clever of Charles Bertram. People don't know what they can do till the emergency arises when they are compelled to do it. But we say it was rather clever of him to compose off-hand a fictitious letter, and appear to read it to his unsuspecting wife, when the epistle he really held in his hand was a very different affair.

While, however, we give Charles Bertram credit for the full amount of talent requisite to accomplish such a feat, we will not forget likewise the amount of duplicity it required to undertake it at all.

That he could so deliberately deceive his young, trusting, and affectionate wife, is not a favourable trait in Charles Bertram's character; perhaps, if the matter had been argued with him, he would sophistically grounded his exculpation upon the fact, real or presumed, that it was all for the best.

There, however, we differ from him, because we are quite certain, from experience in many cases, that the truth never does half the mischief that a concealment of it invariably does, sooner or later, let that concealment be caused by as elaborate and talented a lie as ever passed the lips of man.

Charles Bertram was making himself miserable, because he had a secret. He felt that such was the fact, and yet he never dreamt of adopting the most obvious remedy in the world, namely, the getting rid of the secret. It was, too, a secret which women readily forgive—a secret which a woman, really loving her husband, would certainly hear with pain, but which had far—far better come from his lips than any one elses, and that it might come from some one elses there was always a chance.

The curse which had been launched upon his head on the church steps was the curse of a bereaved mother, whose daughter had died a victim of the unbridled passions of Charles Bertram. He had been the seducer of innocence. Certainly it was not a necessary consequence of such an act that his victim should die, but she had died, and the mother coupled the death with the previous distressing knowledge of her child's shame, and said she wished all to be visited on the head of Charles Bertram, who was certainly the primary cause.

Now, if he had had the courage to tell his wife that, before he knew her, which was the case, he had contracted a liason with one whom he had found reason to desert, Mrs. Bertram might certainly have heard the intelligence with a pang of disagreeable feeling, but she would have forgiven him, and then any more ill-natured version of the story that might have been attempted to be given her by another would have been stopped at once by her declaration that she knew all about it.

This course, however, Bertram had not moral courage to adopt. Perhaps the man who would have had sufficient mind and active power of reflection to do so, would have never had occasion to confess such an amount of criminality at all.

Certain was it, though, that Charles Bertram possessed a mind not of sufficiently high order to enable him to grasp at any great results, and beyond the concealment of anything he had done, he could not get.

As soon as he found an opportunity, he now, in the solitude of his own room, reproduced the letter he had crumpled up so hastily from the eyes of his wife. He spread it carefully before him, and dreading each moment some interruption, he read it as it really was, and not as he had pretended it was to his wife. It was as follows, and no wonder that each word of it sent a pang like a barbed arrow to his breast—

"CHARLES,—If I had wanted to inflict pain upon you, I should not have written this letter. If my object had been that you should suffer pangs of conscience on my account, I should have not written to you. But I have another, and, I hope, a better motive, Charles. I wish to console and to comfort you.

"These may sound strange words as coming from me to you, but yet are they true ones. I have pictured to myself what you must surely endure when you hear that I am gone. You cannot be wholly destitute of conscience That is surely an impossible state. I have heard generous sentiments come from your lips, Charles, and they could not have been feigned. By the time you receive this, I shall be no more. My mother has promised that, sealed up as I shall seal it, it shall be delivered to you when I am dead.

"And now, Charles, for the pang I wish to spare you. Do not accuse yourself of my death. Early in life, incipient consumption showed itself in me. I am dying of that disease. Think so, Charles, and comfort yourself with that thought.

"It was cruel to make me love you, and then cast me from you for ever. It was very cruel; but do not accuse yourself of my death, Charles. Remember, I die of consumption. My mother will have it that your conduct towards me has broken my heart, and, in the bitterness of a mother's grief, she may come to you when I am no more, and reproach you.

"Oh, Charles! as a last and an only favour, let me implore you to be kind to her—not to speak to her harshly—to tell her you regret me. Endeavour to soothe, for remember, that whatever she may say to you is wrung from the bitter anguish of a mother's bereaved heart.

"May you be happy, Charles; happier far than you might have been with me, even had you redeemed every promise which I was weak enough to listen to and believe. If my forgiveness—a forgiveness not offered for the purpose of contrasting my sense of virtue with your conduct, but in pure sincerity—can bring you comfort, you have it. I pronounce it on my deathbed, and I pray to the great God, who sees all hearts, likewise to forgive you.

"Do not, therefore, let this letter sound like a reproach. Do not fancy it is one; but believe it to be, and accept it as it really is, an endeavour to place you upon better terms with yourself than you might otherwise be upon hearing of the death of one you said you loved, and then left to shame, to want, and to despair. These few words come from

"EMMA."

Charles Bertram read this note through three times before he could make up his mind to withdraw his eyes from the letters of which it was formed. Then, with a deep groan, he looked up, and there was an expression for a few moments upon his face of bitter agony. It was an agony he well deserved to feel; for woe—woe be to him, the de-

sure to come for his iniquity, had not before reached him, it surely had begun to do so now.

He groaned again and again, and then sinking into the chair he had so recently quitted, and covering his face with his hands, he gave himself up, for about a quarter of an hour, to a gloomy retrospect of the past. He saw, in his mind's eye, the beautiful creature, whom he could not conceal from himself, by any kind, or by any amount of sophistry, he had sent to an early grave. He saw her, as when first he saw her, radiant with cheerfulness, and with the roseate hue of health upon her cheeks, and then, in the bitterness of his heart, he cried—

"What is she now? what is she now?"

It was a fearful question. What is she now, but the pale, awful-looking tenant of the grave? The thought was horrible, and Charles Bertram buried both his hands in his hair, as he exclaimed, despairingly—

ceiver, who could light up the flame of love in some pure and innocent heart, to the destruction of honour and happiness. Woe—woe be to him, the despoiler, who appreciates beauty, virtue, excellence, and happiness, but to destroy them.

Charles Bertram rose from the chair on which he had been sitting, and staggered to and fro across the room for some minutes, in a state of mind which beggars all description. If the retribution which, sooner or later, was

"Oh, that I were dead!"

Then he sprang to his feet as if he had suddenly been shot, for there was an attempt made by some one on the outside to undo the door, which he had had the prudence, at all events, to lock, before sitting down to the perusal of that most agonizing letter. He flew to a looking-glass, and glanced hastily at it, before he would venture to ask who was there. There was a frightful alteration in his face. The traces of mental suffering he had endured for the last half hour were plainly visible there, and he dreaded that they should meet the eye of his wife.

"Be calm—be calm," he muttered. "Be calm, Bertram, be calm—be calm."

He took the letter hastily from the table, and replaced it in his pocket. Then he gathered courage to move towards the door, at the handle of which another attempt had been made, and to say—

"Who's there?"

"Oh, dear, sir," said the voice of Mrs. Blair, the housekeeper, "I beg your pardon."

He advanced and opened the door.

"Do you want me, Mrs. Blair?"

"Oh, it's of no consequence, sir; I hope I have not disturbed you at all, sir?"

"Not at all. What is it?"

"I wished, sir, to go to tea with my sister."

"Oh, I dare say Mrs. Bertram will spare you."

"Oh, dear me, I ought to have gone to her, of course; but I have been so much in the habit of respecting you, sir, that I came naturally to your superior mind. I do hope, sir, that you will be very happy. You ought to be, sir. A person of your great attainments, as I always said, deserves a wife among a thousand, and one who can thoroughly appreciate you."

"Thank you—thank you."

"Shall I take my orders from Mrs. Bertram, sir?"

"Yes, of course."

"Very good, sir; but when anything should require a superior mind to give the direction about, I hope I shall not make you angry by coming to you, sir?"

There is not one man out of a thousand who could withstand so very artfully contrived an appeal to that personal vanity which every individual possesses, to a greater or a less degree, and Charles Bertram was not the man to be proof against so nicely and delicately insinuated a compliment.

"Of course," he said; "I shall be very happy at any time to hear anything you may please to say."

"Sir, I feel very much obliged to you. I consider it quite an honour to do anything for you, and quite a privilege, of which I ought to be proud, to be allowed to speak to you."

"Well—well, Mrs. Blair, we will not quarrel about that. Of course, I wish you to treat Mrs. Bertram with every respect."

"Of course, sir, I will, for your sake. If Mrs. Bertram, sir, were a very troublesome person indeed, and very ill-tempered, and far behind you in intellect, I should, for your sake, treat her with marked respect, sir, always."

So saying, Mrs. Blair bowed herself out of the room, and it was not until she reached her own apartment that she suffered the faintest smile to pass her lips. Then it was but a very faint one, and she proceeded to equip herself for the visit she intended to pay to her sister, and which she was now resolved to pay without consulting Mrs. Bertram, and if there should be anything said about it, she intended to defend herself by saying that she considered Mr. Bertram had given her leave.

It is quite possible for a domestic, if at all admitted to the least familiarity of discourse, to poison the peace of a whole family; and many a woman, such as Mrs. Blair, has not only made a house too unhappy for any honest servant to remain in it, but has actually succeeded in parting husband and wife.

How far Mrs. Blair will succeed in her machinations against the innocent wife of Charles Bertram, remains to be seen. That she considered her an interloper, and treated her accordingly, is a fact that cannot be disputed; and as Mrs. Blair was a very religious woman, when she did hate anybody she went to an extreme; for as it is a fundamental part of the belief of evangelical people that, for being hard of belief on any particular point of doctrine which it requires a capacious swallow to get down, anybody may be subjected to the trifling punishment of being burnt on a gridiron for countless ages, it is a poor affair in comparison to hate anybody, and wish and attempt to inflict upon them as much misery as possible in this world for the most trifling offences.

Hence do we consider such doctrines, and such blasphemous assertions against Heaven, as that eternal punishment can be inflicted upon any one, as most mischievous; and, while we wield a pen, we shall never let slip a fair opportunity of declaiming against the horrible, brutal, ignorant, and demoralizing superstition which asserts the existence of a devil.

* * * *

This little conversation which Charles had had with Mrs. Blair had restored him to something of his usual equanimity and usual looks, so that he was not afraid now to meet his wife, whose inquiring glance, dictated as it was by affection, would have at once seen the disorder of his mind, had she, instead of his housekeeper, been the person to come to his room.

Fortunately for him, Charles, Mrs. Bertram was engaged with a visitor, who had called upon her with the licence of an old friend, to congratulate her upon her arrival in town, and her prospects of happiness.

This visitor was a lady of the name of Ogden, and a more amiable or good-hearted creature could not have been found in all the world, although we hope there are many like her in mind.

Mrs. Ogden was not good-looking —she was not young. Having lost her husband very shortly after marriage, she had been compelled, with a very small income, to eke out a living in the best way she could, by the aid of such accomplishments as she possessed. Chance had made her acquainted with Mrs. Bertram before the marriage of the latter, and now she called to see her with, to the full, as much pleasure at the prospect of her happiness as if her own had been equally, to all appearance, as well in every respect assured.

In the society of this excellent friend the hours passed rapidly away, and Charles's absence was not commented upon. Hence was it that he had had ample time to read the letter, and to get over the first flush of suffering which it had brought to his mind.

He and Mrs. Ogden were acquainted, for that lady had offered facilities to the meeting of the young people before their marriage, so that when Charles entered the room and found her there, he considered it quite a fortunate circumstance, as it diverted his wife's attention, and made her less likely to see any traces of his recent agitation still in his countenance.

Mrs. Ogden was a little garrulous, and now she began with some degree of volubility to speak to Charles concerning his mode of life, and the happiness he was sure to enjoy with such a companion as Margaret.

"Well, Mr. Bertram," she said, "now have you not found out that the day of your marriage has been the dawn of your happiness?"

"I am making no complaints," said Bertram, with a smile that sat but clumsily upon his countenance.

"As yet, he means," added his wife, laughing. "What he may make is quite another thing."

"Complaints!" cried Mrs. Ogden; "I should like to hear him make any complaints, indeed. Nonsense. But I do believe in my heart that men never know when they are well off."

"I believe that, too," said Bertram, "with one exception."

"And that——"

"Is myself. I am well off, and I know it, and fully appreciate it. Some of these days, Mrs. Ogden, I shall quite surprise you by writing some ode in praise of matrimony, which shall excel anything of the kind ever attempted."

"Was anything of the kind ever attempted?" said Mrs. Bertram, archly. "I thought all the odes went on the other side of the question."

"Well, and so they do, my dear," said Mrs. Ogden; "and the shameful quantity of both prose and poetry that is launched against the married state is a disgrace to civilised society."

"So it is—so it is," said Charles.

"Then do you be chivalrous, and

take up the lance on the other side. A married man might be listened to."

" And why not an unmarried one ? "

" Can you ask? Just see what a look of contempt a married man always casts upon a boy in love."

" True—true."

" It is indeed true. But, by-the-bye, Mrs. Bertram—how odd it does sound to me to call her Mrs. Bertram—talks about your buying a carriage."

" We intend starting something on wheels," said Bertram.

" Well, you know best—but just remember what expenses you may have, that's all."

" Expenses !"

" Yes, to be sure. You will find half-a-dozen little Bertrams will consume bread and butter enough to run a pair of coach horses, and that jackets and frocks will swallow up a carriage."

" Now, really, Mrs. Ogden," said Mrs. Bertram, " do not accumulate our possibilities at the rate of six to one."

" I think," said Bertram, " that half-a-dozen such liabilities would make me pull a face as long as Guy Fawkes in the pantomime last year."

" Do you, indeed ?"

" I am sure of it."

" Ah, but," said Mrs. Ogden, " only consider what a number of pretty little incidents will then disturb the dull monotony of the day. You will be sitting down upon slices of bread and butter on the drawing-room chairs; treading on marbles on the staircase, and so rolling from top to bottom, on the principle of the patent castors. Then there's the measles and the hooping-cough, and the whole family of rashes, of one sort and another. And then——"

" I cry you mercy !" said Charles ; " pray have done; and remember you never said anything of this beforehand, Mrs. Ogden."

" Certainly not."

" Then it was very disingenuous of you, indeed."

Mrs. Ogden laughed, and so did Mrs. Bertram, and Mr. Bertram himself tried a laugh, but the letter of " Emma " was in his pocket, and it weighed down his spirits like a lump of lead.

" I will put it away somewhere," he thought to himself,—" I will put it away somewhere !" And he glided from the room, just as his wife began to tell Mrs. Ogden all about the mysterious box, and its still more mysterious contents.

————

CHAPTER X.

THE REFLECTIONS OF GUILT.—THE VISIT TO THE HORRIBLE LODGING OF THE SEDUCED.

CHARLES BERTRAM determined at first upon destroying the letter, but there came over him inexplicably a dread of doing so, he knew not why. He trembled more at the thought of consigning that reproachful note to the flames, than he did at retaining it. He could almost fancy that the voice of destiny spoke distinctly to him, saying,—

" Destroy that letter, and some more terrible retribution will await you."

This was an impression solely attributable to his nervousness, and guilt is always nervous and full of trepidation, such as never, under any circumstances, can assail the breast of the innocent. Oh, what would he not have given now to recall that episode in his existence, which had begun in all the wild delirium of guilty passion, to end in lawless triumph over an innocent and virtuous heart, and in the death of one who ought, beneath the sunniest skies of Heaven, to have lived long and happily, blessed herself, and blessing, by the benign influence of a thousand excellences and virtues, all around her. But who can recall the past ? Oh, what millions of changes would take place, if the footsteps of a mortal career could be again trodden—if we could each of us, with the acquired experience of a life, be but gifted with the glorious tenure of an ability to commence again existence.

What mistakes of judgment we could then rectify—what errors of feeling we could set all right then—what objects of former pursuit and ambition would be thrown aside as worthless now in the possession, and what new and glorious ones would we take to our hearts as cherished guests. But such may not be, and Charles Bertram is not the only one, by millions, who, in the hour of distress and misery, arising from a consciousness of wrong, has exclaimed, with an anguish only such can feel,—

"If that I could retrace those steps which I have trodden—if that I could undo and blot out for ever from the page of human history those actions, the results of which will haunt me to the grave's brink, and even beyond that —yes, beyond that may I look for the retribution of a life to come—that retribution which, although it may be but of a negative character, is still terrible to reflect upon."

The room into which he went with an intention of destroying the note was quite dark, with the exception of the small flickering light which danced upon its walls from a fire that was in it. The season, although sufficiently advanced to enable any one to have reasonable hopes of dispensing with any means of procuring artificial heat, was still sufficiently bleak and cold towards the evenings to induce the indulgence of a fire in one room of the house, at all events, which could be sought if occasion required, and it was to this apartment which Charles Bertram repaired, with the ostensible motive of burning the soul-harrowing epistle of his victim. Now he stood pale and irresolute in that dimly-illuminated room, with the letter in his hand, and twice he asked himself, in a half choking whisper,—

"Dare I burn it? Dare I burn it?"

A voice as from the tomb seemed to answer him in the negative, and slowly he folded it up again, and turned from the fire, as he said in a solemn whisper,—

"No, no—I—I will keep it, but in some secret place. I will keep it—and, oh Heavens, let it be punishment enough for me that I shall think of it when joy is sparkling at my heart, and dash from my lips the cup of happiness. Let it be punishment enough, that when delicious music is sounding in my ears, I shall think of this letter, and turn the sweetest sounds to discord and to harshness. Oh, let it be punishment enough for me to think of it when the soft kiss of affection is resting on my cheek."

With a deep groan he let his head drop upon his breast, and for some moments he stood like a man upon the verge of eternity, which he was to reach through some dreadful means, which cowed his spirit, and oppressed any mental energy he might otherwise have possessed to enable him to meet his doom as became a man. He raised his eyes suddenly, and in the dim light, which only reached in faint scintillations to the farther end of the apartment, he saw seated on a chair a female form.

Fancy in a moment told him who it was. That the shade of her he had loved to her own destruction had come now to complete the dreadful retribution which the letter had commenced, rushed with the irresistible force of firm conviction across his mind. A strange whirl of sensations came over him, and for a moment he thought he should faint. He gave a loud cry of alarm, and with a desperate energy, lent him by despair, he rushed from the room towards that where his wife and Mrs. Ogden were still in animated conversation, little suspecting the state of mind in which he was.

He rushed into the room at once, crying,—

"Save me! Oh, save me from the dead! Save me, you who have done no wrong! Stand between me and that dreadful form. Surely this is too much. Help—help—help! The apparition is coming. I heard it gliding on behind me like the wind. It comes—it comes to blast my eyes for ever. I shall never see now ought else but that dreadful form!"

Exhausted by excess of emotion, he sank into a chair, and covered his face with his hands, while he shook in every limb.

These words were uttered with such terrific vehemence, and he had rushed so wildly into the apartment, that both Mrs. Ogden and his wife were too much petrified with astonishment for some moments to interrupt him. They looked aghast, as well they might, to see the man who had been but so short a time before indulging in the most sportive badinage of conversation, now in so dreadful a state of alarm.

It was Mrs. Ogden's voice, as she cried, "Good God! what can have happened?" which restored Margaret to consciousness, and she then flew to

Charles, and twining her arms around him, cried,—

"Charles—Charles, for God's sake! what is this? What has occurred to make you so? Speak—speak, or you will kill me, perchance, with unfounded apprehension."

He allowed her to remove his hands from before his face, and then he looked around, as if he feared each moment to see some horrible sight, which would drive his soul to madness.

"No—no," he gasped, "it is not here."

"What, Charles—oh, what?"

"It—it has not followed me."

"He is surely dreaming," said Mrs. Ogden.

"Or mad, or mad!" cried Margaret, clasping her hands. "Oh, Heaven preserve him!"

"No—no," said Charles Bertram; "I am not mad. It was a fearful sight."

"What sight?"

"The dead—the dead."

"The dead?"

"Oh, I have ever scoffed at this—I have ever laughed to scorn such idle fancies, and now—now my own eyes have seen that which is enough to sear them for ever, as well as drive the judgment from its seat."

Mrs. Ogden shook her head, as she said,—

"Don't be alarmed, Margaret. This is only some excitement of the imagination, which will soon pass away, and he will then be quite well again."

"Charles, tell me what you saw?" implored Margaret. "Tell me what it was?"

"In—in the small room adjoining the library, there sits an apparition."

"An apparition?"

"Yes, I saw it. I passed it as I left the room. I thought it followed me, but—if it has, it is now waiting for me outside the door—it may be waiting for me; I have heard that such beings never appear to two people at once; we are three, and so—so it may be waiting for me."

"Now, really," said Mrs. Ogden, "is this worthy of a man of any education or judgment? Really, Mr. Bertram, I was disposed to give you credit for more mind than you now exhibit."

"Say what you will," he replied; "I cannot doubt the evidence of my own senses. I saw it."

Margaret walked to the door of the room, followed by the eager eyes of Charles. She flung the door wide open, and then turning to him, said,—

"Convince yourself, Charles, of this delusion. Nourish it no longer. You see that there is nothing here."

"Then—then it remains in that room where I saw it."

"Charles, if you love me at all, you will come with me now to that room."

"No—no—no."

"I will," said Mrs. Ogden.

"Oh, no: do not just yet leave me quite alone."

"Then accompany us."

"If I dared, I would. I do begin to feel ashamed of this fear. I have seen a sight, though, which might well appal the boldest. In cool, calm, and sober judgment, we may talk of these things defyingly; but when they come before our eyes, then human nature will shrink, despite all the philosophy which education and habit have seemed to engraft upon it. But I will come with you. I know not why I ought to feel so much fear. I—I have nothing to reproach myself with."

He was beginning to fear questions as to his particular motives for being so terribly frightened, and he was racking his memory to remember what he had said when he first came into the room where were his wife and Mrs. Ogden; but so hurriedly and unreflectingly had his words been uttered, that he could not remember one of them, although that their import had been a dreadful fear of what he had seen, he knew full well.

It relieved him a little when Mrs. Ogden said,—

"Was this supposed appearance, Mr. Bertram, that of any one you know?"

"I have not," he thought, "said I knew the form, else such a question would not be asked me. Thank Heaven, I have not so far committed myself as that."

"No, no," he replied, "it was not the form of any one I knew. It was merely, to all appearance, the apparition of a female."

"Then I wonder how you were so terrified at it. I suppose I am a very simple-minded sort of person; but, I must confess, that if I were to go into a room and see what I thought was a ghost sitting in an arm-chair, I should be more interested and curious than frightened at it."

"No—no—no."

"Indeed I am sure I should. I don't believe there are ghosts at all: but, if there were, they certainly, to my mind, would be the most curious and interesting among natural phenomena. I say, I don't believe there are such things, because their appearance is contrary to all we know of the laws which govern the natural universe; but still, of course, we may be wrong, for anything is possible with Heaven."

Thus rationally spoke Mrs. Ogden, while Charles Bertram, leaning upon the arm of his wife, unwillingly accompanied them both to the room where the apparition had been by him seen.

How bitterly he regretted, as he went, that he had not had strength of mind sufficient to keep his fears to himself, instead of making so great a display of them as he had done, especially before Mrs. Ogden; but that again was one of the past things which could not be recalled, and which, along with many others, could only be, as usual, lamented.

When they reached the room door, Charles Bertram evidently hung back a little, and Margaret whispered to him in a tone of gentle and affectionate reproach,—

"Oh, Charles, Charles, is this you? Be more firm, for my sake as well as your own."

Upon this, he strove to assume a degree of courage he was very far indeed from feeling, and just managed not to actually run away, when the door of the apartment, which henceforward he felt sure would be a fearful one to him, was opened.

"There is nothing here," said Mrs. Ogden, as she walked boldly into the room, carrying a light which she had brought with her from the apartment in which she and Mrs. Bertram had been so recently conversing.

"Nothing whatever," said Mrs. Bertram.

Then Charles mustered courage enough to cross the threshold of the room, and to look nervously around him, after which, with a long breath of relief, he said,—

"I—I see there is nothing here."

"Now, I hope, Charles," said Mrs. Bertram, "that you are convinced that this is a matter purely of imagination."

"Yes, yes, yes."

"Where did you see the apparition?"

"On yon chair,"

"What," exclaimed Mrs. Ogden, "here, where my shawl and bonnet are placed? Now, how could you be so desperately foolish, Mr. Bertram? You have just caught sight in the dim firelight, I suppose, of these articles of apparel, and then fancied them to make up the outlines of a human form. Really I am surprised at you."

"Do—do you really think that such has been the case?" said Charles, in so different a tone to that in which he had before spoken, that no one could have believed it was the same person who was speaking at all.

"Do I think?—I am certain."

"And you, Margaret?"

"Of course, Charles; I consider the delusion now as most easily and clearly accounted for."

"That is a relief."

He placed his hand in his pocket now, to assure himself that he had the fatal letter, which had caused him so much disturbance of mind, quite safe; but a new alarm of a far more defined and fearful character came over him, as he found he had not got it about him. He cast his eyes over the floor rapidly, and he was so evidently in a state of anxiety searching for something, that Mrs. Bertram said,—

"What have you lost?"

"Oh, a trifle—a—a letter. Stokes's letter that came with the box, you know."

"The mysterious box?" said Mrs. Ogden.

"Yes—yes."

"Well, now you mention that, I have no doubt that it preyed upon your imagination, and really very much helped to produce the delusion under which you were labouring, Mr. Bertram. As a matter naturally to be supposed, when the imagination is in a state of gloomy excitement or meditation about anything, it is much more likely to receive erroneous impressions; and hence your notion that my shawl and cloak formed part of a female form seated in the chair, on which those articles merely hung."

"No doubt," said Charles, and he thought to himself at the same time, how little they knew or guessed how much, in reality, the letter from the fictitious Stokes, which he had so cleverly read, had to do with the affair.

The loss of that letter was, however, a matter to him of paramount importance, and one which now outnumbered all other considerations. He looked eagerly all over the room, upon and under every chair and table—but it was not to be found. It was certainly not in that apartment. Then again he searched all his pockets with more than needful minuteness, for a letter was not such a very small thing that it could elude him easily, and he found it not.

"Were you looking at it?" said his wife.

"I had it in my hand, and thinking it nearly useless, although certainly something of a curiosity, I was on the point of destroying it by throwing it into the fire."

"Which, no doubt, you did."

"No—no. I am quite certain I did not."

"Then never mind it, Charles. Some of the servants will, no doubt, find it."

So thought Charles Bertram—but far from such a thought being any consolation to him, it happened to be the very thing he dreaded, so he said—

"I wish to find it. I must have dropped it on my way from this room to the drawing-room."

He took the candle, and carefully searched as he went, but no trace whatever of the letter could be found. Somehow or another, it had mysteriously disappeared altogether. This was a circumstance which caused him much disquietude. At one time he was inclined to think that in the hurry of the moment he must have cast the letter into the fire, and then he again considered that such a thing was not likely, as his movement upon seeing the real or supposed apparition was in a directly contrary course, namely, towards the door. Tortured by conflicting feelings, he could make up his mind to nothing but that the letter was gone—but into what hands it had fallen remained a mystery, which, perchance, was only to be unravelled when it might be produced to his confusion and dismay.

"Oh, fool, fool, that I was," he thought, "to hesitate for a moment about the destruction of that letter, which was so dangerous to my peace; and yet now I have tampered with it and lost it. I had the power to put for ever out of the world such a damning piece of evidence against me, and yet hesitated to do so from some infatuation which now appears to me to be the height of madness."

And so, indeed, it was. Had he still possessed that epistle which told so sorrowful a tale against him, perhaps he would still have reasoned as he did when he resolved upon not committing it to the flames. In his possession it was harmless, but now that he had so inexplicably lost it, he would have given almost anything to hold it in his hand once again, and be able to debate within arm's length of a fire upon a means of destroying it.

"Who could have picked it up?" was the question he continually asked himself. "Who could, in this house, with the exception of my wife, feel any interest in it?—and that she has it not I would stake my existence. If one of the servants has it, why is it not taken to her—or to me, for a reward?"

These were questions troublesome enough to answer, although easily put, and in a very painful state of mind Charles Bertram told his wife that he thought a little walk in the open air would do him good. This was a suggestion to which she gave an immediate assent; she offered to accompany him, but he evaded the request by saying—

"I always find that a very rapid walk recovers me soonest from any mental emotion. You could not keep up to the pace at which I shall go for a moment."

"I am not a fast indeed, walker."

"I shall not be long gone. An hour,

or perhaps less. Let me find you here when I return. Mrs. Ogden and we can sup together, if she is not otherwise engaged?"

Mrs. Ogden said frankly she was not, and then, with an assumption of good spirits he was far, very far, indeed, from feeling, Charles Bertram left his own handsome, indeed we may say splended house, with more real unhappiness at his heart than the man who swept the crossing which was almost immediately opposite to it. And yet what would the world have said, if called upon for an opinion upon such a subject?

An undefined, but a growing notion that he should like to ascertain yet some more particulars of the death of the victim to his passions, prompted him to walk in a certain direction, and he soon found himself in the dingy looking neighbourhood of Clerkenwell, and standing by a large chestnut tree, which, for now nearly a hundred years, has occupied a place at the corner of a

row of houses called Cobham-row, and which are opposite the governor's garden of the prison.

CHAPTER XI.

CHARLES BERTRAM'S HARASSED FEELINGS.—THE BLACK MANTLE.—THE GRAVE OF THE BROKEN HEART.—THE PRAYER.

IT is strange, but a no less true than strange thing, as regards human nature, that it always seeks to know as much as possible, even of those events which are calculated to become the greatest stings of memory, and to embitter almost every joy in the recollection of.

Those who have committed great crimes have, almost invariably, been found curious as regards all the little intricate circumstances attending upon the deed they have done, as if to them the interest of the matter really for a time superseded the sting of conscience, which was likely to be rendered so much more severe by such circumstantial details. It was so with Charles Bertram.

A strong and almost uncontrollable desire had come over him to ascertain all he could respecting the last moments of her whom he had brought with sorrow to an early grave. Notwithstanding the assertions in that letter which he had so mysteriously lost, that consumption had claimed that young and beautiful being as its victim, he could not

"Lay that flattering unction to his soul."

Too well he knew that despair, shame, and regret, had sapped the springs of her existence, and although consumption, medically speaking, might be the real cause of her decease—that she could have perhaps, lived long and happily but for his treachery, was a conviction he could not, by any sophistical chain of reasoning, divest himself of. It would appear then very odd that he, of all men, should seek particulars, any one of which must harrow him to the very soul; but, as we have said, such is frequently a part of the mysterious action of the human mind, and he obeyed the impulse.

He stood, then, by that aged tree, and paused for some moments in gloomy meditation. Well—too well he knew that spot. It had been one on which, many and many a time, he had met that too fond—too unsuspicious—too trusting girl, whom at length he had the poor and unmanly triumph of deceiving. No wonder that that spot should awaken in his mind painful feelings. He deserved, amply, all the retribution that such feelings could bring upon him.

With a shudder he passed on, and took his way towards a narrow street in the immediate vicinity. He paused at a house which he knew well, for it was there he had last visited the deceived one, and endeavoured to persuade her that urgent business arrangements called him to the Continent for some months. That was immediately after he had made up his mind to marry Margaret, who, perhaps, owed her good fortune of being a wife to the sterner principle which forbade him attempting to make her a mistress.

Charles Bertram did not expect that she of whom he wished to gain intelligence had died in that house. His only expectation in calling there was, that he should ascertain the address at which she had really passed her last hours. He knocked lightly at the door, and a dirty looking servant girl answered him.

"Do you want to look at the lodgings?' she said.

"No—no. I want to inquire the address of one who lodged here some time since."

"Oh—missus ain't at home."

"But perhaps you can tell me?"

"Who was it, sir?"

"Miss Armstrong."

"Oh, she as was so ill! She went to live down Coppie-row, sir, at number eight."

"Thank you, and—and that's all you know of her;"

"Yes, that's all, excepting that she's gone dead."

The girl added this piece of information as if it were a mere trifle as concerning any one.

"I know that," said Charles, as he walked from the door.

The servant girl looked after him, as she muttered to herself—

"Now, I wonder who he is? He might as well have given me a shilling! but some people is so shabby, like missus, who wouldn't give so much as a cheese paring to save nobody from being hung, I'm sure—no, not if they was her own flesh and blood, she wouldn't. I knows her well."

Charles Bertram was too far off to hear those reproaches, which had begun upon himself and ended upon that universally disliked character to all servants —"missus." He walked hastily towards the street, or rather long strangling throroughfare, which had been mentioned to him as that in which the poor victim had resided and died.

It is, frequently the unhappy disposition of many to repent them of the evil which they do when it is too late to remedy any one portion of it. When their iniquities have produced the most direful results—when all the evil that could possibly arise is consummated, they seem suddenly to awaken to a consciousness of their own cruelty and injustice, and to wish, with all their hearts, those things undone, which, while there was still time, at all events, to ameliorate, they heeded not.

It is not until the grave closes over an ill-used, ill-quittedi object that many persons awaken to a full knowlenge of what they should have done in condistinction to what they have done. Then come all the unavailing regrets—the yearning wishes which never can be fulfilled. Then come those heart sicknesses which might well have been spared by one half hour's just reflections while there was yet time for action.

And Charles Bertram endured all this, and well he deserved to endure it all, for in his conduct towards Emma Armstrong there was not one redeeming trait. He had found her poor, but happy. He left her destitute and despairing,—yes, that was the state to which he consigned her whom he had affected to love.

He had never known what poverty was. It was, to his imagination, a name without any particular signification. True he would sometimes sigh and call himself poor, because he could not conveniently spare money enough to purchase some rich luxury which he really had no manner of occasion for; but poverty in its real, ghastly, terrible reality he knew absolutely nothing of.

And to such real poverty had he left Emma Armstrong, and yet she had written to him to endeavour to still any alarm of conscience he might feel in supposing himself the cause of her death.

Oh, if he had had but one half the heart he had, he must have felt half choked to read that epistle. Had it been contrived by the cunningest hand that ever wielded a pen, it could not have inflicted upon him the fearful agony that reached him through the sheer innocence of the epistle. It was not written to wound him, and yet how, like a barbed arrow, it pierced his heart. It was written to soothe, and yet it was poison to his peace.

And let not the reader of these pages imagine that Emma Armstrong had the least suspicion of the effect her letter would have upon her seducer. She had but one idea in writing it, and that was, to spare him the thought that he had caused her death, and to endeavour to convince him that it was that bane of the gentle and the beautiful—consumption—which had brought her to the grave. She wanted him to think that, and hence she had written those lines which had probed his very heart, and caused him sensations of acute misery, which no time or concurrence of circumstances could ever obliterate.

Oh, why is it that woman's best and fondest feelings should be used as the means of her destruction? The seducer has the sorry boast of deceiving his victim by arraying against her her own virtue, her own innocence; suspecting no wrong of him, because she knows no wrong of herself, she yields to persuasions which are truthless, to promises which are never intended to be performed. And then, when all is lost, how truely does she find, in the eloquent words of one of the greatest geniuses that ever adorned this country, that—

" Man's love is of his life a thing apart—
'Tis woman's whole existence."

This was a mournful truth, which Emma Armstrong soon discovered, and she sunk beneath the harrowing thought. She did die of what is technically called a broken heart—that is, she fell into a state of bodily indisposition, in consequence of deep mental affliction, which soon carried her to the grave.

Charles Bertram knew that he was virtually her murderer; he could not conceal from himself that damning fact; no stultification of his reasoning powers could induce him to think otherwise—the fact stared him in the face. He had, and he knew it, blighted and destroyed one of the fairest flowers in Nature's garden. How could he be happy?

But he is knocking at the door of No. 8, Coppice-row, Clerkenwell, and we will follow him into that house, from whence, so short a time before, the victim of his arts had been conveyed a corpse.

An elderly woman opened the door. She wore a widow's cap, and had upon her countenance that look of patient, habitual suffering which, alas! in this world of sorrow, sits upon many a face which seems formed to pourtray in its speaking lineaments happier feelings.

Charles Bertram could scarcely speak to her for a moment, and when he did, it was in strange, husky tones that he said,—

" Did—a young person of the name of Armstrong live here?"

" Armstrong!" exclaimed the woman. " Dear—dear, yes; but she is dead, sir."

" Dead!" said Charles, affecting a surprise he felt not, but which his general state of agitation enabled him well to feign. " Is she dead?"

" She is, indeed. Did you know her, sir?"

" I am a distant relative of the girl's,

and learning, by more accident, that she was in London, and in indifferent circumstances, I have come to do her good."

" God bless you, sir, for the intention; but it is now too late."

"Too late?" he repeated. " Yes, too late."

His grief and agitation were so apparent, that the woman invited him into the house to rest himself, and as to get into conversation with her, and to hear her account of the last moments of Emma Armstrong, was his object, he at once accepted the invitation, and entered the house.

It was a clean, poor-looking place. Everything was made the most of; but in all the interior arrangements there was ample evidence of that poverty which wages war against an attempt to keep up appearances. The widow showed him into a little parlour, and handed him a seat, saying,—

" I am sure, sir, anybody is welcome here who comes on a kindly errand with the name of Emma Armstrong in his mouth. Poor thing, if ever there was anybody too good by a great deal for this world, it was her."

" Indeed ?" gasped Charles.

" Yes, sir. And, no doubt, God in his own good time will punish, as he ought to punish, him who reduced her to the state she was in, and then left her to die."

" Yes, yes !" gasped Charles.

" Are you aware, sir, of her history ?"

" I—I—heard that she had fallen."

" She was deceived, sir, by a villain. His name is Charles Bertram. I tell it to everybody I come near. A villain, sir, who behaved towards her as no man with the commonest feelings in his bosom would have behaved."

" Was his conduct so bad ?"

" It was, indeed. He seduced her, and then left her to die—to starve—to any fate, in fact, that might present itself to her, poor thing. Oh, I hope I may never see him in this world."

" I hope you never may."

" His name is Charles Bertram, sir. Remember that, sir, if ever you should come across such a man."

" I shall not forget the name, you may depend."

" Do not, sir."

" And so, she died here ?"

" She did, poor thing—she died here in my arms, and, would you believe it, her very last words contained a prayer to Heaven to forgive him who had done her so much wrong."

" She died of—of—consumption ?"

" Consumption ?—stuff ! Poor thing, that was what she wanted everybody to believe ; but she broke her heart. She died of grief to find herself so cruelly deceived by one she had loved and trusted ; and yet, angel as she was, she never would blame him at all, even at the moment of her greatest suffering, and when pain and anguish had possession of her."

" And so she died ?"

" Yes, sir. On the morning before she died she spoke to me, saying, in so weak a voice that I could hardly hear her,—' I shall not be long a trouble to you. I shall not see another sunrise ; but it is dreadful to think what he will suffer on my account when he hears that I am gone. He will fancy himself the cause of my death, and so his existence may be embittered. I would not have that happen. That one should suffer is enough. I forgive him all.'"

" And—and," said Charles, " you combated that opinion ?'"

" I did. I told her he deserved to suffer, and I said I would find him out and tell him so ; but she made me promise not to do so."

" Did she die that day ?"

" She did, poor thing. She got weaker every hour, and the doctor said he could do nothing for her. Her old mother sat on the floor, at the foot of the bed, and never moved except once in about an hour to wring her hands."

" And—and she died in peace ?"

" She did. When her last moment was nearly come, she turned to me, and flung her arms round me, as she cried, in a tone of voice I shall never forget to my dying day,—' And even now I can forgive him, and pray to the great God to forgive him likewise.'"

" What more ?"

" She never spoke again."

" And so the tragedy was over ?"

" You may well call it a tragedy, sir. A sad tragedy, too, was it. She lies in Clerkenwell churchyard, poor thing. And now the mother is dead, too, and

I hear that Charles Bertram is married, and spending his money in all sorts of luxuries with his wife. Oh, if that man can lay his head down upon his pillow at night without a pang, it is a very surprising thing to me."

"And would be to any one," groaned Charles. "What were the circumstances of the Armstrongs?"

"Oh, sir, that's neither here nor there. I am poor enough, Heaven knows; but they, poor things, had nothing. I thank God I was able to take care of her."

"And at your own charge you kept her?"

"It was very little it took to keep her."

"Can you name any amount that she died indebted to you? If you can, I will pay it."

"You pay it, sir?"

"Yes, cheerfully. Would to God I had come here while she yet breathed."

"Ah, sir, I wish you had. It might have soothed her to see before she died some one belonging to her who could have spoken to her the kind words that I am sure you would have done; but I suppose it was the will of Providence. You have made no promise, though, sir, not to go and tell Mr. Bertram what a villain he is, and, if I were you, I would do so, indeed, to his very face. He should not be ignorant of the mischief he has done, or have it in his power to pretend ignorance."

"You may depend he shall know all."

"That's right, sir. I am glad to hear you say that."

"I think it was a pity he was not sent for."

"I proposed once sending for him, but Emma Armstrong shook her head, and in that soft, quiet way in which she spoke always, she said,—' No, no. Had he the wish to find me, he could do so. If he can forget me, let him. I will not send for him—I am content to die without seeing him again now, although I thought not, when last I looked upon his face, it would be for the last time in this world.' "

"But if you had sent, he might have come."

"I send! No, sir. I wouldn't send after that. As she said, if he had wished to see her, he could have found her out easily. It's quite plain and clear he had cast her off, and quite forgotten her."

"You think so?"

"How can I think otherwise? But of one thing I am quite sure and certain."

"What is that?"

"Why, that Heaven will punish him in some way or another. That man will never be happy. Something or another will happen to him, for certain, that will make him one of the most miserable wretches in the world."

Charles Bertram trembled. He thought of the curse which had been launched at his head on the steps of the church, when he was leaving the sacred building with his bride. He thought of the constant state of anxiety he had been in ever since, and he could not but tell himself that the day of retribution then began, and that the words of the widow were but too true as yet, for he had known no happiness since that moment. He had now heard enough—more than enough, to add much to the miserable reflections which had before found so permanent a home in his breast, and he rose to go.

"Accept," he said, "this small gratuity, for the care and tenderness you have bestowed upon Emma Armstrong."

He laid, as he spoke, a ten-pound note upon the little table, and then turned towards the door.

"Oh, sir," said the widow, "how can I thank you? But this is far too much."

"No, no. Take it."

"One-half of such an amount I am not entitled to, sir. God bless you. If you had but come before poor Emma Armstrong had died—"

"Enough, enough. She lies, you say, in Clerkenwell churchyard? Some day I should like to look upon the spot of ground which holds her sad remains."

"Alas, sir, you would not find it."

"True, true, true. Farewell."

"But who, sir, shall I think of, when I think of this visit? You are a relation, are you, of poor dear Emma Armstrong? Who shall I say, if I tell the story to any one, called upon me, and behaved so generously?"

"Never mind. Never mind."

"Nay—but, sir——"

"It can make no matter. Take the money. Use it, fancying it came from Emma Armstrong herself, as it came from one who deeply grieves for her, and sympathises with her fate. One who would have given a hundred times the amount to look upon her face again in life, to hear her speak those words of—of forgiveness."

Deeply affected, Charles paused, and then making an effort to recover himself, he said, suddenly,—

"Good night. Good night."

He walked rapidly to the outer door, and in another moment would have gained the street, when his footsteps were arrested by a cry of surprise from the woman. He turned to know the cause of the sudden exclamation, and he saw her with the bank-note in her hands, and gazing upon it with looks of surprise and consternation.

"What is the matter?" he said; "why do you look so earnestly upon that note?"

"There is a name upon it," said the woman, with a shudder, as she dropped it.

"A name?"

"Yes. The name of Bertram. You are—"

"That unhappy man," cried Bertram. "I am Charles Bertram, and the hell of remorse has already commenced within this guilty breast."

Without waiting for any answer, he dashed from the house, and, in a state of mind bordering upon distraction, he flew along the streets towards his own house.

CHAPTER XII.

MRS. BLAIR'S CONSULTATION WITH MRS. PRIMROSE, HER SISTER, AND ITS RESULTS.

IT becomes our duty, considering the rather important part which Mrs. Blair, the housekeeper of the Bertrams, is destined to play in our little drama of real life, to say some few words concerning that lady, and her own immediate connexions.

There were, then, two sisters of the name of Finch. They were left, by the death of their parents, in a very doubtful and troublesome position in life, without friends, without connexions that felt in the least disposed to be of any assistance to them. In fact, they were, with the exception of what they could earn by such needlework as they were qualified to do, and able to procure, entirely destitute.

These sisters Finch were, however, what the world calls fine women : i. e., they were big, and of the masculine order. Moreover, they had a tolerable portion of ability, which, possibly, had it been better directed by education, would have produced far more beneficial results to society; but being, as they were, both ignorant women, the natural talent with which they were gifted took a wrong course. The imaginations which might have charmed many persons descended to mere lies, and an aptitude for the lowest species of intrigue and chicanery.

Work for the miserable pittance they were earning they would not; and, consequently, these two sisters held solemn council together, as to what would be the best course to pursue.

The result of their deliberations was, that they cautiously embraced a course of life which, however profitable it might be, was very far from being respectable—one went to reside ostensibly with a decrepit old man, named Blair, as his housekeeper; but, in reality, as his mistress. The other, after a more erratic career, succeeded in hooking into matrimony a tradesman of the name of Primrose.

Old Blair died, and the elder of those sisters, who had been looking forward to his decease to become the mistress of considerable property, found then, to her consternation, that she had been deceived, and that he had been living upon a life annuity only, and all she got was what she could lay her hands on that actually belonged to him in the furnished apartments in which they had both for some years resided.

This was a heavy blow for Mrs. Blair, as she now called herself, who was not so young as she once was, and the masculine order of beauty which, if it could be called beauty at all, she possessed, was not of a good keeping quality, but very much deteriorated, and had become, in a manner of speaking, rusty by age.

The sisters now held a long consultation, the result of which was, that, despite some grumbling on the part of poor Primrose, who was very nearly spirit-broken, Mrs. Blair was accommodated at his house until she could do something for herself.

Then, in pursuance of a plan which they had matured between them, Mrs. Blair turned religious, and sought for another situation as housekeeper to a single gentleman. She had hoped, of course, to get hold of some other old man, whom she might possibly inveigle into matrimony; but so long a time elapsed without such a chance occurring, that, at length, she was glad to accept a situation as housekeeper to Charles Bertram, who was too young and gay for such a woman as Mrs. Blair to have any chance of entrapping, and, therefore, she never attempted it, but confined herself to such peculations as were in her power to carry on in a large house where she was trusted with unlimited control.

Now, Mrs. Blair was making money by this state of things, and, taking into consideration all things, was very comfortable indeed, until Charles Bertram's announced marriage gave her a very severe shock. She felt that, from the moment that Mrs. Bertram set foot in the house, her, Mrs. Blair's, occupation was gone, and that, even if she were permitted to continue in her situation, she could have no chance of continuing the successful career of peculation which was rapidly making up for herself a very handsome purse against any emergency. In fact, she felt that she should not be getting on.

This term, "getting-on," in the minds of Mrs. Blair and her sister, Mrs. Primrose, meant getting, by some undue means, more than they ought. If they only had what they were justly entitled to, they did nor consider they were getting on at all. The point of gatting on only began where the roguery and the scheming commenced which produced some profits that they were not in equity entitled to.

Mrs. Blair was forty, or over that age a little, and to have her gradual means of independence quashed by Charles Bertram's marriage, was really, she considered, too bad.

We have said that she and her sister both had a certain amount of natural ability, and at a meeting they had after the announcement of Charles's intended marriage, it was determined to attempt the accomplishment of one of the most infamous and nefarious plans that ever the human mind imagined. The separation of Charles Bertram and his wife was the object which may be said to have been actually resolved upon by these delectable sisters.

Alas! there occurred circumstances which fearfully assisted them—circumstances which, in themselves, would have been nothing, but which, when seized upon by these two bold, unprincipled women, were of dreadful importance. It was while Charles Bertram was hearing, with such agony as he might feel to hear, the particulars of the death of Emma Armstrong, that Mrs. Blair and Mrs. Primrose sat in earnest consultation at the house of the latter.

Mrs. Primrose was three years the younger, and, for a strong-minded woman as she was, it was astonishing what stress and importance she gave to that accidental circumstance. Perhaps she thought more of it as a means of annoyance to Mrs. Blair, than in any other way. Alas! that people of active intellects should so very seldom be at all amiable.

These ladies were not very squeamish, as might be guessed by the glass of hot brandy-and water which was before them, and to which, with great regularity, they each paid attention.

"I am the more resolved," remarked Mrs. Blair, "upon the subject to which we have turned attention, because I am convinced that Mrs. Bertram dislikes me."

"Of course she does," remarked Mrs. Primrose. "I have often asserted it, that the first thing a newly wedded wife feels anxious about, is to effect a complete change in the household of her husband, if he have one."

"Precisely. She likes all the servants to be of her choosing, and of her engaging, as a matter of course."

"You may, then, Blair"—the sisters always called each other, when conversing alone, Blair and Primrose— "you may then, Blair, look out for a discharge on the very first opportunity."

"An attempted discharge."

"Attempted! What do you mean?"

"I mean, that a fortunate circumstance has occurred, which, I think, will induce Mr. Bertram to defend me against his lady."

"What, against his young wife?"

"Yes, his young wife."

"And his handsome wife?"

"Ay, and his handsome wife."

Mrs. Primrose shook her head, as she said,—

"At your age, Blair, you may depend you have no chance against her, if you were ever so much in the right and she were ever so much in the wrong."

"My age!"

"Yes; you know I don't set up to be young, and you are three years older than I am."

"A circumstance which you are resolved, Primrose, never to forget, for I believe I hear it mentioned, every time I come here, twice or thrice."

"Well, we need not quarrel about ages, Blair. We have held together too long, and acted together too harmoniously, now to get up a contention on such a point as that."

"True: I want no contention."

"Then tell me what is the circumstance which you consider gives you such a hold upon Mr. Bertram."

"The knowledge of his intrigue with the girl I have before named to you."

"Emma Armstrong?"

"Yes. You are aware that I found out, by generalship and by perseverance, that he was engaging in an intrigue, and, in fact, that he had seduced the girl."

"All of which he may deny."

"He might have denied it, but now I have such proof as he could never get over."

"Indeed?"

"Yes. Moreover, he has involved himself in such an intricate web of falsehoods, that shame at their discovery and disentanglement will become a stronger feeling even than his dread of his wife getting a knowledge of their intrigue, which, after all, being before his marriage with her, she has nothing to do with."

"Very true."

"Read this, and then judge for yourself. I picked up this letter just before I came out. You will soon see its great importance, and what a very uncomfortable document for Mr. Bertram it would be, were it to find its way into his wife's hands."

Mrs. Blair then handed to her sister the letter which Charles Bertram had received from Emma Armstrong, and which, in his flight at seeing the supposed ghost, he had dropped, and afterwards in vain searched for.

Mrs. Primrose read it with evident interest, and when she had concluded, she said,—

"You are right—this will do; but what an uncommon fool the girl must have been."

"Very."

"Is she really dead?"

"I have ascertained that she is."

"You may make, then, much of this letter. Bertram is not a man of the most resolute conduct, by all accounts."

"He is quite the reverse of a resolute man. He is weak and nervous to excess, and I know, as surely as if such a result had already happened, that when I come to open rupture with his wife, he will shrink before a threat of this letter being produced, and feel himself necessitated to protect me, and retain me, in spite of her, in his service."

"And what immediate course will you pursue?"

"The same as usual. I will falsify every account, and pocket as much money as I possibly can; I care not how soon war is declared between me and Mrs. Bertram."

"But there may be danger?"

"None at all. The only way then will be to commence operations upon the mind of the husband, by insinuating that the reason she wants to be rid of me arises from her fear of being herself found out in some lapse."

"I understand."

"I am as certain, Primrose, as that I sit here, nothing can be easier than to make such a man as Bertram jealous. He might hesitate at my assertions, but all the news coming from you who will appear so disinterested, he cannot refuse to give some credence to it."

"Exactly; and we share, mind, the produce of the next year."

"Which shall be ample. Besides, I have another scheme which wants consideration."

"Have you?"

"Yes; but no more of it at present."

"More! I have heard nothing at all of it yet."

"Well, well, drop it. It would but distract our minds from what at present has to be done."

"Very good, Blair; I am never one to advise too many irons to be put in the fire at once."

"How do you get on with Primrose now?"

"He turns more foolish every day. I don't think he will last long, do you know."

"Indeed!"

"No; but that don't much matter. The business is declining, and, before it gets worse, I want him to sell it and start anew in something else; but he wants enegy for such a course."

"Oh, Primrose, you have certainly got a living by yoking yourself to such a fool, and that is all."

"Not quite all. I have made up a very good purse of my own, with which I should leave him, if his circumstances were to get in any way embarrassed."

"You could not do better, I am certain."

"Oh, I have considered it all closely, and am quite clear about it, I can tell you. So you mean, you say, to take as much as usual out of Bertram's house?"

"I do. As yet, I have made tolerably regularly a pound a-week, in addition o my wages, and I shall go on on the same system, now that I really believe I have such a hold of him that he dare not discharge me."

"You talked of another scheme, Blair; you have made me curious about it. Why should you hesitate to tell me? I shall waste more time in conjecture as to what it may be than in genuine thought upon it."

"That is possible."

"It is a fact. Come now, Blair, be explicit."

"I will then, Primrose."

"That is right. You know, then—"

"My dear," said a man, putting his head in at the door just a little way, "I am going out."

"How dare you, Mr. Primrose," exclaimed Mrs. Primrose, "how dare you, I say, presume to intrude upon me in this way, when I'm engaged? have I not often told you that I will not be intruded upon, sir, in such a manner?"

"Well, but——"

"It is not well, sir——"

"But——"

"Will you go?"

"I am going! but I thought, you know, as I was going out, my dear, that you wouldn't mind giving me eighteenpence or so, you see."

"Eighteenpence, sir!" exclaimed Mrs. Primrose, with a look of the most intense astonishment.—"Eighteenpence, sir! And what on earth can you want with eighteenpence?"

"Why—why, you know, I hav'n't had any snuff for two days, and I don't like to be always asking you for money."

"But you are always doing so, Mr. Primrose."

"Oh, no—no—no!"

"How dare you contradict me? You know, Mr. Primrose, that contradiction is one of the things that more than anything else shatter my nerves, and make me the creature that I am, giving way to anything and to anybody."

"Lor!" exclaimed Primrose.

"Sir, if you had some wives, you would soon have found out what they would have demanded and done. They would not have put up with everything in the meek, mild, gentle way that I, according to my disposition, endure from you."

"Gracious!" said Primrose, lifting up his hands.

"You affect that you are astonished. Do—especially before anybody—make out you have a termagant wife if you can, sir. There's sixpence, and don't ask me for money for some days now, if you please."

"Some days—sixpence!"

"Mr. Primrose, I shall be tempted to tell you a bit of my mind, if you don't be off."

"Oh, dear," said Primrose, who could not call his soul his own in his own house. "Don't get in a passion. I'm going—I was only saying that sixpence didn't go very far, that's all, my dear; but you have a great notion of the value of money."

"Mr. Primrose, say another word, and I shall demand a separation—I shall send my attorney to you, sir."

Upon this threat, poor hen-pecked Primrose hastily withdrew himself from the parlour, and took himself off as quickly as he could, believing really in his own mind, as all men do who have wives of the class to which his belonged, that they could not possibly do without them, and that they are really, as they represent themselves, very wonderful women.

We have found invariably this to be the case with hen-pecked husbands; and their constant excuse to their acquaintance, when remonstrated with on account of their state of domestic subjection, is—

"Oh, but Mrs. So-and-so is a very clever woman, if she has her little faults of temper, and a very fine woman, too."

When he was gone, Mrs. Blair inclined her mouth towards the ear of Mrs. Primrose, and spoke for about two minutes slowly and distinctly. As she continued, her own countenance became flushed, while Mrs Primrose's turned very pale, and a slight shudder pervaded her frame.

"You will think of it," said Mrs. Blair, rising,—"you will think of it. You now know more of me, and of what I am capable, than ever you knew before."

"I tremble!"

"You tremble!—you—you!"

"Yes; but, as you say, I will think. 'Tis bold and desperate—desperate as it is bold."

"And wonderfully profitable."

"True; but——"

"Pshaw! I didn't think you would have shrunk."

"But detection would be terrible. Since you have become religious, Blair, you have become doubly desperate and unscrupulous."

"You would have an equal benefit. There is enough for both—amply enough for both, I say—I know it. I want a carriage, a handsome house, servants, pleasures, and all my own, too. I must feel that they are all my own, or they would be valueless. I must have them, and I care not what I wade through to obtain them, so that the path be short."

"I will think; but I own you have given me a shock. I am getting, however, each moment more familiarised with the idea. The first shock is the worst, I find. I will think it over, and when we meet again, I may be able to talk more calmly of it."

CHAPTER XIII.

THE ARRIVAL OF THE SHIP ATLAN-TIA.—THE YOUNG STRANGER.—HOPES OF HAPPINESS.

IN order, now, to introduce to our readers one whom it is important they should become immediately acquainted with, we must refer to a newspaper which bears date some months before the marriage of Margaret Harrison with Charles Bertram, for a paragraph which ran as follows:—

"There is every reason to believe that the suppositions concerning the loss of the Atlantia, in her homeward-bound voyage from Cape Coast, are too true. The ship Lucy, from Rotterdam, brings in a piece of spar, with the word 'Atlantia' painted on it, so that it is highly probable the ill-fated vessel has gone to pieces during the storm off the coast on Wednesday last; and, as no news has been heard of passengers or crew, we are compelled to come to the sad conclusion that all on board the ill-fared vessel have perished."

In another paper, bearing date a few days later, appeared a paragraph, which said,—

"All hopes with regard to the preservation of the Atlantia are now at an end. We subjoin a list of the names of the passengers, who, no doubt, have found a watery grave."

Here followed a list of the passengers, which we need not occupy our space with, inasmuch as only one of them is of any importance to our story. That man was named Theodore Danton.

His history, although far from being a discursive one, was romantic enough, as pourtraying feeling and sensibility, which, in one so young—for he was but twenty years of age when the Atlantia was supposed to have been wrecked, with him on board—are rarely to be met with.

He was a cousin of Margaret Harrison's, and, like her, an orphan. Three years previous, he had left his native land, penniless, and without bidding adieu to any one. His acquaintance with Margaret was but slight. He had ever been a dreamy dispositioned boy, mild and quiet spoken, shunning observation; but to those who would take the trouble to study his character, and had the tact to do so, he was found to possess a world of latent fire and intellect.

Those who did know him best, all agreed that at the bottom of his heart lay some secret which, they thought, consisted in an attachment to some one whom he would never name.

In person, Theodore Danton was rather under the ordinary standard, but his finely-formed features and gentlemanly address made him universally admired. Such was he when he suddenly disappeared, and nothing further was heard of him until his name appeared among the list of the supposed sufferers by the wreck of the Atlantia. Then numerous inquiries were made; and from other arrivals from Cape Coast, it was ascertained that, during the short period of his stay there, Theodore Danton had been enabled, by a variety of circumstances, to do such good services to various wealthy individuals, that he had amassed a sum amounting to two thousand pounds, with which he had taken his passage in the Atlantia.

This news had reached the ears of Margaret, in common with every one else who knew Theodore Danton. All that she remembered of him was, that he was a shy, handsome-looking lad; and she was much grieved to hear of his death, at a time too when so far in life he had been successful in procuring gold as well as golden opinions.

The rapid transition, however, of her own fortunes from what they were to what they became when she was the wife of Mr. Bertram, was highly calculated to banish every other thought from her mind, and, although she never thought of Theodore except with a sigh and a feeling of regret, yet it was not likely that his fate would produce any more permanent effect upon her mind.

And so everybody made up their minds that the Atlantia and all her crew and passengers were lost, until one morning there came beating up the English channel, with a favourable wind, and looking as spruce and comfortable as possible, this very ship, the Atlantia. She came up to the Downs, and, to the astonishment of everybody, appeared none the worse for a detention, somehow and somewhere, which had extended over some months.

Upon being boarded by different officers and parties, both from the ships and the shore, the captain accounted for his disappearance with his ship, cargo, and crew, by stating that off the African coast they fell in with a piratical vessel, which chased them and took them ; that they were carried up a river some hundred miles into the interior of Africa, and the passengers and crew placed in confinement at a village inhabited by buccaneers and freebooters of the ocean. Then a plan had been made among themselves of escape, and after much preparation put into execution. They overmastered their guard, and, proceeding to the harbour, seized again their own ship, on board of which arms, ammunition, and cannon had been placed by the buccaneers, who, finding her a fast sailer, had determined upon making use of her in their nefarious trade. After a protracted fight for nearly the whole length of the river, they beat off their foes, got to sea, and made sail for England.

At the commencement of the chase in the first instance, when the vessel was captured by the pirates, Theodore Danton had managed to hide his money so securely that it was never found by the huccaneers ; and when the ship became again the property of its rightful owners, he did not find himself minus one guinea of the little hoard, with which he wished to reach his own country, and to amass which for a special purpose it had been his great object in going.

This was the whole of the tale : and hence was it that, with the exception of a few who had been killed in the contest with the pirates, and a few more

wounded, the Atlantia, with her cargo and possengers, came bravely and unhurt into port.

The news of the safe arrival of the missing vessel flew from mouth to mouth with great rapidity, but most of the passengers, landed immediately, reached their friends and relations, who had given them up for lost, long before the public papers could communicate to he world a large the pariculars of the wonderful preservation of the ship, and the hundred or so human souls that had trusted to her shelter.

Among those who landed first, with delighted eagerness, to retread the shores of England, was Theodore Danton. His looks were all animation —joy sparkled in every feature of his countenance, and no one could cast even the most hasty glance upon his handsome, glowing face without saying—

" How happy that young man is !"

He took but slight refreshment at Dover, and then, having ordered a post-chariot with good horses, he made immediate speed to London, which, if he could have reached on the wings of the wind, he would have gladly done so—so great was his impatience to accomplish the one object which had been the dream of his existence, since first he had been able to tell himself that he loved !

Yes—love ! all-powerful love ! was the lode-star of his actions—that feeling was it, which sent him on his errand to the coast which has been the grave of so many Europeans ; that feeling was it which nerved him to be foremost in preparing the plan of escape from the buccaneers' village—and that feeling was it which now made him hasten to the metropolis so swiftly, and yet so tardily, as it seemed to his longing impatience to get there.

Alas ! poor—poor Theodore Danton. You were too late. Happier, far happier for you had you found a grave in the deep ocean, than to reach the land of your birth and your love to feel so sad a blow of fate as that which hung impending over your devoted head.

It was Margaret Harrison—his cousin, Margaret Harrison—who was the object of his love ; she was the lode-star of his fate. It was a deep, earnest, devoted passion for her that made up the secret which lay at the bottom of his heart, unmingled with one base or ordinary feeling.

When first his boyish eyes had gazed upon her, he loved her. He never breathed his passion to her ears; but at home at times he would look the beaming fondness that was in his bosom. He loved her perhaps as none other ever loved—at least, he loved her as very, very few are capable of loving.

But she was poor, and he had nothing. He had no home to offer her. He was penniless, beyond a few pounds that might suffice to take him, as indeed it did, somewhere, where the struggle to live would not be so difficult. And, under these circumstances, with a rare devotion, and a calculation in his passion which few would have felt, he di I not tell her of his love. He rather avoided than sought her, lest, by some chance, he should be thought so selfish as to make her a partner of his poor fortune. He adored her, but he had the sound intellect to know that it would have been not love, but selfishness, that would have sought to make her his ere he had a home, in relation to which he could have said,—

" Welcome, welcome, Margaret. Here is a heart that loves you, and here is a home in which you may be happy."

Till he could say so much, he hid his honest, noble passion deep in the recesses of his heart. And so he went abroad, and Heaven seemed to bless him; for he prospered beyond the most sanguine hopes of the most sanguine imagination.

Three years, only three short years had elapsed, and he was returning comparatively a rich man. Nay, was he not actually rich? for the sum he had would go far, and produce him all his desires. He was rich, and with Margaret as his wife, he would not have envied an emperor his throne, although a thousand cringing vassals stood ready to obey his nod.

But Margaret was married; she knew not of the passion of the romantic boy of genius who had loved too well to tell her that he had loved at all, and so she had married another—another with a heart no more to be compared to that which glowed in the breast of Theodore Danton, than is the dullest flint to the purest diamond that ever flashed from the bowels of the earth upon the eyes of man.

Oh, what a libel it is upon the justice and the goodness of Heaven to say that marriages are there contrived and pre-ordered. Let us not believe so for one moment, if we would preserve our reverence for that which is great, and holy, and good. Would Margaret Harrison have ever been united with such a man as Charles Bertram? Alas! no; or we must deny the prescience of Heaven, or, admitting that deny its benevolence.

Little did she imagine the fearful interest another had in her and her actions; she never for one moment dreamt that such a love as that which Theodore Danton had for her existed at all in the world, and as to imagining that he had such feelings towards her, too well had he kept the secret of his heart for her to have any suspicion of its existence in that casket of pure thoughts and feelings.

Theodore was not one to inflict pain, even upon a dumb creature, who was debarred by nature of the power to complain, because he was impatient; and although he thought the time long and tedious, and that the carriage went desperately slow which conveyed him to London, yet he said nothing, but rather strove to chide his own impatient feelings than to urge the horses to greater speed.

Free and easy, says the proverb, goes a long way; and, at length, Theodore Danton found himself close to that city he had left so poor, and yet so full of hopes, and now returned to with one class of those hopes more than realized. He ought to have been suspicious that fortune had some desperate trick to play him, or he would not have been permitted to acquire the wealth which was a minor object of his young ambition. He ought to have trembled at what slippery trick the goddess was about to play him.

But he was not yet sufficiently a man of the world to be alarmed at success, as a man of the world may well be; for, in all the history of human fortunes, it surely happens that a something will be found which shall dim the lustre of apparently the brightest destiny, and lay up some cankering care in the heart of seemingly the happiest and the purest from all anxieties. Let no one envy the man who is carried through the streets in a splendid equipage. He has probably got gnawing at his very heart some care which would induce him to envy the very beggar who, with whining supplications, solicites alms of him as he steps from his carriage.

Let no man envy the rich, the titled, the powerful—for, so sure as any one posseses advantages of one description, fate, destiny, fortune, providence (call it what you will), takes especial care that there shall be quite enough of bitterness mingled with the cup of human felicity.

We do not know how this is, or why some people call it wise and wonderful, and pretend to like it. We can only say that we feel disposed to grumble most confoundedly at this admixture of the vexations with the sweets of life.

But, to return to Theodore Danton. Towards the close of his journey, he had been indiscreet enough to indulge in some blissful anticipations—we say indiscreet, because he ought rather to have prepared himself for disappointment, as being more consistent with the usages of human life. But he fancied how he would fly to the feet of Margaret —how he would tell her he loved her— how long, and with what fervor he had loved. He could fancy he saw her sweet face pale and red by turns, as she listened to those glowing words which, with all the fervid eloquence of first and only love, he felt sure he should be able to utter. He would tell her how, in the hour of success, he had thought of her, and, for her sake, blessed the happy fortune that had made him so. He would tell her how the thought of her had enabled him to bear up against all dangers; and how, when in the very desperation of evil chances, he was enabled, by the mere pronunciation of her name, to nerve himself to feats of valour and of endurance, which else would have been impossible, and in which he could not have felt sufficient interest to dream of performing.

Then he pictured to himself her reply —her surprised reply, to find that he had loved her so long, and yet—

"Never told his love!"

He fancied how she would feel such a love ought to be rewarded, and then should he not be happy! What evil destiny could touch him? Was he not, in the once dear consciousness of being beloved by Margaret, encased in armour of triple steel against the shafts of fate?

These were the blissful thoughts of Theodore Danton; and not even the aspect of the weather, which usually, if gloomy, lends some of its depression to the human mind, could reach his heart. He arrived in London when it wore its worst aspect.

The dull, heavy, leaden-coloured sky that hung over the metropolis, became denser and heavier, till its already overcharged contents began to descend in the form of rain, that promised a steady and continued fall.

No weather is more wretchedly uncomfortable to the Londoner than wet weather; there is nothing for it but to go through and get wet, for, notwithstanding all that may be said or done, there is nothing that entirely saves him from his share of the shower. All he can do is to mitigate the evil, and escape with as small a share as may be of the rain,—on the same principle that Lord Chesterfield told the waiter, at the country inn, to whom he had complained that there was some dirt on his plate, when he was told he must eat a peck of dirt before he died, that it was quite unnecessary to take it all at once.

Hour after hour passes, and yet the heavy, pelting shower abates not. The streets become washed and cleansed of all the mud and accumulations of filth that had been growing of late. The house-tops were saturated, and the spouts, in many cases, were surcharged with water, and dashed the overflowing element over the pavement below, much to the horror and annoyance of the foot-passengers, who could not avoid the shower without going more than ankle-deep into the kennel to escape the sluice.

The pavements looked well washed, and the roads too; the sewers were heard roaring with the rushing sound of water, but with a deep and mysterious noise that mingled with it something of dread and terror.

All business that could be put off was put off, for who would, that coul help it, venture out in such a heavy, deluging, and continuous shower as that which was falling?—no one. Those only were seen whose hapless condition would give them no choice but the celebrated "Hobson's"—that or none.

The very cattle in the street steamed from the effects of the rain—while the harness was brightened, and the drivers were wrapped up in indescribable coats and caps.

Such was the state of affairs in the out-of-door world, when, with a heart beating wildly and unequally from the excitement of the feelings that filled it, Theodore Danton alighted from the post-chaise at an hotel in London.

"I will seek her at once," he said to himself. "Oh, I shall have happy dreams to-night! for I will seek her at once, and she will tell me that she can love him who has shown how sincerely and how truly he can love her!"

CHAPTER XIV.

THE PAINFUL MEETING BETWEEN THEODORE AND MARGARET.

THEODORE DANTON'S impatience would not permit him to take even the necessary rest and refreshment which he was really in need of, after his long journey and the great fatigue he had undergone. He did have a thought of waiting until the morning before he sought out Margaret; and happy it would have been for him if he had—happy to a limited extent, for he would at least have had one more night of pleasant dreams and dear anticipations.

But when did prudence wage successful war with love? Never—never. He dismissed the thought of sleep before he saw Margaret; and, despite all the disagreeables of weather, and the feeling of exhaustion which even the excited state of his mind could not prevent him from feeling, he wrapped himself up in a cloak and left the hotel, to look for her who might, but for the sad chance that she was already another's, have been with him so happy!

The only clue which Theodore had to were Margaret was to be found, was to go to the house of the poor but amiable family with whom she had been residing upon his departure from England.

"She may still be there," he thought; "or, if she be not, they will of course be able to tell me were she is."

This was a natural enough supposition, and, alas! too true a one. They were able to tell him were she was, as well as what she was now.

He reached the street, which, to his mind, had been graced by her presence, with great speed. Well he knew the way to that house—for many and many an hour had he paraded it, on the opposite side of the way to that on which she whom he loved had resided, and was quite, to his mind, sufficiently rewarded if he saw but the shadow of her form upon the blind, as she moved about the room.

The rain had ceased; but such was now the state of feverish anxiety that Theodore Danton had got into, that he would not have been aware of it even if the most furious of storms had raged about him. His whole thought—his whole soul, was fixed upon one object, and that was Margaret—his dear cousin Margaret, whom he had invested with every grace and every virtue which can belong to woman, and a thousand more besides, culled from the prolific garden of his own rich and teeming fancy. When he actually reached the street, his courage almost failed him. He was too happy—too near, as he conceived, the fruition of all his fondest hopes.

"Well—well I know her principle," he said,—"she would marry no one to entail additional struggles and additional misery upon him. 'Tis only three years since I trod this street. She will not at all be changed. Beautiful and good as ever will she be. I always did receive, in the few times that I have seen her, a most kindly welcome from her. Perhaps even then she loved me a little. Oh, if there be but one spark of such a feeling in her heart, surely, with the devotion I shall convince her I still have for her, I shall succeed in fanning it to a glorious flame."

He paused a moment at the door of the house. He gazed up at the window which was so well known to him—all was dark! a dreary feeling of some terrific mischance came across him, and he shuddered.

"Suspense would kill me," he said, and he knocked at the door.

He watched the fanlight which was over it, and in a moment or two he saw it illumined from within. It grew lighter and lighter—some one was coming. How his heart beat then! It was enough almost to kill him.

The boor was opened by a woman whom he did not know. He looked at her in silence, and she at him. He was too much agitated to speak, and she was waiting to know what or who he wanted.

"I—is," at length he asked, naming the person who had kept the house previous to his leaving England,—"is Mrs. Andrews at home?"

"Andrews!" said the woman. "Did you say Andrews?"

"I did—is she within?"

"I hope not, sir."

"You hope not! What do you mean?"

"Why, considering, sir, as she's been dead and buried for a matter of two years, I should be very sorry if she was within."

"Dead and buried!"

"Yes, sir—just so."

"For two years?"

"About that time, poor woman. She fell into misfortunes, I am sorry to say, and she died."

"She had a daughter, who resided with her, I believe?"

"Yes, she married Nokes, the young, drunken carpenter, who belonged to the Temperance Society, and they've gone abroad somewhere, to emigrate, as they call it, and dig up stumps of trees, and sleep along o' rattlesnakes somewhere."

"Is all this possible in so short a time? Why, I have not been absent from England but three years."

Theodore somehow dreaded, strangely enough, to ask for Margaret Harrison. He was endeavouring to gain courage so to do.

"Three years!" said the woman. "Lor, sir, lots o' things may happen in half of that time."

"They may, indeed."

"Did you want a lodging, sir, that you came here, or did you know the Andrews?"

"I knew them a little."

"Oh, perhaps you lodged here?"

"No—no. In fact, my principal errand here was to discover were one of their lodgers had gone. There was a young lady who resided with the family."

"Oh, was there?"

"Yes there was. I want to know where she is. Her name was Margaret Harrison."

"Harrison—Harrison;—why, you don't mean Jane Bender, do you, who had the attic?"

"How can I mean her when I say Harrison?"

"Oh, lor! I know now; a young girl —quite a girl, with long hair?"

"Yes—yes."

"A pretty-looking girl, who always speaks so low."

"Yes—the same—the same."

"And she used to sing, and be so mild, and so gentle, and so cheerful, that everybody was in love with her."

"She is the person. Where is she?"

"Why, let me think,—I know I can tell you,—Queen Ann—Queen Ann—"

"What on earth can Queen Ann have to do with Margaret Harrison?"

"Bless me, how impatient you are. Queen Ann may have a great deal to do with her, when I believe that's the name of the street where she lives."

"Queen Ann-street?"

"No, no—I'm deceiving of you."

"Good God! why not tell me at once?"

"Well, you are the most impatient gentleman ever I met with in all my life. I always do confuse Queen Ann-street, do you know, with Weymouth-street."

"Not on account of the similarity of names, I should say, madam."

"Well, I don't know that; but, however, I can tell you that it's Weymouth-street she lives in, and the number, I think, is eleven,"

"Where is Weymouth-street?"

"Why, don't you know it's a fine, handsome street that leads out of Portland-place?"

"Fine, handsome——"

"Yes, and fashionable, too, I can tell you, if so be as you are a stranger in London."

"Fashionable! Why—why, what

change can have come over the fortunes of Margaret? She was poor when I left London—she was very poor."

"So she might have been; but she's made such a good match, that she can lift her head up now, they tell me, along with any duchess."

He gazed at her in astonishment, and mechanically walked into the parlour. He sunk into a chair with a deep sigh, as he said—

"Now, tell me all—now, tell me all!"

"All what, sir?"

"Of Margaret. I loved her—God only knows how I loved her."

"Poor young gentleman," said the woman, as she now began to see the real state of the case. "Well, really, I am very sorry indeed, and if I had but known, I would have told you by degrees about her being married."

"Never mind; the worst pang is over. I am trespassing upon you, I feel; but if you will tell me all you

MRS. BLAIR ENJOYING HERSELF AT THE BOTTLE.

know concerning her, it will spare me the agony of telling another one how much I suffer."

"Well, sir, all I know is as she's married to a very rich gentleman, who, some people say, rolls about continually in wealth."

"His name?"

"Bertram—Mr. Bertram—that's his name. I shouldn't have known, I dare say, anything about it, but there was a sort of disturbance at his wedding."

"A disturbance!"

"Yes; and the newspapers had it. It was all about some mad woman, who prophesied something wrong, and tried to put a carving-knife into his inside, but he wouldn't have it, and then she died. It was a terrible row, sir, as I heard."

"And—and Margaret—what became of her?"

"Oh, I can't tell. I understand they live in Weymouth-street in great riches, and all that sort of thing. She's Mrs. Bertram, of course; that's all I know about it."

"Thank—thank you. It is more than enough."

"More, sir?"

"No matter. I—I am better, and will go."

"I suppose, sir, as she jilted you?"

"No—no—no."

"Well, I thought——"

"No; she does not know I ever loved her, or that I am even in existence. Let that suffice, and breathe no word of reproach against her to any one. She is innocent. 'Tis I have indulged in a mid-day dream—'tis I have built an airy castle, which now with a breath has fallen in fragments at my feet, and I am wretched!"

"A castle, sir?"

"Yes—yes."

"And it fell down? Lor! Well, I'd bring an action against the man as built it up for you, sir. My husband had a shed built in the yard. Well, that stood very well, and he employed the selfsame man to build him a thingumity, you know, sir, as we thought would be a great convenience, and the blessed seat broke in in a week, and let somebody in."

"Ah," said Theodore, who was quite unconscious of what the woman said. His thoughts were with Margaret.

"And so," she continued, "my husband wants him to repair it, and he wouldn't, so we brings an action into court, and we produced the round *kiver*."

"Did you?"

"Yes; and so we gained the day. And that's what you ought to do, for a castle is nothing, of course, in comparison with a Mrs. Jones."

"No—no."

"I mean, a castle is a more serious affair, sir."

"Yes—yes. Good morning."

"Good morning to you, sir. If you should want a lodging, we have 'em to let; for we took the concern after the Lord took Mrs. Andrews, you understand, sir; and we heard from one neighbour and another all about what lodgers she had at different times."

Theodore walked out of the house. If we were to say he staggered out, per-

haps we should be nearer the mark. He was perfectly confounded. There was a sense of confusion, mingled with pain, in his mind, which made him almost incapable of thought. He only knew that all he had striven for—all he had lived for—was blighted and gone.

A lad, who saw the disordered manner in which he was walking, thought that intoxication was the cause, and called after him:

"Hold up, old chap. If you take another pint, you'll be all the better."

The thought that he was walking in that such a manner that he might well be taken for one inebriated came instantly across him, and he made an effort to appear composed.

"Be calm—be calm," he said. "All is lost but honour—honour; happiness is denied to me in this world now. Oh, if I had but some duty now to turn to, if there was but some sacred tie which bound me to any one, I would set it up in opposition to this dreadful feeling of despair which is rankling at my heart, and yet hope for victory."

He knew not which way he went. Chance, or some fatality, guided his footsteps. It may be that we are but playthings in the hands of destiny; or it may be that those things which appear strange—so strange that we are tempted to believe them arrangements —are but the accidental collisions arising from general circumstances.

Be this as it may, Theodore Danton walked as direct as it was possible for any human being to do, from the little mean house at which he had obtained such direful intelligence, to Weymouth-street, Portland-place, and until he actually paused at the very house numbered as the woman had told him, he really knew not where he was. Then, with a shudder, as he looked around him, and knew the locality, he said,—

"It was to be—it was to be. I must see Margaret. Even now she must know how much she was beloved, and then I will bid her adieu for ever."

He stood upon the doorstep, and gazed around him for some seconds; any one would have thought he was much interested in the appearance of the street, but he saw nothing of it. His thoughts were far otherwise engaged. Reason was just beginning to whisper to him, "You are wrong, Danton. You should not seek an interview with Margaret."

Had he listened to the promptings of reflection he would never have laid his hand upon the knocker of that door; and, oh, what a world of heart-sickness and sorrow would have been spared had he not done so; but to use the words which had passed his own lips when he found himself in the street, "Perhaps it was to be."

He knocked at the door, and the sound seemed to fall upon his own heart. The knock he gave was not one calculated to excite much attention from the servants of Mr. Bertram, who were used to those thundering appeals to the knocker which were so fashionable, we presume, but now are rated, very properly, so vulgar. Besides, he ought to have rang as well, but he did not; and the consequence was, that the footman, when he did condescend to come to the door, did not fling it wide open as he would have done to a visitor who had announced himself by a more imposing summons, but only so wide as to allow of his own bulky form filling up the gap most completely.

There was, however, about the appearance of Theodore Danton so much of the gentleman, that when the light from the hall lantern fell full upon him, the footman involuntarily stepped aside, and opened the door wider, as a kind of mute invitation to Theodore to walk in.

He did so; and then, in a deep, hollow voice,—it was the only one he could assume with any chance of steadiness, —he said to the man,—

"Is—Mrs. Bertram within?"

"Yes, sir."

"Tell her, then, that—that some one wishes to see her."

"If you will favour me with your name, sir, I will take it to her."

"Yes—yes. Very right—yes. Tell her that Theodore Danton is here, and would fain see her."

"Mr. Danton? Yes, sir. Will you walk into the waiting-room while I deliver the message?"

Theodore did so. The room was handsome, but he saw nothing of it. The superb decorations were all lost upon him; the gilding had no glitter in his eyes; the mirrors no brilliancy He felt not that he trod upon a carpet of rich texture—he knew not that he sank into a chair costly with rare carving. His heart was with Margaret. He was to see her; but what was he to say to her?—that was the question.

It was strange that Theodore never for a moment seemed to comtemplate the possibility of coming across Mr. Bertram in that house, where it was so natural he should do so. He did not give a thought to him, and had he met him suddenly, and been told who he was, he would, no doubt, have started to think that he was in the presence of any one who had dared to love Margaret, and make her his. It was the mere fact that she was married which pressed upon his mind. The individual who called her wife was of no account in the horror of the communication which had been made to him, and which had so effectually blighted all his earthly prospects. Then the footman came into the room, and said, in bland accents,—

"Mrs. Bertram will be very happy to see you, sir, upstairs, if you please."

CHAPTER XV.

THE INTERVIEW.—THE DISTRESS-ING COMMUNICATION.—THE ENCOUNTER WITH MRS. BLAIR.

THEODORE DANTON followed the servant upstairs to the drawing-room. It had no one in it. He had expected to find Margaret there, but such was not the case; and when the footman had ushered him in, he said,—

"Sir, if you will take a seat, my mistress says she will be with you in a few moments."

"Thank you," said Theodore, mechanically; and he stood nearly in the centre of the room.

From the ceiling of this room hung a magnificent chandelier of cut glass, capable of containing a number of lights. Some three or four only of them appeared to have been lighted, so that although, to many persons, feelings, there was light enough, yet in that large and costly apartment it had rather an odd effect.

"And this is her home," thought

Theodore. "This is the home of her whom I fondly dreamt of rescuing from poverty to a mere state of ordinary comfort. I find her surrounded by all the evidences of wealth. In the furnishing of this house, my whole fortune would be expended. My dream has fled. I am alone—alone in the wide world,"

Each moment appeared an age that brought not Margaret to him; but he knew not what detained her. When some months since she had heared of the wreck of the Atlantia, she had made up her mind then that she was utterly alone in the world, and that feeling did not then affect her so much as did the sudden intelligence that such was not the case. She was really agitated at the news of the arrival of Theodore Danton, and the reason why she came not to him immediately was, that she wished to recover as much composure as she could first.

Human nature has a propensity to forget the changes which time produces, or at least not to take them into consideration, and its estimate of people and places. To Margaret's idea, Theodore Danton was the timid, shy lad she had known three years before; she did not calculate that those three years were sufficient to make the boy a man, and, moreover, that he had during then seen enough of life to make the greatest alteration in his demeanour, as well as in his general appearance.

"Poor Theodore," she soliloquised; "what dangers and what hardships may he have endured. I long to hear of the escape he has had from shipwreck; but he must not see me in such a state of agitation as this. How foolish of me to feel so much tremor at the mere fact that I have one relation in the world, when I thought I had none."

Did Margaret, in the inmost recesses of her heart, cherish the least fond feeling for Theodore Danton? Had the question been asked of her, she would have said, unhesitatingly, no, not more than relationship and general esteem may freely warrant. And, so far as her own judgment of the matter went, she would have been justified in saying so; but love may sometimes, under some subtle disguise, lurk in the heart when its presence is least of all expected.

Perhaps she did love Theodore Danton a little, and, had she not been another's, that love might have ripened into a fast and firm affection.

It was about five minutes after Theodore had been ushered into the drawing-room, that she came slowly down to meet him. His eyes were fixed upon the door of the room—his sense of hearing appeared to be preternaturally acute—he could hear her light footstep as she came—his heart told him it was hers. He pressed his hand upon his heart.

"Now, God help me," he said, and in another moment he saw all that he loved on earth.

"Margaret—Margaret!" he exclaimed, and he rushed forward two steps to meet her.

"Theodore!" she said with surprise; "why—why, you have grown a man."

She held out both her hands, and he took them in his, as with trembling accents, of such acute misery that she could not but beware that some fearful calamity was pressing upon him, he said,—

"And you are a wife!"

"I am, Theodore. But how pale you look; you are not well. Tell me of your escape from death on board the ill-fated ship. Good God! Theodore, what ails you?"

"I am mad!"

She started, but quickly recovered herself, as she said,—

"Theodore, shall I guess why you are so unhappy?"

"Guess!"

"Yes. You have lost all by the wreck. You are penniless. Ah, can you imagine that now I have the means to make things otherwise, I will allow one, and the only one, too, to whom I can claim kindred want? Be of good cheer, Theodore. I will speak to Mr. Bertram, and we will contrive for you some path of honest and honourable industry."

"Contrive for me a path to the grave," said Theodore, as he drew his arms up in an excited manner. "That, now, is all I have to hope."

"Theodore!"

"Margaret—Margaret! I ought never to have come here. It was a great fault."

"A fault—why a fault?"

"It is madness! Tell your servants to drive me from the house, Margaret, entertain me not one moment here; speak no kind words to me. I ought not to be here!"

Margaret's immediate impression was that, in consequence of the sufferings he might have, for all she knew, undergone in the wreck of the vessel, he had become disordered in his intellect. A feeling of natural alarm took possession of her, and she was about to ring the bell, when he laid his hand upon her arm, saying, in a calmer tone,—

"Do not—do not! I will soon be gone; but since my fate has brought me here, and since, betrayed by feelings which I have no means of conquering, I have uttered words requiring explanation, I will give it."

"You astonish me, Theodore."

"Before I say that which I feel it may kill me now to leave unsaid," he added, "let me tell you that I will, to-morrow morning, as early as may be, leave England for ever."

"Leave again?"

"Yes, with the hope that I shall soon find a grave on some other land, or in the depths of that ocean whose wrath, now, will have no terrors for me."

"You surprise as well as afflict me."

"Margaret—Margaret!——"

He covered his face with his hand, and groaned audibly.

"What would you say, Theodore?"

"God—oh, God!"

"Nay, speak to me. If you have grief that the hand of kindness can assuage, tell me of it. Speak, Theodore, oh, speak freely!"

"I *love* you, Margaret!"

He sunk on his knees at her feet, and clung to her hands, as he now looked up in her face, which was scarcely less agitated than his own.

"Margaret, I love you!"

"Theodore!"

"I know what you would say. 'Tis madness, presumption, folly, villany, or all combined, and yet I love you. 'Tis hopeless, and yet I love you; criminal in the sight of God and of man, and yet I love you. Destructive to my own happiness, perchance, both here and hereafter; an affliction to you likewise, as well it may be, and yet, Margaret, I love you!"

"Good God! Theodore!"

"Yes, I love you with a passion boundless as the realms of eternal space. I love you, Margaret, as man yet never loved woman. It is not a feeling, it is not a passion, it is my whole life—my soul itself. Margaret—Margaret, I love you!"

Margaret was terrified at such a burst of passionate eloquence. At the moment she had no power to stop him, and now seizing both her hands, he covered them with wild, fervent kisses, as if he would have devoured them. This act restored her to herself; she broke away from him as she exclaimed,—

"Rise, Theodore Danton—rise. This attitude is as unbecoming for you to assume as for me to suffer. Rise, I say, and pursue at once the determination you boasted you had made, to leave me for ever."

He rose tottering to his feet; he spoke in a strange, whispering sort of voice, very different from the vehement one in which he had uttered his last words.

"'Tis done—'tis done!" he said; "I am going. Oh, that it were to death! I am going—and why should it not— why should it not? On far less grounds many a man has hastened to the throne of God, perchance from thence to be hurled to that perdition from whence there is no redemption."

These words excited a new alarm in the heart of Margaret. That, in his present state of mad excitement he should go and commit suicide, appeared but too probable with such a temperament as his, and she said,—

"Theodore, let the past be forgotten, as it shall be forgiven. Think more calmly on this disappointment. I am a wife, and dare not listen to you. After what you have said, I dare not be near you. Go from England, and take with you my good wishes."

He held his head strangely with both his hands.

"Theodore—Theodore, what are you thinking of?" added Margaret. "Be more yourself. Do you want to bring destruction upon us both? What are you thinking of now, Theodore?"

"Nothing—nothing."

"You are not master of your words or actions."

' What have I to think of now but despair ?"

"This is madness."

"It is. It has been madness from he beginning. Oh, God, what a madman I have been!"

"What mean you ?"

" Margaret, when least you knew it, when least you suspected it, the boy loved you—the quiet, sensitive, shy boy, who almost seemed, in his deep idoltary, to shun your presence, as too much happiness, than court it. I loved you then with a passion that grew with my growth and strengthened with my strength, Margaret; but I was poor, and, strong as was my love, I did not lose reflection with it. I told myself that I ought to have something more than the heart of an idolater of your beauty and excellences to offer you. For this reason was it I went abroad, resolved to win a name and wealth to lay at your feet, or to perish in the pursuit. I did not tell you that I loved you; I would not, until I had achieved something. God help me now! what have I achieved but a broken heart ?"

He covered his face with his hands and wept. Margaret was deeply affected; her own tears flowed freely. She could not, for a moment, doubt the sincerity of every word he uttered. There was the god-like stamp of truth upon them all.

"Oh, Theodore—Theodore!" she said; "why did you come here to say this much ?"

" Because I knew not what I did."

"Alas! alas!"

"You can pity me ?"

"I do—I do, Theodore—from my heart I do. I knew not that you loved me."

"No, no. I kept that secret here—here in my heart of hearts; but, oh! how I dreamed of the day when I could tell it to you without a blush; when I could say, ' Margaret, I love you—will you be mine ? for see what I have done to endeavour to take off some of my unworthiness.' "

" You will be happy yet, Theodore."

"No—no. Never—never!"

"Compose yourself. This is a dreadful interview. Heaven might have ordered it otherwise; but we must bow to its decrees. I speak to you now the more freely, because this is a theme which, between us, can never—never be repeated."

"Never—never," said Theodore.

"Think of me, Theodore, but as one you loved—who has passed away from your sight and observation—one whom you may meet in a better world, and under happier auspices, but never again here. I cannot be angry with you, Theodore; the conventional forms of the world would tell me to be so, but I cannot, because I do believe you mean no wrong, but have erred only in judgment."

"As I live, Margaret," said Theodore, mournfully, "I knew not until one short hour since you were a wife."

"I—I guessed so much."

"I went to make means wherewith to bless you; I made them. Fortune, with a seeming kindness, lured me on to think that I was prospering in my intention, and that she was smiling on the efforts I was making. Gold came to my hand; friends, new friends, full of generous feelings and impulses, flocked around me. Along with the bright gold I sought, there came no taint, for with it I gathered golden opinions."

"You have been fortunate, Theodore."

"Fortunate ?"

"I mean, you have been successful."

"Yes, in the accomplishment of my despair."

"Oh! say not so; you are young, and life may yet present to you a thousand charms. Many objects of better ambition than the fulfilment of a dream of love will present themselves to you in your path through life. You have talent; you have enterprise and enthusiasm. Surely, with such qualities, you will accomplish something that shall chase away the deep gloom of this disappointment."

"Oh! no, no, Margaret, ambition is now dead within my soul; the stimulant that first warmed it into life is gone. What is fame—wealth—the world's applause—and homage—now to me ?"

"Much, if extracted from men by the sheer force of goodness, and the nobility of greatness."

"There is now no spark of smouldering ambition which even your breath can fan into a flame. I look along the dreary walk of life—I see no flowers by the wayside that I wish to pluck; but I see the grave in the far distance. Would to Heaven it were nearer."

"These despairing thoughts are unworthy to you; and, I add, that they are, to me, afflicting!"

The tone of voice in which Margaret spoke sufficiently proclaimed the state of her feelings. She deeply, sincerely pitied him who, with so rare and noble a generosity, had forborne even to tell her that he loved her until he had done something to entitle himself to the applause of her judgment likewise.

"I am lost!" he moaned.

"Oh! Theodore, you must leave this house now, and at once; but let me implore you not to leave it in such a frame of mind as that which now possesses you. When you heard that I was another's, prudence should have told you not to seek me, but——"

"Oh! Margaret, prudence did say so much; but I was mad, and knew not what I did. For coming here, now, I feel that I deserve your reprehension, Margaret; perhaps even your contempt."

"Neither, Theodore, neither. I can fancy the state of feeling which urged you to the step; but hear me out. I was about to say that, since you have come here, you ought not to part with such a feeling of despair."

"How otherwise?"

"Let me have the satisfaction of knowing that I have awakened better feelings in you; let me not feel that, for me, you went away despairing, and that some dreadful act of rashness might result. He loves not truly who seeks not the happiness of her he loves."

"Oh, God! am I amenable to that reproach? Sought I not your happiness?"

"You did; but do you seek it now?"

Theodore was silent, and, after a brief pause, Margaret resumed,—

"If, for my sake, you were capable of doing so much, let me implore you, for my sake, to do a little more. Think of me with calmness; although a disappointed man, yet does it become you to be a man."

"Alas! that little more you ask of

me, Margaret, transcends all that has gone before it."

"And, if so, the greater is the triumph."

"A triumph without reward."

"Not without reward—not without reward. The triumph of having done a duty can never be without reward."

"Margaret, I will go—I will strive to do as you bid me. I will try to hide beneath the mask of indifference those feelings which I may conceal, but never, never can forget."

"To forget may be impossible. It is a foolish plan to ask any one to forget; but to remember, and yet control the effects of memory, may be heroic."

"Alas! how little of the hero is there in humanity. When most we fancy we are playing such a part, some motive guides us that makes the seeming sacrifice a pleasure."

"Now, Theodore, you will leave me; you will go now, Theodore."

"Your husband?"

"Is from home now, and I thank Heaven he is so, for—for——"

"For what?"

"No matter. Heaven only knows what jealous phantasy might come over him were he to know what errand brought you hear."

"Then, by the great God, would he wrong you as well as wrong me, Margaret. I loved you because that your soul was pure and good, as well as that my eyes told me you were beautiful. I love you still, because I know you are a piece of virtue. The great God who sees all hearts knows that with no evil intent came I hither on this dreadful day."

"I believe you, Theodore, and you may well believe that I believe you, by according to you so many words upon this subject."

"Yes—yes—yes."

"Farewell now! We must not meet again."

"I—I go; but, oh! Margaret, ere I go, there are two questions my soul pants to ask of thee."

"Say on, and such as become my honour to answer, that will I answer, Theodore."

"Are you happy with him who has placed you in this glittering home?"

Margaret head by the back of a chair

or support as she, in a strange tone, repeated the words,—

"Are you happy with him who has placed you in this glittering home?"

And then she looked around her, as if connecting for the first time with such a question the gorgeous and ample decorations of that magnificent apartment, which, to her, would ever be a means of calling to mind this most painful and harassing interview.

"Ah! you hesitate," cried Theodore. "To hesitate in the affirmative answer to such a question, is at once to answer it otherwise."

"No, no, no!" exclaimed Margaret.

"Well, you did hesitate."

"It was a question you should not have asked me, Theodore. 'Tis scarcely one I ought to answer. But—I—I am happy."

"It is enough—I am convinced. I am very glad—very glad that you are happy. I did not suppose you otherwise; but still, hearing from your own lips an assurance that you are happy is more joy. You are happy, although you hesitated a moment. You are happy!"

"I am happy."

"And now the other question, Margaret."

"Say on."

"If—if you had been now, on my return, Margaret Harrison, instead of Mrs. Bertram—oh, tell me, would the dream of my too fond heart have been fulfilled—would you, Margaret, then—could you have been mine?"

"Theodore—Theodore! is this a question you ought to ask, or I to answer?"

"Yes, yes, yes! Tell me so much?"

"And in either case add a pang to the misery you have declared you already feel."

"I am as one on a bed of sickness, and would know the worst that fate has in store for me."

"I cannot answer you."

"You will not!"

"I will not, Theodore. It is a question I will close my heart against. It is a question I ought not and will not for one moment entertain."

"I am answered."

"Translate this silence how you will, or in whatever way your own imagina-tion may choose to dictate to you. Theodore, answer to it I have none."

He tottered towards the door, and then he turned and said in a faint voice—

"Farewell!"

She could not speak, but she waved her hand in signification of adieu. Another few steps he took, and then with a burst of frantic grief he cried—

"Margaret—Margaret, dear Margaret——"

"Hold, Theodore. Another word and I shall be compelled to call for aid. I cannot, I will not, Theodore, I dare not hear you utter such words."

"My brain burns, Margaret! beautiful, adored Margaret——"

She laid her hand upon the bell. He heard the sharp tingle, which was the result, and in a moment a footstep was upon the staircase.

"Was this well?" he said

"It was well," said Margaret; "and thank God I have had the sense to do it. Adieu."

A footman made his appearance, and Margaret, in a cold, calm tone, which proved that it is true women can control their feelings much better than men, said—

"Show this gentleman out."

"Yes, madam."

Theodore looked bewildered for a moment. He spoke not, but mechanically he followed the footman down the drawing-room staircase to the hall.

He had left his hat in the waiting-room, into which he had been first shown, and he would have gone out without it, so bewildered were his heart and brain with the agitating interview he had passed through; but the footman handed it to him, saying—

"Your hat, sir."

"Yes—yes," said Theodore, "farewell for ever!" and he was about to pass out, when the astonished footman again said—

"Here is your hat, sir."

Then he took it, and placing it hastily upon his head, he passed out of the house. He made a sudden rush down the steps and ran violently against a woman who was ascending them. With an exclamation of impatience he passed on, leaving Mrs. Blair, who was the party he had run against, to recover herself and her bent bonnet as best she might.

CHAPTER XVI.

THE QUARREL OF MRS. BLAIR WITH MARGARET. — THE DISCHARGE FROM SERVICE AND THE MISSTATEMENT.

WELL and bravely had Margaret gone through the agitating meeting with her cousin, Theodore. Perhaps it would have been a higher reach of prudence on her part, had she rejected such a conversation as she had held with him altogether, but having held it, she had conducted it nobly.

The moment he was gone, she threw herself on a sofa, and burying her face in the ample cushion, she wept more bitter tears than ever she remembered to have shed. It was a gush of feeling which might fairly have been expected after what had passed.

"How foolish is this," she said, as

THE QUARREL BETWEEN THE TWO NURSES.

she rose; "how weak and how childish I am. Perhaps these tears I ought almost to call criminal."

The small light that was in the showy apartment, to her, now appeared glaring, for she had had her eyes completely shrouded for some moments, and as she placed her hand across them to spare herself the pain of the glitter, she unconsciously repeated Theodore Danton's words, saying—

"And am I happy in this glittering home ?"

It was with a shudder that she repeated these significant words, conveying, as they did, so very important a question; and yet one she had not before seriously asked herself. Perhaps it was one of those questions which are best unasked, for, like many preparations, it set the mind to work to find food for vexation.

Ask whom we may, who has reached the height of human ambition, to all appearance, the question of, "Can you think of no wish yet ungratified ?" and we shall soon set the intellect to work to think of something as far, if not farther, off the attainable as were some of the ambitious objects which had been already achieved.

"Am I happy in this glittering home?" again repeated Margaret, and now that it had been once suggested to her, she felt that it was a question she should often ask herself. But why did she fear it? Was she not happy? At all events, was she not as happy as any state of human existence could be at all fairly supposed to be? Did she find Charles Bertram exactly all that she had expected? Not exactly: she found him a little selfish; she found that about his character there was a taint of disingenuousness, which, before marriage, she had not been able to discover.

But these were not serious or painful faults. She had no right to expect perfection in a husband; and, besides, Charles Bertram was a man of the world, one who, with sufficient means, had mixed in its follies and foibles—one who, on account of those means, had been compelled to take a totally different view of society from those who had them not.

The question she ought to have asked of herself should not have been, am I happy? But am I as happy as I ought fairly to expect to be?

"I must banish this from my mind," she said; "and now comes another serious question—shall I, or shall I not say anything of this affair to Charles?"

This, indeed, was a serious question, when once it became a question at all, which it should never have become, for a greater error of judgment could not be than that which was involved in the very asking of it.

Margaret's first act upon seeing her husband, should have been to tell him all about it, and to relate to him as nearly as possible everything which had been said by Theodore to her, or by her to Theodore. By such means she would, she must surely have disarmed all jealous feeling on his part, and, although he might have been vexed at the occurrence, his first feeling would have been his worst, and it could not have partaken of jealousy, which from a small beginning will so quickly grow to such a monstrous growth, as to overshadow all other feelings and sensations whatever, in its rank luxuriance. But she

hesitated. She knew that Charles Bertram was of rather a peculiar temperament. and she dreaded to imagine that he was more so now than she knew of.

"What would he do?" she asked herself; "what would he do, if he got, as he might, furiously angry with poor Theodore, who is to be pitied, not blamed?"

The idea that in addition to the affliction of mind he was already in, Theodore should be doomed to receive violence or insult at the hands of Bertram, was to Margaret an extremely painful one, and that such might be the case, she felt was very possible indeed, with such a temper as Charles Bertram's. After all, the fault of Theodore consisted not in loving her, but merely in the mere fact that he called to tell her so, after he knew she was another's. That was a fault, for it would have been more heroic, more noble, and a higher course of virtuous action, had he not done so, but had banished himself at once somewhere were he would never have seen her again, and so ran no chance of vexing her pure spirit with a knowledge of his affection, and the blight which it had cast upon his life.

We say, this would have been Theodore Danton's best course; but he was human, and, consequently, the sport of all those motives and impulses which sway humanity, and he did not take the best course, but the most natural one. There Margaret felt that he was to blame. There was his error, but it was one of those errors which women easiest forgive. He had erred in loving her; could she then not forgive him? Oh, yes, but would Charles Bertram view the affair in the same light?

That was the fearful question. He might be satisfied of his wife's virtue and honour, but not of Theodoe Danton's intentions. And how could she say all she would wish to say, and all that her heart would prompt her to say in his defence? Her tongue would be tied on such a subject for fear of saying too much, and hence she could not be able to speak at all, without fearing to show a partisanship that might produce far more mischief than mere silence.

Perplexed beyond all comparison with any degree of perplexity she had ever before suffered, Margaret could not make up her mind to any course of action, and, consequently, she remained in a state of doubt and irresolution, which was worse than if she had made up her mind to some course which involved an error of judgment, so long as she had really made up her mind to it. Such minds as Margaret's never contemplate falsehood for a moment; but she drew a crude distinction between the perversion of a fact, and the suppression of it.

Hence, although she would have disdained to falsify for a moment to her husband, or even to any one else, what had happened as regarded Theodore Danton, she did think earnestly of not saying anything about it at all. Margaret was in the midst of this perplexity, when the door of the drawing-room was opened, and Mrs. Blair made her appearance. The very sight of this woman was unwelcome to Margaret at such a time, and with more petulance, or perhaps one might call it resolution, than she usually possessed, Margaret, before Mrs. Blair could say a word, said herself,—

"I did not ring."

"I am aware you did not ring," said Mrs. Blair, who, when she chose to be insolent, as she did now, for it was a part of her plans, could be so indeed.

"Then why am I intruded upon?"

"I am sorry to hear my presence called an intrusion, Mrs. Bertram. When I was engaged here, I was told to consider myself in so responsible a situation, that there was no part of the house I might not visit."

"I would rather be alone," said Margaret.

"I hope, madam, we are to be on good terms?"

"Good terms—good terms?"

"Yes, Mrs. Bertram, I hope we shall be comfortable together."

"Mrs. Blair, I believe you are the housekeeper, and as such, I do not see the necessity of our being on any other terms than those of mistress and servant."

"Mr. Bertram has always treated me with the greatest respect, madam."

"Of course he has. Mr. Bertram I do not suppose would dream of condescending to do otherwise."

"Condescending?"

"Yes, condescending. And now, Mrs. Blair, permit me to say once more, that I wish to be alone."

Mrs. Blair would not be shaken off so easily. She had wished to have a quarrel with Mrs. Bertram, and she saw that she was going the right way to bring it about.

"Madam," she said, "of course I shall leave you to yourself. I have certainly not been accustomed to be treated in this manner, because I have always had the greatest respect shown me wherever I have lived. I was engaged by Mr. Bertram, madam,"

"Very well," said Margaret, calmly. "You are now discharged by Mrs. Bertram."

"Discharged!"

"Yes; I never put up with insolence in domestics. You are discharged, and will please to make up your accounts, and leave the house."

"Indeed, madam; and so these are all the thanks I get for trying to do my duty?"

"I cannot," said Margaret, rising, "turn you out of this room: nor do I like, as you are a female, to order the footman to do so; therefore, my only resource is to leave it myself. You certainly have the satisfaction of being fully aware that you had better not send to me for a characrer."

"My character, madam, is in black and white, and I don't want one from you. Perhaps, as you are discharging me, you will not be surprised that I put down in my accounts a sum of money for a new bonnet."

"A new bonnet!"

"Yes, madam. A young man, a visitor of yours, as I understand, must needs leave the house so abruptly, that he ran against me, and spoiled my bonnet."

"It was Theodore," involuntarily exclaimed Margaret.

"I dare say it was Theodore," said Mrs. Blair, drily.

But Margaret was too busy with her own thoughts to notice the imputation conveyed in the words of Mrs. Blair by the tone in which they were spoken.

"What shall I do?" was the anxious question she asked herself. "What shall I do?"

"A lover, I'll be bound," thought

he delighted Mrs. Blair. "I have her now—she is my slave."

"I have nothing whatever to do with any misadventures your bonnet might have come to," said Margaret. "You are discharged, and your accounts shall be looked over."

"But, madam—the young man."

"Well?"

"I don't want to make mischief. I am the last who would say one word to—to—you understand—to breed dissension in families. Wherever I have lived, they always said that much of me."

"I will, when I see my cousin, Theodore Danton," said Margaret, "speak to him on the subject."

Margaret then instantly left the room, which Mrs. Blair most certainly had the pleasure of turning her out of.

"Humph!" muttered Mrs. Blair, "what am I to think? Her cousin! All lovers are called cousins, except where imprudence goes a long way, and then they become brothers. Her cousin—ah! I understand that. I saw her change colour, too, when he was mentioned. He may be her cousin, but if he is not her lover as well, I am very much mistaken. They say a cat watches a mouse well, but no cat ever watched mouse as I shall watch you, Mrs. Bertram. Cousin, indeed! And I am discharged. I—ha! ha!"

This "ha, ha!" was meant as an intimation that she had not the remotest intention of going. Not she; she had a hold of Mr. Bertram by possession of the letter from Emma Armstrong, and she now fully expected that the time would not be very far distant when she would have a hold of Margaret, too, on account of this cousin, who she was so happy to think she had just come home in time to run against.

"She is shy at present," resumed Mrs. Blair, "she is shy and young, but that will wear off. I should not be a bit surprised if she should send for me and make this quarrel up before I can say anything to Mr. Bertram. Well, well," added Blair, after a pause, "I will wait to give her a good opportunity of doing so, for, if she should, I can carry on what robbery I like in the house, and she will, instead of being one whose detection I have had to fear, become one whom I can compel to back me out,

should any one else dare to impeach me. That would be a remarkably pleasant state of things, indeed, to have both husband and wife completely under my thumb, because each was afraid of what I had it in my power to tell to either—and I will, too, or my name is not Blair."

Mrs. Blair, full of these self-congratulatory feelings, walked off to her room, from whence she issued her order for a nice tasty supper to be prepared for herself, which orders were, as usual in the kitchen, complied with, along with the usual amount of grumbling, for nothing aggravates servants to such a degree as being compelled to wait upon a servant.

And what did Margaret, when she reached the privacy of her own room, think of this new aspect of affairs? She leaned her head upon her hands as the question again, vague and indefinite as it was, passed her lips, of

"What shall I do, now?"

Troubles, entanglements, and disagreeables of all kinds and descriptions, seemed thronging up and around her, and she knew not how to steer clear of them. The sudden insolence of Mrs Blair was so unexpected, after the cringing, canting manner in which she had already behaved to her, Margaret, that she knew not what to think of it. That it could all arise from her meeting with Theodore, and a thought that he was a lover come to the house in the absence of Mr. Bertram, she could scarcely think: because, what could induce her to think so, in the first instance? and, in the second, what good did it do her to show so much insolence on the occasion as to insure her own dismissal? Alas! Margaret was no match for Mrs. Blair; she had not the least notion of the policy that unprincipled person was pursuing, and, consequently, she had no key to her actions; and, in her ignorance, likewise, of the hold which she had upon Charles Bertram, the quarrelling with her, Margaret, seemed, on the part of Mrs. Blair, to be little short of an act of positive and sheer insanity.

But, putting aside all this, Margaret felt the necessity of saying something to her husband about Theodore Danon, and, after some time spent in reflection, she exclaimed,—

"I may tell him Theodore has been here, without telling him that he came to make a declaration of love to me."

Here seemed a means of overcoming the difficulty, and placing the affair in such a light that no mischief could result from it at all. The more she thought of this view of the subject, the more reasonable and capital she thought it. She felt much easier in her mind, and she exclaimed,—

"Yes, I will tell him Theodore has been here; but there can be no occasion to breed mischief and uncomfortable feelings by a description of his hopeless passion. It is a theme, too, which will never be resumed, and, therefore, the news of it may as well rest in my breast for ever. The next I hear of Theodore will be his departure from England, no doubt, and there will be an end of the whole transaction."

Margaret breathed more freely, and much she blamed herself, and wondered how, perfectly innocent in deed and thought as she was, she had allowed herself to be so uneasy concerning a matter in which no one could blame her. She bathed her eyes to get rid of all traces of her recent tears, and then, with more calmness than any one would have thought to be possible after so much agitation and excitement as she had passed through, she awaited the return of her husband.

CHAPTER XVII.

MR. PRIMROSE'S STATE OF MATRIMONIAL SUBJECTION.—A CLEVER WOMAN, AND HOW TO MANAGE A HUSBAND.

HAVING incidentally mentioned what a clever managing woman Mrs. Primrose was, we may as well proceed to detail some of that lady's doings, as being of themselves more elucidatory of the fact than any description we could give, and will duly impress the minds of our readers with the power of the female world, and of the actual state of subjection in which Mr. Primrose really existed; showing also to those who are not so blind as those that will not see, that Mr. Primrose's case is by no means a peculiar or solitary one. The reverse is generally the case, for it is a principle of female nature to discover the weak side of the male species, and, attacking them in that quarter, they more or less, according to the obstinacy of the garrison, succeed, sooner or later, in subduing the lords of creation to a state of bondage.

Mrs. Primrose was a disinterested female—at least, so she gave everybody to understand, and Mr. Primrose in particular; she sacrificed herself, that is, her pleasure and happiness, her enjoyment, and her hopes of the sweets of this life, to the management of Mr. Primrose's affairs. She desired to see her husband prosper, and she took a prominent part in all great determinations, and was, in fact, his banker. How this came about was very strange, but very natural, because a very common occurrence with all classes of people.

Mrs. Primrose, during courtship, had always expressed a great abhorrence to interfering with the prerogatives of the men, and said it was very unbecoming in a wife to interfere in matters that she had no business with at all. Mr. Primrose was charmed with such sentiments, so unusual, but at the same time so reasonable; but he was doomed to find out the difference ere long. Indeed, it might be questioned if he did not gradually and imperceptibly fall into his wife's opinions; at all events, he was brought to acquiesce in them, and he found out afterwards what a dangerous thing precedent was. If, therefore, at any future time, Mr. Primrose thought he would act in such a manner, he was instantly met with—

"Why, you know, Mr. Primrose, that it was never done before—it was never so."

"But why not now?" sometimes Mr. Primrose would venture to inquire.

"Well, I never saw such a man as you are, Primrose; you would make your home a mere place for changes, for all sorts of odd notions and out-of-the-way desires. I am really surprised that a respectable man like you, who passes in the world for a clever man, should think of such a thing."

Mr. Primrose afterwards held his tongue; he did not see his way through he maze of argument that his lady could produce to him upon any particular question which he desired to be settled one way or another. It was impossible to contend against such a torrent of eloquence and argument. Mr. Primrose was eminently fond of peace, and occasionally he was not averse to spend a few hours among old acquaintances whom he had met. But there was always a difficulty to get over Mrs. Primrose, who was his cash-keeper, and to escape without a contest with any petty cash was a miracle.

It must not be assumed that there was no money passing through the hands of Mr. Primrose—quite the reverse; but, somehow or other, he was always induced to give it, like a "good man," to his wife. The habit became so confirmed, that he would as soon have thought of keeping a favourite giantess in his house as a few pieces of silver from his wife.

Mrs. Primrose, indeed, allowed him to have something in his pocket; but it was a well understood thing that he was to give a very exact account of how it had been spent; not that there was any possibility, much less probability of his spending it improperly. The amount was the bar, it was so very small, and at this, indeed, Mr. Primrose did rebel; but then he was informed that if somebody didn't look after him, and keep his place together, he would run a course of ruin, and that she, poor thing, was a martyr to his interest, and what did she want to spend? She, forsooth, could live at home without being obliged to spend money when she went out; for her part, she could not see the necessity for Mr. Primrose's keeping the society of those who merely met to eat or drink, or, in fact, to do anything else but business.

To all these tirades Mr. Primrose merely spoke in deprecation, professed he should be sorry to see his wife angry, as, no doubt, good man, he was, for it was extremely unpleasant. Moreover, he always gave in, and Mrs. Primrose invariably treated him to a long lecture afterwards, so that he emphatically gained nothing by his motion, and his retreat was always accompanied by mortification and disgrace. But then he had this one consolation, he knew that

Mrs. Primrose was a very clever woman. Alas! it was the fact.; she was too clever by half for Primrose, who sunk deeper and deeper into the mire daily, and was irrevocably and unequivocally henpecked, as it is not inaptly termed.

It was some time before all this came about; it did not come about at once. On the contrary, it came slowly, and by degrees; had his eyes been open to it all, it would have enabled him to struggle, and, very possibly, successfully, against domestic and female usurpation. No, no; what was too tedious to be borne by a mind unused to contemplate such conduct, was effected by degrees, and as the individual sunk beneath each successive effort, he became accustomed to look upon female domination in this thing, or in that little thing, of no consequence, or not worth quarrelling about, until he looked upon so many things in this light, as matters of no consequence, that it was too late to struggle with his fate.

So thought Mr. Primrose, who was, therefore, now reduced to mean and petty shifts and intrigues to gain any little object that he might be entitled to, but which his clever and self-sacrificing wife did not think he was, or which her caprice caused her to object to. It happened, on one occasion, he had a little niece, who had been left an orphan; he took her home, intending to provide for her, and keep her from want. She was a sweet-tempered girl, and very pretty; her beauty and her forlorn situation had interested him, and so it would have done almost any one else. However, Mrs. Primrose had been out—she was out when Mr. Primrose entered the house with his niece in his hand, and found nobody but the servant, who let them in, and who informed him her mistress had gone out on a round to the tradespeople.

"Then she'll come home in a pretty temper," thought Primrose, "for they are sure to cross her, and if somebody won't bate a penny, why she'll come home and vent her ill humour on me or somebody else. Well, well, I am used to it, and don't mind it; but I suppose others do, and that's the worst for them. Well, well, she's a clever woman, and really manages a house well. She certainly has my interest at heart; but it takes a troublesome form at times. However, I must not complain, we are all with our faults. By-the-bye, I shall want a little more money to-day. I expect there'll be something unpleasant about that. Ah, well, I had better see how the wind blows before I ask for it. If it's any way stormy—anything disagreeable, I'll hold my tongue and save all trouble."

Just at that moment Mrs. Primrose arrived, and was evidently in high ill humour, for she rated soundly the girl for not cleaning the steps properly while she was about it.

"Please, ma'am, I did," was the reply.

"You did not, lazy huzzy."

"Please, ma'am, I did."

"Look at the dirt—do you see it?" said Mrs. Primrose, pointing to the place.

"Yes, ma'am."

"Then how can you tell me such a falsehood as to say you cleaned it?"

"So I did, ma'am."

"Then why is it dirty?"

"That I suppose is master, and——"

"Is he come home at this hour?"

"Yes, and the——"

"The what?"

"The young lady."

"Brought a young lady home, has he?" exclaimed Mrs. Primrose, in amazement.

"Yes, ma'am."

"To stop to dinner, I dare say. And here have I been worrying myself endeavouring to save him money, and he must come home and knock down a week's savings."

As she said this, she walked into the parlour, where Mr. Primrose was engaged in explaining some picture to his niece, and did not see his sweet wife enter.

"Well, Mr. Primrose—oh, dear, you did not know I was in—don't disturb yourself, pray—I'm in no hurry."

"Now, my dear!"

"Oh, pray don't talk so to me."

"Well, then, here is my niece Emma."

"So I see."

"And she is going to remain with us for some time to come."

"Indeed! Mr. Primrose," exclaimed the lady, aghast at such temerity.

"Yes, my dear, she will. Her father and mother are both dead—she is an orphan, and without friends."

"Indeed."

"Yes; and I have brought her home here to be with you."

This announcement completed what the dirty doorstep had begun—the climax of anger and rage was reached, and there was nothing more required; and she flounced out of the room, saying,—

"She could see through it—it was merely a blind. A big girl like that was not fit to be always hanging about a man, and that man Mr. Primrose, of all others!"

Mr. Primrose was much hurt at what his wife had said, but he believed it was a passing fit of ill-temper, and would no doubt go off in a short time. He, therefore, took no further notice of it, but immediately set about, in his own mind, arranging to his own satisfaction various articles of domestic economy. Alas! that Mr. Primrose should have so far forgotten himself as to have permitted himself to speculate upon domestic arrangements that were not his province —it was no business of his, and so he found it.

When he thought that Mrs. Primrose had in some measure recovered from her anger, and had, as he hoped, begun coolly to reflect upon what she had said, he sought her out, and found her in another room.

"Well, Mr. Primrose?"

"My dear," began Mr. Primrose, in a deprecating tone, "I did not see you when you came in; but there was no harm done."

"Oh, dear no, no harm in a married man talking to a great girl big enough to be a woman, and at the same time turning his back to his wife. Of course there was no harm; oh, dear, no; but you must have been deeply engaged—deeply interested in what you were saying. And she, too,—oh, yes! there is a pair of you."

"Surely you cannot mean what you would insinuate against a little girl, my own niece—you are joking!"

"Oh, yes, anything I say is a joke. I always joke, especially when my feelings have received a great shock—oh of course, it must be a joke—it is so funny!"

Mr. Primrose looked very blank; he knew not what to say or to do. It was an unexpected circumstance, and he knew not how to get over it, or what to say.

"I tell you what, Mr. Primrose," said the lady, "you are a good-for nothing man. What if I were to tell th world how you used me, they would believe it impossible; and if I were to tell, by way of climax, how I have sacrificed health and happiness for you, how I have slaved and toiled—and all the reward, all the thanks, I have received is, that you have brought home a young girl to destroy my peace of mind."

"Good God!"

"Oh, there, swear if you will, reprobate that you are; but I deserve all this, because I've been so meek and so submissive."

"What can I do?" exclaimed the unfortunate and bewildered husband.

"Send her away, to be sure."

"But she has no relations."

"Any excuse. I see how it is—all sorts of shifts to keep her by you; and I'm to be sacrificed, because you don't know what to do."

Mr. Primrose saw it was no use in contending against his wife; he must be in prepetual trouble, and he had no strength of mind to keep out of it, until she would listen to reason, and become amenable to it too.

"Well, this is unfortunate. The poor girl has just become an orphan, without friends or money,—I thought you would not have objected to afford her an asylum in the house, and under your own care. She would have helped you, and you could have watched over her, until something could have been done for her."

"Very wisely arranged, and without my being even asked—and a great girl like that! No, no; I'll not go to sleep in the house while she remains under the same roof."

"My dear——"

"Don't dear me, Mr. Primrose; you know I don't like deceit."

"There's no deceit; but she shall go, then, but not to-night—she shall go to-morrow. I will try and send her some-where—she must not be thrust out into the street."

"Oh, a night here, indeed! You'll let her remain one night, will you?"

"If you are alarmed, Mrs. Primrose, I'll sleep out to-night."

This was a climax, and Mrs. P. fainted outright; and fearful of the consequences, he hurried his niece away, and placed her in the house of a friend, who took care of the unfortunate girl, and Mrs. Primrose's peace was restored.

Thus it was that Mr. Primrose was managed—ay, managed very nicely, and so was his house. He went out to business, and when he returned everything was in order—not a pin out of place; it was nicely managed, very nicely managed, and so was everybody and everything that Mrs. Primrose had to do with.

Mrs. P. was a very clever woman in her way; had seen something of the world, vulgarly speaking, and had great aptitude in making bargains, and managing tradespeople generally.

Mr. Primrose managed his own affairs pretty well; but he had to make a report of them to his lawful wife, and had, moreover, to hand over all monies, with any deduction, though upon this latter scorce there were occasionly some little doubts, and books were not always considered as over clear, "Because," as Mrs. Primrose once observed, "you can put down what you like, and you can also alter a figure."

But, alas! poor Mr. P. had no such sins as those to answer for—at least, there were never any found out; if he had been discovered in such a thing, why, his suffering wife's peace of mind would have been totally ruined, and so great would be the remorse, that he would never again sleep in peace.

Thus it was that Mrs. Primrose managed her lawful spouse, and everybody else besides, when they had anything to do at the house with her; and Mr. P. was content to permit the ascendance that had been gained over him to continue, and he wore the yoke of female subjection, perhaps, without being fully aware of it.

CHAPTER XVIII.

THE AGONY OF THEODORE DANTON.
—THE STORM.—THE ILLNESS AT
THE HOTEL.

WHEN Theodore Danton left the house of Charles Bertram, and ran with such precipitation against Mrs. Blair as to commit the ravages he did upon that lady's bonnet, he was in too excited a frame of mind to attend to any of the ordinary courtesies of life, or undoubtedly he would have been the first to apologise to that lady for the unintentional act of violence. He rushed onwards, saying,—

"She is lost to me for ever—she is lost to me for ever!"

The few chance passengers whom he met, and who had an opportunity of seeing his face, got out of his way as quickly as they could, for he had all the appearance of a madman, and they knew

THE VISION.

not what sudden form of violence his mind might assume.

"Lost—lost to me for ever! I shall never see her like again!" was all he said. But he accompanied the words with some wild gesticulations, which were amply sufficient to warrant the idea of his insanity.

By wandering on in this manner he soon began to get clear of the town; and the long garden walls, and the liberality of space given to the roads, proclaimed that he was getting into the suburbs of London. But he knew nothing—heeded nothing, except that he had bidden adieu to his heart's best love for ever, and that never—never more was he to look upon the face of Margaret again in this world.

"Lost—lost—lost!" he moaned. "Oh, Heaven! what have I done to have the only blissful hope of my existence thus blighted? She is lost to me for ever—my beautiful Margaret—she, who nerved my arm in fight—she, the remembrance of whom made the worst of perils seem as nothing—she, for whom I have toiled night and day (fo

Heaven knows all my toiling was for her)—she is another's. Lost to me for ever, and I am wretched!"

He heeded not the swift-descending rain; he heeded not the howling wind that swept among the trees, which now by the road sides began more frequently to rear their stately heads, and afford the agreeable contrast of their sweet, green herbage to the houses they sheltered and imparted so much effect to.

He knew nothing yet; the mind felt not—sympathised not yet with the bodily fatigue, and yet he had walked some miles, and that, too, at the pace which, under ordinary circumstances, would have much fatigued him.

From sheer want of thought and of reflection, though, he was really adopting the very best possible plan of restoring his mind to a better state, for bodily fatigue will often fully succeed in calming down an excited state of the imagination when no other means would produce so desirable an effect upon it.

When once absolute fatigue began irresistibly to make itself felt, he began to get calmer, and at length he paused but to find himself on a country road of which he knew absolutely nothing, and wet to the very skin from the pelting rain which still, in squally showers, kept falling rapidly.

"Where am I?" he said, as he looked round him with surprise, "where am I, and how far have I wandered in this state of mental agitation, which the loss of all I loved produced in me? This place is strange to me."

He turned to retrace his steps, and walked with a slower pace. He thought of asking his way of the first person he met; but it was late, and he had retraced his way nearly a mile before he heard the sound of an approaching footstep. Then he saw the dusky figure of a man approaching, and when he had come sufficiently close, he called out to him, saying,—

"Can you tell me where this road leads to?"

"To Ealing," was the reply.

"Ealing—Ealing; where is that?"

"Why, straight on, to be sure."

"But I want to reach London."

"Well, you will reach it if you walk on; but it's a matter of four or five miles, or more."

"Thank you."

Theodore Danton walked on.

"Alas!" he said, "how bewildered must have been my head and heart to take me so far on such a night as this. I can almost fancy I am mad. Oh, Margaret, Margaret, why are you another's!"

He checked the rising agony of his heart, and saying,—"Hush—hush—hush!" as if he were talking to some one else, he strove to withdraw his mind from the subject that possessed it wholly, and to think upon what course in life he should now pursue, now that the one great object of his ambition was effectually and for ever at an end.

"What is to become of me?" he asked himself. "Let me think. I promised Margaret that I would leave England. Shall I fulfil that promise, or yet linger around the spot were all I love resides? Love—love! dare I love her now? Is not the very thought a criminal one, and at war with common justice? And yet, who can dictate to his heart? I do love her still—I do adore her still, and not all the laws, human and divine, can make me love her less than now I do."

At one moment he thought he would leave England, and then again he fancied he could have the constancy to stay, and yet make no attempt to intrude himself upon Margaret, and that it would be some source of melancholy satisfaction to feel that he inhabited the same city with her, and that the objects he looked upon likewise met her eyes.

"To be near her is something," he said; "but I must not come in her way. I dare not see her; or, if I did, it must be from a far off, where she knew not that my eyes were fastened on her. Why should I be, by my ill-omened passion, the blight of her young existence? No, no; she shall not see me more."

So he thought, and in so thinking, no one, who calmly reflects upon the subject, will be inclined to disagree with him that it would now be most ungenerous of him to obtrude himself upon the notice of Margaret—that by so doing he might be completely destroying her happiness, for the mere gratification to himself of beholding her occasionly, who, to his eyes, was so gratifying a sight.

"No, no—a thousand times no," he exclaimed. "Before I die, or before she goes from this world to her kindred heaven, I should like to see her; but it must not be till such a moment comes that I can bring myself to beg for another interview. Then, when the most malevolent can place no misconstruction on my motives—than I would fain see her, to bid her that long adieu which shall herald one or other of us to the calm and silent grave."

Even as he spoke a storm commenced which seemed to shake the very earth to its centre. It was but of short duration; but the thunder roared and rolled in the sky, and the forked lightning lit up the night with its livid, yet grand and beautiful lustre. Theodore sought no shelter. He had a gloomy sort of pleasure in exposing himself fully to the elements. He looked up to the sky, which was each moment presenting an appearance as if torn asunder by the vivid flashes of ghtning, and he smiled as he said,—

"Fate has done her worst to me. It would be a friendly flash of that subtile power, which thus grandly blazes between earth and heaven, were it to strike me dead. Let it do so—I fear nothing, now—I hope nothing."

In this wretched state of mind he reached London, and it was as he reached the hotel at which he had put up, that he first began to feel the effects of long abstinance from food, intense mentle excitement, and the soaking he had got from the rain. A sudden faintness came over him, and a death-like chill pervaded all his limbs. The cold perspiration, like drops of ice, broke out upon his brow, and he could but just manage to stagger into the hotel, when he fell on the floor of its hall in a state of total insensibility.

* * * * * * *

There was, as it were, a pause in the very existence of Theodore Danton. A raging fever seized him—delirium took possession of his brain—he knew nothing, felt nothing; but he lived—

"The king of a fantastic realm,
Seeing what others saw not."

Weeks collected into months, and still he lay at the hotel in the most hopeless state. The best medical assistance wa procured; for his money was found in the one trunk he brought with him, and the landlord, who was a respectable man, had called in some neighbours, and counted it over in their presence, so that no sort of suspicion of peculation could attach to him.

From some strange whim or accident, the name of Theodore Danton could not be discovered upon anything that belonged to him, and he had been, before taken so alarmingly ill, but too short a time at the hotel for its proprietor to know who or what he was. An attempt was made by advertisement to find out some one who knew him; but the announcement never met the eye of Margaret, and, had it done so, she would not have probably suspected, from a mere description, that it referred to him.

For many days and nights he had raved incessantly, and pronounced so many names, that it was quite impossible for any one to come to a judgment as to whether any one of them was his own or not. The medical men who were called in to attend upon him, at first seemed inclined to think that his recovery was hopeless; but, when he went on for some weeks, they entertained a better notion of his constitutional powers, and predicted that if he continued to battle with the fever a short time longer, he would have a fair chance of eventually getting the better of it.

Nurses were employed to sit up with him night and day, who, as is usual with those functionaries, dozed and dreamt their time away, paying about as much attention to the sick man, when no eye was upon them, as they did to one of the posts of the bedstead on which he lay. But those people seem to be necessary evils, and so form a component part of the elements of society.

Poor Theodore raved of Margaret. He called upon her incessantly, sometimes for the hour together, until, exhausted, he would sink into an uneasy slumber, which was full of frightful images.

To give the doctors their due, every attention was paid to him, and all was done for him that medical service had it in its power to do. The result was that, after a time, although he was very far indeed from recovery, such a state of things was predicted as not only likely but tolerably certain.

His raving was not so frequent. He began to have better and calmer repose; and at length, one day, after the physicians had held a consultation concerning him, they desired that he should be carefully watched, for they considered his disorder was about to take a turn, and, although they were unanimously of opinion that it would be for the better, yet there was a possibility of quite a contrary result.

He had fallen asleep—for more than eight hours he had never moved or spoken, and they would not have him awakened. They left medicines with the nurse, which were to be given to him the moment he should awaken, provided he were calm and serene; if otherwise, they warned the people at the house that he might jump up and be dangerous.

This was not a very agreeable state of things one would have supposed for the nurse, but she took it in quite a business sort of way, and, having seated herself in an arm chair, she placed some tables and chairs so about that if Theodore should get out of bed he must fall over them, and then she settled herself to sleep. And to sleep she went; little heeding whether her patient awoke or not, or was calm or voilent, so long as she had her money and her repose.

Hour after hour passed away, and still the deep sleep continued on Theodore. So calm, so dreamless, and so deep was it, that it might well have been considered as the sleep of death, from which the mortal frame would never again awaken.

Twelve o'clock had struck. The solitary candle that burned in the sick chamber gave but a feeble light. There was a stillness in the room which would have been absolutely profound and solemn, but for the loud snoring of the nurse. Alas! how that nasal trumpet broke the charm. Sometimes a whistling sound proceeded from it, which would then again deepen into a grunt, and go from a grunt to a snort, and then closely resemble what we would suppose a pig to say if he had the influenza.

It was truly terrific, that snore. But bad as it was, and sonorous as it was in its intonation, it completely failed in awakening Theodore Danton. He heard it not; and, until the hour of two in the morning, he still slept on, and the nurse still snored on. Suddenly then he gave a profound sigh, and moaned gently and feebly. A sensation of pain, arising from feebleness, came over him. He was in a profuse perspiration, and he slowly opened his eyes and looked upon the nearly closed bed-hangings for the first time with a consciousness of reason for many weeks.

There was a singing in his ears and a strange bewildered sensation still about his brain; but he had passed the rubican, and soon the organs of thought arranged themselves in due order, and the mental machine began to act with regularity and precision. He knew not where he was, but it was something to be able to ask himself the question, and to feel even the difficulty of answering it.

"What—what has happened?" he contrived to say.

But his voice was so low that it would have required any one to place an ear close to him to have heard the sounds.

He strove to move, but found that he had not physical energy to do so. He held up by a great effort one of his hands between himself and the dim light, and, to his surprise, he saw that it was frightfully thin, being little more than skin and bone. He let it fall again upon the coverlet, as again, in a faint whisper, he said,—

"Good God! what has happened?"

There came upon his ear the loud snore of the nurse, and much he wondered for a time what could produce such a strange and hideous noise. He placed his thin hands over his face, and tried to think. Suddenly, with a strange gush of memory, the name of Margaret came to his lips, and, with a deep groan, he very nearly lasped into the swoon. The name of Margaret was now the key to all that had occurred. He understood and recollected everything but the events of his illness, the nature of it, and the length of time it had lasted.

He ran over in his mind his whole history; how he had loved his cousin Margaret; how he had gone abroad—made money—come home again, and found her wedded to another. The full particulars of the painful interview he had had with her at her husband's house likewise came freshly to his mind, and he recollected how, in the despair of his heart, he walked into the country and then back to town again. The last event which he was quite clear about was, asking a man on the country road where he was, and being told he was near Ealing.

Beyond that point all was a blank, although he could fill it up by supposing that he had been seized with a sudden illness, and that such was the reason why he was in bed, and why he found himself in such a state of weakness and exhaustion as he was in.

"How long have I been here?" he murmured. "Why am I left alone too?"

The nurse gave a loud snore that was enough to awaken the very dead. It produced such an echo in the room, that it actually aroused herself, and, starting wide awake, she cried, in a half-bewildered tone,—

"Eh—eh? Did you say anything? Oh, of course not. Poor devil! he can't say anything. I do wonder now what it was woke me up so all of a sudden. Some blessed presentiment, I shouldn't wonder, as my frame was in wants of something."

The frame soon received about a quartern of gin at a draught, and then the lady felt much refreshed.

Theodore spoke twice, but his voice had no chance whatever against hers, so he tried to attract attention another way. He feebly stretched out his hand and laid hold of the curtain, which he shook, and slight as the stroke was that he, in his weak state, was able to give it, it produced a rattling of the rings at the top.

"Lor bless me!" ejaculated the nurse, "it's him. Is he wiolent, or isn't he?—that's the question."

In order to settle this point, the lady rose, and, having cleared herself a passage among the various articles of furnature she had placed around her as a protection against Theodore, in case he had got out of bed while she was enjoying a deep slumber, she approached the side of the bed and drew aside one of the curtains, quite heedless of whether the sharp rattling sound of the brass rings, by which it was suspended, was calculated to alarm her patient or not

"Well?" she said, "well?"

The sudden accession of light which now fell upon the eyes of Theodore, confused him for a moment, and he did not answer, upon which the nurse added,—

"Come, now, there's a good soul. If you can speak, speak, and if so be as you can't, why, hold your tongue and be quiet, for it's no time o' night to be disturbing a Christian, I can tell you."

"I have been ill," said Theodore.

"Ah! there's news," exclaimed the nurse. "I suppose you ain't a going to be violent?"

"Violent! good God, I am too weak to move."

"And a remarkably good job too."

She walked to the table and got the medicine which he was to take, and which, to his surprise, she at once administered by laying hold of his nose so tightly, that he was compelled to open his mouth wide, upon which she took the opportunity of dashing the medicine down his throat, at the great risk of choking him completely, and so putting an end to all his troubles. Then she said,—

"Now go to sleep again like a Christian, and don't say I haven't done my duty by you."

CHAPTER XIX.

THE COMMUNICATION TO CHARLES BERTRAM.—THE FIRST SUSPICION.

CHARLES BERTRAM'S return on that evening of the unexpected and painful visit of Theodore Danton to his house was most eagerly looked for by Margaret. As hour after hour passed, and he came not, her nervousness and general excitement increased very much, and she almost feared that when he did come home, she should scarcely have nerve enough to tell him, clearly and distinctly, what had occurred.

It will be recollected that she had another subject than that of the visit of Theodore Danton, on which to speak to him, namely, the insolence of Mrs. Blair, which had induced, and, indeed, mposed upon her, Margaret, the uncomfortable but the necessary step of dismissing her. There was a something about this insolence of the housekeeper, which, the more Margaret thought of it, made her the more convinced that it was premeditated, and hence arose a natural anxiety on that head. Most welcome then was the knock of her husband at the street-door—a knock which she recognised as his at once; and yet, when the first feeling of satisfaction that he had come home had passed away, which it quickly did, it gave place to one of alarm and nervousness.

"What have I to fear?" she said: "I tremble as if I had some tale of guilt to unfold to him, instead of merely relating the visit of a relative, and the insolence of a domestic. Courage, courage, Margaret. This weakness is indeed most unworthy of you."

But reason as she would, she felt the weakness, and she felt it the more, because of the hideous suspicion that had now for some time begun to find a home in her heart, that her husband had become to a great degree indifferent to her. This was a suspicion which she had made the greatest efforts to crush, but the words of Theodore Danton,—

"Are you happy in this glittering home?" would occur to her continually, and they were words which contained a question she now dreaded to ask herself, to answer candidly even to herself in the privacy of her own chamber.

But now Charles Bertram had come home, and there was no time for thought. Action must supersede reflection, and she walked hastily from her chamber to seek him. She knew that, upon coming home, he always proceeded to a small room adjoining the dining-room, and thither she sought him. When she entered this apartment, she found him pacing it to and fro, as if some subject of painful contemplation were on his mind, and she dreaded to think it might be one which what she had to tell him might increase. And yet she had no rational grounds for such a dread.

"Charles," she said; "how late you are."

"Yes, yes. I was detained. It is late?"

"It is, indeed."

He evidently made a great effort to assume a cheerfulness which he did not feel, and the smile which he forced upon his face, although it satisfied Margaret that she had nothing to do with the depression of his spirits, yet gave her pain to see, because it was so evidently forced.

"Charles," she said, "I fear you are not well?"

"Oh, I am quite well."

"But vexed at something?"

"Vexed? What is there to vex me? Oh, no! Is not everything, Margaret, *coleur de rose* about me? I should be a most miserable man to be vexed at anything."

"Nothing ought to vex you, Charles."

"Nor does anything."

"Ah, may you always be as serene."

"Amen to that, Margaret."

"But yet we cannot help vexations, and I feared there was a cloud upon your brow."

"That was your imagination, Margaret. I am, it is true, a little worried, and shall not be sorry when this carriage of ours comes home."

"Well, but, Charles, I have something to tell you."

"Say on, say on. Is it serious or mirthful?"

"Why, surely, it ought to be the latter. You recollect that on our wedding day I made the remark to you, that I was not like many who had relations to worry you, for that I was not aware of any one living soul who could claim any kindred with me?"

"You did so."

"It now appears that I was wrong."

"Indeed."

"Yes, Charles. There was but one to whom I was in any way related."

"And who was that?"

"Theodore Danton, my cousin."

"I have heard you speak of him."

"Yes, some time since."

"But you said he was drowned in the wreck of some ship, I think, Margaret."

"I did; but by a strange combination of circumstances, that ship has not been lost. It has returned, bringing with it my cousin, Theodore Danton."

'How became you aware of that, Margaret?"

"Because he has been here to see me this very evening. He came here as soon as he found me out. He—he came here, you see, Charles."

"So you say; I shall be very happy to see him. That is—I—I—never did see him. I suppose he is a gentleman?"

"In every deed and every word a gentleman."

"Then I can have no objection to his acquaintance."

"We shall see him no more."

"No more?"

"No. His visit here was a farewell one. He will leave this country again very shortly. We shall see him no more, Charles—no more."

"It will be but common courtesy for me to call upon him, though."

"No—no—no."

"How eager you are, Magaret, that I should neglect your cousin. Is he a disagreeable person to you?"

"No—yes; that is, I do not know where to find him. He merely came to make me a farewell visit. That is all. I never asked him where he was staying. He will leave England, and we shall see no more, hear no more of him."

"He seems a very mysterious personage."

"He is of rather a romantic and peculiar turn of mind, Charles; but I thought I would tell you myself he had been here, because then—then—"

"Then what?"

"I really know not what I am saying. The sudden visit of one whom I thought dead confused me, I believe, and flurried my spirits a little."

"So it seems, Margaret."

"And then he did not know that I was married."

Charles Bertram gave a slight start as he said—

"Was that displeasing to him?"

"Displeasing, Charles! Displeasing to see me happy!"

"Oh, then, he was inquisitive enough to ask you that question?"

"Call it not inquisitive. He did ask me if I was happy in my glittering home."

"Glittering home?"

"His words, Charles, those were."

"Oh, I could have sworn that. The question was not nicely put, Margaret; and, from what you have said, perhaps it is well I do not call upon this gentleman, whom we will now, if you please, say no more about."

It was a great relief, as may be supposed, to Margaret to drop the subject upon which she was so ill-qualified to converse composedly; so new was anything in the shape of concealment or deceit to her mind, that she could not attempt either without the greatest terrors, and hence she had acquitted herself so very badly in a matter which to many would have been no effort.

"We will say no more of him," said Charles Bertram, with some degree of asperity. "It sounds a simple question, Margaret; but I do not wish people to ask you if you are happy in your glittering home."

"Nor I, Charles."

"Then it is a good thing that this cousin is going."

"A very good thing."

"Is he young?"

"Yes, and handsome."

"And handsome! Well, enough of this. I'm glad you told me of his visit, because some one else might."

"That was my impression."

Charles Bertram sharply turned upon her, and said, in a voice of surprise—

"Margaret?"

"What, Charles—what is it?"

"Do you mean to say that your telling me was a result of reflection merely, and such a train of reasoning as you have avowed?"

Margaret saw in a moment how incautiously she had allowed herself to be entrapped in a dangerous discussion. The colour mounted to her temples as she said—

"Charles, I have no reason to keep this visit of my cousin, Theodore Danton, from you."

"We will drop the subject," said Mr. Bertram, "if you please. It seems as if it promised to be an ungracious one."

"Why it should, Heaven only knows."

"Never mind it; we will not quarrel for fifty cousins, Margaret. He has come, and he is going, you say, or gone; I wish to hear no more of him."

"Nor I—nor I, Heaven knows. And now, Charles, I have another matter to speak to you about."

"Another cousin ?"

"No, I have no more cousins. It is of Mrs. Blair that I would now speak."

"And what of her ?"

"She has been so insolent to me that I have been compelled, in order to save myself from a repetition of it, to discharge her."

"She insolent ?"

"Yes. Most insolent."

"I could not have believed it possible from any other lips than your own, Margaret."

"Nor could I have believed it of her unless I had had, as I have had, the evidence of my own senses."

"In what did her insolence consist ?"

"She obtruded herself upon me, and I was compelled to give up the drawing-room to her, as she would not leave it."

"Indeed."

"It is so. I never saw such overbearing insolence in a domestic in all my life, and when I discharged her she taunted me with the statement that she was your servant and not mine, as if here, in my own house, I were a nonentity—a mere image, which I am sure you, Charles, never intended me to be."

"You at once discharged her ?"

"At once."

"It was well. The climax disarms my anger at the whole transaction, Margaret."

"Then you approve of what I did ?"

"I do, most fully and unequivocally."

Margaret threw herself upon her husband's breast, as she said—

"Oh, Charles, shall I confess that I did tremble after this, my first exercise of authority in your house ?"

"Tremble !"

"Yes, I knew not if you would approve or not of what I had done. Had she been a domestic hired by myself, and trusted by myself, I should not so much have hesitated ; but as she said, truly, she had been engaged by you."

"Which made no difference on earth as regarded her relation to you, Margaret, as her mistress. You did quite right to discharge her, and quite as I would have wished you to do under the circumstances, had I been at your elbow to prompt you."

"Then I am happy."

"And was the dread of my disapproval of such a thing as this sufficient to make you unhappy ?"

"It was, a little ; she seemed to have some threat upon her lips, although she actually uttered none."

"Think no more of her, Margaret ; she shall go, and before she does go, I will assuredly give her my opinion of her conduct towards you, which fills me with as much astonishment as it does indignation."

"Oh, Charles, I ought to have known that you would have defended me in such a case as this."

"She must have been mad or intoxicated. I recollect I was told once by a discharged servant that she drank ; but I pay no attention to what a domestic says after getting discharged."

"You do not ?"

"Not the least. As a matter of principle I shut my ears to everything. So much may be prompted by malice that it would be the most dangerous thing in the world to pay any sort of attention to such statements coming from ignorant people, with excited feelings, and no very strong sensations regarding right and wrong."

"It is an admirable principle to go upon, Charles."

"It is one I invariably have gone upon."

Margaret felt wonderfully relieved and reassured. That Mrs. Blair, in her anger at finding Bertram sanction her dismissal, would tell him of the visit of Theodore Danton, and insinuate to him that he came to her, Margaret, as a lover more than a cousin, she had every reason to believe from what had fallen from the lips of that very religious lady during the short but amazingly decisive dispute in the drawing-room.

Now, however, that Charles Bertram had professed so wise and so in every way admirable a course of action as regarded the statements of the discharged servants, she had no fear, and she fully expected to hear from him that Mrs.

Blair had made the attempt upon his jealous feelings and signally failed.

So rapid and so remarkable was the change that took place now in Margaret's spirits, that Bertram could not possibly fail to take notice of it, and he said,—

"Why, Margaret, your spirits fluctuate very much. But a short time since you seemed depressed and agitated, and now you are full of life and energy."

"And you do not, Charles, object to my being full of life?"

"No, no."

"Then let me be so. And now tell me when the carriage will really come home; and only consider what cruel delays we have been subjected to on account of it."

"So we have. You and I will go to-morrow to the man, and threaten, that if it be not finished by a certain time, we will not have it at all from him."

"It is the only way. All London tradesmen care about is to get an order, the execution of it they leave to chance,

MRS. BLAIR'S PLAN OF BRINGING MISERY ON MARGARET SUCCEEDS.

or some such convenience, which, in some cases, never arrives at all or certainly not until the person whose patience has been so much tried becomes almost frantic, and does, or threatens, something very desperate indeed."

"You are right, Margaret," laughed Charles, "you are right. That is about the way they do business. Twice in my life I have had to threaten mighty respectable shopkeepers with legal proceedings for the recovery of articles

which I had paid for, but which from sheer neglect were not sent home, although I had the patience of Job himself in waiting week after week for them to come."

"And we will have the carriage then to-morrow, Charles?" eagerly asked Margaret.

"Oh, but, Margaret——"

"What—what?"

"There is a serious question,"

"What question?"

"Shall you be happy in your glittering carriage, Margaret?"

"Nay, now, Charles, those foolish words have made too deep an impression on you. What need you care for such a question being asked of me, when you know yourself what my answer must be to it, unless I am the most miserable and dissatisfied person who ever breathed."

"I will mention it no more."

"Do not. Let the remembrance of it, as well as of him who, in a moment perchance of thoughtlessness, uttered the words, sleep together. He meant no ill."

"Possibly not."

"I am sure he meant no ill."

"I am content."

"Do you not remember what a popular ferment there was, Charles, about the loss of a ship called the Atlantia?"

"I do."

"Well, it was on board that that Theodore Danton was. The story of their preservation is most romantic, and would make a perfect romance in itself."

"Indeed!"

"Ay, indeed, it would. How they sailed from the friendly port, full of hope and expectation of soon looking on their native land. Then how the storm came on, and dashed them to and fro, at the mercy of the winds and waves. How they gave up all for lost; and some prayed, and others, with the stupor of despair, looked on, and some anticipated the doom that could but come at last by a mad leap into the foaming sea."

"You paint it well."

"Oh, do I? I can fancy I see such a scene proceeding so full of woe. Then would the natural characters of all come out in strong relief against the artificial feelings which custom and hypocrisy, which had become a second nature, had entwined around them, till they themselves believed they were what they affected to be, and wished others to believe them.

"Go on, Margaret, go on."

"The romance might be heightened by some one among them being jealous without cause, and even at that time of death seeking vengeance. Arrayed in gloomy apparel—Oh, the black mantle that came to you in the mysterious box would do."

Charles Bertram sprang to his feet.

"No more—no more!" he cried. "I—I do not like allusions to that black mantle—no more."

"Charles—Charles!"

"Enough. I—I do not wish it spoken of—enough. Never mention it again, Margaret. Let me have wine—say no more, but let me have wine, to drown the remembrance of——"

"What, oh, what?"

"Hush! 'tis nothing.—I mean, your description of the wreck."

CHAPTER XX.

CHARLES BERTRAM AND THE HOUSE-KEEPER.

PERHAPS now the most important hour of Charles Bertram's life might be considered that which he passed with Mrs. Blair, his housekeeper, while she was giving to him most especial reasons why, in contradiction to the wishes, the feelings, and the opinions of his young and beautiful wife, he should still retain her in his service.

If Charles Bertram had been a man of more enegy of character than he was, he would have spared himself much unhappiness, and we should not have a story. Had he been able to meet evils that really existed, not by attempting to cover them with others, but by a manful candour, which must have disarmed anger, he would yet have known an amount of domestic happiness for which he sighed, but which, alas! he now seemed doomed never to know.

There was nothing in his position to prevent him, if he had had precision of intellect sufficient to make the determination, from at once making a confidant of his wife. True, he had committed an error at which she would have felt much shocked and much hurt; but still, if a woman love her husband, she will readily invent excuses for those lapses of morality which occurred before she knew him, whatever may be her agonized feelings, should she discover any similar escapades after matrimony.

If Charles Bertram, then, had been able to take a rational and a clearer view of his own position, he would have been able to divest it in a very short time of most of its evils. He should have left nothing for malevolence to tell to his wife. By making her himself acquainted with the story of her who now could vex no one, love no one, he would have prevented the possibility of her listening to such a narrative from any one else.

It is a direct fact, which cannot be denied upon reflection by any one, that nobody ever yet told a circumstance to another without colouring it on one side or the other. It is impossible to do otherwise; and however we may wish to relate any circumstance with such a strict regard alone to facts as shall free us even from the suspicion of a bias, the very language in which we couch the facts will be more than sufficient to show where our feelings lie on the matter.

Thus, then, taking such a view of the circumstance, Charles Bertram ought to have been convinced that if any one chose at all to tell the tale of his wife, it would be sure to be told in a way to do him the greatest amount of possible prejudice and evil.

No one friendly to him was likely to tell her at all anything about it; for where would be the utility of so doing? It might be very well for him, her husband, to come to her with such a narration, saying,—"My dear, I tell you of this error of mine, which I committed before I knew you, for fear you should hear it from some malevolent person instead;" but no other person could come to her with the tale without being obnoxious to the reproach of great meddling impertinence, if a friend, or to a wish to do him injury, if an enemy.

He, then, and he only, should have informed his wife of all that had occured; and, had he done so, there cannot be any reasonable doubt but that she, however hurt at the time her feelings would have been, would have conceded to him an entire forgiveness of the act, and found in the very confidence with which he had treated her abundant reason for being assured that she had not to fear a repetition of any such conduct. And, likewise, as confidence begets confidence as much as distrust begets distrust, she would have entered into, to him, the whole story of Theodore Danton, and he would have been spared some pangs of the heart which he was doomed to feel.

Alas! how many domestic tragedies have arisen from want of mutual confidence. If there be contentment and bliss in any family circle—if there be that show of confidence and pure affection, which can never be assumed, he who sees it may be sure that there are no secrets.

It is want of confidence that betrays man and wife as well as the whole world; and ninety-nine out of a hundred of the subjects of contention, or of mutual coldness, which last people a lifetime, might be entirely dissipated by one half-hour's mutual explanation, openly and reasonably, which it would be found would destroy the supposed uncomfortable circumstances of a thousand little extraneous circumstances that had made it look gigantic, but which had really no foundation but in error and misconstruction, or in the malice or the folly of others.

Unhappily, however, Charles Bertram was one of a large class of men who, when they think they have anything to complain of, take a moody pleasure in nursing it up. They have not the candour to say anything about it, but they have the hypocrisy to hoard it up as if it were something extremely precious, and worth the keeping, while they wreathe their mouths with smiles, and endeavour to make observers believe that all is fair and right, and that no subject of discontent is harassing their minds.

Such a man was Charles Bertram, and a more admirable subject for the machinations of such a woman as Mrs. Blair certainly never existed.

And as regards this woman, Mrs. Blair, let not our readers for one moment suppose that in her character there is anything outragous or contrary to reason. She is, we can assure them, sketched from the life. There are many such women, possessing more or less art than she, but imbued with the same feelings and prejudices. We think we hear some reader say that she might have been far more happy, and far more comfortable, at one half the pains she took to lay up for herself what no doubt would do a world of future discontent. We echo that sentiment, and it is the

Principle which we hope and wish to establish by our story.

There are hundreds and thousands of people who, if they were to exert one half the ingenuity to be honest that they do to be thieves, would make fortunes; who, if they were to bring to bear upon any branch of honourable industry one half the skill, the enegy, and the cunning which they exercise to be idle, must succeed most wonderfully.

It is a common error of human nature that it will not be happy in the most simple and easy method of procuring such a result, but it must, from some mistaken and crooked feeling of its own, adopt some tedious mode of endeavouring to accomplish that which might have been done with a most marvellous ease in the ordinary current aspect of things.

And thus Mrs Blair, who might have been perfectly happy, surely, by making herself useful and agreeable to Mr. Charles Bertram, would not do so, but must needs proclaim war against him, and endeavour in vain to accomplish that result by the unworthiest of means.

Surely, surely, such people as Mrs. Blair must think themselves immortal, or they would be content with feeling secure from the ills of life, instead of grasping at what they never can hope to enjoy.

Mrs. Blair had been robbing Charles Bertram of a certain sum, we will say, weekly, but at what period she intended to begin spending it was extremely doubtful. Of that she had no definite idea. All she thought of was the acquisition of the money, and, like such people generally, the strong probability was, that she would never enjoy those hardest of all earned gains which were accumulated at the expense of honour and honesty.

For such a woman as she was, the quarrel with Mrs. Bertram was rather precipitate. But then she was so wonderfully elated at finding out that she had some ground to go upon now to Charles Bertram concerning his wife, that perhaps her usual cunning slept a little, and wanted its activity. And, yet, if she had had it to do again, she told herself, she thought she should do it. She had both husband and wife in her power. The story of the black mantle, she felt convinced, would confound Charles Bertram, and the story of Theodore Danton would have an equal effect upon Margaret, his wife.

Shall we confess it, too, that Mrs. Blair was not always, indeed very seldom, averse to a little stimulent? She never got actually much the worse for the small drains of something considerably stronger than water with which she occasionly treated herself, and she was inclined to think that some of her boldest and most successful strokes of policy were executed when she had had just enough to impart tension to her nerves, and brilliancy to her imagination. And now she knew that the conversation she was going to have with Charles Bertram was the most important which she was ever likely to have with him. Upon what should pass during that interview, she felt convinced, would depend the question of her supremacy in that house, or otherwise. She would either henceforward be protected by her husband, through what she should say of the wife, or be repudiated by both. Like a general, on the eve of a battle which is to decide the fate of a kingdom, and, what is of far more importance to him, his own individual fortunes, she reviewed all her means of attack and defence. The question that arose in her mind was, "Shall I at once tell him that his wife has a lover, or not?"

Now, Mrs. Blair was in one respect clever. Let us give the devil his due. She never, if she was not hurried away at the moment by some strong impulse, wasted her forces. If to let Charles Bertram know that she was aware of what the mystry of the black mantle meant would be sufficient to secure her her position in the family, she did not wish just then to go any further. She would content herself with watching Mrs. Bertram to see if any additional evidence should turn up which might lead to convict her of keeping up a correspondence with the young man of whom she, Mrs. Blair, had obtained so very transient a glimpse. This, however, was a matter on which she could not well decide, until the interview actually took place between her and Mr. Bertram, and that interview she resolved should be with Mr. Bertram alone, when she could say to him, in a very few minutes, should he show any disposition to take high ground in the matter, how very expedient on his part it would be for him to listen to her.

She sought him. He was in a small room on the second floor, which was used as an occasional sitting-room in the event of any indisposition, or other cause, making a sitting-room in close proximity to the bed-chamber a matter of convenience. Charles was then in a fretful frame of mind. Things were getting uncomfortable about him; he scarcely knew why, and, as we have said, he was a man much more likely to get passionate and fretful under any disagreeables, than calmly to meet them, and deprive them of their power to sting.

When Mrs. Blair entered this room, which she did simultaneously with the tap at the door by which she announced her presence, Charles turned with an angry countenance upon her. She had tact enough in a moment to see it, and pausing close to the door, she said,—

"I dare say, Mr. Bertram, that Mrs. Bertram has prepared you for what I am about to say."

"I really don't know, Mrs. Blair," said Charles. "The fact is, a house in which there is any contention will not suit me."

"Nor me, sir."

"Well, then, Mrs. Blair, that there is contention, is a fact which I presume you are going to dispute; therefore, the only plan, I think, is for us to separate."

"I think so, sir."

"Oh, very good."

"But, before I go, perhaps it may be worth your while to know why it is that Mrs. Bertram and I do not agree."

"Oh, I don't care. I don't want to know. Some people's tempers don't assimilate in some way, and then there is an end of all agreement."

"Mr. Bertram, there are reasons why Mrs. Bertran is anxious to rid herself of me, and to get another in my place. You will recollect that, having before your marriage been in your service, I naturally consider myself far more bound to you than I do to her. I am sorry I cannot rid myself of such a feeling; but

my respect for your character, your talents and your conduct towards me, has tended to increase it, and I feel that while I live I shall never get rid of it."

This was attacking Charles Bertram certainly at one weak point, which was personal vanity. That is one of the outworks of the mind, which with by far the greater number of persons is very easily carried by assault, as the resistance it makes is lamentably feeble. It certainly had nothing to do with the question at issue, but it acted as a sort of anodyne to the mind of Charles, and prepared him better to listen to what Mrs. Blair had to say to him. It soothed him down, and it is rather difficult to snub a person who has just paid one a very handsome compliment, a compliment, too, the more handsome, on account of its being undeserved, for people general appreciate compliments in that way. If you say to a man of genius, "What a clever fellow you are!" he knows it is no more than his due; but if your benevolence prompts you to say as much to a fool, of course he is mightily obliged.

We knew a friend of ours once, who had a reputation among all who knew him of being the most universal favourite with the ladies that could well be conceived, and seeing and hearing that he was but a very common-place sort of fellow indeed, we were much puzzled to know the why and the wherefore of this. At length we were enlightened by a mutual friend, who had taken the trouble to study the subject.

"You must know," he said, "Oxendon is the greatest favourite with the greatest number of ladies, because he praises them for qualities which they do not possess. Of course, beauty is not common, and if you go into a room full of company, if you see one pretty female face among them, you may consider that you are fortunate. Now, when Oxendon goes into such a company, he pays no attention whatever to youth, to intellect, or to beauty, but is flattering and attentive to those who have none of those advantages, and as they are by far the greater number, he carries the day as being an agreeable man by an immense majority of votes."

And this, good reader, is the secret of the boasted conquests of many of your ladies' men. Conquests not worth the making. They would meet, as well they know by experience, with nothing but comtempt and repulse, were they to attempt to attack one heart that is worth the receiving, and so they solace themselves with many that are to be had for the picking up; and were you to hear some fellow boasting of his great success with the ladies, and how admired a courtier he is, ask him if he knows one under thirty, or of common good looks, or education, from whom he can obtain even the courtesy of a passing glance. It is not a conquest that is estimable, but what is gained by such a conquest. But to return from this digression into which Mrs. Blair has led us unconsciously, we may say that Charles Bertram was a little pleased, and his reply was,—

"Mrs. Blair, I cannot but feel the justice of what you say, and I can only regret it."

"Mrs. Bertram is right," she added, "and perhaps she does wants many wives would do under similar circumstances, she what a servant who would esteem her more than her husband."

"Indeed."

"That is the whole truth. My devotion to you, to your feelings, and to your interest, is what she does not like."

"But you only suppose so ?"

"Nay, sir, I know it. 'You,' she said to me, 'Mrs. Blair, you seem to imagine that it is quite impossible that Mr. Bertram can do anything wrong.'"

"Did she say so ?"

"She did, sir."

"Humph! that would imply that she thought I might do wrong."

"Now you mention it, sir, it certainly would, although I merely took it as a casual remark, which, no doubt, was intended to wound my feelings; but I have seen that she has her suspicions."

"Suspicions of what ?" said Charles Bertram, lowering his voice.

"The black mantle."

"Ah! speaks she ever of that, Mrs. Blair ? why—why, I told her all about that, and what suspicions need she have ? I do not like a suspicious person. I told her about it, and that ought to have satisfied her, of course."

"It ought; but do you think, sir, it has ?"

"Yes, yes. Surely—surely it is the truth, and, therefore, of course, it not only ought, but has. I cannot help thinking that you must be wrong there, Mrs. Blair. It is so trivial a circumstance."

Mrs. Blair gave a short, dry cough.

"If I must leave you, sir, I must. There is no avail. I will now trouble you no further."

"Nay, stay a few moments, Mrs. Blair. I—I—has my wife hinted to you and suspicions concerning the—the—black mantle ?"

Mrs. Blair advanced closer to Bertram, as she said in a low voice of great apparent confidence;—

"She—has."

"Ah, indeed, and what ?"

"I did all I could to convince her that she was acting foolishly, in giving way to any uneasy thoughts about such a matter, but by some means or another, Heaven only knows how, she has conceived an idea that that box, and the black mantle which was enclosed in it, have reference to some intrigue in which you have been concerned."

"No, no."

"It is so. She is full of suspicion. Can you not guess why she quarrelled with me ?"

"No; why ?"

"You surely understand ?"

"Indeed, I do not."

"She thinks I know all about it, and will not tell her."

"Indeed!"

"Yes, and hence she said that I was one who imagined you could do no wrong. You understand, I am willing —oh, I am quite willing to leave; and you may depend that I was most discreet."

"But—but——"

"Oh, I told her nothing. In vain she offered me money; in vain she pictured to me advantages such as I have never had ; in vain she used every argument she could to induce me to betray you; but I would not, and then anger suddenly took possession of her, and she determined that I should leave the house."

"You—you surprise me."

"I knew I should."

"But, Mrs. Blair, what had you to tell ?"

"Oh, my poor head! how forgetful I am. I have always said that I might have made a fortune long, if I had had more art. I have not told you, Mr. Bertram—"

"What—what?"

"That I found the letter you lost, and that came with the box in which was the black mantle."

Charles staggered back a pace or two and sunk into a chair. He turned very pale, and looked intently in the face of Mrs. Blair, who piously cast up her eyes to the ceiling, as if she were muttering some general and comprehensive prayer for the happiness of the whole human race, coined out of the extreme benevolence of her heart. There was an awkward silence of at least five minutes' duration. Charles was turning over most anxiously in his mind what he should do in this most untoward affair; and so bewildered was he by the sudden piece of intelligence, that he could on the spur of the moment but imagine a host of evils, without any palliating circumstances.

Mrs. Blair was looking at him, although she seemed not to be so, and she was mentally arranging in her own mind not only what she should say next, but imagining what he was most likely, under the circumstances, to say. Truly, it was an awkward state of things, and Charles Bertram's fate was in its most critical position.

Oh, if his good angel—if there be good angels, or bad ones either—could but then have whispered to him to rise and defy Mrs. Blair, and go at once and explain everything to his wife, how much happier a man might he have been. But it was not to be so. Each moment of hesitation was fatal, and, when he did speak, the first sound of his voice convinced Mrs. Blair that all was as she could wish, and that she had accomplished her object without entering at all, just then, into the affair of Margaret's male cousin, which she very much congratulated herself upon having in reserve for some other, and, perhaps, more troublesome occasion.

CHAPTER XXI.

THE CONFERENCE AND THE AGREEMENT.—MRS. BLAIR'S TRIUMPH OVER THE WIFE.—CHARLES'S AWKWARD POSITION.

"MRS. BLAIR," said Charles,—"Mrs. Blair."

"Yes, sir. What may be your commands, sir?"

"You say you have found a letter addressed to me?"

"Yes; and very sorry am I to add that, somewhere among my things I have mislaid it again."

"Mislaid it! Good God! how could you do that? Why, it may be found by some one else now."

"No, sir. It is not, indeed, in the house. Not for the world would I have had it here; so having a number of things belonging to me at my sister's, Mrs. Primrose, I took it there, and placed it away somewhere—where I now really forget; but you may be assured, sir, it is safe."

"You will return it to me?"

"Of course, sir, the moment I find it, you may depend. I will go to-morrow and look again for it. I may find it, or I may not; but if I do, I will bring it to you. If I do not find it now, it is sure to turn up some day."

"But—surely you know where it is. You can find it for me, Mrs. Blair, if you make diligent search for it, you know. Pray do so, and count upon my grateful remembrance, when once that letter is placed in my hands."

"As I am about, of course, to leave your service, sir, I shall have ample time to look for it, and Mrs. Bertram will get some one to fill my place who will play the part of spy upon you, which I have declined."

"A spy upon me?"

"Yes, sir; that's the proper name to give it. I told her I would not, and I could not do so, and thus, of course, we quarrelled."

"Indeed, Mrs. Blair, it is a hard thing for you to leave my service on such a ground as this."

"It is, sir; and many persons, it discharged in such a way, would not hesitate to place that letter in an envelope, and send it to Mrs. Bertram.

Indeed, my sister wished me to do so."

"Your sister? Why you do not mean to tell me that she is aware of such a circumstance, Mrs. Blair? It was highly imprudent of you. You should have kept it, at least, to yourself."

"Oh, I can answer for my sister with my life; she is a woman of strong but amiable feelings—I can fully answer for her. What she said was, 'If you are discharged, I don't know what my indignation may prompt me to do; but if you retain your situation, just let well alone.'"

"She said so?"

"She did; and then, I will confess, sir, I felt sorry that, in the impulse of the moment, I had trusted her with the letter at all. However, it was done, and could not then be undone."

"Mrs. Blair, when I come to consider all things, I am inclined to be of opinion that you must not leave me."

"Oh, sir, I must."

"Nay, why so? Surely you have no desire to leave me, Mrs. Blair?"

"Desire to leave you, sir? Oh! I could live and die in your service. There is nothing that I would not gladly do for you from morning till night; but, now that you are married——"

"Well, what of that?"

"You must consult the wishes of your wife; you must have no will of your own—you must discharge every one from your service who does not exactly fall into her whims, sir,—you must get rid as quickly as you can of every domestic who has not been hired by her, and been made to understand by her that you are nobody, and that she, and she only, can exercise any power or control over them."

"No, by Heaven."

"Oh, dear, yes, sir; you will find that such is the case. Mrs. Bertram will begin upon the footman next, I expect, because he was not hired by her; and when she once gets a new housekeeper in my place, of course it will be easy enough to find fault with the servants and change every one of them."

"This is a species of domestic tyranny I shall not submit to," said Charles Bertram, angrily.

"Then you must be quite prepared, which very few men are, to assert that you are master in your own house, sir."

"Indeed, for that I am fully prepared."

"So you think you are?"

"Who questions my authority?"

"Mrs. Bertram has commenced to do so, as you perceive, by discharging me on the very first opportunity, because I would not be a spy upon you and your actions."

"Then I shall commence an exercise of my own authority by keeping you, Mrs. Blair."

"Oh, sir, you will yield, and I shall be in a worse situation than before —I know how it will be."

"Indeed, you are very much mistaken. If I make a point of this matter, you may be assured I will carry it out. I will not thus easily have the reins of government in my own house taken out of my hands."

"Sir, if I thought would be firm, I would consent to stay."

"I shall be firm, Mrs. Blair, you may depend. Putting aside every other consideration, I shall be firm upon principle in this matter. I feel convinced that if I give way now, my whole authority is completely lost."

"You take, sir, a just view of the subject, but I am afraid a painful one to me. Who knows what slights I may have to endure now?"

"No, no, you will have none; I will manage all that by fair means, if I possibly can, but be assured you shall suffer no slights. If you will stay, stay—but, of course, I cannot prevent your leaving me."

"I will try and find the letter."

Charles started.

"You will oblige me by remaining," he said, "you will oblige me much by remaining where you are, Mrs. Blair. You will find the letter if you can, and let me have it. It is of some importance to me, although not great, of course. I do not pretend to deceive you in the matter—I had an unfortunate acquaintance with a young person."

"Oh, these things will happen, sir,

especially when a gentleman is hand-some, and has such a mind."

"Well, well, Mrs. Blair, we will say no more on that point; of course, you can easily imagine how I may not only be very excusable, but really much to be pitied in the transaction."

"Decidedly so, sir."

"And yet I do not wish to have any words with Mrs. Bertram about it, you know."

"If once she knew it," said Mrs. Blair, oracularly; "if but once she knew it, you would never hear the last of it. In a hundred invidious ways it would be continually brought before you. Depend upon it, Mr. Bertram, that when a wife once becomes acquainted with such an affair, she will make the most extensive use of it in her power, and never let it thoroughly drop."

"You are right: on my soul, I believe you are right."

"Pray, sir, there is one thing which if I remain with you, I must beg of you to allow me to do."

"What is that?"

"To pay out of my own pocket for the little extras which I used to make out a bill of to you once a month."

"Why so?"

"Because I cannot endure the idea of rendering accounts to Mrs. Bertram. I know that were I to do so, her constant aim would be to humiliate me, and you would be continually annoyed upon the subject."

"Well, well, I cannot of course allow you to pay for anything yourself. I will give you, when you require it, a five-pound note, and you need make up no accounts at all."

Mrs. Blair took her pocket-handkerchief with great rapidity from her pocket, and clapped it on to her eyes.

"What is the matter, Mrs. Blair?"

exclaimed Bertram, who was far from expecting any such sudden accession of sensibility.

"Such noble, confiding generosity!" she exclaimed, in a tremulous, broken voice; "oh, sir, it is in another, and a better world, you must look for your reward. It is, indeed, and not here—not here. At the throne of grace we shall meet!"

Then Mrs. Blair shook her head, no doubt at the general iniquity of mankind; and half shutting her eyes, she gave the lids that tremulous motion we have mentioned before as incidental to very pious people, and which, should any of our kind readers observe in any one, we beg they will consider as a warning not on any account, or to any extent, however trifling, to put trust or confidence in that individual.

It was just a little too much almost for Charles Bertram to believe that he was especially entitled to any consideration in another world, so he broke up the conference, by saying,—

"Well, well, Mrs. Blair, you will quite undertand that you continue in your situation, and take no dismissal."

"From anybody else but yourself sir?"

"Very good, let it be so."

"Ah, now, indeed, I feel a holy calm," said Mrs. Blair; "oh, sir, if you were but to hear the godly Mr. Mortimer, or the beautiful Baptists Noel, how happy I should be! That would, indeed, be heavenly!"

"Some day, perhaps, I may; but not at present, Mrs. Blair."

"Well, sir, I only do hope that the day will come when I shall see added to the same flock of lambs in the fold of the Lord which are going to heaven, you, my dear sir, for you are certainly the best of masters, that I have always said. It is not always we find such a mind combined with such grace of manner, and such very good looks."

"There—there, that's enough, Mrs. Blair; you want to make me vain."

"That would be impossible."

"Make yourself easy; I will manage this affair with Mrs. Bertram, and do you endeavour to find me that letter as quickly as you possibly can, for believe me that, for many reasons, I wish to have it."

"It shall be found, sir; I am intruding upon you, and am very sorry you should have thought it necessary to mention about giving me money."

"Oh, by the by, I had forgot; I took out my pocket-book, but did not give you the note; there it is, Mrs. Blair, and when that is done with, you know, without saying anything at all to Mrs. Bertram, you can tell me, and I will give you another, so you will feel quite comfortable on that head. Good morning, Mrs. Blair, good morning."

"The Lord look straight down upon you, sir!" said Mrs. Blair, "and cover you with the manna of his righteousness. Amen! amen!"

CHAPTER XXII.

MARGARET'S REFLECTIONS. —THE ILLNESS OF THEODORE DANTON.

We have taken occasion to say lately in this work, that confidence begets confidence, and distrust begets distrust. So true is that saying, that it may be carried to almost any extent, as regards the motives which govern the conduct of mankind. The passions, the feelings, and the prejudices of an individual, do not alone affect himself, but they have a much more serious influence upon the feelings and the conduct of others than at first sight would appear at all possible. But, in the present aspect of affairs at the house of the Bertrams, we have a most notable example of this.

Mrs. Bertram, as the reader is aware, was as candid, and truthful, and confiding a creature, as was ever created. She was one who abhorred mystery, and secrecy, and designing conduct, quite as much as it was admired by her wily and bad housekeeper, Mrs. Blair. She had always, almost to a fault, been in the habit of saying what she thought, in reference, perhaps, to what it was politic to say. Her truthfulness was great, and well known to all who were at all acquainted with her sufficiently intimately to be able to form any opinion of her character.

And yet, with all this, she did not tell her husband that Theodore Danton loved her. Wherefore was this? Wherefore was it that she thus negatively, for the first time in her existence, gave her mind to falsehood? Why was it that she suppressed a fact which in no way attacked her own character, and which certainly she ought, viewing the matter abstractedly, to have told to her husband?

The reason is obvious. Already had she seen enough of Charles Bertram's character to be fully aware that he had not sufficient control over himself to hear calmly and patiently what he ought to hear, with such feelings. Already she had discovered that peculiarity of mind which led him to brood over simple matters, and convert them into something great, monstrous, and alarming, in the alembic of his imagination. And therefore was it that this fault in him produced the fault in her.

What he could not hear reasonably, she felt that nobler, higher interests, forced her to conceal. 'Twas true that Theodore Danton loved her, but he loved her not as Mrs. Bertram. There was no criminality in his passion, but the mad-brained jealousy of Bertram would have found abundance. As the penniless, prospectless Margeret Harrison, he had loved her; as such he had cherished her image in his heart, and toiled night and day that he might be able to come to her, saying,—

"Margaret, I love you! For your dear sake, I have toiled; and now I come, for the first time, to tell you that I love you, when I can lay at your feet some proofs of my sincerity, and offer to you the home, not a shadow of which I could have begged your acceptance of before."

This was the sort of love which he had had for her; and when he left the shores of England, he left her as Margaret Harrison—when he returned, he found her a wife. There was nothing criminal in such a love as this. He had, with quite as little passion or feeling as could well be expected from one of such an ardent temperament, met her once again, but to feel that his heart was blighted for ever, and his best affections scattered to the winds.

The reader is aware of all he said and of all he did, and that Charles Bertram had no right, in such a case, and under such circumstances, had he even overheard all that passed, to find fault with either Theodore Danton or his own exemplary wife.

But yet Mrs. Bertram felt that, for Theodore's sake, she durst not tell her husband; and it was not from any wish on her part to keep the painful secret. Oh, no! Gladly would she have poured it into a husband's sympathising, right-thinking heart, had she been blessed with such a man, but she was not; and hence, as we may say, the faults of Charles Bertram's character compelled faults in others.

She, however, fully intended that she would take some opportunity, when Theodore was gone, and when she could point triumphantly to the fact that he was gone as a proof of the innocence of his love, to tell her husband all about it, as well as her reason for not sooner confiding the story to him; but, alas! this resolve, like most of the resolves of mortals, was "crossed by fate!" It was doomed never to be carried out, under the circumstances which she pictured to herself, for those circumstances did not occur as she had pictured them.

And yet she was not thoroughly satisfied that she was adopting the best course she could. She was not accustomed to weigh her actions in the scales of cold expediency. This process of mind was perfectly new to her. She had hitherto, without one obtruding doubt of the propriety of the matter at issue, and without disguise, when she chose to speak at all, told the whole truth unhesitatingly; and hence she felt in a most unhappy frame of mind that she could not say to her husband,—

"Charles, Theodore Danton loved me; and now that, upon his return from abroad, he finds me married, he is nearly beside himself with grief."

She could not bring herself to utter those words, for she knew not how they might be taken; and while she considered whether she should utter them or not, of course the time for uttering them properly was passing away, and what at first had been but a doubtful silence became very shortly almost a compulsory one.

If she had several opportunities of telling so much to her husband, and embraced none of them, it would sound amazingly odd, and come from her lips with all the bad grace of a confident guilt, upon after reflection, for her then to commence a speech with,—

"Theodore Danton loves me."

When the mind is nearly on the balance for and against any particular line of conduct, some very trivial circumstances will frequently cause the scale on one side or the other to preponderate, and Margaret had quite intellect enough to feel that, having embraced a particular cause, there was far less evil and danger commonly in pursuing it, than in deviating from it suddenly, and leaving whatever good consequences might fairly be expected to result from it unfound. Thus, then, she firmly resolved that she would allow Theodore Danton to leave England, according to the determination he had expressed, and she had rather than otherwise encouraged, before she told her husband the cause of his avowed absence. The idea of keeping it always a secret from Bertram she would not allow herself to entertain, partly from a fixed aversion to secrets which had been instilled into her in early life, and partly from a strong sense of duty towards him, whom, at the altar's foot, she had sworn honour and obedience.

"Yes," she said to herself; "yes, I will tell him when Theodore has gone, and then he cannot be jealous. When he knows that he who loves me has expatriated himself because he finds me the wife of another, and that he cannot love me with honour, he must be satisfied of the purity of the feelings which actuate poor Theodore. I shall be able to give him the name of the ship in which he has sailed from England; I shall be able to give him such particulars as shall enable him to satisfy himself throughly that such is the fact; and then, let him feel what momentary pang he may at the idea that any one else has those feelings of affection for me which he would himself have wholly and entirely, and which he alone is entitled to have, he must, upon a few minutes' reflection, accord to Theodore Danton the honour he so nobly deserves."

Thus, then, did Margaret satisfy her mind upon the most painful and harassing topic that had everr occured to agitate it, one which not again, through a long life, was likely to take place, and which, when once entirely rid of, by a disclosure of the facts to her husband, she fondly hoped would become faint, even almost to obliteration, in the long lapse of time to come.

"And Theodore, as years increase upon him," she thought, "will get rid of the painful feelings which this disappointment has occasioned him. Other pursuits will engage his attention : men have a thousand resources againt that sickness of the heart from which women can rarely fly. And he will, doubtless, find some other who will engage his fond affections, and make for him a happy home, even such as he strove so nobly to make for me, when I knew not that he loved me."

She sighed deeply as she spoke. Was there some feeling of love kindled now in her bosom for the enthusiastic youth who differed so much in character from the man she had mated with? Did she feel a pang that, when Theodore came home, he found her not as he had left her, but the bride of another?

It might have been so : but, if it were, it was unknown even to herself, for her bosom was too much virtue's throne to enable it to harbour for a moment one injurious feeling. She paused, perhaps, to ask herself the question, if she thought she should have been happier as the wife of Theodore Danton. There are many questions which we all hesitate to ask ourselves, and this was one from which Margaret shrunk, lest an answer might arise from the depths of her own heart which she should never forget. She stifled the rising feeling, and strove with virtuous might to forget that she was beloved by one whom she could but admire and respect, while she had sworn to love one whom she was faintly beginning to tremble to discover she could do neither to. But the matter never assumed so broad a shape in her mind as we have now put it; she would not let it, for, when she found her imagination wandering that way, she instantly stopped it, and forced herself to some other train of thought.

*   *   *   *

And now let us cast our eyes for a few moments upon poor Theodore Danton. There is a darkened room—but one faint light is permitted to come into it from a shutter partially only opened; straw is thrown down in the front of the house; the door of the apartment is passed with slow and cautious steps by those who have to ascend or descend the staircase. Those porters who enter the room do so with a subdued tread, and what conversation is carried on is in whispers. A dim fire smoulders in the grate, while, on the chimney-piece above, is an array of phials, which, from the peculiar shaped lables that hang from their necks, have been evidently used for medical purposes. The room is a handsome bed-chamber, spacious, and well appointed; it is a respectable, but not a fashionable hotel, a hotel which the inmates are reminded that they are well to do, rather from the comforts that surround them, than from the exorbitant bill they are called upon to pay. The curtains of the bed are all but one, drawn closely round it, and, from the rapt stillness that there reigns, he who lies upon the bed might well be supposed to have taken his last farewell of this world and all its sorrows. But such was not the case; he still lived, although, in the opinion of all, Death upon him had set his seal.

It was Theodore Danton—the noble-minded, chivalrous Theodore Danton —the brave, the generous, the gifted Theodore Danton who there lay hovering between life and death.

A fever had seized upon him, which had failed completely to yield to any of the most ordinary remedies. The people at the hotel had got seriously alarmed, and as he became delirious, the first medical aid was called in to see him.

The case was declared to be one of extreme seriousness, and the more so as its cause and first rise were unknown. The brain was evidently most affected, and one of the physicians who had been sent for declared that, in his opinion, the whole system must have received some most remarkable and severe nervous shock to produce such a state of illness as the patient exhibited. It was a form of illness that rapidly developed itself; and, notwithstanding all was done that human skill could dictate, poor Theodore Danton grew rapidly and visibly worse.

He was in no state to be questioned, and when, indeed, it was attempted, all that was got from him were incoherent replies, wandering far from the subject matter of the question.

Under these circumstances, the landlord of the hotel took legal advice, and he was told to do all that could be done for the sick gentleman—for a gentleman he evidently was—and to take an inventory of what belonged to him, and then seal up his effects.

This was done; and to give the people their due, nothing was spared that could in any way tend to recover the sick young man.

For some hours, now, this time had been passed between alternate fits of raving and complete exhaustion consequent upon them. Two nurses now occupied the room, and they were conversing together in low whispers by the small fire which was ordered to be kept in, but as low as possible.

"He won't last long." said one.

"No, to be sure not. When I first clapped my eyes upon him, I says, says I, ' He won't scratch gray hairs."

"He can't scratch none now since his head's been shaved," remarked the other.

"In course not; but you know what I means. The last job as we shall have with him will be the laying on him out."

"Very likely, I say, what sort of a corpse do you think he'll make now, really?"

"Why, it's all as it turns out. Some, as you'd lay your life would make as handsome a corpse as ever you'd care to clap your eyes on, turn out quite t' other, which you knows as well as me."

"To be sure. That often happens."

"I believe you. You never can tell. When sometimes you'd say quite the contrary, the corps turns out as nice as butter."

"Oh, dear, yes; and at others there's a draw o' the face."

"Yes, or a overflow o' the *bile.*"

"To be sure there is, as makes all the blessed difference in life. I often says as you are sure of nothing in this world but death and the quarter day."

"Oh, them you is sure enough of— them you may swear to. I wonder, now, when he means to begin agin?"

"No how, and never, I hope. I'm tired of it, quite, I am. I do wonder who the deuce Margaret can be as he's always talking about."

"Oh, some hussey or another."

"Well, you know young men will be young men, and natur will be natur, do what you may, or say what you will. You was young yourself once, you know, Sally; think of that."

"Young once?"

"Yes, to be sure you was."

"And what do you take upon yourself to call me now, I should like to know, Elizabeth?"

"What now?"

"Yes, what now, woman?"

"Don't you call me a woman, or else I shall just tell you you is a female."

"If you call me a female, I'll soon let you know which is the outside of the door. Recollect as I'm the original nurse."

"The original stuff."

"What's that you say?"

"What, you want me to speak loud, do you, and wake up the patient, and then get the sack from the doctor. Oh, you designing female!"

How far the contention might have gone it is hard to say; but a long-drawn sigh from the patient attracted both their attentions.

"Bless me!" said one; "for all we know that's his last."

"Come and see."

They both rose and looked on the bed at the languid form of poor Theodore. A mass of ice was placed, enveloped in oil-cloth, near his head, and his whole appearance was that of a dying man.

"Margaret, Margaret—my Margaret!" he moaned.

"There he goes again," said one of the women. "I really do wish Margaret was stuffed down his throat."

"If so be," said the other, "she was a wirtuous female, I shouldn't be so much put out as I is."

"But how do you know, Elizabeth, as she isn't?"

"Oh, I know what I knows."

"Yes, but I don't."

"Then, I can tell you that when young men calls anybody *hisen* they can't be virtuous."

"Well there's something in that."

"Oh, I hate to hear him."

"Margaret—Margaret," again said Theodore, and then suddenly altering his moaning voice to one of accusation, he cried,—

"Chide the ship—chide the ship. Oh, how slow she sails; and yet they say, with a flowing sail,—England, England, land of her I love; home of my Margaret, when shall I look upon your shores again? Fly like a sea-bird over the dancing waves. Take me to her. No—no—no. That was a dream. She is not another's—she is not another's. Fiends—fiends, you would whisper me to madness—to madness."

"There he goes again. Well, I never, now. Isn't it worth all the money to hear such nonsense a coming from any lips o' mortality?"

"There—there," cried Theodore, "she stands upon the rock—she nears the brink. No—no—no more. Margaret—Margaret and I fettered. She turns her head—she does not see the yawning gulf; she is smiling on some one, and she sees it not. Margaret—Margaret. She is gone. Gone—gone. God, she is gone. Was there no special providence to save her? Was such beauty made to perish? Help—help—help! Oh, help! Margaret—Margaret!"

"I suppose," said one of the nurses, "I suppose from what he says, as that young woman, whoever she is, has had some bad fall."

"It seems like it."

"He said so. That's the way, as the gentleman said as was a smiling on a Monday, a laughing on a Tuesday, and a corpse on a Wednesday. We is here to-day, and we is gone to-morrow."

"Uncommon true. There he goes again."

"The burning house—the burning house!" cried Theodore. "Oh, how the beams crackle—how the glass shivers to a thousand pieces. There is no one in the blazing pile—there is no one there who is beloved by aught human. We will look calmly at the grandeur of the fire."

"How uncommon reasonable he is all of a minute. Lord have mercy upon us. That was his art, I suppose?"

Theodore, after a moment's silence, uttered a shriek so loud and ear-piercing, that it sounded from one end of the very street to the other, and alarmed everybody.

"I see her now—I see her now!" he cried. "That mass of flame, and she, but as a dim speck of human life reflected from it. There! can no one save her? Help—help! Why am I held by a thousand hands from rushing to her rescue? Help—help! Madness—torture—horror! There—there—there. She cries for aid. 'Tis Margaret's voice. Are you brave? See you not her burning? Release me now, and let me fly to her. Help! Oh, help, God save her. She screams. Have mercy, Heaven!"

"It seems to me, Elizabeth, as that young man has something or another on his mind."

"Well, I shouldn't wonder. One would think now, to hear him a going on, as that young woman he speaks on had been in a house a fire."

"So one would; but, *arter* all, perhaps it's only one of what the doctor called his *allusions*."

"Well, I don't know. He makes noise enough about it to be no allusion. That's all I've got to say about it."

"The sweet fields and scented flowers," said Theodore. "Oh, this is Arcadia. What a scene of love! The dappled deer are straying in the vale. This grateful coolness of the overhanging vine is almost magical—that verdure at my feet. Oh, can the rarest art of man produce a carpet like to this?"

"Bless me if he isn't a admiring of the carpet, Elizabeth."

"Well, it's a Brussels."

"Yes, but a good deal worn in places."

"Ah, to be sure, and the rug don't come near it in pint of a match, leastways in pattern."

"Not a bit. What fancies people as is ill do take. Only to think, now, of his beginning to admire the carpet."

"It's odd enough. Hark to him now."

"And you are here, too, dearest and best?" said Theodore. "Ah! my Margaret, what a new charm now breathes among the flowers. What new beauty has the sunshine now. Let us wander through these groves of Attica, and talk of love."

"What's that he says about the attic, Elizabeth?"

"I don't know, really. He did say attics, that's all I can say about it. I heard that with my own mortal ears."

"And so did I."

"This is Elysium," said Theodore. "And do you love me, dearest? Ah! did you guess the fondly cherished secret of your lover's breast, and tell yourself I would return to say how I adored you, my Margaret? My own, my beautiful Margaret, are we not happy now?"

"Upon my word, Elizabeth, my opinion is as he'll say something decidedly improper soon."

"Do you think so? Don't say anything, then; but let's hear it. I havn't heard anything improper for a whole week."

"Lor, how provoking,—here comes Dr Middleton."

"Sure enough—sure enough Let's put on our sympathetical looks, Elizabeth."

CHAPTER XXIII.

MR PRIMROSE'S OLD FRIEND JACK RODNEY.—A HAPPY MEETING.—THE LETTER.

ABOUT this time a serious blow was given to the supremacy of Mrs. Primrose in the rule of her family and husband, and deprived her of the boast she had been uniformly heard to utter so frequently, and with such pride and triumph, that she ruled Mr. Primrose as easily as she could control a child. How the matter happened, was thus:—

Mr. Primrose had, in his youth, and his subsequent years of discretion—till, indeed, it became manifest that he had committed a great act of indiscretion in marrying Mrs. Primrose — a very intimate and pleasant companion, one Jack Rodney, a very hearty fellow. Some how or other, they had not been intimate for some time. Whether it was that Jack thought marriage wonderfully altered men's minds towards their companions, the friends of their adolescence and their manhood,—

whether it was Jack had an antipathy to babies, cradles, or wives, or whether more important matters of life called him elsewhere, is not known, but certain it is, that Mr. Primrose had not seen Jack Rodney for many a long year.

He had not been seen, he had not been heard of, and his whereabouts was unknown. However, one afternoon he came. Mr. Primrose was seated, after his dinner, with a newspaper, and an empty glass by his side, and considering the propriety of replenishing it, which he began to think he might effect with impunity, as Mrs. Primrose was out, and would know nothing about the matter, unless she had marked the bottle—no very unlikely affair either—he was just in this state of dubitation, considering the propriety of refilling, and reading an article on refunding in the paper, when a sharp rap came at the knocker. Primrose started, and mentally ejaculated, as the sour countenance of Mrs. Primrose crossed his imagination,—

"There's my wife. No more grog, no more chance of it than as if it had no existence. Well, well, fate is against me—it's an empty bucket to the German Ocean against me. What a pity I hadn't been quicker; but never mind, never mind."

Mr. Primrose listened to the hurried step of the servant girl, as she went to answer the door, and expected to hear her sharply reprimanded, for not flying to answer the door earlier.

"Is Mr. Primrose within?" said a loud, heavy voice, that he knew was familiar to him, and yet, for the moment, Primrose could not recollect the individual to whom the said voice belonged.

"Yes, sir," replied the servant.

"Tell him Mr. Rodney wishes to speak with him."

No sooner did he hear the word Rodney pronounced, than a host of former reminiscences sprung up, and in the first emotion of pleasure at the call, he jumped out of his chair and opened the parlour door just as the servant was coming in; and this produced a collision, as is well understood and explained upon mathematical principles. On two bodies coming with equal force from opposite directions, and meeting at one and the same point, they will, all things being the same, come to a state of rest. This was precisely the case in this instance. Mr. Primrose stopped the servant from coming in, and the servant stopped Mr. Primrose from going out.

"Mr. Rodney, sir," spluttered the girl.

"Jack," shouted Primrose.

"Hilloa," said Jack, come forwards. "What's the matter, Primrose?"

"Oh, nothing. Only the girl ran in——"

"Into your arms."

"Oh, no; for God's sake."

"Oh, I sha'n't say a word about it. I have come at an unfortunate moment."

"Not at all; but Jack, how do you do, Jack? come in, my dear fellow."

"With all my heart. And how are you, as you ain't dead? I suppose you are a widower? You ain't in mourning, but I can understand all about that. How are you?"

"Oh, very well, indeed. How are you? what a time since I saw you Mary."

"Yes, sir."

"Some hot water, Mary."

"Yes, sir."

And Mary departed upon her errand.

"My dear fellow, how glad I am you have come. I thought it had been Mrs. Primrose."

"Devilish lucky it was not Mrs. Primrose; had it been, why, she would have been displeased, eh?"

"It would not have happened—it could not have happened; I assure you, it was purely accidental."

"These things are always purely accidental. But what do you mean by its not happening if it had been for Mrs. Primrose?"

"Because, my dear fellow, I should have been in no such hurry to have got to the door. She would have been with me soon enough; and hence it was that I was coming to you as soon as I heard your voice, and she was coming in to announce you."

"I see the cause of the unpleasant dilemma—the juxta-position of the two

planets, Mars and Venus. But joking apart, how have you been?"

"Been?—oh, very well; sometimes a little queer, and at other times well enough."

"And matrimonial affairs——"

"Are as I suppose they are elsewhere. I have nothing to complain of, only Mrs. P. has a disagreeable habit of saying more than I like; but you know, my dear fellow, the best way to disarm such petty annoyances of this kind, is to take no notice of them, and let them pass you by in the same manner as you would the wind."

"That is truly philosophic; but it is, unfortunately, the philosophy of the weaker party."

"Indeed!"

"Ay, it is, I assure you. The stronger governs the weaker, and the weaker, when it cannot help itself, gives in, and says—

"'What must be, must; and the best thing we can do, is to obey without increasing the tyranny of others by unavailing resistance.'

"But a truce to this, my dear fellow. I have called upon you to see you, and to enjoy half-an-hour's chat upon old times—that is, if you have the leisure."

"I never was better pleased in my life," returned Primrose, "than I am with this visit. We will have some grog, and should Mrs. Primrose be out, which is not at all unlikely, for some time longer, we can be comfortable and snug."

"Quite right, my boy; women always spoil a grog party—they make it turn upon one's stomach."

At this moment the hot water was brought in by the servant girl, who seemed rather amazed at Mr. Primrose's temerity and liberality.

"Glasses, Mary."

"Yes, sir."

And Mary brought the glasses, large rummers, and placed them on the tray close to Mr. Primrose, and then left the room, with an air which seemed to say,—"I know what will be the consequence of this—I know what missus will say."

Mr. Primrose at once pushed a bottle and glass to Jack Rodney, saying, as he did so,—

"Come, Jack, I know you used to prefer mixing for yourself, and, if we die for it, we will have a pleasant hour or two."

"With all my heart, Primrose. Take my advice, and when you hear your wife coming, lock the door, and swear if she will go out she sha'n't come in at all, unless she asks pardon."

"But consider the children."

"Oh, ay, the children—well, they don't fret, do they!"

"Oh, no."

"Well, they'll eat their bread and butter just as well if Mary were to cut it as they would under her carving, depend upon it, and thrive just as well."

"That may be, Jack, but——"

"But you would rather not risk the experiment! very well—never mind—there's a time for all things. How goes business?"

"Oh, very well; I must not complain—I am doing decently, decently, Jack."

"That's well, too."

"And yourself?"

"I can't complain, except that I don't grow younger. Do you know, Primrose, what I have been thinking about, as an improvement upon nature?"

"No."

"Why this; a man ought to be permitted to renew his best days again—so that when he is forty, or five and forty, he may suddenly go back to sweet eighteen, and live his remaining years in getting old again; he might die just as soon, if that were considered any obstacle; but it would make the population more vigorous, and better altogether in my opinion, morally and physically."

"That may be all very true, but I can see only one great objection."

"And what is that?"

"The impossibility."

"Granted. But, barring the slight disadvantage, it would be a very good scheme."

"Women would be delighted at it, no doubt, for many a grey-headed dowager would be glad to renew her days after youth."

"So they would; but they are the very individuals to whom I would deny the invention, because nobody would care anything for resuscitated females."

"It's more injurious than anything else; and, therefore, the distinction or exclusion, is useless."

"Unfortunately, very unfortunately, my dear fellow, but somebody may hit upon some plan some day—not in mine I fear— by which they can either explode marriage altogether, or find what is yet barren—some method of compelling wives to keep their oaths, and be obedient."

Mr. Primrose sighed deeply, and touched the glass with his lips, and sipped the contents with much deliberation and relish, and then, after divers sips, he said,—

"Well, wives may be novel to you, and, therefore, entertaining to talk about; but with me they are not in the same odour;—will you be so good as to change the subject?"

"With all my heart; since we have had enough of wives, suppose we go back to the girls."

"Ah, that would be a change."

"And no bad one, either. Do you not recollect those two cherry-cheeked damsels you and I used to take about with us, before you met with Mrs. Primrose? They were hearty and merry wenches, and wanted not much for beauty."

"They did not; many a pleasant day we four have spent together. I thought you intended to have married one."

"Who—I?"

"Yes."

"Lord bless your simplicity, Primrose. I would have as soon thought of offending holy writ, and marrying my grandmother."

"What a devil-may-care fellow you are, Rodney. I never heard——"

The latter part of the sentence remained unspoken, and was lost, in consequence of a sudden and sharp rap coming at the door.

"What's the matter?" said Rodney, as he observed his friend's beaming countenance assuming a more serious hue than it had done since his entrance.

"I think that's my wife."

"Well, Primrose, I don't wish to promote quarrels in families, but I think you should be master. If I were you I would, too."

"Ah, my dear fellow, you don't know what being master is. I am master, but I make it a rule never to interfere with domestic affairs. I never break domestic arrangements—it is her province, and if I threw her out, that would throw me out, and that, again would disturb the harmony of all my business arrangements, and then things would go wrong altogether, and I should be the sufferer."

"Well, then, I'd be hanged or decapitated if I would. But, there, the door's open."

This was true, and the servant was in conversation with the postman for some moments, and then shutting the door, she was about to descend the kitchen stairs.

"Mary!" shouted Primrose.

"Yes, sir," said Mary, in a shrill voice, and in another moment she opened the door.

"Who was that?"

"It was only the postman."

"With a letter?"

"Yes."

"Who for?"

"For missus, sir."

"Then, put it on the mantel-piece," said Mr. Primrose, with the air of a man who had behaved with stern dignity in his own house.

The servant did as she was desired, and then left the room. There was a pause of some moments, and then, after swallowing nearly half a tumbler of grog, Mr. Primrose rose, and going to the mantel-piece, took the letter in his hand and gazed at it, and whistled for some moments.

"Are you going to open it?" inquired Rodney.

"Oh, no."

"Indeed!"

"Oh, no; I never open anybody's letters but my own," replied Primrose, hastily.

"Never open your wife's letters?"

"No; there would be such fuss about it, and she would talk of my want of confidence and kindness, till I should never be at the end."

"But would leave her in the middle of it; that would be very good, and a very capital plan, too. Is it not your place to know all?"

"I wonder who it can be from," muttered Primrose, scratching his head. "It is a man's handwriting:—dear me."

"Open it."

"If I could do it, now, without her knowing anything about it, I should like to know very well about the contents. There seems to be a card wrapped up in it somehow or other."

"Some invitation or other, to some party at the theatre or ball, where she will go and leave you to take care of the juvenile Primroses."

"Oh, no; she would not think of doing that; but the wafer is scarcely dry."

"Pull it open."

Just as Rodney spoke he did pull it open, and out fell the card, which Rodney picked up, and on looking at it, exclaimed,—

"Well, I am a prophet for once."

"Eh? what?"

"Why, it's an invitation to a masquerade."

"A masquerade? exclaimed Primrose, quite aghast.

"Yes, look at it; there it is, plain enough. Vauxhall masquerade—ball—dances—lights—dancers—gentlemen, rum fellows; and your wife, eh! There's a bill of the play, gentlemen, eh?"

"Be quiet, Rodney," exclaimed the bewildered Primrose, "be quiet."

"Oh, certainly, I ain't a husband, and I have no reason to make a noise; only, on the score of old friendship, I did not like to see you so imposed upon."

"What would you do?'

"Bowl her out, to be sure; bowl her out."

"Bowl her out?"

"Yes."

"How?"

"Why fold up the letter, and put it on the shelf; take no notice of having seen it; let her go; she'll give you an excuse for being out, and then you'll follow her, and watch her, unknown to her, and there will be a clean bowl out, and if you ain't master after that you never deserve to be."

"I see it's for to-morrow night."

"Then I'll get tickets and have all in readiness, lest you should be bowled out, for your receptacles may be searched."

"Very true."

"But what is she to dress in?"

"A black domino with a white rope, which is worn round the waist."

"That is excellent, because there will be none other like it. Well, we can go in character, and shall have some glorious fun; at the same time, it will be glorious fun to bowl her out."

"Why, as to that," said Primrose, "I don't know, if anything should be going forward, why, of course, I should like to find it out."

"And you will. Was it a man's handwriting the letter was in?"

"It was; but, here she is."

"Invite me to-morrow evening, and insist upon it. She will not be sorry in heart of the excuse to get out."

CHAPTER XXIV.

MRS. PRIMROSE'S LIBERALITY, AND THE MASQUERADE AT VAUXHALL. —ITS RESULTS, AND THE PRO-MISE OF A QUIET LIFE.

By this time, the door was opened, and Mrs. Primrose walked into the parlour with a loud sniff of the nose, to indicate the scent of an unusual quantity of spirits, and said, as she entered the room,—

"Dear me, somebody must have been throwing liquors about since I have been out for the purpose of waste, and making the place uninhabitable. Oh, dear—faugh!"

She entered the room, and, seeing Rodney, she gave a sort of half saluta-tion, and, turning to her husband, she said,—

"But I did not know you expected company."

"If you mean me, ma'am," said Jack Rodney, with a bow, "you are

mistaken. I have not had the honour of seeing Mr. Primrose since I last saw you, and that is some few years."

"Oh, indeed. I am sorry that we did not know of your coming, we could then have provided against the contin-gency."

"Pray do not let that distress you; I am very comfortable, and hope you will not put yourself out about me—I shall be particularly sorry."

"Oh, no doubt, sir; but I meant not that. I meant to say we had nothing to offer you. It is very unfortunate, very."

"So it is; but this will serve me better than anything else. Pray, who is your spirit merchant? I never drank better spirits."

"My dear," said Mr. Primrose, fearing a storm, and being desirous of seeing if anything would put her in a good temper, "there's a letter for you. I don't know who it is from. It is on the mantel-piece, were Mary put it."

Mrs. Primrose took the letter and examined it carefully, and then went out of the room and read it, but soon after returned, when she had taken off her bonnet and shawl.

"Is that a bill, my dear?" said Prim-rose.

"It is not a bill, Mr. Primrose. I never permit any tradesman to send bills at unseasonable times. I always see them paid, that's my care; but since you are curious, I'm going to a supper party of ladies, who meet to consider some private affairs and some charities."

"Oh, a very good thing. But when?"

"To-morrow night."

"Then, Jack, perhaps you will come and have supper with me, and spend the evening?"

"With pleasure, Primrose, and we'll have some private affairs and charitable affairs to boot, if you are so minded."

"Thank you — thank you, Jack," said Primrose, in a bewildered manner.

"Well, I must bid you good bye, and will be sure to come and see you to-morrow night. I suppose, ma'am," said Jeck, "you have no particular ob-jection if I come as early as six or seven?"

"None, sir. Mr. Primrose does as he pleases about his own friends. Come at what hour you please; Primrose knows it is all one to me."

With that, Jack Rodney rose, and, with a sly look, he shook hands with Primrose, and took a more ceremonious bow with Mrs. Primrose, and left the house with his reiterated promise of being there the next night.

*　　*　　*　　*

The night quickly aproached, and Mr. Primrose was a very unhappy man during the interval; he scarce knew how the time passed, and sometimes answered Mrs. Primrose snappishly, and was answered snappishly in return, and then Mr. P. became like the raging lion, which the artist had drawn with a beaming smile upon his countenance, and thus frustrated the design of the innkeeper.

Matters went on thus—Mr. P. getting impatient, and straining in his bonds, and, whenever he did so, he was reminded by the said bonds and the gaoler that they resisted, and were stronger than he. At length, the time came, and at the same moment, Jack Rodney's well-known knock was heard at the street-door.

"Ah!" exclaimed Mrs. Primrose, "now you have one of your boon companions with you, you will be well enough. 'Tis a strange thing, that a man like you, Mr. Primrose—a married man, and the farther of a family, too—can never be satisfied, save when you are in the company of what you call your boon companions. It won't do, Primrose, it won't do, and I, your lawful wife, tell you so, mind that. I have said nothing about it this time, but, mind, it must not be repeated. Do you hear, Primrose?"

"Yes, my dear, I do hear."

"Then remember it, and don't drink all the spirits up; there's but one bottle of brandy—that you needn't touch, it's too good to be given to people who drink wholesale; and there are two bottles of gin, and now mind, Primrose, I won't have more than one drank. Only think what an expense it is to have liquor drank up in that manner. You ought not to drink up one bottle, Primrose, you ought not; and then there's the sugar. Oh, if you were half as careful as I am you would be a rich man."

"Very well, my dear. Much of what you have told me I have heard before, and the other, I will remember for another time. I hope, however, you will remember much of what you say at your charity supper to-night, and not pay more for it than need be."

"Mr. Primrose," began Mrs. P. in a high strain; but here she was stopped short by the entrance of Jack Rodney.

"How do you do, Mrs. Primrose? Primrose, how do you do?"

Mrs. Primrose returned the salutation with some reserve, and with much haughtiness, and darted one bitter look at Primrose, who rose up and shook Jack heartily by the hand, saying—

"I am glad you have come, Jack—very glad, indeed. Sit down."

"How have you been?"

"Terribly fidgetty. He's not been the same man he was before you were here last night."

"Indeed! Perhaps he's sorry I have come to prevent his being at your charity and family supper; if so, say the word, Mr. Primrose," said Jack.

"Oh, dear, no," said Mrs. Primrose; "he could not go, since there are no gentlemen admitted."

"What do you say, Primrose?"

"What I meant was this," said Primrose: "Mrs. Primrose has been telling me she has left out a very liberal allowance of spirits——"

"Indeed!"

"Yes; and hopes the sugar and lemons will last out the two bottles of gin and one of brandy that she has left us."

"My God! exclaimed Mrs. Primrose, with a start; and then recovering herself, she gave a wife-look at Mr. Primrose, and hastily quitted the room.

"Now, Primrose," said Jack Rodney, tapping him on the back, "I honour you, my boy; you have begun well, and it shall end well."

"What do you mean?"

"Why, you have begun the campaign with vigour, and you will conquer in the end."

"And how about the masquerade?"

"Hush! here she comes again. Perhaps she'll insist upon locking you up."

Mrs. Primrose did enter the room,

and, being full dressed, she was ready to go out.

"I am now about going," said Mrs. Primrose; "and, as it will be late before I am back, I shall wish you good evening. Primrose, you needn't sit up beyond your usual hour, because you'll be unfit for business, and Heaven knows there's no need of that. Mary will sit up for me."

There was no necessity to wait for a reply to any one of these imperious commands that she had been pleased to give, so she sailed out of the parlour, and in a few moments more bang went the street door.

"Hurrah!" said Jack Rodney.

"'Lovely woman is a treasure.'

Eh, Primrose—what say you, my boy?"

"How about the arrangements for the masquerade? Rodney, tell me all about them."

"There's little to tell you, my dear fellow. I have completed them, and as there is plenty of time yet, we may as well season ourselves with that bottle of brandy your wife so kindly provided for us. We shall have ample time to sip it."

"Let us have the tea-things cleared off."

"As you please; 'twill be better. Tea-things are digestive to look at, but a more intimate acquaintance with them gives a man the dyspepsia."

"Indeed!"

"It is a fact, I assure you. I often suffered that way, until I left off drinking tea and took to strong potations, and now I am as hearty as a young bullock, and can't get a head-ache if I were to try."

"What disguises are we to go in?"

"You are going as an Hungarian officer of dragoons, with boots and spurs, all jingling and musical. You'll create a sensation, I assure you."

"And yourself?"

"Oh—I—yes, I forgot. I'm going as the black cymbal-player to the regiment of Fusilier Guards."

"Characters excellently well chosen. But tell me in sober earnestness, when are we to go, and what are we to do?"

"I'll tell you all at the proper moment, but it's no use now. We'll leave here about eight o'clock; none of the com- pany arrive earlier, and, therefore, we should be too conspicuous."

"Very well; and now we'll sit down to the brandy, it will enliven the moments."

"It will, my boy."

*   *   *   *

The hours passed quickly, and eight o'clock soon came round. The bottle was duly emptied, and at length Rodney said,—

"I think we may as well walk down to the river and take a boat to Vaux hall; it will be cool and refreshing."

This was agreed to, and the two friends quitted the house, and proceeded to the river and took a boat to Vaux-hall, where they arrived safely. It was then nine o'clock.

They watched several of the figures go in, and among some of them was a black domino with a white robe.

"'Tis she, by St. George!" said Rodney; "now, Primrose, be firm, and do not precipitate matters; let's be sure of the worst, and then act reso- lutely."

"What can I do? What would you advise me to do?"

"Act like a man. Watch her and follow her closely, and then, when you are satisfied, acknowledge who you are, and how you intend to act, and be reso- lute. Do not let crying and fainting have any effect upon you whatever."

"They shall not—they shall not," whispered Primrose.

Immediately after they promenaded the saloon, where there was a Babel of sounds, and a variety of persons of all sorts and descriptions.

There was an abundance of gentle- men who took upon themselves the military character, and sported swords and spurs in number—men, who would have fainted at the smell of powder, and sooner have led a horse than mount one.

Among the company they were at no loss to discover the domino with the white girdle of rope; but she was not alone, she was with a strapping fellow in the disguise of a Highlander.

They walked, and talked, and pro- menaded the saloons and the gardens, and wherever they went Rodney and Primrose followed them, but most cautiously, lest they should alarm them before the proper moment.

"There," said Rodney, as he saw them dancing,—" there, what do you think of that, my boy—who's in the right, now? Come and join the dance; there are two pretty damsels without partners. While we are here we may as well make ourselves as happy and merry as we can."

Before anything could be said, Jack hurried him forward, and in two minutes he was whirling away in the dance to his own amazement, and crossed hands with his own wife.

He shuddered, but there was no help from the contact, and on he went to the end of the dance, when he found himself with his arms round the waist of the fair nymph he had been dancing with, and gazing abstractedly at her.

"Hilloa, Primrose! what are you about? Follow me—they have again quitted the ball-room, no doubt to retire to some secret secluded alcove where they can indulge in the overflow of love."

"The overflow of love!" ejaculated Primrose, with clenched teeth. "Lead on, I'll follow."

Jack Rodney did lead—he was just the man to lead, he was glorious and happy. Plenty to drink, abundance of company, and mischief in view as a seasoning to the whole.

They walked lightly and rapidly, and Primrose felt the cool air against his excited temples, and he felt equal to anything, even to flatly contradicting Mrs. Primrose to her face. They came to an alcove—a deep, dark place, such as lovers wish to meet in; they stopped and listened. There were two persons in conversation not much above a whisper, but loud enough for them to hear all that passed; it was not much, but it was decisive.

"Oh, Mrs. Primrose, most angelic of women! how I have longed for this moment to come, when no envious husband could look down upon us."

"Ah! ah!" thought the envious husband, "I shall have a word or two to say to you on that subject before the interview is over."

"Ah!" sighed Mrs. Primrose, "he don't treat me as he ought—he neglects me and is always contrary, and, in fact,

never behaves as other men behave to their wives."

"I will for the future," thought Mr. Primrose.

"Oh! then he ill-uses you? Your kindness of heart will not allow you to say so, but I see it—oh, I see it!"

Mrs. Primrose sighed again, and there was some unintelligible whispering going on that caused poor Mr. Primrose to perspire very freely.

"Come to my arms, dearest, and forget the envious world; you and you only I love. I would you were free, I would he were dead."

"Thank ye," thought Primrose.

"If he were—but 'tis no matter—though we cannot be married, yet we may be no less to each other on that account; we will love and live together. I have received proofs of your love; the last letter you sent me and bank-note were quite safe, my dearest angel."

"D———n!" muttered Primrose.

"A kiss of those sweet lips."

"Eh? what! Would you—dare you?" exclaimed Primrose, who broke away from the grasp of Rodney, and bounced into the alcove.

There was a scuffle and a faint scream; the lover dashed out, but he was met by Jack, who administered a severe round of punishment before he could escape.

He then entered the alcove, where he saw Mrs. Primrose in hysterics, and Mr. P. gently knocking her head against the wall, which had much effect towards recovering her. Mr. P. was a perfect Trojan. He talked most eloquently and most learnedly of the duty of wives to their husbands, and quoted I don't know how many texts, to prove what a wretch she was. At this request, Jack fetched a coach, and they all three rode home together.

The whole of the time that they occupied in going home, was employed in severe talking on the part of Mr. P., and Mrs. P. was shamming fainting fits; during the continuance of which, Jack advised all sorts of odd out-of-the-way methods of recalling her senses, the very mention of which did, in fact, recall them, and they were, therefore unnecessary.

They got home, and Mr. Primrose invited Jack Rodney to stay all night, which he did, and they both drank so much grog, and sang so many songs, until they both got so tipsy by daylight that they could not get up stairs to bed, but slept in the parlour, very drunk.

CHAPTER XXV.

THE NEXT MORNING.—CHANGE OF SCENES IN ONE HOUSE.—THE EXCUSE AND RECONCILIATION.

THE next sun shone upon a very different scene in the house of Mr. Primrose, or Mrs. Primrose, to what it had ever done before. Indeed, it appeared as though a mortal revolution had taken place—a mortal earthquake had opened, and swallowed up the former order of things, and again vomited forth a new state of being.

This was easily perceivable by the fact, that when the maid-servant rose in the morning—oh, profanation that she had never before witnessed!—when she opened the shuters, she beheld two tipsy gentlemen snoring in stuffed leather back chairs!

Who could have believed such an occurrence to have taken place in the house of Mrs. Primrose—in the very sanctury that contained her precise and authoritative person? Here, beneath the very roof in which she slept, slept Mr. P. and his friend Jack Rodney! It was monstrous!

And they, too, had drunk up her brandy, and her favourite cordial—the essence of something or other brandy—something stronger than ever came to the lips of mere grog imbibing mortals, men who put water to their drink to spoil its strength; yea, that was gone! all had been desecrated; and had an invasion of barbarians taken place, more disorder and confusion could not have ensued in so well-ordered a house as that was—I should say, had been.

The servant gazed upon the glasses, upon the bottles, and upon the sleeping individuals, as they lay back with their open mouths, snoring most perseveringly and distressingly. She gazed upon the articles one by one, as they stood. There was the candles all guttered and run to waste; the snuffers open, and out of the tray; lemons without their rinds, looking raw; a sugar bason, with only one lump of sugar left. Long did she gaze upon the scene, and it was many minutes before she could believe her eyes; and when she became convinced it was real, and that it was no delusion, she lifted up her hands and her eyes in utter and inexpressible amazement, and said,—

"Lord have mercy on us! What a jolly row there will be. I wouldn't be master—no, that I wouldn't, for all the house holds."

She paused at this peroration, and approaching the table, took up the brandy bottle, and looked very carefully at it, but shook her head, and she replaced it very gently on the table as she said,—

"No, no, not a blessed drop left, not as much as would cure the tooth-ache, or stop the cholic."

She then made a similar examination of the remaining bottles, some of which she very carefully and slowly lifted to her lips. It would have been curious to a looker on to have observed how gently she kissed the lower edge of the neck of the bottle, and with what a steady hand she tilted the bottom end upwards, and the generous fluid poured out without any gurgling sound whatever. Somehow or other, the liquor was stronger than had been thought for, or a little had gone the wrong way, when, in consequence, she had a most violent desire to cough, which she repressed only at the expense of holding her breath, and forcing the blood to her face.

She replaced the bottle, whipped the solitary lump of sugar out of the basin, and then whipped out of the room, and closing the door, she gave vent to her suppressed coughing, and made up for the denial she underwent in the room. Then swallowing the sugar, she set about lighting the fire, and put the water on, and then proceeded about her usual duties with increased bustle and spirit, until it was near eight o'clock.

"What's to be done?" thought she: "master and t'other gentleman are sleeping like pigs, poor people, and missus ain't up yet. What's in the wind now, I should like to know? Something's wrong, and gone queer, I dare say—it must be so—missus going mad, and master's getting the upper hand; but won't he catch it, poor man, when he's sensible, and sensible she'll make him—a precious she-devil she is—but I must go and call her—I don't smell now."

This last observation was applicable to the state of her breath, which might have been affected by the morning dram she had for once indulged in, and which she thought might have made a discovery probable and possible.

"She'll blow up, I dare say, because I haven't called her before; but I must say I did, and heard her answer."

Going, therefore, up to her mistress's room with this determination, she tapped at the room door, and listened for a reply.

"Well," cried Mrs. Primrose.
"Please, ma'am, 'tis past eight."
"Where's your master?"
"Asleep, ma'am."
"But where?"

"In the parlour, along with t'other gentleman. They are both fast asleep in the easy chairs."

"Very well."

"What shall I do, ma'am?"

"What do you mean?"

"Why, please, ma'am, I can't lay breakfast, nor nothing, they are so tipsy, and there's so many empty bottles lying about."

A groan proceeded from the bedroom.

"Never mind, then, clear the table and light the fire, but don't wake them, and when all is ready, come and call me."

"Yes, ma'am."

Away went the drudge to perform the task assigned her, and wondering what on earth was the matter with everybody this morning.

"Master's drunk," she murmured, "and missus ain't out about it."

This put a stop to all further mental efforts—it was a climax, beyond which she could not think or believe —a perfect hyperbolean region of thoughts, beyond which she could not crawl, and would not attempt; she, therefore, set about performing the task imposed, and soon succeeded in completing it.

"Please, ma'am, all's ready," said the girl, after having tapped at the door.

"Water boiling?"

"Yes, ma'am."

"And breakfast laid?"

"Yes, ma'am."

"That will do."

"Very good," thought Mary; "I may go."

And go she did, leaving Mrs. Primrose to follow out some plan that she had thought of, and resolved upon carrying into execution, but what that plan was, can only be seen by the following:—

When Mrs. Primrose was quite dressed, and ready to descend, she went to the glass, and saw she was a little pale. This was pleasing, and she felt quite satisfied with her looks. She left her bed-room, which she had occupied that night by herself, and descended to the breakfast-room, where both the gentlemen were fast asleep. She rang the bell, and desired the girl to bring some toast, and when it was brought, she set herself to the task of tea making.

Jack Rodney, feeling the influence of the fire and broad day-light, was the first to awaken, and opening his eyes, he started and looked at the change that had taken place in the appearance of the room, and the table. Jack looked about, and seeing Mrs. Primrose present, felt confused, and scarce knew what he was about, when he stammered out,—

"Beg pardon, ma'am — shouldn't have gone to sleep, but suppose you were not here when I did. Ay, brandy was good, very good. Hope you are well, ma'am, quite well?"

Jack, just when he got to the end of this, began to recollect the events of the preceding evening, and Mrs. Primrose's *liaison.*

"I am not well, Mr. Rodney," said Mrs. Primrose; and then added in a dejected tone, pointing to Mr. Primrose, "such sights always make me ill."

Jack started, and made no reply, and Mr. Primrose himself now awoke.

"Well, Mr. Primrose, what do you think of passing your nights thus? Are you really not ashamed to be drinking, and then sleeping in the parlour all night?"

"Eh? what?" exclaimed Primrose, sitting up in the chair suddenly, and then putting his hand to his head, he added,—

"Oh, my head, my head."

"No doubt," said the lady, helping herself to some toast; "no doubt; but if you like being intoxicated with liquors, you must expect such results. You ought to have known better."

"But, my dear."

"It doesn't matter, Mr. Primrose, it doesn't matter."

"But you——"

"Oh, yes. I am in fault, because you have the head-ache; that's always the way—it's quite right to say I gave you the head-ache."

"D——n it, ma'am!"

"Oh, goodness, he swears—the barbarian—the wretch, to use profane language."

"It does seem odd to me," said Jack Rodney, breaking in upon this conversation. "I say, it does seem odd to me, that Mrs. Primrose should be the injured party, when she was found with another man, who was—not unwillingly to her—making love to her."

"Ah, Mrs. Primrose, tell me how that happened—yes, ma'am, tell how that happened; tell me before I turn you out of doors, ma'am."

"Tell me, sir, how you became beastly intoxicated—tell me that, sir."

"I sha'n't, madam—I sha'n't. Just imagine—oh, my head!—just imagine my excitement, madam—yes, that's it —I was drunk with excitement."

"And emptying the bottles," added Jack.

"And emptying the bottles," repeated Mr. Primrose, not knowing what he had to say.

"I couldn't help what the man said to me. I'm sure I said nothing to him."

"But how came you there?"

"Why, I suspected you were going

there, and followed you to prevent your ruin."

"But you didn't know I intended going there?"

"I suspected it, though I didn't know. You dream, Mr. Primrose, you dream."

"I dream, madam, I dream! What do you mean by that, madam?"

"You dream, and your sleep has been disturbed of——"

"Yes, when you kick."

"Oh, you ungrateful man! I say, you were disturbed in your sleep, and talked; you mentioned a name, and said something about Vauxhall masquerades, and I determined to go out and give you the opportunity; and the man who spoke to me I believed to be you, you false, wicked man; and so believing, I wished to convince you before your face of your iniquity, and that's how it all happened."

Poor Primrose was completely bewildered, and Jack Rodney said,—

"But the man called you by name."

"He did not, sir," said Mrs. Primrose, so decidedly that he forbore to speak any more.

Primrose was confused, and his head ached so badly that he scarce knew what to say or think about the matter, but said,—

"It is very strange that you should have left the saloon to have gone with a man into those quiet-looking places; it was not only wrong, but many men would never have allowed you to enter their doors again."

"No more of that, Mr. Primrose, if you please; my temper will not let me put up with it. I am a patient and forbearing woman upon all points, save one, and I will not be suspected. Pray, where is there another wife that would have done as I have when she found her husband and friend drunk in the parlour?—Would they have got them a good fire, with tea and toast and ham?"

Mr. Primrose looked around, and saw there certainly was what she had informed him; those dainties were present, and at that moment Mrs. Primrose put into his hand a strong cup of tea, which he really wanted, and felt grateful for.

What could he do?—what could he say? He felt his anger diminishing, and his mental faculties were in extreme disorder; there was not, indeed, any chance for him in his present state of contending against Mrs. Primrose successfully, and he felt it.

"Well," said Jack Rodney, "I can't but say this is very acceptable. My head is a little queer, and if there was a spoonful of brandy in the tea it would settle the stomach."

"It would," said Primrose.

Mrs. Primrose got up, and going to the sideboard, produced a wine-bottle, which she uncorked, and put some in two glasses, and said they had better take it as it was made.

"Neat as imported," said Jack; and his portion had disappeared.

Primrose tried to do the same, but he shuddered several times before he could take it, and when he did, he gulped it hurriedly down.

Then Mrs. Primrose recommended ham and toast, which recommendation Jack Rodney heartily seconded, and gave a practical example.

"I tell you what, Mr. Primrose you'll want a walk after breakfast to compose yourself, and you won't be well till after dinner. I hope you will never drink to excess again."

"Never," said the subdued Primrose; "never!"

"Then I won't say anything more about it."

Primrose felt grateful for this, and took a walk out with Jack Rodney, and after sundry glasses and good adieus, they parted.

CHAPTER XXVI.

THE PHYSICIAN'S VISIT. — THE OPINION REGARDING THEODORE. —THE CRISIS OF THE FEVER.

BUT to leave Mr. and Mrs. Primrose to such tender dalliance as two such characters are accustomed to, let us again return to the couch of him whose heart and brain had been so "wildered" for the love of Margaret —poor suffering Theodore Danton.

For a short period it seemed as if he were about to recover from the serious illness he had laboured under, but unhappily a relapse of the most dangerous character ensued. Two nurses had to be hired to attend upon him instead of one, and altogether the affair, from appearing to have ended, became ten times more serious, because it was now acting upon a debilitated frame instead of a strong one.

Dr. Muddleton was a very great man in his way. He was quite a celebrated man—a man of wonderful parts and attainments—a man who made himself a busy public man, which some people were ill-natured enough to say did no good to his knowledge or skill as a physician. He had been sent for to attend upon Theodore Danton because he kept a large house and a handsome carriage. Of course, everybody thinks a physician who can do so must be a most marvellously clever fellow. It is fancied that other people must have trusted him with their corporeal condition, and have given him many fees, which have furnished the house, and paid for the carriage.

The wholesome proverb, that one fool makes many, is thrown away upon these people altogether, nor are they aware that the carriage and the house have, in most cases, nothing whatever to do with the practice of the physician, but support him, instead of him supporting them.

It is almost invariably the rule in illness that the cleverest man is usualy called in first, and the most fashionable man afterwards. A young practitioner who had attended upon Theodore when first his indisposition seized him, was really a clever man, although a comparatively poor one, but he was not a conjuror. We say, he was not a conjuror, because the disease under which Theodore Danton laboured would go on in spite of him, and then the fashionable physician, who looked sulky if he had not a five pounds' fee, was sent for.

This was Dr. Muddleton, a big, pompous man, with a superficial, showy style about him that was wonderful, and, no doubt, considered remarkably clever by his admirers; but which, had he not been the man of limited intellect he really was, he could not have adopted. It is lamentable that even in such a profession as that of physician a man's success should almost invariably depend upon cir-

cumstances quite apart from his skill in his profession.

The fact is, that the science of medicine altogether is of so uncertain and quack-like a nature, that its professors have to resort to all sorts of schemes and artifices to push themselves forward. Physicians exist upon the gullibility of human nature, and their opinions are very rarely worth sixpence upon anything This they themselves know, and so well aware are they of the fact, that it is to some extraneous circumstances, altogether apart from any professional skill, that they owe their reputations, that we see instances of their daily resorting to all sorts of eccentricities in order to attract public patronage.

One will adopt a pompous and grave exterior, and never be known to smile —another will be always on the smirk, as if it were the finest thing in the world for anybody to be ill—another will affect rudeness in his manner, for which he would be kicked in any other profession — while a fourth will depend entirely upon outside show, and the glitter of the carriage and the horses, and the footmen that belong to him.

We happen now, ourselves, to know several fashionable physicians, to whose skill and judgment we would not intrust the life of a puppy dog we valued, but who are very great men for all that. There is one whom we could name, who, for many years, was what is commonly called toad-eater to the Duke of Sussex, a man of the most limited intellect, and yet who, in consequence of being by that connection thrown into what is called good society, has become, from a half-starved, shifty wretch, glad to do anything for anybody, a fashionable physician.

But let us return to Theodore Danton. The nurses put on what they called sympathetical looks when the doctor made his appearance, but they might have put on any kind of looks, so far as Dr. Muddleton was concerned, for he was by far too much engaged with himself to pay much attention to anybody else. He was one of those bores of society who think they have abundance of talent in small talk, when really the twaddle they utter is beyond everything in the world contemptible.

"Well, well, how are you doing ?" he said, in a louder voice than any one else used in the sick chamber. "How are you getting on ? Charming weather. Ah ! keep the room dark. Ah ! Very good—very good. So, of course, we are not much better. Well, well, we must have patience. Of course, we can't expect to get better all at once. Oh, dear, no. We must have some patience, of course."

"Certainly, sir," said one of the nurses.

"And trust in you and providence, sir," said the other.

"Well, well. Never mind that, we (of course, he meant himself and providence) will do the best we can."

The young physician who had been first called to attend upon Theodore, now entered the room, and was treated with considerable hauteur by Dr. Muddleton, who scarcely condescended to give a nod of his great addle-head upon the appearance of the young man, who at once, after a very slight acknowledgment of the great man's arrogant salute, went to the bedside, and took Theodore's hand in his to ascertain if the fever had in any respect abated.

This young man's name was Russel, and when Dr. Muddleton saw that he was really disposed to see to the patient, he said,—

"He don't seem much better. Ah !"

"The fever is rather on the increase," said Dr Russel. "Nurse."

"Sir," said the nurse, who despised Dr. Russel because he did not keep a carriage.

"Has he spoken lately ?"

"He has spoken rubbish."

"Still delirious ?"

"Quite *deleterous*," said the nurse.

"Of course, of course," said Dr. Muddleton, "of course. I should feel inclined to continue the same course of medicines, most decidedly."

"I should make a decided alteration," said Dr. Russel. "For six-and-thirty hours, now, medicine has been persevered in which has produced no beneficial effect, and, indeed, has failed in producing any of the anticipated effect completely, as you must perceive."

"Well, you must be aware that such is the regular course."

"Regular course !"

"Yes, to be sure, sir; the regular course."

"I am aware that the prescription which, contrary to my judgment, you wrote for the patient, is to be found first in all treatises on the disease under which he labours; but, when it fails, as, doubtless, the best medicines will in some constitutions, in producing its expected effect, of course, we are then called upon to try something else."

"And pray, what would you try ?"

"Nay, sir; as you are senior physician, I shall be happy to hear your opinion. You perceive, by the state of the patient, that the drug has not acted as a febrifuge."

"Ah, well; ah, well."

"What do you advise ?"

"Well, Dr. Russel, if you think a change desirable, of course, I do not wish to stand in your way. I have no doubt these excellent women who attend upon the invalid, will attend in every respect to any instructions you give them."

Dr. Muddleton was always a great man with nurses. They always called him a love of a man, and it is astonishing the influence which such women have over the sick, even to the extent of recommending a physician; so that this great bloated charlatan found it to his account to propitiate them, and always did so.

"If the nurses keep themselves quiet and sober, and do their duty to the patient," said Dr. Russel, "nothing more is required of them, that I am aware of. Their duty is of the easiest, and rather a negative than a positive character."

"What a nice man Dr. Muddleton is," whispered one of the nurses to the other.

"Yes, you may say that," said the other; "but what a unfeeling wretch Dr. Russel is, to be sure."

"Ah, he is."

"Well, my dear sir," said Muddleton, with a grand flourish of his arm, "we will not quarrel about this affair. I shall be happy to hold a consultation with you in another room."

The consultation was held, during

which Dr. Muddleton contrived to fish out of Dr. Russel what he thought best to do under the circumstances of the case, and then declared it was just what he was going to propose; so he wrote the prescription, and had the credit of the remedy.

"I believe, now, that is all we can do," said Muddleton.

"Except to caution the nurses," said Dr. Russel, "that the crisis of the fever is near at hand, and that they must be particularly careful in the attendance upon the patient."

"Oh, yes, yes. Perhaps, as I am rather pressed for time, you will be so good as to say as much to them?"

"Very well."

Dr. Muddleton never liked the job of cautioning the nurses. Well he knew that those persons looked upon any word of caution given to them in the light of a most grievous insult, and he did not wish to endanger his popularity by saying anything of the sort.

Dr. Russel had no such qualms of conscience. He walked at once to the sick room, and said,—

"You will be most particularly careful to keep the patient quiet now, for the next four-and-twenty hours, and attend to the instructions which will accompany the medicine closely."

The women were afraid to say anything uncivil; but, as Dr. Muddleton had anticipated, they felt themselves insulted, and when Dr. Russel was gone, they were loud in denunciations of him, and their approval of Muddleton.

"Dear me, Elizabeth," said her companion, "we must n't breathe now, I suppose. Oh, dear, me!"

"And we are to be cautioned, is we?"

"And by him, too!"

"No real gentleman — where's his carriage? That shows the difference between a real gentleman and a poverty-struck one. You don't find Dr. Muddleton saying anything unpleasant; no, not for the whole world he wouldn't."

"Ah! he knows what a nurse's feelings is, but it's quite clear to me as Dr. Russel has no feeling of his own, and so doesn't suppose anybody else has. It's enough to make one really savage."

"I tell you what it is, Elizabeth, if anybody says anything to me about being quiet, I always feel inclined to make a noise."

"And so do I."

"That's my feeling on the matter."

"And mine too; for we've a right to our feelings as well as anybody else, I should think, if they were all the doctors in the world. Be quiet, indeed! I'll be quiet if I like, and if I don't like, I won't be quiet."

"That's right; unless one has a proper spirit, there's no such thing as getting on in the world."

"Of course not. I won't be spoke to by anybody."

"Nor me."

"We won't be quiet, leastways not because he told us, I can tell you. A nice thing, indeed, that we are to be told what to do by a man as can't keep a carriage, and I shouldn't at all wonder as he lives in lodgings. It's enough to aggravate any nurse as never was, that's my opinion. Oh, I hate him, I do!"

"And so do I."

"Just give me that bottle, and I'll run out to the Black Bull, and fill it again."

"Do, my dear, and be sure you ask 'em for the very best."

"Leave me alone—I'll taste it, and I won't bring it away from the bar, if it isn't the proper thing, I promise you."

One of the nurses went to replenish the gin bottle, while the other sat down again by the fire to drop into that dozy state, which is incidental to nurses and old cats.

These individuals, old cats and sick nurses, lose all perception of time. They sleep when they can, and the only difference between the two is, that the cat is much the more estimable animal, inasmuch as it is sober, which the nurse very seldom is.

There are exceptions — we do not blame all for the faults of many, and in the sketches we feel called upon to make frequently in these pages, we must always be understood to honour the exceptions to any consideration, in the same ratio as we hold up to reprobation those who deserve it.

A sober, intelligent, humane, and well-conducted sick-nurse will rejoice to see the faults and the vices of others perfectly pointed out, considering that she must shine from contrast.

And now poor Theodore Danton might be truly said to be hovering between life and death. The fever, if it should pass a certain point without showing any symptoms of amendment, was almost certain to carry him to the grave.

The crisis was at hand, and however ignorant Dr. Muddleton might be upon that score, Dr. Russel knew it well, and was proportionably anxious.

This gentleman, to the great chagrin of the nurses, called again late in the evening. They had not the least idea that he would do so. Indeed, in their opinion, no medical man, let the case be of what amount of emergency it might, ought to call at any time after two o'clock, because, as Elizabeth remarked, "What right has he to take a nurse at a nonplus?"

Being taken at a nonplus, of course meant being drunk, dirty, or otherwise unprepared for a visitor.

As for the patient, he was of no consideration further than as a kind of peg, on which to hang all the proceedings contingent upon his illness.

It was half-past nine o'clock when Dr. Russel walked into the room, and it was quite impossible for any one to walk into that room with a nose of the most ordinary quality, without being immediately aware of the propensity of the ladies for the cream of the valley.

The first words he uttered were,—

"There is a strong smell of liquor here."

"Liquor, sir?" said Elizabeth, as she held to the chimney-piece with one hand, and waved about the canle with the other. "Did you say liquor, sir?"

"I did, woman."

"Then you're mistaken."

"I cannot be mistaken; you are now in a state of partial intoxication, as is very easy to be perceived."

"Me?—me?"

"Yes. Where is your companion?"

A loud snore proclaimed that the other had resigned herself to repose, and then Dr. Russel at once left the room.

"A good riddance," said Elizabeth, who was too much under the influence of the popular anodyne to place any other construction upon the conduct of the doctor, than that she had got comfortably rid of him. "A good riddance. The idea of coming here at such a time of night as this. It's just like his nasty poking way, it is. Oh, I hate him!—I hate him!—I do, and no mistake. The wretch!—how odd this mantel-shelf moves about, to be sure, bobbing up and down, so that it's quite a job to put the blessed candlestick on it. Come now. Ah, there I have you. Down with a dab. He! he! he!"

She did succeed after several ineffectual attempts in placing the candlestick on the mantel-shelf, and then she sunk into an easy chair, two of which were in the room, one being occupied by the slumbering nurse, and the other now by her who would soon be in the same state of unconsciousness.

But Dr. Russel was on mischievous thoughts intent; when he went from the sick room, he desired at once to see the landlord of the hotel, and when that person, who was really a gentlemanly man, came to him, he said,—

"Are you aware of the conduct of the nurses that are in the room above?"

The landlord looked very much astonished, and a little frightened, as he replied,—

"I know nothing to their prejudice; I sincerely hope they are doing their duty?"

"Not exactly. Will you place a couple of your waiters at my disposal?"

"Certainly, sir, and with pleasure; more than a couple, if you require them."

"No, no; a couple will suffice; just bid them follow me up to the sick gentleman's chamber."

This was done, and the landlord himself, much hurt at the idea that the nurses should not be doing their duty by one who was seriously ill in his house, and towards whom he felt every kind of feeling that it was possible for one man to feel for another, followed Dr. Russel to the chamber of the invalid. The moment they arrived there, Dr. Russel said,—

"Tread softly, and you will not disturb my patient: but look at the condition of the nurses, and you will quickly see why it was I required your assistance."

The laadlord and the waiters did look, and there they saw these watchful guardians of the sick each asleep in her separate arm-chair, and snoring with an aggravated loudness that was enough to have awakened anybody, let their repose be ever so deep or sound.

"This is too bad," said the landlord; " I cannot endure this, it is really too bad; these women, I assure you, sir, were recommended for honesty and sobriety of the first character, and that they should have behaved in this manner, is to me a perfect mystery."

"I have no doubt in the world of that, sir," said Dr. Russel; "they must be removed, but, in their removal, we must have no noise, for your guest is in a most perilous condition, hovering between life and death; and it would be better that these women should sleep on quietly, and not attend to him at all, than that anything like a disturbance should arise in the act of getting rid of them."

" There need be none, sir, I assure you; there need be none—we will soon manage that; there is a spare room just across the landing, and my two young men here can lift them up, chairs and all, and carry them in there."

" A good thought," said Dr. Russel; "let it be done, sir."

The waters received their instructions, and being stout, hearty fellows, the two of them carried the nurses one by one, chairs and all, into the apartment which had been mentioned by the landlord.

Their brains were steeped in the forgetfulness of gin, and, consequently, they knew of nothing that was taking place, the whole affair being comfortably managed without disturbing their profound repose, and without even varying the tune that was played by each lady's olfactory organs.

And there they were locked in, to wait until, in the due order of things, the bacchanalian fumes should have worked off their brains, and they should have recovered their consciousness of where they were.

"We must contrive some means, sir," said the landlord, " of attending upon the gentleman, until a new nurse can be got."

" Leave that to me," said Doctor Russel; " but, in the interim, I shall remain with him. I have got through my professional duties for the day, and as his disorder is at its crisis, I should like to watch it."

He then sat down by the bedside, and gave the landlord the address of a person in whom he knew he could confide, to come and act as sick nurse to poor Theodore Danton, who, but for this Doctor Russel, would most probably have gone to an early grave unknown and unlamented, except by her who might, or might not, according to circumstances, have known he was no longer living.

And there he lay, while she whom he loved imagined that he was, in pursuance of a resolution he had expressed, making such active preparations as lay within the immediate compass of his means, to leave a country which had no further charms for him, a country which he had sought with such fond hopes, but to find them completely crushed by a circumstance he had not even considered the probability of.

Alas! poor Theodore, if you are to be pitied because you are not happy with her whom you loved, how much more is she to be pitied who, in addition to that calamity, is, by a cruel fiat of fortune, united to one whom she cannot even respect?

Poor Margaret, in vain will you attempt to conceal from the heart that the passionate devotion of Theodore Danton has touched you; in vain would you endeavour to persuade yourself that you are fancy free, because you ought to be so; in a tumult of grief and passion shall your mind be tossed; and, although virtue holds so high a place within the precincts of your heart, that never from its precincts will you stray; yet, terrible will be the struggle between duty and feeling, and fearful in its results, and calamitous in its very victory.

But let us return to Theodore. Eleven o'clock has struck, and the solemn hour of midnight is coming.

———

CHAPTER XXVII.

THE RECOVERY.—THE UNASKED-FOR CONFIDENCE.—THE ADVICE OF A TRUE FRIEND.

THEY came in about half an hour to whisper to Doctor Russel, that the nurse he had sent for was engaged, and could not come. This was scarcely a disappointment to him, for he expected it—bad nurses might frequently be disengaged, and good ones seldom—and the mere fact that there was one of that fraternity who could be confidently sent for by Doctor Russel was almost good presumptive evidence that she was likely to be engaged.

"Never mind—never mind," he said to the waiter who brought to him the intelligence "I am a very good watcher, although not much used to it and will remain here myself."

He made up his mind to remain until the crisis of the disorder had completely past, and that was an event which he calculated upon taking place in a few hours. Theodore Danton was in a deep sleep, from which he would

awaken, either just to die, or so much better, that the most reasonable hopes could be entertained of his recovery.

Almost every ten minutes the careful physician looked into the face of the slumbering man, to watch if any change had taken place for the better or worse. He leaned his head down, and listened to the breathings of his patient, and twice or thrice he placed his finger lightly upon Theodore's wrist, to ascertain if the pulsation was equable and full. It was about one o'clock in the morning when a restlessness seemed to come over the young man who there lay combating with the grim destroyer; he moved several times, and tried to pronounce some words, but they were too inarticulate for Doctor Russel to catch the purport of them. The physician looked anxious, for such symptoms betrayed a state of brain agitation he was sorry to perceive. To have been suddenly awakened at such a moment as that would have been death to Theodore Danton. The physician knew as much, and, oh! how he dreaded that some disturbance in the house would suddenly produce such an effect. But all was still, and he congratulated himself that the disturbed symptoms were passing away, when a sudden noise in the street fell upon his ears. The noise arose from three half-drunken fellows, who were, at the top of their unmusical voices, shouting out some boisterous, stupid glee, to the annoyance of those who are well, and, perhaps, to the death of several who were sick. And this brutal, unfeeling annoyance, could only be quietly endured. When a noise is an evil, a blackguard or a fool is sure to have it all his own way, because any attempt to stop him only produces a greater amount of tumult.

On they came shouting, roaring, screaming, and laughing; nothing but braining them could possibly have stopped them; and yet such are the brutes that public hospitals are erected to take care of when they are sick, and for whom the more moneyed classes of society, whom they thus wantonly annoy, are called upon to subscribe a large per-centage of their incomes. We are no advocates for restricting the enjoyments of the humbler classes of society—of course, we must assume that those who behave in such a manner in the public streets are of the very lowest grade—but we do wonder that, with all the efficiency of the London police at the present time, two or three drunken ruffians are permitted, without molestation, on their route from the public house, to awaken perhaps a thousand industrious persons from their repose, and, perchance, produce the most calamitous results where sickness prevails.

Poor Theodore Danton tossed his arms wildly, and seemed more than once upon the very point of awakening; but the physician rapidly extinguished the light, and noiselessly drew the curtain over that part of the bed from whence it had been withdrawn, and then he waited with almost breathless anxiety the result.

The noisy ruffians in the street had got past the hotel, so that the sound of their uproar was on its decrease, and now very gradually it died away, enabling the physician better to hear the low moaning sounds that came from the lips of his patient. But they ceased at last, and the wrapt stillness that reigned around, together with the darkness, had its soothing effects. Once more the sleep of the sick man deepened, and the physician said, in a low tone,—

"There is yet another chance for life."

Cautiously he lit the candle again by the smouldering embers of the small fire, and calming the excitement as well as he could which the noise in the street had occasioned him, he sat himself once more down by the bedside to carry out his benevolent intention of watching the slumbers of him to whom he was a stranger except so far as the great principle of humanity actuated him to consider him a friend. There was a long and dreary silence. Dr. Russel's thoughts were, perhaps, elsewhere, for he certainly started when he heard a low, weak voice say,—

"Alas! is it all a dream?"

"Hush! hush!" said the medical man. "Be still; you have had an illness which will not permit you to talk freely."

There was a tone of emotion in the physician's words, for he knew, by the manner in which his patient spoke, that the alarming crisis was over, and that now, in all human probability, health would again dawn and brighten on his cheeks.

"An illness?" said Theodore.

"Yes, and a serious one; but pray be calm and still; you are better now."

He laid his hand upon that of Theodore as he spoke, and the warm, moist touch convinced him that the fever had left his blood, and he had but the exhaustion of his illness to contend with. There was now a considerable pause, after which Theodore said, in rather a firmer tone,—

"'Tis very strange—the more I try to grapple thought, the more it flies me. A strange confusion of many images comes whirling through my brain.

What has happened to me I know not; I cannot yet separate the real from the unreal."

"Do not attempt it," said the physician. "A time will come for all that, and soon, too. Swallow this cordial, it will much compose, and procure for you a much more healthful slumber than you have enjoyed for some time past."

Theodore took the medicine which the physician had been careful enough to provide himself with, and then he said, in a low tone,—

"Am I in England?"

"In England!" said the physician, with surprise; "most certainly."

"Then some of it is not a dream, and I must have seen her."

"Believe me, my young friend, you are not in a fit state to enter into conversation at present on your own affairs or any one else's."

"I have slept long, and yet sleep is again coming over me."

"I am glad the narcotic is taking effect," thought the physician. "You will be better able to converse in twelve hours time."

"Twelve hours!" said Theodore, "did you say twelve hours?" and even has he spoke his voice grew lower and fainter. What he continued to say was too low to be heard, and finally he dropped off into a quiet slumber.

"That will do," said the physician; "he will awaken weak, but comparatively well."

Virtually, then, his watch was over, and Dr. Russel rose and noiselessly left the chamber.

He repaired to the lower part of the hotel, and the expression of his countenance at once assured the landlord that the critical period in the disease had passed away.

"He is better," he said.

"You may almost call him well now," said the physician, "with ordinary care. Do not let those drunken nurses attend upon him again. Any one will do now who is quiet, sober, and attentive, inasmuch as the danger of the disease has passed away."

"I rejoice to hear it, sir," said the landlord. "I wouldn't have had a death in the house on any account; not that I am superstitiously afraid of anything of that kind; but it casts a gloom over all one's arrangements, and is, take it at the best, a most uncomfortable affair."

"I do not think you have anything to apprehend on such a score as that. It is a case in which a relapse is rare."

"I rejoice to hear it, sir. I have sat up the whole night itself, fearful of hearing some bad news from you, and now I feel well pleased that such is not the case. What will you take, sir?"

"I must confess, now that the danger is over," said the physician, with a smile, "I do feel inclined to solace myself with something: but tell me what you know of this young man; he seems to have some great calamity preying upon his mind."

"Why, the truth is, sir, we know little enough of him, beyond that he came here having all the appearance and manners of a gentleman, and with such luggage as induced us to think he came from some long distance abroad."

"Indeed! He asked me if he was in England."

"Then that confirms it, sir. Come now, James, make haste,"—to a waiter, who had been sitting up with the landlord.

"Yes, sir—yes, sir," said James, and he bustled about; while the landlord went to get his keys, in order to get some choice wines to lay before Dr. Russel.

"Beg your pardon, sir," said James, when the landlord's back was turned; "but I always likes to know diseases. I was brought up in the medical way myself, sir."

"Indeed? I am sorry to see you a waiter, then. How was that, brother brush?" said Dr. Russel, good-humouredly.

"Very much obliged to you all the same," said James; "but many young men as is brought up to our profession has to be much more of a waiter than I is. You see the joke, sir—waiting for patients I mean, sir. What d'ye think of that, sir? Not a bad 'un for half-past three o'clock in the morning."

"Very good indeed, James."

"I thought you'd say so, sir. The doctor waits for a patient till he gets impatient himself, sir. What d'ye think of that?"

"That's brilliant, James," said Dr.

Russel—"positively brilliant. I have heard it before, certainly, James."

"But it's none the worse for that, you know, sir."

"Not the least, James, it only sink deeper into the soul. But how cam you to be brought up to what you ca our profession?"

"Why, you see, sir, my father was a very eminent man, stood six feet two, sir, in his own soles, and he had the privilege, sir, which nobody else in London had at the same time, of letting in and out all the great doctors to Bartholomew's Hospital."

"The gate porter I presume, James."

"Why, sir, you may call him the gate porter if you like, sir, in a manner of speaking; but that's neither here nor there, sir; and after I had finished my studies at the school of St. Botolph's, Aldgate, I went to be assistant to Dr. Dunderhead."

"Why, James, I was not aware," said Dr. Russel, "that there was a medical scool at St Botolph's, Aldgate."

"No, sir; but there's a charity one."

"Oh, ah! to be sure—yes."

"Well, sir, that's how I came into the profession. Dr. Dundeahead supplied me with a plum coloured suit, with a breaking-out of brass buttons upon it, an imitation goldlaced beaver, and a basket with two flaps covered with oilskin."

"Oh, I see now, James you are, indeed, one of us," said Dr. Russel. "I was not aware you had been so nitiated into the mystery of the craft."

"Yes, sir and now you understand it, you can't be surprised at the bias it gives to one's intellected degorgonation."

"Not at all, James. I made up my mind long ago to be surprised at nothing," said Dr. Russel.

"Very good, sir, and that's the reason why I glories in diseases, accidentations and fractures."

"James," said Dr. Russel, "you are too cunning for me."

"No, sir—surely?"

"Yes; they teach more at St. Botolph's, Aldgate, than ever I learnt. You overpower me, James, with the profundity of your professional acquirements."

"No! do I though?"

"Certainly you do. What motive could I have in saying you do, if you do not? I expect no fee from you, you know, James."

"No, sir, that's very true—very true indeed; but what was the matter with the young gentleman, sir?"

"Icipient inflammation of the brain, James."

James looked up to the ceiling for a moment, and scratched his chin, and then, placing his finger upon the side of his nose, he said,—

"Sir, was the *magnum bonum* affected?"

"Dear me, James, how learned you are! I see you have not forgotten your Latin."

"I should think not, sir; but that's a medical secret between you and me and the knowing ones."

"Is it? Then I am not one of the knowing ones, for I don't know it, James."

"Oh, nonsense, sir! Gammon—gammon! That's a sell—a sell only."

"Nay, James, honour bright."

"O, yes, sir, you know well enough; but you think I don't. All you have to do, when you want to speak Latin, is to put a *buss* or *hum* at the end of it."

"James, you astonish me. Pray give an illustration."

"Oh, really, now—really! you make me blush, sir; but just, now, to convince you that I ain't a flat; suppose a chap has a confuxion on the nose, sir, I'd pop that into medical Latin in a moment."

"How, James, how?"

"Why, sir, I should say that the patient was afflicted with a *crackabus* of the *snoutem*, and if that didn't puzzle the natives, d—e I don't know what would, sir. But here's master. Mum's the word, sir. If he thought I was a medical man, he might think I was a humbug, too. No offence to you."

Dr. Russel did not take offence at James's delicate allusion, or his secession from the profession in which he must have been so singular a member; and giving him a good-humoured nod of intelligence, he said to the landlord as he entered,—

"By-the-by, have you sent to any one to attend upon the sick guest of yours?"

"I have not, but can do so, though it is very doubtful if they can be here before the morning," replied the landlord.

"Very well; but you may as well send at once. I should feel more at ease if I knew that he had an attendant ready to wait upon him the moment he awakens. He will be very weak."

"I will send at once," said the landlord. "I have a young fellow yet up that I can send, and who knows the abode of a careful woman, whom I have no doubt will do all that is wanted very creditably, though she is not a professed nurse."

"She will do well enough; send for her, I beg of you, and when she comes I shall leave, with no other thing on my mind that can disturb my ease or reflections."

"Very true, sir."

The landlord quitted the room, and gave the orders which Doctor Russel desired, and then returned to the room in which he had left the doctor.

"You see, sir, I have nothing but what is cold in the way of eating."

"I am not very particular," said Doctor Russel; "anything that is not heavy."

"A little chicken ——"

"Will do as well as anything; you could not have had anything better suited to the time and occasion."

"I am very glad to hear you say so, sir," said the landlord; "and now we may eat, drink, and be merry."

"I do feel as if I could do so without any reproach," said Doctor Russel. "Come, you must sit down and join me, unless you have already satisfied your appetite."

"No; I could not eat, but merely sipped a little out of a glass."

"I see; just keeping your lips moist," said Doctor Russel.

"Precisely."

They both sat down to a very respectable supper, which looked very much like a cold collation very prettily spread.

"Upon my word, landlord, your chicken is so good, and my appetite has suddenly become so keen, that I am afraid I shall break through my usual custom of taking little or no supper, and eat heartier than ever I remember at such an hour."

"Circumstances alter cases, you know, sir, and then having fasted so long is a very good excuse, if not a justification for indulging in the pleasures of the table."

"I feel it so, and shall be guided by my desires, keeping on the windy side of repletion, and then, as I have a walk, I shall not hurt."

"I believe not, sir. You will find some of those wines pretty good, sir; they came out of a particular binn, that nobody's hand but my own goes in."

"Then, I presume, it is such that cannot be quarrelled with."

"You shall judge for yourself, sir; and as far as wine is harmless, this you will find perfectly so, and generous in its qualities."

"Your recommendation is strong, and I will test it, if you please."

"Do, sir."

So saying, the landlord handed the doctor several bottles of different sorts of wine. The doctor chose one of them, and then said,—

"This, I think, promises well, and certainly looks as pure as crystal, though more of the ruby in colour." Then putting it to his lips, he added,—"Yes, landlord, this does not belie your recommendation, or discredit your judgment either."

"You are very good to say so, sir. I have bought them certainly under the impression that they were the best that could be got."

They both drank, and the supper things being cleared away, Doctor Russel, as if he had suddenly forgot something, said,—

"By the bye, I heard no more of the nurses. You got rid of them remarkably quiet."

"Oh, we haven't heard anything more of them ourselves. They are sleeping off the fumes of the strong potations."

"Oh, indeed. They must have drank deep indeed for it to take such an effect upon such seasoned vessels as I have no doubt they are."

"Certainly; but it's a mystery to me how they got it; but it matters not. James, how did you leave the nurses?"

"Oh, snoring, sir, like one o'clock, one agin the other. I wonder they don't wake one another. They can't keep time at all, and when they do wake, there'll be a row."

"Indeed! How is it they have not awakened before this, James?" inquired Doctor Russel.

"Why, the 'soaperriffics' have taken so strong a hold of the sleeping department, sir," said James; "and the blinds and the shutters were put to, thinking they would sleep the longer, and not so soon disturb the patient."

"Very thoughtful of you, James—very thoughtful indeed, and I commend you for it."

James appeared very well pleased; and when the landlord sent him down to inquire for the return of the messenger that he had sent after the nurse, he came back, saying,—

"He's come back, sir."

"And what does he say?"

"That she can't come till the morning, sir," said James; "but she will be here very early indeed."

"Well, then," said Doctor Russel, "it is so near morning now, it wants but a little to five, and your wines are so good, landlord, that I will stay until my domestics are up, and wait till the nurse comes, and then I can give her a few instructions myself."

"I shall be very happy, sir. I am an early man, myself, in business, and I should scarce care about going to bed myself."

"Then we will sit down."

"James, shut that door; there's a draught fit to cut my head off. What are you listening to?"

"I think there's a row up stairs, sir —back attic—there's a shindy. The ladies are falling out in the dark."

This was true enough. The two nurses, having slept many hours, had recovered from the effects of "soaperriffics," as James had termed them, and were somewhat amazed at being all in the dark.

Without speaking, they both began feeling about for the table, and endeavouring to get a light; and, indeed, they wheeled about their chairs, until they came with considerable force together, the fingers of one being caught between the chairs, and almost crushed, and the foot of the other sprained. A scene now ensued—a row and a fight, and it

was this that was heard by James below.

"You'd better have them at once removed from the room," said the doctor.

"Yes," said the landlord. "James."

"Yes, sir."

"Get assistance, and bring those women down stairs with as little noise as you can."

"Yes, sir," said James.

James instantly dived below, where he obtained the aid of several men, who came up stairs, following him to the room-door. The landlord held a light, and they entered.

"Here's pretty treatment to a hard-working nuss—to be locked up in the dark in a Christian country! Ain't you ashamed of yourself to treat poor hard-working women——"

"Hard-working women!"

"Oh, you wretch!"

"Nothing stronger than tea——"

"Water——"

"Come, come," said, James, "you'l, kill the sick gentleman, and then you'll both of you be hung for murder."

"You all deserve to be——"

"Come, come, come, go down quietly, or you'll be thrown into the street."

"Oh, the wretches!"

And then came such a Babel of sounds and voices that would have awakened the seven sleepers themselves.

"Come," said James, "turn them all down. We can't help the noise, but we needn't have it longer than we like. Now, then," said James, flourishing a napkin, "take the word from me gentlemen. Hip, hip, heave oh!"

The assistants at once seized hold of the two nurses, and being powerfully young men, they soon disposed of them, and carried them down in such a manner as produced but little noise, for James dexterously crammed his handkerchief into the mouth of one, and the other was held by the throat, and all she could do was to cough and splutter,

At that moment a policeman came by, and they were speedily consigned to his care; for they would not go away, but turned to and began to abuse the landlord and the whole of the inmates of the hotel, and wouldn't move on, but obstinately disregarded the persuasion of the policeman, who consigned them to a cell in the station, as being drunk and disorderly.

Dr. Russel again sat down, and found this incident disturbed the flow of conversation that was going on before, which the landlord seeing, said,—

"Some months back a gentleman called here, and said if I were fond of reading old manuscripts—we had been previously speaking of legends and other matters—he would lend me one he had purchased of a parish clerk, with his account of finding it written by the gentleman himself; he said he would call again for it. It is some months since, and he has never been for it, nor have I read it."

"Lend it to me," said the doctor, "and I will read it. It will be amusing, at the least."

"So I think, sir, if it be not instructive."

The landlord rose, and going to a cupboard, took out the manuscript. It was wrapped up in brown paper, and he handed it to the doctor.

"One part is very old indeed," said Dr. Russel, who began, after a few minutes, to read as follows :—

In a country churchyard, close by Brixhill, lay three bodies in one grave. It was an ancient grave that, and had not been disturbed or opened for many ages. When that was last opened the yew trees that now nod their heads so mournfully over the last homes of the dead were but young trees—mere saplings, But that was many ages back, so long that no man can tell—not even the sexton, nor the clerk; the latter did once try to find out the date of that grave, and began to search such documents as belonged to the church; but he lost himself among the registers, and found himself at midnight in the vestry.

The sound of the midnight hour struck lonely and solemn on his ear.— He listened with awe, and with much difficulty he rose up, and with a great effort tore himself from his seat, and rushed out of the vestry, locking the door of the church, and scampering home as quickly as he could to his anxious spouse.

He had to pass through the churchyard, and then by the monument of the grave we have spoken of. There was something mysterious in all the iron rails that surrounded the black marble of which it was composed; something equally fearful was cast around by the shadow of that ancient willow tree, the trunk of which had become withered, decayed, and split in pieces, and had eventually been blown down; but still, on the return of spring, a new tree sprung up from its roots, and it grew as fresh and fair as ever for many years, until it again decayed, and became scattered by the winds; but this reproduction went on as surely as ever.

It was a singular thing, but this old willow tree seemed never capable of being entirely destroyed; there was always a germ within the bosom of the earth that sent forth a new stem, and the long leaves hung mournfully over the sable monument of the dead. At one time there had been an inscription, but for ages past there had been none. Time, the envious destroyer of all things, had destroyed this, though he could not fix his envious fangs on the marble— that still retained its pristine form, though much of its polish and the sharpness of its edges were destroyed; but despite all, there stood the black monument.

The iron rails around it had gone, that is many of them, while those that did remain were oxidated and worn, and had an attempt been made, they could easily have been marched off.

There were curious old traditions relative to this old grave and monument, but none of them were the real ones, and many marvellous things had been said of, and countenanced by, the singular reproduction of the willow tree.

When the clerk passed that old monument and mysterious tree, and beheld its moving branches waving in the night air, and when he beheld the sable monument no longer protected by the rails, but looked as though it would walk out from its ancient cage, which it had already broken through; when he saw this, and thought of the task he had been engaged in, he shuddered at the frowning aspect of the group.

He saw the pale moonlight peeping through the trees, and the night-owl gave his ear-piercing scream, and then off started the terror-stricken clerk with all the speed he was master of. Soon was he within sight of his own house, and rushing in, he shut and bolted the door after him, and then threw himself into a chair, and the first thing he heard was the voice of his spouse, who said,—

"A nice time of night for you to keep a decent married woman up; and a pretty way to come bouncing in in that manner. What made you come in such a manner to frighten a body so, Mr. Watkins?"

"Because it was late," said Watkins.

"Because it was late? I know it was late, Mr. Watkins; but that was no reason you should frighten me; but you want to kill me, that you might marry that nasty wench, Nancy Flowers."

"I know nothing about what you are saying."

"Oh, dear, no! that's the way I'm to be treated. You know nothing when I speak; but if anybody else speaks, you know everything."

Watkins made no reply; he knew that however strongly he denied, or affirmed, or excused himself, the stronger and louder would be the good wife's rejoinder; so, with a deep sigh, he swallowed hastily his supper, and crept to bed, devoutly promising himself that if it pleased Heaven to deprive him of the present partner of his soul, he would be very far from showing himself ungrateful for the mercy, by taking another wife under any circumstances whatever.

There is no amount of human charms that can in any way repay the many miseries inflicted by a female temper.— Thus muttered poor Watkins, and then he fell fast asleep, for he was weary.

That night poor Watkins's sleep was much disturbed, and he had visions of a very unpleasant character, and could not banish from his mind the shadow of the willow tree. At one time they appeared like the bodies of two knights in furious encounter, and were dealing each other deadly and terrific blows, and the fire flew from their armour, sparks flew around, and the blows of sword and armour rang like the sound of hammers on an anvil.

Then there was the form of a woman flitted past, and the knights fought more furiously than ever, and being more intent upon mutual destruction, rather than having any regard for their own lives, they both at length fell mortally wounded side by side.

Watkins awoke in a great fright, and found he was alongside of his spouse, and for once in his life he felt pleased; he gazed through the curtains, and saw the moon shining beautifully and serenely upon the earth, and the clouds now and then passing her full round form for a few moments, obscured the radiance of her beams, but they were soon shining full upon the earth again, to the comfort of poor Watkins, who, seeing by that means where he was, fell to sleep again. But, alas! sleep was no better on this occasion than the first, it was disturbed by all sorts of phantoms, and it ended by one that made a very great impression on his mind.

He dreamed that he was in the vestry and looking over the old registers, when a form of most lovely and enchanting aspect stepped forward from behind one of the marble slabs and stood before him.

Watkins was petrified with fear, he could not walk or stand; he sat in the chair leaning against the wall, and gazing with open eyes upon the beautiful apparition.

She smiled—but the smile died on her features, and a look—such a look —that drove the blood from his very heart, and entranced him with horror, and he felt every little hair on his body swell up an lift his clothes—his flesh crept and ran into knots, and altogether he was in a dreadful state of extreme fear.

The figure paused and clasped her hands, and buried her face within them, and deep sighs seemed to escape her bosom, for her breast heaved and fell convulsively. She endeavoured to speak, but could not do so; her speech was turned to frantic gesticulation. She held one finger out extended towards some of the shelves upon which he knew the boxes containing old registers and deeds were deposited, and in his mind he believed she pointed to one in particular.

Behind the figure stood the shadow of the black tomb or monument there, and the willow tree and all.

"Oh, heavens!" muttered the terrified Watkins; "'tis one of the inhabitants of the black tomb; what can this mean? I have done nothing to offend her—mercy, mercy—do not kill me."

MRS. BLAIR SHOWING TO HER SISTER MRS. BERTRAM'S CHILD.

The figure approached the bed, and, in a sorrowful, sweet voice, and with an aspect so woebegone, and so much mental suffering, that even he felt inexpressibly pained to look at her, she said,—

"For my crimes that I committed while in life, I am compelled to revisit the earth once in one hundred years, and to walk and mourn over the graves of those with whom I sleep, and who sleep there through me early,—long before their time had come.

"I come and mourn, and shed tears —such tears that mortals can never know—can never think—can never believe could exist. In that box, among old papers, you will find the recital of these deeds—of the causes that reduced me to this hard necessity,—for an ethereal spirit thus to traverse the cold pale moonlight, and look upon scenes that recall deeds and things to my mind that give me a hell within my heart, and a fire within my brain.

"Read those papers, and give them to the world, and let men by precept and example avoid the extremes to which passion may urge them. Farewell! my hour of departure is come—farewell!"

So saying, the figure slowly receded from sight, and all was silent and motionless, nothing was to be seen. The room was as it had been, and Watkins slept undisturbed the remainder of the night.

Indeed, he slept till past his usual hour, and when he awoke, he found himself in bed, alone, and broad daylight shining in at the chamber window.

He started up, and having hastily descended to the little parlour, found his helpmate busily engaged in her domestic duties.

"So, Mr. Watkins, here's breakfast been awaiting this half hour; the eggs spoiled, and the tea cold; but it wouldn't be you, if it were not so."

"I'm late," said Watkins.

"Drot the man, I know that; haven't I been telling you the consequence of your late hours?"

"I should have been up as early as I usually am, but I was up late last night, you know, my dear," said poor Watkins.

"And that is what I could have told you last night, Mr. Watkins; if you had come home at proper hours, instead of stopping at the Nag and Thistle, you'd have got up in proper time."

"I was not there."

"Don't tell me that; you were late, then, and are late now, and breakfast spoilt."

"Why didn't you wake me?"

"There—there!" exclaimed Mrs. Watkins, sitting down in a chair, and wiping her eye with the corner of her apron, "wake him! as if it ain't as much as my life's worth to speak to you!"

"Well, but I have had such a strange dream," said Watkins, casting about for some time to avoid a scene, and knowing that such a theme was likely to succeed in engaging her attention.

"And what should you dream about, Mr. Watkins? what ought a married man like you to dream about, eh?"

"I can't tell that; if I could, it would be of no use in my telling you what, in that case, you must know; and, besides, nothing strange or wonderful could take place."

'Strange and wonderful?"

'Yes, strange and wonderful indeed!"

"And when are you to see anything strange and wonderful, Mr. Watkins?"

"I don't know yet, but I shall see if my dream comes true, and then——"

"What then?"

"I may gain something by it, and that, you know, will be worth dreaming for."

Mrs. Watkins looked very hard at Watkins, as she said,—

"You know, Watkins, you have promised me a new bonnet and gown, and I want a shawl as well; you know that, Watkins."

"Yes, yes, I know all that; but let us have our breakfast, and I will tell you all about it."

Thus incited, Mrs. Watkins poured out the tea, and performed the duties of the table marvellously well, as Watkins thought, for she said but very little.

Watkins then began to recount how he had been examining the boxes and the registers, and how the vision of the lady had come, and pointed to one box in particular, and told him there were papers which would inform him of all that had passed, and how the inhabitants of the black tomb had come by their death.

During this recital, Mrs. Watkins was completely absorbed in the contemplation of the wonderful, and when he finished said,—

"But do you think there are any such papers as the spirit pointed to?"

"Why should it point to what did not exist? I have no doubt but they are somewhere about in the vestry."

"You will go and fetch them?"

"I shall if I can find them."

"And read them?"

"Yes, I will read them through at home, after dinner," said Watkins.

"And what do you intend to do with the papers when you have them?"

"Take them to some of the publishers, and they may give me something for them."

And thus it was the relation, and the manner in which it was discovered, became known to the world.

Watkins went that morning, as soon as he had finished his breakfast, to the vestry, and, being secure from interruption, he began to take down the old boxes, one after the other, until he came to the right one. Here he found a small roll of paper carefully wrapped up in several substances, and thrust finally into a long glove, or mitten, of a very ancient date.

Having unfolded it, and thrown the wrappers into the box, he replaced them all, and it being near dinner time, he returned to his cottage, where he found Mrs. Watkins in a state of excitement and who had been looking out of the door every five minutes to see if he were coming.

"Have you found it?" she exclaimed, before he could close the door.

"He-he-he-here it is, in my pocket. Is dinner ready?"

"It is."

The worthy couple sat down to their dinner, and this they hurried through with a speed that evinced their mutual curiosity.

"Now," said Mrs. Watkins, "here's a jug of ale and your chair; now sit down, and read the papers; you know you are a dabster at old writing, and deciphering old deeds, and I dare say you can manage this."

"Yes, yes; it is not so bad as a good many I have read," said Watkins, with some pride and self-complacence.

In the time of Edward the Second (began the manuscript, which was most beautifully written, and in excellent preservation) lived two knights who had greatly signalised themselves in arms, and in the more happy parts of their career of warriors and gentlemen, they were friends—men who had done each other acts of friendship, and saved each other's lives. They were brothers in all but the accident of birth, and that often serves to divide those who are united.

Though men of renown, they were yet young, and neither had reached the age of five-and-twenty. They were tall and robust men, who could wield sword and battle-axe with good effect, and were skilled in many matters, that gave them the right to offer advice in council. They were not rich, and yet possessed enough to make them respected, and they both, moreover, were good officers, and bore posts in the army assigned them by the king.

These two gentlemen lived in the greatest amity and friendship, until an event happened which changed the aspect of affairs. Once they were at a tournament; they both acquitted themselves so well, that they won more than one prize, and had the misfortune to lay their prizes at the feet of the same lady. They had openly chosen her as the object of their present devotion, and thought no more of her; yet they could scarce refrain admiring so much beauty and loveliness.

The lady, unfortunately, was a co-quette, and well knew the charms she possessed, and the way to use them for the mere purpose of ensnaring the affections of men whom she never intended to marry, and whom she only cared to see as adding to the number of her admirers. Her heart was untouched by love, and at the best she knew not the evil she inflicted. Her parents were proud and rich; the baron of Charworth Castle had broad lands, and he had no son to inherit them, and he was determined to make no alliance for his daughter save such as she herself made—it should, for her sake, be a love match.

The two knights were invited to spend some days at Charworth Castle, and there partake of the hospitality and sports of that place. Neither of the knights hesitated; and, beyond a casual observation or two respecting her beauty, neither of them intimated the interest they both began to feel in the lady. Ten or twelve days were consumed, and pleasantly and happily enough. There were fallow and red deer in the woods, and hawking by the river, and in these sports they spent their time.

The Lady Maude, too, rode out, attended by the two knights. She was an accomplished horsewoman, and displayed a skill and courage which excited their admiration. The two knights were both equally enamoured, and yet they neither saw the other's love. They had only eyes for themselves; they saw but the object they loved, and could not distinguish the devotion of the other.

Before quitting Charworth Castle they each sought Maude, and declared their love in passionate terms, and begged that some hope might be given to them, however small it might be. Instead of accepting or declining their proposals, she declared that for the present she could not make up her mind to accept of their services; but in a twelvemonth's time she would give them an answer.

But, in the meantime, she loved no one; but she could not help believing she might do so if they persevered. This was enough; they believed they were loved, and could expect no more; for, according to the manners of the age, this was a kind of probation, of her expressed and appointed, before the true knight received the acknowledgment of his lady's love, and in such a light did they each receive and comply with these commands.

They left Charworth Castle, and proceeded in search of adventure, and were not long in finding such. Their prowess was called into action more than once in the wars with Scotland, and in those with France. The twelve months soon came to an end, and then they again visited the castle of Charworth, where they were cordially received by the baron, who welcomed them to Charworth Hall.

Again did the two knights cherish in secret the hopes that Maude had given them as the dearest feeling and thought they could experience; and often would each hug himself with the hope of years of future happiness. There was a secret misgiving as to the fate of their friendship for each other, and neither of them liked to acknowledge the passion he felt.

They had been so long intimate friends and brothers in arms, that any change in their situation would seem like a calamity to the other, because it would tend to sever that which had hitherto been so sure and firm. Neither liked to announce to the other that such a state was about to ensue, that would give the one different hopes and prospects to what his brother could partake in.

This was the reason they spoke not of the passion which grew in all its strength and intensity, and when they returned to Charworth Castle a second time, they repaired to the bower of the lady to claim the performance of the implied promise.

" I cannot tell you how grieved I am," she said, "that I cannot do what you require."

" Indeed! dearest lady, wherefore not?"

" Because there are two claimants."

" Two, lady?"

" Yes, sir knight."

" And who may the other be who prefers his claim to mine? I will compel him to yield or die in the attempt."

The lady hesitated.

" Do you doubt me, lady? I swear by my knighthood and the holy church to make the recreant yield to my pretensions."

" 'Tis Sir Edmund Warner."

" Sir Edmund?"

" Yes, your friend."

" False friend."

" He sought the same promise from me."

" Then be assured, lady, he shall renounce you in my favour, and then my happiness will be complete. Farewell till I can lay at your feet his sword."

The knight left the bower to seek his friend, and he was not long gone before Sir Edmund came to demand the fulfilment of the part promised.

" Indeed, I cannot, Sir Edmund."

" And wherefore not, lady?"

" Because it would bring danger to you. It would deprive me of you altogether."

" You read riddles, lady."

" Well, Sir Philip Melville has just declared he will slay any man, and even you, if you give not up your suit to him."

" Sir Philip?"

" Ay; do you doubt me?"

" Surely no; but I knew not that he sought your love, lady."

" You will soon hear by his own demands, for he seeks you with the intention I speak of."

" Then he will take my life long before I cease to love you, lady."

The knight knelt, and, taking her hand, pressed it to his bosom, and respectfully to his lips, and then he said,—

" This will be a sad trial, but it shall be gone through without fear or hesitation. I sacrifice all to the shrine of love and beauty. Farewell, lady, may fortune prosper me."

Thus speaking, the knight left the lady's presence, and soon met his friend. For some moments neither spoke, but at length Sir Philip spoke with a great effort.

" Sir Edmund," he said, " I love the Lady Maude, and I can brook no rival. I do not wish to break our long friendship if it can be maintained; but you must give up all pretension to her hand."

" Nay, that I will not, Sir Philip, and you can care but little for the friendship you speak of, if you can make such a demand."

"I mean what I say, and make the demand, and insist upon compliance."

"You may, but unless you can tear my heart out, and deprive me of life, you will never get a compliance. I love and will win the Lady Maude."

"Then our swords must cut in twain the friendship that has lasted so long, and with my body I devote myself to the winning of the love of the Lady Maude. Let us meet by moonlight in the old churchyard, and there decide our difference."

This was agreed to, and the knights separated to prepare for the coming combat; and as each was well aware of the valour of his opponent, death they knew could only quench the opposition. They met and fought. Long did the sounds of their swords ring in the night air; the combat was long and furious; wounds were given and received, and yet neither fell; but at length, staggering, faint, and weak from loss of blood and wounds, they ceased to fight, and fell on a newly made grave. At that moment, Maude, who had heard the clangour of the combat, and sorry for having gone so far, hastened to the spot, but too late to stay their hands—they were lying side by side.

They both cast their dying eyes upon her, and then, as if both instigated by a sudden knowledge of the truth, pronounced her name with a curse, and then slept the sleep of death. Shocked at the sight, and the unexpected revulsion of feeling in her two lovers, she was for a moment or two stunned, reeled, and fell, striking her temples upon the helmet of Sir Philip, and died instantly. Next day they were all three found thus, and were buried in one grave, with a marble monument erected to their memory. The willow tree was planted by the Baron of Charworth.

"It is a very singular affair altogether," said Dr. Russel, "and exhibits the state of feeling of the age very truly; devotion to slaughter and the fair sex was all a knight had to think of."

"It is very strange, and such times as those would scarce do now—a few such ladies and gentlemen would do much towards decreasing the surplus population of these realms."

"Yes, indeed, they would, and the only renown they would obtain, would be such as the gibbet confers; but this is removing people out of their age."

James entered, saying, "She's come, sir."

"Very good, James," said the doctor, "I need not wait now any longer, and I shall leave you with your medical knowledge, James, to superintend her operations, and put her in the right way of doing anything that may be too much for her."

"You may depend upon me, sir," said James. "I'll keep a professional eye, sir, upon the whole of the proceedings. It's a great advantage, sir, in a hotel, though my master never will see it, to combine the waiter, sir, with the professional man."

"I should say it was; and now, landlord, I think I can go. Do not allow any one to hold any conversation with my patient. I will come again in about six hours from now, when I shall be able, no doubt, from the state in which I shall find him, to order him some nourishing diet, for he will need sustaining now, as of course he must be in a state of great exhaustion."

"Everything, sir," said the landlord, "shall be as you order. I am extremely thankful that there is no likelihood of a death in the house. Apart from the disagreeableness of the thing, it of course would have done me a great injury, for people will not willingly choose a hotel where a dead body is lying, and I could not very well have received any one without alluding to the fact."

"Certainly, certainly; but you may, as far as human judgment can speak upon such matters, dismiss such fear from your mind. You see the young man has had one dangerous relapse, which his constitution has successfully fought through, and I don't think he is likely to have another."

"I am happy to hear it, sir."

The physician saw and spoke to the woman who had been sent for to nurse poor Theodore Danton, instead of the two hags who had undertaken that duty, and, by their violence and intemperance, shown themselves so very unfitted for it. He found her quite the nurse in every respect, and was much pleased that, during the anxious period of his convalescence, the young man should have so intelligent a companion as this person seemed to be.

Theodore was still soundly sleeping, and after giving the nurse whispered instructions, Dr. Russel, who had not had any sleep now for a day and a night, left the inn, with the consciousness on his mind that he had saved the life of the interesting young stranger.

CHAPTER XXVIII.

MR. BERTRAM FALLS COMPLETELY INTO THE SNARES LAID BY MRS. BLAIR, AND DETERMINES UPON WATCHING HIS WIFE. — THE MONTHLY NURSE, AND THE STRANGE DISCOVERY.

WHILE these things were taking place, as regarded the heart-stricken Theodore Danton, Mr. Bertram was falling deeper and deeper still into the toils of that fiend in human shape, Mrs. Blair. It was not exactly what she said that implanted so deeply in his heart the seeds of suspicion against his wife; but it was what she had the art to seem to leave unsaid that produced the worst effects.

Like Iago, when stirring up the jealous feelings of Othello to the pitch of frenzy which deprived him of the power to reason correctly, and so made him so easily the tool of a villain, did Mrs. Blair by hints, inuendos, broken sentences, and half words, as if she were repenting that the candour of her disposition compelled her to speak—drive him nearly to distraction. Suspicion once aroused will soon find materials upon which to strengthen itself, and Bertram began to imagine, from every word his innocent wife uttered, and from every one of her actions, that he could gather something confirmatory of the idea that she loved him not. Every one of these feelings and virtues which before, in consequence of his placing a liberal and a correct construction upon them, tended to make him love her, were now, to her prejudice, arrayed in his mind, seen as they were through the new medium of his jealous feelings.

She had now, to him, became like the man's wife in the lines—

"Some wives have many faults,
Mine has but two—
There's nothing right she'll say,
And there's nothing right she'll do."

If any one's conduct is but once viewed with the jaundiced eye of suspicion, let their actions, thoughts, and language be each as pure as unsullied snow, they will not escape detraction; and thus it was that Mr. Bertram, as he adopted the reprehensible practice of watching his wife's minutest actions, and weighing her most careless words, was continually wondering he had not seen so and so before, and not remarked such and such a trait in her disposition, which told to her disadvantage. Then his mode of conversation with her was all of a character the very reverse of that which would have tended to bring into activity the best feelings of any one. He spoke always dubiously to her, and he watched her changes of countenance as she answered, and always suspected that what she said was not really what she thought. This was a state of things which could not last very long, but which, so long as it lasted, was calculated to inflict upon both parties incalculable misery and annoyance.

Whatever Bertram himself suffered, in consequence of his own folly, we cannot pity; but the unmerited sufferings of his innocent and really exemplary wife, demand our warmest sympathy. What was likely to be the result, Heaven only knows; but many tears were shed by Mrs. Bertram in secret over the thoughts of how unhappily situated she was. She knew herself to be blameless, and, therefore, did it seem to her hard to be subjected merely to the caprices of a man who, whatever affection he had for her, had contrived to emerge it all into jealousy instead of tenderness. That she had committed an error of judgment in not at once communicating to him the visit, and the reason of the visit, of Theodore Danton, she knew; but it was only an error of the head, not of the heart, and Mrs. Bertram was as pure, as innocent, and as sinseless, notwithstanding that, as any wife could possibly be. Therefore was it that she felt how peculiarly hard it was that she should suffer as if she were some guilty thing.

Mrs. Bertram could go nowhere now without her husband either dogging her himself, or sending some one else to do so. She did not know this, but she had reason to suspect it. Probably she, like the man in the play, felt sure of it, and if she had been very sure indeed, would have done something desperate contingent thereon. There may be many circumstances of which we may feel tolerably assured, and yet which we are in so bad a condition to prove, that, if the party whom, with a perfect conviction of the truth of the accusation, we could accuse, chose to deny the imputation, we should be at fault. Thus, when Mrs. Bertram met her husband repeatedly out, and found that, let her go to whatever part of the town she might, he, by some extraordinary means, knew of it; and when, from such a combination of circumstances, she felt convinced they could not be accidental, and was told herself that she was watched, she had all the pangs of feeling that such was the case, and yet, if Bertram chose to say "it is not so," what real proof had she to adduce that it really was? This was, indeed, a wretched state of affairs, and there was Mrs. Blair, too, in the house, in defiance of her. Bertram had told her that, in consequence of the length of time Mrs. Blair had been with him, he wished her to remain until she had suited herself with some other situation. This was the most insidious plan that Bertram could possibly have adopted for the purpose of securing Mrs. Blair indefinitely in her situation. He rather shrank, certainly, from saying to his wife, "Mrs. Blair shall remain here, whether you like or not, and in defiance of the notice to quit which you have given her," because that would have been to come to open war at once; but, since it was by Mrs. Blair thrown upon his shoulders to find some means of retaining her in her place, in defiance of Mrs. Bertram, he adopted that which we have stated.

"Of course," he said, "as you have given Mrs. Blair notice to quit, that is quite enough for me, and I could not think of keeping her, or of entering at all into the causes of your dismissal of her. It is sufficient for me that, in the exercise of your legitimate authority here, you have dismissed her; but then, of course, I know her better than you do, and I am quite convinced, from my previous knowledge of her, that her faults are those of temper more than of actual disposition. I, therefore, have, with a hope that you would acquiesce in the arrangement, promised her that she should remain here until she suited herself with a situation which, of course, I have only to say I hope she will do soon."

This was a kind of speech to which Mrs. Bertram could make but one reply, and that consisted of a consent to the arrangement which her husband had made. Thus, then, was this serpent continued in the house, to the destruction of all domestic comfort, and ultimately to the destruction of Bertram himself nearly, and everything he held dear in the world.

There was, too, a circumstance which, while it ought to have awakened every feeling of tenderness which was ever an inhabitant of the heart of Bertram, only under his present state of mind tended to give him more and more uneasiness. This was the prospect of Mrs. Bertram in due time presenting him with an infant pledge of their affection. This, instead of being the source of pleasant anticipation, one would have expected it to be, was really the reverse to both the parents. To Bertram it was new food for his jealousy, and he would walk about now moodily, with his arms folded, as he kept muttering to himself, in an undertone,—

"Humph! a child—a child. Of course, whether it is like me or not, I must keep it—oh, dear, yes. D——n!"

To Mrs. Bertram the prospect of becoming a mother, although far distant, was by no means pleasurable or encouraging. She found herself a wife without possessing the confidence or affection of her husband; and no wonder, therefore, that her eyes filled with tears as she asked herself what would be his conduct to the child when it should see the light. She found, however, some solace in making preparations for the coming of the little stranger, and she diverted her thoughts from many an uneasy circumstance by superintending those tiny garments which were to adorn the new denizen of the world.

Like all very young and inexperienced mothers, she was terribly anxious about a thousand things which she had no occasion to have been anxious about at all. Among other arrangements, a nurse must of course be engaged immediately, although months must elapse before her services could be required. One of the gin-drinking, lying, ignorant, hideous fraternity was recommended to Mrs. Bertram by a female friend, and on the very day on which poor Theodore Danton was by Dr. Russel declared to be in a state approaching to convalescence, the nurse who had been recommended called upon Mrs. Bertram.

She was a thorough specimen of her class, of enormous roundabout dimensions, and with a great, white, flabby-looking face, that showed up in vivid contrast the ruddy, purplish hue that played about the tip of her jolly nose. Her black bonnet surmounted a curious specimen of a cap that can only be found on such occasions; her gown and shawl were sufficient to tell the passers by her profession. For the remainder, she was a big, bony, and heavy-looking woman—such an one as would induce people to think she would suit, because she was strong and hearty, and capable and willing to work. When admitted to Mrs. Bertram, she dropped a curtsey, and began by saying,—

"How do you do, ma'am? I called as I heerd you were likely to want some one to attend upon you under certain interesting circumstances. Ah, many's the ladies as I have attended afore this. I have always been fortunate in my ladies—they all do so well."

"Indeed!"

"Yes; you see, ma'am, all's right when the doctor once turns his back, and then all depends upon good nussing. Yes, ma'am, that's what it is, depend upon it."

"There is, I dare say, much truth in that, and I hope it will prove so."

"And so do I, ma'am."

"I am told you have often acted in this capacity before, and are, therefore, fully competent to all the duties of such a situation?" said Mrs. Bertram,

"Yes, ma'am, I am; that is, always under a doctor, you know—always under a doctor."

"Of course."

"Then, ma'am, though I don't like speaking of myself,—yet, in a manner of speaking, we can't sometimes help it, otherwise people wouldn't know nothing about me,—I may say there is nobody more attentive or more lucky than I am. I mustn't say it's all through me, ma'am; but I must suppose it's owing to a kind of providential-like luck that attends me."

"Indeed!"

"Yes, ma'am; and my ladies always profits by it, as in course they must, else it's no good luck to me, is it?"

"That depends much upon taste," said Mrs. Bertram; "but, if Heaven pleases that I am spared to get over it, you shall not complain of my want of liberality, provided you are all that you say you are during my illness."

"Yes, ma'am, oh, dear yes—certainly, ma'am, it always depends upon satisfaction given and received; that's the main thing, ma'am."

"I need hardly ask you respecting sobriety, because it would be an instant disqualification, if it were otherwise."

"Oh, yes, ma'am; sober!—yes, catch me otherwise, I'll give you leave to have me pilloried. Yes, a person who's given to drink, ma'am, ought to be burned at both ends—that's my opinion, and the opinion of many of the doctors as knows me, and well they knows it, too. Temperance, ma'am, is a wirtue—a wery great wirtue; and so's abstinence another. I wouldn't break one of them, ma'am, for the walley of all you could give me."

"I am very glad to hear it, indeed," said Mrs. Bertram. "You are sober, skilful, and attentive;—what more can we do or can we want? There only remains the experience to prove it all."

"Exactly, ma'am, and I shall be ready as soon as you are; for, you see, if I ain't here, I'm somewhere, and that's how we do it."

"Precisely."

"And then, you see, I'm so attentive; indeed, I may tell you one instance of it, of a Doctor Russel. He sent for me to attend upon a poor young man, and he tried all the underhanded ways he could think of to get me away again;

he couldn't, because he couldn't say anything to my face."

"Indeed! and why not?"

" Because I was taking such care of the young gentleman, that he was getting well too fast; and I know now that he's going back, if he isn't quite dead now."

"Is he so bad?"

" Yes, poor Mr. Danton!"

"Who?" exclaimed Mrs. Bertram, with such a start that the nurse started too.

" Danton, ma'am; yes, ma'am, Danton I said."

" What is his Christian name? Oh, was he a young man—dark?"

" Yes ma'am, very dark; they pulled

down the blinds; he was a young man, ma'am."

" His Christian name—his name was——"

"Theodore, I believe, ma'am; yes, ma'am, Theodore Danton was the young man's name. Bless my stars

and garters, what's this all about? I shouldn't wonder if we don't have a miscarriage, now."

This was caused by Mrs. Bertram falling down with a loud scream; she had fainted on hearing the name of Theodore Danton.

CHAPTER XXIX.

THE PARTIAL RECOVERY, — THE CAUTION —THE CONVALESCENT.

DOCTOR RUSSEL was true to his word, and after the lapse of six hours returned to the hotel to visit his patient, which brought it to near mid-day; and upon quitting the house he met James, to whom he said,—

"Well, James, how does your patient get on now? You have so much of the medical profession at heart, and love it for its own sake, that I dare say you are quite ready to issue the bulletin?"

"Oh, quite, sir. He's much better, all things considered—as well, you understand, as one can be who has just turned his back upon the undertaker and the mute."

"I understand you, James; you are expressive and explicit."

"I always wish to be so, sir, though I can't always be so with a cus'omer. They are such rum fellows sometimes, there's no knowing what they say or what they mean, or what to say to them again; and then their tempers are very bad, and you don't know when they joke and when they don't, and there's the chance of rows."

"That's very disagreeable."

"It is, sir, and I often wish I was their medical attendant, and they were my patients."

"Why, James, why do you wish that? —it's very extraordinary!"

"Oh, I'd physic them, sir."

"Surely you would if they required it, but not else, James, eh? Enlighten me."

"Well, sir, I'd give them draught after draught, and a blister on the nape of the neck, with another on the stomach, and that should cure them of all their vagaries."

"Very effectual. But where's the patient?"

"This way, sir, this way;" and James led Dr. Russel to the apartment where the patient he knew lay. Before, however, he came there, he met the landlord, who said,—

"Good morning, sir. I am happy to say that I think the unfortunate gentleman is recovering; he has awoke, and speaks very rationally, and appears to have something of a craving for food."

"This must be very cautiously tended to at first," said Dr. Russel, "because his stomach is in no way fit to perform its accustomed functions as if it were in full vigour and health, and we must begin very gently in exercising it by degrees, to bear the proper place in the recovery of the frame. We must give him all that is nourishing, and at the same time of easy digestion."

"Exactly, sir."

"Beef tea and broth, and then a little chicken; but don't let him have so much that he can say, 'here is more than I can eat;' rather stint him in the quantity, and allow him to have it oftener if he desire it, because he will most likely be willing to eat more than he can well digest."

"Very good, sir," said the landlord.

Dr. Russel then entered the apartment where the patient lay, and the nurse, as soon as she perceived the doctor, said, with a curtsey,—

"I am glad you have come, sir, for my patient has been anxious about you."

"Has he been long awake?"

"About half an hour."

Dr. Russel approached the bed of the sick man, and stretching out his hand, he took that of the patient in his own, saying,—

"You find yourself very much better, do you not?"

"I am better, sir, thank you," he replied, in a weak voice, "but I seem almost unable to move; I feel hunger."

"No doubt you do, and shall have something—it is a very good symptom; but you must be cautious how far you indulge yourself."

"I may make a few inquiries now, sir, may I not?" said the patient.

"Hardly—besides, there is little that can be said; I would advise you to employ your mind upon other matters than your own—a day or two can make no difference to you, because you cannot hurry on a cure, but you may retard it."

"How came I here?"

"All that is known is, you were very ill and insensible, and you are now better; therefore be satisfied, and all will be well, and I will come and see you again; but all you need do, is to be perfectly quiet, and cautious in your diet.

" May I read ?"

"You may, but have as subdued a light as you can see by. Good day."

Then shaking his hand kindly, and giving some directions to the nurse, Dr. Russel left the room. The patient at his request had some mutton-broth given him, and was then propped up on pillows. As he lay thus relieved upon the bed, he read the following tale. It was an old book he had chosen, because the print was large and clear, adapted to the weak state of the patient. The blinds of the room were left down, but there was enough of light to enable him to read :—

Encircled by its own grounds, and nearly hidden from view by large and ancient looking trees, stands Belmont-house, an old Tudor-looking place, with many windows and buttresses, and surrounded by a low stone wall, and a well paved yard in front of the main building, with wings at either end, and an old fountain in the space between, which used to play, but which had ceased, as being useless, seeing that there were no inhabitants.

This ancient house had long been uninhabited and falling to decay, but it looked beautiful even then, and showed the grandeur of its former owner. The cause of its being uninhabited was singular and distressing, such as indeed but few ever knew, and those few have long since disappeared from the face of the earth. Many, indeed, who passed that ancient and venerable pile, used to look up and wonder what sort of people once inhabited such a place,—they must be almost princes,—and why they did not now live in it.

This was what but few knew, and those scarce knew it, save by tradition. It was strange that the heir to such a property, the owner of such a splendid house, should permit it to fall to decay ; but there were reasons that were sufficient for that individual to act as he had done. He resided abroad, and had not been there for years, and there seemed to be no possibility of his ever returning.

Sir Robert Chambers, the former owner, in fact, the last who resided there, had been a stanch royalist, and had suffered much for his adherence to the royal cause, for which he fought with all the desperate bravery of those unfortunate cavaliers. But as their fortune declined, his possessions became forfeited and seized upon by the prevailing party. Some time before the war actually broke out, Sir Robert loved and won the daughter of one of his neighbours, Alice Gordon, the daughter of Sir John Gordon, another gentleman of property, within a few miles of this place.

She was extremely beautiful, but she was haughty and proud, fond of riches and the glitter of wealth, and the adulation that it produced from others. Alice was at the same time treacherous and deceitful, though at that time nothing was known of this—it had not made itself manifest even to herself. It takes years often to develop the different characteristics of a person's mind—it may be the absence of the necessary stimulus that is wanting, but the quality or capacity still exists, though it be unknown and unseen. Such was the case with Alice Gordon.

The marriage was celebrated in great style and magnificence—there was open house for many days both at Belmont-house and at the residence of Sir John Gordon, and a numerous retinue of guests and vassals crowded around, and spared not the viands and the strong liquors, for those were the days of extreme prodigality in hospitality, a time of profusion. There was no stint here, and, moreover, Sir Robert Chambers quitted the hall on the morning of the feast, when he took leave of the guests, after having introduced his bride to them, and then set out for London, where he intended to pass a few weeks.

This passed ; he returned to the hall, where some very pleasant months elapsed, and a happier time had never been than that ; but there is always something to mar prospects of happiness, and prevent the fulfilment of those pleasing anticipations of the future, that are often cherished in the mind, but to be disappointed in the future. The quarrels between the parliament and the crown broke out, and each party watched the progress of the other with much anxiety ; but the royalists regarded any act of the parliament with great care and jealousy. Thus some time elapsed before anything happened to disturb the public tranquillity, and the prospect of violent commotions did not begin to be perceived until they were close at hand.

There were several people who watched the progress of events with some interest; but few of them more so than Sir Robert Chambers and Sir John Gordon, but both with different sentiments; the former with unshaken loyalty, the latter with a strong predilection for the parliamentary interest.

Thus the two families soon discovered strong opposite interests, and by the time the young wife had borne Sir Robert a son, the first of these unhappy differences broke out.

For some time, however, neither party took any part in the coming struggle; but they both prepared to do so with determination, and with all the force they could each muster. Sir Robert Chambers armed all his tenants and retainers, and they both had so much attachment to their landlord and to the cause, that they flocked to his standard.

His father-in-law, Sir John Gordon, took the parliamentary side of the quarrel, and he endeavoured to do all that he could to defeat the object of his son-in-law; this purpose, although it was kept secret, and but little communication was held between the two families, was defeated by Sir Robert Chambers's wife, who held all the principles and opinions of her father; and forgetting her duty to her husband, she sent information to her father of all that had occurred, and enabled the parliamentary party to prepare to dispute his passage.

The morning that Sir Robert Chambers and his tenantry, to the number of about thirty, who would follow him anywhere, were ready to start, he took an affectionate leave of his wife, and of his infant son, then scacely two years old, and then riding to the head of the company, he gave the word, and they were soon in motion.

He had scarcely travelled a mile from the place they started from, when they found themselves opposed by a similar body of men drawn up across the road, ready to dispute the passage with them.

Sir Robert was much enraged at this,

for he believed his purpose was unknown to but very few, and none of the enemy knew aught of his intentions; and he could not help exclaiming to one who held a sort of subordinate command under him for the time,—

"I did not expect this, and yet I know not whether to look upon them as enemies or friends; they may be the latter, who, seeing us approach, are desirous of learning our purposes; if so, we shall ride along in greater security, and in more company; but keep close together, and I will ride ahead to learn their object."

So saying, Sir Robert rode beyond his troop, and the same was done by the person commanding the other party, and then, for the first time, he recognised his own father-in-law.

"Good heavens! Sir John Gordon?"

"The same," said Sir John.

"What may I understand by this array—that you intend to join the royal cause? If so, I shall be happy with your company."

"Such is not my intention."

"What may it be?"

"I have heard that bodies of royalists are stirring about, and I have authority for stopping and dispersing them."

"As for dispersing them, Sir John, you must wear a better sword than the loyal hearts by whom I am followed; we intend to join the royal cause, and do not draw a rebel's sword upon us."

"I will do my duty, were you my own son, instead of my daughter's husband; you must turn back, Sir Robert."

"I will not."

"Then we must come to blows. I am here to intercept any one who may attempt to pass on such an errand."

"I should have thought you would have sought some other occasion to have displayed your disloyalty to your king."

"The king has turned traitor to his subjects, and not his subjects traitors to him."

"You lie, Sir John."

"Ah!—but 'tis no matter; the kingdom was not made for the king; but he is king no longer, and I owe him no allegiance. But this is not a place to dispute in; are you prepared to return to your estate, and remain neutral?"

"I am not."

"Then I bar the road."

"And I must force the passage. There is no other road that I can take now, else I would not draw my sword against you, Sir John Gordon, but there is no alternative."

"None at all."

Then riding back to his own troop, Sir Robert Chambers drew his sword, saying,—

"Now, my brave lads, here is an opportunity to try your mettle; these good neighbours of mine will not let us pass; we must pass, and the consequences be on their own heads. Hurrah, my boys, for God, your king, and your country!"

When he had done speaking, Sir Robert placed himself at the head of his men, and giving the word, they all rode at a hard gallop, increasing their pace as they neared the opposite party, who were drawn across the road.

The word was given, and the whole party were presently in a gallop, and came thundering down on their charge, while the enemy received the charge quietly, and in about ten minutes they were completely overthrown and scattered, leaving nearly half their number dead and wounded on the earth, while the victors scarce lost a man. They chased them along the road for some distance, till they contrived to escape, and when there was no enemy to be seen, Sir Robert called a halt.

"There, my lads," he said, "we have begun well, and have done some service, though a small one, in destroying so many enemies of his majesty; when we join the royal army, we shall be so many more, and they so many less."

After a short rest, they again resumed their journey, and Sir Robert was employed, in his own mind, in endeavouring to find out how it was his father-in-law had learnt his intention, for he had evidently done so.

"He might have learned my general intentions," he said to himself, "for these men could hardly be expected to keep such a secret, but I had not told any one save my wife that this was the morning on which I should start. It must have been her, and yet she would scarce betray her husband; it is monstrous—she could not do it."

He contrived to join the royal army after many struggles and difficulties, and then went through with credit all the different battles fought by that unfortunate monarch, until the fatal battle of Worcester, where all hope vanished.

From this field Sir Robert rode to his own residence, weary and faint, determined to take leaf of his wife and child, and then either hide about the old hall, or attempt an escape. This he did, and arrived at the hall. which he found filled with visitors and rejoicings. Many of his old enemies were present, and among others was his father-in-law.

"I must not show myself to him," he muttered. "He will make a prisoner of me."

He stood alone in the gardens, and threw himself into a seat, and could scarce refrain from uttering a sigh and shedding a tear, to think his home should be a scene of rejoicings upon, to him, a most distressing and melancholy occasion.

"She might have had more delicacy," he muttered; "for she cannot be forced to do this; her father would be able to prevent that; but she and he are both well pleased enough."

As he muttered these words to himself, he heard the sound of approaching footsteps, and drew himself up in a corner, so as to remain unobserved by any one who passed. He soon heard the voice of his wife and that of her father, as they came walking gently towards him, engaged in earnest conversation. It was some moments before he could distinguish the words that were uttered, but as they came nearer, he could hear his wife say, in reply to something,—

"I have not seen or heard from him yet. He has not ventured here."

"I know that. I have intelligence of him as being at the fight of Worcester, and that he was among those who had escaped."

"That's unfortunate."

"Very."

"But he will have many dangers to encounter before he can get out of the kingdom. Indeed, they are all so many chances in our favour."

"They are so; he was wounded, too, and that will be another chance against him."

"So it will."

"I think he will come here, and then, of course, he will be secure."

"Certainly," replied his wife. "I shall know how to act; I will persuade him to conceal himself about the house, and then he can be dispatched, and it can easily be accounted for; these things, now, are soon done."

"They are."

"And when he is once out of the way there can be no bar to the contemplated, marriage. I wish that young bastard was out of the way."

"There can be no occasion to hurt the child; he is not in the way."

"He will come into the property."

"Oh, no; he can be brought up in ignorance of who he is, and yet I can have him always near me. I will send him away, and then, when old enough, make him an attendant about me."

"Very well—very well; it will be a good thing when Sir Robert's death is certain. I'll never forgive him the overthrow he gave me that morning. I had no idea he had so many men."

"I told as near as I heard, and that was near the truth."

"It was, but I couldn't credit it; and I did not charge as he charged. Indeed, my men were scarcely fit for the job, they had no heart in it; they would have followed him rather than me, if he had been wise enough to challenge them to do so."

They now passed out of hearing, and left Sir Robert a prey alternatively to fury and anguish. He could hardly believe his own senses; he could hardly believe his own wife could behave with so much vileness and treachery; and yet, could he doubt it? He had, more than once, resolved upon rushing out and destroying them both; but a recollection that he would soon expose himself to inevitable danger, from which he could make no escape, his own wound and all, were motives that deterred him, but to take a surer and more certain revenge.

He walked about the garden, but no one was near at hand, and he determined to entrust some of his own domestics with his safety; for he believed them incapable of the same treachery as his wife had been capable of. For that purpose he waited until midnight, and then, knowing where the gardener slept,

he determined to awake him. He accordingly went to him, and awoke him, and when the man became aware of who he was, he expressed the most extravagant joy; but suddenly he said,—

"Oh, Sir Robert, what made you come here?"

"Where could I go better?"

"Any place—no matter where, Sir Robert; this place is filled with enemies."

"How so?"

"My lady—but Lord, Sir Robert! I beg your pardon. I didn't mean——"

"Nay, speak plain. I have heard something of my lady, and I do not wish she should know I am here, or else I should lose my life."

"Then, since you say so much, Sir Robert, I must e'en tell you she intends, as soon as you are dead, to marry some Roundhead churl, who has lots of money and land, the spoil of loyal men."

"Very good. Now where can you hide me; in the house or outbuildings?"

"I must think, Sir Robert. But come into my place, and I will get the cellarer up and the groom; they would, I know, die before any harm should come to you."

Sir Robert entered the place, and some good cheer was placed before him, and while he was eating, with an appetite that could only be acquired by fasting and exertion, the three servants were employed in holding a consultation as to what was to be done. They agreed that he should be concealed in the stables, for the groom asserted that he could hide at least a dozen men there, and defy all the Roundheads in the country.

"And besides," he added, "there's means of getting into the house from there, and then back again. I know the place well. I have had occasion, to tell the truth, Sir Robert, to secrete more than one unfortunate lately, and they have been searched after, but it was no use."

"Then that will do for me," said Sir Robert, "and here I'll remain, despite all that can be done, until times change."

With this determination he rose, and told his domestics that he now depended upon them, and not they upon him. Upon which the old cellarman burst into tears, and swore he would never taste wine again if anything happened to him; and he would blow up the house, and set fire to the whole neighbourhood.

Sir Robert Chambers remained in his own house for some years, and during all this time he was faithfully tended by these three individuals, who were as true as steel. During this time Sir Robert had twice appeared to his wife, who believed him to have been an apparition, from the fact that he could not afterwards be found.

This for a time alarmed her, but this feeling wore away, and she began to rejoice at the prospect of hearing he was dead, as she felt he must be dead, else he would have sent to her for money, and as it was, she had not even heard of him directly or indirectly since he had left the fight at Worcester.

Often did Sir Robert lay and see the enemies of his country, of his king, and his own personal enemies, enjoy the best his estates were capable of producing. This often made the sturdy old knight swear and menace the visitors with his clenched fist, but when they could not see him, it availed nothing; but he felt relieved by the exertion—it was a kind of satisfaction, the only one of the kind that he felt or was capable of exerting.

The times were changed, and the death of the Protector came like new and joyful tidings. That evening Sir Robert drank plentifully of wine to the health of the king and the eternal perdition of old Noll and his fanatical followers; he indulged deeply, and compelled his three faithful servitors, the only beings who held communication with him for years, to join, not unwillingly, in his potations, and the result was almost a discovery. However, the affair was got over, and the landing of the king gave such universal joy, that the Roundheads hid themselves.

Sir Robert, having made himself known to his vassals, armed them, and enjoined them to keep the secret, and in the midst of a feast, he walked into the midst of them in his ragged and torn vests, with his cavalier bonnet and sword.

There was a terrible consternation, and swords were drawn, but the servants rushed between their old master and his enemies; and the lady fainted, and eventually died from the effects of fright.

The book fell from his hands, the fatigue of reading had almost induced sleep, and he lay in a state between sleeping and waking. The tale conjured up several reflections that employed his mind, and then his thoughts reverted back to past scenes, to the one whom he loved, and who was now another's, who must be hateful to her. While he lay thus, he heard the nurse enter the room; she walked quietly and stealthily to the bed, and drawing the curtains aside, she looked to see if he were awake. He opened his eyes, and looked at her.

"I beg your pardon, sir; but I thought you were asleep. How do you find yourself?'

"Better. I was not asleep."

"Do you think you are well enough to receive a letter that has been left for you this morning?"

"A letter for me?"

"Yes, sir."

"Yes, I am well enough to read that certainly, if I am well enough to read anything else,"

"Well, but I mean you will not let it disturb you, else Doctor Russel will blame me for letting you have it at all."

"No, no. Give it to me."

The nurse handed him the letter, and as soon as he saw the hand-writing, he tore it open, and read as follows:—

"THEODORE,—Chance has informed me of your state, and where you are. Had I known your danger before, I would have flown ere this to have whispered some words of consolation in your ear, and be assured that if we are separated by the hand of death, in losing you I have lost the only being whom I could truly and fondly love. I will come and see you by sunset, and if fate so ordain it, take that farewell of you that will for ever remain indelibly imprinted on my heart.

"MARGARET BERTRAM."

Theodore wanted to rise, and begged the nurse to aid him to dress; but she succeeded in persuading him of the impropriety and danger of such a step, and also in allaying much of the agitation by which he was moved. She, however, promised that the person when she called should be shown up, if he conformed to the doctor's rules.

Having thus gained her point, Theodore lay back upon his pillow, and indulging in pleasing and painful reflections, he fell into a light slumber.

CHAPTER XXX.

THE INJUDICIOUS COURSE PURSUED BY MRS. BERTRAM.—MRS. BLAIR DISCOVERS THE WEAK SIDE OF THE MONTHLY NURSE, AND PROFITS THEREBY.

THE shock Mrs. Bertram had experienced by hearing thus suddenly of poor Theodore Danton's situation, in all the exaggerated colours in which the disappointed and malicious nurse dressed it, was more than enough to produce the most serious indisposition in her delicate frame. She remained in a state of insensibility quite long enough to alarm every one in the house, and particularly to awaken in the mind of her husband the most serious apprehensions.

It is a homely, but none the less true saying on that account, that we never know the value of anything or anybody until we are placed in circumstances that warrant, or seem to warrant, the supposition that we are about to be separated from it or them for ever. So it was with Mr. Bertram as regarded his wife. While she was in health, and there appeared no probability that death was about to step between them, he was so full of jealous anger that he could almost have imagined her dead with a feeling of satisfaction; but now that real danger appeared at hand, he forgot in a great measure his jealousy, and all the latent tenderness of his heart towards her rose up again to reproach him for what he had already done to make her unhappy.

He began now to consider—which, for a man of his jealous temperament, was going a great away,—that she might be innocent; and, as he looked upon her insensible form, he almost wondered how he could ever have uttered a harsh word to one so helpless and so beautiful. He took the nurse aside, while Mrs. Blair was busy in applying such restoratives as were at hand, previous to the arrival of a physician, who had been sent for, and asked her what had been the cause of the sudden and severe indisposition of his wife.

"Lauks a *mussy*, sir," was the reply of that lady, "young wives, sir, with their first, is always a making a unkimmon fuss about nothink. It's all in the way o' natur', sir. I dare say she felt flurried, and we all knows what flurry will do."

"Then you think she will recover?"

"Recover, sir! I should think so. Look at me. Now, sir, I'm as delicate a female woman as never was. You'd be amused and bamboozled, sir, if you know'd half o' what I'se gone through; and, you see, here I is yet."

There certainly could not be two opinions upon that point, for if the nurse had been about a third of the circumferential dimensions she was, no one could have had any difficulty in at once recognising her presence.

Mr. Bertram felt a little relieved in his mind at the cool, off-hand, professional sort of way in which the nurse treated the matter, and he began to think he was tormenting himself without sufficient cause. Then, as the nurse gave him a hint to leave the sick room, by saying, that the lady would be agitated when she recovered, if she saw him, he went to his own study, desiring to be informed directly Mrs. Bertram had recovered consciousness.

If he, Mr. Bertram, wondered at the sudden indisposition of his wife, Mrs. Blair wondered still more, and could not but believe that there must be some special reason, which perhaps the nurse was aware of.

A woman of such an intriguing disposition as Mrs. Blair was always apt to fancy that there was a great deal more in any circumstance than ever met the eye, and she resolved that the monthly nurse should not leave the house until she had detailed to her, Mrs. Blair, all that had passed between her and poor Mrs. Bertram.

When the physician came he soon succeeded in restoring the lady to consciousness, and declared there was no danger.

"I will look in again," he said, "in the course of the day, as it would be injudicious just now to question her as to the cause of her fainting, even if she is aware of any cause. Let her be kept quiet, and questioned by no one. She will probably go to sleep."

The curtains of the bed on which Mrs. Bertram lay were accordingly drawn, and as she really showed some disposition to sleep, the room was darkened, and she was left to herself.

The physician politely asked for Mr. Bertram, and was shown into that gentleman's study, for physicians have no idea of going away without their fee;

but, as he can have nothing to say to Bertram which can be at all interesting to the reader, we need not detail their conversation, but will proceed at once to state what passed between Mrs. Blair and the nurse, and what steps the housekeeper took contingent thereon.

When the arrangements were made in Mrs. Bertram's chamber which left her to herself, Mrs. Blair turned to the nurse, and in her most winning accents, she said,—

"Pray walk into my room; I am sure you must be tired.l'

"I thanks you was y, mum," said the nurse, "and as I is to be Mrs. B.'s monthly, why, in course, I likes to be on good terms with everybody, mum."

"Certainly, certainly. This way, if you please."

"Thank you, mum"

"I am only so glad that Mrs. Bertram has entered into an arrangemen- with so respectable a person as your self."

"You are wastly polite, mum. Oh, werry."

By this time they had reached Mrs.

Blair's own room, and when the door was closed, that lady made at once an experiment which her knowledge of human nature generally, and of nurse nature in particular, enabled her to know would in all likelihood be eminently successful.

"I don't know how you feel, nurse," she said, "but for my part, anything of this sort flurries me to that extent, that I don't get the better of it till I have taken a little drop of something to settle my nerves."

"Lor!" exclaimed the nurse, lifting up her hands and turning her great yellow looking eyes to the ceiling, "how very strange. Well, I never, now. How very strange."

"What's strange?"

"The *similitatitory* of our dispositions. Anybody would say as we were sisters. It's really one o' the oddest things in the world, but I feel just the same pain, and no sort o' difference."

"How very odd."

"Yes. I feels a kind o' sinking here, and when I does feel it, I could take my oath, unless I gets a drop of something, I goes on getting *worserer*."

"No doubt, no doubt. What would you prefer?"

"My dear creature, I prefer never a one thing over another; but constitution, of course, is everything, and one's bound to take what agrees with one, and not to be on continual bad terms with one's inside."

"Certainly not."

"Then, if there is anything o' that nature that makes me feel more comfortable nor another, I must say it's gin."

Scarcely had the words left her lips, when a bottle of the soothing liquid was produced, and after one glass, the nurse declared herself to be wonderfully better; and Mrs. Blair having thus discovered that even a monthly nurse had her weak side, at once commenced her inquiries.

"Did Mrs. Bertram complain of indisposition before she fainted?"

"Not a bit—not a bit. She went off like a lamb."

"Indeed."

"Yes. She was a talking as comfortable as needs be; and I was remarking to myself and saying as it would be September afore I was wanted, which is a comfort, because Mrs. Entwhistle is agoing to be down with her eighth in November, and all this will be over afore then."

"Yes, of course. What were you talking about? Allow me to fill your glass?"

"No, no—now really——But it is mild, and so I dare say it won't do no harm, or else I would not venture; I'm not the woman I was."

"Yes; and so you were talking of nothing particular?"

"No; I can't say as we was. Really I was just a-talking about the sick gentleman as I was attending to, and she asked me if his Christianity name was Theodore, and, when I says 'Yes, ma'am,' says I, 'it were,' down she goes, in a faint away situation, like any flounder."

Here was news for Mrs. Blair! Now she understood in a moment why Mrs. Bertram had fainted, and she congratulated herself at the tact she had displayed in detaining the nurse to get from her a communication of so much importance. She, however, controlled successfully any indication of exultation, and, with a calmness of manner which showed that she was no bad actress, she said,—

"And who is this Theodore?"

"Oh, a good-looking enough young man. He's been uncommon ill, and is now dead, I shouldn't wonder."

"And his name is Theodore?"

"Yes—yes."

"But of course he has a sirname?"

"Oh, dear, yes, he has; it was me as found out what his sirname was. Nobody know'd it till I found it out; and then, quite promiscuous one day, as I was moving some of his things, there comed open a leather desk; in a writing case, and inside, was his name, Theodore Danton, and then I told some of 'em at the hotel, cos they hadn't the least idea of who he was."

"Indeed. Did you say he was a fair young man?"

"Oh, bless you, no—quite the other way—dark he was, most decided, and black eyes he had as never was seen."

"It must be he," thought Mrs. Blair; "it is Mrs. Bertram's cousin; it is he whom I encountered at the door of the house. Here is material now to influence the already enkindled jealousy of Bertram with. What will Mrs. Bertram do? What course of conduct will she adopt?"

"One would almost have thought she knowed him," said the nurse, "she went off so complete when she heard his name."

"Oh, I don't think that," remarked Mrs. Blair. "She's very delicate, and, no doubt, was a little excited at seeing you, which made her more ready to faint at anything which awakened her sympathies."

"Well; I can't say; it may be so, or it may not. No—no—not another drop. What if it was to get into my head? I should never forgive myself; no—never."

Notwithstanding her horror of intemperance, she now contrived to take another glass, and even another glass after that, so that, at length, when she rose to go, which was a movement necessarily waited for by Mrs. Blair, she moved to the door in anything but a straightforward manner.

Mrs. Blair, herself, left her out, for she did not wish any of the servants to perceive the condition of the nurse; but that was a feeling which arose from no consideration towards that personage, only she knew well that they must know it was in her, Mrs. Blair's, company that she must have got drunk, and she did not wish to lie under such an imputation.

The moment she had got rid of her, Mrs. Blair proceeded to Mr. Bertram's study door, from whence the physician had not long emerged, for it being that gentleman's first visit to the house of the Bertrams, he had given some time to making himself as agreeable as he could, in the hope of making a good connexion.

Mrs. Blair's countenance wore a wonderful air of triumph as she tapped at the door of the study, but the moment Mr. Bertram said "Come in," she altered its expression to one of serious concern; and, opening the door very gently, as was her custom, she entered the apartment with that cat-like tread which always characterised her movements when she was not in a pas-

sion, and forgetful of her usual caution and duplicity.

The politeness of the physician had been rather a bore, as far as Mr. Bertram was concerned, and, probably, had he not stayed, Mrs. Blair's conference with the nurse, short as it was, would have been broken up. But it so happened just then, that everything had played into Mrs. Blair's hands, and every little circumstance had conspired to make her successful in the diabolical manœuvres she was so intent upon.

Did she believe, for one moment, that Mrs. Bertram was guilty, or that she harboured one thought of guilt? No, no! a thousand times no. Mrs. Blair was by far too good a judge of human nature for that. She knew virtue, when she saw it, well, and if she had been so situated that it was for her advantage to do so, she could have freely staked her life upon the innocence of Mrs. Bertram, and yet that very circumstance seemed, if possible, to add to the bitterness of her feelings against her.

But it is, and has always been, a characteristic of vice to hate virtue—of honesty to abhor dishonesty. The sort of hatred which those fallen angels that are debarred the bliss and the glory of the presence of the Almighty may be supposed to feel against those who shall dwell in such sunshine of joy, may, on a smaller scale, be supposed to be felt by those who traverse the paths of vice against those who still sit in the light of the majesty of virtue.

As religious fanatics of all grades and denominations are ever mad to make proselytes, so are those who have fallen from the high estate of innocence ever anxious to pull down who they can with them. The next satisfaction to that in their minds, is to make some one who is really innocent suffer all the consequences of imputed guilt, and such was what Mrs. Blair was attempting as regarded Mrs. Bertram.

"Well, Mrs. Blair," said Bertram, eagerly; "how is Mrs. Bertram now? The physician told me she had recovered."

"She has recovered, sir."

"Is she sleeping?"

"I believe she is, and I am happy, of course, because you must naturally, from the kindness of your disposition feel anxious, to be able to assure you that she will soon be as well as before, and that it is no physical ailment."

"What do you mean?"

"I mean, sir, that it was a mental shock that produced the attack of faintness, and such being the case, it will not occur again, probably. She will, no doubt, now summon presence of mind sufficient to conquer any outward exhibition of feeling."

"You speak in riddles. What mental shock has she experienced? I have just now assured the physician that it was impossible such could be the case."

"You were wrong, sir. But, so far as he is concerned, that makes no difference whatever as to what may ensue."

"Mrs. Blair, explain yourself. You have something to tell me, I know, by your manner. Let me know it at once, that I may decide how far my peace of mind may be affected or compromised thereby."

"Sir, I fear to tell you."

"You fear?"

"Yes. Because it is natural that you should feel indignation, and I dread that, in the excitement of such a feeling, you may take some hasty step."

"Good God!"

"Nay, sir, express no emotion. Consider the present situation of Mrs. Bertram, and to what serious censure you would expose yourself. If you will promise to me that you will be calm——"

"Yes, yes, yes."

"And that you will not adopt any hasty course—that you wait, at least, twelve hours before you do anything at all in the matter, I do not mind telling you all I know of the affair."

"I promise, I promise," said Mr. Bertram, in a voice half choked with emotion; and then Mrs. Blair proceeded, in a low tone of voice,—

"I had some conversation with the nurse, in whose presence this fainting fit occurred, and from that woman, who can, of course, confirm to you my words, you will hear that the fainting arose from the sudden shock Mrs. Bertram received upon being told of the serious illness of one Theodore Danton."

"Theodore Danton?"

"Yes; her—*cousin.*"

"Yes, yes; her—perhaps pretended cousin. It is a convenient tie of relationship—one easily wrapped up in mystery. D——n! what of him?"

"Hush! hush! You promised to be calm."

"I—I am calm—very—d—d calm. Go on."

"It appears that he has, unknown to her, been seriously ill—nay, in a dying state. He may, indeed, be dead."

"Dead! Thank Heaven!"

"Nay, I do not say he is dead; but it was the thought that he might be which has produced Mrs. Bertram's indisposition."

Bertram clasped his hands over his head for a moment, and then he said, suddenly,—

"How did that nurse know so much?"

"She nursed Theodore Danton."

"Vengeance! Curses——"

"Hold! Is this being calm? She may be innocent."

"Innocent — innocent! and faint away at the mere mention of his name, in combination with a statement of his illness! Innocent! No—no—no! Impossible!"

"Do not decide too hastily. You have not sufficient proof. Your wife may admire Theodore Danton—she may pity him—perhaps for feeling an attachment towards her which she cannot reciprocate, but she may not love him; and notwithstanding all that points in her conduct towards an assumption of her guilty thoughts, she may be innocent. Nay, all the more nobly, gloriously innocent, because that she has been placed, perchance, in the way of deep temptation."

Probably this speech, every word of which was so strictly true, presents the character of Mrs. Blair in its most wily aspect. She knew that in uttering it she did not dissipate one of the wild, mad, agonizing feelings that had found a home in the breast of Mr. Bertram; but by uttering it she not only absolved herself from any consequences of what might occur, but she got up an impression in his mind that she was rather inclined to be the eloquent advocate of Mrs. Bertram's innocence than her accuser, and hence anything she might say that was calculated to rouse his jealousy would have a far greater effect.

"This comes," he would say, "from a friend, and, therefore, is not made the most of. There may be yet the most serious particulars concealed."

And Mrs. Blair could afford to be eloquent in speaking of the presumed innocence of Mrs. Bertram. Any fact, or assumed fact, conducive to a belief in her guilt, she knew required no dressing up, but came with far greater force upon the mind of Bertram when told distinctly, and in as few words as possible. Hence she now added,—

"It is impossible, of course, sir, for me or any one else to hope so far to blind your judgment as to attempt to convince you that Mrs. Bertram is indifferent to that gentleman, Theodore Danton; but yet her affection for him may be of a perfectly innocent character."

"An innocent character!" exclaimed Bertram, vehemently, "an innocent character! when a woman faints away at the mere mention of the indisposition of some man who is not her husband!"

"Nay, but, sir——"

"Indeed! D——n! I wonder what amount of indisposition on my part would induce such a result? But I will have revenge. Yes, I will take good care to have ample and speedy revenge."

"You must be, sir, most specially careful. These circumstances, of all others, are such as require the greatest care and vigilance. You must do nothing hastily, or you may do what you may all your life repent of. Let me implore you, sir, to be careful."

"Careful! Careful of what?"

"Of your own peace. If you are convinced, or if you should be convinced that you have just cause for grievous complaint, it is yourself that you should then look to, so that in after years you should be able to say, ' I have acted with firmness, and, at the same time, with moderation.' "

There was something so judicious in this advice, that at once Mr. Bertram could not help being struck with it. After a few moments' silence, he said,—

"Mrs. Blair, I am so thoroughly convinced of your devotion to my interest, and of the accuracy of your intellect, that I shall, without hesitation, adopt any line of conduct you will point out to me."

Mrs. Blair took out her handkerchief and wiped away an imaginary tear from each eye, before, in a voice which had all the sound of being broken by emotion, she replied,—

"Sir, I cannot sufficently thank you for this great mark of esteem. Heaven knows that I have endeavoured to do my duty by you, however difficult, in consequence of recent events, it has been to me. My tears have flown in secret, sir, because of the unworthy manner in which Mrs. Bertram has thought proper to treat me; but while I have the happiness of enjoying your confidence, I shall care for nothing else, but continue to do my duty."

"There, there, Mrs. Blair, do not be affected. This marriage of mine will, I see, be the bane of my existence; but you cannot help that; it is done, and cannot now well be undone."

"As you say, sir."

"Let us reflect camly upon the future. What can I do?"

"Why, sir, of course, in your present frame of mind, you are most anxious to discover how great a degree of intimacy Mrs. Bertram may have with this cousin."

"Yes, yes."

"And you will not forget one circumstance in her favour, which is, that she could not have seen him lately, or heard from him, or else she must have known of his illness, and she would not have been taken so much by surprise as to faint away at the news."

"Mrs. Blair, you are ingenious at finding excuses for Mrs. Bertram."

"Matters are getting serious now, sir, and it is requisite that there should not be the shadow of a doubt upon your mind with regard to any decision you may come to. I hope that you will join with me in endeavouring to find out any imaginable plea that can be urged in Mrs. Bertram's favour."

"And yet you are the woman whom she would gladly have turned from her house!"

"Of course, whenever Mrs. Bertram felt thoroughly convinced that I intended to do my duty by you to the utmost, she hated me."

"Of course—of course, she did; I can easily understand all that; you would not be a confidant and a creature of hers, and, therefore, she takes a dislike to you, because, as a matter of necessity, you must be in her way."

" We will not say that, sir."

" It is the truth, and, therefore, ought to be said. Did this nurse tell you where the—the—cousin was lying ill?"

" Yes, I got that information from her."

" Then—then, I will go and seek him, and demand an explanation of everything. I feel that I ought not to delay another moment."

" Demand an explanation from him! Why, Mr. Bertram, are you mad? What sort of an explanation can you expect at his hands, pray? Go to him? —oh, no. What could he say, but, with as much show of mock solemnity as was in his power, at once attempt to hoodwink your judgment by declaring to you the innocence of your wife. But what am I saying? She may be innocent. Go—go !'

" No—no. I perceive, Mrs. Blair, the struggle that is going on in your mind. You feel certain of my wife's guilt, but you yet hesitate to condemn her to me, and hence this hesitation of manner and these different observations. Your first feelings prompt you to speak the truth, and then, upon reflection, your wish not to be harsh to Mrs. Bertram induces you to say all you can in her favour,"

Mrs. Blair again mopped up some imaginary tears, and looked as if she would have said, " Ah! what penetration ! There is no deceiving you ; you perceive in a moment the kind and benevolent struggle that is going on in my mind."

After a pause, during which Mr. Bertram was resting his head upon his hands, and presenting a complete picture of hopeless despondency, Mrs Blair said—

" My dear sir, compose yourself. The thing will be now to take notice if Mrs. Bertram does anything contingent upon the information she has received of the illness of this young man."

" Yes, yes, yes," groaned Bertram.

" Leave that to me. I will take especial care to find out if she writes to him or visits him."

" Visits him !" exclaimed Bertram, springing to his feet.

" Nay, now, sir, you will remember that it is quite a matter of impossibility

for me to act if you perpetrate any violence. If you will consent to repress your feelings completely, and trust to me to do the best I can, all may be discovered ; but unless you consent to such a course, you will allow me to decline acting at all in the matter."

" Well, well, you know, Mrs. Blair, that I have confidence in you. Do as you please —do as you please."

" And you will attempt nothing, sir ?"

" Nothing—nothing."

" If you see Mrs. Bertram, pray be calm, and say not one word which shall induce in her mind an impression that you suspect the real cause of her fainting."

" I will not."

" Then you will either be convinced by her silence respecting that real cause that there is something connected with it to conceal, or, by a mock confidence, she will seek to lull those suspicions which she may fear others should excite."

With this speech, which she knew would, of course, leave a rankling impression behind it, Mrs. Blair left the room, and Bertram sank into a chair, in a state of mind compounded of such a whirl of conflicting emotions that, for more than hour, his thoughts presented a complete chaos, and all he felt distinctly was, that if, in his present state of mind, he sought his wife, he should be certain to commit himself in a manner which would prevent him having what he supposed to be the great advantage of Mrs. Blair's services

---

CHAPTER XXXI.

PRODUCES MRS. BLAIR IN A NEW LIGHT.—THE LETTER AND THE DISCOVERY. — THE PROJECTED SURPRISE.—THE AMBUSCADE AND THE SPY.

MRS. BERTRAM, poor thing, we were going to say, was ill advised ; but we should rather say that she was not advised at all.

She had but one friend upon whom, in the greatest and strictest confidence, she might have thrown herself for advice and consolation, and that was the Mrs. Ogden whom we have before made mention of. She, however, was now out of town, so that poor Margaret was now left entirely at the mercy of circumstances and an unhappy disposition, which was wanting in that "sterner stuff" that would have enabled her to take some decisive steps that would soon have defeated Mrs. Blair.

Our young readers will not fail to perceive that all the machinations of Mrs. Blair, and all the cleverness with which she contrived to sow the prolific seeds of dissension between Bertram and his wife, might have been rendered nugatory and complete failures, had Margaret Bertram but had resolution enough to have no secret whatever from her husband.

It was in that point that she gave power to the housekeeper, and when once the latter found that such was the case, she looked upon the condemnation of poor Mrs. Bertram as quite certain.

The evils of keeping secrets could not be possibly made more apparent than by the disastrous condition in which Mrs. Bertram was now in. She had hesitated at first to make a confidant of her husband, and now it was too late to do so with any grace. She had herself, too, by such a line of conduct, induced such behaviour on his part towards herself which was calculated still further to repel any confidence on her part, and thus she not only strengthened the bonds of the wicked and most unscrupulous Mrs. Blair, but she made it more difficult still now to extricate herself from the difficulties to which she was subjected, and the still greater ones which were dimly crowding around.

Without mutual confidence in married life, there can be no permanent happiness; it is one of the vainest things in the world to seek for it; and here, in this case of the Bertrams, we see how mutual dissatisfaction, and how mutual distrust arose on both sides, as a consequence of secret keeping.

When Mrs. Bertram recovered from the swoon into which she had fallen when she had so suddenly heard of the severe indisposition and the probable death of Theodore Danton, she easily listened to the physician's counsel to be quiet, and not to engage in any harassing conversation. The fact was, that nothing could just then have given her so much uneasiness as any questioning regarding the real cause of her fainting,

and she was thankful to be left alone to think concerning what had happened.

And oh, how bitterly painful was thought now to her! How it appeared as if, day by day, as evidence thickened upon her mind that her husband loved her not, there came about proofs that some one else was ready to die to prove the deep sincerity of his affection. If anything could bring despair and agony to the breast of any female, this would assuredly suffice to do so.

Affection always, to a certain extent, begets a similar feeling. At least, no one can be ever thoroughly indifferent to any one who loves them; and although Margaret was purity itself as regarded any real thought of evil, yet, could it be expected that she should be able to hear unmoved, that Theodore Danton was dying, when she knew that it was the agony of his disappointment at finding her another's that was hurrying him to the grave?

"Poor Theodore! poor Theodore!" she moaned; "alas! and are you to go to that dreadful grave of hope, and life, and love, uncheered by even a word from me! Oh, God! oh God! what can I do? what can I do?"

A flood of tears came to her relief, and after that gush of feeling had subsided, she began, with as much calmness as she could, to reflect upon what she could possibly do under the circumstances. The idea of remaining in a state of complete ignorance as to whether he, Theodore, was dead or alive, was one which she could not tolerate. Know that much she must, at all events; and when she came to consider that it was just possible that the nurse might have been discharged from attending upon him for other reasons than what she had stated, and, that, although perhaps dangerously ill, he might yet, before death closed his eyes for ever, be sensible of the kindness of a few words from her, the desire to attempt to see him became so strong, that in a few minutes it overwhelmed every other consideration. Then it was that she wrote the letter which has been already laid before the reader, and the worst concerning which that can be said was, that it was an imprudent one to write. And the more especially was it imprudent under the circumstances in which she was placed, when any sort of evidence of that character was calculated to be made the most of against her, and to redound greatly to her prejudice. But when people have their feelings warmly interested, they are not so well qualified to draw accurate conclusions like mere lookers-on. We can see where Mrs. Bertram made serious mistakes, because we happen to know something of the snares that environ her; but the reader must bear in mind that, although she, Mrs. Bertram, had every reason to believe Mrs. Blair to be her enemy, she could not have the remotest idea of the dreadful nature of the plot she was getting up against her, or of the hideous lengths she was inclined to go for the furtherance of her wicked designs.

It was not till the letter was written that Mrs. Bertram recollected that she had had no time to ask the nurse where it was that Theodore Danton was lying so dangerously ill, but we are aware that Mrs Blair possessed that requisite information, and we shall quickly see that she made use of it. To the further progress, however, of Mrs. Bertram, this was a complete stopper, and she, after sealing the letter and directing it to Theodore, laid it down on her dressing-table in utter despair.

For some time no idea occurred to her how to get over this difficulty. There were by far too many hotels in London to send a letter from one to the other on the wild-goose chase of finding a Mr. Theodore Danton. Besides, she could not, let her employ who she would, rely upon their taking that amount of trouble. At length, when nearly exhausted and maddened by their conflicting emotions, she thought of an expedient. She had the card of the monthly nurse, and she of course could direct the letter safely, and at once, to its destination. This no sooner occurred to her than she wrote within a new envelope, in which she enclosed the note to Theodore,—

"Please to address the enclosed, and send it on at once to the hotel where Mr. Danton is staying. He is a relative.

"Yours, &c.,

"MARGARET BERTRAM."

Here, then, was a chance of the letter

reaching Theodore, and by a circuitous route, too, which promised secrecy and safety. She immediately rang her bell, and desired that a footboy who had been recently engaged, and whose name was Thomas, should be sent to her. Upon this lad coming, she handed him the letter, which was now on the outside addressed to the nurse, and said,—

"You will take this letter, Thomas, with as much diligence as you can, and come to me when you return for your reward, which will be in proportion to the speed you make."

This was a sort of promise which was highly calculated, as may be well supposed, to put Thomas on his metal, and he would have been off directly, only that Thomas held in that household rather a peculiar and delicate position. He had been introduced by Mrs. Blair, and to Mrs. Blair he looked for all the good that was to come to him in this world. He was named Thomas Chiffinch, but who Mr. Chiffinch ever was remained a profound mystery; perhaps Mrs. Blair considering that Thomas had good reason to believe that she was his mother. She told him she was his aunt, and coupled the statement with the threat that if ever he divulged that she was even so nearly related to him as that, she would turn her back upon him altogether, and he might starve, or go into the workhouse, just as he pleased.

To Master Thomas neither of these contingencies presented a very alluring aspect, so he rather declined both, and declared himself a firm partizan of his aunt Blair, and wished as he might "stick to the blessed spot where he stood if ever he told nobody as she was nothing to him."

One of the duties of this hopeful youth was, before he went out of the house on a message for anybody or anything, to come to her first with the particulars thereof. Accordingly when he received Mrs. Bertram's note, notwithstanding the reward which was promised him for expedition, he had too great a fear of Mrs. Blair to disobey her injunctions, and he took the note to her at once.

"What is that, Tom?" she said.

"A letter, with a little one inside of it. Missus wants me to take it cuick, and I wish you'd let me be off, for she says as she'll come down handsome in proportion, which, I supposes, means five shillings, at least."

"Silence!" cried Mrs. Blair, as, without the least hesitation in the world, she opened the letter and read what was addressed to the nurse. "Silence, Tom—don't interrupt me, as you value your life."

"Lor!"

"Humph! to forward this immediately," muttered Mrs. Blair. "She don't know his address it appears. Oh, it shall be forwarded, madam, you may depend. I would not keep it back for a trifle. Of course it shall be forwarded—directly, too; but first we will see what it contains."

This was opened as systematically as the first one, and then Mrs. Blair read those few words which Margaret Bertram had, in the agitation of her mind, written to poor Theodore. A smile of most malicious and demoniac meaning came across her face as she muttered,—

"I have her now—I have her now. She is in my power. I have her now, most surely."

"Have who?" said Thomas.

"What is that to you?"

"Oh, I only——"

"And what business have you to only! You ought not to presume even to hear what I say, unless I say it directly to you, much less to make a remark or ask a question about it. Let me have no more of this insolence."

"Well, I never! I'm sure I didn't mean nothing."

"Silence!"

"Very good."

Mrs. Blair re-sealed the letter addressed to Theodore Danton, and then she wrote the name of the hotel and the street in which it was situated, in pencil on the back, after which, turning to Thomas, she said,—

"There; you need not go to the nurse at all. This is the exact address to which you must hasten. Ask if the gentleman named Danton is staying there, and how he is. If he be not dead, you will leave the note; otherwise, you bring it back to me; but, in either case, you come to me before you see Mrs. Bertram."

"Ah, to be sure. I knows—I knows."

"Now, then, be off, and earn your five shillings, if you think there is that amount to be earned, with what diligence you may."

Thomas needed no spur. Off he set, as quickly as he could, to the hotel, where, as we are already well aware, he delivered the note, which set poor Theodore in such a flutter of expectation.

"Now," reasoned Mrs. Blair, "she is completely in my power. She cannot now possibly escape me. Mr. Bertram shall have ocular demonstration of the fact of his wife's visit to her lover and cousin. He shall see her with his own eyes enter a public hotel. My only difficulty now will be to restrain him from committing some act of desperation, which will either involve him in such serious consequences that he shall be compelled to break up his establishment, or some explanation will ensue that will give him confidence in his wife's innocence."

She thought deeply how this could be effected, and the more she though the more she felt convinced that, unless she bound him very solemnly indeed by some promise which he dared not break, he would, upon actually seeing his wife enter Theodore Danton's hotel, rush after her.

"Still," she said, "he must see her. I cannot forego that intense satisfaction. No words and no other species of evidence can have one half of the effect of his seeing her himself. After that I would say nothing, insinuate nothing. All I shall then have to do will be to get a separation between them effected as quickly as possible, so that each shall think themselves so much ill-used by the other, that all attempt at explanation would be degrading."

She could see no way of keeping Mr. Bertram at all within bounds than by extracting from him beforehand some very solemn promise so to do, and then keeping so near to him at the moment when he himself should be perhaps, in the excitement of his jealousy, unable to control himself, as to exercise over him that amount of moral control which she had already succeeded in acquiring over his imagination.

"That is all I can do," she said; "and if even then he should become so ungovernable that I cannot keep him out of the hotel, I must even go in with him and take care that the scene which shall ensue is not one to create anything in the shape of an explanation."

In this kind of reflection she awaited anxiously the arrival of Thomas, who, to do him justice, accomplished the distance between the house of the Bertrams and the hotel, and back again, in much shorter time than could have been at all reasonably expected, considering that Thomas carried upon his bones ample evidence that the Bertrams kept a good kitchen. He made his way at once to his aunt's private room, and the moment she saw him, she said,—

"Well, well—be quick. Have you found him ?"

"Oh, yes; he ain't dead, but they say as he's precious bad."

"Indeed !"

"Oh, ah, I believe you. I seed one o' the waiters, and he says as it's a infection o' the something with a *spine* and a *menbrain*. A precious learned fellow, that waiter. I tried to say some o' his hard words, and loosened two o' my front teeth, I can tell you."

"Peace ! I want none of your buffoonery. You will now go to your mistress and tell her that you got the address from the nurse, mind, and then took the letter on yourself. You understand ?"

"Oh, yes ; oh yes."

"Let her put what question to you she may, mind you stick to that. You will ruin yourself if you make a blunder of this."

"A blunder ! Lor, it's as easy as lying ; I should think I'll make no blunder, aunt."

"Silence. If I hear you call me aunt again, within the walls of this house, out you go, and I will take no further trouble about you. You are well aware that I have no desire that our relationship should be known."

"More have I," said Thomas, as he left his aunt's room, and hastened to find his mistress. "If the servants knew as I was any relation o' yours, a nice dog's life I should lead in the kitchen; they do love you so, and so don't I; oh, yes, above a bit, no how, with the fat end up'ards."

Thomas found Mrs. Bertram in the room where he had left her. She was so agitated when she saw him that she could not speak, so, without having any questions asked him, he told her, in his own way, that he had been to the nurse, and then to the hotel, and that he had not seen the gentleman, but he had left the note for him.

Margaret then had just power to gasp,—

"Thank God, he lives."

"Yes, ma'am; but they say as he's jolly bad, ma'am."

"But he lives! but he lives, and he may yet recover!"

She wrote upon the back of one of her own cards the name of the hotel and the address. Then she presented Thomas with only half-a-crown instead of five shillings, as he expected; and, surely, that was enough, considering that Thomas was paid as well in the aggregate for his services.

CHAPTER XXXII.

THE VISIT OF MRS. BERTRAM TO THE HOTEL, AND ITS CONSEQUENCES.

WHEN Mrs. Bertram was alone, her first impulse was to look at a bracket clock that was in her room, to see what time must elapse before she could keep her self-imposed engagement with Theodore Danton. She found that only two hours must pass away ere it would be time, at all events, to leave home, in order to get to the hotel at the appointed hour, and the reader may well imagine in what a state of intense agitation those two hours were passed.

At one moment she would blame herself for making the agitation, and feel that she not only ought not to have done so, but that she should not have strength enough to carry out her intention. Then again she would call herself barbarous and cruel that she hesitated for an instant in imparting to Theodore such consolation as was possible in his great affliction.

"A visit from me will, by such a mind as his," she said, "be considered in its proper light. He will place no misconstruction upon the circumstance of my coming to his sick chambers. Besides, he is a relation of my own— the only one I now have in the world— and common feeling and common humanity should dictate to me the course I am now pursuing."

An hour elapsed, and she looked from her window upon the night. She shrank as she did so, for it was a most unpropitious one—one upon which her going out at all was certain to produce remark.

The rain was coming down fast, and the wind blew around the chimney tops, and roared and howled down them, sometimes sending down clouds of smoke that were prevented from rising by the strength of the wind. The rain pattered against the windows, and each raw gust of wind brought an accession, that sounded mournfully and dismally, and caused a melancholy, saddening feeling to the heart.

She looked down upon the streets— and listened to the damp, pattering sound of feet, and the click and screech of the patten, more than which nothing conveys so strong an impression of the bad and inclement weather that may reign, or at least all those signs produce so gloomy a feeling in the mind, that nothing but some strong and urgent motive could induce any one voluntarily to brave the evening.

She listened to the sound of the passers-by—but they were few and solitary; now and then a carriage would roll by, probably a hackney carriage; for who would allow their horses to be out in such weather, unless, indeed, some powerful reason existed? The rich care not for human cattle, they are more careful of their brutes.

Such an evening was not one on which Mrs. Bertram would have gone out, almost under any circumstances that could be named. She looked out on the weather, and shrunk from it; but she had resolved to go—she had written to say so; he might be dead, but she would go. The thoughts that occupied her mind were more than sad and melancholy, they were gloomy and full of grief, and a deeper shade of sorrow was thrown by the sounds and appearance of the weather.

The sky was overcharged with one mass of dark clouds, the sunset was no moment of beauty and pleasure—the sun sank without a lingering trace of his course, and the only difference in colour was when some cloud more surcharged with rain than others came over, pouring out a greater deluge of rain than those hanging around it. Thus passed the hour of sunset, and, the sun once below the horizon, the night set in gloomy, dark and bleak. Margaret could imagine easily all these evils of the weather, although she saw them not, but still she would not be deterred from the expedition she had undertaken on such a ground, and she said to herself repeatedly—

"I will keep my word—I will keep my word. I will go, since I have pledged myself so to do. He shall not have to say that I promised something on the impulse of a generous feeling, which in my calmer judgment I would not perform. No—he shall not accuse me of that."

And then all her reflections, let them assume what character they would, came round to the point that she would go, and she must go, although she trembled so much as the time approached that she feared after all her courage would fail her, and she should be unable to proceed. Again and again she looked to the weather, and she had the consolation of, at all events, seeing that the rain had abated, although the state of the streets was not likely to be improved by that circumstance. Then she wondered much that her husband had not been to inquire how she was, and when she rang for lights, which she did earlier than they were really required, she asked if he was in the house. The answer was in the negative, although the servant said he had not been gone out long. Margaret breathed more freely when she heard he was out, and she said—

"In a quarter of an hour from now, have a hackney-coach at the street-door for me."

"A—a hackney-coach, ma'am? There's the carriage, ma'am, if you please, I can order it."

"I do not want the carriage," said Margaret. "The distance I have to go is very short indeed."

This was no argument for a person keeping a carriage not so to use it, but of course it was not the footman's province at all to argue the point with his mistress, so he merely bowed, and said—

"Certainly, madam, certainly. A coach shall be ready at the time you mention;" and then he went down into the kitchen to put on his hat to go for the vehicle, and as he did so, to expatiate to the servants generally upon the oddness of his mistress wanting at that hour a hackney-coach to go out in by herself, too.

"Now, I'll tell you my opinion," said the cook, looking as wise as the learned pig; "she's a-going to look after master."

"Lor! you don't mean that?" said John.

"Yes, I do. Where I lived once before, there was the same thing. Missus was jealous o' master, and she used to drive about after him."

What a mistaken hypothesis was this. Poor Margaret Bertram had but one fear now in the world, and that was, that by one of those extraordinary accidents that do sometimes get the better of all likelihood, she should meet her husband. Poor Margaret, had she known it, but she did not even make the inquiry, would have been glad to hear that Mrs. Blair was out likewise. Alas! how little she guessed the errand upon which both her husband and the housekeeper had gone.

John got the best-looking hackney-coach he could find, and that was not a very good-looking one, for on a decidedly wet evening, vehicles are sent out into the streets of London, which otherwise would never make their appearance, and this happened to be one of that occasionally used number. Within ten minutes or so of the time when she judged Theodore would be expecting her, Mrs. Bertram descended the staircase of her house, and crossing the hall, was assisted into the lumbering vehicle that stood at the door.

"Where to, ma'am?" said the footman, touching the front of his forehead.

This was a question which Margaret had forgotten to prepare herself to answer. She did not wish to name the hotel actually to which she was going, so she just on the impulse of the moment gave the name of the street in which it was situated. This was duly communicated to the coachman, and after swagging a great many times from side to side, the vehicle got fairly in motion.

*   *   *   *

During these two long and weary hours to Mrs. Bertram, Mrs. Blair was not idle. When she had completed all her arrangements as regarded the letter, and ascertained from Thomas that all was right, and that he had delivered the epistle to Theodore Danton, she smiled to herself, as she said—

"Now is the time for action. Now I shall have my work to do with this enraged husband. What a storm I have raised. Why, any one but me would shrink appalled from it. But what care I? Ha, ha! What care I, so that I compass my own ends? All will be well, and I shall triumph over every obstacle, and at last completely overcome this virtuous Mrs. Bertram. She and her husband shall separate, and I will reign supreme mistress of his house, and of all his domestic expenditures, or never more let any one attempt such a project. If I fail, let all others despair."

With a confident step, so different from that of Mrs. Bertram, that any one who had gone superficially into the mysteries of the human mind might have been inclined to transpose the relative positions of the two, and that she, Mrs. Blair, was the innocent party, and Mrs. Bertram was the guilty one, the fiendish housekeeper now took her way to the study of Mr. Bertram, whom she was so "fooling to the top of his bent."

But innocence often trembles while guilt is bold, and it was truly so in this remarkable instance. Margaret Bertram, who was the very soul of honour and rectitude, was going with trembling nerves to do an act for which an angel in its purity could not have blamed her; while Mrs. Blair with a confident mien was about to perpetuate a piece of villany such as, let us hope, for the sake of human nature, there were few indeed who would even have contemplated.

Mr. Bertram was expecting her with a feverish anxiety that made him as wretched as any human being could possibly be. Each minute had appeared to him to be an hour of agony, and yet but five-and-twenty minutes had elapsed since she had left him, and during that time Thomas had been with the letter to the hotel and returned.

This interview between Mrs. Blair and Mr. Bertram, the reader will bear in mind, took place during the time that Mrs. Bertram was passing those two hours of intense anxiety which preceded her starting to keep her appointment with Theodore Danton at the hotel. She repressed the look of triumph that had made her eyes sparkle as she walked from her own apartment to that of Mr. Bertram, and she wore rather, when she opened the door of his study and entered it, which she did without an announcement, a look of deep dejection. She seemed to him as if a dreadful and a stern duty only impelled her forward, and that she was most unhappy in having to be the means of convincing him of his own dishonour.

He advanced a step to meet her, as he said,—

"Speak—speak? Have you ascertained all?"

"I have."

"Keep me not in suspense! Oh, keep me not a moment in suspense! What have you learned?"

"Mr. Bertram," said Mrs. Blair, with such a serious countenance that he found himself compelled to listen to her—"Mr. Bertram, before I shall enter into the subject upon which I now come to you, I must exact from you so solemn a promise that it shall not be in your power to break it."

"A promise of what?—Good God! a promise of what?"

"A promise that you will abstain from a particular course, which I know, and which it is natural you should be much tempted to pursue."

"Go on—go on. You have but to demand and I will promise. What is it you require?"

"Plainly this. You must promise me that you will not to-night, let you be placed in what circumstance you may, seek an interview with Theodore Danton or with your wife?"

"Good heavens! then you have some news to tell me which ——"

"Nay, sir; I answer no questions. What I have to say remains unsaid unless you promise me that which I have required of you as solemnly as one human being can promise anything to another."

"As solemnly?"

"Yes, as solemnly. I wish you to use the name of heaven even in the promise which you shall make to me, for I wish that it should be binding on your very soul."

Mr. Bertram looked surprised, and Mrs. Blair, with her arms folded, schooled her countenance to an expression of calmness, which did, and was sure to give her a great power over so irascible a man.

Nothing can tend more to give one person a kind of moral control over another than temper. Let an individual be in ever so irascible a state of mind, he or she is sure to feel the influence of calmness in another; and now Bertram felt that he was mentally inferior to the woman who fixed her glance upon and camly demanded of him so solemn an asseveration. He was, however, too impatient to know that which she acknowledged she had to communicate to him to haggle about the terms in which the communication was to be couched, and he said,—

"Dictate what oath you will, and I will take it, though its weight shall sink me to the lowest depths of perdition."

"It will not do so, because there is nothing to prevent you from keeping it, Mr. Bertram. Its being kept depends entirely upon yourself. You must swear that you will see that which shall be presented to your observation to-night, and not to-night take any steps connected therewith."

"I swear."

"By all your hopes hereafter?"

"By all my hopes both here and hereafter."

"That will do."

"Well—well?"

"I will take you to where you shall see your wife cross the threshold of an hotel."

"An hotel?"

"Yes; to visit ——"

"Who—who?—God of Heaven, who?"

He started up, and laid his hand with so firm a clutch upon Mrs. Blair's arm, that his finger-nails dug into her flesh, and it was with a half scream of pain that she added close to his ear—

"Her *seducer!*"

Bertram staggered back as if he had been shot. All his violence of manner in a moment deserted him. Those words seemed to deprive him of the power of action; and yet, surely he must have expected them, or something to the same purport. Still, there was something in the actual words themselves which at once, and for the moment, completely unnerved him.

Mrs. Blair saw the effect she had produced. Perhaps she really did not intend to be so very energetic; but she was not sorry that she had been so, now that she saw how completely she had prostrated him. This state of inaptitude for everything, however, was sure soon to pass away, and when she saw that the colour was again revisiting his cheeks, she stepped close up to him, and said—

"Remember your oath."

She was determined that these words should be the first that rung in his ears when he did recover himself sufficiently to understand what was said to him.

"Yes, yes," he gasped.

"You will be guided by me?"

"Like—like a child."

"'Tis well, Mr. Bertram, and for your own benefit. I am the best, perhaps I ought to say the only friend you have in the world. You shall know all now, and see all. There shall be no doubt upon your mind, because now there is no doubt upon mine."

"None—none."

"And you will do me the justice to say that I have fought hard against coming to this, to me, most painful conclusion."

"You have, indeed. I can do you that justice. You have acted to me as her counsel. Be under no apprehension that any one can blame you. Your conduct is most unimpeachable; I will stand between you and all calumny."

"I am satisfied. God help us all. The fellowship of grace be with us. Now, sir, if you will come with me, I can place you where you will see quite enough to at once satisfy you that Mrs. Bertram visits this Theodore Danton at his hotel in secret. She will be there about sunset."

"If this be so," said Bertram, as he held up his hand solemnly, "I take another oath."

"To what?—to what?"

"Never to sleep another night beneath this roof."

"Oh, that is folly—madness. Had you taken, now, an oath that she should never sleep another night beneath your roof, there might have been some sense in such an arrangement."

"No—no—no, I swear to that I have said. I am heart-broken, and yet dangerous. Let him beware who has made me what I am. I say, let him beware."

"Remember your oath to me."

"I will not forget it. You shall find that I can be calm—that I can, when I please, school myself to calmness. You shall find that I will keep my oath to the very letter. My revenge must be a matter of reflection, not of impulse. Oh, I shall be wonderfully cool and collected."

"Come, then, at once."

He snatched his hat from the table where he had placed it.

"I am ready," he said. "I am quite ready—quite—quite."

Mrs. Blair soon equipped herself, and, with Mr. Bertram, she left the house on the worst errand mortal ever ventured on before the face of Heaven.

CHAPTER XXXIII.

THEODORE DANTON'S IMPATIENCE.—THE NURSE'S ALARM. — DR. RUSSEL'S COUNSEL.—THE HOUR OF THE APPOINTMENT.

THE sleep that Theodore Danton fell into after the receipt of the letter that was written by Mrs. Bertram, lasted some time. The excitement he had felt at the time had exhausted him much, and the slumber was the consequence. The nurse began to congratulate herself upon the turn things had taken, for at first she feared it would have been otherwise; but the present sleep, which had become deep and lasting, would more than repair the evil that might have been done by the previous excitement.

It was now about an hour to the time that had been named for the meeting, and Theodore Danton showed some uneasy signs in his movements and breathing. He turned once or twice, and muttered some words that were inarticulate, and the nurse looked upon him as he lay thus uneasily, and a few moments more scarce elapsed before he opened his eyes, and looked around as if to collect his thoughts.

"Is she come?" he muttered "Is she come?" And he looked around uneasily.

"There is no one here," said the nurse; "but compose yourself and remain quiet; so much depends upon that."

"Is she come?" he muttered, in a low tone, and seemed scarce to comprehend the answer that was given.

"No one is here," again replied the nurse, calmly; "no one at all."

"And yet she said she would come; yes, she wrote to say so. Is it a dream? Did I dream that beautiful vision? It must have been a fond imagining of fancy; and yet I must have heard more than this. Did I have a letter, nurse? Did I not receive one?"

"Yes," said the nurse, "I gave you one."

"Then 'tis no fancy—no vision. She will come, then; she will come. Where is the letter—the letter?"

"You had it sir. I did not notice what you did with it."

Theodore searched about, and found he had placed it beneath the pillow on which he lay. He took it up, and read it through and through.

"Ay," he said, "she said sunset. It is that within an hour—ay, an hour, and then I must see her, yes—once again, I must get up—I must get up and see her."

"You cannot get up, sir," said the nurse.

"Cannot get up?"

"No, sir; it would be dangerous, and, for aught I know, more than dangerous. It may cost you your life."

"It may," said Danton; "but I would not mind that. I must see her —I must rise."

"Indeed, sir, you must not. Recollect the injunctions of Doctor Russel; and, besides, you would be unable to keep up a few minutes, even if you could succeed in rising, which I very much doubt, for I do not think you have strength enough to do so. You are not aware of what you have suffered, and how truly weak you are."

"You may be right, but I am stronger than you think for. I can rise —I will rise; if death be the penalty, it shall be paid; but rise I must and will."

"Well, sir, but you do not consider——"

"I do consider, and it is consideration alone that prompts me to do what I have resolved upon. I must rise."

The nurse was much alarmed, and tried various methods to soothe and persuade him. He was much agitated, and he trembled; there was a heightened colour that stole to his pallid cheeks every now and then, but it fled as quickly as it came. This caused the nurse much inward pain, for she felt that, should he succeed in getting up, and perhaps going out, there would be the greatest danger imaginable.

"If you get up, sir," said the nurse, driven to despair, "all I have to tell you is, I will not be answerable for the consequences, and I can with safety predict that you will be too weak and faint to see the lady."

"If my strength do fail me," he said, "all I can do has been done; and yet I feel too strongly, and have too urgent motives for doing this, and that alone would give me strength."

"Ah! you know not what you do."

Theodore made no reply, but began to dress himself, and in part succeeded: but when he came to stand on the floor, then it was that he began to feel his weakness; his knees knocked together, and he found himself unable to stand without support. He paused for a moment or two, and then the nurse said to him,—

"You are too weak by far to make this attempt. Are you not deceived in yourself? Let me persuade you to return to bed."

"No, no," said Theodore, falling on the bed in an almost fainting condition, "I must rise and see her; you know not the feelings that urge me to do it."

"I can understand their strength," said the nurse, "and believe that they are stronger than you are; but here comes Doctor Russel."

At that moment Doctor Russel, unseen by Theodore Danton, entered the room, and appeared much amazed to see his patient lying on the bed, on the coverlet, half dressed.

"What is the meaning of this, nurse?" he said; "how came Mr. Danton up like this?"

"Indeed I could not help it, sir," she said; "he has had a note, and he has not been the same man since."

"Mr. Danton," said Doctor Russel, "really this is not only imprudent in you, but it is positively hurtful and dangerous; you must permit yourself to be placed in bed again."

"Indeed I cannot."

"You have had a note; it was imprudent to give it to you in your state."

"No, no; had it been otherwise, I should have rendered all your kind aid and skill useless. I could not have survived."

"Well, tell me what it is that you wish done, as far as you deem necessary to a stranger," said Doctor Russel, kindly.

"I was about to leave England, and leave her I loved more than life. She has heard I was dying, and is coming to see me; let me see her, and then, if my life be the penalty, I will cheerfully pay it."

"Come, come," said Dr. Russel, "you must not agitate yourself so much; and if it will restore your calmness, I will give you my opinion, that this interview, if not too agitating a one, will not be so hurtful as denying it you."

"Thank you, sir. I must see her— I should die did I not. I will merely sit up in a chair in another room."

"No, you had better not quit this room nor your bed, there is danger in that; and, should you desire it, you can be dressed, and lay on the outside of the bed; but you must do this, because, in fact, you cannot see her at all otherwise,—you'll faint, and be insensible."

"I will adopt your counsel so far," said Theodore, faintly; "but, oh, if you knew, sir, the state of my mind, you would not throw any obstacle in the way."

"Neither will I; but you must be guided by what I say, if you wish to succeed in your request; you must not allow this interview to be more agitating than you can help."

"I will not, sir."

Here the nurse aided him in putting on a few more garments, and he lay expecting momentarily the appearance of Mrs. Bertram.

Dr. Russel, after kindly reiterating his caution and advice, quitted the room, and immediately going to the landlord of the hotel, he informed him that he desired possession of some small ante-room near the door; and that when a lady came to inquire for Mr. Danton, he begged he would give orders to the waiters to inform her that he desired to see her before she was shown up into the room where Theodore Danton lay. This was at once promised.

* * *

Such was the state of affairs at the hotel with poor Theodore Danton, while so much mischief was in preparation for him and for her whom he loved with a devotion which was as sincere as it was destitute of guile, or thought of guile.

Theodore loved Margaret because she was, in his estimation, the pure and the virtuous creature he had always believed her to be. Had she been otherwise, she would not have been the idol of his worship, but at once she would have fallen from the pinnacle she stood on in his affections, and grovelled in the dust far, far beneath his notice.

He is waiting for Margaret. The heavy lumbering hackney coach is conveying her to the hotel. But where are Mrs. Blair and the infatuated, deceived, wretched Mr. Bertram? We shall see.

Exactly opposite to the hotel was a private house, with a deep portico entrance. At night it was involved in the greatest shadow, for the inhabitants of the house apparently did not see the necessity for either the ornament or the use of a hall lamp. There were two persons. Mr. Bertram stood with his arms folded across his breast. It was a strange and hideous thought of his; but after he had left the house for some moments, he had sent Mrs. Blair —and for what? For the black mantle. Yes, on that night he arrayed himself in that black mantle which had been sent to him, accompanied by so fearful a malediction.

Mrs. Blair saw that he was in no fit state to be argued with. To her it mattered not whether he wore a black mantle or no mantle. She knew where to lay her hand upon it at once, and she got it for him. He threw it over his shoulders, and then, with a gloomy satisfaction, he walked wheresoever she chose to lead him, had it been to perdition—and God knows it was nearly to that awful doom, for she was the cause of his committing crimes which might well jeopardise his immortal soul.

But we must not anticipate. Sufficient for the day is the evil thereof; and too soon we shall come to occurrences of a character that will need no adventitious aid from the author's pen.

And there he stood, as still as though he had been the statue of a mourner at a funeral, in the deep shadow of that doorway. He spoke not, unless to respond to something which his companion occasionally said to him, and she spoke with an idea of ascertaining his state of mind now and then. He moved not at all. Gloom was at his heart, despair at his brain. He waited for the dreadful moment when his companion should tell him to come from his place of concealment, and blast his eyes with a sight of such damning proof of his own dishonour as she promised him.

Mrs. Blair was a few paces in advance of Bertram. She was waiting and watching for the arrival of her victim. Now and then a fear came across her mind that she might not come; but a second thought always sufficed to correct that first one. She believed Mrs. Bertram to be too rigidly good and truthful not to come, since she had given her word.

And this fiend in human shape, with such an appreciation of the virtues and the excellencies of the young wife, was so intent upon her destruction. Oh, what a chaos of hideous and fearful feelings must have been that woman's mind! Surely in her composition nature forgot those seeds of virtue which produce in some disposition such glorious fruit. For the honour of human nature, we would indeed be most unwilling to suppose there were many characters such as Mrs. Blair, and we own that we should have hesitated a little before we drew such an one, had it not been from the life. But it is so. We have known a Mrs. Blair, and therefore it is that we are, perhaps, the better enabled to enter into the minute varieties of such a character. And who, in the general experience of human nature, could have failed to know a Mr. Bertram? Such characters are, alas! for the peace of all connected with them, but too common. There is no city, no town—nay, no petty hamlet, without such individuals. We might even say, that there were scarcely any hundred married men from whom there might not be picked some one or two who would have acted precisely as he did. These are men who are ever suspicious, ever jealous; men who, let the purity or innocence of those with whom they are thrown into contact be what it may, are ever on the look out for some little circumstances of suspicion; men who would turn the most guileless and innocent language and actions to some evil purpose; men who, in their own minds are so intricate and artful as regards all their dealings, that they can never for one moment be brought to believe but that every one else has some covert object in the most commonplace observation.

But let us return to that doorway in which was Charles Bertram and the Mephistophiles of his fate—the artful, designing, yet foolish woman who was hurrying him to destruction.

We say foolish woman, because, of all follies, the folly of guilt—let it come in what alluring shape it may to the vitiated imagination — is surely the greatest. He or she who is successful in chicanery and falsehood, is most to be really pitied by the philanthropist; for, so surely as that the sun will rise after being for a certain number of hours excluded from our sight, so surely will some awful moment of retribution come which will be more than sufficient to convince the most hardened and sceptical of the children of vice that they have made a most lamentable error, and indeed chosen the wrong course.

Charles Bertram stood like a statue, with the sable cloak about him, and now Mrs. Blair came close to him, and whispered,—

"Do not be impatient. She is sure to come."

The only answer he gave her consisted of a shudder, and a gesture to signify that he heard her. Then again she stepped forward in advance, to watch for Margaret's coming, which she had not long to do.

It seemed as if now the ordinary course of nature had been suspended, to allow these persons, in whose fate we feel ourselves so much interested, to enact a scene which to them was full of such amazing and awful importance, and yet how simple and commonplace it looked. The street was, as we have said, by no means a noisy or a bustling one, and but few vehicles of a public or business character came down. Had it not been for now and then the horrible rattle of two or three ill-made and half-disjointed cabs, as they were driven along by their savage, reckless drivers, the streets would have been quiet enough; but now they suddenly seemed to abandon the thoroughfare, and as a lazy, asthmatical-looking hackney-coach turned into it, all was calm and still.

"I think," said Mrs. Blair, in a whisper just loud enough to reach the ears of Charles Bertram, "I think she comes."

Some sound, between a groan and a sigh, came from his lips, and he drew the black mantle closer around him.

The coach made its way along the street, and then paused. The driver was evidently asking of the person he had within the vehicle where he should stop, and having received some direction, he put the horses again in motion, and halted at the door of the hotel.

"Now!" said Mrs. Blair.

"Yes, now!" said Charles Bertram, in a deep sepulchral voice, and he stepped forward about two steps.

"She has come."

A bewildered sensation came over him, accompanied by vertigo, and he had for a moment to hold by the rails near which he was for support. This feeling, however, was only momentary, and then he was himself again. He stepped across the pavement, and then

Mrs. Blair took his hand and led him forward.

There was only one passenger who took any notice of what was going on, and he did certainly look with astonishment at the singular appearance of a man with a funeral cloak on him being led so stealthily along by a woman who had hold of him by the hand. There was plenty of time, for a hackney-coachman does not get off his box in a very great hurry. He has to collect together all the odds and ends of the multifarious great coats and wrappers in which he is enveloped, and then it takes him some time to open the nearly impracticable door, and let down the steps.

By the time all this was accomplished, Charles Bertram had been brought by Mrs. Blair almost on a level with the side of the coach, and then, as she tightened her hold upon his hand, she said,—

"Now, Mr. Bertram, remember your oath to me. I implore you to remember your oath."

"Yes, yes," he said, abstractedly; and she feared, as she looked in his face and saw how his eyes were rivetted on the door of the coach, that he did not comprehend what she said, but would, despite all his promises previously made to the contrary, commit some act of desperation, in which she would find it utterly impossible to stop him, or even to contend with him.

The fear of her soul showed itself in her countenance; she clutched his arm as tightly as she could, and yet, with a conviction of how easily he might be able to tear himself from such a grasp.

She began to apprehend the very worst—to tell herself that she had gone too far; that she had raised a demon she could not quell again; and that, whatever might be her control over Charles Bertram, so far as it consisted in arousing his worst passions, she was lamentably deficient in the means of quelling them again.

But there was no time for deliberation now. The steps of the coach were lowered, the coachman presented his arm, and, in another instant, the eyes of Charles Bertram were blasted by the sight of his wife as she descended from the vehicle. Mrs. Bertram said nothing to the coachman as she gave him some money, and then walked across the bit of pavement to the hotel, the steps of which she hastily ascended, and then disappeared.

There can be no doubt but that Bertram actually had not the power of action during these brief moments, or he would have committed some frightful extravagance, which would not only have at once upset all Mrs. Blair's plans and projects, but which, likewise, would have produced to himself the most awfully calamitous results.

Had he been armed, and had the power to use arms, he, perhaps, on the spot, would have murdered his innocent wife; but she was reserved for more suffering even than the deprivation of life would have inflicted upon her. Heaven had yet its own designs to fulfil. Charles Bertram stood like a man in a trance for a few moments. He seemed changed to stone, and Mrs. Blair had twice said,—

'You saw her enter?" ere he manned himself sufficiently to move.

Then, as if from his momentary reaction he had gained accumulated strength and power, he forced himself from her hold in a moment, and, uttering a shout of rage, he rushed forward with the strength and speed of a maniac.

Not well calculating where he was going, he came full against the coachman, and flung him down as if he had been a child, falling himself then over the prostrate form of that astonished individual several yards, and bringing his head so forcibly in contact with the edge of the pavement, that he was at once, by the force of the blow, rendered insensible.

CHAPTER XXXIV.

THE INJURY OF BERTRAM.—MRS. BLAIR'S PRECAUTIONS.—THE ASTONISHMENT OF MR. PRIMROSE, AND THE EXPLANATIONS OF MRS. BLAIR.

AT the moment that Charles Bertram thus sprang forward to, no doubt, rush into the hotel, and seek for vengeance on his wife, and him who he considered her seducer, the state of agony and apprehension that Mrs. Blair was in may

be easier imagined by our readers than described by us.

There can be no doubt but that, for an instant, she considered that something was about to happen which would at once dispel all her dreams of ambition, and, indeed, that she would be most uncomfortably dragged forward to public odium and reprobation for what she had done.

When, however, she saw what had occurred, and that Charles Bertram had, by what she could not help considering the fortunate fall over the coachman, stunned himself, she was as delighted as if some of the anticipated gains of her new position—that new position she looked forward to in Bertram's house, when his wife should be expelled from it—had already fallen into her hands. Perhaps for the first time in her life, she, with anything approaching to real sincerity, uttered the exclamation of,—

"Thank God!"

She then walked forward to ascertain, if possible, what amount of injury Charles Bertram had received, and to adopt immediate measures for getting him away from that spot before Mrs. Bertram should again appear upon it.

"D—n my capes," said the coachman, as he sat burdened with that article of hackney dress, and scarce understanding what it was all about, but sat wildly glaring around him.

The street was perfectly quiet, and the whole affair was so sudden and unexpected, that Jarvey was completely smothered in judgment, as he afterwards expressed it to his companions; hearing, however, the words of Mrs. Blair, he felt, when he could recover from his surprise sufficiently to understand anything, exceedingly indignant against that very virtuous lady.

"D—n my capes, here's a go! A man is suddenly upset, and almost sent to immortal smash, and somebody else says, 'Thank God.' Well, I'm blowed if this ain't a pretty go. Who's up in the monument now, I wonder, a stargazing? What's to become of us? I say, what's the matter, that a man can't shut up his own cutch steps without being busted in this here sort of way? Is paving stones cushions? though, if they were, that'd be no reason why a man should be made to set on 'em against his will. It is an old saying, ' you may lead a horse to water, but you can't make him drink;' and I have know'd some hosses as wouldn't go if they didn't like—that's what it is, any how. But I never heard o' sich a way of making a man into small meat without axing his leave. I have set down, whether I will or no—neither with your leave nor by your leave; and there's somebody ahead there as has been floored too. Happy go lucky; here's work for the gemmen of the long robe, as they call them chaps with the big wig. Who won't stand up for his precious rights as an Englishman?"

While he was speaking he swung his capes about him in a great passion, and he seemed by this to be visibly recovering, and his voice began to increase.

"I say, ma'am, why should you thank God I got knocked down? and why should a cutchman be knocked down and flummoxed in this here manner? I say ma'am—d—n my rags!"

"My good man," said Mrs. Blair.

"Good man!" echoed the coachman. "Who's a good man, I should like to know? I'm not to be knocked down for nuffin, and then told I am good man. That don't suit Dumpling Bill, any-how."

"Yes, but——"

"No, but, ma'am——"

"Will you listen to me a moment?"

"Listen, ma'am! and what am I to gain by listening? There's no good in listening, ma'am. I have been feeling, ma'am—that's what it is."

Seeing there was no probable chance of getting the coachman to listen, she pulled out her purse and opened it.

"Will you listen to me?"

"Anything in reason, ma'am," said the coachman, getting on his legs again, by some singular and odd kind of movement. "Yes, ma'am, I'll always listen to a lady as is a lady, and does as a lady should do under such circumstances; 'cause you see, ma'am, it's a great aggravation to hear anybody say, 'thank God,' 'cause a poor cutchman is floored on a sudden in that manner. How should you like it, ma'am—eh? That's the kevestion, ma'am. I thought I'd got a fat customer. Blow me, if all

the blessed breath ain't pumped out o' my inside, and no sort of a mistake."

"You shall be remunerated for what has occurred."

"Be what, ma'am? I'll see you all into the middle of next week first. It's bad enough to be took unawares and floored, without enumerated, or done anything else to arterards."

"You do not understand me. All I wish of you is, that you should accept some money to recompense you for being thrown down, and then assist me to get this gentleman home. He is not in his right mind, therefore you need not be at all angry at what has happened with regard to him and yourself. If your coach is now at liberty, I will hire it to take him home, and probably a crown for your unfortunate fall will enable you to forget it."

The coachman cast up his eyes in a kind of amazement as he exclaimed, holding up his hands,—

"What a uncommon sensible woman! Ma'am, you is a out-and-outer. You knows what's what, you does. You is a lady, and behaves as sich, and no sort o' mistake. Did you say five shillings, ma'am?"

"Yes."

"Very good. If so be, you see, ma'am, as you pays me that ere now, we shall start fair again."

Mrs. Blair felt but too anxious to get Mr. Bertram away from that place to stop any proceedings for the sake of five shillings, so she at once handed to the coachman that amount, and then said,—

"Come, now—you are strong enough, I dare say, to do so,—lift him into the coach at once."

The little scene which we have described had not gone off wholly unnoticed by any one, for although the street was a quiet one, yet some people occasionally came down it, and, more-over, one of the waiters from the hotel, seeing through the half-glass doors of that establishment that the coach was not gone, came out on to the steps to see what it was waiting for.

This was no other than our learned friend James, whose medical and surgical studies were of such moment and importance, and when he saw, as he supposed, that an accident had happened, he was quite delighted at such a capital opportunity of showing the amount of his professional acquirements. And here we must beg the reader not to suppose for a moment that we laugh or are inclined to raise a laugh at James's knowledge of medicine and surgery; on the contrary, we think him quite as useful as in most cases any member of that profession, which contains the greatest number of charlatans and humbugs, not even excepting the church or any other.

James, if called in to a sick man, would be just as likely to do him some good or some harm as what is called a regular practitioner. We do not mean to say but that there are a few circumstances under which a practised medical man can decidedly do some good, but they are extremely few indeed.

"Hilloa!" cried James, "what's the *accidents?* (this was James's Latin for accident); anything the matter with the *nuccus membrane,* eh?—Let me see. Ah—oh! I'm afraid this is a bad case. Been run over, I suppose, by a *coachibus* and kicked by the *horseus,*"

"Lor!" said the coachman. "How long have you been in that ere way, eh, young fellow?"

"What way?"

"Rummy about your head-piece, I means. I s'poses as you're just got out o' some lunatic asylum?"

"You are a low, ignorant fellow," said James. "I despise you. As a medical man, I of course despise you."

"What folly is this?" said Mrs. Blair to the coachman. "Will you assist me, or will you by yourself lift the wounded gentleman into the coach?"

"Come," said the coachman to James, "if you ain't quite cracked, lend us a hand here."

After a little hesitation, James, who was a good-natured fellow enough, assisted the coachman to place the insensible form of Mr. Bertram in the vehicle, and then Mrs. Blair immediately herself got in.

"Now, ma'am, where to?" said the coachman, as he stood with the door in his hand, after he had banged up the steps and pushed in the ends of the straw with which the bottom of the coach was duly provided.

This happened to be a question which Mrs. Blair had not duly considered.

All she felt was that she by no means intended to take Mr. Bertram to his own house, in his present condition. Her great policy, she now felt, was to keep Bertram and his wife separate, and so prevent the possibility of any explanation taking place between them. It occurred to her for a moment, that to take him first to a hospital, in order to ascertain the nature and extent of the injury he had received, would be a good thing; but then she dreaded that the authorities there might insist upon his friends being at once sent to, and so she made up her mind that that would not do at all.

Thought is proverbially rapid, but yet the coachman got impatient while Mrs. Blair was engaged in her mental cogitations, and once more said—

"Where shall I drive to, ma'am?"

A more fertile brain than that of Mrs. Blair's could scarcely have been found, and now she at once decided upon taking him to the house of her sister, Mrs. Primrose, and she gave the coachman the address.

"That will do," she said to herself, as she propped up the insensible Mr. Bertram in a corner of the vehicle, to prevent him from pitching forward against her. "That will do. Primrose may say what he likes, or think what he likes; his sayings and thoughts are of no consequence whatever. Although the house is nominally his, I can thoroughly depend upon my sister."

Mrs. Blair was right; she could thoroughly depend upon her sister, for anything that was vicious, tricky, or despicable; for two more unprincipled women than they both were, could not, by any possibility, have been found. Just show either of them that there was anything to be got by any proceeding, however wrong, vicious, or unjust, and they were the persons to blink every other consideration and at once carry it out.

In addition to this, when Mr. Bertram had recovered somewhat from his hurt, she, Mrs. Blair, would still be at hand to reassume her control over his mind, and thus finally, and to her own satisfaction, work out the termination of her diabolical plans. It would be necessary, too, for her to return to Bertram's mansion, and to whose care could she so well confide the deluded, unhappy victim of her arts as to Mrs. Primrose?

"He shall remain at my sister's," arranged Mrs. Primrose, in her own mind, "until to-morrow, at all events, when I can consider how the affair stands in all its bearings, and arrange precisely what is to be done. He cannot be much hurt, and, at all events, a great deal of what I may decide upon must depend upon what state of mind I find him in upon his recovery from the effects of the accident—that will be to-morrow, no doubt, and then, if I can but persuade him to take some harsh steps as regards Mrs. Bertram, so that he gets up in her mind such a feeling of ill-usage that she cannot look over it, all will be well, and my expectations will be answered."

Thus reasoned this perfectly guilty woman, during the progress of the coach towards the house of the Primroses. The distance was not great, and soon the vehicle stopped at the door of the house, and Mrs. Blair immediately alighted, telling the coachman to wait until she came to him again before the hurt gentleman was lifted out.

Mrs. Primrose was at home, but Mr. Primrose was not, and this was just the state of things which, had Mrs. Blair arranged them herself, she would have liked best; not that she, or Mrs. Primrose either, cared one straw what Primrose thought or said about anything, but his being out of the way, at all events, spared them the trouble of issuing any commands to him upon the subject.

Mrs. Primrose felt rather alarmed to see her sister come in a coach to the door, and she was eager in her inquiries as to what was the matter.

"You will be surprised," said Mrs. Blair, "when I tell you that Bertram is in the coach at the door."

"Bertram?"

"Yes; but in a state of insensibility, in consequence of a fall on his head. I have the most particular and special reasons in the world for not taking him home."

"Indeed?"

"Yes: and there is nowhere but here that I can bring him with any degree of safety to some plans, of which you already know something, but concern-

ing which I can now tell you muc more."

"Then by all means bring him in."

"Have you a spare bed?"

"No. But let him lie down upon Primrose's bed for the present. I shall be able to arrange matters soon, when you have him in the house, and got rid of the coach."

"Very good."

Both the sisters now proceeded to the door, and, by the assistance of a man who was passing, and whose services were retained at the price of a pint of beer, the still insensible Charles Bertram was lifted from the coach and carried into the house.

"You had better take him upstairs at once," said Mrs. Primrose, as they were about to place him in the parlour, and this opinion being echoed by Mrs. Blair, he was carried upstairs by the coachman and the other man, and laid down upon Primrose's bed.

"Precious heavy he is, to be sure," said the coachman; "it always makes me as dry as dust, carrying anything up stairs."

"So it does me," said the other man; and, as they both went down the staircase again, they talked so loudly and eloquently in praise of beer, that Mrs. Blair, who knew the value of small gifts at the proper time, was induced to add a pot of beer to the pint promised; and then the coachman said "as he saw, from the werry fust moment as he clapped his precious eyes on her, as she was a real lady, and not one o' them as was only wamped up to look like one, and then grudged a poor fellow a extra drop o' beer, all for to wet his whistle."

Could even Mrs. Blair be insensible to such delicate and courtly compliments?

CHAPTER XXXV.

THE INTERVIEW BETWEEN MRS. BERTRAM AND THEODORE DANTON.— THE PARTING. — AN AFFECTING SCENE.—THE LAST GIFT.

THE state of mind of Mrs. Bertram as she went in the coach to Theodore Danton's hotel, was of so confused a character that she would have found no small difficulty in herself describing it, but yet she never for one moment wavered in her resolution of visiting him.

"I am right," she told herself, "to visit him. He is sick; and no foolish scruple shall keep me away from him. If he were to die, and I had not spoken one word of cheering kindness to him before the grave closed on him for ever, it would be a sore place at my heart while I lived."

Little did she suspect when she ascended the steps of the hotel what real danger she was in, or how strange and excitable a scene she was leaving behind her. Little did she suspect the proximity of her husband, or of the arch fiend, Mrs. Blair; she walked into that house in the consciousness of innocence as well as in fancied security.

Alas! how miserably was she mistaken—what an awfully frightful step, as regarded its possible consequences, had she taken. But now it was done; the crisis of her existence had arrived. She was no longer a wife but in name; and he who had sworn to love, to honour, and to protect her, was henceforward to cast her off to despair.

When fairly within the hall, if it might be so named, of the hotel, Margaret felt confused, among the number of personages whom she saw passing to and fro, which to ask concerning Theodore; but one of the waiters observing her hesitation, and probably being struck instinctively with the conviction that she was a lady and ought to be treated respectfully, came up to her, saying,—

"Madam, do you seek any one here?"

"Yes—yes, Mr. Danton."

"Oh, the sick gentleman, madam."

"He is here?"

"Certainly. Dr. Russel desired me that if a lady should call for Mr. Danton, she should be shown into the room where he is waiting."

"Who is Dr. Russel?"

"The doctor, madam, who has been attending upon Mr. Danton—a very clever man, madam; give me leave to assure you, our James here, who knows something of such things, says he is a remarkably clever man. This way, if you please madam, this way. You will find, madam, Dr. Russel in that room, if you please. Coming—coming—coming!"

Some bell had rung rather violently, and the waiter rushed off with the quick shuffling gait of that class of gentry, leaving Mrs. Bertram at the half-opened door of a room, from which there issued a stream of light.

Margaret hesitated a moment before she went into the room, and then she pushed the door completely open, and found herself in the presence of the calm, gentlemanly, and self-possessed Dr. Russel, who had been anxiously expecting her, and who wished to catch her before she saw Theodore, to combat her feelings, and to make the interview as short as possible, in consideration of the still very weak and debilitated condition in which he was.

There was a moment's silence, and then Dr. Russel, advancing, said, respectfully, and in a tone of voice which was highly calculated to assure Margaret,—

"Have I the honour of addressing Mrs. Bertram?"

"That is my name, sir," she replied. "I presume you are the Dr. Russel of whom I have heard honourable mention?"

"I am Dr. Russel, madam, and I trust that you will excuse me for the liberty I have taken in requesting you to see me before visiting your friend, Mr. Danton, on account of the reason I can give you for so doing."

"Oh, certainly," said Margaret, "certainly. I fear I am very much intruding upon you."

"Not at all, if you will be guided by prudence in this matter. I am quite sure that this visit will either do good or ill to my patient; and I am likewise quite sure that it is in your power so to regulate it, that it shall be the one or the other."

"Indeed, sir?"

"Yes, madam; he earnestly and ardently desires to see you. The idea of your visiting him at all, is delightful to him; but if the same be of an agitating character I fear it would do him harm."

"Is he very ill?"

"Not so ill as weak from former illness. If you will satisfy him by seeing him, and talking cheerfully to him, for a short time, and then leave, you will confer a benefit upon him; but, otherwise, you may do him a mischief."

"I understand, sir, and will be very cautious, indeed. Believe me, you shall have no cause to censure me. I will be careful to say nothing which shall produce anxiety or irritation. Mr. Danton is a relative, sir."

There was a slight flush of colour upon Margaret's cheeks as she uttered these words, and with the ready tact of a man who had seen much of the world, Dr. Russel at once knew that she said so much to take away from his mind any impression to her prejudice that might arise here from the fact of her visiting Theodore at all.

"I am quite aware of that, madam," he said, "and think your visit dictated by the best and the kindest of motives."

"Margaret felt more thankful than she could have hoped to express, and when Dr. Russel added,—

"I will now conduct you, if you please, to the sick chamber," she allowed him to take her hand in silence, and passing through a door-way they together ascended the staircase that led to the sleeping chambers of the house.

The state of agitation that Mrs. Bertram was now in, would have prevented her from making any remark, even if she had wished so to do; but there was no necessity for her to speak, for Dr.

Russel said nothing to her before they reached a closed door, which now only separated her from the chamber of him with whom she might have been so happy had fate united them together in those holy bonds which death alone can sever.

"Will you allow me to announce you?" said the physician.

"Yes—yes, if you please."

Dr. Russel left Margaret on the threshold of the door, and went up to the bedside of Theodore Danton, to whom he said,—

"The lady whom you expect has come."

Theodore, with an exclamation of joy, would have risen, but Dr. Russel said at once, and firmly,—

"Mr. Danton, as your physician, I am of course placed in a situation of very great responsibility. It would have been easy for me from the first to have prevented this interview from taking place at all, and even now such a course is in my power. If you do not consent that it shall be a short one and a calm one, I cannot possibly permit it."

"Let me but see her," said Theodore; "Let me but look into her eyes again; let me but hear her speak, and I shall be content."

"Very well—she is here."

He went to the door and led in Margaret. In another moment her hand was clasped in Theodore's, and she pronounced his name. Then tears came to her relief, and she wept bitterly.

"Margaret! dear, dear Margaret;" he said, "this is kind and good of you, indeed. Oh, if I had dared to hope, dear Margaret,——"

"Hush, hush!" she said, "I cannot hear this. As your relative, Theodore, I have come to visit you in your sickness."

"And may Heaven bless you for so doing, Margaret! You are looking pale, and not so well as when I last saw you."

"And you, Theodore," faltered Margaret. "There is a great change in you."

"Yes, yes! I have stood upon the brink of eternity. I am not what I was. Oh, Margaret, Margaret, some evil star has ruled my destiny."

"Speak not so," said Margaret. "Do not impugn Heaven's justice thus. You know not what you say. You will be well again."

He shook his head mournfully, as he said with a deep sigh—

"Never—never what I was! The light of my existence has passed away from me. I may live, and I may appear among men, but the ambition to be what I was is dead within me. The grave will be welcome now."

"Nay, Theodore, this desponding will pass away with the indisposition that has produced it."

"It cannot. The dreams of my hopes can visit my imaginations now no more. All is darkness now—without a hope—without a scintillation of joy. Dear Margaret, we might have been ——"

"No more of this, Theodore—no more. I have but to hear that you are better—to wish you well—and—to leave you—for ever."

"For ever, Margaret?"

"Yes, for ever! This meeting, perchance, has far more of heedlessness in it than reason. Oh, Theodore, live on and forget you ever knew me. Let the dim cloud of oblivion sweep across the past. Let us be to each other as we were years ago, Theodore, and then you, at least, will be happy—happy with some one who can love you."

Theodore was silent for a few moments from excess of emotion, and then, in a low, earnest tone, he said—

"Margaret, to be as we were even years ago is for me to adore you, as I then adored you, although I spoke not of my love. It was a boyish passion, but, unlike such passions usually, it grew upon me, strengthening each day as I strengthened, until it became the one absorbing pursuit of my existence. Oh, Margaret, Margaret; I then made the fatal mistake of supposing that the fair flower I had destined for my own bosom would remain unpicked by any other hand. Alas! it has been plucked, and I am desolate."

Margaret would fain have interrupted him while thus he spoke, but she really lacked the power so to do. Her own feelings were too much affected to allow her to speak; but when he ceased, she made an effort, and, in saddened, broken accents, which fully betokened what she suffered, she said—

"Theodore, this must not be. I can hear no more of this. I am a wife, and if I have made to Heaven a vow that—that was not quite sanctioned by my heart, I still must keep it—I cannot—I dare not—Theodore I will not hear you talk of love to me."

"I—I have no more to say. God! —oh, God! that I were dead!"

"Such desponding is criminal. You have no right, Theodore, to make such a wish—it is not just—it is not fair of you. To yourself—to your maker it is not just."

"But I despair——"

"Despair is the coward's subterfuge. Do you suppose, Theodore Danton, that you are the only one against whom fate's most envenomed shafts have been levelled? Do you imagine none but you can be unhappy?"

He looked up in her face with inexpressible grief and affection, as he said—

"Margaret, I would die a thousand deaths to make you happy."

"I—I have not said I am unhappy."

"There needs no words to tell me that."

"Hush, Theodore, hush. Once again, farewell."

"No—oh, not yet. Another moment spare to me. Oh, you know not how dear, how precious, in after times, the recollection of this scene may become. I may live,—and I will not play the coward so much as to die by my own hand—I may live to bless you, Margaret, for wasting yet another moment upon the poor, desolate Theodore Danton."

"What would you have me say?"

"Margaret—I—I will not call you dear Margaret, for you have forbidden me—I will pursue my intention. That intention which the stern hand of disease only has stayed. I will leave England for ever."

"'Tis better," she said faintly.

"Yes, I know 'tis better, and it shall be done. But when I am far away, Margaret—you hear, I do not call you dear, dear Margaret—when I am far away, will you, when you look on this small gem, think of him who last looked upon it in this chamber?"

He took from beneath his pillow a curious bracelet of gold, made into the form of a serpent, in the head of which were two small diamonds, representing the eyes of the creature. The trinket would probably have fallen from the nerveless grasp of Theodore Danton, had not Margaret taken it from him, but she did so without an intention of retaining it, although the action had all the appearance as if she accepted it.

"No, Theodore," she said, "I cannot accept of this. I need no such artificial aids to memory."

"Nay, Margaret he said. "Please me by taking it, and think me selfish if you will, when I own that I have a hope that in return, you will bestow upon me some trifle which has belonged to you, but which will have a dearer value in my eyes, upon that account, than the costliest gem that man ever envied the possession of."

"I cannot exchange gifts with you now, Theodore," said Margaret. "You totally forget, surely, when you ask so much, how very differently we are now situated to what we once were."

He sank back on the pillow in a state of exhaustion, as he said,—

"Yes, yes, it is true. God help me! It is true. We are, indeed, differently situated; but yet, Margaret, can it be possible, that knowing, as you do, that my affection for you is as pure and sinless as is a child's, you can imagine aught wrong in bestowing upon me some trifle which I can carry with me to a foreign land, as a memento of the past, or fancy that by accepting from me such a bauble as this, you are in any way compromising that stern principle which makes me love you?"

There was sufficient reason in these words for them to have some effect upon Margaret; and when she came to consider that she knew she could rely fully upon the honour of Theodore Danton, her scruples for the moment vanished, and she drew from her finger a small gold engraved ring, which she had possessed before her marriage, and to which, therefore, Charles Bertram could attach no claim.

"Take this, Theodore," she said; "my judgment scarcely approves what I am doing."

"But let feeling sanction the act," he exclaimed, "and judgment will forgive the seeming error, and decide that it is but a seeming one."

"Now, farewell!"

"Nay—not yet, not yet! You will accept the bracelet?"

"Yes, yes! But I must begone. This, remember, is to be our last meeting, unless by some unavoidable accident, in the world. You will remember that, Theodore?"

"Yes—yes!"

"You will promise, too, before I go, that it shall be so."

"Oh, Margaret, when would I form my lips to utter that promise were you remaining here to be the dear reward of my not making it? I could never make the promise, Margaret."

"Is this generous, Theodore?" said Margaret, reproachfully.

"No, no," he said, "it is not. But you acquit me of meaning that which I uttered. The words passed my lips without a moment's reflection. You are my better angel, and recall me to myself."

"You promise me, then, before I go,

that never again, by your own presence, or by a messenger, or even by letter, will you again seek to know that there is such a person living as myself."

" Is so stringent a promise necessary, Margaret ?"

" It is—for my peace and honour, and for yours."

" I promise."

" Theodore, I will not say I thank you for the promise, because it is a most proper one for you to make, as well as for me to exact; and now I must bid you farewell !"

" And for ever ?"

" Yes, for ever !—unless——"

" Oh, Heaven be thanked !" exclaimed Theodore. " There is yet a hope, then, that the cruel sentence may be recalled. Oh, I breathe again—I live a new life—I have now some hope."

" Nay, Theodore, do not hastily place a rash construction on my words. I was about to add that the separation would be final, unless you found some other heart to love; and then, if your condition was altered, if you were the husband of another——"

" Never—oh, never !" he exclaimed, passionately; " my heart is widowed. Never, oh, never !"

" Then we may never meet again.

" But, Margaret," he said, after a pause, " there may be circumstances affecting your own destiny which may enable us to meet again."

" What circumstances, Theodore ?"

" You—you will not be offended with me Margaret; but you might, in the visitations you know, of existence—you might be left alone."

" Hush, Theodore, hush ! I cannot hear this."

" You are right—you are right ! Forgive me, Margaret."

" There is nothing to forgive, Theodore. I am quite sure you meant not to speak selfishly or offensively. Life and death are in the hands of Heaven, and we know not what may occur. This, however, is one view of our condition upon which I must not—dare not speculate."

" No, no ! I agree with that—I agree with that. You are right, Margaret. I am blinded—too blinded by passion, and by the bitterness of my disappointments to think or act correctly."

" No, Theodore, do not accuse yourself. You are not blinded; but I can perceive that you are freely uttering whatever thoughts come to your mind, without the slightest reference to their effect. And now, once again, let us utter that word which, come from what lips it may, is ever a mournful one, of —Farewell !"

" Oh, most mournful !"

" And yet it must be uttered. Farewell ! Theodore, Farewell !—perhaps for ever !"

She held out her hand to him, which he clasped in both of his, and at that moment of feeling she let him carry it unbidden to his lips; she felt his tears fall upon it, and her own chased each other down her cheeks from very sympathy.

" Farewell ! Farewell ! if it must be," he said; " oh, word of anguish—dear, dear—Margaret ! Let me call you dear unblamed for the last time in the world. You do not chide me, now ?"

" No, no," gasped Margaret.

There was a silence unbroken save by sobs, and then she drew her hand away from his grasp. She tried to speak again, but she could not; she listened to hear if he spoke, but all was still, and she thought that he considered the distressing interview had ended then where it was, so she walked, or rather we ought to say she tottered from the room.

She did not know that Theodore Danton, in the excess of his anguish at that moment in which he was to bid her whom he loved so truly adieu for ever, had fainted and lay perfectly unconscious if she went or strayed, upon the couch where she left him.

Dr. Russel and the nurse were both outside the door. The former offered his arm in silence to Margaret, which she accepted with a feeling of thankfulness, for she was too blinded by her tears, and to much overcome by her feelings, too be capable of supporting herself. He led her down the staircase, and across the hall, to the door-steps of the hotel, and then he said, respectfully,—

" Madam, can I get a carriage for you, or place you any distance on your way; if so, pray command me"

She only shook her head in reply. Dr. Russel bowed and then she walked down the steps into the street like a moving statue more than a creature of life.

CHAPTER XXXVI.

THE HAPPY THOUGHT.—STEALING A MARCH UPON MRS. PRIMROSE, AND ITS UNEXPECTED RESULTS.

AT the moment that Mr. Bertram was placed in Mr. Primrose's bed, that gentleman was with a few friends, who had induced him to take a little more than the usual quantity; indeed, just enough to enable him to throw off the natural fear he had of Mrs. Primrose; and she not being present, had not the same power when absent as when present. He was in so happy a state that he had thrown off all recollections and disagreeables at home. He had met an old friend—Jack somebody—who insisted upon treating him, and then he could not do less than do the same thing in return, and the result was that of a healthy and joyous state of *in vino*; and when he parted company it was much later than usual; and when he was hastening home, he was hunting his brains to death to find out some excuse by means of which he could appease the wrath of his spouse.

"Ah," said he, "it's no use, excuses are all alike; even if they have the uncommon merit of being true, they are never believed; indeed, I don't think wives ever think much about the truth; all they think of is, what kind of turn the excuse can give to their reproaches, and whether they cannot get an extra account of matter, for a good scold can be squeezed out of it.

"Ah, well, they must have their scolds out, I suppose. Never mind, I can but bear it; and it is very disagreeable, after such a pleasant evening. I wish I could go to bed without her knowing anything about it; but that is impossible—I might as well endeavour to catch a weazel asleep as to catch Mrs. Primrose a-napping."

And so he might. Poor Primrose! there are many such wives as you could boast of possessing—who will give themselves such trouble about their husbands, and who boast of their duty and devotedness, and who *will* sit up

for them, despite all they can say to the contrary. No—though they say it makes sad inroads into their health, yet they say they cannot sleep if Mr. —— is out—they are sure to keep awake, and they would rather keep up, and so forth; and all the while, if what they say be true, it would be infinitely better if they were to go to bed. But then there is the latent feeling of fear that they should go to bed and sleep, and be defrauded out of their knowledge of the exact hour their truant spouses think proper to return home at, and deprive them of the superiority such knowledge usually bestows upon them.

"Ah," thought Primrose, "if Mrs. P. would only go to sleep, I shouldn't be home any later, but, but I am sure it would increase my happiness, and she would be much more amiable—if she can be so at any time, if it were only that she had been less than usually disagreeable.

"I wonder what she is about now," he said, as he entered the street in which they lived; "it has been a very pleasant evening—a very pleasant evening indeed, but I wonder if it will have the usual unpleasant termination. It is a melancholy reflection that so much happiness is to be so broken in upon by one's own wife."

He came to the door, and he listened attentively for some minutes; he could hear nothing, and he pulled out the key and gently opened the door, and closed it after him.

He was almost struck dumb with astonishment, when he heard voices in the parlour, and when he came to look he could see a light through the keyhole, and underneath the door of the room.

"Oh," thought Primrose, "I am caught oh? Well, she can't say more than she is used to. Ah, well, it ain't worse than it might be, though it almost gives me the stomach ache."

He paused and could hear the murmur of voices in earnest conversation, and some other sounds occasionally.

"I wonder who it can be?" he muttered; "who can she be talking to in that manner? They keep it up, too; that's pretty good proof they are all women."

He listened again, and could distinctly hear the sounds of his own wife's voice, and that of Mrs. Blair, in earnest and continued conversation.

"Ah," he thought, "they are at it now; nobody's safe now, and everybody they know, or have known, however slightly will be called over the coals, as they call it. Oh, lor'! oh, lor'!"

"He knows nothing about that," said Mrs. Blair to Mrs. Primrose.

"Nor will he know anything about it," rejoined Mrs. Primrose.

"It was a very singular occurrence."

"Yes; it doesn't happen every day."

"No; I'm sure it needn't."

"However, it would not be without its effect, if that there can be no doubt."

"I dare say."

"It grows late."

"That is very likely."

"Husbands are all alike.'

"Women always get ill-used.'

"After they are married."

"Oh!" thought Primrose; "there she goes, she's getting ready against I come in—well, there's no taking her by surprise. What a piece of fun it would be to go to bed first and swear I had been in bed all night long, and breaking my rest by waiting for her. Capital!"

This was capital in Mr. Primrose's idea, and therefore he lost no time in putting such an artful dodge into practice. For this purpose he crept up stairs, at the imminent hazard of breaking his neck, and of risking a discovery, which if it had taken place, would have placed him in a very awkard position, for Mrs. Primrose would, doubtless, have said, that he only desired to escape observation because he was not in a fit state to be seen. A very pretty reflection, but at the same time he could not aid or help himself; however, as it turned out, he was not caught in the fact, but he got up stairs and entered the bed-room, which was all in darkness. He shut the door, and walked about, and quickly divested himself of his clothes, and then he walked to the window and looked out into the street at the gas below.

"Yes," he muttered, "I have the advantage of her to-night, and shall have the pull in the morning.—I'll go to bed at once."

So saying, he walked to the bed and jumped into it. Judge of his horror and amazement when he found there was something in that bed, and that something a human body, perhaps a female. Poor Primrose got into a sweat; he must have made some tremendous mistake.

"What will Mrs. Primrose say?" he muttered, as the dreadful supposition came across him, that he had gone to bed with the maid.

It was really a dreadful supposition, and one that for a few moments perfectly paralyzed him, and he could not rise and quit the dangerous proximity. This, however, gave him time to recollect himself, and then he began to remember each event as it passed, and he looked round the room and saw so many things to remember, that he came to the conclusion that after all he had made no mistake, and that he really was in his own bed.

"What can be the matter?" he muttered to himself; "there is evidently somebody here."

He rose up and looked around him, and a few stray rays of light fell on the bed, and a very odd kind of head met his gaze.

"Why, it ain't a woman, after all," said Primrose, his courage returning with this discovery, though, at the same time, it cost him some other pangs that altered the whole aspect of affairs.

Yes, there was no distinguishing the affair; there was a rough-looking head of hair, and whiskers to match, lying on his connubial pillows. Yet it was melancholy, but as undeniable as melancholy, and there was as unquestionably a head, and a body belonging thereto—that also was a settled fact.

"Well," muttered Primrose, "this is rather too much of a good thing; I'm d—d—yes, he said so—If I stand this."

Then, with a great jump, he jumped out of bed, and, in the anger of the moment, struck the supposed invader of his domestic happiness (?) over the head. Finding, however, that he did not move, he dressed himself quickly, and rung the bell the while most violently.

Mrs. Primrose and Mrs. Blair, both suspecting Mr. Bertram had risen, and had taken this mode of ascertaing where he was, immediately ran up stairs with a light to assure the unfortunate individual that he was safe. Judge of their astonishment when they saw Mr. Primrose just in the act of putting on his last garment, with anger and fury in his countenance and manner.

"Well, Mrs. Primrose!" he began.

"Well, sir?" she replied.

"You'll say that's my fault, I suppose?"

"That you keep late hours, sir, do you mean?"

"No, madam; but the company you keep. I'll not stand it." Then he exclaimed, ringing the bell again. "I'll have the servant, and she shall be a witness of your infamy."

"Upon my word!"

"Mrs. Primrose!"

"Sir."

"Go on," he cried; "go on."

"Are you mad?"

"I have been, but I mean to alter."

"The sooner the better; there's plenty of room for improvement."

"Shameless woman!"

"What do you mean, Mr. Primrose?" inquired Mrs. Blair. "I have heard of much, but I wouldn't have believed as much as this."

"I dare say not," said Primrose, jerking his arms into his coat in a great rage; "I dare say not; you are what I call a d—d artful lot. However, thank God, you've gone too far, and have left me a remedy to get rid of the whole of you."

"Goodness me! the man's ill; he must be sent to a lunatic asylum."

"Poor Primrose; I always thought his behaviour was very peculiar, and can make great excuses for his conduct now that I see his malady in this shape so plain."

"D—n it, madam, you would make a saint swear, or mad, or creep out of his skin to escape you, you wretch—oh! you vile, profligate woman!"

"Quite mad—quite mad, I think," said Mrs. Blair; "he had better be put under restraint this very evening."

"That's right, that's right; go it," said Primrose; "but I'll turn you out of the house, adulteress, base, ungrateful woman!"

"What do you mean, Mr. Primrose? what do you mean? I will not put up with such behaviour from such a troublesome, good-for-nothing-fellow like you."

"Oh! you complain, do you?"

"And well she may."

"There, look!" said Primrose, as the servant entered. "Look, and see, shameless woman, see, I have found you out; there is your paramour. Do you think I am so dead to everything that I will quietly put up with this?"

At the same time he pointed to the bed on which lay Bertram,

"Yes; I see," said Mrs. Blair.

"And so do I," added Mrs. Primrose.

"Do you?" inquired Mr. Primrose of the girl,

"Yes, sir."

"Then, madam, you see your guilt?"

"Oh, dear!" exclaimed Mrs. Primrose; "did you ever see such a man? You only see a specimen of the trouble I have with him. Bless you, he's always taking some vagary or other into his head, and now you see."

"And so, Mr. Primrose, you have the audacity to accuse your wife, much less suspect her? If I were her, I would not live with you.'

"I'll take care she shall not."

"Well, I am the cause of all this," said Mrs. Blair; "but you must insist on your legal rights, and cannot want friends."

"Your fault?"

"Yes; you know the capacity I live in at Mr. Bertram's house?"

"I have heard."

"Well, that is Mr. Bertram."

Mr. Bertram?"

"Yes."

"And what's Mr. Bertram to me?"

"Oh! nobody, of course."

"I find him sleeping in my bed when I am out; it matters not whom it is, it is the same to me; my injury is the same be it whom it may."

"Very well, sir, Mrs. Primrose is an injured woman. I brought Mr. Bertram here because he was insensible, and unable to speak, and I know nowhere to take him. He fell down and struck his temples."

Mr. Primrose felt there was a strange sensation creeping over him as the explanation was given, and found that he had very probably discovered a mare's nest.

"And now, Mr. Primrose, what do you think of yourself, sir?"

Mr. Primrose looked very foolish, and

knew very well what kind of situation he was in, and now saw which way the tide set.

"Well," said Mrs. Primrose, "I have had a life of it in my time, and have heard of other people being tired of life; but no poor wretch ever led such a life as I have led with that man—it's perfectly dreadful!"

"It must be. He ought to go down on his knees and beg and entreat your pardon."

"So he ought."

"But how could I tell who he was?" asked Primrose.

"Why couldn't you have taken the trouble to inquire?" said Mrs. Blair. "Is that an unreasonable expectation?"

"But to put him in my bed!"

"We couldn't put him in any other; and, besides, he is a gentleman, and he's insensible."

"And has been so for some time."

"Yes."

"Then why not have a surgeon to attend him? or he'll die, and we shall have the trouble of a coroner's inquest here."

"You wretch! go down stairs and sleep below, in the kitchen. If you are wanted, we will call you; but do not, as you have any shame for the past, come in sight again."

Mr. Primrose was glad to escape and hide himself below in the kitchen—thankful enough for the mercy extended to him.

They sent for a surgeon, who came, and who, after seeing Mr. Bertram, cupped him behind the neck, and after some time he returned to a state of consciousness, when Mrs. Blair assured him he was safe, and, as she was by him he could be well taken care of.

CHAPTER XXXVII.

MRS. BERTRAM'S MIDNIGHT WATCH. THE OMEN.

WHEN Margaret Bertram left the hotel to proceed homewards, all the scene of bustle and excitement which, during her interview with Theodore Danton, had taken place outside was over. The street was restored to its usual quiet and decorum, and those who could have told her what occurred, did not dream of doing so, in consequence of not having the least suspicion that she was in any way interested in what had taken place. Even James, the waiter, with his vast imagination, had not the least idea that the melancholy-looking lady who had come to the hotel to visit the sick gentleman, could be at all interested in a *fracas* which had taken place outside the door with a hackney-coachman and a madman.

Mrs. Bertram did certainly, when she reached the door of the hotel, look to see if the coach was waiting, but when she found it was not, she walked slowly homeward. Now that she had paid this visit to Theodore, she felt far easier in her mind. She felt that she had, at all events, whether he lived or died, performed a duty, and that if she and he should never in this world meet again, which was more than probable, they had neither of them anything for which to reproach themselves.

"Thank God, he is recovering," she said to herself. "He will not die. I shall not now have the melancholy reflection that despair has killed him. He is recovering, and when he does so, he will, in pursuance of his word, which he passed to me to do so, leave the country, and all will be well. In another land, the now too vivid impression of his disappointment in this will pass away, and he will perhaps find some other whom he can love sufficiently well, at all events, to ensure to him far more happiness in married life than, alas, I am likely ever to enjoy."

When she reached her home, she at once repaired to her own room, and then she sat down to think. She seemed to have so completely now settled the whole affair connected with Theodore Danton, that she felt far happier than she had been for days, and after some time spent in calmer reflection, she said,—

"And now I feel convinced that the best thing I can do, as well as the most correct thing, is to tell my husband all that has occurred. He will not blame me. He cannot. If I can but get him to hear me out, calmly and dispassionately, I am convinced that at all events, and whatever other grounds of contention may arise between us, we shall

never have a word concerning poor Theodore Danton."

Acting upon this determination, which, although a wise one, was, alas! too late, she rang the bell, and when the page came in to answer to the summons, she said,—

"Is your master within ?"

"No, ma'am."

"Very well. When he does come home, say that I am up and that I want to see him."

"Yes, ma'am."

"Before I sleep to-night," added Margaret to herself when she was again alone—"before I sleep to-night I will tell him all, and that I have been to see Theodore Danton; nay, I will endeavour to persuade him to go and see him likewise, and to be friends with him. Why should he not? Theodore is my only living relative, and surely, as he is incontestibly a gentleman, my husband can have no manner of hesitation in making his acquaintance."

Margaret Bertram by no means positively connected the coldness which had arisen between her and her husband with Theodore Danton. Indeed, had she been suddenly asked by any one why it was that she and Mr. Bertram were not such good friends as they had been formerly, she would have found the question a very difficult one to answer.

That Mrs. Blair was a ground of contention, or, at all events, of coldness, and that she was likely to continue so as long as she remained in the house, Mrs. Bertram could have found no difficulty in stating ; but, beyond that, she certainly would not have known what to say.

She began to suspect that the excuse

given to her for the continuance of Mrs. Blair in the house was merely an excuse, and nothing more, and that that crafty individual had a good perception of when she was well off, and that she was not at all likely to suit herself elsewhere as long as she was so well suited where she was. This, however, was only a suspicion, and as such, until time should tend to positively confirm it, Mrs. Bertram felt that it would be beneath her to notice it to her husband. If, however, after some length of time, she should find that Mrs. Blair remained, and likewise that she was making no exertions to obtain another situation, she fully contemplated again speaking to Bertram upon the subject.

Eleven o'clock came, and no announcement was made to Margaret of her husband's return. She waited another half hour, and then she rung to inquire if he had left any message when he went out. She was told none and that no member of the household knew where he had gone.

"Still I will sit up for him," thought Margaret. "Surely he will be in shortly. I must and will see him to-night before he goes to bed."

To beguile the time, and, if possible, to forget her own anxious thoughts, she took up a book and commenced reading therefrom an anecdote, which, as she proceeded with it, insensibly arrested and claimed her attention.

* * * *

One dark night in November, a private chariot was seen going rapidly along the Tottenham road. It might have been a hired one, but it could as easily have been termed private, save that the coachman was scarcely such an one as would have been kept by any gentleman. They turned up by the side of a green on the left, and before the chapel or church on Tottenham Green, and proceeded about a couple of miles, when they stopped before a handsome cottage residence.

The roads were soft—it was summer time, and the dust, which lay thick, was slightly damped by a falling shower, so that the sounds of the wheels were scarcely heard.

The house they stopped before was one of those square white-looking cottages of not more than three stories high, but with five or six long windows on a floor. The front had a kind of lattice-work nailed over it for the purpose of enabling the climbing plants to run over it, and to support themselves. The front was secured in by a dwarf wall and some railings, with a large iron gate that was securely locked and bolted in the inside. The man who stood in livery behind jumped down and opened the door of the carriage, and then two more came out of the carriage, one of them saying—

"Here's your crape."

The presumed footman took the crape, and bound it over his face, and they all walked to the gate. A new key was placed in the lock, and it turned quickly and quietly. The one then walked to the street door, and finding it was secured on the outside, he clambered up the wall with much confidence, and, opening a window, disappeared.

This was done in silence, and not a word was spoken by any one of the individuals present. A few moments elapsed before anything was heard or seen of their companion, and they waited in silence for him. At length they heard the chains and bolts carefully withdrawn, and the bar removed. When this was done the door was opened, and the man on the inside said, in a whisper—

"All right—be quick!"

The door was immediately closed, and those on the outside hastened back to the coach, and took from it some heavy burden between them, and then hastened through the gates, when the door was immediately opened by the confederate on the inside who was waiting.

A dark lantern was used by the man who got in first and he led the way towards an upper room; the door was ajar, and he went first and gently pushed it open, and his companions followed him. The burden was laid on the floor, and a large thick cloak quickly taken away, and discovered the dead body of a female.

They next approached the bed that was in the room; it was hung round with curtains, which were both drawn, one on one side, and the other on the other. They peeped through the curtains, and then he with the lantern placed the light upon a chest of drawers, and, taking a gag from his pocket, he stood ready.

All this was done with the most noiseless celerity that can be imagined, and then they paused for a moment as they gazed upon the beautiful girl that lay unconscious of the presence of such men as they who stood around her.

"Now!" said the man.

In a moment they fell upon her, and the gag was thrust into her mouth. Then each one secured her on the side he stood, so that she could not move, or utter a sound even of the most suppressed character. A large handkerchief or shawl was bound over her eyes, and then her whole head, after the cap and comb had been taken off, was enveloped. The reason of this will be seen presently.

This done, she was lifted out of bed, and most ruthlessly did the men deprive her of every article of clothing, without one exception. The poor girl struggled, and put up her hands in an imploring attitude, but it was all disregarded by them; and then the cloak was wrapped around her, and so tightly, that she could not get up her arms.

This done, while one man was holding her safely and securely in his arms, the other two took up the corpse, which was of a girl about the same age and complexion, and not much unlike the other, especially in make and size, and dressed it up in the night-dress they had just taken off the young lady they had stripped. Having placed the comb in the hair and even taken the precaution of placing a couple of rings on the fingers, which the living one wore, they arranged everything, and, seizing her between them, they carried her out of the room, the man with the lantern going before.

When they got to the door, he said in a whispering voice to his companions—

"Put her into the carriage and gently turn round. I will come out the same way I came in." Then, closing the door, he locked, bolted, and barred it, so that none could believe it had been entered. Returning up stairs, he was careful not to leave a thing moved out of its place to tell the tale.

He got out of the same window he entered, and closed it after him, and descended without accident or trouble; and having locked the gates after him, he hastened after his companions, who were awaiting him at a little distance.

They rode off at a rapid rate, and, within a short hour, they were in London.

* *. * *

The next morning was a fine summer's morning; the sun rose beautifully, and the trees were dripping with the heavy moisture deposited during the night; the birds sang joyously, and flitted past the window; the thrush, too, sat on the tall trees, and sang most melodiously; and the sun shone through the openings of the tall trees into the breakfast-room of the cottage, which had been the scene of the outrage that had been there perpetrated.

Ashton Cottage was the residence of Mr. Bentink, a widow lady, and her daughter Mary, a beautiful girl of about eighteen, whose loveliness and beauty were only equalled by her good sense and amiable disposition. Mrs. Bentink was a person of a genteel independence — who, in fact, possessed enough to keep off all the ills of life that could be kept off by such means. She was, in fact, in person and purse, altogether a very respectable and respected person; and Mary was the object of ambition of many of the younger portion of the community, who had the good fortune to meet with her; and, moreover, she had even at that age had more than one offer of marriage.

This morning Mrs. Bentink sat alone at her breakfast; she did not eat, but seemed to be musing and listening to the song of the thrush that kept singing most musically and cheerfully. She appeared to be enjoying a pleasant reverie. Suddenly she looked up as the time-piece chimed, and exclaimed,—

"Bless me, half-past eight, and Mary not down. Surely she must be ill."

She then rang the bell that was placed by her side, and when the servant entered the parlour, she said to her,—

"Have any of you seen anything of Mary this morning, or know why she is not down?"

"I have been in the room, but she lay asleep, ma'am, and I didn't like to waken her, she seemed to sleep so comfortable and sound."

"It is very strange. She usually gets up early.?"

"Yes, ma'am."

"Here's Mr. Henry Prosser, too; how he will be amazed to hear she's not up."

"Ah, yes, he will, indeed, ma'am. Shall I go and call her, ma'am?"

"Not directly. Wait a little while; she may have had a bad night, and may have fallen asleep towards morning."

At this moment Mr. Prosser entered. Mrs. Bentink saw him coming up the garden walk. This was the only one towards whom Mary showed any preference of all her lovers.

"Good morning, Mrs. Bentinck; this is a fine morning, and I could not resist the pleasure of walking over to you"

"I am glad to see you; but I am afraid we shall have the pleasure of taking our breakfast alone this morning."

"Indeed. And how is Mary? I hope she is not ill. I hoped to have seen her in her favourite walk this morning."

"She is not up yet."

"Not up yet? You surprise me. Surely something is the matter."

"Well, I hardly know what to think. I will send up and inquire what is the matter."

Mrs. Bentink again rang the bell, and the servant once more entered the room, when Mrs. Bentink gave her directions to go and ascertain if Miss Mary was yet awake, and too see if there was anything the matter. The girl had not been gone many minutes, when they heard a slight scream, and in another minute more the servant re-entered the parlour, looking pale, and trembling violently.

"Good heavens, what is the matter?" inquired Mrs. Bentink. "Is she ill?"

"Oh, ma'am! oh, goodness! oh, gracious!"

"What has happened?" inquired Mr. Prosser, in some trepidation.

"Tell me what has happened?"

"Oh, ma'am!—well, ma'am, I went into the bedroom, and listened, but I couldn't hear nothing, and I couldn't see nothing."

"What, is she gone away?" exclaimed Henry. "Impossible! there must be some mistake."

"Oh, dear! oh, dear! I wish she was," said the girl. "I shall break my heart."

"If you do not instantly tell me what is the meaning of all this, I will go and ascertain myself, and dismiss you from my service."

"Well, ma'am, if you will but listen, I will tell you. I listened and could hear nothing, nor see nothing, and then I opened the curtains, and then I saw her."

"Well, I thought as much."

"Yes ma'am. There she was, poor thing, but I could not hear her breathe, and I could not see her move. At first I thought it must have been her, but while I looked I thought it must have been somebody else; she seemed so altered and so strange, that I could scarcely believe it was the same."

"Well, well. What did you do?"

"I called to her, but she made no answer, and I then placed my hands on her. Oh, ma'am, she was stone cold."

"Dead?"

"Yes, ma'am—dead, quite dead. Poor dear Miss Mary is as dead as a door nail."

The conclusion of this eloquent description was not heard, but both Mrs. Bentink and her visitor rushed up to the room, and there saw the account given was too true. A scene of grief and sorrow ensued; the mother fainted, and wept—she could not contain her grief —she could not even control it, or guide it by reason, it was beyond her strength, and she eventually went into strong convulsions, and it became necessary to send for a surgeon to attend to her.

Henry Prosser felt his hopes dashed from him, and experienced all the grief of a sincere and ardent lover. He looked at the countenance he had so often gazed upon, and yet he could scarce believe himself that it was Mary that lay before him. She was much altered.

"Death alters the countenance very much, and yet I never saw such an alteration as that—it is truly wonderful."

He took her hand. It seemed a stronger hand and arm than what he had noticed, and yet it could not be otherwise. There was one of the rings he had given her, and the other he had often seen her wear.

"Yes, yes," he said, "'tis she, poor girl—how sudden, how unexpected."

When Mrs. Bentink came to herself, she looked upon the body, and thought the change was very wonderful, and she began to doubt; then the servants were called up to look at her, but they thought it was her, and they could swear to her hair-comb, and the linen. Mrs. Bentink herself recollected the rings, and therefore there could be no doubt of the fact whatever, and then how could it have been otherwise?—there was no possibility of its being otherwise. The perfect absurdity of doubting upon such a subject was so apparent to them, that they at once dismissed the thought. The body was buried as that of Miss Mary Bentink, and many friends were present at the ceremony, among whom was Henry Prosser.

It was a heavy blow to Mrs. Bentink, and she was unable to reconcile herself to the cottage, and determined to leave it. Everything put her in mind of her lost daughter, every flower, every tree; she had been so used to attend to them, that they recalled her to her mind so often that she found her health and spirits sensibly decay, and she resolved therefore she would soon leave.

A day or so after she received a letter from an attorney, saying, that her brother's wife, who was also a widow, had recently died, and had left her daughter, if she survived, a moiety of her fortune, and another moiety to her cousin, Charles Hargrave. If either of these two died, the survivor was entitled to the whole.

"Ah!" thought Mrs. Bentink, "this would have been good news had poor Mary been living, but she is dead, and Charles will benefit by it. It would have been a nice little fortune for her, poor girl. I would I had died for her. I never liked Charles; he was a bad youth, and grew up a worse man, capable of anything. I regret she had no better or worthy relative to leave it to, but I suppose she did not exactly know the character he bore."

Mrs. Bentink accordingly wrote to the attorney, that she had now no daughter living. Charles Hargrave was her nephew, and had at one time been very intimate with them, until his conduct towards Mary was so bad that he was forbidden the house. He had run through a career of dissipation of the most brutal and degrading character, and he had been known to act, in one or two cases, with so much violence and dishonour, that he was discarded by his own family.

Mrs. Bentink, not finding any one likely to make any offer for the house, determined to leave it as it was, and at once to go to London, and lodge at some respectable house, or in some family where she could receive that attention she so much required. She felt she was lonely; she had lived out all she loved, and life seemed no longer to have any charms for her. Death was to close the career she had run, and she cared not now how soon it came. In her walks, she more than once saw her nephew, Charles Hargrave, but he decidedly did not know her. He passed her and looked her full in the face without the slightest signs of recognition. She noticed that once or twice he went to a house at the back of that she herself lodged in. It was in Islington, and was one of those old-fashioned houses in which there are so many things to admire, but there are very few of them that now remain. The house he went to was equally old and strange in conformation, but it was by no means so substantial; it had been uninhabited for many years, but Charles had taken it, and went there occasionally. The house was in a very dilapidated condition, because the rain had gone through the roof and rotted the rafters, and there were many places in which the weather could not be kept out, and very often the place, in winter time, had been the refuge of beggars who were houseless.

Hargrave had taken precautions against them; indeed, he had had shutters and iron stanchions put before the windows—the doors were made good, and new locks were put on and the place made secure. The roof had received a temporary repair that would throw some of the water off, and keep the interior very dry.

This house Mrs. Bentink could see from her bed-room window as she sat sometimes by herself, as she would often do, and, indeed, it was a favourite place with her whenever she had any friend who came especially to see her.

One day Henry Prosser called to see her, it was the first occasion he had ever called, and the people with whom she lodged having some friends with them, she had retired to her bed-room, where she had a fire, and sat looking at the old house at the back. She desired him to sit down by the window, and for a few moments she continued to gaze upon the old house.

"I don't know what it is," she said to Henry Prosser; "but that old house opposite always chains my eyes, and I cannot help looking constantly at it; it quite fascinates me."

"Indeed!"

"Yes; I have seen Charles Hargrave enter that house yonder twice."

"Have you?"

"I have."

"Then I have had a most singular dream, and I scarce can tell what to think of the affair. It may seem as silly to you as it seems strange and inexplicable to me."

"A dream, Henry?"

"Yes, a dream."

"Of what?"

"Tell me again, did you say that Charles Hargrave entered an old-fashioned house, or uninhabited place, several times?"

"I have."

"Good heavens! how singular!"

"What is singular, Henry? Seak."

"I have had a dream. I have dreamt the same dream on three occasions. I must tell it you, though you may blame me for recalling events that have caused you much sorrow."

"Speak on, Henry."

"Well, I dreamt that this Charles Hargrave had taken Mary away, and concealed her in such a place as that one you are looking at."

"Ah, poor Mary! hers was a sudden and inexplicable fate. She altered so strangely, that I almost doubted her identity."

"And so did I. I could not believe it was her; and had I not seen the rings, I would have disbelieved her death."

"There were too many proofs of that, unfortunately," said Mrs. Bentink; "and yet it can scarce seem more than a dream, and I have often thought there was some great mystery about it."

"I cannot pretend to understand it, or throw a doubt upon the events. The impossibility of its being otherwise is so great and so glaring, that I know not what to think, and yet I must own that I would give any sum to see the inside of that house; not that I have any hope or expectation of seeing anything; and yet the strangeness of the dream, and the coincidence with the fact of his going to a dilapidated house, appears so very mysterious."

"It is singular."

"Most strange."

"And yet, what motive could he have had to commit such a deed, were it possible?"

"He came into possession of a considerable property by her death?"

"He did; and yet she died before we knew that she had become entitled to it."

"Very true; but he might have known it earlier, because he had been forbidden the house, and I dare say he could execute any project of revenge, if there were a possibility of doing so."

At this moment a tremendous and piercing shriek came upon her ears with startling distinctness, followed by two others. They looked at each other; it seemed to come from the very house they had been looking at.

"It is dreadful," said Mrs. Bentink, with a shudder; "surely something horrible is being perpetrated; it makes my blood run cold to listen."

"I cannot remain here any longer; and I cannot sleep until I have been over that house yonder, by fair means or foul."

Saying this, Henry Prosser rose, and bade Mrs. Bentink good morning, and promised to call upon her at the earliest opportunity, and let her know what he had done.

The first thing he did was to go round to the house, and ascertain its locality; and he had scarce done so, when he observed Charles Hargrave leave the house, very much excited.

This determined Henry; he went home, and procured the aid of a servant of his own—a stout courageous man—and arming themselves with a brace of loaded pistols and several implements, they sallied out, and were soon in the neighbourhood of the old house. It was difficult to gain access, but there was a court on one side of it, and the wall skirted a bit of a waste or yard, and this they both contrived to scale. Once in the yard, they were satisfied, and could make use of the tools that they had with them, without exciting observation.

In about five minutes they had effected an entrance into the house, and were within its walls, and, having secured the doors on the inside so that they should be free from interruption of any kind should Charles Hargrave return, they soon ran through the rooms, and then they came down stairs and proceeded to the cellars, and here they found one strongly secured by an iron bar and a padlock. Besides this, there were two strong bolts, one at the top, and the other at the bottom.

"What can this be for?" said Henry, as he gazed at these fastenings.

"Not to keep people out sir," said the servant, "because the bolts would not be on this side, but to kept people in "

"It would seem so, indeed."

"Shall I break the lock, sir?"

"Yes; put the crowbar in at the staple—that will be the best, I think."

This was done, and the bar fell back with a clank, and a groan came from the inside. The door was thrown open, and they both entered the cellar. It was dirty, and the smell was strong enough to have destroyed life almost, and yet there was a living human being in it. Henry sprang forward to look at the miserable object that lay huddled up on some straw before him. He threw the rays of light upon it, and saw it was a female, chained against the wall, and her hands so fastened down that she could not raise them. Her hair was dishevelled, and she had scarce an article of clothing upon her, and fresh marks of blood seemed smeared over her person. He could not distinguish her features clearly. She was gagged, and could not speak; she looked up to him, and moaned. He immediately released her from her horrible situation, and the next moment she exclaimed, in a voice that filled the dreary place, and thrilled through his very nerves,—

"Thank God! Henry, you come in time to save my life."

He staggered back, and would have fallen but for his servant.

"What do I hear—whom do I see? God of Heaven! it cannot be. Oh, no—no! it cannot be," he said; "she died and was buried!"

"Oh, heavens! do you forget me, Henry Prosser?—at least, do not leave me here to perish, but aid me to get back to my mother, and to escape the horrors of this place and the brutality of Charles Hargrave. My God! what have I not suffered!"

"'Tis her voice. Oh, heavens! what shall I do? Your mother believes you dead; but come, you shall see her, and we will endeavour to make something out of this affair. Get a hackney coach, and then we will hence."

The next ten minutes were spent in the most agitating conversation; and when the coach came, they both carried her into it, and then went home to Mrs. Bentink. A strange scene took place, Mrs. Bentink not knowing what to do, and being dreadfully agitated; and when she saw her daughter, she fainted away, and Mary too.

It was with difficulty that any explanation could be afforded, and when it was, she could but relate all she knew of her abducation—that she was hurried away to London, where she was placed in the cellar and chained up by Hargrave, who came to her frequently, and made the basest proposals to her, but she would never submit, and that night he had more cruelly ill-treated her than he was used to do, having struck her till the blood flowed. She stated that her rings and clothes had been forced off her person.

This, at once, accounted for their being upon the dead body that was buried.

The next day Charles Hargrave was secured, but not before he was allowed to go and make the discovery of the escape. He was secured, dreadfully agitated, and was then taken before Mrs. Bentink. He was compelled to restore all the property he had taken, and make over the greater part of his fortune to the poor. However, he committed suicide. Henry Prosser and Mary Bentink, in six months afterwards, were married.   *   *   *

Margaret Bertram looked up with a sigh from the book she had been reading, and she was surprised to find that is was one o'clock, as indicated by the time-piece, which was on the mantel-shelf of the small but elegant apartment in which she was sitting.

"One o'clock!" she exclaimed. "What can have become of Bertram, at such an hour? This is insulting me in the eyes of my servants for him to remain out all night, as now most probably he will, without letting any one know that such was his intention."

A flush of naturally indignant feeling crossed her face as she uttered these words, and she much regretted she had resolved to sit up for him, or that she had spoken to the servants at all upon the subject.

"If I had said nothing," she thought, "they might have supposed that I knew where he had gone; but now I have announced that I do not, and of course it will become a common talk among them of how much I am insulted and neglected."

To any wife this was a state of things calculated to produce a disagreeable feeling, but still she could not take upon herself quite to say that Charles Bertram would not be at home for the whole of the night. It was but an assumption of her own, after all, founded on the lateness of the hour, and he might yet come in.

Another hour, however, of anxious waiting, during which each minute seemed lengthened out to at least twenty, sufficed to bring a settled conviction to her mind that he would not come home, and suddenly starting from the sofa on which she had been sitting, she exclaimed,—

"Far better would it be to part with him at once than lead a life like this. Oh, Theodore, Theodore! Hush!— Why do I pronounce that name? Oh, why does the name of Theodore Danton always occur to me when my feelings are distressed, and I feel the unhappiness of my situation? Alas!—alas! what will become of me?"

She hid her face in her hands, and a dreadful picture of the future presented itself to her. She saw herself the neglected, despised, humiliated wife, and she knew how very different would have been her lot with him whom she had been to visit on that most eventful evening, and who loved her with a love so far exceeding any that Charles Bertram had it in his nature to feel.

These were dreadful thoughts. Thoughts concerning which she might have truly said with King Lear,—

"That way madness lies."

And yet how natural were they in her situation; and who can blame her that they found a home in her heart? Can the most rigid moralist that ever breathed do more than accuse poor Margaret of a want of that worldly wisdom which would have enabled her to play her cards with more tact, probably, but less honesty, single-mindedness, and honour? If she had merited suffering by the indiscretion—to give it the very harshest term it was susceptible of—of which she had been guilty in visiting Theodore Danton, most grievously was she doomed to suffer for it—to suffer to an extent which even those who were her worst enemies must pity. Indeed, we should hardly despair of extracting a few drops of kindly sympathy from the eyes of even Mrs. Blair herself.

"I will retire to rest," said Mrs. Bertram. "I will now retire to rest; I can endure this state of cruel suspense no longer. I will retire—but can I insure repose? Alas! no—I would I could. Oh, for some friendly opiate now, that would steep my senses in forgetfulness."

She shuddered then as she added,—

"I could wish to sleep the sleep that knows no waking. What is life to me? Where are it charms? What have I to look forward to, or expect, but an existence of protracted misery without a hope?—an existence which will only become to lerable perhaps towards its close, whe n the torpor of despair has taken the place in my brain of more active misery, and I have ceased to feel

so acutely, because I have ceased to have the capacity so to do."

She lit a small chamber-lamp. She would not summon an attendant, for she dreaded that her looks would tell tales of the state of affliction and heart-sickness she was in.

Oh, how the rich furnishing, the gilding, the gorgeous hangings, and the general aspect of graceful luxuriance which that house afforded, now palled upon her sight. In her mind's eye she contrasted them with the humble home, but the happy one, she had lived in before the wealthy Mr. Bertram sought her hand; and like many more before her, and as many more will do after her, poor Margaret made the discovery that it is not wealth, a costly house, carriages and servants, that constitute happiness, but that calm contentedness of spirit which may be far more readily found beneath the humblest thatch, than dwelling under the gilded roofs of palaces and in halls of state.

She was unaccustomed to be up so late, and now a chilled feeling came over her as she left the room where she had been sitting, and went out to the corridor. Her bed-room was on the same floor as that small boudoir which she could call her own; but when she left it, the change of temperature on the landing was very great.

We do not take upon ourselves now to say that what occurred to Margaret was real or merely the result of a heated imagination acting upon a brain which at the moment, was full of distressful images, and which had been making the most painful comparisons which it was possible for her situation to suggest The hour, too, was one at which it was unusual for her to be up, and, therefore something must be allowed for the amount of weariness which might be well supposed to have come over her.

She had got half-way between the door of the boudoir and the door of her bed-chamber, and, consequently, she was on a level with the head of the staircase which was just between. She felt a strange fear creeping over her, which, for the moment, she attributed to the change of temperature; her heart beat more quickly than usual, and from some impulse which she could not define, but which she did not attempt to resist, she raised the chamber-lamp she was carrying as high as she could above her head, and turned her eyes towards the staircase. She made an abrupt pause as she did so, and then the blood seemed to retreat from all her veins with a frightful gush towards her heart, and then again, with a tingling sensation, to fly like fire through each artery.

She saw some form coming slowly up the stairs. It made no noise, no footfall was heard. It didn't seem to be walking up at all, but it had the strange appearance of ascending as if it were being lifted bodily through a trap-door. She saw the head, then the shoulders; the breast, and so on, till the whole form became visible on the landing, and there it paused, and stood perfectly immovable as a statute. And there, likewise, stood Margaret for some moments, as immovable as that figure; she seemed to be turned to ice by the presence of it, and unable to move or speak. And yet she knew it; she knew the face—the pale deathlike face which was before her; she knew the eyes that were bent upon her with so sad and melancholy an expression; she had not looked upon that face for years; for years those eyes had not beamed upon her; but it was a face, and they were eyes which she could never forget.

It was her mother! Yes, her mother; who, years before, she had followed to the grave. It was the form of her mother as last she had seen her in life, which stood before her! Was not this a sight to freeze the young blood in her vein? Was not this a sight to turn her heart to stone?

Margaret was not superstitious; she had always prided herself upon not being superstitious; but here, whether it was an optical delusion or not, was an appearance presented to her senses which she could not contradict. She strove to speak—she felt that she must, that she ought to say something, but as often as she attempted to do so, the words died away in her throat in indistinct murmurs. How long she stood confronting that apparition she knew not; it might have been but a few brief moments; she had no means then or after of telling.

The feeling that she must speak to this dreadful appearance grew upon her each moment; she felt that, until she did it, it would so confront her with those melancholy eyes fixed upon her face. By a great effort, she did at length utter, in something like an articulate manner, the word

"Mother!"

The utterance of this word seemed to dispel the charm. The figure slowly faded away. The outlines of the form became each moment more and more indistinct, until at last it faded completely from Margaret's sight, the last vestige of it seeming to mingle with the air in the shape of a thin fleecy vapour.

When it was entirely gone, Margaret turned, and went back to the room from whence she had come. She knew not why she did so; she had no motive in going back to that apartment, but still she did go. She placed the lamp upon the table, and then, with a deep sigh, she seated herself upon the sofa. She wrung her hands for a moment, and then, in a sobbing, hysterical tone, she said,—

"Oh, Heavens! what have I done? what have I done to merit so much suffering?"

Exhausted nature then gave way, and she sank back upon the sofa in a state of perfect insensibility.   *   *

"Well," said the cook to the footman in Mr. Bertram's kitchen, as half-past twelve was indicated by the kitchen clock; "well, John, I shall go to bed; they won't have the assurance to want any supper to-night, I should say; what do you think?"

"Why," said John, "the trouble of thinking is great, and I don't intend to do it. Do you think I should have come into service if I had chosen to bore myself with thinking?"

"Well, I declare you are the oddest fellow ever I come near. Don't you think he is, Sarah?" said she, to the housemaid.

"Peculiarly and rationally so," said Sarah, who prided herself upon always speaking with the strictest propriety upon all possible occasions.

"Oh, bother thinking," added John; "I'm going to have some of missus's ale, to keep me awake."

"Well," said the cook, "it would put me to sleep; but really, now, John, how do you manage to get that ale? You know, as well as all of us, that it's dreadful expensive."

"Oh, a dodge—a dodge."

"But what peculiar and illustrative means has your intellectual horizon," said the housemaid, " of persuading Mrs. Bertram that she has drunk it, when you drink it?"

"Ah," added the cook, "we all know it only comes in two dozen at the time. How do you manage, John?"

"Easy," said John, "easy—nothing easier."

"Well, tell us."

"Ah," said Sarah, "enlighten the profound mystery, and enable the human mind to be enigmatical."

"If I understand you, Sarah," said John, " d—n me!"

"Oh, gracious!" exclaimed both the ladies, "John, don't swear."

"I cannot stand it," said Sarah. "My nervous systematics won't stand any swearing."

"And it puts me all over of a chill sweat," said the cook.

"I suppose," said Sarah, "you mean a *prespiration?*"

"Whether I does or whether I doesn't," said the cook, " is my business, and not your'n, I rather believe."

"Very good, ma'am, as you please."

"It is as I please, I rather believe, in this here kitchen."

"Oh, indeed."

"Ladies, ladies," said John, "don't now, don't. You are a-going it again, you two, hard and fast, like hammer and tongs. You asked me how I got missus's ale, and if you will but be a little quiet, now, I'll tell you honestly and fairly. But really, ladies, do not quarrel, do not.

Two such lovely females quarrelling is really dreadful. It's just to my mind as if the angels in the heavenly spears was to begin a scratching each other's eyes out, and a rumpling each other's blessed petticoats."

"John!" shrieked Sarah.

"What?"

"Oh, good gracious! You mentioned a word, sir, which I cannot sit still and hear unmoved!"

"Move, then," said John—"What was it?"

"It was petticoats, sir! I can inform you that a virtuous and right-minded female don't know what petticoats means!"

"You don't say so. You'd better not wear any, then."

"Oh, save me! Cook, do you hear? The idea of no petticoats!—oh, isn't it too dreadful for the human intellectual imagination?—Oh, dear! oh, dear!"

"Well," said John, "don't make yourself uneasy; you can wear 'em or not, you know, just as you like."

"Well, but about the ale," said the cook; "never you mind about Sarah's petticoats, John."

"Very good," said John; "about the ale, then. You know that particular bottled ale was ordered for missus by the doctor, but it's all imagination. I know that, howsomdever, it is prime ale; light, and sparkling, and dear drinking; leaves no bad taste in your mouth, and not a head-ache in a hogs-head of it."

"Well, well, John."

"Well, I'm a coming to it. There comes in a whole two dozen of this ale, and I says to myself, ' What an order! I must look sharp if I get any out of this lot.'"

"So you'd need, unless missus leaves any."

"Leaves any! Do you think I'd take anybody's leavings? No, indeed! I think I see me."

"Well, John," said Sarah, "you is no more nor right there. I don't see why we should take anybody's leavings, not I, nohow, when we consider the human mind, and all that. You is uncommonly correct in your notions, John, except upon delicate subjects, such as petticoats."

"Oh, am I?"

"Indeed you is; but we'll let that drop now, if you please."

"I never touched 'em, so I haven't any occasion to let them drop, you see."

"Oh, goodness!"

"Ah, it is oh goodness!"

"But I want to know about the ale," cried the cook.

"Well, then, you know, I had in a small cask of that at fourpence a quart, on the same day as missus's bottled came in."

"Yes, for yourself."

"No such thing."

"Who for, then?"

"For her."

"What! for missus? But how do you make her take it, John?"

"Why, the first bottle of her own bottled ale she ordered I tapped down here, and drank myself; then I filled the bottle out of my cask, you see, and sealed it well up again, and she never knew the difference, cos she never had her own, and I dare say, now, she fancies it does her a deal of good. After that first one I got on famously, because, you see, I had always a bottle ready in advance, and whenever she orders one of her own, I give her one of mine, and change with her. A fair change, you know, is no robbery, and she is none the wiser."

"What a headpiece you have got," said the cook, " to be sure."

"Ah, to be sure I have! We would need a headpiece to get on in this world; but I suppose now I shall have a late sitting-up job of it to-night, which will be remarkably pleasant."

"No doubt you will."

"Confound Bertram! why don't he keep good hours, or have a latch key? I must speak to him about it. This is a sort of gammon that I can't stand at all, and I won't. If he don't come in in another half-hour or so, I shall go to bed, and he must take his chance of awakening me to let him in or not."

CHAPTER XXXVIII.

THE DREADFUL NIGHT.—DESPAIR.
THE TAUNTS OF MRS. BLAIR.

JOHN the footman might go to sleep with the most perfect security, so far as regarded any chances of his master coming home; but that, of course, he could know nothing of, and, consequently, it was not without some misgivings that he took his candle and ascended the staircase.

He had no business or occasion to go up the principal staircase of the house; for there were two—one for the servants, which led directly to their sleeping-rooms, and another to the apartments belonging to the family. The domestics, however, were not so particular as always to choose the former mode of reaching the top of the house, and, just as chance or the whim of the moment directed, they would go up one or the other of these staircases.

Now, John, on this occasion, ascended by the principal flight, as it was called, and as he went on he felt certain fears and terrors coming over him which he could not account for; at least, so he afterwards declared, and we are bound, of course, to believe John.

He went on until he reached the second-floor landing nearly, and then he felt chilled and uneasy, as if something was in the very air of an uncommon and odd character. He shaded the light—he covered it with his hand as well as he could, and so he got fairly on to the landing before he saw anything which looked out of the way. Even then it was but a trifle; on the landing there lay a handkerchief, which, from its colour and texture, John guessed belonged to his mistress.

"Well," he said, in a low tone, "I'm scared a little, but I really don't know what at. What is there to frighten a fellow in a handkerchief? Of course missus has dropped it as she was going to bed most likely, so I'll pick it up. That's all—eh, eh! I thought I heard something."

There was some strange sound, something between a groan and the utterance of some word of supplication. John's face turned very pale, and his hair, as he declared, began to move of itself on his head, a sufficiently alarming circumstance to be sure. It was not to be supposed that he could stand that long, so as soon as he could at all recover strength sufficient to do so, he turned and fled down the staircase again with great speed and precipitation.

There is nothing in the world half so contagious as fear, and when John, who was rather a great gun among the servants, showed himself in the kitchen, with his ghastly-looking countenance, and trembling so that the candlestick shook in his grasp, as if it had been an especial object to keep it in a state of perpetual movement, he was received with a shriek of dismay, which at once induced the cat to make a desperate attempt to rush up the chimney, failing in which she went head foremost through a pane of glass in the window.

This was far from having the effect of allaying any fears, and the scene of confusion that ensued for a few moments baffles description.

Everything, however, as some philosoper says, somewhere, must have an end, and, therefore, the excited condition of the cook and the housemaids at length yielded to time, and comparative tranquillity was restored. John sat as close to the fire as he could, and ever and anon he cast an uneasy glance towards the door, as if he thought it far from improbable that some grisly spectre would walk in at once, and cut some extraordinary and ghost-like capers of a horrifying tendency. But, as he himself said, and we like to quote John,—"The more he looked, the more nothing came."

"John," said the cook; "good gracious! what was it—what did you see, John?"

"I—I—saw a groan," said John.

"Where—where?"

"Up stairs. I tell you what it is, something strikes me as something's happened to missus."

The servants looked at each other with dismay, and then all of a sudden the kitchen clock commenced that curious purring sound which many clocks preface the act of striking the hour with. Familiar, however, as they were with the kitchen clock, and its peculiarities and modes of expressing itself with regard to the lapse of time, the moment they heard the sound begin, they with one accord rushed from the kitchen, and, with a frantic eagerness that knew no respect of persons or of property, made their way to the hall. Then, and not till then, the cook said she thought it was only the clock, but

the idea was at once, on its own merits, repudiated by everybody, because it was by no means a pleasant or a great idea to have been half frightened to death by a kitchen clock.

"No," said John, "oh, dear, no; it was like the clock a little, I grant you, but it wasn't all the cock—oh, dear, no, by no means—the clock, indeed! Do you think that I should have walked away on account of the clock?"

"Well, but, John," commenced one of the housemaids, who had an immense respect for his opinion, "you know, John, that when——"

There was another scream of dismay from every one, and John at once dashed into the back parlour and shut himself in. And what was the cause of this new alarm? Just nothing in the world but a knock at the door.

Fear will convert, however, the most familiar and ordinary of sounds into those of terror and dismay, and such was the nervous state of the domestics, that anything whatever was amply sufficient to produce a perfect paroxysm of terror. The full conviction that after all it was only a knock, did not come across them for several minutes, and then, when it was repeated, they began to have an idea that it would be advisable to open the door.

They knew it was not Mr. Bertram's knock, and yet it was a double knock; but it sounded like the double knock of some one who rather arrogated to themselves the right to make such an appeal to the knocker, than felt that there was an undisputed right to do so.

John emerged from the parlour, where he declared he had only been to see if the window-shutters were made properly fast for the night.

"Will you open the door John?" said the cook, as now, for the third time, there came the knock, and of a much more decided character than before.

"Open the door?" said John; "oh, yes; of course I'll open the door. Why shouldn't I, eh? You know there can be no danger in opening the door, not the least. It must be somebody, of course, or else they could not knock, you know — ahem! — of course, I'll open the door. Stand aside all of you, and you'll see that I'm afraid of nothing and nobody."

John advanced in an extremely cautious manner to the street-door, and stationing himself behind it in such a way, that when it opened it would enclose him between it and the wall, as if he were in a sentry-box of confined dimensions, he drew back the latch.

Mrs. Blair walked at once into the passage with an angry frown upon her face.

"How dare you keep me waiting?" she exclaimed. "What is the meaning of all this?"

"Oh," said John, as she shut the door, "it's you, Mrs. B., is it?"

"You insolent fellow, how dare you have the presumption to address me with so much familiarity?"

"Familiarity?"

"Yes. The insolence of servants is beyond all conception in this house."

"Hoity-toity!" cried the cook; "if it comes to that, Mrs. Blair, pray what is you?"

"What am I?"

"Yes, to be sure, what is you? that's what I say. You is but a servant yourself, you knows, though you gives yourself such airs and graces."

"I discharge you," said Mrs. Blair. "To-morrow you have a month's wages and go."

"Oh, I don't wan't to stay; but before I does go, I'll be discharged by a lady, and not by a stuck-up piece of goods of a nousekeeper, who is no better than she should be."

Mrs. Blair's eyes flashed with fire for a moment, and then, by a great effort, she subdued her rising passion, and said, rather in a sneering than a passionate tone,—

"I shall be very shortly able, I believe, to convince you all who is really mistress here."

She then commenced ascending the stairs.

"Don't say anythink," whispered John; "I should like her to meet with the devil himself on the second floor landing."

Had there been any cause of alarm, Mrs. Blair would, no doubt, have encountered it, but whether or not the apparition which had shown itself to Mrs. Bertram were a creation of her over-wrought brain, or some real phenomenon of nature of that class, the instances of which are too rare for us to decide positively upon, then most certainly Mrs. Blair saw nothing, but passed on, without a tremor, to the second floor.

There, on the landing, she saw the handkerchief, which she was in by far too haughty a mood to pick up from the floor; but she passed at once into the apartment where, on a sofa, lay poor Margaret Bertram in her trance, and moaning slightly, as if her imagination were troubled with some sad and melancholy images.

"Oh!" said Mrs. Blair; "so she has come home at last, has she? Humph! what a triumph now is mine. I have at lenght succeeded—fully succeeded. Of course Mr. Bertram, when he recovers sufficiently to think and act, will separate from her. Her pride, too, will induce in her such a spirit of resistance, that she will widen the breach which has been created, and all will go on evenly and pleasantly for me. I have achieved now a complete triumph; I shall be mistress of this house and all that it contains; I shall be able to dictate what I please to Bertram, and my condition will be so far bettered from what it was before his marriage, that I shall no longer live as I then did, in constant apprehension that he would make such a connection. Hush! hush! she recovers."

A slight movement on the part of Mrs. Bertram checked any further manifestations of Mrs. Blair's triumphant feelings. In a voice indicative of exquisite anguish, Margaret spoke,—

"Oh, God! oh, God!" she said.

There came over the countenance of Mrs. Blair a change. Was there yet some lingering consciousness of wrong-doing in her heart that made the name of God a terror to her?

"I—I will awaken her," she muttered; "I do not like ravings."

"Spare him, Heaven!" moaned Mrs. Bertram; "oh, spare him, in thy mercy!"

"Mrs. Bertram!" exclaimed Mrs. Blair; "Mrs. Bertram, you do not know what you are saying."

Her voice aroused Mrs. Bertram, and, opening her eyes, she exclaimed,—

"What have I seen—oh, what have I seen? Mother—mother, do you come to bless or to curse?—do you come in sorrow or in anger, mother—dear, long lost mother?"

"Mrs. Bertram, what are you speaking about?"

"Oh, are you here?"

"Yes! don't you know me?"

"Too well—too well."

"I am Mrs. Blair, Mr. Bertram's housekeeper."

"You are my evil genius."

"I don't pretend to know what you mean by that, Mrs. Bertram. I am no one's evil genius that I am aware of. I like what's right, and will not see any one's confidence abused. Is Mr. Bertram at home, madam?"

"I know not. When I require your services I will command them. You understand me, Mrs. Blair? I wish to keep this room strictly private. As you have remarked, you are Mr. Bertram's housekeeper; therefore I desire no service of you."

"Very well, madam, as you please. You see I am very humble, and I have only to hope that you never may require any service of me or of any one. I wish you joy—much joy, Mrs. Bertram, of what is to come."

"Humility from you is hypocrisy, and your wish of joy I translate into a pre-knowledge of some evil. Leave me!"

"I will leave you, madam; but before I do so, since we are alone, I tell you that in the fight for supremacy in this house, which you cannot deny that you and I have had, I am the victor."

"I do not understand you, nor do I wish to do so, Mrs. Blair, nor am I in spirits to hold a conversation with any one whom I cannot esteem."

"Esteem! What is your esteem to me?"

"This is insolence!"

"I know it is. Who said it was aught else but insolence? I know it is insolence, and fully intend it as such. What then, I say, Mrs. Bertram—what then?"

"My husband will surely protect me for his own honour's sake from this," exclaimed Margaret, as she walked towards the bell-rope and rang.

"Did you say for his honour's sake?"

screamed Mrs. Blair. "Well—well you do surprise me, there, I must confess. He will for his own honour's sake, perhaps, have to take a very different step to any you contemplate."

Margaret looked astonished. The remote supposition came across her that, perhaps, Mrs. Blair had been sacrificing to the rosy god rather too freely; but she at once said,—

"You or I must leave this house."

"Then do you leave it," cried Mrs. Blair, who now no longer seemed to feel the least necessity for reserve or caution—"do you leave it and go to your paramour."

Mrs. Bertram's eyes, as well as they might, sparkled with indignation; and she turned upon Mrs. Blair so suddenly, and with such an appearance of dignity—the dignity of virtue—that the latter involuntarily stepped back a pace or two.

"Infamous woman!" said Margaret. "Now I understand you—now I know what your speech alludes to—now I can see, as though some veil were suddenly rent from before my eyes, the odious plot you have got up against me; but truth and honour shall yet confound you."

"Indeed! and so that is your reliance? You will find both fail you, Mrs. Bertram. You came here, and you clashed with me; there you made a terrible mistake. You might have made me a friend — you chose to make me an enemy; and you shall now reap the consequences of such a step."

"Did you ring, ma'am?" said a young girl, who had been recently taken into the service of Margaret to answer her bell.

"Yes, Alice; stay with me."

"Yes, ma'am."

"Ah, you can stay," added Mrs. Blair; "I have said my say. I have no more to add now. Do what you will—strive how you may, Mrs. Bertram, you cannot now escape."

She did not seem inclined to say anything of a very decided character before the young girl who had answered Margaret's ring, and so she now left the room, poor Margaret, what with one anxiety and another on that eventful night, being nearly driven mad.

"Oh, Alice, Alice," she said, "stay

With me. Do not leave me to myself, for if you do I know not what would become of me. I might do some desperate act."

The girl burst into tears as she implored her mistress to tell her what distressed her; but Margaret only shook her head as she said,—

"No, no, I cannot—I may not. I am sure that something most dreadful will happen soon; but, be it what it may, Alice, never do you believe me other than innocent of all wrong. I avow it in the name of Heaven."

CHAPTER XXXIX.

THE MYSTERIOUS DISAPPEARANCE OF BERTRAM FROM MRS. PRIMROSE'S.

IN the morning, after snatching a few hours' brief repose, Mrs. Blair went to her sister's. She hoped by that time to find that Mr. Bertram was in a state which would enable her to induce him to take some immediate steps for the repudiation of his wife.

We have said it was in the morning, and we are right in so far that it was before midday, but it was not earlier by any means, for the various events which had occurred, and the results of which were still so undeveloped, had occupied much time.

"I am quite certain now," reasoned Mrs. Blair, "that I shall be able to accomplish a separation between Bertram and his wife. He entertains, now, no doubt whatever about his own dishonour; and if he be but half as frantic as he was last night, I can persuade him to any measure; and, be that measure what it may, so long as it is a violent one which cannot well be retracted, I care not. What fools these people are to allow me thus to triumph over them, what puppets they become in my hands. I can turn them and lead them any way I please. Talk of people being the victims of circumstances. It may be so with the mass of human beings, but I create circumstances for myself."

Thus did Mrs. Blair flatter herself that, like some evil genius, as Mrs. Bertram had not unaptly called her, she could ride upon any whirlwind, and direct any storm; but she had yet to learn that, in such undertakings as those in in which she had engaged, the hour of greatest danger was the hour of greatest fancied security. She had yet to know that some trivial accident might yet derange all her calculations, and topple to the dust her air drawn castles.

She reached her sister's door in a very agreeable state of mind, for she already considered herself mistress of Mrs. Bertram's house and fortune. Mrs. Primrose met her in the parlour, to whom she said in rather an imperious tone,—

"How is Mr. Bertram?"

"I suppose much as usual," said Mrs. Primrose. "The last time I went into the room he had covered himself up with all the bed-clothes, and he would not move or speak to me, though I asked him a dozen times if he wanted anything that I could bring him."

"Psha! you should not have troubled him. I will go to him myself."

So saying, Mrs. Blair walked up stairs to where Bertram had been left; she found that the curtains of the bed where all drawn, and by the profound stillness that there reigned she conjectured that he must have gone to sleep. This supposition, however, did not in the least deter her from disturbing him, and proceeding at once to the bedside, she said—

"Mr. Bertram—Mr. Bertram!"

There was no reply, and upon drawing one of the curtains on one side, she saw that, as Mrs. Primrose had stated, he was completely covered up by the bed-clothes—head included.

"Mr. Bertram!" she said, "I must speak to you It is absolutely necessary that you should take some immediate steps with regard to Mrs. Bertram. Do you hear me, sir—are you awake?"

Still there was no reply, and Mrs. Blair made up her mind that she would awaken him whether he liked it or not. She laid her hand upon, as she supposed, his shoulder; but found in an instant that whatever it was that lay so snugly ensconced among the bed clothes, it had not the substantiality of flesh and blood.

The thought at once flashed across her mind that Bertram was not there, and, in another moment, she convinced herself of that truth, by discovering that it was to the bolster she had been speak-

ing, which was placed in the bed in lieu of its human occupant.

But where was Bertram? Bertram, who had to all appearance been quite sufficiently injured to prevent the possibility of his removal for some days—where was he? That was, indeed, to Mrs. Blair a question of vital importance, and she went down stairs to propound it.

"Where is Mr. Bertram?" she exclaimed.

"Up stairs."

"No, no. The bed is vacant.

"Vacant?"

"Yes,—and what you supposed to be him is the bolster covered up with the bed-clothes."

Mrs. Primrose gave a faint shriek, and Mrs. Blair laid hold of her by the arm with force fully sufficient to justify it, as she screamed rather than said to her—

"You know something of this. Tell me this moment where he has gone to, or I will bring consequences upon your head which you little dream of."

There was some of the family spirit about Mrs. Primrose, and she replied, in a scarcely less loud tone,—

"How dare you threaten me, you viper? Take your hands off, or I'll tear your eyes out,"

"Where is he?"

"How do I know what becomes of your men? Don't ask me, I've had trouble enough, and little profit, Heaven knows."

"Do you mean seriously to tell me, said Mrs. Blair, who began to see how impolitic it was to quarrel with Mrs. Primrose, "that you don't know where he has gone?"

"How should I know where he had

gone, when I did not know he had gone?"

"Excuse me then—at the moment I was excited. I did not mean to say anything unpleasant."

"Oh, don't mention it," said Mrs. Primrose, in that tone of voice which implied that she should not readily forget it.

"We must find out what has become of him," added Mrs. Blair. "In his present state of mind there is no knowing what he may do ; but, most of all, I dread his going to the hotel where Theodore Danton is staying."

"Then you may depend upon it," exclaimed Mrs. Primrose, "that that's just where he has gone, and nowhere else."

"How it takes my breath away to think what may have happened," said Mrs. Blair, as she sunk into a chair and turned pale at the thought of some occurrences which might, after all, set the whole of her calculations on one side. For example, it was just possible that, in the mad state he was in, Bertram might murder Theodore Danton, and so bring himself to a scaffold : in which case, what was to become of her, Mrs. Blair, and all her fine schemes which so short a time since she had been deeply congratulating herself upon the complete success of ?

Mrs. Primrose was not accustomed to see her masculine-minded sister much moved at anything, and when she now observed how powerfully affected she was at the disappearance, so strangely and mysteriously, of Mr. Bertram, she, Mrs. Primrose, felt quite in a state of alarm.

"I cannot believe that he is gone," she said. "You may yet find that he is in the house. Do not make yourself unhappy about what, after all, may not be a fact."

"Yes," said Mrs. Blair, ' he is gone. I know he is gone. I am certain upon that point, else why would the bed have been arranged so as to seem as if it still had an occupant?"

"Well there is something in that."

"There is everything—and I am ruined !"

"Ruined ?"

"Yes. Can you not imagine that it is for revenge he has gone to the hotel where Theodore Danton is staying? Of course that is the place of his destination. He has, by this time, crossed that threshold which only an accident prevented him from crossing last night, and for all we know, murder may have been commited."

"Murder ! Good God !"

"Don't say 'good God' to me. I am in no humour to be preached to ; and if I were I should not come to you to officiate. What is to be done ? That is the question—what is to be done ?"

"I know not. You are so much better acquainted with all the circumstances that it would be folly for me to attempt to advise you."

"You are right. I must, as I have ever done, act for myself and by myself."

"Command me in any way."

"No—no. There is nothing to do but to ascertain facts. Do you remain here until I come back. Say nothing to any one about Bertram—we now stand upon a mine, and we know not a moment when it may explode beneath our feet."

While she spoke Mrs. Blair arranged her dress for the streets, and in another moment, without waiting for any reply from her still terrified sister, she was gone.

She walked rapidly till she got to a coach-stand, and then she took a vehicle, and desired to be driven quickly to the hotel which she named, where she feared to hear intelligence of some terrible tragedy having occurred. She was carried with rapidity to her place of destination, and by the time she reached the quiet street in which the hotel was situated, she had worked herself into a perfect fever of intense excitement.

Retribution, as regarded Mrs. Blair, had already begun, in the full sense of the word—she was suffering now far more acute pangs than the innocent can suffer, for she had no one feeling of a better tendency to fall back upon.

The carriage stopped, and she sprang from it into the hall of the hotel. The first person she encountered was a waiter, whom she seized be the arm, and of whom she demanded, in loud and peremptory accents—

"What has happened—what has happened, I say ? Tell me at once ?"

"Happened!" exclaimed the alarmed waiter; "what do you mean?"

"Speak! speak!"

"I am a speaking, Hilloa, here's a mad woman."

"A mad woman!" said the scientific James, stepping forward. "Did you say a mad woman? Something the matter with the brainous system. I believe I know a thing or two about such matters. Let me see her."

"Cease this folly," said Mrs. Blair, "and tell me at once if anything has happened here of a disheartening character."

"Nothing till you came, ma'am," said the waiter, who had been in the first instance laid hold of so unceremoniously by Mrs. Blair,

"Thank——" Heaven she was going to say, but, somehow or another, she could not bring herself to repeat the word.

"What is all this about?" said the landlord, coming forward upon hearing sounds of disturbance in the hall.

"We don't know, sir," said James; "Thomas thinks as the lady is a little cracked."

"What does she want?"

"She wants to know, sir, if anything has happened."

"Peace, peace, all of you," said Mrs. Blair; "I want to know if any one has been here to see Mr. Danton?"

"If they did," said the landlord, "they would not see him."

"You are right, very right. You would not permit them to do so on any account?"

"I certainly should not have permitted them on any account; but now it happens to be out of my power to do one thing or the other, for Mr. Danton is no longer in this house."

"Not here?"

"Certainly not."

"Why—why—I thought he was by far too unwell to leave."

"So we all thought; but, for all that, he has mysteriously disappeared."

"And you know not where?"

"We have not the least idea. Can you afford any clue?"

"Not the remotest," added Mrs. Blair, and she abruptly left the hotel, much inclined to think that, at all events, there had not been anything in the shape of a collision between Bertram and Theodore Danton. Had she, however, remained a little longer where she was, and asked quietly a question or two more, she would have obtained some more extended information.

CHAPTER XL.

THEODORE'S RESOLVE.—THE VISIT OF BERTRAM TO THE HOTEL.—THE STRANGE DETERMINATION, AND THE LITTLE LODGING IN SOHO.

THAT Theodore Danton loved Margaret with the greatest devotion, there can be no doubt, and that she felt towards him now feelings of the tenderest character, is equally certain. From these circumstances much misery might, accompanied with much self-reproach, have resulted, had not Theodore's love been of that character which far preferred the happiness of Margaret to all other considerations. When he had in some measure recovered from the excitement which the visit of Margaret had occasioned him, he felt much better than he had done for some time, and while the nurse thought he was sleeping, the blissful idea came across his mind that he might possibly yet be happy with his Margaret in some quiet spot, where they would be secluded from the world's eyes, and live but for each other. Soon, however, his better judgment and better feelings corrected this error of thought, and he said to himself—

"No, no! I will love her, for it is madness to say that I will not; but I will not be the bane of her yet young existence. Rather, a thousand times rather, would I tear myself from her for ever, and consent never again to look upon her face, than I would disturb her pure thoughts by one evil suggestion."

He then began to think what he could do, and what he ought to do, and a voice seemed to whisper to him that he ought to fly from even the possibility of danger to her, who was so dear to him. As soon as the mental suggestion had found a home in his heart, it gathered strength each passing moment, and he said to the nurse who attended him—

"I think I am able to get up now."

"Do not think of doing so," was the reply. "The doctor is most strongly against any such thing. Let me implore you not to think of moving yet."

"Well, well," he said "be it so."

But still the idea grew upon him of leaving, and each moment that it did so, it seemed to him as if Heaven, in approbation of such a course, was intent upon granting him the strength to carry it into execution. But how could he? That was the question. How could he? If he announced his intention, he knew it would meet with strenuous opposition, if, indeed, it were not frustrated by what would be considered friendly violence.

In such a case, of course he could not succeed, because he could not hope to contend against the power that could be brought to bear against him; and therefore was it that by communicating his wish to leave the hotel once, he was in great danger of having that design effectually frustrated.

"I am certain I am strong enough," he said to himself; "I know I could walk; and if not, it will be sufficient to place me somewhere else where she cannot find me, for I will banish myself from her for her sake. I could not stand another interview."

After a time, however, he thought of a plan by which he might escape the vigilance of his nurse. She had had very little repose, but in the adjoining chamber was a bed on which she had lain down when he was slumbering.

"Give me yon book," he said; "I will read for an hour, while you get some sleep; and pray close the door of communication between this chamber and the next, for I fancy there is a draught."

"Here is the book," she said, "but I prefer remaining in the room where there is a fire, and I dare say I shall be able to take a nap in the arm-chair."

This was provoking, but what could he say to it? His only chance now lay in the possibility that she might take the nap, and, in such an event, his only chance was to take the book and read on until he could with security slip out of bed, dress himself, and be off. He accordingly affected to acquiesce in the arrangement, and the nurse seated herself by the fireside in the easy chair, while he commenced reading the following narrative:—

Of all the haunts of vice and misery that this great city abounds in, none have been more frightful and serious than some of those now being pulled down to make room for the new improvements in the neighbourhood of Field-lane.

As the circumstances which led to the perpetration of the crime we are about to narrate were of themselves interesting, the whole affair, and all connected with it, have been thrown into the form of a narrative for the convenience of telling.

The one part a mere relation of cruel crimes, would be unintelligible without the other, the motives that led to the commission of offences so repugnant to our nature.

There was a mercer some years back in the city, who had two sons, the elder John, and the younger Edwin. He was a rich man, and these two sons were his only children, and he regarded them very much, and no indulgence was too great for them. They seldom troubled themselves about business, and they amused themselves with learning how they could most luxuriously and expensively enjoy life in the most fashionable manner and quarter.

The two brothers lived in great amity, though they were of different temperaments and habits. They were by two different mothers. They were the children of the same father, but not of the same mother.

They both expected to share alike in their father's riches, and they seemed equally well pleased at the future prospect thus afforded them.

At length a cause of dissension sprung up between them in the following manner:—

There was a certain notary, whose only child was a rich heiress. She was, moreover, very rich and beautiful, amiable, and young; indeed, there were few who could in London compare with Eveline Montague, for such was her name.

It so happened that the two brothers were sent there upon business when the notary was out, and then they saw Eveline for the first time, and were much stricken with the beauty and charms of the young girl.

"Has not the old notary got a beautiful girl for a daughter?" said John.

"He has indeed," replied Edwin; "I never saw a rarer creature in all my life; she is a perfect gem."

"She is a gem worth the winning and wearing most nobly too."

"Yes, yes; she is a rare jewel."

"And one of price, too, for old Montague has not lived all these years for nothing; he is a rich man."

"No doubt of it, I have heard so from many; moreover, he has plenty of business, and he lives very abstemiously."

"I tell you what, brother John, I feel much inclined to woo the maid for myself, and I tell you now to prevent mistakes."

"And I," said John "shall do the same to prevent mistakes. I am perfectly charmed with her at first sight."

"It seems," said Edwin, "we shall both be after the same game."

"Precisely so."

"In that case, may he who wins wear her," said Edwin.

"Certainly," replied John; "who could desire more of any one? I am willing to subscribe to such a wish as that."

"Then we will visit the house in each other's company," said Edwin, "and we may be sure that we act fairly."

"As you please; I agree to it, save when one of us obtains an invitation without the other; then he shall be entitled to accept of it without the other."

"Very well; very well."

Thus the two brothers agreed to court the same young lady, while they at the same time laid the foundation for the great calamities in life that at least one of them would endure.

They often visited the notary, and became intimate with him and his daughter, and were often invited to stay with them.

The two brothers were young men of attractive parts; they sang, danced, and played music; were engaging in their manners, and more particularly pleasing among females than men, by the nature of their pursuits and education, which fitted them to shine in the drawing-room. It was no wonder, then, tha Eveline Montague felt much pleased a the two young men, and spoke to them with all the confidence of a sister. She had scarcely turned her thoughts so decidedly towards them as to begin to think of one before the other. She did not put the question to herself thus—"Which of these two young men do I like the best?" She had not yet thought so much of either of them as that, but yet she showed an insensible preference to the younger. On one occasion she presented Edwin with a purse of her own making, and gave none to John. This, as may be imagined, estranged the elder from the younger.

"Well," exclaimed Edwin, "I think I may now claim the entire interest in Miss Eveline Montague—she evidently favours me."

"Does she?" sneered John.

"She does; you must be aware of that, brother John."

"I am not aware of that, brother Edwin, replied John. "I admit you have the purse; perhaps it is the fabled purse."

"You may sneer, but it ill becomes you or the subject."

"You are upon the stilts because you have a dubious present."

"I am not. I have the purse, and keep it as an evidence of her esteem."

"Perhaps she only meant it as a hint that a fool and his money are soon parted, and the purse might tend to mend the evil."

"I see you are chagrined at the circumstance, and hence you sneer at what you would gladly have received yourself. It is useless to pursue this subject any further."

"I perceive not, since it disturbs your dream of superiority in the eyes of Miss Eveline Montague," said John.

Little more was said, but enough had been said to show the brothers they thought and felt at variance with each other. This was, indeed, their first difference, and those feelings which had hitherto remained dormant were now and hereafter aroused from their latent state, to all the life that disappointment and jealousy could lead them. It was strange to see the seeds of evil spring up in the breasts of two youths, to see them germing and developing themselves, and taking the place of better feelings. It was lamentable as well as strange. John was certainly doomed to be a disappointed man in this case, and of this he seemed to be perfectly aware, and yet he would not allow himself to show that he was at all conscious of the fact. Moreover, he was madly in love with Eveline himself, and he judged that, but for his brother's suit, he would stand almost a certain chance of gaining her affections, her heart, and hand. To this end he determined to devote all his energies, and to stop at no crime, as will be seen eventually.

John Watts had on many occasions spent his evenings alone, in the company of some of the lowest and most degraded of human beings—he became acquainted with them by means of a female, and, once introduced to this society, he could at all times enter their haunts.

He made an acquaintance with one man, a Jew ruffian, who kept a house in Field-lane, who, in fact, kept five or six houses, all adjoining each other. There was known to be a number of cellars, and other places of concealment, that the police had no means of discovering. It was often said by the officers, "Oh, if he has got to Fagin's, the Jew's, it's no use going there after him."

Criminals of all kinds were concealed there, and it was said that crimes and deeds of blood had been done in those cellars—deeds that never will see the light of day, for those who suffered and those who committed them were alike a prey now to death. To this man John Watts proceeded, believing that he could aid him in the affair in some way or other. It was night when he arrived at an almost concealed door, for there were all sorts of goods exposed for sale. He gave a peculiar tap at the door, which, after some delay, was opened by Fagin himself.

"What," said the Jew, "you here, master John? I didn't expect to see you."

"May be not, Fagin, but I wish you to give me a little counsel and advice."

"Counsel and advice, master John! I cannot promise you either, at present, for I am up to my neck in business."

"Well, the more you have, the more you'll be able to do. I know that from experience." said John.

"I must know what it's about; but come this way, and let me hear all about it—come into my own room."

He followed Fagin into a small back room where there was a fire and a few articles of furniture, but very scantily furnished, and of the commonest character. There was no appearance of comfort, save there was a bottle with a glass, and some mixed spirit, and a strong smell of rum.

"There, sit down," said Fagin, pointing to a deal chair by the side of a blazing fire; "sit down, and tell us all about it."

John sat down, and Fagin went to a cupboard, and pulled out, after much clattering, another glass, which he placed upon the table, saying—

"There, mix for yourself; I have done so for myself."

"Thank you, Fagin," said John, and he mixed himself a tumbler of the spirits and water, and drank a draught, and then said—

"Fagin, I am in a particular situation, and want you to undertake a job."

"You just now said you wanted my advice, and now you have determined upon having the job done, practicable or not; now, my tear Shon, you shee you only vant assistance."

"I want advice how to do the thing."

"Very good—go on."

"You must know my brother?"

"Your brother, my tear—your brother Edwin, do you mean him?"

"Yes, I do; he and I are rivals."

"An affair of the tender passions, my tear. I see! a voman, of course."

"Of course, as you say, Fagin. Well, my brother, you know, is a milksop."

"Yes, my tear."

"Well, he has the way of winning over the girls to his side. Now, I had been rather sweet upon a girl myself, but he must step in and take her from me."

"Ah, my tear, if anybody was to serve me sich a scurvy trick, why I'd——"

"What, Fagin—what?"

Fagin made an expressive gesture, by drawing his hand across his throat.

"Would you?"

"I would, by God."

"It would make a mess," said John.

"Clean it up, my tear,"

"There's more ways of killing a cat besides one, you know."

"What would you do?"

"Why," replied John, "give him some sleeping draught, a poison, or anything that will lay him flat, and then you can smother him, or strangle him, or, in fact, anything you may like."

"I don't like poisons much," said Fagin; "the fact is, my tear, I was so near being poisoned myself, that I have determined to have none in the house."

"I don't care what becomes of him so long as I get rid of him."

"Don't you?"

"Not a bit."

"Well, then, listen to me."

"Go on."

Fagin spoke in a low tone, as he said to John Watts—

"Bring him here."

"He wouldn't come in if he came to the door," replied John.

"Make him drunk, give him laudanum, or anything, and we'll take him in somehow or other."

"Well, I must manage that; but will you manage the other part of the business?"

"Can I not? but mind I will have nobody else in the affair but myself and you."

"Such is my will."

"What will you stand, my tear, that's the thing—the consideration, you know. I am moderate; but you know it is a serious piece of business; it is, you know, very serious—'tis murder, and nothing short."

"Nonsense; murder, be hanged! it's only business; you've an ugly way of calling names, Fagin, but that's neither here nor there. I'll give you fifty now, and another when the job's done, you know, and he'll have a few things about him."

"You must double the sum on the second occasion, recollect, or it's no bargain."

"Very well; you shall have it done. Good by till I see you again."

"Will you say to-morrow night?"

"Yes; I'll try it on, and bring him out. I'll say I have a case of real distress—you'll feign sick, or something of that sort."

"Leave it to me; nobody can hear here if there should be a rumpus."

"Very good."

"The two next houses are empty—one each way—or as good as empty, there's no living soul in them but full of lumber."

With this, Fagin let John out, and when he had gone the old Jew cunningly remarked, with a smile of satisfaction, as he mixed a strong tumbler of rum and water—

"It's all very well, but Master John is a rich man, or will be one, and if he thinks that when this is all done, I'm to be pensioned off for my silence, he's cursedly mistaken. I don't know yet if I will even kill him, but even if I should it won't matter, or I can keep him a prisoner safe enough. But no matter—no matter; it shall all take it's own way, and if he escape death, then he shall live, but down below, upon exceedingly low diet."

*   *   *   *   *

"Brother Edwin," said John, the next day after the above conversation.

"Well, John."

"I had an adventure last night."

"Indeed!"

"Yes; what do you think it was?"

"Some absurdity or other; perhaps a row, and got the worst of it."

"Oh, dear, no; but one that even you would take pleasure in."

"You alarm me—what is it?"

"Why, I met with a most curious and strange case of distress in a female—all alone and unprotected, but very young and beautiful."

"Did you?"

"Yes; and I want you to come and see if you can make it out."

"I'd rather not."

"I don't want you to spend anything there. I'll stand the racket; but I only want your opinion as to whether she be a fit object or not to relieve."

"The money is no object to me more than you, John; however, I will come with you to aid your good intentions."

*   *   *   *   *

It was night when John and Edwin

arrived at the door of the Jew's house, and Field-lane was in a bustle and excitement.

"This is a strange place, Edwin," said John.

"I was thinking so."

"But it is a yet stranger place than you can imagine, and so you will say when you come to see this beautiful unfortunate."

"Indeed!"

"Yes; but here comes some one."

At that moment the door was opened by Fagin, whose eyes glistened when he saw Edwin.

"Well," said John, "how is the unfortunate young girl, my good man?"

"Oh, sir," said he, with a shrug of the shoulders, "she is very bad; but come into my room first, and I will see if I can ascertain if she can be seen at present."

"Do so," said John, and the old Jew hobbled forward, and went up a flight of stairs itno a room over head.

"What a wretched place this is," said Edwin, looking about him.

"It is; but I daresay the inhabitants never knew anything better."

"Probably not."

At that moment they could hear the old Jew come back, and presently he opened the door, saying,—

"One of you can come at a time; and, if one will do, the better, for she is not to be disturbed more than possible."

"You go, Edwin," said John: "I have seen her, and I wish you to do so."

Edwin assented, and followed the old Jew, who let him go along the passage first, and he followed him with a light.

He had not gone far when he fell through a trap-door, which closed after him, and the Jew returned to the room in which Edwin had been left.

"It's done," he said, with a hideous grin. "It's done."

"Have you disposed of him?"

"Yes."

"But how?"

"Come, and you shall see;" and he led the way to a trap-door in the passage, which he opened, and then listened attentively, but no sound came up—nothing but a disagreeable odour came from that place.

"Is he there?"

"Yes, he fell through quite by an accident, you know," said the Jew, looking down.

"Indeed! and do you really think he is dead, Fagin?" he inquired.

"I don't think, Master John—I am sure; this trap has been used before, and it never failed; besides, if he were to escape immediate death, he would be dead in a few hours—this place ain't fit to breathe in."

"I think not, too."

"A lighted candle would scarce burn."

"Indeed!"

"See, there he lies all of a heap! Oh, yes, he's dead—quite dead—don't you see him lying with his head on the stones?"

As he spoke, he moved the light to and fro, and cast a reflection on the body, so that he could see it.

"I see it now," he muttered; "I see it now. But are you sure he is dead?"

"Am I sure I am living?" said Fagin.

"Well, I think he is so, too," said John; "and do you go down and see what he's about."

The Jew turned sharp round at this speech, but he was too late—for John had seized him by the leg, and thrown him off his balance in an instant, and then, giving him a violent kick in the stomach, which caused the Jew to relax his hold in an instant, he fell headlong down the hole.

John listened for a moment or two; he heard the head of the Jew come in contact with the stones, and it cracked with a dull, heavy sound.

"That will do," said John; "now no one lives to tell the tale. I knew master Fagin well enough to believe that, had he lived, I should never have paid him enough—he would have cleared me out—extorted every penny-piece I had, and, besides, it is more pleasant to have nobody alive that knows one's odd tricks. Now for beauty and fortune—for both are mine."

*   *   *   *   *

The fall had never been intended to prove fatal by the Jew; no, he had taken such precautions as would only ensure a stunning fall, which would scarcely become mortal, and that was all in this instance that was produced, for after

THE QUARREL BETWEEN THEODORE DANTON AND BERTRAM.

lying there half or three quarters of an hour, he showed signs of life. Fagin, too, had not met with so severe a fall as John had supposed, but he was stunned, and lay insensible, and had it not been that he fell with his head on a piece of an old hamper which lay in the way, he would have fractured his skull, for he fell with the weight of his body on his head.

When Fagin recovered, he scrambled to his feet and climbed up the side of the wall and got over an opening at the top, which could not be seen, but it was known by him. He was soon safe, and by that time he could hear the footsteps of John as he went along the passage and let himself out.

"Ah, you think yourself safe, do you?" he muttered; "but I will tell you another tale before a week's out."

He then secured the doors, and pro-curing a light, he went into the cell or cellar, and just then Edwin began to come round.

"Where am I?" he exclaimed.

"Just where your brother Shon sent you to, my tear," said the Jew, in insinuating tones; "it was he who planned to murder you because you had the best shance with the gals, my tear, that was it."

The word liar was on Edwin's lips, but the latter part of the Jew's words seemed more than to confirm what he said. Some further parley took place between them, and the Jew said,—

"If you'll swear not to betray me, and to remain here a week, I'll give you life and liberty, and aid you to take vengeance upon your brother, but only on that condition."

Edwin took the oath, and the Jew helped him to get out of the place he had fallen into. He had been dradfully shaken and bruised, save his head, for the Jew had fallen upon him, and so saved himself.

The Jew's object now was to bring down a vengeance upon John Watts's head, and he could think of no other save of hurting him in his affections; as he argued, he would never have consigned his brother to death, had he not been heart and soul in the affair; a baulk now would be worse than the loss of his whole fortune. He even forgot his own passion of avarice in the prosecution of the affair.

"He will," he said, "escape a prosecution; for I could not appear very well in any prosecution; too much would be known, and my occupation gone."

*   *   *   *

About a fortnight after the above, two strangers called to see John Watts. They were shown into a private apartment, and, in a short time, John Watts entered the apartment.

"You wish to speak to me?" he said.

"We do."

"I am at your service."

"Thank you. You had a brother, had you not, called Edwin?"

"Do you know ought of his fate, sir?" said John, with a hypocritical whine.

"I know anything of his fate! how should I possibly do so?"

"I ask your pardon, but you said I had a brother; I hope I have one still, though we cannot tell what has become of him."

"You think he is living?"

"I hope so."

"He was last seen alive in Field-lane, I believe, was he not?"

John gave a start, and said he did not know where he might have been.

"You don't think he has met any foul play, do you?"

"No, no."

"He hasn't been thrust down a trap and a Jew after him?"

John could not speak, but staggerd to a seat, and sat staring with his eyes almost bursting from his sockets.

"Do you know me, my tear?" said the Jew, assuming his natural voice, and divesting himself of his disguise; "are you not pleased to see me? You don't welcome me, though."

"And me, too," said John, throwing off his disguise.

"Mercy—mercy!" said Edwin, and he arose, and for a moment or two staggerd about, and then fell senseless on the floor. The brothers were for a long while in conversation, and the result was, that John Watts entered the army, and was sent abroad, where he fell in an engagement; the Jew was afterwards hanged for some crime. Edwin Watts, after a time, was married happily to the notary's beautiful daughter, Evelina.

CHAPTER XLI.

DANGER IN THE STREETS.—THEODORE'S NEW REFUGE. — THE HOSPITAL.

THEODORE DANTON laid down the book. All was still in that chamber, and he could hear, by the equal and regular breathing of his nurse, that she was fast asleep.

"Now, now is my time," he said; "now is my time to make one effort for love, for virtue, and for honour. Margaret! Margaret! I love you, but it is with a love that shall bring with it no pang. We shall never—never meet again. I will be cruel to you and to myself, in order that I may be kind; come what may of this hopeless passion that now fills my breast, there shall come with it no reproach."

As he spoke, he slowly slipped from the bed, and, feeling a kind of strength fnom the excitement of mind in which he was, he succeeded in pulling on his clothes, which had been brought into the room again, and lay neatly folded on a chair, in expectation of his convalescence.

Exaustion had taken possesion of the nurse, and she slept soundly. She was a kindly disposed woman, and not likely to neglect her charge; but she knew that her patient was all snug, and indeed that he was sufficiently well to let her know if he required her services; therefore, she slept soundly and serenely, little dreaming of the elopement of one who had so little cause to go.

Probably in a healthier state of body, and consequently a more vigorous condition of intellect, Theodore Danton would not have adopted his present plan of proceedings. He had taken a farewell of Margaret. They had agreed for their own peace it were better not to meet again. Strong principle might have enabled both to keep the determination; surely, at least, it would have enabled Margaret to keep it; for her visit to Theodore at the hotel was no proof of weakness or wavering of purpose. A hundred such visits, dictated by such motives, could not have made her otherwise than pure and innocent; so that by leaving the hotel, Theodore accomplished nothing, inasmuch as it did not deprive him, should he feel inclined to exercise it, of the power to visit Margaret, although it might leave her without the knowledge of where to apply to him. But to an enthusiastic mind, nothing is more alluring than the apparent opportunity of carrying out some great principle of truth and honour. He believed that he was doing something that went far towards proving the purity of his affection for Margaret, and hence he persevered in the course he had laid down for himself.

His only difficulty now would be to get through the hall of the hotel without observation; in that attempt he might be fortunate, or the reverse; and as he glided from the room, and slipped gently down the staircase, he trembled as if he had been guilty of some heinous offence, and was making some almost hopeless effort to escape from the clutches of offended justice. He began to feel that his strength, too, was not near so great as he had thought it was; his limbs seemed to sink under him, and a faintness momentarily came over him that compelled him to pause occasionally, and hold by the rails of the staircase for occasional support.

When, however, there is a stern determination, how much more than seems at all possible may be accomplished! Who could have supposed that Theodore Danton, after the dangerous relapse which had so recently come over him, would have had strength, unaided, to leave his chamber? But so it was. In low accents, he repeated to himself—

" For thee, Margaret, for thee—it is for thee !"

Then, as if the repetition of her name

had given him fresh power, he moved onwards.

He came in sight of the hall; it was vacant. A glorious opportunity, and with a feeling of excitement, that almost for the moment imparted the hue of health to his cheeks, he passed on, and without the shadow of a difficulty left that house, in which friendly force would have been used to detain him, had he been observed.

He thought for a moment when he reached the open air, that its pure freshness gave him strength, but how sadly weak he found himself before he had proceeded half the length of the street! He tottered like a drunken man, and the sensation came over him with the conviction, that it would be quite out of his power to proceed much further.

Then, for the first time, it occurred to him that he had been so heedlessly forgetful as to come out into the streets of London without the means of getting a meal's victuals, a state of things; which he might have provided against ; for he believed, that in a drawer of the room in which he slept some of the cash he had had about him when he was first taken ill was placed. But there was now no resource for that carelessness; for to return was a thing he could not think of, and so, with blind reliance upon fortune, which in a healthier mood he would have rejected, he walked on till he could walk no further, when he clung to some area rails for support, and felt as if the whole world were swimming round with him at a prodigious rate.

His helpless situation soon attracted the attention of some chance passengers, and he received timely assistance, or he must have fallen to the pavement, and possibly been seriously hurt. As it was, he was supported in the arms of two respectable persons, who at once carried him to the nearest chemist's shop, where, in a state of perfect insensibility, for he had fainted from sheer exhaustion, he was placed upon a chair.

Active stimulants soon restored him to consciousness, but it was some time before he could speak, and when he did, he merely said—

" I have been extremely ill, but fancied myself sufficiently strong enough to venture into the streets; I was wrong, and now feel my utter inability to proceed."

"You shall be conveyed carefully home," said the chemist, "if you will state your name and address."

"I have no home," said Theodore.

"No home!" exclaimed the chemist, and he glanced at the superior apparel in which Theodore was attired; "you must surely be mistaken; think again, will you favour us with your name?"

"My name is Danton, but I have no home, being comparatively a stranger in London. I feel that I am incapable of taking any measures for my own preservation; my only resource just at present is to some public hospital, where I may remain until I have gained sufficient strength to act for myself."

"I should be the last," said the chemist, "to combat such a resolution. I can place you in one of those asylums, and will make it my care to do so."

A coach was procured, into which he was lifted, for he was now quite incapable of walking. In another half hour, Theodore Danton was in one of the convalescent wards of Bartholomew's Hospital, and there we will leave him, in order to connect that portion of our story which treats of the disappearance of Bertram from Mrs. Primrose's, an event which had filled Mrs. Blair with so much despair, and concerning which she had with considerable precision of thought, came to an astonishingly correct conclusion.

CHAPTER XLII.

THE FEARFUL RESOLUTION OF BERTRAM.—THE IMPENDING CATASTROPHE.

IT is well known to all that are acquainted with the physiology of the human frame, that apparently serious injuries on the head sooner right themselves than any other class of physical afflictions. The fall which Bertram had had at the hotel door when he rolled over the coachman, was no doubt a serious one for the time being, but the remedies that had been applied, combined with a few hours' repose, had enabled the system wonderfully to rally,

so that some time before the morning had fairly set in, Bertram found himself quite in a condition to move, and to take whatever steps his judgment or his imagination might dictate to him. He lay for half an hour revolving in his mind what he considered his injuries; for he really considered himself a most ill-used man, and one against whom evil fortune was playing some of her worst pranks.

The proofs of his wife's guilt appeared to him self-evident and abundant. What stronger proof could he hope or wish for, so he asked himself, than what had already met his eyes? Was not the whole of her conduct consistent with the opinion concerning her, which had been infused by Mrs. Blair? There was no hiatus anywhere —the chain of evidence to his mind wanted no link for its completion. There was no mistake about the individual. She had deliberately left her house secretly, to visit Theodore Danton in a hotel—that he had seen with his own eyes.

"Shall I be so weak," he said, "as after this to let a foolish fondness overcome me, and to doubt? No; the period of action has now arrived; I am assured of my dishonour, and I will be equally assured of my revenge."

He lay in silence for some time, and then, not to be annoyed by conversation with Mrs. Primrose, he pulled the bed clothes over his head when she came into the room and affected to be sleeping.

She had no wish to disturb him, but had merely come to see if he wanted anything; so finding him sleeping as she supposed, quietly and slowly left the chamber.

Then Bertram looked up again and in a hissing whisper said—

"I will have revenge; it shall be deliberate, because it shall be complete. I am now perfectly calm—calm enough to think, and calm enough to act, not from impulse, but from reflection. I must have revenge on both—revenge on her who held my honour in keeping —revenge on him who has enabled her to make so light of the possession. Let me think—let me think."

After a time, he now rose and dressed himself completely. It was very strange, that both he and Theodore Danton should be, nearly at the same time, both intent upon leaving what, as regarded each, was presumed to be a sick chamber, and that secretly, too.

It was then that he placed in the bed the bolster instead of himself, so as to give the appearance of his being in the state of repose in which Mrs. Primrose found him.

Nothing was easier than to leave the house unobserved, because it contained lodgers, and the private door adjoining the shop was free to so many persons, that its being opened or shut, was a matter which no one took any notice of.

It was a strange fancy of Bertram's to put on that mourning cloak, with which he had left his home; but he did so, and with it wrapt around him, he sallied forth into the street. No one could mistake, for a moment, what that garment was. It was a funeral garb, and by some strange hallucination of intellect, Bertram seemed to think that every important action of his life must be performed within its sombre folds.

Men of passion and imagination, rather than of judgment, often take these strange fancies, and from this time henceforward we might almost be justified in considering Bertram insane, so singular a view did he take of his own position and of society. Without, however, dictating to our readers those reflections which they are well enabled themselves to make, we will follow Bertram's footsteps.

He walked on till he came to a gun-shop, and there he purchased a pair of pistols, which he requested to be loaded for him, saying, that he was going a long journey into the most desolate parts of the country.

This was not so unusual an occurrence in the way of business as to induce any doubts about it on the part of the gun-smith, so he complied with the order at once, and handed the weapons, loaded, to his customer. The price demanded was paid at once, without cavil, and, so far as the gunsmith was concerned, the transaction seemed to be a *bon a fide* one, and to be concluded.

With a calm and passionless look,

Bertram walked towards the hotel, where he expected to find Theodore Danton. There can be no doubt but that his intention was to murder him, and Mrs. Blair was never so right in her life as when she considered the mysterious disappearance of Bertram from Mr. Primrose's was likely to be the herald of some fearful catastrophe.

It is said that somewhere in the east there is a lake, the surface of which is calm and motionless, while far down in its depths rages furious storms. Morally, Bertram resembled that fabulous phenomenon: outwardly, he looked cold, and unruffled; but what pen could paint the flow of angry passions that was really raging in his heart?

He was ghastly pale, and the black cloak he wore imparted a strange solemnity to his appearance. People might have supposed that he was so immersed in grief as to have caused its excesses beyond the bounds of sober reason, but no one would have thought him intent upon a deed of blood.

He ascended the steps of the hotel with a quiet firmness, and accosting the first member of the establishment he saw, he said—

"I have come to see Theodore Danton, if he be within."

"Yes, sir," said the man; "he's staying here. I will speak to my master."

At this moment, the landlord was crossing the hall; he heard the question and answer, and stepping up to Bertram he siad,—

"Sir, if you can give us a hint of where Mr. Danton is, you will relieve us of much anxiety; he has mysteriously disappeared from here, within, I should say, the last quarter of an hour."

"It is false!" cried Bertram, with such a sudden passion, that both the landlord and his waiter started back amazed, so strikingly in contrat was it to his previously serene manner.

"Sir," said the landlord, "that is not the politest way of doubting a fact; but I can tell you Mr. Theodore Danton has left my house most unexpectedly, for he was not in a state of health to leave it. Whither he has betaken himself I have not the slightest idea."

Bertram seemed inclined, at the moment, to burst into some furious outbreak of passion, but there is something about truth which carries the stamp of conviction along with it; and, angry and excited as he was, he felt irresistibly inclined to believe what the landlord had said.

"I am a friend of Mr. Danton's," he said; "I wish to do him a service, which I know he sensitively shrinks from. I owe him something; therefore, should you discover where he can be met with, I shall feel greatly obliged by the information, and will call again."

Without waiting for an answer, he wrapped the cloak about him, and quietly left the room, muttering to himself, as he went,—

"It is but deferred—it is but deferred! Vengeance shall yet be mine!"

He had no fixed plan of proceeding, and for a short distance he turned his steps towards his own house; then he paused, and then entered a mean coffee-shop, where he sat for more than an hour, with his head buried in his hands, apparently in deep thought. He had ordered something, which he paid for, and left untasted; and then he walked out, and as he strolled through the quiet streets, he thus gave utterance to the meditations of his soul:—

"The time will come when upon him—upon Danton—I shall be bitterly revenged; but, as regards her against whom I cannot lift my hand, I will adopt a different course. From her, from all that know me, and from the world I will disappear; living somewhere in privacy and in secrecy, I will know all and see all, being myself unknown and unseen. I will leave her to misery, to want, and to destitution! She shall sigh in vain for my return, and one by one shall slip from her those luxuries which I have heaped around her; so will my revenge be certain and secure, and I shall see it—I shall be able to watch the gradations of her despair. This is my solemn determination: I withdraw myself henceforward from all who know me—virtually, my name may be struck off the muster-roll of humanity; and yet will I live for her—the epitone of a terrific retribution. This is my decision! I am not mad! my pulse beats calmly—my brain is cool and healthful! I swear it!—by the Heaven above I swear it!"

CHAPTER XLIII

BERTRAM'S MISERABLE LODGING.—THE WASTING AWAY OF HIS HOME.

BERTRAM did not defer the execution of his plan for one hour; he was resolved never to return to that house which contained what he deemed his dishonest and false-hearted wife. No; he resolved never to see her again—at least that she should be aware of—not again should she look upon his form; of that he was resolved, and he would only see her to note the wasted form, and the signs of poverty and misery which he was about to bring upon her. He thought, too, that would be a pleasant sight—a sight he could look on with pleasure, but one she had deserved.

Bertram's money lay chiefly at his banker's and to withdraw the whole of the balance he had there, was to him an object, and he went there in person, and presented a cheque for the whole amount.

The cheque was looked at carefully and handed about; but Bertram was known, and in an instant it was cashed. It was a heavy sum, and the bulk was in large notes; many thousand pounds were thus at once placed in his possession, and he quitted the banking-house with the whole of his fortune in his possession.

"Now, now," he thought, "I shall be dead to the world, and yet I shall live and watch how the world wags. I shall see her sink, slowly and by degrees, from one state of misery and uncertainty to another, and then my revenge will be slow and sure, such as I can see, and feel, and know it is my own doing. But now to dispose of my property. I have it. I will place it in the hands of another banker who shall not know my name. I will take another, and then deposit my money; then I shall be able to remain in secret, and unknown."

He smiled to himself as he thought it would be a very clever thing to live so and cheat the world. He could live so cheap, too—so very cheap, and in a way that could never be suspected from his habits and manners. There was something, to his diseased imagination that was pleasing to him in the speculations he indulged in concerning his future mode of life. It was so novel that he began to be entertained. In the meantime he continued walking onward until he came to a banking-house that he appeared to fancy.

"This will do," he muttered; "there is something about this that pleases me. It will do, and I am entirely unknown."

He walked up the steps, and pushing open the strong doors, he entered the banking house. For some moments there were so many persons at the counter, that he could not catch an opportunity to speak with the cashier, so he stood and watched them in silence for some time At length, the greater part of them being dismissed, he stepped up to the counter, and seeing the cashier, he said,—

"Can I speak with you, sir?"

"Certainly, sir; what is it you wish to say?" said that individual leaning forward.

"I wish to open an account, but I am a stranger. Can you inform me how I am to proceed in this matter?"

"It is usual to bring a recommendation with you," said the cashier, "from some one of our customers, and then an interview with our manager settles the business."

"I am a stranger from the country, and have no recommendation of the sort you speak of; but can I see your manager?"

"Yes, certainly, sir; walk this way."

So saying, he led the way to a waiting-room, where he pointed to a seat, saying—

"May I trouble you to take a seat for a short time, sir? I will return immediately."

Bertram sat down, and the cashier disappeared, and he was not kept long before he returned, saying, as he entered—

"Will you favour me with your name, sir?"

"Yes; my name is Raymond."

"Will you walk this way, sir? I will introduce you to our managing partner."

Bertram rose, and followed the cashier into a handsomely furnished apartment, where was the managing partner.

"Mr. Raymond, sir," said the cashier, "of whom I was but just now speaking."

The partner pointed to a chair with his pen, at the same time he arose from his seat, saying, in a bland tone—

"Your servant, Mr. Raymond; be so good as to take a seat. Mr. Cabill, our cashier, informs me you desire to open an account."

"It is the fact, sir. I have none of the usual recommendations."

"It is very unusual to open an account with an entire stranger to us."

"It may be, sir, and I must bow to any decision you may come to upon that point. I may merely remark that I am a stranger in London. I have not come from Canada long, and intend to take up my residence in England for some time. I can pay a heavy deposit, some thousands, from which I shall take but little; but, of course, anything on that head is very uncertain and worthless to you. This, however, is the state of the case: if you think proper to accept the account, I will pay to the amount of some thousands at once."

The manager hesitated for a moment with the idea of impressing the new customer with a notion of the reluctance they felt in departing from their usual course of business, and if they did so, how great the favour ought to be considered by him.

"Well, sir," said the manager, "as you are a stranger, we may, perhaps, with propriety, depart from our usual course of action, and accept of the account."

"Very well," said Bertram; "I will now hand you over the money."

"First, sir, there will be some documents to sign, for form sake."

Some papers and books were placed before him, and having done what was usual in such cases, the money was paid and entered in his pass-book, and a cheque-book was given to him; and then Bertram was bowed out under the appellation of Raymond.

"That is done," he said; "'tis the first step, but it shall be quickly followed by others. Let me see—I have nothing else, and would have nothing I would trouble myself with. No, no, I have ample means, very ample means to last out ten such lives as that I shall lead."

He walked away from the banking-house, and directed his steps towards the more densely populated part of the town, or, rather, to a less wealthy in-habited part. How he seemed to gloat upon the prospect of the misery that was to accumulate upon his wife, and to chuckle over his own cleverness and the constancy of his revenge !

"I must have a lodging," he muttered —" yes, a lodging—a home—a strange home, where I can sit and conceal myself all day, and at night I can creep out for air and exercise, and to see the alteration in the appearance of my own home and my own wife. And they'll both change—oh, yes, they'll change. I wonder how long 'twill take to get through all that's there ? Some months —if she were to sell the furniture. How long will it be before a seizure takes place ? Not very long; but yet it is one consolation to know it is not now; but it will be—it will be !"

Thus his morbid excitement every now and then broke out in unmirthful glee, or, rather, joyless pleasure; for he only expressed satisfaction in what was misfortune and misery to another.

He now came to a little street very near Soho-square. It was a street that at once bespoke the general poverty of its inhabitants. The houses were tall and dingy; there was a look of dirt and misery about it, and many would have shrunk from entering such a place, even out of curiosity. He looked at one house, it was a corner one, and there was a lodging to let.

"Well, well," he said, " I'll go and sell these things; I shall get others more in taste with my intended mode of life. I intend living here; 'twill be rare sport to think that the wealthy Mr. Bertram is living in a St. Giles's lodging-house; few, very few, would think it—none, not one, would say I do so. But my revenge will keep; it will grow and be nourished by the food that will be daily created for it. I will call here as I come back."

He left the place, and proceeded to one of the many shops in the neigh-bourhood of the square, which are chiefly inhabited by the Jewish people, who are so disinterested that they are continually living upon the losses they sustain in aiding and obliging the Christians to deal with them. To one of these places did Bertram repair, and having paused, he was immediately pounced upon by one of these indivi-duals.

"Vat shall I serve you with, my tear sir? Walk in, walk in! fit you with anything, from a pair of Wellingtons to a scratch wig. Vat shall I do? fit you with a fresh suit or a new umbrella?"

"Nothing, nothing; I merely want to ask you a question."

"A kevestion, my tear, a kevestion ?"

"Yes."

"Well, vat is it ? Anythin' in my line?"

"Do you buy as well as sell?"

"Yes, my tear, when I can, or ex-change, or anythin', or nothin', as the case may be; now vat shall I have the pleasure of doin' for you?"

"I want to sell these clothes that I have on, and to buy others."

"Oh! a case of exchange—I see, I see! Well, my tear, I'll use you well; walk into the crib, there's an out-and-out show there; I'll sell yer as regular a suit of come-over-me-properly as ever you vore, and as von't vare at all like these seedy-looking togs."

"I don't want much of a suit."

"You shall have vatever you likes, my hearty! so just valk into the crib."

"What will you give me for this suit ?" inquired Bertram.

"Why, that 'll depend much upon what we can agree to. You see them are Sunday togs; but they ain't the things poor people vare; now I can get a higher price for vorse things, cause you see I have got a petter temand."

"You want to cheat me."

"Cheat !" exclaimed the Jew, opening his eyes in utter amazement. "Cheat, do you say! Cot plesh my heart, man ! vat can you be thinking of? but let me know how you get on, what you will have, and vat you axes for these shiny things. Cheat ! Cot plesh me, nobody ever said as much as that to Ebenezer Moses afore."

"I want any old rusty suit you may have; no matter how shabby and poor."

The Jew was puzzled, and looked into his customer's face with much doubt and astonishment, for he thought, at first, this must be a joke; but Ber-tram's face exhibited too sad an ap-pearance to leave any room for doubt.

"I hav'n't got a pad thing, my tear," said the Jew, hesitating for a few

THE DREAM OF CHARLES BERTRAM.

moments, "in my place.   Some on 'em is of course petterish den others, but that is all; no pad—no pad—never buy that, it is no use—can't sell pad, but I can petter."

As he spoke he produced some clothes he had lately purchased. There was out of the lot an old brown coat, a shabby waistcoat, and a pair of black pantaloons, of a somewhat threadbare description.

"How much?" said Bertram, pointing to the articles he had selected.

"Cot plesh me!" said the Jew, looking at Bertram. He was in a disagreeable dilemma,—if he asked too much he would be compelled to offer a higher price for those Bertram had on, and he was desirous of doing business and gaining profit upon both transactions. However, he thought he had better not ask too little at first going off, for fear it was only a do, then he would lose all.

"Two pounds; and very sheap they are—very sheap, indeed, they ought to be."

"Never mind the cheapness or dearness of the article, it is a price I won't give, and there's an end of it; there are other shops, you know, in this neighbourhood."

"I know that, my tear; but they have all got bad characters."

"And, perhaps, with reason."

"It may be so, but I'll use you well. Come, come, tell me what your price is?"

"Fifteen shillings; and plenty of money."

"By father Abraham, and all the prophets!"

"Ay, you have profit enough, then. Do you take my money?"

"Let us see if we can agree about these things you have got to sell."

"No, no, finish one transaction at a time," said Bertram, "we may not agree about the other, you know."

"Oh, yes, we will, if you are at all reasonable and willing to do business."

"Will you take this money?"

"No—thirty shillings."

'No—fifteen."

"Twenty-five."

"No."

"Well, you are tammed hard. A pound is the lowest farthing."

"No."

"Then we can't do business," said the Jew; "but tell me what you vant for them?"

"Six pounds."

"Tam my heart!"

"They are of the best make and material."

"It may pe, put my customers want things that'll wear. I'll give you one pound ten and the other suit,—come, that's a good offer. I shall never get anything by it."

"You will not,—because it won't do."

After much chaffering with the Jew, he got a complete suit, hat included, and drew two pound ten in addition, though Moses declared he should be thirty shillings out of pocket.

Bertram, upon the spot, changed his clothes, and walked away in his new suit very much like, in point of looks, an object of charity and commiseration. It was strange this kind of trafficking, so unsuitable to a man of his taste and habits; but with the sudden change of prospects and objects in life, he had acquired new habits and tastes, and it was with a kind of pleasure that he bargained with the Jew. It was a decided hallucination of intellect, but from such things, and the gloomy contemplation of his injuries and his revenge, he received all the pleasure he could feel. He left the Jew-salesman, and then walked towards the place where he had seen a room to let announced. The house was very wretched in appearance, and but for the number of people going in and out it might have been deemed uninhabited. Bertram walked up to the door, and pulled a bell which he saw on one side.

"Well, what now?" said a gruff voice, after he had waited some time.

"I want to see the room you have to——"

"Go to the devil, or the landlady—I don't care which, it's all the same."

He then gave a single knock at the door, and a long, skinny-looking woman came out into the area—a coarse noisy woman she was, with a face of brass.

"Well, what do you want, old man?" she cried, seeing only Bertram's back, and he did not look unlike an old man.

"I want to see this room you have to let, my good woman."

"Good woman? what do you mean by good woman, I should like to know, you insolent pauper?—good woman, indeed! Well, good man?"

Bertram had forgotten to alter his demeanour with his clothes, but this incident gave him a hint.

"I wish to see your room, if you have one to let."

"Yes, we have."

"Then I wish to see it."

The woman deigned to make no reply, but disappeared, and presently came up the stairs, with a key in her hand.

"If you'll come up stairs, I'll show you the room."

"Is it very high?"

"No; only a five-pair back."

"Oh! is the rent very low?"

"Yes, for such a room and accommodations."

They got, after incredible fatigue, up to the five-pair back room; when there, the landlady unlocked the door, and flung it open.

It was a curious place. The beams ran across the room, from one side to the other, while that next the street, in which was a small tattered window, shelved off from half the height to the roof, depriving the room of a part of its proportions.

The room, otherwise, was very small; it had one table, one chair, a low truckle bedstead, bed and rug,—or something of the sort,—and altogether it had the appearance of wretchedness, and extreme poverty.

"Well!" said the woman, after she had let her visitor survey the room with an air of scrutiny for some minutes, "will it suit?"

"That depends upon the rent."

"Oh, you can't have it for nothing!"

"I know that. But how much do you ask for this—this—" Bertram sought for some qualifying word between attic and hole, but could find none, and the landlady said,—

"Apartment?"

"Why, yes—what rent?"

"Three-and-sixpence, only," she said, and screwed her mouth up.

"Three-and-sixpence!" repeated Bertram, looking around him. "Three-and-sixpence!"

"Yes; no more."

"And no need."

"If you think so, there's plenty as don't; look at the accommodation!"

"Truly! I see the accommodation, and it is very easily seen, too. I can't afford so much for so little, and that's the truth."

"So little and so much!" screamed the landlady; "what would the man want? Isn't there all that he can desire? and yet he ain't satisfied! I tell you what it is—you don't want the room at all."

"Yes, I do; and am willing to make you an offer, if it's any use."

"I don't bate," said the woman.

"Then it's no use my stopping," said Bertram; "the rent's too much."

"Too much?"

"Yes."

"What will you in conscience offer, now—I should be glad to know what you'll offer, now?"

"I will give you the three shillings, but no more; I can pay that, but I can't do any more."

"Can't pay any more?"

"No!" said Bertram, as decisively as if the whole world depended upon it.

"You shall have it for three-and-three."

"That ain't my money."

"It is worth it."

"I don't think so."

"Three-and-three ain't too much for such a room as this; feel the bed—it's soft, and all does not come to more than fivepence-halfpenny a day—day and night; and liberty to light a fire, and go in and out when you like."

"Thank you," said Bertram.

"What do you say?"

"Three shillings."

"Three-and-three."

"No."

"Well, you must have it your own way, let it be three shillings; I hope, however, you'll be a good lodger, and pay regularly to make up the deficiency of the money; it is strange what trouble people sometimes give. I had to prosecute one for pawning, to imprison another, and to do I don't know what besides. People are so perverse,—and now we have come to the determination not to let the rent run at all."

"I don't want it; I am poor, very poor, but I always pay my rent."

"Then you are an honest man."

"When can I come in?"

"Now."

"Very well. I will take possession on this instant," said Bertram, laying his hat down on the table; "and the room is mine."

"But the deposit?"

"I deposit myself."

"But that won't do."

"What do you want?"

"You wretch! I want a deposit—money in earnest; else you'll not take possession, until you have paid something on the account of rent."

"What will do?"

"A couple of shillings, or half a crown."

"I can give you a shilling, and that is very good deposit—a third of the rent."

"Ay, ay; it's little enough, but it will do for the present; pay regular and no trust for anything."

"I do pay regular," replied Bertram; "if I did not I should get into debt, and then I shouldn't be able to pay at all; however, if you'll lend me the key, I'll lock the door, and fetch some coals and wood in."

The landlady gave him the key, saying—

"I haven't asked you for a reference. I s'pose you are respectable?"

"Very," he said, "for my means; however, I couldn't have given you one, so it is no matter, and nothing has been lost."

The landlady knew not exactly what answer to make; she had not even asked his name, and only thought of it when she saw him going to the door.

Well, she thought she could rectify that at some other opportunity, but she could not help thinking he was a very odd man. There was a strange something about his manner she could not make out; and there was something in his gaze that seemed almost preternatural, such as might be found in the insane. However, she got a lodger, and that was all she cared for or thought of.

When Bertram returned to his lodgings, he came back loaded with, besides the necessaries of coal and wood, some articles of food, which it would have been considered absurd to have looked at if he had been at his own place.

He lived in a miserable style—what is called from hand to mouth; he ate and drank of the meanest food—a red herring and a piece of bread would often be his only supper, and the smallest portion of cooked meat his dinner—things he could at no other time have endured for a moment. But so it was; Bertram was quite an altered man, in aspect and in habits.

He never went out during the day, but would go out and walk about the square at night, and take air and exercise. He would go and contemplate his own house, too, in the night, as though by looking at the bare brick walls in the moonlight he could tell what were the acts and thoughts of the one being within whom he had doomed to such an end. Day after day was spent in his miserable attic; he would stand before the window and gaze into the street, and chuckle to himself as he thought of the clever manner in which he had proceeded.

It was a revenge that could not fail; by degrees she must come to poverty and want. What could she do? The furniture of the house, he knew, would be seized for rent, or for some debt or other; the creditor would soon become insolent when he could not see him, Bertram; he would become alarmed, and seizure would take place.

"Yes, yes," he muttered, "she will be reduced from a large house to a lodging, sooner even than I anticipated."

At night, he would again walk about, and then, at a late hour, he would pass his own house, and speculate upon the state of the inmates, their thoughts, their fears, and hopes. Then, when he had satisfied himself, he left the spot, returned to his own miserable abode, and retired to his pallet.

It was a strange life—a life that could only be supported by one whose reason had lost its sway, and who now possessed only such an amount of intellect and cunning as gave an appearance of reason to those with whom he came in contact; in all else, he was decidedly insane.

It was only such as he, and so circumstanced as he was, that could have endured such a life of voluntary privation and distress, and a mode of life so very different from what he had hitherto led.

CHAPTER XLIV.

THE UNACCOUNTABLE DISAPPEARANCE OF BERTRAM, AND THE STATE OF HIS HOUSE.—THE DISCOVERY AT THE BANKER'S.

THE relative positions o the cunning and unscrupulous Mrs. Blair and the unfortunate wife, were suddenly changed towards each other; for whatever the latter might be doomed to suffer, yet that was known, and the disappearance of Mr. Bertram was so sudden and complete, that Mrs. Blair now felt she was bereft of the only support she had against the injured and insulted lady.

When she found that Mr. Bertram had quitted the Primroses, had been to the hotel, and then had not been heard of, she was utterly dismayed, for she then went to his own house, where she found he had not been either.

This utterly confounded her, and she, in her own mind, felt assured that he had been driven to despair at the supposed infidelity of his wife; and instead of revenging himself upon the faithless woman, he had gone, and in a fit of desperation made away with himself—a state of things that boded her no good. On the contrary, it was the only thing that could, as she saw, have any effect upon her position.

As it was, she saw clearly enough that she had been too clever; she had destroyed all the hopes she had reared upon such a foundation; the death of

Bertram by violence was a contingency she never for a moment dreamt of. However, she was not a woman that would readily yield to circumstances; she could flow with the tide, and at the same time, could trim herself for any course. She had hitherto been arrogant, treacherous, and intriguing; now Mr. Bertram was gone, she could, since there was no other hope, become mean, servile, and abject, and she determined, at all hazards, to make an attempt to ingratiate herself with Mrs. Bertram.

"But," she murmured to herself, "I will wait another day first, and see if Bertram does come home, though I think suicide has been his refuge; silly man, who would have thought he would have been so absurd? but he was the object of all my plots and plans, and he is the only one who has done anything to thwart them; and he has not only done that, but he has entirely destroyed them, and now I am at the mercy of his wife. He is a very foolish man."

No doubt, in this point of view, he was; but we will return to Mrs. Bertram.

The absence of Mr. Bertram was, to her, for some time inexplicable. She could not conceive what could be the reason why he so acted. If she were to blame, why did he not visit his wrath upon her, and not abstain from coming or sending to his own home? She, too, thought that some dreadful accident had happened, and what to do she knew not, but sat in lone expectation of seeing him enter the house.

Since she had entered the house, Mrs. Blair and herself had not spoken, nor was it at all likely she would do so; and she looked upon that person's stay in the house as an event that must, sooner or later, be put an end to; and it was not one of her least resolves that if Mr. Bertram came not home, she would herself take care she went.

While strange thoughts were passing through her mind, Mrs. Bertram was surprised by the entrance of Mrs. Blair into her own apartment. This was an intrusion she was about to resent, when the altered mien of that person struck her attention, though it by no means engaged her favour, for she was too well aware of the hypocrisy of Mrs. Blair's acting; but the change affected

was so great, and so complete, that it was interesting.

"No doubt," said Mrs. Blair, "you are amazed to see me come to you, Mrs. Bertram."

"I am, indeed," coldly remarked Mrs. Bertram, as she fixed her eyes on her.

"No doubt; but you see the continued absence of Mr. Bertram gives rise to so many conjectures, and your situation——"

"Has nothing whatever to do with you, Mrs. Blair."

"That's very true, and therefore it is, I hope, you will appreciate my motive in thus coming to you."

"Indeed; I do not understand you."

"Why, under your present circumstances, it will be very disagreeable for you to fall into the hands of strangers, with no one by you in whom you can trust."

"I am not so reduced yet; and, if I chose to be so, surely I have a right to choose whether I will have a stranger or an enemy."

"Oh, Mrs. Bertram, I perceive you do not properly understand and appreciate my character. I am not what I seem."

"I could have made the same remark," said Mrs. Bertram, drily.

"But the absence of Mr. Bertram——"

"Cannot alter anything, Mrs. Blair, and I trust you will not compel me to put an end to it myself."

"I beg, Mrs. Bertram, you will hear me out, and not be hasty in drawing conclusions. I assure you, you do not see my motives in their proper light."

"Indeed!"

"No, ma'am; and I am sorry, very sorry, if ever I have done aught, or said anything, that could give you a moment's displeasure or uneasiness; believe me, when I say——"

"Mrs. Blair, if you come here with the intention of imposing on my credulity, your time is thrown away; after what has passed, this style of conversation is wholly without an object. I cannot understand it.

"Allow me to say, that the continued absence of Mr. Bertram, at this moment, must make you very uneasy."

"I cannot understand the cause of

it," said Mrs. Bertram; "however, you may."

"I do not, ma'am, and yet I cannot be without my own conjectures upon the subject, my own fears and suspicions."

"Indeed!"

"Yes, ma'am, I am, I am sorry to say, not without apprehensions."

"And what may they tend to?" inquired Mrs. Bertram; "but no matter."

"I cannot help thinking Mr. Bertram must have met with some fatal accident."

"What! How?"

"Suicide."

There was a pause on the part of both. Mrs. Blair watched with piercing eyes the effect of this on Mrs. Bertram, but the latter endeavoured to conceal her emotions, for she was well convinced of this woman's selfishness.

"You see it is possible, and, I am afraid to add, it is probable."

"It is but supposition."

"True, it is but speculation," said Mrs. Blair; "but his absence at such a moment is otherwise perfectly unaccountable."

"Well, I have nothing further to say to you," said Mrs. Bertram, turning away.

"But I have a few more words to say; should this melancholy supposition turn out to be correct, what a situation you will be placed in, without any one by you upon whom you can depend; it will be melancholy."

"Mrs. Blair, will you inform me what my unfortunate condition, as you are pleased to call it, is to you?"

"Certainly, ma'am, anything you please, with pleasure; it grieves me to see it, and it is, therefore, because I see all this with regret and sorrow, that I ask you to bury in oblivion all the past, and allow me to stay and attend upon you till you are once more able to be about."

"No, no—I will not permit such a thing for one moment."

"But, Mrs. Bertram ——"

"You waste words."

"If I have offended you, I regret it. I am sorry, very sorry."

"Very likely."

"But what more can I do than acknowledge an error? It would be but Christian in you to forgive; and, if Mr. Bertram were here, he would be well pleased with the arrangement."

"No, no."

"I am quite disinterested, madam—quite. I don't want fee or reward, and my duty to Mr. Bertram induces me to make you this offer, which I implore you, for your own sake, to accept; for your child's sake, consider."

"Mrs. Blair, this interview has already lasted too long; it is high time there was an end to it. I beg you will leave my apartment, and remember, that your past conduct is an utter bar to any hope of future connection between us; and this is the last time, I hope, I shall find it necessary to hold any communication with you; begone, madam, and let the past be a lesson for the future."

Mrs. Blair had penetration enough to see that there was, at least, no hope for the present, but she curtsied with a look of humility and sorrow, as she said—

"I will obey you, madam, though you act unjustly and harshly towards me. You will, I am sure, upon reflection, see this, and acknowledge it; and I may yet have it in my power to show you I bear no unchristian feeling, and shall ever be ready to contribute to your welfare and happiness."

Having uttered these words, she quitted the room with that stately, slow, and cat-like tread, that women of her class generally adopt; and she retired to what she was in the habit of calling her own apartment.

When she had reached this, and had shut the door, the placid, humble, and hypocritical aspect she had just worn, speedily gave way to one more consonant to her nature and to the occasion.

Disappointment and rage seemed for some moments to agitate her whole frame, and her countenance became inflamed, and her eyes expressed anything but the beams of pleasure.

"So," she muttered, "all is up, if Bertram be dead; she will have all the property, and I shall be where I was. I shall have gained nothing; all my plotting, and planning, and watchfulness, go for nothing; or rather, I should say, for something worse than nothing, since she has become my determined enemy. I shall have lost all, instead of gaining anything. What a fool that man must have been to commit suicide on such an account! and yet, what else could he have done, under the circumstances of such a mysterious disappearance?

"Well, well, the game has been played, and skilfully, too; there were chances against me, and they might have turned up against me at any time; and why not now, though I made sure of a successful termination? And so it would have been, but for the incomprehensible stupidity of this man, who would kill himself at a moment when he ought to have freed himself from this woman, and all would have been right; but now she'll have freedom and riches; she'll have the means as well as the inclination to enjoy life; and he who felt most at her infidelity, has, fool-like, given her more power and opportunity to do the same once more."

* * * * *

As Mrs. Bertram sat alone in her apartment, various thoughts crossed her mind. She knew not what to think of Bertram's absence. It alarmed her, and she felt fearful lest he had committed suicide; at least this was what she fully believed he must have done.

It weighed heavily upon her mind; the cause of it, no doubt, rendered this doubly heavy, and her sadness and sorrow left her no room to hope or think of what a future was open to her. She could only think of the calamity that seemed to impend over her through Bertram; not but there were moments when she thought of him whom she had loved, and whom her heart told her she was not even then indifferent to at that moment.

"If he come not to-night," she said, "I will summon his friends, and induce them to make some inquiries about him; they may know, from his early habits and manners, what is likely to have happened; and, if there be any chance of his return, or if he really have committed any fatal act, his body may be recovered and buried."

These thoughts of Mrs. Bertram were sincere enough, and it was with a heavy heart she rose next morning, and found that he had not yet returned.

She rose with a saddened brow; grief, too, she felt, for when the past came before her mind, she could not but be aware, however innocent—and Heaven knew how innocent she was—that she had been the primary cause of the terrible catastrophe she feared to contemplate. This made her sad, and caused deep grief to sit on her brow.

She, however, did as she had resolved to do, and that was to write to some of her husband's most intimate friends, and request they would exert themselves about his disappearance, and either ascertain how he was, or where he was; in fact, if he were living or dead.

During the day, several of his friends called and consulted with her on the circumstance. They all agreed it was a most extraordinary one, and they could not understand the motives of his disappearance, nor could they at all account for it.

"The only thing that I can advise you to do," said one gentleman, "would be to advertise him, and issue printed bills, offering a reward for his discovery, alive or dead."

"That shall be done," said Mrs. Bertram; "anything that will at all tend to the discovery of himself or his remains, should he unhappily have committed any rash act."

"Exactly; and I think to that precaution may be added the police—for after that, there is nothing, that I am at all aware of, that will be of any service."

"Thank you, thank you for the advice; I will adopt it."

"In that case," said the gentleman, "if you will permit me, I will cause the advertisements to be inserted, and handbills to be printed and distributed."

"Exactly. Thank you."

"And I will send an officer, whom I know is an experienced man, to see you, and take what instructions you can give him."

"You are very kind, and I accept your offer with thanks," said Mrs. Bertram; "I cannot go to these places myself."

"Oh, no, no! there is no need you should," said the gentleman; "no need at all—I will send him to you. If I can be of any service to you, in any way whatever, I shall be most happy to be so, Mrs. Bertram."

She had many more offers of the warmest friendship from those who came to her, that they would do anything that she could desire. This was so far gratifying, and she saw the bills were posted that day, and the next morning the advertisements were printed. The officer was sent for, and when admitted, he made many inquiries of Mrs. Bertram that showed his penetration.

"Did Mr. Bertram, madam," he said, "ever stop away from home before?"

"Never."

"Have you any reason to believe that anything hangs upon his mind? Are his affairs in a good state?"

"Everything, so far as I know."

"Pardon me; but have you had any words with Mr. Bertram lately?"

"I have not."

"It is most inexplicable; but we will do the best we can; but here is nothing to go upon; no clue to his habits and manners, such as would lift him above the sphere of observation of our men, and there is less chance of a discovery; but, as I said, we will do our best; but you must not expect much."

"No—no; but still I thank you, and your exertions shall not be unrewarded."

"He is not a man, I suppose, who might suddenly take a whim in his head, and go abroad, or anywhere else?"

"I think not."

"Have you made any inquiries at his banking-house, if he has drawn out any money?"

"No. I never thought of that."

"Then I will."

After some further conversation with Mrs. Bertram, the officer left the house. It was too late to prosecute inquiries at the banking establishment, but he resolved that he would the next morning, to ascertain if he had drawn out any money, as that would probably lead to some discovery, or give a direction to conjecture. Until that time he could do nothing, for he knew nothing.

Police officers are like all human beings—unless they know something, they can do nothing; and thus it was on the present occasion, and should anything turn up, such as a body found drowned, or anything of the kind, he could then effect something by finding out the friends of the deceased.

The next morning the officer walked to the banking-house of Mr. Bertram, and saw the cashier, and then said—

"Does a Mr. Bertram bank here?"

"He did."

"Did—does he not do so now?"

"No."

"How long has he withdrawn his account? I am an officer, and have particular reasons for making the inquiry."

"It was but the day before yesterday, or the day previous to that."

"Indeed?"

"Yes; he came and presented a check for the balance of his whole account."

"It is very singular."

"Indeed! What has happened?"

"Only he is missing, and his friends are anxious about his fate."

"He gave us no reason—he presented his cheque, and, as there were assets, of course it was duly honoured."

The officer, after a few more questions and answers, left the banking-house, and returned at once to Mrs. Bertram, whom he found with several of Mr. Bertram's friends about her.

"Well," said the gentleman who had sent him to Mrs. Bertram, "well, Thompson, how have you got on in this affair? Have you learned anything respecting Mr. Bertram?"

"I have just been to his banker's, sir."

"Eh?"

"Yes, sir; I went there to inquire if he had been there since he left home."

"And has he?" eagerly inquired one or two, among whom was the gentleman who had made such disinterested offers of service to Mrs. Bertram.

"Yes, he was there the next day."

"And—and ——"

"He drew the money."

"Eh, money?"

"Yes, the whole of his balance—every farthing in one cheque, and then left the counting-house, and made no remarks."

"Why, his whole substance, to the amount of many thousands, was there."

"And they are gone."

"God bless me!" said one.

"Here's a discovery!" said another.

" I can scarcely believe the evidence of my own senses," said the gentleman.

The whole party were struck with consternation at this discovery. It was so unexpected, they were confounded. The loss of Bertram was one thing, and the loss of fortune was another ; the former rendered Mrs. Bertram an object of affectionate solicitude and interesting attention, but the loss of fortune as well, changed the aspect of affairs, and Mrs. Bertram became something in their eyes very much like a bore—an ordinary woman likely to have a child in a short time, and become an expensive and disagreeable acquaintance to all who had professed any friendship, or offered their services.

"Ahem," said the gentleman, "it seems to me that nothing more can be done than to continue to look out for him—that's all, positively all, I say.

THE SERVANT BOY DELIVERING THE LETTER TO BERTRAM.

I have an engagement I had forgotten. I bid you good-day, Mrs. Bertram ; pray let me know how you get on, and if you hear anything of Bertram."

So saying, and without waiting for any answer, he hurried himself out of the room.

The remainder of the guests took their departure, and left the house as quickly as they decently could, and at length Mrs. Bertram and the officer were left alone in the parlour.

" It seems to me," said the officer, "the intelligence I have brought has caused much consternation among these people ; they are quite changed."

"They apprehend a change of fortune in me, and hence their sympathies are so strong that they change likewise ; but I have no means, now, of rewarding you, save for what you have done. The matter must drop ; here is a guinea for your trouble."

The officer calmly and unaccountably

refused it, saying he had been at no trouble, and should he hear anything more of Mr. Bertram, he would let her know, and then left the house and Mrs. Bertram, in a state of mind difficult to be described.

CHAPTER XLV.

THE DEPARTURE OF MRS. BLAIR. —THE DESPAIR OF MRS. BERTRAM, AND HER ILLNESS.

MRS. BLAIR, who had made such an unavailing and abject submission to Mrs. Bertram, was under the impression that Mr. Bertram had committed suicide, and left her in full possession of all his property. Then, indeed, she thought there might be a chance of inducing Mrs. Bertram to overlook the past.

She thought, too, the change of position would, perhaps, bewilder Mrs. Bertram so much, that she would be glad to have her about her; but she had been grievously disappointed, for Mrs. Bertram, whether alone or with any one, would have her, Mrs. Blair, less about her than anybody else. She had offended beyond hope of forgiveness, and hence it was she was dismissed with reproach.

Mrs. Blair was scarce affected with any fresh emotions when she heard, for the first time, that Bertram had taken all his money out of the bank, save that she despaired of all success.

Now she saw there was no hope, because if Mrs. Bertram had the inclination, she would not have the power to keep her; she would in time be reduced to want, and, therefore, there was no hope. It was with a pang of rage and disappointment, which is almost indescribable, that she saw how completely she had been foiled, and every effort she had made, was only a failure.

The only consolation that she at all felt was, that Mrs. Bertram had been involved in ruin; but this was a feeling that had no relief. It would be but a poor gratification to know she had done evil, without obtaining any good herself.

She was a bad woman, but yet she would not have done great and irreparable mischief, and that, too, with great danger to herself, had it not been in accordance with some preconceived plan or plot of her own, to obtain a selfish end; and for this she cared not whom she sacrificed. On this score she was quiet unscrupulous; it mattered not to her; but it did startle her; it did, in fact, form a great disappointment, and more especially when she found the evil she had committed so plentifully recoiled upon herself.

Great was her chagrin, and great was her mortification, when she found that instead of Mrs. Bertram being deserted, and turned adrift, she herself was reduced to the same position, with the additional aggravation that hers was brought upon herself in pursuit of another object. She was the authoress of her own misfortune, and that, too, by being so very clever.

However, she reasoned with herself the game was up. She could understand that Bertram's feelings had been wounded beyond what she anticipated, that, indeed, it had been overdone, and his resolutions had all gone into another channel. If he were living, it was quite certain that he would not return now, and the probability was that he was a dead man—a suicide—and had bestowed his money away where it would never come to light. At all events, it would never be discovered by them.

This was a reflection that had but little that was pleasant in it.

"However," muttered Mrs. Blair, "I must make what use I can of my time; 'tis no use to neglect the present opportunity; and I shall help myself to whatever is worth having, and is portable; and this rosewood dressing-case is one of the most valuable that I can find."

To the rosewood dressing-case Mrs. Blair added many other little valuable articles. Nothing came amiss; a few small pictures—that were of any value; and they were carried away by that amiable person.

Having taken such things as she could or dared, she turned her back upon the house that she had brought ruin upon, with a gesture of impatience, as though that ruin had inconvenienced her, and had been the fault of the owner, with the pithy remark of—

"A falling house is no safe abode."

Thus she quitted the place—a house that was marked, by her intrigue, with desolation, and ruin, and misfortune incalculable.

Poor Mrs. Bertram, after the communication of the officer, became somewhat more awake to her situation. She began to fear, and with justice, that a time of pain and sorrow was at hand—a time when she more than ever wanted the protecting hand of friends true and kind; but, alas! she might in vain look for them.

"Bertram has doomed me to misery and poverty," she said; "but I have one friend; I would hardly apply to him, but all others have failed me; they find I am poor, and hence I am deserted by all. They think I shall become an object to be shunned, one that will require the fulfilment of some of the many promises they have made in the days of my prosperity. I will go to him. I will see, at all events, if he be yet better than he was. Alas—alas! what a fate might have been mine. But yet I have not swerved from my duty, nor ever would I. Why, then, am I doomed to such a fate? Alas! Bertram, you have committed a fatal error, and you have not only made me your victim, but you have become your own likewise; and at what a price have you done this! Oh, Heaven forgive you! you have been cruel—you have been unjust. But that is buried in the grave. You are now where nothing can be added to, or subtracted from, the sum of your mortal deeds; praise and censure are now alike to you—all is as one to you."

She arose from her seat, determined once more to go to the hotel where Theodore Danton was staying, to secure the advice and countenance of one sincere friend, for all others had completely deserted her. He might afford her consolation, and, at least, the horrible thought of beggary which now haunted her would be less terrible, because either more distant, or probably because it would be wholly dispelled by Danton. However it might be, she dressed herself for walking, and left the house for Danton's hotel, where she arrived in due time.

It was some moments before she could summon courage or resolution enough to enter. She had been there before, but it was after the streets had become somewhat dark; her motions could not then be seen so readily, nor her features marked; but then she was well aware now she was not under the same fear. She had become suddenly husbandless, and in about a month would become a mother.

This last consideration urged her on, and she walked up the steps of the hotel, and seeing a waiter advancing, she said—

"Is Mr. Danton within?"

"No, ma'am; he is not."

"Indeed!" she exclaimed, much surprised, for she had not dreamed of his having left; it was by far too unlikely —nay, almost impossible, in her mind, an occurrence to be thought of, and now it came upon her like a clap of thunder. "Indeed!" she repeated; and then, after a pause, she inquired—

"When did he go?"

"Several days back."

"Can you tell me where he is gone to?" she timidly inquired.

"That we cannot, for he went secretly, and at a time when we were believing that he could not have had strength enough to walk out of the house, but yet he did go."

"It is very strange."

"Yes, ma'am; it is very strange."

"Then you know nothing of where he is, or where he is likely to be heard of or found, do you?"

"We do not, ma'am; and if you can give us any of the information you ask, we should be obliged to you."

"I should hardly come to seek him here if I knew where to find him elsewhere. He went secretly away, say you?"

"Yes, ma'am, and master would have been glad to see him perfectly recovered before he left. Indeed, he is much interested in the gentleman's recovery, I assure you."

Mrs. Bertram paused a few moments. She could neither speak nor go, but at length she contrived to say—

"I am obliged to you. I should have been glad to see him, but I suppose there is no probability of his return?"

"We can say nothing about that, ma'am, because we know nothing."

Mrs. Bertram staggered from the door. She walked home, Heaven knows how, but her heart throbbed with emotion; it throbbed fearfully, but yet she spoke not, nor did a tear fall till she reached her own door; and then, in the sanctity of her own room, she gave vent to her grief

"Then," she exclaimed—for the feeling first came over her, "then I am doomed to poverty and want. I now see it—I feared it, but now I am certain to fall into misery and squalid poverty. I did think I had one friend, but, alas! I know not now where to apply to him!

"Oh! Danton, if you knew but where and how I am situated, would you not fly to rescue me? Would you not place me beyond the reach of those horrors I have now every reason to dread, and which I may now watch slowly surrounding me?

"Day by day will my means become less and less—day by day will the period of total want come upon me, a time I cannot avoid or elude. I shall be less able to escape the infliction, or lessen the pangs to be endured; for then, perhaps, an infant will claim my cares and my affection. Alas—alas! misery on misery! My troubles will be increased by that, for my responsibilities will be increased. Ah! that the little creature should be born to such a scene of sorrow and misery!

"To think that it should become a pauper's child! Oh, God! what a fate have I been reserved for! Why—why should this be? why should I suffer thus? It is beyond my mind to conceive; but, alas! it is so."

Alas! Mrs. Bertram's reasoning powers were affected; she could not think on all that had happened with calmness; her grief was too poignant; but she had a strong and vivid notion of the perils of her unfortunate condition. She knew well what must be the end of the present state of things.

The house was well stocked with furniture that was valuable, and would last her some time after all the petty debts were paid; but it was with horror that she contemplated the approach of poverty—a poverty which, though not immediate, was not very far distant—a time, a very short time, would elapse before it would arrive. She could count the weeks and days.

A few months seem but a very short period, when at the end of them some great and serious change of fortune takes place, in which we are reduced from independence to poverty, indigence, and unfriended distress.

Day after day did these thoughts press upon her mind; she thought of what she had been and what she was; the many friends who had been feasted in that house were now strangers to it, because they knew that poverty had overtaken one of the inmates.

How misfortunes try one's friends! There are many who willingly come to the well-filled tables and wine decanters —men who will feast with you; but when the power of feasting them has departed, they depart also.

With the migration of means flock one's friends, who follow them elsewhere. Nay, he who has become in his poverty the friend and companion of others of his then own class, or a little above him, feast at their table, and becomes their friend; and yet, when fortune changes, he either does not condescend to look at those who were his equals, perhaps superiors in circumstances, or if he do it, it is with the nod of a man who seems to condescend, and would not do it before any of his new acquaintance at all. How many instances do we see of this! and if this be the case, how much more likely it is that Mrs. Bertram, who was suffering from distress, and who was soon likely to become a victim of misfortune, should also be deserted by those who now swarmed, or had swarmed, around her! She was now destitute. She had determined to give warning to the servants, and hire but one till the period when she should be enabled to again be about and aid herself.

In this purpose she was anticipated by the servants themselves; and one of them entered her room in the morning at breakfast-time, saying, as she handed her some hot water,—

"Oh, if you please, ma'am, my time's up to-morrow, and I should be glad to go."

"Indeed!"

"Yes, ma'am."

"Very well," said Mrs. Bertram. "I need not ask you the reason; but you shall go, though I could detain you if I chose. It is inconvenient to go at such a moment as this, and you may depend I will give you no character without fully explaining your conduct."

The girl flounced about, and declared all she wanted was to leave, and she would leave. Her master was gone she didn't know where, and people said all sorts of things, and a poor servant's character might soon be lost under such an awful dispensation of Providence.

Mrs. Bertram said no more, but she felt this trifling incident severely. It caused her to think yet more seriously of her situation. All the petty insults and inconveniences that could possibly arise came more strongly before her eyes, and she could see herself, day after day, sinking into the depths of misery.

She could see, too, that there was no one human being in whom she could repose any confidence, or who would, in fact, lend her the least aid or friendly consolation in her affliction.

Danton—Theodore Danton—the only one whom she dared have trusted, too, was not to be found; and she was without the aid or countenance of one human being.

"Yes, yes," she would sigh and murmur; "Bertram has destroyed himself, and he has determined to leave me a living monument of his displeasure and revenge. I know I am reserved for a horrible fate, for a fate too dreadful to contemplate. Want and misery stare me in the face. Yes; I know it now—I know it now."

Then hysterical fits of grief and tears would come on, till she was nearly reduced to fainting, and it very often did occur that she fainted away and was left to herself till nature alone aided her in a recovery.

These fits could not but have a highly prejudicial effect upon her health, and she became aware of these facts in too unequivocal a manner to have any doubt about what course she ought to pursue; and yet, how could she suddenly assume a tranquillity of mind that she was very far from feeling?

Indeed, had she succeeded in the outward semblance of such tranquillity she could not feel, it would not have saved her from the effects she desired to escape.

"I am doomed—I am doomed! I see it all—all. A terrible prospect lies before me, and, to add to my misery, I feel each hour that I shall be less able to bear up against this accumulation of horrors."

She would sit by the window, and watch the passengers as they passed, but not one did she recognise as those whom she desired to see; though, on several occasions, she saw those who had been constant visitors and intimate friends go by the house, and turn their heads as they passed it, as if they dared not be seen.

They now never came nigh, and the gentleman who had been so liberal of advice and offers in the first instance had never been seen or heard of since the communication of the Bow-street officer.

True it was, that, on one occasion, a lady and her daughter called who had been out of town for some time, and thus she knew not of the misfortunes of the unfortunate Mrs. Bertram, and she began to greet her in the usual familiar and kindly manner, which had such an effect upon the mind of Mrs. Bertram, that she burst into a flood of tears.

This produced an explanation, during which all came out, and the ardour of the visitor strangely cooled; and, though she preserved her presence of mind, and made no remark, yet there was a very sensible diminution of kindness. There was oceans of talk, but then it was merely talk, and she left, promising to call again; but she never gave an invitation in return.

When she was gone, Mrs. Bertram was so sensibly affected that she went into a more serious fainting-fit than usual. Several followed, with violent hysterics, and medical aid was called in, and a premature accouchement took place.

It was a sad time for the unfortunate mother, who lay there in the care of the most mercenary part of the creation. There was no father present to receive the infant, and give a kindly look and word to one who more than ever stood in need of it. She had no relation and no female friend to whom she could look for the smallest sympathy or kindness. She was emphatically alone, ill, depressed in feelings, and had not even a hope in the future. That future promised nothing but poverty, sorrow, and sadness, without prospect of mitigation.

CHAPTER XLVI.

BERTRAM'S LIFE AT HIS LODGING.—
THE LONELY WALKS.—HIS EXULTATION.

SOME weeks had now elapsed since Bertram had first entered his lodging, and became the inmate of a garret. Perhaps he was the first inhabitant of such a place with a banking account, with, in fact, a fortune; nor would he have been in such an abode, notwithstanding all that had occurred, but that his mind had taken a turn that might be properly termed decidedly on the wrong side of eccentricity; he was certainly insane, and hence all his faculties being concentrated upon one point, one object, he persevered in it beyond what the imagination can conceive a human being capable of.

Few, indeed, for such motives, could conceive and carry out such a conception as that nurtured by the brain of Bertram, one involving so much personal sacrifice and privation. A mere desire to revenge injuries and insults is felt by most people; however they may have had their passions schooled, yet they do desire to do so; but there are few, indeed, who would go to such a length to obtain a gratification; indeed, it was arrived at a point that might safely be called insanity.

However, Bertram had conceived such a plan, and he had fairly commenced the carrying out of such a plan.

He usually sat at home during the day; indeed, it might be safely said he did not go out at all during the day, but only at night; and he lived in that curious manner that imbued everybody in the house with the notion that he was a very old man, but also a very poor one.

"Ah," said the landlady, "he's a funny man; I never saw such a man afore; he's perfectly rumbustical: but then it is in a serious way; he's got such odd looks."

"But he's very uncivil," said the first-floor lodger.

"He don't speak," responded the landlady, "that ever I heard, at least much, and then it's very short, that one's compelled to feel for the end of one's nose to be sure and certain it's not snapped off."

"Ay, but he don't say bad, good, or indifferent; and that's what I calls uncivil."

"Do you?"

"Yes; when a first-floor lodger condescends to say good-morning to the five-pair back, I think the five-pair back ought to say good-morrow too,—that's my way of thinking; it may be wrong, but it's mine."

"Well, I don't say as it isn't; but he is out of the way, now, and that accounts for it," said the landlady.

"Out of the way, or in the way," said the indignant first-floor, "I'll never say another word to him, with his fizzled up pantaloons—who's he, I wonder?"

"That's what I doesn't know; but he does nothing, that I can see, but stay at home all day, and out at night."

"Depend upon it, there's some mystery about it; such people don't come in and out at all hours for nothing, I am sure; it's very strange, and besides, he's such a funny face."

"Funny face?"

"Yes."

"But how do you mean?"

"Why, sometimes I think he looks an old man, and care-worn; sometimes I thinks he's a young man, and then I don't know what to think of him; he's a proggy."

"A what?"

"A proggy."

"And what's a proggy? anything good to eat?" inquired the landlady.

"No; but when anybody's uncommon, and out of the way, and like no other body, my husband calls them proggies; and, I am sure, if anybody's a proggy, he's a proggy."

"Maybe," said the landlady; "but that's neither here nor there: he sometimes has a red herring for dinner, and sometimes a 'tater; but I'll say this, that he be very poor, yet he always pays his rent to a day."

"Well, I am sure you never had better lodgers in your house nor us, and if I do owe you twelve and sixpence, it's not that I can't pay, only I don't choose people should have it just as they please, and it ain't civil to have a low fellow like that crammed down my throat that way."

"Well, who did? If that's your temper, it ain't mine, and don't think it; nobody spoke to you of your twelve and sixpence. I can better afford to wait for it than you can to pay it, so I'll stand none of your slack; so don't think it."

It will be unnecessary to follow the conversation of these two, since they had fearfully merged from the subject they first began upon, no unfrequent occurrence among rivals who diverge at a tangent, strike into any new idea which may be productive of comfortable exercise of the passions until they get thoroughly warmed.

Thus was Bertram looked upon as a very singular man, but very poor; and as the landlady had no reason to say to the contrary, she could repeat her motto, " would speak as she found, and for her part, 'handsome was as handsome did,' and that was all about it!"

This was very well; but the reflection is naturally wakened as to what kind of life that was which has caused such a discussion, and which he led. It was very different to what he had lived but a very short time before it; it was the life of a miser and of a maniac combined. Miserly in the manner of it, and maniacal in the object.

As the shades of evening closed around, and began to dim all objects that were to be seen in the streets, then Bertram walked to the window; and, from the great height at which he was lodged, looked down upon the little yards, and the backs of a number of houses, and watched the merging of daylight into darkness.

Pent up as this was, there was even something to contemplate; and as the evening drew in, he could see the various rooms dimly lighted up, and every sign of night could be seen.

Now and then, a flash of light would reach the attic window—a flash from some candle that had been carried across one of those little pent-up styes, called yards; or sometimes it might come from a staircase window, as the inhabitants passed to and fro.

Yet he would stand there, and look out upon the darkness below; and then he would more than ever gloat over the misery and wretchedness he was causing, by his strange and unaccountable absence, to Mrs. Bertram.

"Yes, yes," he would mutter; "'tis best—'tis best; a better revenge could not be devised. He was gone, and surely she will not know where to find him. She must by slow degrees come to want; yes, the sufferings she must feel will be great—yes, great, very great! So much the better, so much the better—I would it were so, and would always remain so. A state of constant misery and apprehension. She shall never know an hour's repose! Yes, by this time they think that I am dead, and that she will be free. Yes; but how free? Free to walk through the wide world a beggar! Ay, that is the jest of it—the chief excellence of the whole plan; yes, free as a beggar; but no otherwise, no otherwise. She and her child—there is an additional pang for her — a great and deep wound was there inflicted; yes, she will be mad! Mad, did I say? Ay; mad, or nearly so—nearly so, that is. The beauty of the plan is her suffering; and she must be on this side of madness, or she would not then feel the full weight of all her misery. I will go, now; yes—I will go now, and perambulate about. My friends will not know me—I might beg at their doors, and they would be unable to recognise me. My hour for exercise and contemplative enjoyment has come —a time when I can pass my own door, without fear of being recognised by its inmates—and I can see and observe all the little changes that have been made! The signs of poverty, too, will come on apace; they must show themselves, despite all the unwillingness of the inmate to show it. It is stern and relentless, and will show itself. At the moment that I see the first sign of poverty then shall I rejoice; for then I shall know the first downward step taken, and the next will follow in rapid succession, until, day after day, they follow so rapid, that she will be swept away by the force of the irresistible torrent of misery !"

" I will now take my evening perambulation," he muttered, after a pause; " and see what I can that indicates the approach of that moment which will make its appearance, though for some time it will be slow, but increasing its speed, like the rolling stone."

He turned from the window, and throwing over himself some extra clothing, of the shabbiest materials, he left the room; locking the door, he slowly descended the stairs, and left the house.

For some time he walked around Soho-square; that was his principal walk, and here he walked for some time every evening.

He passed through, this evening, several streets, and walked at length into Oxford-street; here he walked up and down for some time, unnoticed among strangers, and unknown. The many individuals passing to and fro completely hid him as effectually from observation as if he had been in his own room.

At length he passed a baker's shop several times, and saw several bills in the window, but for a while he took no heed of them.

At length, however, the thought struck him that there might be something about himself, and that he might have been advertised for in this manner.

Impelled by curiosity, he walked up to the window, and the very first printed placard he saw was one headed— " Missing, a gentleman," and went on to describe himself, offering a reward to any one who should discover him, dead or alive, and information was to be forwarded to the police, who would take the necessary measures for his security.

Bertram smiled as he read the handbill, and thought of the exertions they were unavailingly making to secure him —to find out in what quarter he had hidden himself, or, more properly speaking, they were making exertions to secure the body, for none were there who did not fully believe in his death.

" So," he muttered, " half the police are on my track; the famed Bow-street officers are after me, too. Well, well, let them; they will look a long while,

ere they think of looking for me in a garret in Soho."

This was a fact, for the simplicity of his place of concealment, and its completeness and unity, were well calculated to deceive and throw out men used only to another class of men, who adopted means of secreting themselves that at once fixed suspicion on them.

However, with Bertram it was quite another thing, for they had no scent of him, in the first place; and, in the second, they had no means of judging of the probable course he would pursue; and, finally, they deemed suicide the most probable fate he had come to, and accordingly looked for his body.

" Yes, yes," said Bertram; " they think me dead; I would have it so. They might meet and see me, but they would not know me. I am safe—very safe, and I can contemplate my own windows and yet they shall not know me."

He walked, then, towards his own house, and he walked backwards and forwards, gazing at the windows.

It was getting late, and he could see in the bed-room there was a light. He looked long and steadily, but yet the light continued there, and occasionally a figure passed across. The shadow on the curtain showed him it was a female; could it be the form of his wife? No, it was not her, he could see that; but then what was the supposition it conveyed to his mind? He paused, and watched for some time.

However, fearing to be noticed lurking about, he left the spot, and walked about the quiet and retired streets for some hours. A suspicion of the truth flashed across his mind, and the dark spirit of exultation and revenge had come over him, and yet with a new flush of those feelings which had been to him for some time a stranger.

He felt a new fluttering of the heart; a momentary feeling came over him which he had never before experienced; and then doubt, and the deep maniacal desire of revenge, drowned them.

" If—if," he muttered, "it be as I supposed, my revenge is beginning sooner than I anticipated; sooner than I hoped is the plot beginning to produce its results, and the tree bringing forth good fruit and early."

DANTON'S ENCOUNTER WITH THE TWO FARM LABOURERS.

It was long past midnight when he returned to the same spot, but he was anxious to be assured that it was true that his conjecture was not a creation of the brain, but a substantial fact; a thing that would leave no doubt upon his mind of what he hoped—ay, hoped, because it was an additional misery and misfortune to Mrs. Bertram.

It would hurry her down that steep descent of misery, he thought, much quicker and more surely than before. He did not wish to see the very acme of suffering and misery reached at once; no, no—he desired to gloat over each step, and watch the effects of it; and yet at each step he could not help feeling joyful when the next step was taken. Then a feeling would come over him that it might all end too suddenly; this produced a damp to his *Joy*—to his wild—almost unearthly ecstasy of delight.

"Yes, yes, she shall suffer," he muttered, "she shall suffer—she does suffer—and she ought to suffer; ay, more than I can inflict. But no matter; the catastrophe — the catastrophe is distant; yes, yes, that is distant; there is time enough to wring every heart-string, to sever every tie of affection, to destroy all hope of the future, which crushing tortures shall be all that remain of the present to her!"

He looked up again at the window, but there was yet a light, and he felt confirmed in his suspicions.

"Yes, yes," he said, "a premature birth in consequence of terror and torture of mind. It works well—it works well; who would have thought my plan would have begun to work so well. It is true she suffers.

"It cannot have been any other illness, because she would have been ill before; she would have had a light burning and an attendant waiting upon her. That—that is the nurse, but this is the first night there has been a candle; that's the cause of the change, no doubt. See, there are other lights now; some one comes towards the door to leave."

He stood back, and saw the fanlight of the door illumined by the rays of a candle which was being brought into the hall. The door opens—a female lets a gentleman out.

Bertram knew this man to be the accoucheur whom his wife had chosen, and now there could be no doubt as to the nature of the change that had taken place in the health of his wife. Yes, there was no doubt now on his mind, and he exulted; not because he was a father, but because the infant would be an additional misery to her.

He remained a long while on the same spot, and then he left reluctantly, lest it would have excited suspicion.

He returned slowly to his lodging, filled with reflections of a new cast, but all tending towards the same object and end.

" She will be robbed and deserted by all," he muttered; "ay, that will do well to begin with; she will scarcely know what the world is; while there were means, she would have friends, but now it is quite the reverse."

He came to the garret-door and left himself in, and then locked himself in.

It was a moonlight night, and he stood in a full flood of moonlight as it fell through the small attic window on to the floor. He stood still and gazed out upon the mass of buildings that lay behind, and mused upon his state—upon the approach of that revenge which he felt was even now becoming a thing that he could look upon and watch in its results.

" I have," he muttered, " done a good thing; I have baffled their searches, and I have made, and am now making them feel the effects of my revenge. What can they all think ? It is a strange thought, but it is one that amuses me; they must be thoroughly confounded, and believe me dead—they must believe me dead.

" What can they think I have destroyed myself or hidden my money for ? That is a matter which they cannot speculate upon, since they know not the true reason; but she knows—her heart must at once tell her why it is, and why she is left to herself. Even she must believe me dead."

He threw himself upon the miserable bed that was placed in one corner of the room, and, after some time spent in deep thought, he fell into a slumber.

Thus he employed himself watching the house of a night, and conjecturing within his own mind the nature of the mutations and changes that were then going on.

Thus day after day passed on, and thus the time passed with Bertram.

During the day he kept close in the attic, and then he brooded over the deep-seated passion that was centred in his soul. He gloated over his wrongs, and the means he had adopted to revenge himself upon the authoress of them. He saw the house began to assume that appearance which houses will assume when any change of means has taken place, or owners, for there was something that bespoke poverty. Some of the furniture had been removed and sold, and the house itself was not clean.

Indeed, there was enough to assure Bertram that means had begun to fail, and that, sooner or later, the house must become vacant of its present occupant; for no doubt the rent could not be paid, and he knew of none who would ever advance so much to one in the lamentable situation of Mrs. Bertram.

CHAPTER XLVII.

BERTRAM'S DREAM.—THE FIRE.— THE RECOGNITION,

WITH such gloom brooding at his heart, that it was not to be wondered at that the chance passengers whom he encountered slunk back from him with dismay, Bertram sought his miserable home. Several times he paused and trembled, as if some feeling of repentant emotion had crossed his heart; but if such were really the case, those better impulses were but very transient, and he walked on with his usual settled look of despair, when he reached his lodging. He felt, now, that in the fortunes and, perhaps, the very existence of his wife, an important crisis had arrived. He was not quite mad, and therefore it was not in human nature that he should be utterly callous as to what might occur. And yet there seemed a fiendish kind of rejoicing now and then, which lit up his countenance most frightfully, as he muttered to himself—

"She will suffer—she will suffer now. Now she will discover what it is to have trifled with a man like myself. It is a great revenge I am taking—a revenge invested to her with the most terrific bitterness."

He sat by the light of a solitary candle in the gloomy attic, and he felt that there would be but little chance of rest for him; moreover, too, if he could have gone to his bed with a hope of repose, the very elements themselves appeared to conspire against him. A loud and boisterous wind arose, and gusts of rain dashed against the casement, as if it would shake it from its frail fastenings. There seemed to be something ominous in this state of the weather under such circumstances, and a kind of presentiment came over Bertram that something unusual might occur. With the hasty impatient gesture of some caged animal, he paced the confined dimensions of that attic, giving up at once all idea of repose as utterly futile; and thus more than an hour must have passed over his head, after which a feeling of exhaustion crept over him, and, dressed as he was, he threw himself upon the miserable couch, so different from the costly bed he had once reposed on, to rest, but not, as he thought, to sleep.

A lethargic feeling, however, soon steeped his senses in forgetfulness, and after apparently slumbering soundly for a time, visions of terror and dismay began to haunt his imagination.

It might have been that on that night a watchful Providence yet sought to turn him from the evil which was on him, and, indeed, it would seem so, for had he not perversely scorned the lesson which the visions of his slumber taught him, he might even yet have been happy.

He fancied that he was walking in a delicious garden, and that Margaret was by his side; he thought she spoke with a voice of deep melancholy and wailing supplication, saying—

"Bertram, this garden will become a wilderness; the fragrant flowers you see around me are born of hope, sincerity, and trusting fondess. While these best and noblest feelings remain, you will see a perpetual summer. No nipping blasts shall wither one of these fair flowerets; but you have but to be suspicious of the innocent, you have but to accuse wrongfully those who never were, even in thought, otherwise than just to you, and as if the breath of pestilence had swept across this magic scene, all shall perish!"

Then he thought the vision of her whom he had loved, and made his bride, slowly passed from his sight, and he heard the roaring wind spreading devastation in its progress (no doubt the actual storm without mingled with the visions of his slumber).

He looked around him, and he saw the fair scene changing, as by the touch of an enchanter's wand: the trees were stripped of their verdant foliage, the flowers withered, the air was no longer filled with the odorous perfume of sweet vegetation — the very paradise became a wilderness; and then, as if dragged onward by some unseen power, he fancied he stood upon the banks of a stream of water. It was dashing and foaming onwards, as if swollen much beyond its natural limits. It was night, and a tempestuous one, and then he thought he saw a form gliding along the stream, and something seemed to whisper to him—

"'Tis Margaret—'tis Margaret!"

Her hands were upraised, and in their frantic grasp she held an infant, which, with an appealing look to Heaven, seemed asking for that mercy which its earthly parent failed to grant. Then the same mysterious voice that already appeared to have spoken to him, said—

"Bertram, you are a father. Your innocent child cries to you for justice; pause not, but for your own happiness, here and hereafter, be just!"

Bertram started up from his sleep, and he shook like an aspen, as he sat on the edge of his miserable bed. He clutched hold of the side of his bedstead with a convulsive effort, as he endeavoured to assure himself that all was not as he thought it was, but a flight of the imagination.

He glared into the darkness by which he was surrounded, but the straining of his own eyes caused them to emit an unnatural fire, that for a moment caused him to half doubt the reality of where he was. He shook, but he clenched his teeth, as though his will were at war with his nature; he would not attend to the warning voice of the vision; his nature seemed to revolt at the scheme of revenge he had conceived.

"No, no," he muttered; "I will not forego my revenge. I would die—yes, I would meet an early end, if I were forced to look coldly on my own disgrace, my own dishonour and indignity. I will have revenge. I will obtain it by a sure and slow process. God of Heaven! what have I done, that I should be deprived of that only consolation, that only satisfaction the injured can know? Never! never! never!"

It was some minutes ere he could move, so strongly had he been moved by his vision.

"It was but a dream—ay, a dream," he muttered, "an unconnected chaos of things almost forgotten—bygone hopes of happiness raised with the pleasant youthful dreams of early love, blighted by the faithfulness of one that I had loved. Yes, yes; it was this that disturbed my brain, and almost unmanned me. Many such dreams, and I should go mad—yes, quite mad; but, mad or not mad, I will not forego my revenge."

He rose from his pallet, and walked about the room for some time, and then he walked to the window, and gazed out upon the night. It was a boisterous night, or rather morning, but all was dark and gloomy. He could not see anything. The dim outlines of some houses, indeed, were visible, but he could not tell what they were. He knew, however; but notwithstanding his knowledge of them and their shapes, he could barely follow their outlines.

The wind, too, came in sudden gusts, and drove the rain against his window. Little recked he if it had been beaten in; he was hardly conscious that there was any rain. He heard the wind howl and the rain beat; he saw the gloom that enveloped the night, and yet his thoughts were rather influenced by the general character of the night and occasion, than that he took any especial notice of the elements. For some time he stood in silence, and no sound broke the stillness of that hour in that poverty-stricken room—nought could be heard save the strife of the elements.

"It boots not thinking," he muttered; "she is guilty, and I will have the satisfaction of knowing that she who has caused me all these pangs suffers in return."

He walked about the room for some space of time, until he felt again wearied—even more wearied than before—and he sank upon his pallet. For some time he lay in a waking mood, and his thoughts seemed to turn upon the scenes that had passed in earlier and happier times; and in the midst of these he fell fast asleep, and forgot the cares and sorrows of life.

How long he had slept he knew not, but he had some oppressive feeling, he knew not of what character; he breathed heavily, and found some difficulty in doing so at all, until he began to think there were strange noises in the house. There was a strange smell, too; but then he had a vision, the reality of which, for the time, he fully believed; and why should not the present be the same? However, the difficulty of breathing becoming greater and greater, until he was thoroughly awoke, he started up, and found the room full of smoke.

"The house must surely be on fire," he muttered; and he rose from his bed, and staggered back for a moment or two.

Then he heard the sounds of a mob below and some one shouted, "Fire, fire!" He walked into the passage or landing, but there was no hope of escaping that way. The smoke came up hot, and in dense volumes: there was not even time to seize upon the trap-door, and open that—no, nothing remained but the window of the small attic. Could he have got up to the trap-door, it is questionable if he could have made his way up, because the smoke was so dense.

As it was, however he had presence of mind to shut his own door, recollecting that, if he could get out of his window, he would be safe, for he thought he could scramble into the next house, and so on.

Shutting the door, he rushed to the window, and this he threw open; but, alas! it would not admit of his passing through! What was to be done? He could hear the roaring and the crackling of the flames!

Rendered desperate by the terrors of his situation, he tore from the grate a loose bar, and the aid of that, and the great energy and strength with which he used it, enabled him soon to displace the wood-work around, and remove the middle bar; and then he was free.

He scrambled into the parapet. Fortunately, that was deep and large, else, from the haste with which he fell, rather than let himself into it, he would have rolled over, and fell on the stones below, and have been inevitably crushed to pieces.

As it was, he was safe for the time; but he had somewhat miscalculated the means of escape, for, when he had got thus far, instead of finding an easy access to the next house, all he found was a high stack of chimneys, that projected over the coping.

This was another cause of haste and alarm, as he had to scramble up a steep roof of red pantiles. This was a matter of much difficulty and danger, yet he was successful, and reached the top; but then, he had to displace a brick or two, to enable him to smash some of the red chimney-tops, that stood so close together that he could not pass by them.

This effected, he stepped across, and in doing so heard a terrified scream ascend from the depths of the chimney. This, no doubt, was owing to the broken pieces falling into some room, and terrifying the inmates out of their lives.

At that moment, too, Bertram looked around him, and saw a red glare below. He could hear the loud huzzas of the mob at the engines; the cries, screams, and the hoarse howling of the men, sounded as if the gates of Pandemonium had been suddenly opened, and out rushed the uproarious shouting mob of wretches.

The red glare of the flames ascended, and showed him the mob below; at the same moment the mob saw him.

A tremendous shout arose from the spectators, but for what purpose it was difficult to tell, except to warn him of his danger, or, probably, because they knew not what else to do. However, Bertram did not remain here long, but turning towards the next house, the tiles of which he could very indistinctly see, he saw that he must jump down.

As there appeared to be no danger, but an instant necessity to do so, as the flames were rising over the coping stone, he, with a light spring, jumped on the next house, where he safely alighted.

For an instant he thought all was safe, and he had escaped; but the hope was deceptive, for he had scarcely felt that he had alighted on the right spot, when crash went the frail supports that held up the roof, and he was precipitated below.

"Murder!—murder!"

"Fire!" shouted one voice.

"Oh, mother!—mother!" exclaimed a boy, "here's the devil, mother! Oh, good Lord! what shall we do?"

There was an immediate rush towards the door of the apartment, and Bertram found himself lying in a heap on the floor, amid the ruins of the roof, a table, and the supper that had been laid.

It was a moment or two before Bertram sufficiently recovered his consciousness to be aware of the danger he ran from the falling materials above, and he was struck by a tile on the shoulder. Warned by this, as well as the red glare of the flames, that had now risen high above the house, and the falling embers, he made a precipitate retreat towards the door, which was at that moment opened by the man who belonged to the place.

This individual had scarcely seen the glare of the fire through the broken roof, than he felt himself borne backwards, and forcibly thrown down the stairs. With a yell, that might have alarmed a garrison, the man went rolling from stair to stair, and Bertram, the innocent author of all the disturbance and fright, came down at a desperate pace after him, adding new terrors and dismay to those already felt.

When he came to the street door, the people all got out of the way, thinking that the house was falling, so terrific was the noise and disturbance made, and offered him no opposition, and he soon got clear into the street. He was rescued by some of the firemen, who said, as he came out—

"Here's another saved. You're all right, ain't you, old man?"

"Yes, I am safe," said Bertram, "quite safe. I have run much danger."

"You have; but go in over the way, with the door open there, and a fireman before the door—you can go there for the night; they have offered their house on purpose."

Bertram, confused and much fatigued, instinctively walked across the road, and was very kindly received by the owners.

However, Bertram hung back, and when invited to come forward and warm himself, declined, saying he was warm as it was, and felt more fatigued than cold.

A make-shift bed was offered, and accepted, when, in passing through the passage, he met one who was well known to him.

"Mr. Bertram!" exclaimed a voice close beside him.

Bertram looked amazed.

"How! good Heavens! what has happened? where have you come from?"

"The fire," said Bertram.

"And this garb?"

"Misery."

"I lodge here," said Mrs. Ogden—for it was she. "I lodge here, Mr. Bertram; come in, I would speak with you,"

"With me?" said Bertram.

"Yes, with you. Why, how strange you speak and look."

Bertram mechanically followed her into her own apartment, and then motioning him to a seat, she said—

"I came to town but last night; tell me, for Heaven's sake, what has happened; your appearance denotes something very extraordinary. Is—is— Mrs. Bertram alive?"

"Yes, I believe so."

"You believe so! and do you not know?" inquired Mrs. Ogden, in surprise.

"No. I have not seen her these three weeks, or near a month."

"Good Heaven! what is the mean-

ing of this? Has any misfortune happened to you?"

"The worst."

"Loss of fortune?"

"No, honour."

"I do not understand you, sir," said Mrs. Ogden, somewhat offended at the disjointed manner in which Bertram answered, or, as she believed, tried to evade answering her questions. "Pray inform me what has happened; there can be no objection, surely, to telling me if any great grief has fallen upon you? Margaret and I were bosom friends, and I hope shall continue to be so now."

"Margaret has proved false."

"False!" exclaimed Mrs. Ogden. "False! utterly impossible!"

"Alas! no," said Bertram; "not impossible. She is false and faithless, and I have not seen her since that fatal night."

"And do you intend?"

"Never. She thinks me dead, and I am dead to her and to the world; my hopes and my happiness are blighted for ever."

"There is some fatal mistake in all this, Mr. Bertram. I will never believe that Margaret has done wrong; some fatal jealousy has been the cause of this; you yourself have most probably been the cause of the misery you complain of. Margaret is not guilty."

"I the cause of my own misery?"

"Yes, your jealousy."

"No, no. I have seen that which will convince me to my dying day."

"And I know Margaret too well!— by far too well, to believe her capable of anything that was dishonourable, or that would injure the happiness of one whom she had sworn to love. I say there is some mistake."

"I say there is not."

"Where is Margaret?"

"Where she always was, in her house."

"And you ——"

"Have quitted it, never to return."

"And this is the way you repay the affection of such a one as Margaret, whose high soul could not demean herself to baseness? Oh, no, Mr. Bertram; all the feelings of a man and husband will cry shame on you."

"No more of this," said Bertram.

"I'll hear no more of this—I will not hear such things explained as a mistake. No, no, Mrs. Ogden, that is too palpable, unfortunately; there can be no mistake. It is all too true."

"And what does Margaret say—what does she say? Has she fled you? has she sought an asylum from your suspicions in the arms of another?"

"She is now at home; she has not seen me since I made the discovery, else she had put on as fair a face as need be. I never trifle on such matters, and will not submit my judgment to the results of an altercation."

"Your judgment, sir, would have been no loser. However, it seems to me you are wrong, entirely wrong, and I will stake my existence upon the innocence of poor Margaret."

"I would not stake the smallest coin that ever was produced, because I know she is guilty; but we do not concur—you know nothing, and I, alas! know all too well."

These words were uttered in a short, abrupt tone of voice, and Bertram, evidently much excited, turned round suddenly upon his heel, and flung out of the apartment.

―――――

CHAPTER XLVIII.

MRS. OGDEN'S VISIT TO MARGARET.
―THE OFFER AND ITS ACCEPTANCE.

THE sudden departure of Bertram left Mrs. Ogden time to think over what she had heard from him, though at the same time his sudden departure was what she would have prevented, could she have done so.

"Margaret faithless," she murmured to herself. "Oh! no, no; that cannot be—that cannot be. I know every pulsation of her heart, and know there lurks not falsehood there. She has been the victim of some fatal false appearance, which the jealousy of this man has magnified into a reality, and built a superstructure of unhappiness for himself, that will not bear the test of examination; however, I will see Margaret and learn all—she cannot conceal anything from me; she cannot, she will not; and then I shall see if this mad-headed man be not wrong, entirely wrong."

Mrs. Ogden was much disturbed about her friend Margaret; she knew that she was sincere and affectionate, she knew her sense of rectitude was so strong that she could not be induced to pass from the path of virtue by any sudden impulse; and what could have given the impulse to Bertram's jealousy she knew not, nor could she imagine. These and many other thoughts pressed heavily on her mind, until she fell fast asleep; for, as she said, she had but come to town that afternoon, and this was but a temporary lodging she had taken upon an emergency.

The morning came, and the fire was subdued, after destroying the house in which Bertram had lodged, and the one through which he had made his escape.

Where Bertram had gone no one knew or thought of, and it's questionable if any one was assured of his escape; it mattered not to him, nor indeed to any one else.

It was at an early hour in the day, soon after breakfast, that Mrs. Ogden quitted her lodging to visit her early friend Mrs. Bertram, and offer what consolation she could to one who had been so strangely used as she had been by Bertram.

"Poor thing," she thought, "she must be very dull and miserable; she does not, I think, know he is living—the brute, to let a young wife sit and imagine all kind of things, as she must have done. I should not be surprised if, after what he has said and done to her, she was to do wrong; at all events, I must say, there is not one woman in ten who would not do so; and who would be to blame? nobody but himself—a suspicious, jealous man; they are the worst of men, for they make a happy life ridiculous and miserable."

She now arrived at Mrs. Bertram's, and could not but look at the place in some amazement; it seemed dirty and desolate, as if everything had been neglected and allowed to run as it would. She knocked; if she was surprised before, she was more surprised still, for a big bluff-looking man opened the door. The man was not uncivil, he was rather good-natured for his class than otherwise; and throwing the door open, he awaited her questions.

At first Mrs. Ogden thought she might be mistaken, and said, inquiringly,—

"Does Mrs. Bertram live here?"

"Yes, marm," said the man, in a gruff voice.

"Is she at home?"

"Yes, marm."

"Can I see her?"

"Yes, marm," said the man, turning aside his bulky person to permit her to pass into the passage; then he shut the door. Somewhat puzzled, she said,—

"Has Mrs. Bertram any servant that can show me into her apartment?"

"Yes, marm; but I don't know where she is now."

"Which room?"

"I think you'll find her in the front room, second floor."

Mrs. Ogden was filled with fears and apprehensions, she knew not wherefore, respecting the situation of Margaret, and hastened up to the best bedrooms, where she had been directed to by the strange-looking man.

"He's no servant," she thought; "there's an execution in the house; poor Margaret, she shall not want a friend while I can afford to be one, and while I live."

She now entered the front room, seeing no one near to announce her. This was evidently a sick room, and the faint cries of an infant were heard. She entered, but the bed-curtains were drawn closely round, and she walked round until she came to the fire-place.

"Margaret," she said softly.

"Ah! who calls me by that name? I think I ought to know that voice."

At the same moment she drew the curtain on one side, and their eyes met.

"Ah, Margaret, what's all this I see?" said Mrs. Ogden, gently embracing her.

"I can hardly tell," she said; "the whole seems like a dream; but—but I have no friend now; I am in poverty."

"Say you so to me, Margaret? I have never deserved this of you; but I will not upbraid you. You are ill—you are wretched—confide in me; I will do all that a friend and sister can for you."

"These are the first kind words I have heard spoken to me," said Margaret, faintly; "they are so different to what I have been used to of late, I cannot hear them unmoved."

"Nay, do not take the unkindness of others to heart."

"I do not; 'tis your kindness."

"That must not be. Come, Margaret, ease your mind and confide in me. You have a little one here—I heard it but now."

"Yes," said Margaret; "a poor little wanderer in this world of sorrow and distress. I love it, and yet, as I am now, could wish it had never received its being, poor thing."

"It is a pretty little thing," said Mrs. Ogden, "and you, Margaret, will find much pleasure in administering to its wants, watching its budding, beauties; it will employ your thoughts, and give a direction to your affections."

"I need it—I need it."

"And why, Margaret—why?"

"Because Bertram is dead—he is missing; it must be near a month since I have seen or heard of him."

"And why is this?"

"I cannot tell; as Heaven's my witness I have not wronged him."

"I thought not—I thought not."

"Grief and dismay have laid me here before my time, and when I rise I shall have no home to go to."

"No home?"

"No; there's an execution in the house, and I am only allowed to remain here till I am able to get up and am fit to be turned out. A medical man's certificate has compelled them to permit me to stay until I can be with safety removed hence."

"Poor Margaret, your fate seems a sad one; it seems as if Providence sent me to town, at this particular juncture, that I might comfort and console you."

"Thank you," said Margaret; "my time, since I last saw you, has not been happily spent."

"I feared so."

"I have seen Danton."

"Theodore Danton?"

"Yes, yes!" said Margaret; "he has returned, and is now a wealthy, but miserable man."

"Indeed, Margaret; but was this prudent?"

"I now not. I could not refuse the first interview."

"You had more than one?"

THE EXAMINATION OF DANTON BEFORE THE MAGISTRATE.

"Yes; two; he sought me, hoping to find me yet single. He had left England to procure wealth, that he might become my husband."

Mrs. Ogden listened, and Margaret proceeded.

"You know my former affection?"

"I do."

"Then you can guess the feelings that must have come over me; but I was the wife of another, and I stifled them as well as I could, and as effectually as I could. I discovered, by accident, after we parted, that he was dying at an hotel, and, in the evening, I went there and saw him. Oh, Heavens! what an alteration; he was almost wasted to a mere skeleton."

"Poor Danton!"

"Ay; he was ill—very ill; could scarce sit up. Our meeting was, as you may imagine, sorrowful, and thus I left him. I never saw him afterwards."

"And that is all that passed?"

"Everything!"

"And where is Bertram?"

"From that night to this, I never beheld Bertram; the cause of his absence I cannot tell; it is mysterious and singular—he has committed suicide."

"Has he sent you a note, or anything, to tell you what he complains of?"

"Nothing—nothing. I know nothing of him, or of the reason of his absenting himself; but it is from some anger with me, else, why should he take his money from his banker's, and leave me penniless?"

"I cannot tell. Does he know of this visit to Theodore Danton?"

"I know not. I saw no suspicious circumstances that induced me to suspect it at the time, nor do I now think so; and yet it must have been something. Be it as it may, I am destitute—I have no means."

"You need none, while I have a penny-piece, Margaret. I believe in the rectitude of your conduct—in your innocence, and am convinced that Bertram has ill-used you."

"He has behaved very cruel, and very unjust; but, perhaps he is dead—no doubt he is dead—he must be dead!"

"He is not dead, Margaret."

"Are you sure?"

"I have seen him."

"You?"

"Yes, I."

"And when?"

"Only last night."

"Good heavens!" exclaimed Margaret, a sudden faintness coming over her.

Mrs. Ogden gave her some salts, and, after a few moments, the emotion passed away; but still she was affected.

"Alive—you saw him alive?"

"I did."

"And did he speak? Tell me what he said—tell me what he said!"

"That he was dead to you and to the world, and would persist that you had been unfaithful to him; but I could obtain no explanation from him of what it was that had given him cause to think so, or, indeed, of anything. He appeared in a state of poverty, voluntary of course; but he said you would never see him again; and when I told him I believed in your innocence, and insisted that his jealousy was the cause of all his misery, he flung out of my lodgings, and left the house, without saying another word."

"What a singular interview! What strange vagary could he have taken into his mind to build up such a conclusion as that? Why, had he seen me go to Danton's, he could scarcely have deemed me guilty, without the slightest inquiry—without, indeed, accusing me face to face. No, no, he would have burst upon us both, and then he would have seen a sick man; he would then, had he been ever so angry—he must have been convinced of his mistake."

"I cannot imagine what can be the cause of it," said Mrs. Ogden; "but it may have arisen from some suspicions he may have entertained; a jealous temper is always making food for its own suspicions."

"It must be so," said Margaret; "but it is very dreadful; he has left me and my infant to starve — he must surely be mad, and this is the cause of his cruelty."

"He certainly cannot be much less; but have you seen Danton again?"

"Alas, no!"

"Indeed, I would advise you to do so."

"The advice is too late," said Margaret, with a sigh—"too late!"

"Indeed! How so?"

"He had left a day or two before I called there. They say he left secretly, while too ill to take care of himself; he left without a single person being aware of his departure; indeed, no one would have believed it at all likely or possible."

"Another strange and inexplicable circumstance," said Mrs. Ogden. "One would think that the demon of mystery had run riot through the whole of these affairs, causing one to play at cross purposes with the other."

"It would seem so, indeed, and that most fatally, too. I am sure the events of the last few weeks appear to me more like some terrible phantom in a dream; they cannot be real; and yet, alas! there is not room for doubt, if you knew the anguish I have suffered."

"I can easily understand it—easily; it must have been terrible. I need not ask who these men are down stairs, Margaret."

"They are in possession of the house and goods for debt, and I cannot pay it."

"You know I am not rich, and all I have is a small annuity. Come to my lodgings, and we will be as two sisters, and live together, when you can be removed with safety; and then we can employ our time in endeavouring to trace these two fugitives, both Bertram and Theodore Danton."

"Oh, Mrs. Ogden, you know not how this kindness reminds me of days long gone by. I cannot tell you all I feel and think, I am too weak to express my thanks and gratitude."

"Do not try it, dear Margaret, do not try it; but accept it, and that will assure me of all I can desire or wish."

"I do accept it; I have no other re-source. I would accept it had I other hopes, for none could give me so much pleasure. Nothing can tend so much to soothe those wounds I have received, as the expressions and acts of kindness of a friend like yourself."

"Then I shall look upon this as settled," said Mrs. Ogden, kindly; "so all you have to do is to get well as fast as you can, and then you will leave this place, and those which it contains."

"And truly glad shall I be to do so, for everything I see reminds me of all that has happened, and makes me yet more and more unhappy."

CHAPTER XLIX.

THE HOSPITAL NURSES.—THE SCENE IN THE WARD.—THE MIDNIGHT DEED.

WE now turn from the contemplation of the unmerited sufferings of Mrs. Bertram, and the gloomy and vengeful madness that had seized upon the brain of Bertram, of his desperate and his miserable mode of life, to watch the events that occurred to the unfortunate Theodore Danton.

As the reader well knows, he was taken at his own request to the hospital, whither he was accompanied by a young man from the chemist, with a note which procured him an immediate admission and attention.

He was placed somewhat apart from the rest, and eventually removed from the room into which he was first taken, and accommodated at the upper end of the ward, where there were a few empty beds, at some distance from the other beds in the ward; and so situated as to render them much more comfortable and select.

This place was reserved for such individuals of known respectability as were from any accident or sudden illness brought in on the emergency.

There was a recess, and into this recess his bed had been placed; and, besides that, there was a large screen that was placed around the foot of his bed, so that, though he could see all that passed, yet none could see him.

Here he was left to the mercies of the nurses, who before they undertook the office, have long since become deadened and callous to every feeling of humanity, and now, when they have entered upon these duties, the whole sum and substance of their conversation are the probabilities of human life or death, and the devising new schemes of plunder, or uttering some vile, coarse jest upon the agony of the miserable and dying wretch.

Theodore was decently attended to, for his appearance promised them some plunder, and that was something towards ensuring their respect. He was not decidedly ill, but he was recovering, and had all the weakness and symptoms of illness about him; he could not rise in the bed, but lay there without motion.

He had no wish for motion; he did not desire to move out of his bed, or go out into the street; no, he was there safe from discovery, and Margaret could not again see him.

He lay there quiet, reflecting in his own mind on the past, and the prospect of the future. Neither was such as could give him much hope or promise; he had but little satisfaction in the reflections that arose from the remembrance of the past or the thoughts of what was to happen.

One thing alone was satisfactory to him, he had saved himself and Margaret from peril. That was an inexpressible satisfaction to him. It was painful to think he had seen her for the last time, but it might save many a bitter pang.

Her happiness was all he now cared for—while she was free from reproach and calumny, he cared not for himself; she was yet dear to him—too dear to risk any misadventure in which she might suffer, even wrongfully, for his sake.

Yes, he might suffer—suffer he expected in his own mind, by his blighted affections; but she was innocent of all she felt the same pang, but she could not find any means of alleviation.

Such were the thoughts of Theodore Danton, but he was frequently interrupted in the course of these thoughts by the conversation that went on in the ward-room—conversation neither the most edifying nor the most refined, but occasionally of the worst character— almost always unfeeling.

The nurses, too, took their share in

it. They were not above their occupation, nor above the class they had to attend upon. That was easily seen and understood from the lightness of their conversation.

"Jane," said one of the nurses to the other, as they sat by a fire behind Danton's screen—"Jane!"

"Well, what do you want, now?" answered a large, gross, leviathan female.

"What, asleep again!" exclaimed the first speaker with a sort of laugh.

"What's that to you? You don't have to sleep for me."

"No; but you sleep enough to refresh the whole ward. I wonder how long you would sleep if left to yourself. Why, if somebody did not take some compassion upon you, you would starve, for you'd never wake up to take a meal's victuals."

"Well, never mind. If you have nothing more to say, I shall finish my nap out until the old fool with the lock jaw has died, and rid me of his trouble."

"Exactly; that is what I wanted to speak to you about."

"Eh?"

"He's dead."

"Bravo! Come, there's one less for the night. He was of no use at all; he hadn't got a sixpence in all his pockets."

"He had a friend come to see him to-day," said the first.

"Ah, well! I must get up and go and visit him myself, and look over his clothes. A stray shilling may have crept in among the pockets, you know."

"That made me give you the news," replied the first.

The large female rose, and walked quietly towards the bed, and was there some few moments rifling the pockets of the dead man. This could not be seen, as it is usual to draw a screen around the beds of those who are dying.

"Ha! ha! ha!" laughed one of the nurses when the other was gone, and then she said in a whisper, loud enough for Danton to hear every word of it,—
"I have sent her on a wild-goose chase."

"Isn't he dead?"

"Oh, yes; but I have taken care of his pockets myself."

"Did you find anything?"

"Yes."

"How much?"

"Only eighteen pence, blow me! It wasn't worth the trouble of searching over his clothes. I never did see such a plaguey, beggarly set as come here."

"Yes; it's worse than a poor-house. I wonder they don't send many of 'em to the workhouse infirmary."

"They ought. A poor nurse, now-a-days, can't make what she could make at one time. It is a shame."

"So it is. I wish I could get a windfall; it would be just the thing for me. I want money."

"A very common occurrence."

"There's that fellow with the cracked skull making a hullaballooing. If he ain't quiet, he must be removed."

"Yes, the sooner the better."

"Well, Jane, what have you got, and what are you going to stand out of your gleanings?"

"Ah!" said the fat woman, "curse me, if I have a single mag. He ain't worth a farden. A pretty generation, this!"

"So it is. Did you give an eye to the bed next to the one you went to just now?"

"Yes."

"How is he?"

"Oh! he's tossing and twisting about."

"It'll be all over with him before morning, I should say."

"No doubt, no doubt. He's been a good sort of a fellow. He paid as long as he could; but it wasn't much."

"He's going, though, now. There'll be a bit of picking there."

"Very little, I'm afraid. He hasn't many friends, you see."

"D—n 'em! they very few on 'em have, as I see. There's that fellow that died the day before yesterday. You recollect him, do you not?"

"Oh, yes; with the fractured leg and arm from a fall."

"Yes. Well, he was here for three weeks, and hadn't a friend to come and see him the whole time—not a soul. Talk about feeling; if that ain't coming out strong at the last, I don't know what is."

"Perhaps he was a trouble to his relations, and they are glad he's gone. I'm not sorry; there's another bed empty, and that's another chance, though a bad one."

"So it is; but the young fellow you speak of was a carpenter—was he not?"

"Yes; he was."

"Young as he was he ought to have friends, I think—some shopmates, or something of the sort."

"Why, yes; they must have known where he was—if he wouldn't let his relations know."

"Nobody came to claim him?"

"No,—none."

"Then he's taken to the dissecting-room, and the young surgeons are chopping him about to find what is, and what isn't."

"What did you make by him—eh?"

"Something about six or seven shillings I think."

"That's not so bad."

"There's the bell; something amiss —I suppose more fractures, or wounds, or poisoning—I dare' say," said Jane, the fat nurse.

There was now a silence of some minutes, and then a bustle was heard in some part of the building; and after a time some persons approached the ward in which Danton lay.

"What's the matter, I wonder, now."

"You had better go and tell them to come and carry the dead 'un out of the ward," said the nurse.

"He's hardly cold yet; but, I suppose, it will be quite time enough if I tell them by-and-bye."

"Very good,—only it's no use keeping the cold meat in the ward, you know—the doctors don't like it."

"They won't be here to-night."

The nurse, however, rose and walked away, apparently for the purpose of informing the proper person that the man had died; and then he was soon after removed to a room, where it was usual to deposit such persons as had died. This, of course, was a hospital regulation, and a very proper one too. The persons who had entered the ward when this conversation took place now approached the bed where Danton lay.

"Is that bed occupied behind the screen?" inquired a voice.

"Yes, sir."

"Well, then, this is not?"

"No, sir."

"Just place him in this," said a voice which Danton now recognized to be that of the resident apothecary.

There was some little shuffling of feet; and when the individual moved on one side, Danton could see they were undressing a foreigner—a gentleman, whose apparel, at least, bespoke that he was one of a wealthy class.

"Attend to him," said the apothecary, to one of the nurses; "and should he become sensible, apprise the surgeon of the fact; or, if he be not in the way, let me know."

"Yes, sir," said the nurse; "is there anything else to attend to, sir?"

"Nothing."

The apothecary, and the assistant-surgeon who accompanied him—because the house-surgeon had some friends, and could not attend any further upon him—now quitted the ward, leaving the nurses alone.

"What's the matter with him, I wonder; He's quite insensible—he breathes very hard!"

"Oh; perhaps it's a *plexy*—that's how people do fall down insensible like, at times. The blood goes tingling up to their ears, and confuses the head; and so, in a little while, they become insensible."

"Oh! it doesn't matter, as long as they are going, how they go, or why they go; it's all one in the end."

"So it is."

"Have you seen his clothes?"

"I think I have; you don't often see such as them come into the ward, I'll swear. I couldn't be off seeing and noticing them too; they are beautiful, and must have cost a pretty penny, I dare say."

"No doubt—no doubt; but I say, Margaret, don't you think his pockets are well lined—he has a heavy purse, eh?"

"Yes, he has; I felt it as I took off his clothes."

"Did you?"

"Yes; and I'll almost take an oath that it is well filled with sovereigns; the weight alone convinces me of that."

"You don't say so?"

"Yes, I do; and more than that, we shan't get any of it."

"And why not?"

"Because, you see, he's a gentleman, and his word will be taken against ours, you know; and there will be a bustle and stir, and, rather than have anything said about it, the surgeon will discharge us."

"They may, but they seldom attend to any complaint that is made against us; though, to be sure they don't trouble themselves much about those who haven't money, any more than we do."

"They don't; but I have a better way than that; we can do it all safely—get the money, and nobody be the wiser."

"Ay! and how can that be done? If we clear his pockets out now we may be observed, you know, and then we are booked; he may not see us, but it will be talked off afterwards."

"Exactly; but my plan will avoid all that, for nobody knows him, and he will not be owned; and if he be, why, no inquiries can be made about what he might have had about him."

"Well, but what has all this to do with the man there?" pointing to the bed.

"This much—if we can stop his breathing in the night, why, we shall soon be in possession of the contents of his purse."

"I see—I see," said the other; "but it is a very dangerous plan."

"It may be, if it be discovered," she replied; "but who is to do that, I should like to know? No one, you may depend upon it. It will look as if he died from the same cause that rendered him insensible."

"So it will."

"That is agreed, then, between us; we shall share the contents of his purse; it will be quite a windfall."

"It will, indeed; we ought not to let such an opportunity slip by unimproved, you know. Lost time, they say, is never recovered; and, certainly, a lost chance never comes back again—so we'll make sure of this one."

"That's well resolved upon, at all events; then we'll do the job about midnight, eh?" said the other.

"Why, yes; that is the best hour; there will be nobody awake in the ward, and no one will come into the ward by any accident whatever."

"That's good; at any rate, it is a settled thing;"

"Yes, quite."

"Hush! no more; here comes Sleepy Jane, and we may as well do this job by ourselves; the money won't have to be divided into so many shares."

"True; all right; I understand. Here she comes again."

Sleepy Jane, as she was called, now came and sat down by the fire, and, after a short time, she said,—

"I have been in the next ward."

"Ah!"

"There's Mother Jones dropped into a nice thing. Drat that woman, she's always some windfall or another! I do believe she is the luckiest devil alive."

"Indeed!"

"What has she got now?"

"Oh, you know the old man who was brought in the other day with a broken leg—he was a beggar, and had been run over."

"Yes; he was very old, wasn't he? I thought he would never get over it."

"They say he was very hearty and healthy, and would have got over it but for his own obstinacy in refusing to undergo amputation."

"He wouldn't suffer it then?"

"No; though they assured him that there was every probability of his getting over it safely and in a short time.

"'No,' muttered the old man, to the head surgeon, who stood arguing the matter with him, 'no—no; I'll die with the same number of limbs on I had when I was born.'

"'Then you'll be dead in two days," said the head surgeon.

"'And how do you know that?' said the little old man.

"'Because the flesh will mortify, and, after that, you cannot last four-and-twenty hours.'

"'Very well,' he said, 'let me have some pens and paper; I'll make my will. Let me see, it's a quarter to twelve now; my bed will be vacant at a quarter to twelve the day after to-morrow.'

"'You are resolved, then?' said the surgeon.

"'Yes,' said the old man; 'quite; no disrespect to you, sir, but I will rather die than be hacked about by large knives and saws, and be made an example or show to the young gentlemen who study the art of carving people up in pieces scientifically.'"

"What did the surgeon say to that? It was a rare blow for him."

"Oh! he only laughed, and said, he could do as he pleased, but he would die; while, if he submitted, there was a chance, and if he should change his mind within six he was to let him know and he would come to him. He then passed on to the next bed."

"But what has that to do with Mother Jones, eh?"

"I'm coming to that; the old man made his will, and to-day, about a quarter past one o'clock, he died."

"The surgeon was out by half-an-hour, then; but it wasn't a bad guess."

"Not at all—not at all; he was as good as dead some hours before; but when they came to read his will, he said that he had no relations, and as Mrs. Jones had behaved very kind to him, he would leave all he had to her, and named the clothes he wore, as well as a leather belt he wore around his body."

"That isn't much of a ketch, any how. What was the leather belt?"

"It was a shot belt, but the top had been broken off, and it was stuffed full of sovereigns and half sovereigns, so Mother Jones came into a nice little piece of luck."

"Indeed she has, upon my word; a canting, religious beast."

"Why, how many sovereigns had she then, I wonder?"

"I really don't know, but I think I heard her say there wasn't much short of one hundred and seventy pounds."

"Oh, my gracious! who would have believed in such a thing? I shouldn't, I'm sure."

"Nor I."

The nurses now engaged in some low conversation, and Danton fell back on his pillow utterly exhausted.

"Can such things be?" he muttered; "God of heaven can such things be? Do we, indeed, live in a Christian community, in a civilized age and country? My God, what a prospect! who is safe in the hands of these creatures? it is horrible to think of it. Here are women paid for the performance of certain duties which, when they do perform, they do in the most brutish manner imaginable. Who is to tell what the unfortunate wretch—who lies helpless and unable to complain, and, save to groan, he cannot indicate when he is pained—whom she attends may suffer from the acute anger of his wound, or from her mode of attending to him.

"No one can tell that; they make the poor wretches give them money; it may not be asked for, but if it be not voluntarily forthcoming, why, woe betide the unfortunate being, for he will assuredly suffer in neglect and bodily pain. The nurse will find a thousand different ways to plague, pain, and neglect him; and what can he do? He has no remedy, and the best thing he can do, for his own sake, if he have the means, is to comply with the exaction."

Theodore Danton was perfectly horrified at the conversation he had heard; indeed, there is no word strong enough to express his feeling; but he was perfectly powerless. He was so reduced in strength that he could do nothing; and he was persuaded that to make an alarm would be useless—perfectly useless, and worse, because it would not save the unfortunate man's life. Again, if he could make it known, it would be denied *in toto*, and he would be looked upon as a maniac for his pains.

Indeed, the extreme debility that had come over Danton since his arrival at that place, rendered him totally incapable of arising himself; he could turn from side to side, and that was all. He was at the mercy of these women. He lay there the unwilling confidant of these wretches; the powerless recipient of their vile and inhuman schemes. What was he to do? was a question he more than once asked himself, but he had no means of making an answer.

He lay there thinking for some time, and having been awake for some hours now, he felt drowsy, and the dull, drawling tone of the nurses' voices sounded in his ears like a mere hum, or indistinct murmuring, and it lulled him insensibly to sleep.

He slept some hours soundly, but then, after a time he began to think that some horrible events was about to take place; and then, by degrees, he began to have some perception that there was some motion about him.

He couldn't tell if he were dreaming or awake; he was indeed in that partial state of consciousness in which the mind had but a very dim consciousness of what was passing, or during which the perceptions are so doubtful as even, when thoroughly aroused, the sleeper still remains in doubt of what was.

By degrees, Theodore Danton recovered from his drowsiness; he saw a light was gradually being moved away from his bed, and heard one of the nurses say to the other,—

"Oh, he's fast asleep."

"That is all right; I have examined the others—there's nobody about—now is the time; everything is lucky, and we shall be lucky, too; all is quiet and still, and nothing but the snoring of the sleepers disturbs the silence."

The other nurse beckoned to her, and Theodore Danton now rose on his elbow, and could distinctly see the old beldames as they whispered together. The light stood on a table beside them —the farthest from Danton—and it threw the figures and countenances of the two women up in strong relief.

Harsh and forbidding were the profiles thus strangely presented to his eyes; they seemed well fitted for such a deed as that they now had in contemplation, and which, in fact, they were about to commit.

They stood for some moments thus; their lips moved—he could see every motion, however slight; they had an unearthly appearance; like the impersonation of some fell fiends that plotted woe to mankind, stood they in whispered consultation.

It was over, whatever was the subject of their whispered converse, and they turned towards the bed in which the sick man lay. All was still; the man lay quiet; he now and then slightly moaned, but otherwise he showed no signs of life.

"He is in a nice quiet humour for us now," said one; "he won't have sense enough left to struggle."

"How shall it be done?" inquired one of the nurses, as she felt in her pocket for some time, and then pulled out a small flask, and she shook it close to her ear; and then she took a small wine glass from a nook, and poured out some of the liquid, which she presented to her companion, saying,

"Come, here's a drop to keep the cold out; it's some of the right sort."

"That's the thing; come, here's a toast—'May the evening's amusement bear the morning's reflections.' I'm sure there's nothing but what's proper in that, and the sentiment is well worth the liquor."

She drained the glass off to the same toast, adding, merely by way of a rider,—

"The evening's amusement, Margaret, you know, is innocent, and why shouldn't the morning's reflections? And when I can put my hand on my pocket, and hear the sound of the sovereigns, I always think the evening's amusement must be innocent; and as for my morning's reflections, why, I always has 'em in a glass, you know, so when I turn my back upon it, I know nothing about 'em."

"Well, come along, then; we'll put him out of his misery at once. Leave the light there, it will enable us to see our man better than holding it; for, though I don't expect it, yet he may struggle."

"How will you do it?"

"Smother him."

"With the pillows, as somebody's babbies was at some time or other before we was born?"

"No; with a towel."

"A towel!"

"Yes; but no, he has a silk handkerchief, has he not?"

"Yes, he has."

"Then we'll have that, and wet it, and lay it over his face, and, if need be, a towel also; and if we hold it over his face tightly, he'll soon give up the ghost."

"I have heard as much; but never believed it before."

"You shall see now. I will show it is no joke."

"Where did you learn it?"

"When I was in the West Ingies: my husband was an unbearable plague, and he caught the fever; I attended to him myself, and, when the crisis came on, I put a bandanna over his mouth, and he never got the better of it."

"Have you seen it used in this country afore?" inquired the nurse.

"To be sure I have; more than once. So, come on; be quick."

Danton could see the two nurses go to the foreigner's clothes, and take from them a large silk handkerchief, and soak it in some water, and a towel was used in the same way. Then the nurse took

the handkerchief, and folded it four times double; then she gently laid it on the sick man's face, and then a strong towel was placed over that.

"Now," said the nurse, "now lay hold of your side of the towel, and hold on tight, and it will soon be over."

The other nurse immediately strained her end of the towel, as it was called, and then a perceptible motion took place in the body of the unfortunate gentleman.

He shook visibly, and then by degrees his chest heaved, while he strove hard to free himself from the oppression that he felt was choking him. The effort was but a transitory one; it did not recall his senses to him, but it died away in faint struggles, without any effort to direct them, and in a very few moments more he was a corpse.

"There; that's over."

"It was done precious quick," said the other; "it was quite a mercy for him."

"Quite; it does well, and leaves no trace behind; but quick, take the handkerchief away, and dry it."

"Oh, yes; there will be time enough for all that, you know; let us see what's in his pockets first."

"Very well," said her worthy companion; "we'll take it all out and share it alike. I have no doubt but his pockets are well lined."

They now emptied the pockets of all that was in them, save a few halfpence.

"This purse is full and heavy."

"Here is some loose sovereigns."

"Yes, yes; this is all; come, let us sit down by the fire, and then we can divide it."

Then, creeping like two cats, Theodore Danton saw them approach the fire-place and sit down, with their feet raised, and then they emptied the purse into the lap of one of them.

"There," said the nurse, as she finished counting them—"there; I think this is a very decent windfall, and very well managed—eh?"

"I think so, too. How much is there in all?" inquired her companion.

"There is forty-one pounds ten shillings. I dare say he had been to a banker's, or some such place, and that accounts for his having so mnch about him. Let me see, that is twenty pounds fifteen shillings each."

"Yes, that is fair."

"If we were to have many such windfalls as these, a few years would see us free of the hospital."

"I believe you—if we only had one a week it would do, wouldn't it? Let me see, one a week, that would be twenty pounds—not taking the odd shillings, because we could spend them."

"To be sure we could, and as much again, I should think."

"Ay; but then we shouldn't get independent. Let me see, twenty pounds a week would come to one thousand and forty pounds a year. Why, about five years, at the outside, would be a fortune. We could live like gentlefolks all that time."

"With the experience of hospital nurses," remarked the other.

"In course we could; but then it's no use speculating. There's no such a run of luck in the universe as that—it's all gammon—moonshine; but still it would be a most comfortable thing."

"So it would," said the other with a deep sigh; "but then, you see, there's no continued run of good luck in this sublimary spear; it's all wanity and wexation."

"Oh! none of that. I enjoy things as they go; I don't take things to heart in that manner; it's all d——d gammon, you know; that's only what I call the livery of talk. You chapel goers are all known by that ere way of conwersing, just the same as if you wore a livery over your clothes."

"Well, well—here is twenty good sovereigns. I think they'll pay us for our trouble, and we can now sleep in comfort."

"Yes; that's it."

"I wonder," said the other, thoughtfully, "if we could manage to grab the watch, chain, and seals—eh?"

"Oh, no, no! that would ensure detection, because it's a chance if they have not been noticed; and then they are too costly."

"Why, I suppose there would be some difficulty in disposing of them after we had got them, and so I suppose we must give up all thoughts of them."

"Yes, yes—we must. I am sorry for it, but it ain't worth while running chances of being bowled out."

"No, no; soft and sure, that's my motto; and fair and easy goes a long way."

"So it does. Well, I suppose we may as well have another drain, and then we can sit up in the corner and sleep till morning."

"There's the old man I ought to dose at one clock. Yes; I dare say I'll give myself all the trouble about that. Oh dear, no; a little natural rest will do him much more good than their stuff."

"So it will. Here's to you, and may the present moment be the worst of our lives."

"Amen!" said the other. "It is an ill wind that blows nobody any good."

So saying, the two hags tossed off another glassfull of Geneva each, and resigned themselves to the arms of the sleepy god, as novelists would say. It was not long before they were both fast asleep and snoring, one on each side of the fire-place.

"God of mercy!" ejaculated Danton, "do I dream? and is the scene that I have witnessed real, or some wild imaginings of a disordered brain? It cannot be a delusion; it is all too real —too real. There are the two hags, the midnight murderers, who sleep as sound as though they had committed no such fearful and aggravated a crime—a crime the blacker, because they had such facilities for its commission—a crime the blacker, because they were employed and paid for using all care and tenderness towards the objects of commisseration that were placed under their charge; and yet blacker still, because the unfortunate gentleman was entirely at their mercy. Oh, God! what have I not seen—what have I not beheld? Murder! yes, of the foulest and most unchristian character. Sordid and bloody-minded wretches! could not there have been one spark of human feeling remaining in your hearts? Could you not have thought for one moment that he held life as dear as you? that there were probably others who held his life much more dearly than even he himself could hold it? There may be both wife and child to mourn his loss—to be irreparably injured by the death of their father. But supposition is useless; the speculation as to whom they had deprived of a protector sinks the great and damning act of murder. He shall be avenged. I will denounce the murderesses before their face when the visiting surgeon shall come round, and then we shall see if such a crime as this can go unpunished."

He lay back on his pillow, exhausted by his own thoughts. His feelings had been harrowed up beyond belief; he thought himself almost an accessary of the fact, and that some of the guilt rested upon his shoulders, and that he was to blame because he had not made some effort to save the unfortunate foreigner.

"And yet what could I have done?" he muttered. "Nothing—literally nothing. I could not get out of my bed even; I could not have staggered to his bedside; and, had I even done that, what was to prevent their carrying me back to my own bed, and there securing me? Nay, it is beyond a doubt to me, but they would have murdered me to save themselves any trouble about the matter. Yes; and even knowing the fate that awaited me, could I have saved myself? Oh, no, no, no!—I am too much at their mercy; I have no strength, not even that of a child, and how could I prevail against such wretches? Impossible! I could have shrieked; but my voice would scarce be heard, and it would certainly not have deterred them. Such sounds are common here, and I am by no means sure that it would not facilitate my death as well as that of him who now lies a corpse!"

Thus did thought after thought whirl its rapid course through the brain of the unfortunate Theodore Danton. The deed he had seen done created a horror in his mind difficult to be conceived, and for some time he was in a state of nervous excitement; but, weak as he was, this could not last long, and, from sheer exhaustion, he fell again into a troubled doze. Thus he remained till the movements of the nurses in the ward awoke him to a state of conciousness.

He was calm now, and he began to doubt the reality of the scene he had witnessed on the previous night. He thought it must be some hideous phantom, some terrible dream, that appeared so vivid while it lasted, that it was difficult to dispel what was illusory, or understand what was real.

"It must surely be a dream," he thought. "A dream—yes; there cannot be human beings capable of such deep wickedness."

The nurse approached his bed now to speak to him. He looked at her—there was the same harsh lineaments in her face that he had noticed during the night.

"Is—is," stammered Danton, "the gentleman who was brought in last night insensible, dead?"

"Yes," said the nurse.

Danton shuddered, for now he knew that what he had seen was reality.

"What, did you know him?"

"No," replied Danton; "I did not."

"Ah, poor fellow! he never recovered his senses; and it was as well, I am sure, he did not, for he had nothing on his mind to mak his last moments unhappy; for he couldn't understand anything, poor soul!"

Danton spoke not, but turned his face towards the wall, and remained so until the surgeons should make their round.

In the meantime the nurses pursued their occupation as though nothing had happened of an extraordinary character. Indeed, nothing appeared to have happened at all but what was usual and ordinary.

There was much covert joking among the nurses, at least the two that had been engaged in the murder. They seemed in high glee; many remarks being made to the effect that there were more ways of killing a dog than hanging him, and that all was fair in love and war. It would all be the same a hundred years hence, and therefore they might as well look to present comforts and take care of themselves.

"Such callousness of heart," thought Danton, "I could not have thought could have existed in the most abandoned of mankind. I had yet to learn that woman surpassed man in iniquity, and to make it look worse than in him it ever could appear. But this triumph shall be short-lived. I will denounce them, and that may serve as a warning to others; if it make them no better, it may, perchance, instil fears into them, and thus be the safeguard of some unfortunate being who may be brought here in a helpless state."

But Theodore Danton little knew the women he had to deal with; he little dreamed, even after what he had seen, of what they were capable; and that they who had been guilty of committing so base a crime so deliberately and so coolly were not to be so easily scared by an accusation.

These women were not easily thrown off their guard, and those who were thus far steeped in guilt, could not object, when their safety or interest was concerned, to take a step more up the ladder of iniquity. Oh, no, hospital nurses, as a class, are not the sort of people who will by any means stop at trifles, and not a few of them would stop at anything.

The time passed on, but with leaden wings, to the mind of Theodore Danton; and oh! how he watched the entrance of the surgeons! Oh, how he watched their progress from bed to bed! how he thought they wasted the precious moments in their inquiries and their explanations to pupils!

Yes, the time seemed to grow slower and slower as they approached the bed on which he lay, fevered with anxiety, and a desire to utter his accusation.

At length they neared his bed, but they stopped a moment or two at the bed of the murdered man.

"Dead?" said the surgeon to the nurse.

"Yes, sir," she replied demurely, with a curtsey.

"Did he recover the use of his senses before he expired?"

"No, sir; he went off quite quiet; we didn't know that he was dead for some time—not till we examined again, as we did repeatedly, sir."

"That was right."

"What was the cause of death?" inquired one of the pupils, in a low tone, of the surgeon, as he gazed on the body.

"It is difficult to say; the symptoms he was first seized with are unknown; he was brought here insensible; restoratives were administered, and then cupping behind the head, but to no purpose. Apoplexy was the immediate cause of death."

"No," said Danton, exerting himself; "it was not, it was——"

"What!" exclaimed the surgeon, turning round sharply to Danton; "what, sir, do you practise here, or I?"

"I say the man died because he was cruelly murdered."

"Murdered!" exclaimed the surgeon, thinking that this was a most presumptuous attack upon him in particular, and the profession in general; "I know, sir, the treatment was correct."

"I do not dispute that, but I say the man was murdered, and that he died not the death you impute."

"And whom do you charge with murder?" inquired the surgeon; "it is a serious charge; recollect yourself, and think a little."

"I have thought, and hoped it was a mere delusion; but he was murdered by those two women there; I saw them at midnight do so; they smothered him, and he ceased to breathe; they murdered that man."

"What is the meaning of all this?" said the surgeon; "it's very extraordinary;" and he walked up to the corpse.

"Oh, sir," said the nurse, "the meaning of it is this; that unfortunate person has been raving all night; he has talked in the most frightful manner."

"Indeed?"

"Yes, sir. I don't know what to think of it, sir, but if it be not that he is mad, I should be afraid to listen to him; murder and sacrilege are the best words that come out of his mouth; I only hope he's not distracted with any thoughts of what he may once have done."

"Ah, no, no; the man is mad, I dare say," said the surgeon; "and there's no accounting for the odd fancies they may take; you mustn't suppose him criminal because he talks incoherently at times."

"I am not mad," said Danton; "but what I have told you I saw done with my own eyes. They took money from him; they murdered him first, and then robbed him."

"You will find everything as it was left; he had a beautiful gold watch and chain, and some rings."

"Well, well."

"You will see they are there now, and his money, if he have any."

The surgeon looked at the clothes, and saw it was as they stated it to be, and turning to Danton, gave him a look of commiseration, as he said to some of the pupils,—

"The poor man is mad, I fear, incurably; he shall be properly looked after,"

"He's quite mad, sir; his head seems entirely turned, sir," said the woman: "and my companion here can tell you the same. It's almost too bad to let him remain here, sir; the rest of the patients will be frightened out of their lives."

"He shall be removed to the asylum as soon as possible," said the surgeon, who then, followed by his pupils, turned away and left the place, leaving Theodore Danton in a state better imagined than described.

"God of Heaven!" he mentally ejaculated, "surely, surely such a crime as this will not be permitted to be perpetrated in vain? No, no, the decrees of Heaven's justice forbid it; they cannot act thus—impossible!"

The nurses continued their avocations, and took but little notice of him (Theodore Danton), except once, when they both had occasion to approach him; and then one of them whispered in his ear, audibly enough,—

"You have done a fine thing for yourself; there's the lunatic asylum for you, now. Oh, rare sport! what fun! how you will enjoy perpetual imprisonment. I shall enjoy it—it will be such fun; you'll suffer, and we shall, in a manner of speaking, have killed two birds with one stone."

"Monsters! wretches of the vilest character, can you thus deny your guilt and act with yet more guiltiness? Can you make me the object of your revenge?"

"And why not, good sir?" inquired the nurse, in a mock tone of respect. "Did you not think to consign us to gaol? Did you not think we should be hanged for our pains?"

"And richly would you merit it," said Theodore.

"Ay, that is a matter of opinion. But you wanted to do all this; you have failed, and now it is our turn to try what we can do for you."

"Wretches!"

"Fool!"

"He, he, he! ha, ha, ha!" laughed the two hags, in so low a tone, by his bed-side, that they could not be heard by any others but himself; and then, after a while, they added—

"Another hour or two, and you will be placed in the infirmary of a madhouse —how like you that, most excellent gentleman?"

Danton made no reply, but turned away from these detestable creatures; he would no longer speak to them, nor look at them. It was useless, he would await his fate in silence. It was useless to supplicate their mercy, or to appeal to their justice; for he saw that they had neither, much less would they save him, at the risk of exposing themselves.

With a short malicious chuckle, the two nurses left the bed-side of the unhappy Danton, who now saw what a lamentable position he had placed himself in.

"God's will be done," he said to himself; "I am unable to see my way out of this. What will be the end of it, Heaven above knows, I do not. Oh, Margaret, Margaret, may you ever be free from such sufferings as those which afflict me; may you be happy, as your innocence and beauty most surely entitle you to be; but as for me, I may end my days in a madhouse—horrible thought!"

The hours passed on, and Theodore Danton lay there a prey to all the agony of soul that such a man so circumstanced could feel; and to add to the poignancy of his feelings, he was again

disturbed by his nurse, who came with a frightful grin of satisfaction, saying—
"Come, come, there's good news for you, your carriage is in the courtyard. We'll dress you—they have come for you—you must be quick, for they are in haste to carry you to a madhouse; you, whose only act of madness was to accuse us of murder. Ha! ha! ha!"

Danton was soon ready, and borne along between those two women he abhorred; he was hurried through the wards, and down the great staircase, and placed in a spring van, and secured in an easy chair. A few moments more, and he was on his road to the asylum.

CHAPTER L.

MR. PRIMROSE'S MYSTERIOUS CONDUCT.—THE BREAK UP OF THE HOUSEHOLD.—MRS. BLAIR AND MRS. PRIMROSE'S QUARREL AND SEPARATION.

MRS. BLAIR, when she took her departure from the house of Mrs. Bertram, which she did, feeling assured it was no longer possible, or profitable, to hang on the fortunes of Mrs. Bertram, went, as we then informed the reader, to her sister, Mrs. Primrose, and there we shall find her the same individual, with the same propensities, the same love of power and mischief, that has always characterised her, and without one jot less selfishness than heretofore.

Mrs. Blair, of course, was Mrs. Blair, under all the circumstances that can affect herself; it would have been as difficult for her to have changed her identity as her nature or her disposition.

It is, therefore, not difficult to imagine what kind of life Mr. Primrose was likely to lead, when he had such an adviser and companion to such a wife as he had. The situation of a toad under a harrow was not to be compared to it, for comfort or enjoyment, for quietude or ease.

Even here, where she was quite an intruder, and upon sufferance, she could fancy herself the obliged party, and could not refrain at least from interfering in their private affairs; but no, she would not only not do that, but do it ostentatiously, too, so that it would be quite impossible to mistake the source of the annoyance.

Mrs. Primrose herself was but the second personage in the house; but then she had been so much in the habit of looking upon Mrs. Blair's tactics and advice as the best of their kind, and perfect, so that she did not find it so disagreeable as the unfortunate Mr. Primrose, who was always the end and object of the concentrated venom of the sisters, and not a party conveying the same, but the recipient.

Could any house be in a worse situation for affording comfort to a man, than Mr. Primrose's own house? He paid for it; he worked for it; and, having done so much, what did it give him in return?

Absolutely nothing—yes, shelter, and a place where he could eat and drink at a much dearer rate, with far more discomfort, than he could at a tavern; but, then, to do that, he must have been a brute—an irreclaimable man, who had no heart for his home; as, indeed, under the circumstances, he had not, nor was it a matter of much surprise he had not.

Affairs came to such a pitch, that Mr. Primrose was glad to sneak in and out of the rooms as quietly as he could. He feared to be heard, least it should bring down some matrimonial lecture upon what subject and why he knew not; indeed, it was a thing he had long since given up any hope of finding out, as to why he was thus attacked; for both females asserted, upon such general grounds, that he was not deserving of half the comforts he enjoyed. Both concurring in this assertion, he almost believed it himself, and began to think he must be a bad man.

Affairs, however, did not go on very prosperously with the Primroses; business did not go the right way—the house was empty—there were no lodgers —and, altogether, a gloomy prospect presented itself, which wonderfully soured Mrs. Primrose, who stood in no need of any additional acerbity of disposition.

"Primrose," she would say, "you are a brute—you don't exert yourself as a man—you have no spirit, or you would have been a better man than you are."

"Very likely, my dear," said Mr.

Primrose; "but a man's a man for a' that."

"Mr. Primrose, I am ashamed of you. What do you think will come of you? Here are people coming every day after money. What am I to do?"

"I give you money when I have it. I cannot give you what I have not got. I do my best; what can I do more?"

"Do more! Do you expect that I can keep house upon nothing? Do you expect I can give you food if you don't give me means? Do you——"

"There, my dear. I can do no more. You have all I can gain. I have no more; and I don't have too much in return."

"You don't deserve half the comforts you do get. What you can be thinking of, to expect any, I can't think."

"As for having any comforts," said Mr. Primrose, who appeared to be contumacious, much to the astonishment of both ladies—"as for half my comforts, it would be a difficult matter to divide them, seeing it's impossible to add too, or substract from nothing; and that is the precise sum they amount to."

"Oh! gratitude!" apostrophized Mrs. Blair; "it's not to be found in married men, that's clear; for, after a woman has sacrificed her best days, what is she in his eyes, I wonder?"

"Ah!" said Mrs. Primrose, "I have been a fond, foolish woman—too fond of my home, and confined myself too closely in making it agreeable."

Mr. Primrose groaned, and turned his eyes upwards.

"It's all very well, Mr. Primrose, for you to go on in that way, but I'd have you to know, that if your poor wife is deceived in you, I am not."

"I am sure that is no fault of mine," said Primrose; "but it does seem to me she can say enough, without having any assistance of yours."

"I tell you what, Mr. Primrose, it strikes me that you must have been drinking."

"Drinking!" exclaimed Primrose, in amazement at the accusation.

"Yes, sir; you never dare talk as you do if you had your senses about you. It strikes me, too, that my sister ought to insist upon a separate maintenance; she cannot put up with this; I am sure it's too much for any woman that ain't a horse or mule."

Mr. Primrose seemed as if he wished she was one or the other; and so she seemed to imagine herself, for she said,

"And I dare say he does—I dare say he does; and then he wouldn't be ashamed or afraid, or both, of taking me to Smithfield, and selling me. What do women come to, after they have done all they can for a man? Why, it comes to this."

"Certainly; and now you have come to this, we may as well talk about nothing else; but it don't seem to me very clearly that I have been any great gainer. I have more to support."

"Well, and ought you not? Don't every married man support more, a great deal more, than a single man?"

"And his comforts are——"

"Greater."

Mr. Primrose shrugged up his shoulders, as much as to say that he had not been at all aware of the fact, for whatever other men might do, he had had considerable less to boast of since his marriage than before it; but he said nothing; her arguments were all against him, and he would have been made to believe that he was a base, vile man, so he let all opportunity to retort pass by like golden opportunities he dared not take, for fear of the consequences.

Finding there was no chance of peace that night, Mr. Primrose determined, since he could but endure lecturing for something or for nothing—he was sure to have it both ways—he, therefore, determined upon choosing the former, for two reasons. The first was, it would be satisfactory to have enjoyed something, and make it a set-off against the scolding. The second reason was, it would abridge the period that had to be endured, which was another great object.

In consequence of this determination, he suddenly arose, and taking his hat —without any previous notice or intimation of what he was doing—suddenly made for the door, and then for the street-door. Before, however, he reached that, he could hear Mrs. Primrose exclaiming,—

"Ah, there, he's off to a public-house! Was there ever such an unfortunate creature as I am, to be treated thus? But I won't have it, and that's the fact."

"You ought," said Mrs. Blair, "to have talked him out of that long since. I am sure a man must be vicious, who can withstand the repeated admonitions of his wife. Oh, dear, no——"

"Ah!" thought Primrose, "there they go, a pretty pair; upon my soul, I don't know what to do. This kind of life is very dreadful, and for more reasons than one it must have an end. I will take advice. I am quite clear of one thing, that had I married a couple of tigresses in Wombwell's show, I should not been more perfectly matched than I am, I shouldn't run more danger; it's about the same thing, only the tigresses are handsome, and don't know any better, whereas my wife and her sister do; and yet it makes no odds in the end; there's gratitude in one case, and none in the other."

It was very late indeed before Mr. Primrose returned home. He found there was no one up; not even a candle left out for him, and no supper.

"Oh! very well," said Primrose, as he felt the bottom of his pockets; "it don't matter; no, no, not a bit. I ain't hungry, because I have had supper; but no thanks to them. I do hope one thing," he continued, in a low whisper, and then he paused, "and that is, that she may sham sleep. I know she ain't asleep; oh, no; she never will sleep when I am out. Suppose she should have a fit of the sulks—by Jove, it would be excellent; but I can't hope for it. Oh, no; she likes talking too well—a great deal too well—especially when it's scolding; and when I am the object, it's more relished than under any other circumstances; but it can't be helped, and I must endure it for some time longer. I'll go up and chance all about it."

Mr. Primrose walked stealthily up stairs in the dark. It was quite dark; and, despite his care and caution, he could not avoid stumbling once or twice over things that he never found there before, and which had no business on the stairs and in all the old corners.

"She's turned extra vicious," he muttered, "and put these things in the way because I shouldn't come in without making a noise, and to break my shins,

if possible. I know it; it's exactly what she'd do—she and her sister."

Thus feeling his way, and soliloquising as he went, Mr. Primrose reached his own apartment, and this he found locked. He paused a moment, and had almost made up his mind that he would burst it open, when he recollected there was another bed in the house, and he would go to that, and sleep by himself.

Nothing loth, he turned from the door, and found his way into another room, which, when he entered, he turned round, and locked the door.

"There," he muttered, "I shall sleep alone; but I shall have no curtain-lecture to-morrow morning, and I'll get up in time for breakfast, but no earlier."

With this determination he went to bed, and fell fast asleep.

He awoke not till late in the morning, and then he arose with alacrity. He seemed cheerful, and quite another man. He wore quite another aspect. Who would have known him?—nobody. He washed and dressed, and then he descended the stairs; and he could tell where the breakfast was by the sound of the tea-things, and the sound of voices. He opened the door, and walked into the room.

"Oh," said Mrs. Primrose, "you're come at last."

"I came home as usual, my dear," said Mr. Primrose, in a very mild voice, but it betrayed no fear.

"Very late?"

"Early."

"Yes—this morning, sir."

"Why, it was getting on that way, I must admit. But then I couldn't help it; it was early."

Now, this was dreadfully aggravating; and Mrs. Primrose looked unutterable things, and glanced at Mrs. Blair.

"Don't wait for me," said Mr. Primrose, handing a cup, "You can pour my coffee out without ceremony."

"Do you imagine, sir," began Mrs. Primrose, almost maddened, "that I have made this coffee for you?"

"And why not?"

"Because you are not deserving the slightest notice, sir. Go—go where you had supper last night. Go there, sir."

"Why, you see, my dear, answering

THEODORE ATTEMPTS TO COMMIT SUICIDE FROM THE PRECIPICE.

your first question, all I have to say is, no one has a better right to things purchased by my money than myself. To the second, all I have to say is, that I feared you would not like my staying out all night, or I might have stopped there till breakfast time, and that would have saved you the trouble; but I feared your feelings would be too much hurt, and here I am."

"Wretch!" said Mrs. Primrose.

"Monster!" said Mrs. Blair; "can such things be? Oh, if you were a husband of mine, and treated me so—oh, I'd ——"

"It's no matter—you ain't my wife, thank God!"

"Thank God, indeed!"

Mr. Primrose would hear nothing more, or, at, least, if he did, he would reply to nothing, but took his breakfast very coolly, and sat longer than anybody, and would say nothing; they migh abuse and scold, but he would have nothing to do with it, that was a settled thing with him. There was no accounting for this behaviour upon ordinary principles, save that he was become obdurate and would conquer them, and they resolved that they would conquer him, and thus they rose from the breakfast-table.

Matters went on thus for nearly a week, Mr. Primrose keeping late hours, and being utterly insensible to all the scolding they could find words to express, and appeared to be enjoying their anger as a good joke. He thrust his hands to the bottom of his pockets, and endeavoured to screw his features into all sorts of shapes and convulsions; he would gaze, smile, and wink at the ceiling, and hold imaginary intercourse with nothing, and be pleased.

This was not understandable; human nature, especially female nature, couldn't stand this long; but it was no use; he would keep in the same even course, until Mrs. Blair began to think he was crazed.

At the same time, a variety of articles that were at all valuable and portable were missed out of the house, such as plate, &c., spoons, knives, and other matters that would make money, even to wearing apparel and ornaments.

All this was mysterious, but we will let the reader into the mystery, both of this and of Mr. Primrose's conduct, which had caused much conjecture, if not alarm, in the minds of those whom he was wont to dread, and who held him in awe and subjection.

Mr. Primrose, be it known, in default of domestic comfort, sought the cheering and enlivening society of a tavern, and succeeded, as many have before him, in making himself comfortable. Here, however, he met with a friend whom he had known at school, and whom he had at various times met as hale fellows well met.

On the second night of their meeting Mr. Primrose was rather melancholy, which Tom Stiles, his friend, noticed, and pressed him to say what was the matter.

"You may as well say candidly, Primrose," he said, "for I can see that there is something wrong about you— you ain't right, and that's the truth of it."

"Well, I am not quite right, as you have said, Tom."

"What is it, then, that's wrong— money affairs or domestic?"

"Both."

"Bad case—very bad case. Can't see any way out, though, till I know the particulars."

"Oh, d—n the particulars," said Primrose, suddenly. "God forgive me for swearing; but they are enough to drive one mad."

"Then it's no wonder you look melancholy and sad over them."

"No, indeed. But you shall know all, and then tell me what you would have done under such circumstances."

"Ay, that I will."

"I have resolved upon some desperate course, and yet don't know what or how to begin it."

"Go on, and make a clear breast of it; if I cannot aid you by counsel, I'll keep your secret, Primrose; so never fear me, though I am a bachelor. You know the old saying, Primrose ?"

"What saying ?"

"Ah! no wonder you forget; merry and free are a bachelor's reveries."

"Ah!" groaned Primrose; "those times are all gone by, especially since my wife and her cursed sister have got together. I do believe they would murder me, and rob me afterwards."

"You don't say so ?"

"I do. You must know things are going very queer with me of late, and I don't expect a house over my head many more days, I tell you."

"That's enough to make you uncomfortable," said Tom; "but how is that ?"

"I can scarcely tell you. My wife, you see, has had the whole control of the money, save a little that I have retained for personal exigencies."

"D—n it, man, you should never have allowed her to have held the purse for one day."

"Ah! it's all very well, but women will get the better of you sometimes, and the devil couldn't resist them always."

"Very well, they haven't circumvented me as yet."

"No; your time is not at hand, but it is known; of that be assured."

"Ah! ah!"

"Well, how the monies have disappeared, I know not. Suffice it to say, that they are gone, and I have had a most disagreeable proof of that."

"Have you ?"

"Yes; besides that, my wife has a most awful temper; there's no being in her presence more than ten minutes without being powerfully reminded of her presence; and to add to my misery, she has invited her sister, or her sister has come without it — I don't know which, and don't much care, it's all the same to me, unfortunately."

"It's a most desperate case."

"So it is. Now, what would you do in such an infernal dilemma? Where to go, or what to do, I cannot tell."

"I should cut it—mizzle—evaporate,

and disappear entirely, like an actor through the trap-door of a theatre."

"But—but——"

"But what?"

"What's to become of the house and the wife, Tom Stiles?"

"Oh! let the house take care of the wife, and the wife of the house; there will be a reciprocal affection, I dare say; but if not, it doesn't matter much, as I see. You can't live with one, nor in the other. You only do by choice what must be done after all; and, as for your wife, what has she deserved? Nothing."

"Nothing!" repeated Primrose. "That is the truth; and she is incurable; her life never will mend, come what may."

"Then there is no use in making the attempt, is there?"

"None, certainly; but what am I to do for means?"

"Settle one thing at a time; that is the best mode of doing business, I believe. Is it not, friend Primrose?"

"Certainly it is."

"Then allow me to go on. You must leave the house, at all events?"

"I must."

"Then that is settled. Can you take your wife comfortably with you, wherever you may go?"

"No; I don't think she would go; at all events, her sister would come with her; she is a complete shark. Really, it is quite terrible to think of it."

"Keep up your spirits, and throw off the whole affair. Come, have another go, and you will be all right."

Mr. Primrose did have another go, which considerably enlivened him, and paved the way for other goes, which he took before he left the house.

"Take my advice, Primrose, and leave the whole affair. Come to my lodgings for a day or two, till you can shift for yourself; but, before you leave, take good care of yourself."

"How do you mean?"

"Why, take everything quietly away that is portable and valuable."

"Oh!"

"Everything that is convertable into money. You may as well have it as your creditors, who will take you with them, if they can catch you."

Mr. Primrose shrugged his shoulders, as much as to say;—

"There is no mistake about that; and if they do catch me, I can't help it."

"You see, if you fortify yourself with money and resolution, Primrose," said Tom Stiles, "you will take him by the forelock. Go before you are taken, and you'll have the means of carrying on the war for some time. What say you to it?"

"But what will become of me?"

"Now, or afterwards?" suggested Tom.

"Why, it is pretty well the same thing, I suppose; and so I may as well get rid of all my evils at once."

"House, wife, and creditors?"

"Ay; and that'll be the benefit of the act with a vengeance."

"You will have the benefit of the riddance, in my opinion."

"I shall do it," said Primrose; "they don't care anything for me; they have led me years of misery, and now I'll be a new man, and throw it all off. I'll not submit to it any longer."

"That's a trump, Primrose; I respect you. Here's to your good health; better fortune, and may this moment prove the worst of our lives."

"Amen!" said Primrose; "then I'll begin to-morrow, and cast about for what I can catch. I'll make money; and Mrs. Primrose, who is such an excellent manager, and Mrs. Blair, who is yet better, can surely manage to shift for themselves."

"Certainly they can; who could doubt it?" said Stiles; "and, what is more, you'll see that they will, too."

"Then I can be doing them no harm, and myself much good."

"You'll be a single man again, Primrose! Oh, what a chance! Never give away your liberty again; oh! no; secure that, and keep it as a jewel. Merry and free are a bachelor's reveries, eh? Primrose—eh?"

"Oh, yes; that's the thing; and now it's past one, we must part for the night. I shall be shut out, I dare say—shouldn't be at all surprised."

"Then set to ringing all night, until they are all alarmed; if I were you, I'd set to kicking so, that, if I didn't sleep, they shouldn't."

"I will," said Mr. Primrose, with the full determination to do so.

"Shall I come and help you?" kindly volunteered Stiles.

"No, thank you; I can manage that much by myself; and, as I have made up my mind upon the other matter, I can easily do so on this, I believe."

"I am glad to hear you say so. Good night to you, Primrose, my boy—good night; keep your weather eye open; look out for squalls, and be off before the bums are on the alert."

"I'll take care of that; a week or eight days is all I want. Good night."

Mr. Primrose did, as we have seen, follow the advice of his friend Tom Stiles, and he began from that moment to lay his hand upon all things that were profitable, and that could be converted into money readily, and they very mysteriously disappeared.

This went on for a week, and Mr. Primrose's conduct became more hardened than ever; nothing in the way of talking would do any good; indeed, he did nothing but look at the wall, wink at nothing, and hold communion with nobody.

This was a most provoking state of things, and though Mrs. Primrose and Mrs. Blair both laboured hard to alter it, yet they could not provoke him to a reply; he would hold no argument with them, and he would not even look as if he were vexed, but always wore a smile on his countenance.

This was dreadful, and at length one night he did not come home at all, and the two ladies sat down to breakfast together without having heard of Mr. Primrose at all.

"Well," said Mrs. Blair, after an unusual pause; "well, I am not surprised at all—not in the least—it's only what I expected."

"What?"

"Mr. Primrose staying out all night. It's shameful, when a married man begins to desert his home, keep late hours, and then stay out all night, then there is something wrong; you may depend upon it, he has got into no good company."

"Oh, dear, no; no good or respectable person could think of advising him to stay out to this hour of—all night, I should say—it's really monstrous."

"I hope you won't forget to tell him of it; indeed, you had better turn him out for some time longer."

"Well, well, I don't know but what I will; he deserves it; to stay away from his lawful wedded wife—it's monstrous. I'll never forgive him; I won't live with him any more. I'll have a separation."

"But he has got bad lately so very fast; to be sure, the downward path is more rapid as you approach the bottom, and now he has become worse than ever."

"Yes, he has; but what surprises me is his making away with all the plate and movables.

"Indeed!"

"Yes; it must be he who has taken them; they have been going day after day for the last week. What the reason may be I don't know."

"If that's the case, depend upon it he has some scheme in his head; you may rely upon it that men are always scheming to get rid of their wives, or to do something or other."

"I have no doubt of that. He's been making away with things, that's certain, and what for I don't know."

"You ought to have inquired and insisted upon knowing, because it concerns you much to know."

"That's very true, and I will not allow him to go out of the house again without giving a true account of everything that has been carried away; but perhaps, after all, he's only removing them lest there should be an execution put in."

"Will there be one?"

"I don't know; things ain't as they ought to be lately."

"That is through keeping late hours, and spending his substance in a tavern, as if he wanted to escape from them."

"And that's true again, sister. I've been too kind and affectionate, and too indulgent to him; but I'll alter that plan."

At this moment there came a great dab of a single knock at the door, that made both ladies start, and they exchanged glances for a moment or two.

"What's that?" exclaimed Mrs. Blair.

"A knock," said Mrs. Primrose.

"I know that; I heard it."

"And so did I—but such a knock;

it seems as if it were coming through the door. Dear me, what a knock!"

She had scarcely said so when the knock was repeated with emphasis, and Mrs. Primrose started up, saying,—

"God bless me! my heart is in my mouth. I must go and see what it means; I suppose I must."

She accordingly went to the door, and saw an odd-looking man leaning upon the area rails, by way of support.

"Well?" said Mrs. P.

"Well?" said the man.

"What do you mean by knocking in that way, eh? It's enough to frighten anybody out of their lives."

"Indeed, ma'am, I shouldn't a thought so; they couldn't hear the first, else they'd a come. But is there one Mrs. Primrose lives here?"

"Yes."

"Where is she?"

"I am Mrs. Primrose."

"Oh, here's a letter for you."

At the same time he handed a small note to her, and then left the door.

Mrs. Primrose took the note, wondering much who could have written it, when a glance at the handwriting told her it came from her husband.

"Oh, the wretch!" she exclaimed, as she entered the room; "he has written to me to forgive him, I suppose, before he comes home, I dare say, I shouldn't wonder!"

Mrs. Primrose was engaged in opening the note; as she read it she exclaimed,—

"Oh! oh! oh!"

"What's the matter?"

"The villain! the monster! the wretch! the—the—the——"

"What's the matter?"

"The matter?—the—the——"

"Yes!"

"Why, he has deserted me—left me unprovided for, and unprotected!"

"Left you?"

"Yes; he won't come home any more; see the letter. Oh, the inhuman monster; I'm clean done; oh! oh!"

Mrs. Blair took the note, and read as follows :—

"MRS. PRIMROSE,

"To save you any unnecessary speculations on my account, I write to tell you, you need not sit up for me, or leave the street door unlocked, or the things on the stairs for me to tumble over ; no, I shall never break my shins in that house any more.

"Yes, ma'am, you and your sister can have all you find; it is all yours, and you can make one another very comfortable and happy. I feel no uneasiness on your account; it will not make you unhappy; my presence never was required for any purpose, much less for your happiness. You may as well take care of yourself, though I suspect this notice is hardly necessary. I am very happy—no scolding—and go quietly to bed, and eat and drink in peace.—Your loving husband,

"PRIMROSE."

"Loving husband, indeed!" repeated Mrs. Blair; "a loving epistle truly ; he must have premeditated this for some time. I could see it in his manner ; but who would have thought of his being so bad?"

"No, nor nobody else. I thought I had got him quite under my thumb; but it seems he has got bad advisers."

"What are you going to do?" inquired Mrs. Blair, suddenly.

"I don't know," said Mrs. P.; "it seems to me that he may yet come back."

"Never; he dare not—that's plain. Oh, no, he'd have come here and told you his mind if he dared! Oh, no, he's gone, and gone for good too, and no mistake."

"Well, I'm sure, it's a pretty situation to be placed in. What can I do?"

"Sell all you can, and stay here as long as you can, and when you can't, go somewhere else."

"But where?"

"That I know no more than you do ; but sell, sell, sell, and provide yourself with money, that's the chief want."

"I must adopt that advice," said she, "and that quickly, too, else some one will come and take them. I had several rows with the tradespeople, yesterday; and there are three summonses."

"Be quick then; I would do what you could to-day."

"I will; but he has taken the best things, such as could be carried and turned into money, the wretch!"

"No doubt; but take all that remains,

and if he should come back, he'll find a clean house of it."

"No doubt. He might repent—the villain, and then he'd find how he was punished for his baseness."

Mrs. Primrose took her sister's advice, and was for a day or two busily engaged in selling and parting with a variety of things to raise money. Nor was the sister idle; she followed the other's example, though she forgot to give her the proceeds of what she had disposed of; but the other considered it was as safe in one pocket as the other, though she would have preferred her own, had there been a chance, which it seemed there was not.

About the fifth day afterwards another bang came at the door, which made them start as when Mrs. P. received the letter from Mr. Primrose. She hastened to answer it, and was thunderstruck to see three men enter the house.

Their business was soon known; they came to take possession of the house and effects under an execution for rent.

This was the break-up of the establishment—the last stroke, and now Mrs. Primrose and Mrs. Blair had no home at all; and fearing that some awkward question might be put, or discovery made, that would be very disagreeable in its consequences, they both determined they would leave the house.

They did so, and by some fatality they began to quarrel with each other. Mr. Blair wanted to get possession of the money; and when she could not do so, she abused her sister, and abruptly left her in the street, and they, too, were thus parted.

CHAPTER LI.

THE DEATH OF MRS. OGDEN.—MARGARET'S DESTITUTION.—THE UNEXPECTED RECOGNITION.

WITH what gratitude towards her friend, Mrs. Ogden, did the unfortunate Margaret Bertram seek the shelter that the former had promised the latter when she was able to leave the chamber in which she had been compelled to abide so long! Little comfort could she have expected in a house so situated; indeed, it is questionable if she would not have been turned out to beg without a shelter.

To Mrs. Ogden, then, she walked. It was the first place she went to after she quitted the house. Oh! with what sensations did she now move about! She clung to life more than she ever would have done; she had now another to support and to look to her for nourishment and care. She pressed the little being closer to her bosom as she thought of the difficulties she would have to encounter in doing for it all that a mother should.

Mrs. Ogden's apartments were but mean, but they were only such as she could afford to occupy under the limited state of her finances; indeed, in choosing them she had an eye to the fact that her income must, at the least, support one more, even had she not made the offer to her friend of her assistance.

With this view Mr. Ogden hired these rooms, and forthwith took possession of them, and awaited the moment when her friend, Mrs. Bertram, would come.

That time came, and Margaret entered the house her friend had provided for them. Mrs. Bertram sat down in a chair. She looked into the face of her friend, but she could not speak; her heart was too full.

Mrs. Odgen saw her emotion, and felt acutely for her, and endeavoured to soften her emotion by saying—

"I know what you think, Margaret, and what you would say. We know each other too well, and our friendship is too sincere to make it necessary that we should treat each other than as sisters, and, remember, you have now an infant; therefore, pray do you calm yourself."

"I will be calm, my dear friend," she replied, in almost choking accents, "that is, if I can; but I know not which affects me most at this moment. Your generosity and sisterly kindness, or the remembrance of Bertram's unkindness and injustice."

"Think of neither, my dear; but just let me assist you to undress. Depend upon it we may be very happy under even worse circumstances than those if we be so inclined."

"I am sure that there can be nothing better that I can desire now. Your society and my child's is all that I now covet. My wants and wishes are few, and may God bless you for thus gratifying them."

She could not help bursting into tears as she concluded these words, which were uttered with great feeling and fervour.

"You must not go on thus, Margaret," said Mrs. Ogden, sensibly moved herself; "how could you think of speaking thus? You will make me as weak as yourself presently. Come, come, be calm, and make yourself as much at home as you can, or I wish you."

"Thank you—thank you—I will; for I feel as if my heart would burst; but I hope it will go off."

They conversed for some time together of former friends and occurrences until the evening came, and darkness reigned around. They sat by the side of the fire, conversing for a long while. In this intercourse of feeling and thought they both lost sight, for a time, of the misfortunes they encountered—at least, active grief was settled—and a more equable feeling pervaded the minds of both, and of Mrs. Bertram in particular.

Days passed on; the same events succeeded each other with great regularity. There was but little change; and yet there was none much desired, save in one particular, and that was with regard to Bertram only, but nothing was heard of him.

How long this life might have lasted it would be difficult to say; but there was a change to come over the calmness and tranquillity of the two friends.

Mrs. Ogden fell ill. At first she caught cold, which being only partially subdued, with a slight accession of causes, the same complaint broke out into a more virulent character.

For some time she battled against the effects of the disease, which each day showed more malignancy, and at length it appeared in the form of a malignant fever, that prostrated her bodily powers, and obscured her mental faculties.

It was at a moment like this that Mrs. Ogden felt the benefit of such a friend as Mrs. Bertram, for the latter attended upon her like a sister.

Day and night was she constantly by her bedside, and at her lucid intervals she would thank her for her kindness and attention, and a few brief sentences, from time to time, would be exchanged.

Mrs. Ogden had been confined to her bed for three weeks, when one afternoon, as Margaret sat by her bedside, she woke from a deep sleep, perfectly sensible. She lay for some moments in deep thought, and, turning her eyes towards where Mrs. Bertram was, their eyes met.

There was much in that momentary glance; it was an exchange of a world of thought and feeling, and it seemed to reach the soul of both, and each knew the feelings that were passing in the other's breast.

"Margaret," said Mrs. Ogden, as she feebly stretched out her hand towards her, as if she would speak to her.

"Yes," said Margaret, "I am here; can I do aught for you?"

"You have done much, very much for me; how can I thank you?"

"Are you not entitled to it from gratitude alone, if not from friendship? —but, when I have such powerful motives, life itself I would lay down for you."

"Nay, Margaret, that would be too severe a tax upon your kindness—remember your little one."

Margaret looked at the little sleeping infant, and a pang shot through her heart, and she said—

"It might break my heart to leave that dear innocent, but, if you were gone, what would become of us both? My sufferings would be little compared with hers."

"But you have been kind, Margaret, very. Margaret, what would have become of me now had you not been with me? I shudder to think."

"Do not think, dear, at all; you require more rest and quietude than anything else. If I but once more see you about again, I shall be much happier than ever I was before. Since you have been ill, I have become more aware of the fact than ever I had, that I have yet much to see, and I begin to grow more contented with my fate. I might even in time begin to get quite reconciled, if you were well. Let me see you as you were, and then one of the greatest sorrows I have will be relieved."

Mrs. Ogden smiled and shook her head sadly, as she said—

"I fear, Margaret, that there is not much in the future for me. I cannot but think that this illness will be my last."

"Do not talk thus; it is but the feelings or fears that arise from the weakness consequent upon illness."

"No, no," said Mrs. Ogden; "were it otherwise I should be glad, were it only for your sake, dear Margaret, and your infant; but I think I shall never recover from this illness—it is my last."

"I hope not, I hope not," sighed Margaret; "if you go, I shall have no other friend in the wide world. But I do not mourn such an event from such selfish motives alone, but for your own sake, my dear friend; your goodness of heart deserves a longer career than this."

"Say no more, I would sleep a little; even this has fatigued me."

Mrs. Bertram, with a sigh, drew the curtains around her friend, and walked to the fire, where she sat down to meditate upon the misfortunes that seemed to surround her and those who attached themselves to her.

It was a melancholy reflection, but one that forced itself upon her, that, had she not been situated as she was, her friend would never have been the sufferer she was; she would have escaped that which she now considered an infection she herself raised about her, that produced all the misfortunes that could befall her.

And, as she bent over her child, she thought of her own sad condition; the desertion of Bertram, and the unexpected disappearance of Danton seemed events that were of themselves sufficient to bring about all the evils which she had suffered, and which she could not escape from. The future, too, was full of gloom, and promises of ill to her and her little one.

"Oh, my child, my child!" she said. "What will become of thee? Thou art not guilty of aught against humanity, or even thy father, and why art thou to suffer?"

She paused to gaze upon its features, and a tear stole to her eyes as she thought of the hard fate that awaited it.

"If I had done aught to incur hatred and punishment—and Heaven knows I have not—what can be said of the justice that consigns thee to beggary and want? God help me! I am going mad, I believe, for I question the decrees of Providence when I look upon the helpless innocent that lies and sleeps so calmly; and wherefore should it suffer? but no answer is returned, and that which seems to come unbidden to my mind, makes me shudder to think of."

Overpowered by sleep and fatigue, she dozed for some short time, and was lost in forgetfulness.

That was a happy moment, for then she forgot the miseries that surrounded her, and, when she awoke, a consciousness of all was to her the worst misery that could be inflicted upon her.

Surely she was punished enough to satisfy all the most inhuman mind could desire, or the most insensate fate could wish for. Why was she not snatched from despair? Why was she allowed to linger on, day after day, in wretchedness and misery? Why were both mother and child consigned to the same scene of wretchedness and misery?

She awoke, and stole softly to the bedside of her friend. She slumbered, but she moaned in her sleep, and seemed to be dreaming, or a slight accession of fever had rendered her delirious.

"Poor Mrs. Ogden!" she murmured, "she deserves a better fate than this. She was truly good and amiable. I would I were in her place! If I could take her place, and save her, I would most willingly do it."

Mrs. Ogden awoke, and looked up, and saw her friend bending over her.

"Do you know," she said, "I have had a confused dream. I do not know what it portends; neither can I repeat what I thought—my mind is in too great a state of confusion."

"Calm yourself, and think nothing about it. You will be better when you have rested, and become calmer.

At this moment a creaking of boots on the stairs announced the approach of the doctor. Mrs. Bertram opened the door, as that individual entered the room.

"How does my patient to-day?" he said, as he approached the bed.

"She seems a little calmer, sir."

"That is good."

"But very low-spirited, indeed."

"Oh, we mustn't expect much else,

when we come to consider she has been very ill, taken medicines, and abstained almost entirely from food: we may well expect that she will be low, and weak in spirits."

He drew the curtain on one side, and looked upon her for a minute or two. He took her hand, saying,—

"How have you slept?"

"Pretty well, sir."

"Much?"

"Not very much, sir."

"Were your slumbers disturbed?"

"I had some confused dreams which I could not remember, but they annoyed and terrified me much."

"I see," said the medical gentleman, "you have had a slight accession of fever, therefore do not worry yourself about any of your dreams; they are common enough; they are, in fact, only an indistinct vision floating before the mental faculties; and as soon as we subdue the fever you will have few or none of them."

"I hope not; they have disturbed me much. But tell me, sir, what is your candid opinion of my case?"

"It is difficult to judge, or give any opinion of a disease in progress. If all go on well, the end will be well; but there are incidents that may happen that will change the whole aspect of affairs. I do not see any particular reason to despair."

There was a seriousness about the doctor's manner, as if he had more doubts and fears than he liked to express.

"I cannot say," he added, "that you

are in much danger; it is not of that character which renders any immediate measure necessary; but keep calm and quiet, and take your medicine with much regularity, and then we have done all that lies in our power."

The doctor left, and the two friends were alone again, and they gazed at each other in silence, as if to catch the expression of the other's thoughts.

"Margaret, what do you think of the doctor's opinion?"

"I know not what to think, but while he hopes we ought not to despair. I do hope you will recover; there is every chance for you."

"I know not, but it seems to me my danger lies beyond his skill."

"Do not think so."

"I have no choice. I cannot help myself, Margaret. I cannot think what I choose, and that would not help me if it were possible to do so."

The two friends conversed much together, until fatigue again sent Mrs. Ogden to sleep, from which she awoke not for many hours, and then she was perfectly delirious. The fever had now seized upon her; she was like a burning coal, hot, dry, and delirious. It was difficult to administer medicine, and sometimes impossible.

Things continued thus for some days, the unfortunate woman daily losing strength, while the fever was gaining ground. At length the final moment arrived. Reason returned, but for a very short time, and then fled with life.

It was a moment of extreme terror and misery to Mrs. Bertram to see her friend lie thus stretched, cold and lifeless, on her bed. Her reason did not fail her, but it was so near gone, that she scarcely knew what she did.

Her tears seemed to have been dried up by the greatness of her grief, and she felt her head throb as though it would have burst. She immediately, with more strength and resolution than was at all to be expected, set about doing the last office that can be performed towards any human being.

Determined that, come what might, her friend should be decently buried, she, with a strength of mind that appeared as if sent her for the sole purpose, made all the necessary arrangements for the purpose.

"It is a hard duty," she murmured, as she looked upon the dead body—"a sacred duty, which I will not neglect, despite of my wants, or even my infant's. I will see her to her last long home myself; and if I fall dead on her grave, and my child, then indeed I should think I was favoured by Providence. It would be a mercy to take us from this train of misery and horrors."

The funeral took place. It was decent; for Margaret had raked up everything that would have fetched money; and everything had to be paid for beforehand, for these people would give no credit. Yet she did it without assistance, and it left her perfectly penniless.

Margaret was the only mourner that followed, and the one real mourner that lived to regret the fate of her who was consigned to the grave.

Margaret tottered back to the lodgings in hopes of sleeping there that night, at least, for she had nowhere else to go.

"Well, mem?" said the landlady.

"I want to get up stairs to rest—don't you know me?"

"Why, yes, mem, I rather thinks I does," said the landlady.

Margaret stood and looked at her, and paused before her.

"Will you not let me pass?"

"No, mem, unless you can pay me for three weeks' rent, and give me security for the future."

"You know I am alone and helpless."

"Can't help it, mem, though I am very sorry. I live by my rent, and should soon be alone and helpless myself; besides, you are no lodger of mine."

"I have lived with the late Mrs. Ogden, poor creature."

"She was very poor, since she couldn't leave you a legacy. Mind, I don't disrespect anybody, and don't want words; but you ain't my lodger, and now she's gone, she ain't any of mine; but I must look after myself, or I find I gets nothing for nothing. Good-day, men. Don't collect a mob, or you'll obstruct the highway, and I pays for the highway, and can't have it stopped up. You had better go to your friends, my good woman—you had, indeed, before it grows late, because it is late now."

"Allow me to sleep this night—have some pity on my helpless infant!" she exclaimed, in an imploring tone.

"Ah, I catches me at it."

"You will?"

"Oh! dear, no such thing. Only think, I'm up to the dodge of lodgers; they doesn't come over me with their gammon; once in, and the what-do-y'-call-'im can't get 'em out again. Oh, the artfulness of some people—why, they are as deep as any two people."

"I will go in the morning quietly, and thank you for your humanity. Consider my poor unfortunate infant; it will perish in the cold streets."

"Ah, people oughtn't to have infants who can't take care on 'em; they are an expensive luxury, and a bother too. I wonder you ain't ashamed of yourself."

"Were you ever a mother?"

"What—do you mean to insult me, you baggage?.. I'll let you know I am a mother, and an honest woman to boot."

"Cannot you have some pity for my poor child, and grant me the shelter of your roof for one night only?"

"Feel for you, hussy! I'll have you know I have enough to do to feel for myself and family. Go and feel for yourself, or to those who have a right to feel for you; don't come and disturb me."

"You are an unfeeling woman," said Margaret, bitterly. "I could not have believed that any woman could have had such a hard heart, or have been so insensible."

"Go along; or if you come any of your abuse here, you will get the worst of it, I tell you, 'cause I won't put up with it, and I never could when a child, and will not put up with it now. I am a lawful wedded wife, you good-for-nothing thing."

Having talked till Margaret had turned the corner, she went in and slammed the door after her, congratulating herself that she was now "free from all them set."

Margaret was too much affected to speak; she pressed her little one close to her heart, and walked on for some distance; the tears fell fast, while deep sobs almost choked her. Her grief was extreme, for the prospect was dire and sad, both for mother and child—it was utter destitution that now stared them in the face.

"Yes, yes," she muttered, "I must beg now. I could starve and die, but not my child; no—no—no, not my child; that shall be preserved if I have the power to do so. Yes, yes, I will beg—I will—we must not perish thus. All are not alike; we shall find some charitable."

With this to her terrible but necessary resolution, she walked along the street. That day she had eaten nothing; the last farthing she could find, or make up by pawning or selling, had been given for the burial fees, and now she was destitute.

Yes, destitute of everything—of food and of shelter. She had nowhere to go, no one to speak to, and no one to afford her the slightest consolation and comfort.

At length she determined to make an attempt to solicit aid of strangers.

She had looked at a great many before she could summon up courage to make the attempt; but she, each time, turned her eyes to the almost famished child beside her, and felt convinced that her hunger was becoming fatal to the infant.

She now determined to make the appeal to the next passenger she met. It was a female, and she hoped to excite pity in the breast of one who might be a mother herself.

Margaret Bertram besought her in a few humble words to afford her some succour for the sake of her child.

"Oh, the brat!" said the woman, "to think that such people should have children. Come, go along; take it home."

"Alas! I have no home."

"Then you had better go to the workhouse; everybody pays for the workhouse, and that's the place for all poor people."

"I have but just become entirely destitute, and I know not how to apply; but it is immediate shelter and succour I want. I have had no food to-day; I have no home, and my child will perish of want."

"Then go to the workhouse or anywhere; I can't pay poor-rates and support idleness. There, go away, my good woman; you ought to know better than to stop decent people; but you've no respect to person. I have nothing, so go your ways. Young woman, if you really are in want, there is the work-house."

Margaret turned away, more disgusted than hurt. Thanks to the woman's utter heartlessness, she had taken from her refusal half the sting of the refusal.

The next time Margaret made an application for charity, it should not be of her own sex, but of men.

In this she was unsuccessful, for they paid her no attention, but pushed on, and passed her heedless of her pleadings.

"Alas—alas!" said she, "I am doomed to suffer; this night, alas! will be my last, and then all will be over, for I cannot, will not survive my child."

It was now late at night, and a sense of utter loneliness came over her. She was desolate and deserted.

Upon a door step she sat down exhausted, and weeping bitterly. It was late, and there were very few people about; and the only lamp that was near shed but a feeble ray, and scarcely illumined dimly the spot where she sat.

Suddenly a man stood opposite to her; he was enveloped in a large cloak. It was some time before Margaret looked up, but at length she did, and their eyes met. The recognition was mutual, and in the glance that met her eye, Margaret knew it was Bertram who stood before her.

CHAPTER LII.

THE INTERVIEW OF TERROR.—THE ACCUSATION.—AND THE ATTACK.

YES, it was indeed Bertram who stood before her, he who had been the bane of her existence, the evil genius that stepped between her and what should have been happiness.

It was Bertram, the man who had induced her to trust to him her future fate, and who had betrayed that trust in a manner which should bring upon him the reprehension of every thoughtful mind.

Was it nothing that he should seek her out in early life, and by such promises and vows as had come from his lips, create in her mind a trustfulness in him, which, at the first breath of adversity, was to be scattered to the winds? Was it nothing that he should become, as it were, the canker-worm in the bud of that young girl's dearest hopes and happiness? Did he never consider for one moment that while brooding over what he considered to be his injuries, he had committed none, and that she had not suffered?

The merest lingering suspicion, the veriest shadow of a doubt, concerning the presumed facts upon which he had proceeded—and surely, surely, there was room for a doubt—ought to have filled his mind with a shrinking terror of meeting her whom he had judged so harshly, and towards whom he had exercised a retribution which surely should have come from no hands but the unerring ones of Heaven.

The haughty aspect that he wore was misplaced; he should have remembered that, after all, he was but a mortal judging mortal; most especially careful should he have been, under such circumstances, to inquire if, while seeing the mote in her eye, he overlooked not the beam in his own.

That maxim of Christianity, which says, "Judge not, lest ye too be judged," should have been more present to the mind of Bertram than it was.

And yet, by some strange perversity of reasoning in human nature, we find that the most violent indignation on the part of individuals is always exercised in judging of these lessons of morals and integrity with which they have themselves been the most familiar.

The thief looks upon petty larceny, exercised against himself, as one of the worst of offences. Nothing is so aggravating to one who passes his life in the midst of intrigues as being made the victim of one.

Assuming, therefore, for one moment, although we know the contrary, and our readers know it with us, that Margaret Bertram was guilty, he who had betrayed such a vast amount of iniquity, should have been the last to do so. Some whisperings of his own conscience should have told him to be merciful to another; like a galled jade, he should have winced, feeling that his withers were not unwrung by every ungracious remark which might be uttered concerning the particular quality of crime with which he fancied himself in a condition to accuse his innocent wife.

He should have recollected, that if he had erred, forgetting discretion for a moment in that gush of tenderness that comes across the heart upon the recollection of some early affection which has only slept within the chamber of the brain, she had not, as he had done, been the systematic seducer of innocence, and the betrayer of a guileless and an innocent heart.

Yes, he, of all men, hard as will appear the task, should have sought for extenuating circumstances; and, even if he had believed her guilty, should have allowed gentle mercy to have walked hand in hand with indignation, and smoothed its savage front.

But to hear him talk—to look upon his face—to see him enveloped in the black mantle of woe, and looking so stern—so resolute, and so defying, one would have imagined him a very pattern of the sublimest virtue, treading the earth with so much holiness and purity, that those offences which, to poor humanity, looked but trivial, stunk horribly in his pious nostrils, and admitted of no extenuation.

Thus we say that the harshness, the brutality, and the cruel desertion of his wife, of which Bertram had been guilty, ill became him, of all men, even had she been, to the full extent, all that the demoniac Mrs. Blair and his own fevered imagination pictured her.

But she was innocent, and yet had suffered so much—innocent even in thought, for not for one moment had she yielded to the temptations which had surrounded her. No! with the very heroism of virtue, she had done all that a gentle, trusting, affectionate woman could do, and she had stopped short at the slightest act which could jeopardise her right to that title.

Oh! if right could have been done, and if she had possessed a sufficiently strong antagonistic mind to assert that which was due to her, she should have stood up in the majesty of injured virtue, while Bertram should have crouched at her feet, and begged forgiveness for his deep sinfulness.

But such was not the case: there they were, that husband and wife, who had commenced life together, under such apparently happy auspices; he stern and implacable; she shrinking and aghast at the presence of him who had been her evil genius.

"Bertram, Bertram! it is Bertram!" she said.

"Yes; it is Bertram!" was his reply. "You know me. We have at last met again. Can you look upon my face?"

"Yes; but that it is shrouded by darkness, I could look upon it unflinchingly, although with terror."

"Yes, with terror; so looks guilt upon innocence, because it dreads retribution."

"No!" said Margaret; "so looks innocence upon guilt, because it dreads injustice."

"Say you so? Can you be so bold as well as so bad?"

"So bold, because not bad. Bertram! in the face of Heaven I defy your accusations, and, oh! but that I pity you, for some hour of mental anguish, which will surely come, I would call down upon your head such denunciations from Heaven, as might make you tremble to hear them."

"Indeed; you carry this boldly off. You pity me?"

"Yes; from my soul I do."

"'Tis well. Woman, I have a question to put to you."

"Man, I will answer no question of yours."

"Will not, and yet have sworn to obey."

"But who has broken that holy bond? Who has broken the tie which else had bound me to you, not only in obedience, but honour?"

"You have broken it."

"No, by Heaven! you; and I will not answer."

"Margaret, if my words were full of passion as you're are—if I spoke intemperately, and looked the anger of my soul, you might be bold with the feeling that that anger was subsiding, by its very exhibition; but let me tell you there is something dangerous in a calmness like unto mine. Do you not dread it?"

"Most surely not; for what have I to dread that has not already been accomplished, and that, too, by your means?

From honest toil, the reward of which was sweet, because fully earned, you tempted me. You took me from a humble but happy home, and with a luring tongue, you painted to me such fair pictures of new delight—the consequences of love and wealth, to attire it in its gorgeous hues, that like the giddy moth, which leaves distractedly a sylvan shade to flutter in the brief radiance of some destroying flame, I gave all for you. What is my reward, Bertram? Look upon me now."

Bertram was silent; but it was not with sympathy. He gloated in her wretchedness—the words that painted the distraction of her spirits were music to his ear—the misanthropic life that he had led, had nursed into a kind of frenzy his worse passions, and now he knew no touch of human kindness.

"I repeat, Bertram, what am I now? Wretched, an outcast, a destitute and homeless wanderer; and this is your work."

"It is my work. I hope I have done it well. Tell me, Margaret, since you're disposed to be so confidential, have you suffered much?"

"Heaven only knows how much!"

"Have you seen, one by one, those glittering gauds that surrounded you, disappear?"

"I have! I have!"

"And do you see the choice friends of your prosperity shrink from the house one by one, as they discovered that no longer it glittered with a halo of entertainments that shed a lustre upon them and their sleek audacity? Did you feel all this, and did it bring no pangs to your mind?"

"Oh! I have felt it all; more than that."

"It is well; and thus you found what a bitter world it was you lived in. Perhaps those lips which had been most wreathed in smiles, were the first to curl with scorn and with contempt."

"Some there were who acted so."

"Ah! by the great God, I know it, and those with the greatest candour on their brows, had looked, and talked, and moved as though they could not harbour one selfish thought; those you found, like birds of passage, took their flight when the summer of their prosperity was gone.'"

"I did—I did."

"I glory in it. First came the difficulty—that was fought up against; the flimsy veil of respectability was soon seen through; at last it was cast aside completely, and then came absolute poverty, and the next spectre in the train of evils was destitution.'"

"You're quite right, Bertram," said Margaret; "you have studied human nature: you're quite right, and there was one whom I trusted most—upon whom I most relied."

"Ay, who betrayed you most; 'tis ever so."

"In this instance it was truly so. I was not child-like, or was my experience of the world quite so foolish as to believe that a smiling face might not conceal a hollow heart. I knew that it was easy to ape candour; I knew that it was easy, with great courtesy, for those who chose, to seem far different to what they were; but still I fondly clung to one."

"I'm glad on't—very glad."

"I trusted one, and looked upon my trust in that one as my defence against the duplicity of all others."

"And who might this phœnix of perfection be, who for a time deluded you, and then betrayed you?"

"The only one," said Margaret, rising, "who had called upon God to witness to the sincerity of his truth—yourself, Bertram. Thou art the man."

Bertram recoiled a step, as she pointed in his face.

"D——n!" he muttered, "have I come here to be an accuser, or to be accused? Margaret, I have a word to say to you."

"What word?"

"Your last hour has come."

"Then let it come—I am prepared. Bertram, look on that step from whence I have but just arisen—see you there no living thing?"

"Not one—ah! your child."

"Your child, Bertram."

"No, by Heaven!"

"Yes, by Heaven!—look upon its face. Oh, Bertram, if anything can melt you yet, it should be the sight of that young helpless being—a gift of God to you, though scorned too long. You have yet time for hope—yet time for reparation. Oh, Bertram, it is the .... your child that speaks; you are not—

you cannot be so dead to human feeling as to affect indifference to this appeal. Bertram, I am innocent; and now I tell you boldly to your face, no longer will I endure the stigma of unmerited reproach. I will proclaim my wrongs to all, and in all places, and their proclamation shall likewise be the assertion of my rights. I will make your name—and justly too—a by-word and a scorn, as you have endeavoured to make mine. Now, Bertram, I warn you and defy you!"

"Fool!" he said, "you have sealed your own doom! Some lingering touch of ancient recollection might have palsied the arm of vengeance, but you have made it firm again. We are alone—a deserted street—no one to see the deed—the deed of justice—of retribution! Margaret, look your last upon the world you have made to me so hateful!"

"No! no! mercy—mercy!—yet a moment!"

"Not another instant. Have you a prayer to offer?"

"Yes; may Heaven forgive my murderer."

Bertram clutched her by the wrist. It seemed as if he felt in his breast for some instrument of destruction. Oh, that was an awful moment; nature clung to life. Oh, could she die thus?—young yet, and a life before her that might bring sweets—sweets for the bitterness that had preceded them? No, no, it could not be; she shrieked for help.

"Murder! murder!" she shouted, and she struggled with the assassin.

That struggle was of short duration; some stronger arm than either Bertram's or Margaret's terminated it with a grasp that seemed superhuman in its power. Bertram found himself borne down to the ground, as if a hand from Heaven had been stretched down to crush him.

CHAPTER LIII.

THEODORE DANTON'S ESCAPE FROM THE MADHOUSE.

WE would gladly pursue the particular narrative which at so inopportune a juncture we feel ourselves for a brief space compelled to suspend, in order to attend to another and an important episode in our veritable history, were it not that that episode becomes necessary in its details, in order actually to account for the interruption which Bertram had received in his murderous intentions.

We feel, likewise, that for too long have we left one, in whose feelings and misfortunes we cannot but sympathise, in a position which should awaken for him, and which we are certain has awakened for him, all the best sympathies of our readers.

We allude to Theodore Danton.

Alas! poor Theodore! not so great in thy adversity as a mind moulded of sterner stuff than thine might have been, but still great enough and suffering enough to command the best feelings of every one at all acquainted with thy history.

The inmate of a madhouse!—that intellect which should have been an example and a pride to humanity—that mind which should have lifted its possessor far above the petty storms of adversity, and which would have done so had fortune been kinder as regarded its best and dearest affections.

But, alas! his dream of joy was but of short duration; he struggled for that which should have been attainable as a consequence of such a struggle.

But the bright hope was crushed by fate, and all was lost.

We will not, we cannot blame him that he sank beneath the blow of destiny. It would have been perhaps nobler to have arisen superior to it, and have triumphed over circumstances; but, that he did not do so none the less entitles him to our best wishes, and our warmest, dearest sympathies.

That partial suspension of due reflective power, which had enabled those who wished to do so to place him where he was, soon passed away, and he had then awakened to all the gloom and all the horror of being the inmate of so dreadful an abode.

A madhouse!—words of horror. Let any man, sane as any saint, awaken at any hour to a consciousness that he is obnoxious to such a doom—let him feel how difficult it must be to draw the fine line of distinction between sanity and insanity, and he will awaken to a hopelessness which is enough in itself to produce the result already suspected to be in existence.

So it was with Theodore. Assumed to be insane, he found himself placed in all the proverbial difficulty of proving a negative; and there he lay, revolving in his mind the past, which presented to him but one huge chalice of bitterness, in which no sweetening drop found a place.

Oh! with what a wondrous and enduring love he must have doated on her who, surely if marriages are really made in heaven, would have been his wife, for he and Margaret must have been happy.

Two more congenial souls a divine omniscience never yet created; the very romance of affection would have been theirs, and in their lives they would have personified some poet's dream of what happiness should be.

Whether it was the cool air and regular living of the lunatic asylum in which he had been placed, or that his constitution was yet sound, he began to rally again very rapidly, and to gain strength every day.

The diet was wholesome, and not too much of it; but they were treated harshly, though in his case he was, after a time, allowed some extra indulgence.

This arose from the fact of his being orderly and well conducted. Indeed, his manners and education made some impression upon them, and he was allowed to walk in the gardens for some hours a day unmolested, and this gave him time and opportunity to think deeply upon what had taken place, to recover the right tone of his mind, and the health of his body.

He meditated long upon the means of escape; but that was difficult. He could not do it, for he was so well watched, and the place was so well built, with an eye to security, that there was but little chance of escape. Indeed, the walls were of great height, and were commanded by the windows of the establishment, and then there was no means of gaining the summit.

So he considered it was altogether a mad scheme, and not to be effected, save after a long course of watching and cunning, for they were very vigilant.

On one or two occasions, one of the head keepers, taking a fancy to Theodore Danton, invited him to supper with him, and this passed off very well.

Theodore Danton had a deep-laid scheme of his own. It was rather a determination than a scheme, because there were no details he had been able to form more than what he hoped would be the result of his attempt.

One night he lay listening to the ravings of some desperate maniac not far from where he was confined; but in a more secure place, and confined to his bed, for he had attempted to commit suicide on the day previous.

"Poor wretch!" thought Danton, "little did he once anticipate such a fate as that which now awaits him—death in a madhouse. But then who thought—who could have foretold the same of me?

"Yes, my life is a chequered one, and it has come to an end different from that which, when fortune was at the worst, I could have dreamed of; and yet hope whispers in my heart it will not end, but there will come a time when I shall be free from this. Poor wretch—poor wretch! how he howls and raves."

This was said in consequence of the unfortunate maniac bursting out with a fresh stream of words.

Theodore Danton listened; he grew more attentive, and presently his attention became fixed, for the wretched man's narrative was interesting, and he could not help saying—

"There seems but little madness in that. At times a stream of sentences rush from these maniacs; they cannot help it. A beam of sanity shines upon the whole, and were it so that the rest of their conduct was unknown, they would be deemed perfectly sound in mind. I never could have credited so much. But there again ——"

The man now broke out into a clear strain of eloquence, and each word was plainly and distinctly articulated.

"Curses—deep—deep curses upon those who have placed me here; who have robbed me, and plundered me of all worldly goods and blessings!

"Curses upon them who have robbed me of my beautiful wife, my own adored Amelia: and curses too upon her, who could desert a fond and affectionate

husband, for the adulterous arms of one, who, when he is satiated, will throw her off like an old garment! Curses upon—ay, deep and burning curses upon all who were engaged in this most foul transaction!

"The deed is done—they have gained their day—their victory is won, and here am I, a raving maniac, one who lies almost face to face with death—his hideous jaws are not far from me—I can see him, with the dart which he holds in threatening attitude. It will not be long ere he has me for a victim.

"Once I was happy and contented. I was young and loved; I thought I was beloved again. I might have been; but who will believe in woman's constancy? Not I—not I.

"Yes; I was happy and contented. I had lands and a fortune—a moderate fortune. I was respected and beloved by all who knew me, and was likely to be so for aught that I can tell.

"In an evil hour I loved. I say an evil hour, because it turned out to be evil after all. I was happy while I loved. She was beautiful and fair, and seemed the very impersonation of innocence. Oh, God! how I loved that woman. I could have sacrificed my life for her; I could have lain down and met death cheerfully, did she but love me—and I believed she did.

"Courtship ended in marriage, and I became the happiest bridegroom that ever yet lived, or breathed the wedding vows at the altar to which I led my adored, my all but worshipped Amelia.

"The days glided by in unbroken happiness. I may say those months were one unbroken stream of extatic pleasure, flowing from day to day without measure, or the prospect of a cloud.

But the cloud came at last—unbidden—but it came.

"I had been out shooting, as was my wont at certain times in the year; but they were uncertain. Sometimes I would not leave the side of my wife; and, after having prepared myself, I would suddenly relinquish my intention of going altogether.

"On one occasion, I remember having suddenly given up my intention of shooting, resolving to stay with her whom I loved so passionately, instead of shooting.

"I thought that this was not received with any demonstration of pleasure; on the contrary, I thought that the contrary was the case, and a shade of displeasure and vexation passed across her countenance.

"It was but momentary, for she afterwards said, with a smile—

"'For once, I must entreat you to go out to-day.'

"'And wherefore?' said I, much surprised at such a request from her.

"'Because you promised me one of those hares you spoke of the other day. You know where I mean?'

"'Yes, I do.'

"'Well, one from that place I think I should like so well. Will you go at once? You promised me.'

"'And I will keep my word,' said I. 'I shall go and get one.'

"I left the house, and took a couple of greyhounds, and started onwards towards the place indicated.

"My suspicions were aroused, but yet I determined to go to the place I had promised. When once the demon of jealousy takes possession of the breast, then there is no more happiness, cause or no cause; the mind never recovers the shock.

"I walked rapidly—reached the spot, and in a few minutes found a hare, which was caught; when another was started, and off went the dogs. I raved, for I wanted to get back; however, they were not long, and then, with hasty strides, I turned homewards with the brace of hares, and my dogs at my heels.

"I was dreadfully heated, but I got home within half the time it usually takes to walk the distance.

"My wife was not to be found, and I saw her maid, who caught sight of me, and rushed up stairs. I ran after her as fast as I could, and urged by such motives, there was little doubt but I made good use of my limbs.

"She, however, gained the room in which my wife was; I heard her say I was coming. Before the words were well nigh out of her mouth I burst open the door, which she in vain endeavoured to secure against me.

"There I beheld a sight that at once confirmed all my fears. My wife was unfaithful.

"I stood irresolute for a moment or two, but my looks were terrible, and they were both terrified, and seizing my gun, I ran at them.

"The treacherous wretch, her servant, put out her foot and caused me to fall, and I was immediately seized by her paramour; servants were called in, and I was charged with attempting to murder my wife and her cousin, so she called the man I saw in her arms.

"I raved and swore; charged them with adultery; this they denied, and appealed to the servant who had so thwarted me, and she unhesitatingly declared I spoke falsely; and that, moreover, I had attempted her life, and she ran she knew not whither to save herself.

"My God! my God! that was an awful day! that was a moment that I can never forget were my life lengthened beyond that of the oldest man who ever lived. No, no; it will haunt me whilst I live. God of Heaven! she was beautiful, but an accomplished hypocrite, and a base, cold-blooded wretch.

"I was given into custody for an attempt to murder, and by her whom I loved so passionately.

"I was sent for trial; my servants were all arrayed against me; they deposed to various acts that of themselves might appear singular or odd, but when taken along with the many little circumstances that took place, were perfectly explainable and in keeping.

"These, however, and the fact of my servants having seen me rush after my wife's maid up stairs, confirmed the opinion they entertained of my insanity. Then came the evidence of my wife, and her so-called cousin, to the effect that I made an attempt to murder one of them, but by the divine interposition of Providence, in the shape of a stumble, they were saved from destruction.

"I was found not guilty, on the ground of insanity."

There was a pause of a few moments, and Theodore Danton listened for the conclusion of the maniac's tale; but he waited some time, and then a few groans were all he heard; then all was silent again, but after a while he began again, saying—

"Ay, ay; they placed me here, and here I have raved occasionally. I have been mad, indeed. I have been driven mad, and now I am dying. May Heaven curse them, and send them misery on earth, and torments hereafter!

"Here have I been confined for years, and my adulterous wife has been enjoying herself upon my property, and in the arms of her paramour.

"Is not that enough to distract my mind? Is not that enough to drive a man insane? Ay, it is; and to destruction, too. I am dying!—I am dying! May the curse of a blighted soul rest upon them to eternity!"

Theodore heard no more of the maniac that night; a few groans, indeed, reached him, but beyond that all was still, and he heard no other sound.

In the morning, when the keeper came to him, he said—

"Did you hear the man raving in the next cell all night?"

"I was with him," he replied, "during the greater part of the night."

"How is he?"

"Dead!"

"Poor fellow!" exclaimed Theodore Danton. "Is his tale true?"

"Did you hear it?"

"Yes, I did."

"I believe every word of it."

"Then you think he was not mad?" said Theodore Danton.

"I do; but since he came here he has shown symptoms of insanity, which were purely caused by his treatment. He was sent here, but we could do nothing with him; he made an attempt to escape, and then went off into paroxysms of violence, which compelled us to confine him."

"And what was the cause of death?"

"Suffusion of blood on the brain."

"Who was he speaking to?"

"To me."

"I thought he was raving, and that no one was near."

"No, I was there; and I believe every word he has uttered."

"And what will be the result of all this?" said Theodore.

"I know not, except he'll be buried, and his wife marry her cousin, as I daresay they are all but so already," said the keeper.

"I thought my case was bad enough," remarked Danton; "but it is, perhaps, worse than mine."

"Yours?"

"Yes."

"What is yours, then?"

"Have you not heard?"

"No."

"It is this, then. I was taken ill, and carried insensible to the hospital, where I was placed in bed, and was getting round, when I saw the nurses commit a cold-blooded murder, and then rob their unfortunate victim, who was a foreigner."

"Indeed!"

"Yes; and I had the temerity to charge them with it before the surgeon; and they coolly declared I had been raving in that way all night, and I was sent here in consequence, where Heaven knows how long I am likely to remain."

"Ah, we are none of us without our troubles," remarked the keeper; "but there's nobody that interests themselves about you."

"And, I presume, I may remain here till I am old."

"Why, as for the matter of that, maybe you may, and maybe you mayn't."

"'Tis a poor consolation, though," said Theodore, mournfully, "to be shut up like beasts in a cage."

"What can't be cured must be endured, Master Danton," said the keeper, as he left the room; "but you can take your walk, if you please."

Danton emerged into the open air, and proceeded to take his accustomed walks through the gardens, and during his walk he pondered over what he had heard that morning.

"No," he muttered, "I have not got any one to interest themselves in my fate, and I may remain here to the day of my death, which will be accelerated by the reflection that I am a prisoner here for life—that I have no soul breathing who cares for me, or who knows even my fate. 'Tis, indeed, a gloomy prospect."

He paused; thoughts rushed to his mind of a chequered character. At one moment he gazed at the sky, at another he looked at the walls, and then passed hurriedly onwards, as though he recollected himself suddenly, and would not be observed by any one.

"No, no—I will die," he muttered; "but not here, unless it be in attempting to escape. Should I obtain any weapon, I will not hesitate to make my way out, despite all opposition."

As he gazed around him, he observed a small iron bar; it was about two feet and a half long, and nearly an inch square, like a crow-bar, but used for a lever.

Looking carefully around him, to ascertain if he were observed by any one, and finding that he was not, he suddenly seized the crow-bar, and plunged it into the earth at a certain spot, which he marked, and which he knew very well.

"I shall know that again; and now to observe the times and places—when there are fewer persons about, and when they are all collected. I must and will escape, and should death be the result, why the result must rest with them, and not with me. I am innocent of intentional crime: my liberty is worth contending for, and I will contend for it to the last."

With this intention, he walked about for some time, until the hour at which they all breakfasted, and then they were arranged in a large hall—such as were known to be harmless.

The keepers' eyes were upon them, who would soon have detected if anything had been wrong, and the man who betrayed any symptoms of a fresh accession of madness would in an instant be overpowered by the keepers in attendance.

It was with a wary and cautious eye that Theodore Danton now noted down all the particulars relative to the place; the usual position of the keepers—the doors and the windows.

All these things Danton had never before observed, for he was not strong enough to think of an escape when first he came, and afterwards he felt the utter inutility of attempting one in the face of so many men.

Now, however, he felt his strength revive, and his mind elated, by the possession of the crow-bar.

This made a wonderful deal of difference in his hopes.

Several days passed without anything occurring to give him any chance or prospect to make an escape, and he lay awake night after night, devising means of getting out of the asylum.

He was locked in every night, and thus secured; if he could have got out of the house during the night he might have got off clear, but not without encountering a man who kept watch all night round the house. But that he would not mind doing; at least, it was an alternative he would embrace rather than not make the attempt.

A thought suddenly struck him, as he lay one night revolving the matter over in his own mind.

The idea rose to his mind, that if he could get out and set fire to the place, he should have double chances of escape, because the attention of the keepers would be then distracted.

"I will not do that," said Theodore to himself, "if I can by any means effect my escape without it. It would cause too much danger to others. If," he muttered to himself, "I could contrive to secrete myself, then, indeed, I could do some good. I might take any opportunity of escaping."

He thought that, if he could hide himself in any place about the premises, say for a day or two—then all danger, or much of it would be over—the search would be useless. There was, however, one objection to all this, and that was, how was he to exist all that time? He could not do without food. He must make himself master of the means of existence, and then the scheme could be tried.

He sometimes accompanied one of the keepers to other wards, or parts of the house, and he failed not to observe that there were plenty of means of concealment. In the kitchen there were great stores of flour and wood piled and heaped contiguously to each other, for the convenience of bread-making and lighting the oven.

"I should like to see you make and bake bread," said Danton to the keeper who was with him.

"Would you?"

"Yes. I have often heard it spoken of in the country. I have seen it done abroad, but never saw it made in this country," said Danton.

"Well, we are going to make some to-day, and you shall see it," replied the keeper; "that is, if I can obtain permission."

"Thank you—thank you."

The keeper kept his promise, and in the afternoon he said,—

"If you will come with me, Danton, I can show you how they make bread. I have got permission."

"I am greatly obliged for so much indulgence," replied Danton.

Then he followed the man down stairs into the kitchen, where he saw several men and females at troughs, making bread.

Here they were all at work, and the keeper took pains to explain the whole process to them; and then going to the ovens, he there showed him how they contrived to heat it, and the time it took.

"And how often do you bake?"

"Once a week."

"And can you make enough to last this establishment for a whole week?" inquired Danton.

"Yes; the bread keeps well."

"And how long does it take making and baking?"

"Oh, somewhere from sixteen to twenty-four hours."

Danton had now got what information he desired about the operations carried on in a part of the building he desired to know something about. He returned to his own room, and there, in the quietude of his own cell—for such it was, in fact—plotted and planned within his own mind various means of escape, and weighed their various degrees of probabilities of success.

"If I can once secrete myself there," he thought, "then I shall be all right, because I shall be near where I can obtain some means of subsistence. The larder is close at hand, and I can then help myself to what I want."

This was consolatory, and he deter-mined that he would forthwith make the attempt the next night.

"I must," he muttered, "not let them think I am in the house, else my re-capture would be certain. I must make them believe I have got out."

How to do this he could not for a moment imagine, but determined to trust to the chapter of accidents. which would be sure to throw up something of a character that would aid him.

The next day he got possession of the crow-bar which he had thrust into the earth, and then hid it in his garments, until he had an opportunity of going into his cell, where he secreted it among his bed-clothes.

With what impatience did he await the approach of night—of that time when he could put in execution his plan of an escape from his prison!

How he listened to the bolting and locking of the cells! What music was it to his ears, when he heard the heavy footsteps of the keepers retiring for the night, to sit for a while, and then to carouse, and after that they sought their beds.

It was with the utmost impatience that he awaited until the solemn hour of midnight struck upon his ear. Then, indeed, he felt a new joy thrill through his veins. He arose, and taking the crow-bar, he felt about until he came to the door, which he wished to open.

He had some difficulty in inserting the end of the crow-bar between the chinks of the door, for it was well made, and it took him a long time before he could effect his purpose at all.

At length he succeeded in getting the instrument properly fixed, and then it yielded slowly, but gradually, until it gave way beneath the powerful lever he was making use of.

He stood without the door in another moment, and then made towards a window which was at some height from the ground, but secured by strong iron bars, built with the windows.

To these he fixed some sheets and blankets, and let the end hang out of window, as though he had got out that way.

He was looking very carefully at this, and considering what was next to be done, when a hand was laid upon his shoulder, and he heard a voice say—

"I always thought you cunning, but hang me if I gave you credit for this. But you must come back."

Theodore Danton started, and a sickening sensation came across him, as he saw the keeper with a bludgeon in his hand.

"Come along—come along. No nonsense: you must come, you know."

"Indeed!" said Danton, somewhat recovering himself.

"Yes, you must."

"Then I will not," replied Danton; at the same time he swung the crow-bar in the air, and struck the keeper on the head; and he staggered, and then Danton struck him again, and he fell senseless.

Immediately after that he made for the lower story, and, with some difficulty, he contrived to secrete himself between the wood and the flour-bags.

He had secured a bottle of wine, a loaf, and some cold fowl, before he ensconced himself; and it was well he did, for, before many minutes had elapsed, there was a dreadful stir in the house—the alarm-bells were rung, and feet were heard hurrying to and fro in all directions.

"Ah!" thought Danton, "had I gone out I am sure I should have been retaken, and then all hope would have fled. I should never have had another chance. While I am here I shall be safe, and if I do get out it will be without pursuit."

There was much stir within and without the place; doors were opened and shut, until all was quiet; but then they came to the kitchens and basement story to search there, and Danton could hear them close to him, endeavouring to ascertain what had become of him. But he was secreted in such a manner that he left no traces, and no opening presented itself where he could have got in, and they believed he must have got out of the window, which they were unwilling to credit.

"He must have got out of the window," said one; "there can be no doubt of it—it was open."

"There is much doubt of it," replied another; "for how the devil he could have squeezed himself through those iron bars I can't think, hang me!"

"You may depend on it he's made like a cat, and will go into any compass, just to suit circumstances."

"Well, it's a rum start."

"How's Hicks?"

"Oh, he's shaking his head to and fro, and feeling for it with his hands every now and then. He's had a gentle tap, I know, for he don't notice trifles."

"He doesn't, indeed; he's staggering about as if he were drunk. I wouldn't have had his visitation for a trifle."

"No, nor any one else. But he must have got clean off, that's clear."

"Oh, they'll have him before morning; thay have sent off several men, and he's safe to be taken."

"Come along, we may as well get to bed again."

The men then quitted the place, and all was quiet for the night.

Here Theodore Danton remained concealed all that night and all the next day, and he could hear the conversation of the menials, who did nothing but talk of the extraordinary escape that had been made by himself.

The next night, Theodore Danton came from his hiding-place and helped himself to the contents of the larder, and regaled himself with the best he could find.

Afterwards, he walked about for exercise for a couple of hours, and then, having secured enough provisions to last the next twenty-four hours, he again crept into his hiding-place, where he fell fast asleep until the next day, when he was awakened by an exclamation from one of the servants, who declared that something had been in the larder and eat all the governor's pie, and there would be a pretty shindy.

"Who could have been there?"

"How can I tell?"

"It must have been the cat."

"Then the cat can play a good knife and fork," returned the cook, "and, moreover, she can enjoy a bottle of wine!"

"Ay—ay!"

"Yes; here's one that wasn't uncorked, and she can use the corkscrew, I find."

"Well, I'll put a watch upon the place, if I sit up all night."

This was a dangerous hint to Theodore Danton, who began to fear he should run a great chance of discovery, and he resolved now he would make his escape that very night if the coast were clear.

It so chanced that this night the cook sat up, and he dared not move from his place of concealment, so he made his stock of provisions last out the next day, and that was no hardship.

However, the cook, not finding any one attack her provisions, and finding also that it was fatiguing, gave up the watch, and the next night the coast was clear; and, after provisioning himself, he found his way to the back door, which, being the weakest in the whole house, was easiest to break open.

This he did easily, and then stood in the open air. Then, after considering where there was a way out for some time, he determined to cross the beds of the kitchen garden, and then break through the hedge.

There was a large ditch to leap, but he successfully accomplished this, and then made across the open country, till he emerged into the high-road to London.

"Thank Heaven!" exclaimed Theodore Danton, "I am now free again!" and he here flung the crow-bar into the hedge. "I am free from that dreadful place! There will be no search for me—I have got clear off, and have no relatives to keep me there for the sake of my property. I am free!"

CHAPTER LIV.

THE STRANGE EFFECTS OF THE STRUGGLE UPON DANTON.—THE INTERVIEW IN THE STREETS.

THE struggle in which Bertram was so suddenly and unexpectedly engaged in with the stranger proved desperate, indeed. He lay on the ground beneath the powerful strength of his opponent, who seemed to hold him in the grasp of a giant.

Driven to despair, he twisted and turned, and exerted himself with all the energy of a madman; but no; the blows fell as heavy, and the almost death-grasp that tightened upon his throat remained as fast as ever, despite all his efforts to free himself.

"Madman—idiot! leave your hold, you will choke me—you—you will strangle me. Curses—curses! unhand me, villain! Hold off, will you?"

"Inhuman wretch! take the punishment your crime deserves. I'll not leave you while you have strength to resist. Wretched man! what could induce you to attempt the murder of one so helpless?"

"Help, help!" gasped Bertram, as he endeavoured to shield himself ineffectually from the blows of Theodore Danton.

Yes, it was Theodore Danton whom chance or fate thus threw in the way at a moment when so little was the prospect of rescue afforded to the unfortunate Margaret Bertram, in this most urgent moment of need. He had wandered about, and the fresh air had much contributed towards his recovery from his recent illness; the excitement of his escape, and the exertion necessary for that purpose, had had this beneficial effect upon his health.

Bertram, in consequence of Danton's shifting his hold, contrived to shake himself free of the grasp upon his throat, and threw himself over. Making a desperate attempt to rise, he struggled to his feet; but Danton still followed him close, and beat him over the head and face with his clenched hand, until his face was covered with blood.

"Mercy! mercy! Hold off—curses!" muttered Bertram, as he staggered about under this infliction.

"Hound!" exclaimed Theodore Danton; "dare you ask for mercy—you, who refused it to a woman? Curses on you, cowardly wretch! Curses on you!"

These words were accompanied by such a shower of blows, that Bertram reeled and struck himself against a lamp-post, and then made a desperate rush to escape from the unequal struggle with one who was so much his superior in physical strength and in energy.

Theodore Danton, seeing that the man was about to escape his hands, and thinking he had not been punished enough, made a grasp at him, and caught him by the black mantle he wore; but, nerved by desperation, and the fear of death before his eyes supplying the place of strength, he dashed away, leaving a portion of the mantle in

Theodore Danton's hand, who stood gazing after the fugitive.

Margaret Bertram stood terrified at the struggle that was going on; she knew not whether she were safe or not. Once or twice she was about to hurry from the spot, but she was by some unaccountable motive or other induced to come back again.

She now saw Danton beneath the lamp, looking in the direction which Bertram had taken, and then at the piece of the ominous black mantle which he had in his hand, alternately, as if he were debating the propriety of following.

"No, no; I will not follow;—no, no; I will not follow. Who knows where he may lead to? I may fall into the hands of the madhouse people."

A shudder passed over his face, and he seemed to have a strange excited feeling rush over him, his eyes glaring wildly around him.

"Ay, ay; the fight is over. But where is she for whom it was fought?" he muttered to himself.

Theodore Danton turned round to look after Margaret, who had watched his actions, and became convinced that he was strongly excited by the scene that he had just been an actor in, and she determined within herself that she would devote herself to him, and would sacrifice the remainder of her days to secure the health and comfort of one who had become thus affected in consequence of his love for her.

The fact was, the struggle between Danton and Bertram had deranged his brain; the sudden excitement he had suffered acted upon his brain, and produced an action dangerous to his intellects.

"Danton—Theodore Danton!" she exclaimed; "you have saved my life."

"Ah!" he exclaimed; "I should know that voice—'tis one I should remember well."

"It is that of Margaret."

"Of Margaret Bertram?"

"Yes, Theodore; yes, it is."

"I should, indeed, know that voice; and, were I dying, it would recall my life—my fleeting soul would revisit my eyes to enable me to see that form. Ah, Margaret! what do I behold? Is this you?"

"Yes, Danton; 'tis I."

"And in this garb? How—what has happened—who—who was that? Who was he that would have laid his hands upon you but now?"

"That, Danton, was," said Margaret, with some hesitation—"that, Danton, was Bertram."

"The villain! he would have murdered you—he would have killed you, Margaret. I will go after him—I will follow him to the end of the world but what I will overtake him, and be revenged upon him. I will do you justice, Margaret—I will."

"Nay, Danton—nay, leave him. Let him seek safety where he will—he will not return here."

"But you, Margaret—you—where have you come from? Why are you out thus at night? Has he driven you from home?"

"It is the same, since he left me and the place to go slowly to ruin. He left me to come to distress and beggary."

"To beggary, Margaret?"

"Yes; to beggary, Theodore. I am in extreme want. But you are ill—you are ill, Theodore; let me attend upon you as a sister. You are very ill, I see."

"I—I— am not ill, Margaret; but I think I shall go mad to see you in this state. I—I, too, have no home. I have just escaped."

"Escaped?"

"Yes; escaped."

"How? You do not mean you were in prison, Danton? That could not be."

"But it was, Margaret, a much worse place than a prison, that in which I was confined, from which I have escaped."

"And where was that, Danton?"

"A madhouse, Margaret."

"A madhouse! Good God! you have not been confined in such a place as that?"

"I have."

"And why? You have suffered in health. I need hardly ask you the cause."

"Alas! Margaret, I have suffered severely. I accused the guilty, and my reward was an accusation of madness while in the hospital."

"You in a hospital, Theodore?"

"Yes; I left the hotel, Margaret, and became ill in the street, and was sent to

THE IRACAS IN THE GIPSY ENCAMPMENT.

the hospital; and because I could not calmly see murder done, was sent to a madhouse, where I was kept for some time, until at length I got out."

"And wherefore left you your hotel?"

"Ah, Margaret, it is useless to inquire—quite useless to inquire," said Theodore Danton; "we have met again, and I believe there is a fate."

"It is the first time I have seen Bertram for some time; he left me to want—to starvation, and he would have murdered me."

There was something in Theodore Danton's manner that assured Margaret Bertram that he was much excited by the contest he had been engaged in for her sake with Bertram. It had disturbed the equilibrium of his mind, and he gazed vacantly about; but he preserved an affectionate manner towards her, and

a certain share of reason in all he said; but there was a vague, unsettled gaze in the eye, which seemed particularly lighted by the fires of insanity.

He paused some moments without speaking, but stood irresolute, and undetermined what to do.

"Margaret," he said, "which way do you go—where do you intend to seek shelter?"

"Alas! Theodore, I have none."

"None, Margaret—none?"

"No. I am a wanderer—alone and deserted."

"God of Heaven! do I hear aright? You deserted, Margaret—no home, and in distress! Oh, what a fall is that which hath beset us both! Come, Margaret, we are both wanderers—we have both of us been ill-used by the world; let us seek some place where we can pass our days in quiet."

"Be it so, Theodore; but as your sister be it. You are not well, and I will spend my life in the dear task of ministering to your wants. To see your health restored would be all I should care for."

"But I should desire your happiness, too, Margaret; that and nothing else I should desire. What would be all the world to me, and I know that you were suffering? No, no; your health and happiness must ever be my object."

"My happiness, Theodore, is for ever broken. I may attain tranquillity of mind, but never happiness. That is gone, and there is no hope—no hope. I would there were, but it has left me. Here, this very night, Bertram met me as I sat here—my only shelter. I am reduced to beg for food, and to lie in the open air for want of the shelter so necessary to me and my little one."

"Ah!" said Danton; "the child!"

"Yes, I have it," she said, as she showed it to Danton. She had it wrapped up, and close to her own breast, to keep it warm.

"You had not that when last I saw you."

"No, Danton; the unfortunate child has seen the light since our interview at the hotel, and it has been deserted, with its mother, by its natural protector; and we have been left to perish or live by the hand of charity, and even such a miserable life would have been cut short but for you."

"Then come away from this spot; 'tis no place to stand and talk in. 'Twill be day-break in a few short hours, and the streets are now empty; we will go forth together, and consult means of safety and of living—'tis our destiny."

CHAPTER LV.

THE MIDNIGHT WALK—THE RESOLVES OF MARGARET AND THEODORE DANTON.

MARGARET BERTRAM and Theodore Danton walked side by side for some distance without speaking a word, both were engaged deeply with his or her own thoughts.

Danton was endeavouring to form some plan of future conduct, but he could not. His thoughts seemed confused—a mistiness floated before his eyes, and objects appeared in a different mental light than formerly.

"Oh, Heaven!" he muttered, "what has come over me? I am not the same man I was. God forbid that I should suffer from mental disease, or that the accusation of those hags at the hospital should have been prophetic, and my mental disorder should follow! Oh, God—oh God! what am I reserved for?"

Margaret, too, had her thoughts. What were her prospects? Bad enough. Her infant and herself reduced to beggary, and she had just escaped being sacrificed to the fury of a jealous and enraged husband, who had no cause for his suspicions.

She was rescued by her former lover—the man of all others she could have been so happy with, but whom she now looked upon in the light of one who had saved her life, and entitled to her gratitude and love; for him she could lay down her life, or make any sacrifice she could to benefit him.

Thus they walked for some time, both occupied by thoughts that were none of the happiest, though happiness was their object. At length Margaret, said—

"Theodore, where are you going?"

"In truth, I cannot tell, Margaret. I know not where I am going."

"Then why walk at all, Theodore? You will be fatigued before you have made any settled plan; before you have begun to do anything towards a conclusion, you will be tired."

"I am tired, Margaret; but what of that? What must you not have suffered before this?"

"Yes, yes; never mind that, Theodore—never mind that; think of yourself."

"I am not so lost as that; but, dear Margaret, you are starving. Stay, I have some of the provisions with which I stored myself from the madhouse; they will serve to stay the cravings of hunger till the morning; but, alas! I know not how to provide against the contingencies that may then arrive."

"Do not think of that. Endeavour to meet the present moment alone: that past, and the next will come on in succession."

" Ay, that it will, Margaret, in rapid succession, and faster than I can meet them with any chance of successfully doing so."

" I hope not; but do not despair."

"Despair! I have often. But yet, when you are nigh me, I ought not to do so—you whom I have loved so long and affectionately."

"No more of this, Theodore; the time for that is long since past. Think of me as one you have loved, and as a sister; as one who could devote her whole life to your service, in the hope of, in some measure, repaying the sufferings you have endured for my sake; think thus, and I ask no more."

" You are my better angel, Margaret —you have been the load-star of my existence; but envious fortune always deserted me. But your counsel is good, and it shall be as you desire."

"Then," said Margaret, "hadn't we better seek some place where we can lie concealed? for Bertram will, no doubt, endeavour to find me, and trace me out; then, indeed, my life is not safe, nor yours, should he get an opportunity of injuring you."

"Yes, yes, Margaret; I understand that well—very well, indeed. He who would injure you would injure me, too. But heed not that; I shall be by your side, and as he has fared, so will he fare again, if need be."

" I do not doubt that, dear Theodore; but where will you seek an asylum?"

"We will walk on until we find one," said Danton; "we can rest when we have gone on until we tire. But what is this?"

As he spoke, he held up in his hand a piece of the cloak he had torn from that which Bertram wore. Margaret shuddered as she looked at the ominous piece of the mantle.

" It is a portion of the black mantle that Bertram wears. It must be a sign of madness, I believe, for it cannot be worn by any one who is alive to the usages of life. It is strange and ominous: I cannot bear the sight of that funeral pall."

" It is strange."

They walked on for some time. The morning was beginning to lighten; a gray streak of light was in the east, and by degrees the clouds began to lose the inky blackness that hung over the earth. They walked on until they came to the outskirts of the town.

"Now," said Theodore Danton to Margaret, "we will sit down here for a while, and await the rising of the sun; then we can make our way into the country."

" Into the country?"

"Yes; we are now on the outskirts of the town; do you recognise the place?"

"Not by this light, Danton. But why do you leave London?" inquired Margaret.

" Because we shall be sought there, and shall not here; and I think, also, the air and scene will do you and me good. We can remain unquestioned. Moreover, at present I have no means, and there may be the possibility of obtaining some temporary shelter."

"Yes, I see."

" And then, Margaret, we should find it impossible in London to obtain a lodging upon any terms. They would not take us in, and the people there must know the business of every one as well as their own; they would require money down, and ere I could do that we should both starve."

" We should so, Theodore. Do what you deem best: I am content to follow you."

They again resumed their walk. The day was now advancing, and the sun shone upon the mists that hung upon the earth, and they were gradually drawing off, leaving a clear and pleasing landscape, so different to the miseries of the few previous days, that they could scarce believe they were in the same climate they had been in. The birds carolled gaily on the hedge-thorns, and the larks rose in the air, as their footsteps disturbed them.

" You see, Margaret, all nature seems most happy, and why should not we?"

" Yes, yes; all are happy, Theodore."

"We are?"

"Yes, yes; say no more—say no more on that subject now, Theodore. I have not slept for a long while, now, and can scarcely stand for fatigue."

" Dear, dear Margaret, what shall we do—where shall we go? Any place you see that you say stop at, there will I do so; or say that you wish me to do anything, and I will not hesitate."

"I know it, Danton—I know it."

"But will you remain here, and let me go on, and seek for some such place as that which will shelter and conceal us both?"

"No, no; we will not part—we will not part. We have parted once, and we met only by accident. The same may happen again. Oh, no—no, Theodore Danton; go on, I will follow you; though my limbs refused to move, still I would follow you with my eyes and good wishes."

"But I will not leave you, Margaret; though he who should have protected and cherished you in the hour of distress and need has left you, yet will not I. No, no—now I know you are destitute, my fortune shall be your fortune."

"I know your heart, Theodore, is ever generous and kind. We may not be so mistaken in the purposes of Heaven, as to suppose that we are entirely deserted —that neither aid or help of any kind are to be afforded us in our extreme poverty."

"Poor Margaret, how I pity you, and sorrow and regret your state. It must be a dreadful thing to be so deserted, and left with one so young. But I will do my utmost to make it up in the way of kindness and protection to you."

"I know you will, Theodore; but where are we now? Do you know what part we are in now? This seems all new to me."

"And so it is to me, Margaret; it is new, and it is even beautiful; and yet I think there is much that is strange and awful."

"Strange and awful, Theodore?"

"Yes."

"And why?"

"I cannot tell. It may be fancy; but I hear something like a death-knell."

"You?"

"Yes, I do. I might say I feel it rather than hear it. It is here."

And as he spoke, Theodore Danton put his hand up to his head.

Margaret noticed the action, and a pang of alarm shot through her brain, as she found that her first surmises were but too likely to turn out correct as regarded his sanity.

They continued to travel thus for an hour or more, until they both felt wearied and exhausted. For some reason or other, Theodore thrust his hand into his pocket in a moment of despair, as he looked upon his companion, who dragged her way along by his side, with evident signs of fatigue and distress.

For some motive—he could not tell why, but from a sudden impulse he could not resist—he commenced a very narrow search through all his pockets, and the result of which was, he discovered that he had yet a small piece of silver about him.

How it had escaped the hands of the hospital nurses, or the people at the madhouse, it was beyond his power to conceive.

CHAPTER LVI.

THE ROAD-SIDE HOUSE.—THE FIRST REST.—THE UNINHABITED COTTAGE.

ALMOST a smile of joy crossed his countenance as he looked at Margaret in silence, and then towards a small road-side house not far ahead. It was a little humble-looking place, but clean and neat; there was an air of prettiness about it that would take mightily with any one; and as Theodore Danton looked at it, his heart was elated, and he said to Margaret, in a tone that caused her to look up at him with surprise—

"Margaret?"

"Yes, Theodore."

"Do you see yonder road-side house?"

"I do."

"We will rest there."

"Do you know the people?"

"No."

"Will they allow you to do so?"

"Why, yes, Margaret; I find, thank the fates for your sake, I am not entirely without money."

"Indeed?"

"No. I knew not that before, nor can I at all understand how it is that I am not. But see, I have at once what will pay for some refreshment, and ensure you a few hours' rest."

"Thank God, indeed, for such a mercy! for I am all but quite sinking."

"Take my arm, and we will cross the road, and enter yonder room, where there seems to be a blazing fire."

Cheered by the prospects of such a

rest and the hope of food, induced her to struggle along, and they soon came to the house. It was called the Haymakers. There were seats outside the house, and hay-crates, and horse-troughs.

They entered the little parlour—they were alone—no one else had yet come in—it was early; but there were seats, and there was a good fire, and Margaret was chilly and fatigued.

They sat down, and soon after the host entered the room, walked up to the fire, which he stirred very carefully, and said, after a pause—

"Fine morning, sir, after so unpromising a day as yesterday was."

"Indeed, you are right," said Theodore; "but can we have breakfast here?"

"Yes, sir."

"And how soon?"

"We shall have some tea ready in half an hour, sir, and then you can have it."

"That will do."

The landlord paused, and pretended to be looking about, and dusting the various articles in the room, and then suddenly stopping, he said—

"It's cold this morning."

"Yes, it is."

"Have you come far?"

"Yes."

"Oh," said the landlord, somewhat puzzled and bothered at this answer, which was given in a very decisive but short manner, as if Theodore desired not to be annoyed with questions; still he was determined that he would not be thrown aback by this, but said—

"Come from town, sir?"

"Yes."

"Oh," said the landlord, again. "It's unpleasant walking this time in the morning."

"Yes, rather."

"Going far, sir?"

"Yes, rather."

"Oh," again said the landlord, who was now ashamed to push his questioning to any greater lengths, lest he should put what he called his foot in it; but having learnt so much, he quitted the room.

"Now that fool is gone, Margaret, how do you feel now? Are you any better?"

"I am thankful for the rest; and I feel so drowsy, that I can scarcely keep my eyes open."

"Then sit in that chair with the arms in it and sleep; you want it, and it will do you good; do so. I will remain here, and when the breakfast comes, I will awake you."

According to this advice, Margaret sat in the large arm-chair, and leaning back, she was in a very few moments sound asleep.

Theodore Danton sat brooding over the past, and reflecting on the future; but he was unable to point out to himself any precise course to be followed out with success and happiness.

He was completely abroad; but at the same time he never for one moment dreamed of altering the end or object of his life, viz.: to live and to benefit as much as he could the unfortunate Margaret.

He gazed upon the pale and wasted form of Margaret, and sighed as he looked at her, and he thought how different it would have been had she been the wife of another, and that other himself.

She would yet have been beautiful—she is yet beautiful; but there are the marks of distress and sorrow stamped upon her features that tell a tale indeed.

Thus he reflected, or rather thus his thoughts wandered, from subject to subject, until the breakfast was brought in.

The half hour in which the breakfast was to have been brought lengthened out considerably, and was as near an hour and a half as possible, when a mass of different people came in.

It was fortunate for Margaret that this was the case; for though so dreadfully fatigued and tired, yet she now woke her up; but she felt considerably refreshed by this sleep.

"Theodore," she said, "I have slept long, I fear, and you have been sitting watching here."

"I have," said Danton; "and it has given me more pleasure to see you take the rest that you so much need, than as if I had been to sleep myself."

"How long will it be before we have the breakfast in? We must have been here some time, and he spoke of half-an-hour."

At that moment the door opened and several labouring men, and carters, and such like, entered the room, and in a few minutes more they were followed by the landlord, who brought in a large tray, with a number of pint mugs, or pigs, filled with tea, and a plate to each, with some large slices of bread and butter.

These he placed upon the table, and began to serve round to each individual in his turn. Theodore Danton and Margaret were served along with the rest.

"You take tea, sir?" said the landlord, inquiringly, as he handed it to him.

"Yes."

"And your good lady?"

"Yes, certainly."

And forthwith they were accommodated with the viands so much in use.

They all sat in silence for some time. Theodore and Margaret both felt grateful for the refreshing beverage, and eat and drank in silence, and continued to gaze from time to time upon each other, and then upon the individuals who filled the parlour.

For some time all was silence, and few words were spoken among the countrymen, they being too much employed in eating. But when the edge of their appetites became a little blunt, one of them said,—

"Why, you are all so busy, you can't ax a fellow how he does."

"I suppose you've only found your tongue now. You are getting full—eh?"

"Well, and time, too—ain't it?" remarked the other with a broad grin. "I'm done; but if you ain't, why it's your fault, and not mine."

"That's very well of you, Carter; but Smalls is as good a hand at a bean feast as yourself."

"I think there's a pair," said another.

"Oh, yes; but Smalls likes to take things easy; he chews as if he wanted the taste twice over, and wouldn't be contented with one tasting."

"Oh, yes!" remarked the victim of their jokes: "Oh, yes! I like to have the most I can get for my money, and you are content to swallow all you get given to you, as if you were so many crocodiles, without regard as to what goes down."

"Ha! ha! ha! I wonder what sort of a fish a crocodile is; has he got horse hairs for a tail?"

"Yes, to be sure; and a pair of specs, like our parson, on his nose, which enables him to see while he's sleeping."

"I'm danged if our parson bean't always awake," said another; "you can't do him."

"Nor our'n."

"Have you tried?"

"Once or twice, a little; but it was no use; he was too many for me."

"Was he, now?"

"Yes."

"By the way, have any of you come down the road lately?"

"What road?"

"The road that runs off from the left yonder, before you come to the next turnpike-gate. The hard blue road as I call it."

"I know which you mean. It runs right ahead for many a mile, and then runs into the great north road, I think."

"Yes—the same."

"Well, what of it?"

"Only this. There's an empty cottage there, that I have seen to let for I don't know how many years—it is quite empty."

"Have you been in it?"

"No."

"Then it's a lucky thing you didn't."

"And why?"

"Because it is."

"But why?"

"Haven't I told you?"

"No."

"And haven't you heard?"

"No, I ain't."

"Why, it ain't been inhabited for scores of years. I never recollect any one living in it."

"Nor I."

"Nor I."

"But it was so once, for all that; but something happened there once—I may say twice or three times—that would prevent any one from living in it again. I wouldn't, and yet I don't care for much."

"It's a pretty place, too," remarked one of those in the room.

"So it is; but that don't make it any better. Why, what do you think was the cause of its being so long unlet?"

"I can't tell."

"It's a very unlucky house."

"And why?"

"Because the last three families had great misfortunes that befel them there —one after another, as fast as they came."

"What happened to 'em—eh?"

"The first family were nearly all poisoned, and yet nobody could tell how it was done; every search was made, but they could never detect the person who poisoned them."

"That might have been an accident, you know; and nobody might have been to blame."

"That is very true; but it couldn't be found out; and more than that, there were several who were poisoned who didn't eat or drink the same things."

"Ay, ay!"

"No. Besides, they would scarce any of them have done this themselves: they were different in habits, and their ages were different."

"It was an odd thing; but, at the same time, the house wasn't to blame."

"Oh, dear, no!—not at all; the house wasn't to blame, as you say— only there's no knowing the reason why a place is unlucky; if you could tell that, all would be right, and then one could guard against it; but here it was not; they couldn't tell nothing, only that people died, they thought from poison—but even that was only guess work."

"Oh! they didn't know they died of poison?"

"No."

"Oh! that makes a difference."

"So it does."

"And a great one, too."

"Exactly; for they may not have been poisoned at all, and nobody, then, could be found out."

"No; we know that; but they couldn't find out even the cause of death, and that made it so very suspicious."

"Well, go on."

"The next family that came had about two-thirds of its members carried off in a malignant fever of some sort, that nobody could tell anything about it, and the doctors could not cure it. Six out of nine persons died there."

"The devil the did!"

"I tell you that is a fact."

"It really was an unlucky house. Upon my word, I wouldn't live in such a place where there had been so many unaccountable evils taken place."

"Nor I."

"That's just what I said in the beginning," said the other; "and this is not all, neither."

"Not all!"

"No. There was another family, who took it after all this had happened."

"The deuce they did."

"They must have had some pluck, however."

"It is most probable they had never heard anything about it."

"Ah! that is likely now. Some strangers to the neighbourhood, I dare say."

"Yes, yes."

"Well, they came and took possession of the place, and lived happy enough, when one fine morning, three out of five of them were found dead in their beds, and nobody knew why."

"God bless me! what can be the cause of such a dreadful state of things?"

"Are you sure you aint joking?"

"Yes, quite sure on't; and, moreover, you may ask anybody in the neighbourhood if that ain't right, and they'll tell you that they believe that it is all true—quite true."

"I have heard something of the same sort myself," said the other countryman.

"You have?"

"Yes; but it's many years ago since the place was inhabited."

"How long?"

"A matter of five-and-forty, or maybe fifty years," he replied, "as far as I have heard say."

"Then this did not happen before that?"

"Oh, yes! but not long, though. Somebody was after it, but they heard all about it, and wouldn't have anything to do with it at all."

"They were in the right not to have anything to do with it; that would be to run a great chance of being done for easy enough."

"You may say that."

"Well, my time's up."

"And so is mine."

"Yes; and I must be on the road, or I shall have my master after me; and that won't do, considering I came away an hour and a half before he did."

"In a long day that may be made good, you know, and he may pitch you up,"

"He may; and he is just the sort of man that would, too, I tell you."

"Good morning."

"Good morning."

And thus, one after the other, they left the old inn, and each proceeded on his way.

Theodore Danton and Margaret were both seated by the fire, and had listened attentively to all that had passed, but had said nothing. Before others they shrank from conversing; but, at the same time, their minds were busily employed respecting each other; and now they were alone, Danton broke the silence.

"Margaret," he said, "you have heard what these men have been conversing about?"

"I did."

"About this deserted cottage?"

"Yes, Danton, I heard."

"Well, do you believe in the superstitious fears of these men, that it was the habitation that caused the death of these people, if they ever died at all, or anything of the kind took place?"

"No; I cannot, will not believe anything of the kind," said Margaret.

"Then we will go and live there for a time, at least; it will suit our plan of concealment very well. We shall be undisturbed. It shall suit our means until I can get money, and then it will suit our tastes and prospects of future life."

"I am satisfied," said Margaret; "let it be where it may, I will follow you, and there remain."

"Then we will at once proceed; for having paid for the breakfast, I have but a small sum left—a very small sum, not equal to a day's food."

"God's will be done, Theodore; but we cannot do more than resign ourselves to our fate. Heaven will surely not desert us entirely."

"Not entirely, perhaps, though so nearly so that we may perish; and yet in the meantime we must live, and attempt to get food and shelter; those are wants so purely necessary, that we cannot avoid doing. So we will go at once."

"I am ready, Danton, whenever you feel inclined to go. My rest and breakfast have so much refreshed me, that I feel hardly the same person. I was nearly starving."

"We have met, Margaret, and I am thankful for it, since you required help. We may make each other happy; and yet I feel as if in the future there was hope, and yet, again, I have fears."

"Your mind is disquieted. Think no more; but let us leave this place at once, and proceed towards this cottage."

They now arose, and, having paid the landlord, Theodore Danton and Margaret Bertram left the Haymakers, and proceeded towards the road in which the cottage was situated.

CHAPTER LVII.

THE DESERTED COTTAGE.—THE ILL-NESS OF THEODORE DANTON.—THE DESTITUTION OF DANTON AND MARGARET.

THE sun now shone warmly, and the day presented a cheerful and happy appearance; the mists of the night had been drawn up, and the view across the country was beautiful in the extreme, True it was, the foliage was off the trees, the hedgerows and branches were all bare of foliage; but there were the green fields to relieve the eye.

The green fields, even in winter, have a beautiful and gay appearance, especially when enlivened by a little sunshine and a cloudless sky. At such times the birds sing, and nature seem to rejoice, and the heart of man rejoices also. How could it be otherwise? for when was not the example of such a place contagious?

The heart of him who cannot rejoice in nature, must be woe-worn, or steeped in guilt too deeply to feel the genial effects that such things have upon the souls of more favoured mortals.

Such was not the case with Theodore and Margaret, though Heaven knew they had enough to weigh them down to the very earth, in the way of affliction. They had had enough to have destroyed mind and body in many; but yet they lived. This, however argued no insensibility on their parts;

quite the reverse; but their feelings were so well balanced, that they did not seem to carry passion to so great an excess that it blinded and subdued all other faculties.

Grief sometimes sharpens the senses, and renders them more than usually acute. So it was with Margaret Bertram, and so with poor Theodore Danton, whose mind, however, was so much confused, that at times he was scarcely in a condition to take care of himself.

"Yes, yes," he would mutter; "all are beautiful—heaven and earth—and yet what can man enjoy of it, unless he have other things? These things are given us in a state which we cannot enjoy. Circumstances must concur, else we cannot enjoy that which is given us. 'Tis a pity the enjoyment of one thing should depend upon so many others."

They walked onward for some distance, and after a time they came to the road where they had to turn off as they neared the turnpike.

Here they went some distance. All was cheerful and happy, save these two; and yet their unhappiness consisted in the feeling of sorrow for each other, rather than for themselves.

"Well, Margaret," said Theodore, "all around seems happy and bright; why should not we?"

"Oh, Theodore! we may be so yet, and should be so if many things that have happened had not; but we must bear our lot, and do our duty, then we may have happiness at last in reflection."

"That is true; and yet reflection sometimes employs memory, and then something like unhappiness will peep out. But there is the cottage, I think."

"Yes, yes," said Margaret. "I see it is very lonely."

"I am glad of that."

"Yes; it will be more convenient."

"And safer."

"Would you go in now?"

"Yes, unless you wish it should be otherwise."

"No, no. I am fatigued, and shall be glad to sit down."

They once more proceeded on in silence, until they came to the cottage, when they paused to look at it, and examine its exterior.

"It is very old and crumbling, but not very large," observed Theodore.

"No; but large enough to have held a tolerably numerous family."

"It has held such."

"So we heard at the public-house."

"And it will hold us."

"I wonder if ever the owner comes to examine it, or if any one walks over it."

"Some one comes," said Theodore, "Well, we'll ask whose cottage it is' and some few questions."

In a few moments a kind of labouring man came up, and who noticed them.

"Whose cottage is 'that, friend?" inquired Theodore Danton, pointing to it.

"That cottage there?".

"Yes."

"Whoy, that be Mister Gubbins's."

"Where does he live?"

"Not very far. Maybe four or five miles like; but he beant there."

"Where then?"

"Whoy, they say he be somewhere in Hungry! but where that be, whoy I don't know; but it's a plaguy long way, as I've heard."

"Who has the place to let, then?"

"Whoy, nobody, as I knows; but it lets itself, cause nobody won't live in it."

"I see."

"Nobody won't take care of it; or it's a nisish place after all; but people die do so plaguy oddly, that they can't live an they will."

"Indeed."

"Oh, yes; I know one or two who've died there; and nobody never even goes into it."

"Quite deserted?"

"Oh, quite—quite. Nobody goes there. 'Tis a great pity, after all,

'cause the place is a good 'un, though I'd sooner live anywhere else."

"Why do people die in it?"

"Oh, I can't say."

"How do you know the unfortunate house is the cause of their deaths? Does it arise from sinks or anything connected with the place?"

"Yes; it must be something of the sort, 'cause they never died afore, you know, leastway in that way, which makes a world and all a difference. There's something in the place. The fact is, it's an unlucky house, and he who goes in there will be a dead man as I look upon it."

"Indeed."

"Yes, master; I don't say the house is bad, or the place at all bad; but it is an unlucky house, and that's saying enough, master, for anything. 'Better be born lucky than rich,' say I; that's my motto, master."

"And a very good one too. Good day."

"Good day," said the man, and he walked on, leaving them alone, yet gazing at the cottage.

"Do you fear to go on, Margaret?" inquired Theodore. "Say but the word, and I will turn aside, and seek some other shelter. It will be but temporary, you know, at the most. When I can be assured of my safety, I will secure the means of life; for I am alone in London, and I fear I shall not obtain what is my own for a greater time than we can subsist. To think that I should have fallen into such a train of circumstances at such a moment as this!"

"Do not let these considerations, at such a moment, give you unnecessary uneasiness. I have no fears of the terrors of the place; they are doubtless exaggerated, if they exist at all; but I think they may altogether prove untrue."

"Yes: or if not, easily explained by natural causes."

The place was well fenced round, and though it might be rotten in places, yet it had not been broken down, and it was difficult to choose a place where they could easily get in at.

After some time spent in walking about, they found a place that was not observable at once to any one, only they who had been at pains to search, as they had been who now discovered it.

"Margaret," said Theodore, "let me aid you. I will get through first; then give me your child, and I will take it while you get through."

Margaret did as he had said, and they both soon after trod in the garden that surrounded the house everywhere, as it were, with rankness and weeds. There was scarce a foot of it but what had its appropriate weed, that overran the spot. The whole place looked like a wilderness.

"Here, at least, Margaret, we shall be safe from the fear of interruption; and now to get in if we can. There must be some means of entrance. We will go round to the back of the house."

They both walked round the cottage till they got to the back.

It was a pretty Gothic cottage; but one that had had no settled plan of building, for there was no order or regularity of plan. It was the more picturesque and convenient for this, no doubt.

After some search, Theodore came to a small door, which, however, seemed not to open until he put his shoulder to it and forced it in.

"Here we have now shelter. Margaret—enter. Heaven knows how tired you must be—enter. 'Tis a poor welcome, this—a very poor welcome."

"Do not talk about such things; but do you come in, and obtain some rest yourself; I am sure you are ill."

"Nothing — nothing, Margaret; I assure you, I'm only grieved for your sake."

Margaret saw, or thought she saw the lingering traces of long illness in Danton's countenance — he seemed flushed since he had breakfasted—his eyes were dilated, and a strange expression came from them that she did not like. It seemed something like the signs of insanity; indeed, he was flighty, as it was termed, even then, and he seemed to be wandering every now and then; and it was only by fits and starts that he now addressed her, and then he abruptly ceased to speak. He every now and then gazed upon

her with sorrow and tenderness, as if he lamented her fate, but said nothing respecting it.

They now entered the house, but such a cloud of black dust arose as soon as they set foot into it, that they were compelled to tread very cautiously.

"This has, indeed, not been entered for some years," exclaimed Theodore Danton.

"No; such a layer of dust could not accumulate without a number of years passing over in solitude. How damp it smells."

"Damp!"

"Yes; do you not smell it?"

"Oh, yes, I do; that comes through the flood."

"The flood!"

"Yes, the deluge."

"Good heavens! what are you taking about, Danton?" said Margaret, half terrified.

"Yes, dear Margaret; I was speaking of the forty days' rain, when the deluge happened. Doctor Johnson might, indeed, well inquire if it always rained in those parts; but Noah was too far gone in wine to give him any answer, you know."

Margaret Bertram, when she heard these words, could have fallen to the earth. She groaned deeply, as she said to herself—

"It is as I thought—it is as I thought; his mind has given way beneath the load of affliction and illness he has suffered. Poor Danton—poor Danton! what an undeserved fate have you met with. God grant me strength, and I will attend upon you, and do all in my power to restore to you the use of those faculties that now seem wavering."

"We must have a fire, Margaret."

"Yes, Danton; it will be necessary."

"I will make one; I will go and find materials for a fire, somewhere or other."

In a few moments Margaret heard him walking about from room to room, and then came a tremendous crash, as if something had been thrown down and broken.

Margaret was seated on a kind of settle, near the window, and waited until his return, which was not very long.

"See," he said; "I have taken an old door that was hanging half down; it is good fuel, because it is dry, and most fit for such a purpose; we will soon dispose of the damps."

He set about laying some of the smaller pieces of dry wood, and some paper, and then having done that, he paused.

"Were is the light to come from?" inquired Margaret, doubtfully, as she watched his actions.

"From my pocket."

"From your pocket," she replied, slowly. "What can he mean? Alas —alas! he is worse than I thought him."

"When I escaped from the madhouse I provided against any want of that kind; I have some instantaneously lighting matches;" and as he spoke, he produced them, and soon obtained a light by their means, and in a few minutes more the wood was crackling and flaring in the grate of the deserted house.

CHAPTER LVIII.

THE SEARCH THROUGH THE DESERTED HOUSE.—MELANCHOLY AND GRIEF OF MARGARET.—THE FIRST MEAL IN THE HOUSE.

THE feelings of Margaret Bertram when she saw the bright gleams of the fire, and heard the flames crackling from the wood which was in the grate, were gratifying enough. She could rest, and Heaven knew she was fatigued to an excess: and Theodore Danton felt relieved from apprehension when he seated himself in that long empty apartment.

Those were trains of reflection that suggested themselves to the minds of each. Margaret congratulated herself upon her escape from the injustice of her husband.

"He would have killed me," she said to herself, "he would have killed me; and Theodore Danton has saved me from such a fate as Bertram would have inflicted. Heaven is merciful, and I will endeavour to repay him by tenderness and care for his few wants.

While I live, I never will leave him, nor cease to be grateful for that service; and he will never be what he was once. I tremble to look at him, lest I should hear something that shows the mental disorder that has seized upon his mind.

Then she looked upon the infant she carried in her arms. What a life its father had left her to live! And what prospects had the innocent, helpless babe before it? None, but such as its mother had provided for it—or such as the unfortunate Theodore Danton might be able to give it; or such as the peculiar tenor of his mind might induce him to afford.

A thousand thoughts such as these crossed her mind; were Danton free in his intellects, she was convinced he would not hesitate to act even a father's part towards the child, for it was her child; but as it was—as there was a prospect of his becoming worse, and in that disordered state of mind caused by such a train of misfortunes and adventures, she knew not what she could expect from him.

However, she would act her part— do her duty towards her child, and be a faithful and disinterested nurse and attendant upon the unfortunate Theodore Danton.

He too, had his reflections. He saw in the future a round of events that he thought might be in store. The wheel of fortune had many turns yet to take ere his adventurous life could be closed.

"I have passed through many adventures, many reverses, and, lately, many terrible events have occurred around me—things that have been a scourge to my mind, an infliction upon my reason to think of them—and yet I live. I have been in a madhouse, but they little thought I deserved my fate. They who sent me there little thought that my crazed imagination would have, had its state been known, justified them in sending me there.

"But I am free now. They will not now find me; they will not seek for me here; they will not, in fact, look after me. I was there but a hospital patient, for whom nobody cares, and no one will inquire about me."

Thus Theodore Danton sat employing his thoughts, while his eyes were fixed upon the fire that blazed in the grate, and threw out a warmth in that apartment where such a sight had not been seen for many years.

Margaret Bertram sat watching him, fearful lest she should disturb the tranquillity of mind that seemed to pervade him at that moment. When she saw him look up, she then spoke.

"Theodore," she said.

"Well, Margaret ?"

"I am thankful—very thankful; we have, at least, a place of rest and shelter, where we are free of interruption and intrusion of all kinds."

"Yes, yes," he remarked; "we are safe—quite safe here; no one will think of looking after me here. I am sure just such another place cannot be found within the three kingdoms. I would not change it for any money."

"I wonder if the old place contains any articles of furniture, or is perfectly empty ; that there are, in fact, no other persons here but ourselves."

"Eh ?" said Danton; "no one else here but ourselves ? Oh, no; we are quite alone."

"Have you been over the house ?"

"No; but I could tell if there had been any human being in here recently. Traces of it would have been left which it would have been impossible to efface under something like, at least, a month's favourable circumstances."

"Indeed, Theodore ?"

"Yes ; I am sure of it; and yet I will look over the place before dark, because we shall want some firewood ; if there be any conveniences we shall need them. Now I think of it, I will go at once."

"Do, Danton; but be sure you come back."

"Do you imagine I could desert you? Oh, no, no, Margaret. Now I know you are ill-used, I will do my best to protect you from evils of all kinds and character. True it is, the home I here have to offer you is little better than that of a beggar's, yet I shall have, by-and-bye, a better."

"Name it not, Danton. We have been thrown together in the midst of misfortune. Do not, then, speak to me of what may be in your power. I trust you may have all that you hope and wish."

"I have it, Margaret, but cannot at this moment go and seek it. I fear lest those people who had me secured within their vile place should institute a search, and offer a reward; and for the sake of a few pounds, some persons may secure me, and consign me to the same horrible cell again. That would, then, be the last of my connection with the world."

"Think not of it, Danton—think not of it. While we are here, I will get all that can be wanted by us at some distance from this place. They can have no suspicion of my knowing anything of you."

"Oh, no, no; that will do; I shall be safe enough, without doubt. I will now go and look over the place from one end of it to the other."

He arose and left the room, and his footsteps sounded through the hollow house with dismal sounds and mournful echoes. The windows vibrated ; and yet, strange to tell, there were but few panes of glass broken ; but through these the wind came in fitful gusts.

Room after room he entered, but they presented nothing but the black dust that so soon collects in empty houses. Here it lay on the floor more like a carpet ; and, save where the winds had swept across in one particular channel, and cleared the dust away, the sound of the footsteps were subdued ; but elsewhere the hollow, reverberating sound rang through the whole house.

Room after room did Theodore Danton enter, and yet he found nothing. The house had been thoroughly cleaned out. No article of any utility had been left to the mercy of any individual who might come at a future time.

"It is all empty," said Theodore, as he entered the last room, and gazed around, — "all empty. They have cleared out very clean, indeed. Oh ! this is a closet—empty too, of course ; but I may as well look."

He walked up to the closet, and then opened it; but he found some trouble in doing so. He forced the door; it was old and mouldy from decay, and soon came open, despite the small lock that held it together.

He looked in, and then beheld, to his surprise, an old mattress and a rug, and some things connected with the bedding; he laid hold of it, and found it all very damp and mouldy from long keeping.

"Come," he thought, "this, at least, is a convenience; for to sleep on those dusty boards is more than what is proper, or can be done for any length of time; fatigue might, indeed, induce sleep; but, beyond that, you must not expect rest upon the bare boards, however soft they may be. But have we not a fire? Put it before that till night, and I'll warrant it will be pretty dry; and, if not, it will be safer than these boards."

Being satisfied about this, he pulled them out of the closet, and placed them at the head of the stairs, and was about to descend, when he espied a ladder that led to the loft above the rooms he was then in.

"I will go up here, and see what there is to be seen," he said; "and then I can say I have seen and know the resources of the house."

So saying, he stepped up the ladder, but he was compelled to use much caution in doing so, for the ladder was very rotten, and he was by no means sure that he was not doomed to a fall, in consequence; however, he got to the top, and lifted the trap up, and pushed it on one side, and then looked into the vacant space.

For a few moments he could see nothing; but, at the same time, he was aware that the change of light to dark by no means aided the eyes, and so, remaining for near five minutes, he began to distinguish objects.

The red pantiles presented orifices enough to let in small beams of light, which seemed to render the place just visible to the eyes, when they became a little accustomed to the subdued light that entered the loft.

Here was not much—a couple of old chairs, that seemed as if they had been thrown up, because they were useless lumber.

"These may as well come down," muttered Theodore, as he pulled one out and dropped it down, and then the other came rattling and bumping along, stopping only when it got to the bottom.

There was nothing more, and Danton descended the very doubtful ladder, and when down he began to descend with his spoil to the room below, where he had left Margaret and her child.

"Here, Margaret," he said, "I have found some few things; they will serve to make this place more convenient than it would be without them."

"They will, Theodore; undoubtedly they will; it is fortunate, I am sure, very fortunate that you have found them."

"Yes; this is damp, and will require drying; the fire is gone low, I will replenish it from below."

So saying, he arose, and throwing on the fire the few remaining sticks there were, he went down stairs to procure more, from what source there was—the old doors and other matters below promised an abundant supply for some time to come. Having broken up as much as he could carry, he took it up, and then returned to Margaret Bertram.

"Here," he said, "is fuel enough to last four-and-twenty hours at the least."

He then laid it down, and placed some more on the fire, and then he placed the mattrass and the rug, so that they would be dried before night.

He looked around, and saw the sun was sinking towards the west, and then, for the first time, he remembered his own wants and those of Margaret.

"Margaret," he said, suddenly.

"Theodore," she replied.

"The sun is setting, and it was not very long after sunrise that we took our last and only meal during this day."

"It was, Danton,"

"Then it is time that we had another."

Margaret was afraid of saying it was, for she knew that there was nothing there that could be had; and she knew that the small change that Theodore had received at the Haymakers was hardly sufficient to buy bread.

"I know not how we shall get one," pursued Theodore, "but we cannot go to bed supperless; the money that I have with me is so small in amount that I almost fear to say I could get anything."

"We must be content, Theodore;

we cannot do impossibilities, none can do that; what we cannot obtain we must truly do without."

"But I will try and obtain something, be it ever so poor; that will, at least, be something to prevent the cravings of nature till to-morrow."

"Then we must hit upon some plan of support; if nothing presents itself I will beg."

"Do not name such an alternative. I cannot listen to such an alternative; you shall never do so. Things will not come to such a state."

"I hope not: but the worst can but happen; the best may come to pass."

"We will not hope or expect, but believe that all will be well yet."

"Never again, Theodore; but no more of that. Let us be thankful that we are so far safe and clear of enemies."

"There is much in that," said Danton; "but keep up a good heart, and I will do my best to make things as well as they will admit. I will now go to the nearest place where I can obtain some kind of food."

So saying, Theodore Danton left the old house, and Margaret Bertram could hear the sound of his footsteps as he quitted the house, and then along the path belonging to the garden, and then all was still. She could not hear those sounds any more; he had left the cottage, and was in the main road in search of some place where he could obtain food.

CHAPTER LIX.

THE DISTRESS OF MARGARET, AND THEODORE DANTON'S ILLNESS.— THE LAST RESOURCE.

WHEN Theodore Danton returned, he found Margaret Bertram in tears. She was so absorbed in her own grief that she heard him not when he entered the room. He stood for a few moments gazing upon her. She sobbed violently, and Danton felt that poor Margaret had much—very much, to grieve for.

"Margaret," he said, in a low voice, "Margaret, dear Margaret, why do you weep?"

But Margaret heard him not.

"Margaret," he said, in a louder tone, "Margaret?"

Margaret lifted up her head, and gave a start at seeing him in the room.

"I heard you not," she said; "you came in very quietly. Have you been in long?"

"No, Margaret; neither did I come in quietly; but you have been weeping."

"I have."

"And yet weep?"

"I do."

"Cease, dear Margaret; you have nothing about which you need weep."

"Much, much."

"Not that you need blame yourself about. Your acts and deeds have all been such that you need not weep further; you are purity itself."

"I know I have wronged no one; but then it is the heavy penalty of another's mistakes and crimes that I am to be under, and to conquer them or perish."

"Conquer them, Margaret."

"But the power may be wanting."

"No, no; it must not be so—it shall not be so; if you sink, Margaret, I shall never survive."

"We will not talk of it; forgive me, Danton, but I knew not you were present, or my grief should not have been visible; but there, 'tis gone now."

As she spoke, she dried her tears, but she could not destroy the traces of them; they were too deeply marked upon her features to be so momentarily eradicated.

"I have obtained food, such as it is; it is simple, indeed, but it is all I could obtain."

They both sat down to the poor and simple meal, and both ate sparingly, for there was something upon the mind of either of them that seemed to fly from conversation.

The night now came on, and the sun was set; darkness seemed to pervade all nature.

"Theodore?" said Margaret.

"Yes, Margaret, what would you say?"

"Are there any fastenings below?"

"I believe so."

"Will you not use them?"

"If you desire it, though there can be no use in doing so, since you may rest assured that no one, not even for a very large sum, would come to this house, of which they are so much afraid."

"Well, as you think proper, Theodore. I thought our fire might attract some one."

"It would scare them."

"But some may not be fearful, Theodore; and if we should have occasion to be disturbed, we had better hear them before we see them."

"That is true, and I will secure the doors, then."

Theodore Danton secured the doors, to satisfy the fears of Margaret.

In a short time he returned, and said, "How my head aches and swims."

"Indeed, you are ill."

"I know not; there seem noises in the air, and the room seems to go round. God of Heaven, this must be madness! Margaret, tell me, am I in command of a thousand legions of spirits, or am I dreaming?"

"You had better seek rest, Danton; you require it—you are very ill."

She laid her child down in one corner, and drew the mattress from its position, and threw it down, saying,—

"Come, Theodore, sleep; you want it. Try, for Heaven's sake, to obtain rest. All depends upon your health."

"It does, Margaret," said Danton, and he threw himself upon the mattress.

Margaret Bertram sat by the fire with her infant in her arms, and she gazed upon its bright flickering flames as they shot upwards. She thought of the destitution that had assailed her and her infant, the murderous attempt of her husband, from whom she had only escaped with life by the aid of Theodore Danton. He was indeed her saviour, while she had been the rock upon which he had been wrecked. His love for her had been the cause of all this mischief.

As these thoughts passed through her mind, she looked upon the sleeping form of Danton, who lay overpowered by fatigue and weakness from his recent illness.

His slumbers were disturbed—he was restless. Half-formed mutterings came from his lips, and his hands were clenched, and he threw them about from side to side with frantic gestures.

"He sleeps but ill," she said; "he is yet disturbed in his mind. I would he were calmer, but he is alternately flushed and then pale; his eyes dull, or lighted up with more than mere intelligence—

by a frenzy almost amounting to madness."

She paused and rocked herself to and fro. The night was far advanced, and poor Margaret, overcome with sleep, fell into a doze, after having made the fire up, leaning her head against the wall.

She was aroused after a time by some frantic exclamation of Danton. Half terrified, and fearing she knew not what, she started to her feet, utterly unable to understand what had happened; half asleep too, she did not recollect where she was, or how she came there.

"In Heaven's name!" she exclaimed, "what has happened? Oh, tell me what has happened!"

No one spoke, and she looked upon the mattress where Theodore lay, and saw him there in a deep sleep, but motioning with his hands, and his lips were moving.

"I see, I see," said Margaret. "It is a dream; and yet I thought I heard a dreadful shriek."

She rose and threw some more fuel on the fire.

"The room is damp and ill aired," she said, "and a fire is the greatest comfort we can know under the circumstances; it will warm us, and draw off the damps."

She examined the door, and the fastenings were as they had been; and she became satisfied that she must have dreamt, and awoke in the midst of her dream.

"I see I must sleep for the sake of my child," she muttered; and taking the rug, she wrapped it round herself and child, and lay down on the mattress, and soon fell into a deep slumber.

*   *   *

It was morning. The sun shone into the chamber, and the two sleeping fugitives were yet deeply drinking of the draught of oblivion that was given them in the form of sleep, and their cares were buried with their consciousness.

Happy moment! Who would be awake and feel misfortune, want, and misery, while sleep would refresh the body and ease the mind for a time of the heavy burden that weighs it down?

The unfortunate Margaret Bertram awoke, and looked around her from side to side; she sat up and saw where she was;

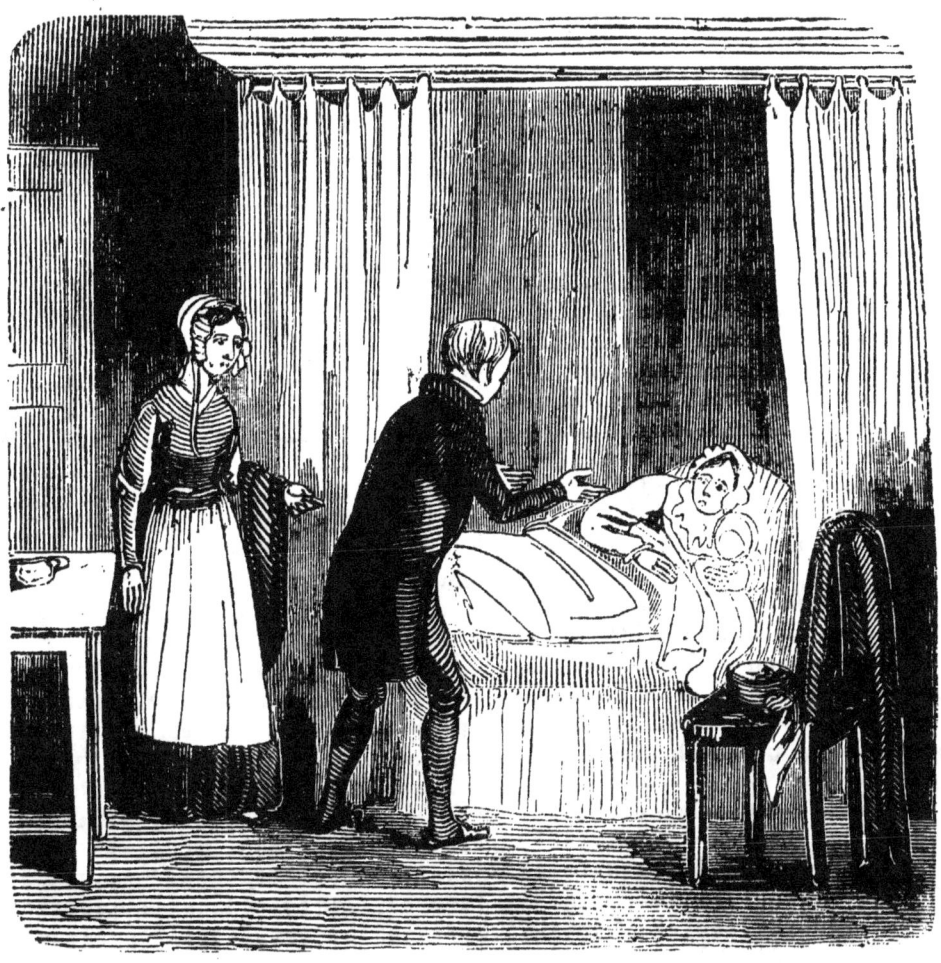

MARGARET IN HER ILLNESS ATTENDED BY THE OLD GENTLEMAN.

and then her eye fell upon the form of Danton. She started, and looked in his face.

"He is ill," she muttered "very ill."

She arose softly, and laying her child down, lit the fire as cautiously as she could, and then proceeded to examine the state of her unfortunate companion.

"Theodore!" she exclaimed, "Theodore!"

But there was no answer.

"Theodore!" she called, in a louder voice, as she laid her hand upon his shoulder.

"Are you awake, Danton? Do you hear me?"

Danton turned himself, and looked vacantly for some time, and then said, with a ghastly smile,—

"Water, Margaret, water!"

"What has happened?"

"Water!"

Margaret rose. She knew not what to do; but after a careful search, she found a jug that had been thrown away, because the spout and handle had been broken off. In this she obtained some water and gave it to him. He drank it, and fixing his heavy eyes upon her, he said,—

"Thanks, Margaret, thanks. I am very ill—very ill, indeed. I know not what is coming over me, but the room seems to go round, and I can hardly see. I am hot—burning hot—my brain seems burning."

Here he groaned aloud, and seemed to fall asleep, or in a state of insensibility.

This continued the whole of the day, and Margaret waited on him as a sister. The only food she took was what remained from that which Danton had brought in the preceding evening, and some water.

In the garden she found some fruit

that was ripe, and had fallen from the trees; these were all she could offer to Danton.

Theodore remained insensible nearly all the day; he was sensible a few hours during the day, but only at times, and he was completely prostrated; a fever had seized upon him, and his delirium seemed to increase.

The next day she was reduced to an extremity for food. Not a morsel of any kind was to be found in the house. However, fortune favoured her this much; Danton had yet a small ring on his finger. Driven to desperation, she begged him to give the ring to her, but he was unable to comprehend her wants, till, driven to extremity, she drew the ring off his finger while he was insensible.

Scarcely knowing what she did, she left the house and made the best of her way to London, and sold it. With the produce of that she procured some necessary articles of food, and something especially for the use of Theodore in his disorder.

It was nearly night before she was able to reach her destination. She entered the house as before, and found the fire was out, and Danton raving.

"Margaret," he said, "Margaret, where is the long-cherished and deeply-loved one? Where is she for whom I toiled, and who was torn from—— Ay, where is she?"

"Danton, Danton, I am here. Look up!"

It was useless. Danton continued insensible, and thus remained for many days, Margaret being in extreme want and destitution. Sometimes even food was very scarce and difficult to be had; so much so, that her appearance became greatly altered for the worse.

Day after day passed thus, and yet there was no apparent abatement in Danton's illness or in Margaret's distress; but she still continued her untiring exertions in waiting upon the unfortunate man.

CHAPTER LX.

CONCERNING MRS. BLAIR. — HER FIRST ADVENTURES AFTER PARTING WITH HER SISTER, MRS. PRIMROSE. — HER PROBABLE COURSE.

MRS. BLAIR parted with her sister, Mrs. Primrose, under circumstances of considerable aggravation, in the open streets. They had both been turned out of house and home, or, rather, Mrs. Primrose had, and as Mrs. Blair had no better title than the former, she was compelled to follow; having got into her own possession the greater share of the produce of the things sold from the house of her sister, as well as those purloined from the house of the unfortunate and much injured Margaret Bertram.

Thus it was Mrs. Blair was in possession of some funds, to which she was by no means entitled, to carry on the war for some time longer.

Nothing daunted, though considerably embittered, if that were necessary, by the mishaps that had already taken place to baffle her, she determined to assume a high hand, take a lodging, and seek out for some new engagement elsewhere.

The past was no experience to her for the conduct of the future, only to induce her to exert greater fraud and cunning than before; for such people always attribute their failure to the fact that they have not been wily enough, and not that such palpable acts of injustice cannot possibly go on without detection, or that the uncertainty of human purposes can be controlled and directed into a channel, especially directed to carry their own schemes to the desired harbour.

Thus it was that Mrs. Blair determined, and when she should get another chance — and another chance she promised herself she would have, despite her present uncomfortable circumstances, to exert a greater amount of cunning and duplicity than she had hitherto done.

She obtained a lodging, and began, as much as possible, to feast on whatever friends she had left. She had made a good many what you may call friends—visiting acquaintances—who received her because she was one of their sort. She was particularly religious, and so were they; but these, after a time, found out how matters stood, and gave her the cold shoulder.

That, however, was just the thing Mrs. Blair could very well put up with. She wouldn't see anything that she didn't like. She became, consequently, the more and more religious.

She was perseverance in the extreme. She could not see the coldness of this one, or the neglect of that. It was useless for them to look at the clock, get fidgety, and wonder what sort of night it was, and express their opinion, that, although it didn't rain then, it would soon.

All was to no purpose. She always stopped till supper was disposed of, and then she went home to her own lodgings, to sleep but not eat.

It was thus things went on for some time, until at length one of the principal feasting houses would put up with it no longer. It so happened that Mrs. Blair had been busy in fomenting a quarrel between man and wife, and incurred the dislike of both parties.

Soon after, the quarrel was made up, and Mrs. Blair incurred the most special dislike of both parties, especially the head of the house, who determined to be revenged on the lady the next time she came.

It was supper time; an hour Mrs. Blair frequently took advantage of, and called in to finish the day with less expense to herself than convenience to others.

"Ah!" exclaimed Mrs. Blair, as she entered; "how do you do? You're looking charming, Mrs. Bent."

"Pretty well, I thank you."

"And you, Mr. Bent?"

"Much in the same mind as before."

"What regular people you all are."

"Yes, we are; but why?"

"You always sup at one hour to five minutes. There's no passing your house: and when one calls, it is sure to be at your meals."

"That's very true."

"Don't let me disturb you. I can talk, you know."

"Yes, I am quite aware of that; but we cannot see you sit out there. It's quite uncomfortable."

"Oh you always make me so welcome."

"Yes, indeed, you are welcome."

"I am sure of it."

"You do as we do?"

"I shall be most happy."

"Then, Mrs. Blair," said the gentleman, in a calm, quiet tone, "you are very welcome to do as we do—sup at home."

"Eh?"

"Sup at home."

"When I next call at your place, sir, the invitation shall be the other way."

"I mean it to be so, madam."

"Irreligious wretch!"

"Oh very!"

"Impious mortal!"

"Singularly so."

"Mrs. Bent, I will call and see you at some other time, when we can have that consolation left us of conversing on religious topics, and the welfare of the soul."

"I have ceased going to chapel," said the lady.

Mrs. Blair was staggered.

"I don't intend to go any more."

"Dreadful!"

"And I consider the Reverend Jeremiah Shark as a great impostor. I don't go near him again."

"Merciful Heaven! how great is thy goodness, when least it is apparent. The utter destruction of this man and woman is to me the removal of a stumbling block I never, until this moment, thought or imagined to exist. But," she added, "the removal of the stocks and the stones, in the path of the righteous ——"

"The sooner you remove yourself, Mrs. Blair, the less chance there will be of your being personally inconvenienced by the aid of the servant."

"You are a wretch!"

"Yes, of course."

"And ought to be pounded alive."

"And made into a paste to anoint suffering souls with," remarked Mr. Bent; "and in the meantime I shall sit down and enjoy my mutton."

So saying, the gentleman began to cut away at a very handsome leg of mutton.

There was no help for it; but out

she went, and the street door was closed for ever upon her.

This was something of a vexation to Mrs. Blair, for at that moment her funds were very low.

It was some time since she had seen her sister; and, despite all she could do towards eking out her funds, yet they gradually diminished, until the last five shillings were alone in her purse.

It was now a matter of calculation as to how long she could exist; but, all she could do in that way, under very favourable circumstances, and pursuing the sponging system to the full, she could not hope to last out a week.

Her rent had not been paid for a month, and the landlady was becoming more and more urgent, and things wore a very threatening aspect altogether.

She had striven rather hard to obtain a footing in some family, but they all shrunk from it, and viewed her approaches with suspicion; and now that she had become more abject, mean, and cringing, she was viewed with more suspicion than even when she bore herself differently.

"She is only more pressed by necessity," they argued; "not that she is not at all altered in her aims and objects; they are the same, but she is pricked on more sharply than ever; the danger threatened in her approach is just the same, perhaps greater than ever."

Thus it was with Mrs. Blair.

One evening when she came home, the landlady met her on the stairs and said, holding her hands towards her,—

"The week's up, now."

"What week, Mrs. Bennett?"

"Why, my week; my rent's due now.

"Oh, yes, it is. I didn't understand you."

"You do now, though?"

"Yes, Mrs. Bennett, yes."

"Well, then, hand us over the rent."

"I really haven't got it, but——"

"You haven't got it?"

"No, but——"

"Then how dare you go for to take for to occupy my 'partments, and give me no rent?"

"I don't mean to do so."

"But you do."

"Indeed I do not, Mrs. Bennett."

"Then give us the rent."

"I haven't got it."

"That's just what I say; it's all blessed gammon, and I won't be done this way—my room ain't a-going to be okepied by people as pays no rent."

"But I will."

"Oh, gammon."

"Well I have not got it now, but to-morrow I will either borrow it, or raise it somehow or other."

"Oh, I des-say; you very religious people always intends a do at the last; you comes it so very strong in the prayer meeting line. Now, people as pays their rent may pray, and with a good face, too, but not them as don't. It's no use your going up stairs, now."

"Why not?"

"Because you can't—you'd better toddle."

"Well, but I must sleep in my own apartment; you drive things too hard. I must enter into my own room; I am, by law, entitled to do so."

"Oh, very well; if you sleeps there, you'll sleep along with my man, that's all."

"What!"

"You'll have to sleep with my man —I don't mind, it's only once in a way, and nobody'll know anythin' about it, when you are fairly gone."

"What horrid depravity! Woman —woman, I thought you—even you, had some sense of shame."

"If I have, you ain't."

"To think of offering me her husband, as if I'd——"

"What!" exclaimed the landlady, furiously; "who said anythin' about my husband? He's a hard working 'dustrous man, as ever broke bread or dusted shoe leather."

"Did you not say I must sleep with your husband?"

"My husband, you hussy!—no, my man."

"Your man! oh, horrible wickedness! She is not content with her husband, but she must have a very improper connexion with some man— Oh, fie, fie!"

"Well, I'm blow'd," exclaimed the enraged landlady, "if this ain't coming it. I tell's you what, you're a good-for-nothin' hypocrite; blow yer, you wagrant, as can't pay yer rent; why, I should be ashamed of myself, if I was you."

"But who, then, do you say is to sleep in my bed? I'll pay no rent, if I have not the possession of my own room."

"You can go in."

"But nobody else besides?"

"Yes; a broker."

"You don't mean to say you have put a broker into your own room?" exclaimed Mrs. Blair.

"I shouldn't put him into anybody else's."

"But there is only your own furniture," said Mrs. Blair, "for I have none, as you know."

"But you have some boxes and odd matters that will pay a trifle over the expenses, and better have that than nothing at all; so, you'll find my man up stairs."

———

CHAPTER LXI.

MRS. BLAIR'S STRANGE VISITOR.— SHE LEAVES HER LODGINGS.

MRS. BLAIR heard this announcement with something like terror. It was the first occasion of the kind she had ever encountered; and though she had expected something of the sort, yet it came sudden, and staggered her.

She would have replied to Mrs. Bennett's last words, but that worthy and exemplary female had quitted the field, and slammed the door of her apartment to, so that she had no alternative left her, but to go up stairs and see what was to be done there, if anything.

As she approached her own room, which was a back room, second floor, containing a bed and appurtenances thereunto belonging, she heard a singular sound proceed from her apartment, such as she had never before heard.

It was a deep, male voice, giving out sounds that were not very unmusical it is true, but, to her mind, terribly out of place, profane and indecorous.

She listened for a moment with a sickening sensation at the stomach, and heard some words given out by some one who was within; and, while she stood there, a consciousness came over her that she had slept her last night in the apartment that the musical individual had become an occupant of, and one, too, she could not very well endure.

Again the man burst out afresh, and she heard distinctly the following words, sung as if the individual were singing in character upon the occasion—

"How happy am I,
No cares to annoy;
Why are not all
As happy as I?"

This might have been a very polite and appropriate inquiry from a bacchanalian monarch who had nothing else to do but to eat, feasts, and to drink out of golden goblets, but, in the present case, it did not at all apply to Mrs. Blair, nor perhaps truly to the individual who uttered them on this occasion. However, outward show went far to say that they were very appropriate indeed.

Mrs. Blair could scarcely wait to hear so much of the song, when she slowly opened the door and beheld a sight that chilled her heart to behold.

There, on the dressing-table, stood some beer, and a dip all guttered, with a cocked hat on the summit of the wick, beautifully illuminated, like a night scene round Mount Vesuvius.

On the bed, too—on the very white counterpane—was seated the individual who had sung the song, and who was then pouring a libation of beer down his own throat, and, as he placed the pot down with a bang on the dressing-table which was beside him, he congratulated himself by singing—

"A werry good song,
And werry well sung,
Jolly companions every one.

Hilloa, my lady, how do, eh?"

This was said to Mrs. Blair, who entered the apartment with a kind of mist before her eyes; she felt a swimming in her head, and could by no means feel comfortable.

"Take a seat, my dear; you are as welcome to it as if it was all your own."

Mrs. Blair did sit down, not in consequence of this invitation — she couldn't help it; had nothing been between her and the floor, on to the floor she must have gone.

"Well, my dear, how is you."

"What do you do here?" exclaimed Mrs. Blair, not knowing what to say, but finding it necessary to say something.

"Why, I came to make myself comfortable; do you do the same; will you have any heavy?"

"What?"

"Beer."

"Wretch!"

"Well, I'm d—d," said the man taking the pewter pot in his hand, and swinging it round in it; "if that ain't the height of incivility; well, ma'am, though you don't know any more manners than Mike David's sow, I does, so here goes—

"'Here's health to all good lasses.'

But that don't do; you're too old a gal; but never mind, you've had your day, and now it's somebody else's turn; don't be down upon your luck."

"Are you going to stay here all night?"

"Yes, I am, thank heaven; between you, and me, and the post, how are we to sleep?"

"What?"

"Will you sleep inside and I out, or you out and I inside the close?"

"Monster!"

"Oh, no, I'm a tidy man of my inches; but without gammon, what is to be done?"

"What can I do? the rent shall be paid."

"You wouldn't let me in in the morning."

"Yes, I would," said Mrs. Blair, a flash of hope gleaming over her countenance, as she imagined the man would be induced to grant her request to leave the room; "I'd give you the key."

"And you'd put the bedstead against the door; oh, I'm up to a dodge or two; it's no go, old gal—no go. I'm as artful as two people. Have you got any tobacco about you, eh? I'll give it you another time."

"Miscreant!" muttered Mrs. Blair, as she in vain endeavoured to think what was to be done.

"Will you tell Mrs. Bennett that I want some beer and tobacco? I'm quite out."

Mrs. Blair paid no regard to this request, for she was incapable of making any attempt to argue or converse with the man in possession, whose peculiar eloquence and mode of thought were such that she was completely driven off the field, and unable to stem such a torrent of words.

"Mrs. Bennett, Mrs. Bennett!" shouted the man in possession, with stentorian lungs; but it produced no response until he had shouted for about the fortieth time, and then Mrs. Bennett came.

"What do you want, Dobbs? She's not a-going to begin any violence, is she?"

"No, ma'am; only I wants some beer and two screws of the best tobacco."

"You'll be drunk."

"No, I shan't; besides, I'm a-bed."

"You'll set the place a-fire."

"No, I won't. I'll smoke in my hat, and make a spittoon of the wash-hand basin."

Tempted by these offers of cleanliness and carefulness, Mrs. Bennett was induced to send for the beer, tobacco and pipe, which were duly sent up stairs.

"Then you will not let me sleep here?" said Mrs. Blair in a desponding tone.

"You can have half the bed; what can I do more, I should like to know? You can't have it all."

"Then I shall sit here," said Mrs. Blair, who had bethought herself only how she should pass the night, for to go out at that time of night was too much out of the question to be thought of.

"You can stop there or here, my dear," said the man in possession; "I shan't disturb you; I shall sit here and smoke until I've smoked all my baccy, and then, reserving one pipe for the morning, I shall go to sleep where I am."

*   *   *   *

It is useless to pursue this scene any further; Mrs. Blair had on this occasion lost all that volubility of scolding which had on several occasions carried her through several disagreeable scenes; on this occasion it seemed as if all would be wasted upon this man, who had much too high a notion of his "convivial powers," as he called them, to feel angry at what she said.

She endeavoured to sleep in the arm-chair where she had seated herself, but it was a vain endeavour, for so long as the man in possession had his tobacco, and could keep awake, for so long he kept up his snatches of songs.

When he left off singing and smoking, he slept; but this was no cessation from annoyance—far from it, because it only produced a change in the nature of the music, for he began to snore most outrageously; and then he would wake up and talk to some imaginary person who was not present.

Not the least annoying of the affair, and which terribly derogated from her dignity, was being addressed as "old gal." This she was compelled to bear with what - fortitude she could; for, indeed, it may be well imagined, that to a woman of her disposition it was a very great aggravation to feel herself thus constantly insulted, and at the same time to have no remedy—not even the gratification of being able to say something spiteful in return.

But the longest night has an end, so had this, and morning broke on as ill an assorted pair as could be well imagined. No one for a moment can conceive the nature and the virulence of the pent-up feelings of Mrs. Blair; and when she saw it was daylight, she looked as though she would have changed it to darkness.

"Well, my darling," said the man, who woke about seven o'clock; "how are you, my old gal? I wish you hadn't been sulky, but taken half your bed. Lord love you, I should have as soon thought of injuring my grandmother as you. There warn't nothin' to fear; but you are as dignified as a pew-opener on a Sunday morning. I'm blessed if I don't think that's what you are."

Mrs. Blair made no reply to this insulting supposition, but seeing it was time, she arose, and having dressed herself for walking by putting on every article she could, or rather that her tormentor would permit her to take possession of under the circumstances, she took a last look of the room, and slowly descended the stairs.

"So you are going?" said Mrs. Bennett; "bad luck go with you, you black-looking baggage."

"I'll punish you for forcibly taking possession of my room in the way you have," said Mrs. Blair; "it will cost you as many pounds as you may hope to gain shillings."

"Ha! ha! I'm glad you're going. Put that into your pipe and smoke it. I tell you what, don't be so grand, and people won't mind a slight loss—at least, they won't be angry with misfortunes; but you deserve all you have got."

Instead of replying to this speech, Mrs. Blair walked out, leaving the street-door wide open, to the intense aggravation of the landlady, who was obliged to shut it after her.

CHAPTER LXII.

MRS. BLAIR AND HER FRIENDS.— CHANGE OF CIRCUMSTANCES.— MISFORTUNE'S NO LESSON.

MRS. BLAIR'S situation was as bad as it could well be—at least, she had never been so near destitution before, and there was no apparent means of getting out of the unfortunate dilemma in which she found herself placed. She was sinking deeper and deeper in the mire each day, and in a short time there would be a depth beyond which she could not go, and at which even she shuddered to think.

But she hid this view of the case from herself, or blinked it over, by saying—

"Surely, surely, some of my acquaintances will give me a temporary lodging, until I can procure another engagement. They cannot, will not refuse me so small a favour."

It was just possible that Mrs. Blair overrated the complaisance of her acquaintances, and underrated the magnitude of the favour—or it may be that she was a woman who was generally feared, and by all discerning persons kept at a distance, lest, if she became intimate, there would be no shaking her off.

It is a fact, that there are some persons who, when they fall into misfortunes are never pitied; while others deserve them less, and yet receive the helping hands of friends.

In this case, we must look for something that determines the friends of the party in something more than the mere blamelessness more or less of their conduct, but in their general manners being free, frank, and open; but let such a one as Mrs. Blair fall into misfortune, and none pity her, no not one.

That eventful morning in which she had been turned out of her lodgings, she resolved to commence the most determined system of sponging she could adopt, and thus feast, vampyre-like, upon her friends, until the source should be dried up, and exist no longer —that, in fact, she should be forbidden every man's door.

And, when a bar had been so placed to bar her entrance, then she had the presumption to hope and expect that, to use her own words upon the occasion, Providence would open some other source of comfort for her.

Truly if Providence had, Providence would have aided and abetted a very indifferent character.

The first house she came to was that of an old acquaintance, a Mrs. Beard, who had lately been married a second time—one who had some experience of her before, on a former occasion; and who now fancied she would have something uncomfortable said or done at table, and in the presence of her new husband, who, by the way, had seen Mrs. Blair on one or two occasions, and conceived an unutterable dislike to the woman.

As may be imagined, there was no much to be got out of such a couple; but Mrs. Blair was not aware of the fact; she could not see it, though it was plain enough to any one else; but Mrs. Blair, though an acute woman on some points, was by no means so on others.

Mr. and Mrs. Beard were at break-fast when Mrs. Blair was announced to them by the servant.

"Show her into the back-parlour,' exclaimed Mr. Beard.

"What can she want at this time of day?" exclimed Mrs. Beard. "Why, it's not nine o'clock yet—there must surely be something the matter."

Before the servant could get out of the breakfast-room, Mrs. Blair walked in, and, in a very solemn manner, said—

"I wish to speak to you very particularly."

"Well?"

Mrs. Blair pointed significantly to the servant, who stood gaping at this piece of assurance.

"Susan, you can leave the room," said Mrs. Beard. "I can call you when I want you."

Susan did leave the room, and then Mrs. Beard said, in a short tone with a cough—

"Will you have the goodness, Mrs. Blair, to proceed, and say what you have to say, as you see we are at breakfast."

This was cool, but Mrs. Blair was equal to it, and replied, in an undertone—

"I do not wish to disturb your breakfast. Pray, go on; you can hear me just as well. I am, you know, at this present moment, out of an engagement."

"We do know that, Mrs. Blair."

"Well, I have abstained from asking my friends for assistance, but I am now really reduced to that necessity. I am unable to go on any longer."

"Dear me! I thought you had a very good place at Mr. Bertram's, and that you did as you liked there."

"Not exactly. I had much to do there; my salary was small, and many things that ought to have been found me I was compelled to buy. The Bertrams were ruined, and I did not get all I was entitled to."

"Indeed!"

"Oh, dear, no!"

"Then, there's your sister."

"Her husband's left her, and she's removed."

"Where is she?"

"I don't know."

"It appears that misfortune has stuck

to you both, and not left either of you any room to envy each other."

"Certainly, that is in some measure the case. But what I wish to know is, if you would assist me with lodging and partial board, until I can get another engagement?"

"I am very sorry, Mrs. Blair," said her friend, "that I cannot, in this instance, oblige you."

"Indeed!"

"No; it is entirely out of the question."

"You would be no loser by it in the end, for I would pledge myself to repay you, and to take the first engagement that offers itself in any way to me," urged Mrs. Blair.

"I am sorry that it cannot be complied with."

"I thought," said Mrs. Blair, as a last argument, "that we who had always been friends, and worshipped in the same pew, sung psalms out of the same book, and uttered the same responses together, had been almost as sisters, and such a favour as this would not have been refused to me."

"No; I don't go to the chapel at all, now. I've got married again, you see, and have got no time to sing psalms, utter responses, or do anything, save sit at home, or go to the theatre."

Mrs. Blair was aghast at this. She had not expected any such admission, great as was her knowledge in the hypocrisy of the sect she belonged to.

"Can you aid me, then, in any small way? I am destitute, and have not even a lodging to go to. I have been turned out this morning, and a man put in my room all night. I have nowhere to go that I can call a home."

"Really, I don't know. We've been

to so much expense lately, that I haven't got anything to spare."

"If it be ever so small a trifle, it will be acceptable, very acceptable, indeed."

"Well," said Mrs. Beard, feeling over a purse full of silver, and at length finding a sixpence, she dropped it into the palm of the beggar's hand, saying—

"Really, Mrs. Blair, that is all I can give you; lending is out of the question. Good-morning."

"Good-morning," said Mrs. Blair, not knowing what to say.

"And, Mrs. Blair," said Mr. Beard.

"Sir?"

"We are going out of town for six months, after to-morrow, and so, of course, we shan't expect to see you any more."

Mrs. Blair felt she was not a match for these people. As long as she had any hold upon people—as long as she had what is termed the upper hand of them—then she could make them feel; indeed, her power to do mischief arose chiefly from two circumstances—viz., in situation and opportunity.

She arose, and walked to the parlour door, looking back upon her former friend, who had turned round towards the fire, and was sipping her coffee. She was about to speak, but Mr. Beard arose, and followed her to the door, and let her out without another word passing.

She left the house almost stupified. She began to see that she was not generally admired—that something must have caused this; for people, however bad, don't desert an old friend all at once. The usual mode is to let them down gently, and by degrees; whereas, she had been deserted all at once, and by all who knew her.

She now regretted that she had parted with her sister; she yet might have had funds—she might, in fact, have helped her, provided she got any help herself. At all events, it would have been one more chance.

House after house did she go to, but she found that, so soon as she mentioned the extent of her wants, she found no sympathy, but much anger.

Thus it was with her until night came, and then she knew not where to lay her head. That night, however, she found a lodging, by paying for it, which she was able to do; and the next day she had to part with some of the things from off her back.

Thus she went on for several days, and occasionally calling upon her friends; but this at last failed her, and she became, in less than ten days, really and truly a beggar. She used to take up her stand at the corner of the street, and when anybody came she thought was not one who would act harshly, or an officer in disguise, she would solicit alms. To this state had this bad woman reduced herself at last. Had she been other than what she was, she would never have sunk thus—not certainly wholly unpitied or unaided as she was.

Day after day, wretchedness and misery became more and more familiar to her. Hunger and cold were bitter companions, as she could now tell, by experience. Her strength daily decreased, and she had a bad cough that sorely troubled her. She used, however, hail, rain, or shine, to be seen begging in one quarter of the town. She could sometimes see her former friends and companions pass and repass, pretending not to know her; but she knew too well that they did know her.

Never, or scarcely ever did they give her a penny piece—that would have been too much, too great a stretch of charity. No; they preferred rubbers and points at whist to giving alms to a beggar.

Day after day did she drag herself about, in the old black gown she wore, which seemed an emblem of herself and her fate—that the one would last the other out, and be in existence at the death.

So it was; but what could she look back upon to derive any comfort from? There was no one act that she could look back upon with anything like complacency, though she thought the occasion justified everything she had formerly done, and which now seemed only unfortunate, and not at all wrong or criminal.

So it is with many minds; they cannot conceive it possible that they have been to blame—quite the reverse; they think it is the world, and, despite that which ought to be more palpable to them than any one else, they continue to look upon themselves as the injured parties.

CHAPTER LXIII.

THE PERISHING WOMAN. — THE DARK LANE SCENE, AND THE INFIRMARY.

ONE cold winter's morning, as two men were passing along a narrow street —it was early in the morning; the shops were not then open—they came to a small archway, from which proceeded a deep groan.

"Did you hear that, Bill?"

"No; what was it?"

"Wery much like a groan."

"Didn't hear it."

"But I did. There it goes again."

"Oh, I hears it now."

"What's to be done?"

"Don't know."

"You had better call, or go in and see what's the matter. Somebody may be dying, for all you know."

"Hilloa! hilloa! Who's there?"

There was no answer; the echoes of the shout only sounded on the ear.

"Well, we can't say we haven't asked. Hilloa! hilloa! who's there? Blest if it ain't almost dark."

"It is. There—there!"

They listened, and a groan came distinctly upon their ears, and caused them both to start.

"Bill, let's go on."

"B—but if anybody's dying?"

"Well, we shan't be blamed for it; so come on."

"Yes, I will. But let's go under and see."

"I'll follow, if you go first."

This arranged, they both entered the archway; it was a long arch, or covered way, under a house, and leading into a court or alley at the back, and was very dark. However, their eyes got accustomed to the light, when, near a door that opened from one of the houses, they espied a dark object, it was darker than the surrounding gloom of the place.

"Bill, look yonder. What's that?"

"It's werry like a woman, or a bunble of rags, I can't tell which. But it's precious dirty."

"Ain't it!"

The two worthies approached the unfortunate object, who was lying perishing from cold and hunger. She lay huddled up in a heap, incapable of motion, but groaning every now and then from pain.

"Good Lord!" said Bill, "as sure as I'm a livin', breathin' soul, it's a woman! She's perishing with cold and hunger. What shall we do with her? We can't leave her here."

"Go to the workhouse and tell them."

"Oh! they wont't stir themselves. It's too early for any one but a beadle or a porter to be about."

"Well, they are all as is wanted, Billy. Come on; we can't do any good if we was to try, and we should only waste time in doing so."

"Come on, then," said the other, and the two men hastened off to the nearest poor-house they could find, and that was not far off at that moment. In a few minutes they arrived at the gates, where they remained for a quarter of an hour before anybody appeared, and then the porter, in his shirt sleeves, came to intimate he had been hurried while dressing, and considerably ruffled in mind by the noise.

"I tell you what it is, young fellers," he said, very impressively, "if you don't know how to handle a bell, don't touch a bell handle. Do you hear?"

"Ay, ay."

"Then mind."

"Yes, yes; but there's ——"

"No, no; there's no buts in the case."

"A woman's a-dying!" shouted one of the men. "Do you hear? a woman's a-dying!"

"Very likely; d—n 'em, they always do die at very inconvenient hours. Anything wrong, and it's sure to be a woman. I wish they were all a——"

"Are you going to let the woman die?"

"I cannot help it; if she will she will, you know. In the God's blessing! am I to help a woman's dying, I should like to know? as if she would pay any attention to my request not to die, if she were so inclined!"

"But she's perishing with cold and hunger."

"I didn't do it, old feller. Mind your own business."

"Very well; since you take it so coolly, I shall apply to a magistrate, by which time the woman will be dead. I have no doubt she will die in the meantime, and then you will be answerable for her death."

"You will, will you ?"

"I will."

"Ah, before you get there she'll be here, and you'll take nothin' by the motion."

"Where are you going for her ?"

"You haven't told me yet."

"Then get ready, and we'll wait for you."

"You'd better come inside," said the man, who began to think a complaint on this score might not be well met, and that his tenure of office might be infringed upon. "Where do you say she is ?"

"Lying all of a heap against a door in a court. I'm sure she's dying."

"God bless me !" said the man, "what a night to sleep out in! But then, there's no knowing what these paupers can bear until you try 'em; it's positively annoying."

"Shall you be long ?"

"No. Here, you paupers—here, I say, Bill."

"Hilloa !" said a gruff voice.

"Just send down two o' them new hands. I wants 'em strong, 'cause there's something to carry."

This was a secret, that, however strong they might be when they first entered the place, their strength speedily became lessened upon the diet of the place.

In a few minutes the two men came down stairs, and then, appealing to the great man, wanted to know what they were to do for him ?

"Go with these men, who'll show you where there's a woman as is kicking the broom."

"Kicking the broom ?"

"Yes."

"What's that—eh ?"

"Why, it's the same as kicking the bucket, as far as I can see. But go on, and make haste."

"Have you the master's order ?"

"No ; but I'll make that all right. Go and get the woman. It's a case of emergency; and I can do all that's requisite, for the master is not about yet."

"Very good."

The two men then left the workhouse to proceed with the two sent by the authority of the beadle to take the unfortunate creature to the infirmary of the workhouse on a stretcher, where she would be attended to.

It was but a few minutes' walk to the spot, and they arrived there before any one had been by, either to disturb her or to hear her groans.

There she lay all of a heap, precisely as they left her, without a movement. She must have been too helpless to move her hands ; they were numbed.

"Here she is," said one of the men.

"Open the machine," said another.

This was done, and all four aided the unfortunate creature into the machine ; they lifted her quietly and carefully, but her groans increased with each movement they made in lifting her, which showed them that even motion increased her pain. She was as gently placed in the coffin-like convenience as they could, for the men were not yet hardened to human sufferings—they were but recently thus employed.

"Now," said one, as they covered over the top ; "say, are you ready ?" and he lifted up the end of the poles, by which it was carried, and, his companion doing the same, they commenced their return to the workhouse.

Before leaving, the two men who had first found her said they would call in a day or two to see how she was, whether she lived or not.

The unfortunate creature was taken into the workhouse, and the beadle having inspected her, declared he could do nothing with her, and that she must go into the infirmary.

Into the infirmary the miserable creature was taken, were the medical officer happened to be, and at once gave directions for her recovery, which he declared was very problematical; she must have been exposed many hours.

Small quantities of wine and nutritious food were given her, and after several hours labour they succeeded in partially restoring her senses.

She gazed around her for some time, almost vacantly; she seemed to be endeavouring to recollect herself, and ascertain where she was, but she was evidently unable to speak. The doctor considered that it was much better she should not be spoken to or questioned; she was, therefore, left to herself for some time and she fell asleep.

Occasionally she would awake, and then small quantities of liquid food were given at these times, but she spoke not, and soon relapsed into a slumber.

"What do you think of your patient?" inquired the apothecary of the doctor.

"I really cannot understand it; that is, I cannot quite make out the extent of mischief that exists; she takes small quantities of food, and sleeps,"

"It seems as if the stomach would retain it then."

"Yes; but one may be deceived even here, for it may act so languidly as to be over-burdened by a small quantity of the lightest food."

"It may so."

"And then again, she sleeps without any waking to inquire after anything; but just takes her food, and then sinks into a slumber again."

"Shall you give her anything?"

"A stimulant, or someting of the sort."

"Have you inquired her name?"

"I have not."

The woman now opened her eyes and appeared to be looking about for a time; she fixed her eyes upon the surgeon for a moment or two.

"Do you want anything?" inquired the surgeon.

She shook her head, and the surgeon continued,—

"Is there anything you can take? say so, and you shall have it." This would have alarmed an old pauper to have heard this, for he would know his case was a desperate one, indeed, when a workhouse surgeon should offer to let him have what he wanted.

She again shook her head.

"What is your name, good woman?"

"Blair," she replied, in a low tone.

Yes; it was the unfortunate, but bitter enemy of all who opposed her, that lay there in the last extremity. Her fate was in no respects better than her victims.

CHAPTER LXIV.

THE MISERIES IN THE DESERTED COTTAGE.—THE LAST HOPE.—THE RING.

IT now became evident to Margaret Bertram that the unfortunate Theodore Danton was very ill—that, indeed, he was entirely helpless; he was even, at times, entirely insensible, and incapable of doing the least thing for himself. Sad and silently passed the hours with Margaret, as she watched the sick bed of Theodore, in that deserted house.

Three days had now elapsed since she first came there; and how the time had been passed she could not tell, save in the saddest and most melancholy manner imaginable. Sad, indeed, are the hours that are spent in watching the bedside of the sick, when poverty and want are at the door.

Such was the case with these two unfortunate victims of an unkind fate; for Margaret had once left and purchased some small necessities that were indispensable to prevent absolute starvation. Poor Margaret watched him with a sister's care: his ravings and moanings were to her sounds that carried pangs to her heart.

"He would have protected me," she muttered—"he would have kept me from want; and that last deed he did for me—the rescue and protection I received at his hands—is the cause of his present bereavement of sense. Until that moment he was well in his mind, but that conflict has had a maddening effect upon his brain; it roused those feelings of hatred and revenge that had lain dormant within him; and, though they were felt but momentarily, still they have left a withering effect upon him, from which he may never recover.

"Thus I have to answer for this unfortunate state. It is, indeed, my place to devote the remainder of my days to his service—to the restoration of his intellect and health, if it so please Heaven; if not, while I have strength left, I will endeavour to make up, in some measure, the loss and misery he has suffered on my account.

"And thou, too, thou unfortunate little one! I would to Heaven thou hadst never come, coming, as thou dost, into a scene of misery, wretchedness, and want; but, being here, thou art a part of myself, and as I live, so must thou. But I will be a good mother, at least, if not such a one as I could wish. If I were a richer one, then thy young days would be spent better and more happily; but, thank Heaven, thou canst not feel the wants and deprivation thy mother feels! No, no; before thou canst feel them, may better fortune be thy fate!"

Pressing her infant closely to her breast, she kissed its innocent lips; at the same time, a tear coursed its way down her cheek, and a deep sigh escaped her.

Her attention was next called to Danton, who now woke from a sleep. He had been for some time delirious; he was no better now, and appeared to talk of scenes that had happened while he was abroad, and which she seemed unable to understand. Then, again, he would revert to the days of his childhood—to those days when first he saw her; and then to the scene between her and Bertram, when he had nearly killed her.

"Margaret," he said, suddenly.

"Danton," replied Margaret, leaning towards him, and catching every word he might utter, hoping each time he awoke that he might have recovered from his mental disorder. It was possible, she had heard, that such cures should take place.

"Margaret do you remember when first we met?"

"Yes, Danton—yes!"

"We were both different, then, to what we are now, eh? Times have changed—sadly changed!"

"Yes, they have," replied Margaret, bitterly, for she felt that it was too strikingly true.

"We have both seen the vicissitudes fortune."

"We have."

"Margaret?"

"Well, Danton?"

"Is this home?" he inquired, looking around him at the bare walls. "Is this home, Margaret? I thought I had means, riches—that I had provided luxuries for you, Margaret—all for you; and yet where are they?"

"Danton, Danton! do not talk thus; you will break my heart to listen to you. You know not the agony I feel when I see you thus, and know that I have been the cause of all this."

"Yes, yes—all for you Margaret! I have done all this for you; and, had you not been living, I should not have done it! But it's all for you—all for you!"

Poor Margaret burst into a flood of tears: she could not hear this unmoved. The words were constantly on his lips, and their repetition seemed most melancholy and sad.

"Good heavens!" she exclaimed, "what have I done that I should thus suffer, or that he should suffer such torments as these? Surely we have not deserved such terrible punishment, unless for some involuntary or unknown deed!"

Sad, sad, was the prospect in that lone house. Day after day passed by, and no change took place. Danton seemed no better. He was often delirious; never thoroughly sensible; but slept much; feverish, and cried incessantly for water.

On several occasions Margaret had left the cottage, and taken some article of apparel that Danton had (in their distressed state, they might have been deemed superfluous), to purchase food; but it was food of the commonest description.

Indeed, little more than bread passed her lips. She was grateful for that, so that she did not starve; but, at the same time, there was a little fruit that remained in the garden—a few winter apples, and some of those that had been left on the ground, and had been preserved from wet by some accidental circumstance of situation.

These, indeed, formed the chief ingredient of Danton's food. It was cooling; and when he had them placed before him, he took them in preference to any other.

There were, besides, some vegetables that had grown wild almost, having been left to grow without cultivation. These, indeed, formed a great portion of the food that Margaret herself lived upon; but, though it kept life and soul together, it by no means prevented a growing weakness and emaciation of the body to take place.

Indeed, there was not one person

who could have known Margaret Bertram, had they met her. Her friend, Mrs. Ogden, had she been living, would not have done so ; and it is doubtful if she could have been recognised by Bertram himself.

It at last came to an extremity; there was nothing else to part with, —nothing that she could think of that would procure food of any kind, however coarse or small in quantity ; when suddenly, as she gazed upon the sleeping form of Danton, she observed a small ring—one that had escaped the eagle eyes of all those through whose hands he had passed.

She herself had not seen it; but there it was. Perhaps he had had it concealed about him, and now, in a moment of insanity, he had put it on.

" For his sake, as much as my own," she said, as she gazed upon it, " I will take it, and procure the necessaries we so much need."

She, without any difficulty, took the ring off his finger, which was so thin, that the wonder was it had not fallen off, which assured her he must have but lately put it on.

With this ring, the last thing that was left them, Margaret determined again to make her way to London, and there dispose of it—how, she had not thought; but to obtain money for it was the only thought she had, though she was so weak that she could hardly hope to walk the distance; and what made it more difficult was the carrying the child with her all the way.

This there was no avoiding. She could not leave it, without any aid or care, for so many hours, or what was worse, to any accident that might befall it in consequence of Danton's state of mind; for her fears pictured to her the possibility of his getting up and injuring the child, without being able to judge of what he was doing.

It was midday when she left the house; and then, watching a moment when she was not observed by any passengers—of whom at all times there were very few—she entered the road, and took her weary way to town.

Poor Margaret was very weak—very weak; indeed, she could hardly walk with her burden; but yet her own mind told her of the necessity that existed for the exertion she was called upon to make; and, however unwilling nature might be to respond to the call, yet the will urged her on; and, after a long and toilsome walk, she found herself once again in London.

It was with a timid step she sought to dispose of it. The shopkeepers generally run things down they intend to purchase, or, rather, all things that are offered to them they decry ; and she found that her helpless state was easily gathered from her outward appearance, and all advantages were taken.

" What do you want for this thing ?" inquired one, as he weighed the ring on his finger. " It is of little esteem, and very light."

" I want to sell it for its value."

" Ah, but I can't be buyer and seller too. You have a price, I suppose ?" the man inquired, contemptuously.

" It is worth a pound."

" Ha—ha! a pound !"

" What will you give me ?"

" Two shillings."

" No ; that is not a tenth of its value —not a twentieth of its value—I am sure," she said.

" Then take it where you will get that money for it," said the man, rolling the ring across the counter to her.

Margaret took the ring, and left the shop with a heavy heart, and found the same kind of reception in two other shops, and at length she came to a fourth.

The usual question was put of—

" How much do you want for it ?"

" It's value," said Margaret.

" I don't know what it is," said the man, carelessly.

" You can tell better than I."

" Where did you get it from, young woman ?"

Margaret hesitated.

" Honestly come by, of course ?" said the man.

" Yes, certainly," said Margaret, her cheek glowing with shame at being compelled by circumstances to stand by and hear such an insinuation.

" Oh, well then, as you have come by it honestly, then—that is, as honesty goes in these hard times—I will give you five shillings for it at once," he said, carelessly.

"Not five——"

"Well, do better, if you can."

"It is about an eighth of its value."

"We may keep it a year before selling it; but I don't mind giving you seven, as you've come honestly by it."

Margaret was compelled to accept this offer, it being the highest that had been made, and the transfer was speedily made; and Margaret possessed a larger sum than she had yet possessed for many days or weeks.

She was compelled to obtain rest and refreshment before she could return to Danton, for her weakness would have prevented that taking place—she could not have walked it.

* * *

The unfortunate Danton still lingered, and Margaret patiently waited on him, day by day, performing every office that need or kindness could suggest to her, but still he seemed to get no better. A constant fire was kept up, and the room they lay in now became well aired and warmed, though it was cold enough.

In little more than a week Margaret found herself again reduced to extremities; but how she was to escape the absolute starvation that was advancing towards her she knew not—there seemed no hope and no prospect.

The days were spent in retiredness, sorrow, and lamentations; and Margaret herself began to feel her health and strength decay.

———

CHAPTER LXV.

THE DEATH OF MRS. BLAIR.—HER CONFESSION OF THE PAST.—HER USEFULNESS AFTER DEATH, AND UNCEREMONIOUS FUNERAL.

THAT evening Mrs. Blair seemed to come to her senses. She gazed a long while about her for something, but little heed was taken of that; indeed, the duties of those who attended were divided—when they thought proper to attempt to look after them. She lay there groaning and moaning; and as the sounds that came from her throat were feeble, they were not considered urgent.

The food that was given her, as we have said, was in a liquid shape, and ordered to be given frequently, was done only now and then, at distant intervals; and, indeed, it was fortunate that it was given at all, and purely accidental, for the attendants had to be up from other causes.

"I wish some of the paupers would die," said one to the other.

"So do I."

"They are such a plague—there's no getting rest, night or day, for them —they are worse trouble than if they paid for all that was done," said the old woman with a short cough.

"Indeed, they do make more fuss. I wonder, since they have so many likes and dislikes, that they don't stop away."

"They ain't got no friends; that's why they come here."

"Then they should learn to be satisfied."

"So they should. Paupers, you know, are the most ungrateful people in the world; they are always doing something they shouldn't do, and vexing somebody in authority."

"What is she groaning about?"

"I don't know; and don't intend to trouble myself about inquiring, yet awhile," said one.

"No, it will soon be daylight."

"It is now."

"We shall be relieved shortly, then."

"Yes; and not before I am tired."

"Nor I, either."

The two old drones sat before the fire, and dozed off to sleep, and the wretched woman now groaned more audibly than before, and evidently wanted to speak to some one; but her voice was evidently too weak to make known her wants.

"Oh, God!" she exclaimed, "this is punishment enough. I know I am dying. Yes—yes—I am dying—dying from want and poverty. What agony! I would that I could speak to some one, and confess the mischief that I have done, and endeavour to make some reparation. But, oh, no; I am here a dying pauper, and nobody heeds my moans."

This as true enough : nobody took any notice of her, and she was left to repent or die, which she pleased, or couldn't help. She had all the attention she could expect in such a place.

*   *   *   *

The morning came, but the hours passed slowly enough, and she felt exhausted long before the hour at which the attendants generally move about.

At length they did move about; fires were lit, and things assumed something of the air of life, though many were upon the verge of departing life. The nurses came round and administered a little food to Mrs. Blair, who could scarcely swallow.

" How are you, now ?" inquired the woman.

" Dying," she replied.

" Ah ! everybody as is ill, thinks as how they are going to die, though it's more t'other, I should say ; but then there's extra allowance, and that's a great temptation."

" I cannot eat."

" Oh !"

" Is there a clergyman ?"

" Eh ?"

" A minister ?"

" A clergyman or a minister to a workhouse ?"

" Yes."

" Oh, dear, no ; why do you want to know ? Are you particular about your burial ? 'cause Jack Jones reads the burial service, so you needn't be uncomfortable about that."

" I have something to say before I die."

" Well, say it. I'm here."

" No—no."

" Well, leave it alone, will you ?" said the nurse, angrily, at not being deemed worthy of a pauper's confidence; "a destitute wretch," as she afterwards observed, "as didn't ought to live, as she didn't do so with without being a trouble and expense to other people as oughtn't to be troubled."

"There is no minister, then?"

"None."

"The surgeon?"

"He won't be here yet awhile."

"I wish to see him directly."

"You can't."

"Good Heavens, I am dying."

"Well, do it quietly, and don't make all this fuss about nothing. Do you think you are the only person as is dying? Hasn't nobody ever died before you? What do you think as come of Cain and Abel, Gog and Magog, and all them old men, even the pratiarks? Do you think them's a living, like so many wandering Jews?"

This was unanswerable, and Mrs. Blair lay at the point of death, but unable to express the contrition she felt, and confess the mischief she had done to some one who might take the trouble to endeavour to undue what she had done, so as at least to prevent some portion of the evil that was likely to occur from what had been already done by her.

But nobody came for nearly three hours, and then surgeon and apothecary both came their rounds to visit the patients early, as there were several paupers in a desperate condition.

"How is this woman?" said one to the nurse.

"She says she is dying," said the nurse, in a tone as much as to say it's all gammon.

"Do you want anything?" inquired the surgeon.

"I wish to say a few words," said Mrs. Blair, enunciating her words very slowly, but distinctly. "I have something on my mind, which I wish to confess, for I am dying."

"Anything you have to say we will listen to; and, if possible, we will do anything you may desire."

"Thank you," said Mrs. Blair; "it is nothing I want for myself, but I have committed some wicked deeds, and I wish, if possible, to undo as much evil as I can, that I have caused."

"That's very proper."

"Go on," said the surgeon.

"I was in the service of Mrs. Bertram, a lady recently married. I knew something of the husband before; he was a gloomy, hasty man, and I had some power over him."

"Well?"

"I was there as kind of companion or upper servant, and had it in my power, when all things were left to my management, to peculate a great deal."

"Ah, very likely."

"I had done so at other situations, and always with impunity; and I endeavoured to do so here, but Mrs. Bertram seemed determined to check all this, and see to many things herself, which caused a great hatred to spring up in my breast."

"Yes—yes."

"Well, I became possessed of a secret concerning Mr. Bertram; he had seduced a young lady and refused to marry her. She died of grief, and he was invited to the funeral. Knowing the violence of the parent, he refused, and in return she sent him a funeral dress—band, gloves, and cloak—all to his house, with a deep and bitter curse.

"At his marriage she cursed him, and caused him such dread by predicting evils, and told him his marriage should be unhappy, and his wife should be unfaithful."

"I see."

"This fear I saw actually took possession of him; he was a gloomy, superstitious man, and it was the thing of all others that would make an impression upon him. I knew all this, but his wife did not."

"Exactly."

"This gave me some power with him, and when she complained she did not like me, and desired me to be dismissed, he objected; and I, in my turn, did her all the damage I could. It was not long before I found an opportunity of injuring her.

"A Mr. Danton returned from abroad, and came to see her, not knowing she was married."

"Yes—yes."

"Danton had formerly been her lover, but he had never declared himself to her. His circumstances were not such at that moment that he could do so, as he thought, with propriety, or with any hopes of success with her family."

"I see—I see," said the surgeon.

"He came to her, and when he found what had happened, and all his hopes blighted, there was a very affecting interview, which was intended to be the final one.

"Theodore Danton had determined again to quit the country, and never to return to it again. I am well acquainted with the purity of conduct and intention of both parties."

"But represented it in another light?"

"I did; for Theodore Danton fell ill at the hotel at which he was stopping. This was caused by the state of mind under which he was labouring, and he became delirious.

"By a singular accident, Mrs. Bertram learned what had happened to him, and she was told he was dying, by a nurse whom she was about to engage."

"I understand."

"Then she determined to go and see him, and for the last time take a farewell of him."

"Exactly."

"My object was now to ruin Mrs. Bertram, so that I might have the entire management of his house, and commit any peculation I chose."

"Exactly; but it was a very bad design."

"So it was, and that is why I unfold it. I acquainted Bertram with his wife's intentions, and fomented the natural jealousy of his disposition, and persuaded him it was the fulfilment of the curses wrapped in the black mantle. He went to watch the motions of his wife. I persuaded him when he got there, that to see her enter Danton's hotel was proof enough of her infidelity.

"This he believed, and when he saw her enter, he left; but what became of him after, for he got up and went away the same night, no one knew, while he took all his money out of his banker's, and has not been seen or heard of since; and I believe Mrs. Bertram and child are straying or begging about the streets. If you would do a dying woman an act of grace, find out Bertram and let him know the part I have played, and that next to myself he is to blame, but that his wife and Danton are incapable of wrong."

As Mrs. Blair spoke she sank back, and became speechless from exhaustion, and in that state, in a few minutes more, she died.

"Well," said the apothecary, "this is a very pretty woman. What can be done?"

"Draw up a memorial, and sign it, then advertise for Bertram," replied the surgeon.

This was done, and Mrs. Blair was buried, after being of some service to the surgeons in the way of a scientific demonstration, and then her remains were popped into a shell, and not even Jack Jones took the trouble to read the burial service over them, which, as he truly remarked, couldn't "save or make her soul."

CHAPTER LXVI.

THE TEMPTATIONS OF MARGARET.—THE DANGERS OF TOWN.—THE BURGLARS.

Days had now passed, and yet no change appeared in Theodore Danton, save that he fluctuated—sometimes better and sometimes worse. Occasionally, too, he was sane; sometimes almost raving. All this was most trying and harassing to poor Margaret, who, however, bore up with fortitude. strength, and devotion, unequalled and unexpected in Margaret, because, from all the concurrent circumstances of her habits and character, she was presumed to be uneqal to the task.

But, with her, the task was one of love and choice. She would not, she could not, have left him to perish there by himself—far from it; she would have perished to save him.

It was a great hardship to be required to do so much, but there was no help for it; and what was demanded by the necessity of the case she fully accorded.

Then there was her child. She yet had strength to fondle and caress an object that, while it demanded her love and attention, was the source of great unhappiness, because she could not do for it what she desired; for food, and all other necessaries, were scant, and some totally wanting. She was destitute of all those little things that tend so much to children's comfort and well-being.

This, to her, was a thing she could not bear to look upon, and yet could she not blame herself as being the cause of all this. It was not she who had done all this; it was the perverse and morbid nature of Bertram, whose insanity had reached such a pitch, that he would have deprived her innocent babe of the only efficient protection it could know.

Day after day passed slowly away, and yet no change seemed to come over the spirit of the scene.

No hope beamed forth from Heaven or earth—no one step was made towards improvement. The reverse was indeed glaringly the case; for each day brought with it a succession of fears and necessities, that she could not see how she was to combat them.

There was no fighting against starvation. This was a thing so real, and had its evils so immediately felt, that it appalled the mother, who looked upon the face of her babe with horror, as she saw the thin, lank visage of the infant plainly speaking the want of what, under happier circumstances, she could have afforded it.

What was to be done? She could not stay there and starve; she could not see him die of hunger who had loved her so much, and who had suffered, and who was suffering at that moment; neither could she see her own babe die in her arms.

No; she had but one alternative left, and that was what she before unsuccessfully attempted—begging.

She shuddered, as she considered there was but little hope in that; and, when she remembered what had occurred when she was reduced to that state before, she trembled at the thought that such might happen again, when there was no protecting arm near to save her from the destruction that then threatened her.

However, there was no helping it.

Do something, she must. They could not be fed by any miracle. Food came not through the heavens, however it might have done so in the days of old.

She arose, after some deep thought, and determined once again to dare the world, and beg.

It requires some courage to beg, and and Margaret received hers from despair. To the last extremity indeed she had come. What more could happen than the pang of actual starvation?

A greater necessity impelled her forward this time than before, and she yielded to it. What might be the result she could not tell; but this much she knew, that to live at all she could not be brought to endure more.

She once more left the cottage by the accustomed route, and determined that, if it were possible, she would bring something back to the unfortunate Theodore Danton.

She proceeded towards London, that being the spot she had pitched upon; indeed, there was no other place where there was any chance or prospect of success; for, if one refused, another was at hand—there was a chance of even a mendicant's picking up a living among the charitable.

And yet it is remarkably true, that a really poor and reduced person never gets a chance of obtaining a crumb, where the professional beggar makes a good thing of it.

There is something about the reduced unfortunate that does not take with the charitable; they are not unfortunate enough, they are not abject, and do not show the same amount of making up to attract the eye, as he who is an adept.

Thus it is that those who shrink from beggary—from importunity—never have any chance, or such a chance that it is mere risk or accident—the amount of probability being in favour of death, among such, on an average, to nine out of eighteen.

So much for the charitably disposed.

Margaret's thoughts, as she walked towards London, were of the most painful character. Her fears and apprehensions were so great, that she scarce knew what to do, or where to go.

"God help me!" she said; "but for him and the child, I would lie down by the road-side, and die. I could feel it in my heart to do so; and wherefore should I not, but for thee, my unfortunate babe? What could induce me to live this wretched life? Ah, Danton—yes, Danton cannot be left to perish! And yet, God knows what I may not yet have to suffer myself. Yet, if I cannot get food somehow, we must all starve, Danton and all."

These reflections urged her on, and she neared the great city; and as she did so she could not but feel a hope, that amongst so many, she could not be left to perish.

"There must be some superfluity that is wasted in this large place, that can be spared us, to keep life and soul together."

Thus buoyed up by a momentary hope, even of such a character, she pushed her way into the suburbs of the metropolis.

Here she looked about her. Everybody seemed busy and in a hurry. She knew none, and could hope for nothing but scorn from strangers. And could it be called hope? The feeling she had in her breast was not hope; nor did expectation and anticipation have any share in that feeling.

She looked at a great many, but they gave her no encouragement to begin; but she stationed herself where some shop-lights came full upon her, and stood in an attitude expressive at once of humiliation, fear, and want.

Margaret Bertram, the young and beautiful, had indeed fallen to a depth below what she could ever have believed it possible she could have sunk, ere death closed her eyes. Yet, despite her misery and wretchedness, she was yet young and beautiful; but that beauty was obscured by want and famine.

After some time, a woman came by, and suddenly stopped. She looked at her for a moment or two, and then said—

"Young woman, are you begging?"

"I am in great distress—very great distress."

"Oh, I dare say."

"I am starving, and my child too."

"Is that child yours?"

"It is. I had not brought it out had it not been mine."

"It strikes me you had better take it home, poor thing! and not bring it out here in the cold. You can't be a mother, or you'd have left it at home in the warm."

"Alas! I have no home."

"Oh, I see, you are one of those worthless hardened things that lie about the streets at night. Ah, you are an abandoned creature. I wish they'd put you in a watch-house, for the sake of the poor little child. You ought to be ashamed of yourself."

"I cannot help my poverty," said Margaret.

"Oh, nobody ever can," said the female, who immediately walked away, having insulted the poverty and wounded the feelings of the unfortunate sufferer.

Alas! how many characters such as these are there in a large place like London! Many, many!

Poor Margaret pressed her babe to her breast, and she could have sobbed aloud, to think she should be accused of a want of feeling towards one that had come to her in the midst of want and suffering, as this had. She loved it dearly, and one great portion of the suffering she suffered was on account of its troubles. She, however, remained where she was; and soon after a penny piece was placed in her hand by a young man and woman, who were probably about to be or had been but recently married; and their sympathies were excited on account of the child and the appearance of a young mother.

To Margaret, placed as she was, this was a relief; for it showed her that there were at least two persons whose hearts were not entirely callous to human suffering.

"Young woman," said a tall, genteel-looking man, with a harsh expression of countenance, "I am afraid you are an abandoned sinner—I am afraid you are begging."

"What are those to do who are destitute of home and food?" inquired Margaret, in despair, as she shrunk from the man's inquiring looks. " I have neither."

"Oh, it's melancholy to see the state to which many of us are reduced. Let me tell you, young woman, you are offending against the laws of your country."

"I was not aware, sir, I was offending against any laws; to ask for bread is no crime; even want, I hope, is not considered a sin; if it be in the eyes of men, it is not in those of God, and may He aid me, for his creatures will not."

The tall man paused and seemed to think this a personal reflection, and then entered into an argument to show that indiscriminate charity was not charity at all; which, in effect, he proved began not in the highways and byways, but in a person's own heart, in his breast and at home; meaning, no doubt, that the individual who partook of the greatest number of creature comforts, was the most charitable, of which class this individual was a most distinguished member.

"If you will attend next Wednesday evening," he said, "at the New Bethlehem Chapel, or on Friday at the old Jericho Meeting-house, I will endeavour to teach you the evil of your ways."

"No, no," said Margaret, who listened to him without heeding him. "No—no; I want food."

"Ay, for the soul."

"I cannot subsist upon it," said Margaret, in despair; "my babe will die, and I shall too."

"Think of your immortal—"

A hollow sound followed, almost like a kick at a cask, and the tall gentleman was now in worse than Egyptian darkness, for a young man coming by, having left his work, was attracted by the sound of voices, and listened to the conversation, and becoming convinced of the fact, that the speaker was, in his own words, a religious vagabond, so he determined to put the kibosh upon him.

"Here, my good woman," said the mechanic, "here's all I have got; you shall have fourpence; keep clear of that man; he's all talk, and has as much wind as a pair of bellows, and no more compassion."

Margaret looked at the young man who uttered these words to her, but she saw nothing but the ordinary set of features of a hearty good-natured young mechanic.

She had not time to utter a " thank you," before he was gone, and before she could think of what she had better do, the infuriated gentleman had, by hard exertion, extracted his head from the awkward made cylinder, which served the place of covering for his head; but this was not done without tearing out the lining, and scraping the skin off his nose.

"Where is he—where is he?" he exclaimed, turning round and round. "Where is he? I'll have him transported."

"Thankee for nothing," said a boy.

"Only tell me where he is; I'll give five shillings to anybody. Where is he?"

"I'll take your money; hand it over."

"Where is he?"

"There."

"Where?"

"There."

"I don't see."

"'Cause you don't look high enough. I can see both eyes, his nose, and his mouth, and part of his face, shining like Warren's out of the moon up yonder."

"You rascal."

"Oh, come, none o' that, if you please; come, come, don't rascal me; I'll fight you for sixpence."

"I'll call an officer."

"You may call two, and tell 'em I offered to fight you after you had insulted and aggravated me. Who are you, I should like to know? A nice man at a tea-party, where muffins is plenty; why, they'd never get a pair of stockings long enough for your legs. Where did you come from, and who's your mother?"

The tall man was quite overpowered by the eloquence of the butcher in the red nightcap, and seeing he was likely to get the worst of the argument, as he had very few patient listeners, he could not make any head against this line of argument, and he thought of moving away.

Exasperated, however, and anxious to wreak his vengeance upon somebody, he turned towards Margaret, and said—

"It is some of your companions; you are all alike. I'll have you all punished. You shall be sent to the House of Correction for an improper character."

"You are an improper character. I saw you talking to the young woman, and I dare say you got what you deserved. The young man wot hit you, wouldn't have bonnetted you if you hadn't said something wrong."

"Come, go on, or you'll get put in Newgate. You are no good and after no good. You had better make off while the play is good. Take my advice; you won't like a pumping upon, I dare say."

"Go on! Hit him on the nob," said another.

The tall man was borne down by public opinion, and glad to sneak off, not the less irritated that he could not injure any one; but he looked back most maliciously upon Margaret.

"Young woman," said a man, "just move away. He'll come back when we are all gone, and then he'll be sure to have you grabbed for asking for food, and sent to the House of Correction for begging. He's one of the right sort for that."

"Ay, ay; he is."

Margaret, seeing she was likely to become an object of notoriety, and, perhaps, unpleasantly so, willingly walked away, not before, however, she had received a few more halfpence from some of the more compassionate portion of the crowd.

She walked away, thinking in her own mind there was no refuge from misery for those who were once unfortunate. To be wretched was a sufficient passport for the unprincipled to seize hold of the opportunity to indulge in their propensity for trespassing on the feelings of others who were less fortunate than themselves.

Margaret had scarce gone the length of a couple of streets, when she thought she observed that she was followed by an elderly man. She recollected now that she had seen him in the crowd, and she became alarmed lest he should have some similar design against her.

After a time he came up to her, and peered in her face, and then he looked round to see if he were watched; but seeing no one near, he said, in an under tone,—

"Did I not see you in the crowd yonder?"

"I dare say you did, sir."

"Oh! you are a-begging?"

"I was," said Margaret, ashamed.

"Oh, it is a poor trade."

"I have no other. I am destitute."

"Is that child your own?"

"Yes, it is."

"You are married?"

"Yes."

"Oh!" said the old gentleman, and he seemed to be thinking about something, but couldn't make up his mind to it; but after a few minutes spent in tumbling over his pockets, he said,—

"I pity your case, for I think yours is one of real distress. Is it not so, my child?"

"It is so, unfortunately," said Margaret.

"Ah, well! I have no money with me now, but if you were to come home with me, I would give you temporary relief, and my wife could find you something for the child, I dare say."

"Thank you," said Margaret, surprised and overjoyed at the intelligence; for she had nothing on the child, other but what she wore, and she now had hopes of being able to return to Danton that night with food, for she had left him but a small portion of bread and some water, the only food she herself had had for several days.

"Nay," said the old man, "save your thanks till you see that what you have is worth them."

Margaret followed him at a short distance, and they went up one street and down another, until they came to a back street.

The old gentleman paused before a house, and looked back to see if any one were following, and, seeing no one about, he beckoned to Margaret to come up to him.

"If you will wait in the passage," he said, "I will send the servant with a light."

"Thank you, sir; I can wait here."

"As you please; but I dare say my wife will like to see you before she gives you anything."

Margaret made no answer; but at this speech, she at once followed the old gentleman into the passage, for he had opened the street door with a key he had about him.

"Wait a moment," he said.

Margaret stood still, and heard the old man go into a back parlour, and there ring a bell, and a servant answered it. A few words were spoken, and then the old man went out, and went up stairs, and then the servant came out.

"Oh!" she said; "my mistress wants to speak with you."

Margaret followed her into a small back parlour, where she saw a lamp suspended from the ceiling.

"Sit down," she said. "You are tired, I dare say."

"Very," said Margaret.

"Walked far?"

"Many hours, and have not rested once."

"Oh, poor thing! The old gentleman is very good, and when he once takes a fancy to anybody, there's no knowing the end of it. He will not leave after once relieving you."

"I am sure I am very grateful to him for his kindness, which has not come before it is wanted, for I am at the last extremity, I assure you."

"He's a little odd now and then, but that's only his way; and missus, she's a good soul; but she's not so generous as he is; but she'll do what she can."

"They are very good."

"Oh! uncommon—uncommon."

"Is she at home?"

"Yes; shall I take the child a little while? I will warm it before the kitchen fire."

"It will cry."

"Oh! dear, no! Poor little thing, it is perished with cold. You can come down for it, and then I will have a hot cup of tea ready, and some meat. It will do you good."

"The child will be a trouble."

"Not a bit,"

"It is not used to strangers."

"Never mind that."

"I would rather not."

"You don't think we can injure the poor little thing so?" inquired the servant, in a tone expressive of regret.

"Oh, dear! no. I am only fearful the poor little thing is ill, and unused to look upon strangers."

"Oh! never mind that; it will rest you, and enable you to speak more at ease. I'll take great care. Come, now; I shall think you really think I mean harm by the little innocent, if you will not part with it."

"Oh! I have no such fears," said Margaret; "and since you are so kind as not to mind the trouble, you can take it."

"Trouble! Oh, no!—no trouble at all. What a sweet face; but it is very thin."

"Yes, I can account for that."

"Very likely; but it will not want a friend in old Mr. Barnes, I am sure."

"Is his name Barnes?"

"Yes, it is."

"I shall never forget that name."

"I am sure he'll give you good cause to remember it."

She took the child in her arms, and began talking to it as she left the room, and walked down stairs.

A kind of alarm seemed suddenly to take possession of the mind of Margaret, for which she could not account. She looked round the room; it was not furnished as rich and comfortable people would have it furnished—at least, she thought so; and this again made her uneasy.

Why did they take away her child? She could not say; and yet she was very sorry she had permitted it.

They could have no design against the child. Surely they could not injure it? and yet, why else did she feel alarmed?

This was a puzzling question.

"They intend to kidnap it," she thought; and without waiting to ascertain, or to think upon the absurdity of the supposition, she arose and went to the door, with the intention of going down stairs for the infant.

In doing this, however, she encountered the old gentleman.

"Oh! you are here," he said.

"Yes, sir."

"Oh! very right—sit down."

Margaret sat down, without knowing

MARGARET'S VISIT TO THE SICK-BED OF THEODORE DANTON.

the reason why she did so, and the old gentleman continued to speak,—

"Oh! you have suffered much?"

"I have, indeed, suffered very much."

"You are married, you say?"

"Yes, sir."

"Do you live with your husband?"

"No, sir."

"What is the cause of that?"

"Alas! my husband has gone mad, sir."

"Where is he?"

"I do not know," said Margaret, who began to dislike this kind of examination, for it tore open wounds she had rather have allowed to fester in silence, without the prying eyes of strangers to examine them, and cause them to bleed afresh.

"You do not know?"

"No, sir.",

"Is he not in a place of confinement?"

"No; he is at large, wandering about insane."

"Ah; very uncomfortable for you to have a husband and no husband," said the old man with a leer.

Margaret did not see him.

"There," he said, "is some silver; it is all the small change I have about me now."

Margaret professed she was grateful, and desired to be allowed to have her child.

"They have it down stairs, I suppose."

"Yes, they were kind enough to take it for me."

"Very good; they wished to ease you. Now, wouldn't you like to have it in your power to do well for your infant—at least, better than you can do now?"

"Heaven knows how glad I should be if I could by any honest course procure the means of subsistence for myself and child."

"You may do this if you will."

"I would do it most willingly."

"Then listen; you have no husband, 'n point of fact."

"That is true."

"And I no wife."

"Indeed, sir, I thought," stammered out Margaret, "that you had; you said so, I thought."

"I did, because I wanted to speak seriously with you. You are young, and, despite your distress and misery, are very beautiful—very beautiful. Will you remain here and live with me?"

When he had said these words, he leered at Margaret, who was too confounded to speak, but remained trembling in silence for more than a minute. The old man misunderstood her silence, and said,—

"You will do well to consider over it; it is not an offer that is every day made to one in your condition."

"And will never be accepted by me."

"What?"

"I would never have entered this house had I dreamed for a moment of what was the object in enticing me here."

"Enticing you?"

"Yes, you have induced me to enter this place, that you may with safety insult my misery and wretchedness; but, though poor—ay, poorer than you can conceive—I have not fallen so low; I am not so abject as that, and never can be."

"But you can come to no harm."

"I do not understand you."

"Who can blame you?"

"My own conscience."

"Fiddlestick about your own conscience; how comfortable you would live, and how comfortable you might make your child."

"Oh, my child!"

"Would be better fed and clothed, protected from the cold, and in all respects more comfortable, and better taken care of."

"Very likely. I would do any honourable and creditable thing for the sake of my child, but what you offer me is neither."

"Come, come, my good creature," said the old man, laying his hand upon her arm; "sit down beside me, and talk the matter over; you sem frightened."

"I may be, since you hold such different language now to what you used but a little while since."

"You were in the street, then, and would not have listened."

"I know it; and because you think I am now obliged to do so, you venture to say that to me you dare not to a beggar in the streets."

The old man was somewhat annoyed, and not a little confounded; he had not anticipated such an opposition, especially thus argued; but he was the more inflamed, and he said,—

"That may be all very well; but I do not see why you object when you consider all things; you have no tie, nor I ——"

"I have my child."

"Which would be benefitted," said the old man.

"And I have my good name."

"Which will not procure you bread or a friend; you are altogether wrong, my good girl," interposed the old man.

"I am right; therefore, let me go; give me back my child—give me back my child."

She attempted to arise, but the old man seized her by the waist, saying, as he pulled her down again,—

"No, no, you must not go yet; I have more to say to you. Do you hear? Now come, don't be violent; I must tell you at once you cannot get out till I choose to let you."

"You cannot, dare not, keep me here longer than I will stay; you cannot mean it."

"I not only do, but walk to that door, and see if it be not locked."

Margaret the moment she got loose, flew to the door, but found it closed, and resisted her utmost efforts.

"God help me!" she said; "what have I done, that I should suffer in this manner? whom have I injured? what wrong have I occasioned by one artful, criminal act?—none!"

"Ah, that's where it is," said the old man—"people don't suffer because they have done wrong. Oh, dear, no. It's because Providence makes 'em do so without any reason of ours. Come,

come—accept a good offer, and be happy."

"Happy!" said Margaret; "and can you, who have plenty, an abundance, and who require nothing, but who have so far over and above what is absolutely necessary to gratify every want and legitimate desire—you who have all this and enough to gratify even vices—can you talk to any one in my condition and say 'here you are starving, you and your child; commit this bad act to please me, and I will relieve your distress'—can you do this and think you belong to humanity?"

"And why not?" said the old gentleman, in whom the recapitulation of the catalogue of the things he had it in his power to do, produced no other feeling than that of pleasure and gratification.

"Oh, man, man, can you, who are verging towards the grave ——"

"D—n it, what put that in your head? I ain't verging towards the grave—I ain't near it; I'm strong and hearty. I ain't likely to die. Pho—pho; it's all d—d stuff!"

"You may be nearer than you imagine."

"I—I—confound—I—eh? what do you mean?"

"You are mortal."

"I know that; well, what of it? We are all mortal, ain't we? What of it? I've a good life yet."

"And you are old."

"No such thing."

"Your looks—your grey hair ——"

"Well, I'm sure—a pauper to talk thus—a beggar out of the streets; and my grey hairs, too!"

"Yes, you are old."

"I am not fifty-eight yet, and that's no age. When I'm thirty or forty years older, then, indeed, I may think about being old; but not at fifty-eight —not at fifty-eight."

"You may be nearer the end of your life than you think for. God may cut you off in the midst of your wickedness; you may not even have time to repent the grievous sins you have committed and contemplate committing."

"Well, of all the cursed impudence that ever I heard ——"

"Think of all this, and then consider if what I have said is not the truth. I hope you may never be betrayed into

the commission of acts so unsuitable to your age."

"Oh, this is all d—d stuff!" said the old gentleman, rising in a great rage, and ringing the bell. "I made you a good offer, for which in return you talk to me about age, and I don't know what. I see it—I see it. It won't do with me; my money is as good as anybody else's. But you have a choice, I suppose. Thank God I'm independent, and don't care a button. for anybody—that's my sentiments."

The servant now came.

"Here, give this woman her child."

"Eh?" said the woman.

"Give her her brat."

"Yes," said the woman. "What's the matter?"

"Oh, an infernal saint, that's all. She's particular as to age."

"I'd stand little about that, if I were you; I wouldn't have asked her the question."

"Oh, there are plenty more where she came from."

"Ay, to be sure."

The woman left the room, and while she was gone, the old man said to Margaret,—

"So, you won't accept of my offer?"

"No."

"You may do worse."

"I cannot."

"Pho—pho! you don't know: starvation is worse for yourself and child; but you can choose your own fate. It's nobody's fault but your own if it does die, though it is young."

"I hope not; but you cannot save it if it is to die. Its fate cannot be retarded by you."

"Yes, good living would do it."

"And if I cannot get that honestly and honourably, I will not obtain it by other means."

"Very well; I might have taken means to convince you there was nothing of that kind in it; but I'm not going to be told I'm old by one whom I oblige. Oh, dear, no, not at all—quite the other way, I assure you, so you may walk."

At this moment the woman returned with the child, and gave it to her, saying, as she did so,—

"Well, I am astonished. I fully expected to hear a blessed riot, to say the least of it. I am conflobbered."

"Oh," said the old man, "she's a fool, or she'd know her own interest better than that."

"To be sure; who could be so silly? But I suppose she thinks too much of herself."

Margaret took her child, and felt her mind relieved of all anxiety on the account of the infant.

It was evident the old debauchee had been terribly vexed this time, for she had touched upon a subject that wounded him sorely, and upon which he was irascible and sensitive. His self-love had been wounded; he could not recover his ruffled temper.

It was fortunate for Margaret that she had by chance touched upon a subject that freed her so well from the old man; for the probability was, or rather the certainty, that violence would have been offered her ere she escaped from that house.

Margaret got the child, and she cared for nothing else in the world. The possession of her child caused Margaret's courage to rise; she felt herself better able to resist any attacks that might be made upon her, when she knew she had her child, and the knowledge of that gave her greater strength.

"Now, ma'am, troop, bag and baggage," said the woman.

"Yes," said the old man; "she don't know who's old or who's young, I'll be sworn. She must have a very young man for her husband. Come, ma'am, I'll show you I can make better bargains."

Margaret made no reply; but was about to leave the place, when the old man said,—

"Have you made up your mind?"

"Yes."

"You will not stay?"

"No, no."

"You had better consider of it. You are yet young and pretty; you may have many years of enjoyment yet, which you are likely to lose, as you are now "

"Can an old man like you desire to tempt one wretched, like myself, to evil? You who are more fit, as regards age, to be my father or my grandfather. Can you ——"

"There, there; that'll do. Push her out. D—n her father and her grand-father, and all her relations, and herself into the bargain. What infernal insolence! I am hale and hearty."

"Ay, a great deal better man than the young ones, I'll warrant. Give me a hearty, middle-aged man, one something older than a mere boy, before all your neither one thing nor another young fellows, as don't know their own minds."

"Ay, to be sure; but she don't see that."

"I can see that."

"Come, out with you."

"Out with you, ma'am," said the woman.

Margaret needed no second invitation; but walked past them both with great swiftness.

"There goes a fool," said the woman.

"To be sure," said the old man, who was yet in a great rage, for he had not cooled down.

The street door was only on the latch, and this Margaret lifted up, and in another moment, she stood in the street, and her breath came and went more freely.

"Thank Heaven for this escape!" she said. "Thank Heaven for all its mercies, and especially for this! Who could have believed that so much wickedness could exist in human nature?"

She turned away, and went through several streets; she knew not where she was. Her thoughts and recollection had been alike confounded, and she wandered on, not knowing where.

Suddenly she found herself near a large house; it was a corner one, and, before she was aware of it, she found herself in the midst of three or four men.

"Hilloa, Missus!"

Margaret paused.

The voice was a very gruff and brutal one; but she knew it was suppressed, and only used in a subdued tone.

"Hilloa, Missus!" repeated the man; "what do you do here?"

"I am merely passing along."

"Where to?"

"I don't know."

"Come, come, none of that gammon."

"I don't know where I am."

"Where do you want to go to?"

"I cannot tell the name of the place where I want to go. I only know it by sight."

"D——n nonsense! Do you think we are to be gammoned by such stuff as that? Oh, no!"

"It is the truth."

"You've been set on by the traps."

"I don't know who they are."

"Well, I'm blessed! You've cheek enough, at all events, and, were it not for the child, I'd give you a dowser."

"A what?" said Margaret.

"A smack of the mouth that would send your ivories down your throat, and you after them."

"I am sorry if I have offended you."

"Oh, stuff! You are wide awake and on the look out. Come, you must consent to be quiet and go with us. We've a job in hand, and won't be disturbed."

"I'd rather go on."

"No doubt,"

"I don't wish to stay here."

"I dare say not; but you must."

Margaret knew not what to do, she saw the men were brutal, and ready to commit any act of violence they might be willing to set about.

"What shall I do?" said Margaret, trembling.

"Go in there, and sit down, and don't hear, see, or say nothin,' or you'll get stunned in a second. We are too wide awake to be done so easy as all this."

Trembling with apprehension and fatigue, she walked up the steps of the house, at which the man tapped gently. It was opened, and a voice said, in an under tone,——

"What's the dodge now?"

"Here's a woman."

"Well?"

"Let her come in."

"I don't want her," returned the voice.

"Very likely; but she must come in and sit down till all's right. She mustn't go on and tell tales."

"Very well."

The door was opened, and a man seized her by the arm, and hurried her along into a large room. All was dark, and he said, as he pushed her into a seat—

"Sit still, and utter not a sound, as you love your life; for the first sound you make will be your last—you will be a dead woman in the next moment."

All was then silent, but she could now and then hear stifled sentences, and the creaking of places, as if doors were being forced in some parts of the house.

She had no doubt but they were robbing the place, and she was thus made a party to it.

In about an hour the men all assembled in the room, when a dark lantern or two were placed upon the table, but with their light upon the wall, so as to avoid going near the shutters.

"All right?" said one.

"Yes."

"Where's the swag?"

"Here."

As he spoke, he produced a quantity of plate, which they all hid about them, and where they could with safety; and then the rest was placed in sacks, and some money and jewellery were amongst them.

"This will pay," said one.

"I believe you."

"Let's have some wine."

"Don't be a fool, Jack."

"Why, you don't think I'd make a hass of myself, do you? I know that one must be sober on such an occasion as this, or else all goes wrong."

"It just does."

"Well, am I wrong?"

"No; go on."

"Well, here's fortune."

The men drank an ale-glass of wine a-piece at a draught, and then one of them said—

"Give the young woman some."

"Here, drink this; it will do you good."

"I would rather not."

"I see, you bear malice, because we have caught you. Now, don't be a fool; it will do the young 'un good."

"But it is not mine."

"Well, it don't hurt the wine."

"I would rather not have what don't belong to me."

"Now, I'm d—d, if you don't drink

it, I'll smack it in your face," said the man.

Margaret, fearing some act of violence, took the glass and drank half the wine, and then said to him—

" Do not make me take the other. I am unwell, and have not had any food for many hours. I am afraid of the wine."

" Why hadn't you said so before? Here are some biscuits—take them and eat them."

" Well, Walter, how about the time?" inquired one of the men; " is it time to be off, think ye?"

" I think we had better be ready to start at a moment's notice, for I think it is daylight now."

" That it is," said one of the men who had been on the outside, to look out; " I'll tell you what I think, we had better go at once; the street is entirely clear."

"Then, let's be off."

This was at once agreed to, and the whole party assembled, amounting to about six or seven, and having among them several hundred pounds' worth of plate and jewellery.

They all left the room, and cautiously treading along the passage they reached the street door, when one of the men inquired if the coast was clear.

" Yes, all right," said the man on the outside of the door; " come out as quickly as you please."

" Come on, then," said the foremost, and they all made their way into the street, and then immediately crossed it, and went down a lane not far on the opposite side of the way.

After passing some distance at a rapid rate, they came to a cart, into which they all jumped and drove away, leaving Margaret Bertram in the streets.

" Thank God!" she muttered, " I am free from these men; robbers though they be, they are not so disgusting, nor so wicked as the old man who had an abundance of everything."

She knew pretty well where she was, and now determined to make the best of her way to the place where Danton was. He had now been twelve or sixteen hours without any attention, and it would be some time before she could reach home.

She thought of the few pence the people had given her and the little food it would buy, when she suddenly recollected that the old man had given her some silver.

This recalled the fact to her recollection that she had forgotten to give it him back, which she would have done had she thought of it at all; but, as it was, she had been so full of fears that she had scarcely any power of thought left.

She, therefore, determined that she would wait in London until the shops were entirely opened to procure herself some food to take to the cottage for herself and Danton. This she accomplished in about two hours, and returned to the deserted house.

CHAPTER LXVII.

BERTRAM'S WANDERINGS. — THE DREADFUL DREAM.—THE SPECTRE BRIDEGROOM.

WE will now take a glance at Bertram, who escaped from the grasp of Theodore Danton, after the latter had rescued Margaret so opportunely from the murderous assault of the former. The dark cloud still hung over him, and his thoughts were as gloomy and sombre as the funeral mantle in which he enveloped himself.

It was with mixed emotions of fear and fury that he rushed from the spot where he had been so suddenly seized, and so signally defeated, in an object which he had compassed, and in which he believed he had succeeded—indeed, he had almost accomplished his diabolical purpose of murdering Margaret.

But how had he been foiled? By a stronger arm than his own. This was a galling reflection to him—a reflection he could not bear to think upon. Ay; a stronger man than himself had interposed between him and his wife.

Ay, so it was; but who was that man? That was a question that jealousy and suspicion always found a ready answer to; for no reason was there, other than that, why he should suspect the truth. Who was it, indeed, who would stand between him and his revenge—his chastisement of his wife? Some such an one as Danton, whom he believed to be the seducer of his wife. Who so fit? Who so likely? None; not one.

And why? Because nobody else, he argued, would have ventured to interfere in the quarrel between man and wife.

This was a weak argument, and Bertram, even in his state of mind, felt it to be so; but it was not enough to prevent him adopting it the more earnestly, because he blindly shut his eyes to the fact that it was unlikely and improbable.

It was not the less likely and improbable, because it really had happened. So far from that being any argument in favour of the probability, as a mere matter of speculation, it was improbable, and very unlikely to be the case. That it was so, must be considered one of the surprising facts which occur but rarely—that are only reckoned within the bounds of possibility; such a thing as a large prize in a lottery—the return of a comet after an absence of a thousand years of travel.

This, however, was unknown and unthought of by Bertram, who was only actuated or maddened by jealous fears and suspicions; so that, in fact, he was ready to adopt any opinion that came uppermost in his mind, at the same time that it favoured the peculiar bent of his intellects.

Thus it was he believed it must have been Danton who used such violence, and yet he thought that people could not stand still and see a murder committed before their very eyes. No —no; they could not do that.

On the night in question, he rushed Heaven only knew whither, for he neither knew nor saw. He fled for some time, believing himself pursued by the man who had struck him down; but finding after a time he was unmolested, he slackened his speed, and when at the corner of a street, he paused and looked back, and breathed fast and heavily.

"Not followed—not followed!—I thought I had been; but I suppose I have outrun him."

He paused, and panted for breath, and he wiped the blood and sweat from his face, for he had received some hard blows from Theodore Danton, and his features had been disfigured and distorted; and they had bled much from the blows and bruises.

"Fool—fool—fool! that I am," he suddenly exclaimed; and he struck his forehead with his hand.

He paused a moment and looked around him on all sides, and then stamping his foot, continued—

"Yes—yes; fool that I am, I ought to have guessed this; he would not have left her to follow me. No—no; he would not do that; they are together sure enough, and are conversing upon my flight. Yes—yes, they have succeeded, and I am foiled."

He ground his teeth.

"Yes; I have been foiled, beaten, ay, and frightened. Yes, frightened; ay,—I have been frightened."

He stamped his heel.

"And they, too, are laughing at my terror and flight. Oh, curses—curses! What would I not give to have them here now this very minute. I would crush them both—ay, they should die together."

Again he paused, and shook his clenched hand menacingly in the air, as he exclaimed—

"But—but they are gone, they have escaped me now. Another time they may not be so fortunate.

" I will leave the country—I will leave the country, and never return any more. That will be the best revenge I can take. Let sharp and bitter poverty overtake her and her brat. Let her linger and die—it will be a slow and terrible death. Ay, that will be obtaining the greatest revenge, because it is obtaining the greatest amount of pain from her.

"She was begging—I am sure of that; and she had not been in that place had she been able to go elsewhere. She had not been, with her child, at midnight, on a cold door-step had she any home—any shelter; but no, no, no. She is a houseless wanderer—truly, a beggar of the most abject class."

He paused, turned, and walked away slowly and solemnly, as the same turn had come across him.

* * * *

He wandered about the whole of that night, and early in the morning he paused before some mean place, where the earlier portion of the London populace can purchase cheap provisions, from a cup of coffee to a rasher of bacon, or a cup of tea to a plate of water-cresses.

He paused for some moments, and seemed as if he were uncertain in his resolution to go in or not.

The shop-door opened, and some men came out. They had been having some refreshments at the place. They looked at Bertram as they passed him, and one of them said to his companion—

"Jem!"

"Well, Bill."

"Did you see that cove's face?"

"What, that undertaker-looking sort of man? Yes."

"Ain't it beautifully ornamented?"

"It's pretty considerably bloody and black, if that is what you mean," said the other.

"Yes; he's got it last night somewhere, and he seems as if he were rather less sober than he ought to be."

"Ah, he's been at a funeral party; and having got miserably drunk and quarrelsome, has had a bit of a scrimmage, I'll be sworn. Look at him! Why, his back's all over mud."

"Ah, he's had a fair back fall, and that's the consequence of it; or else he's been taking a nap in the gutter."

"No; it's been a scrimmage, depend upon it; he's had a rough tumble for it."

"And got the worst, I think."

"You may be sure of that."

Bertram would hear no more, but walked into the coffee-shop, where there were many rough-looking men luxuriating over a compound by a singular perversity of language called coffee, although the real berry was, in all human probability, innocent of producing the slightest effect, as indeed it might reasonably be said to be absent.

He sat himself down in one of the little places where he was pretty well screened from those who were seated in the same box with him.

"What shall I have the pleasure of doing for you, sir, this morning?" said the landlord.

"Breakfast."

"Yes, sir."

The landlord hesitated; but seeing that the customer said no more, and feeling desirous of a more particular description of the article, he ventured to add,—

"We have several sorts, sir."

"Eh?"

"We have tea, coffee, rolls, toast, eggs, ham, bacon, bread and butter, and water cresses."

"Very well, let me have them."

"Eh?" said the landlord, bothered at the idea of his guest having all breakfasts at once.

The fact was, Bertram had only heard his last words—his thoughts were wandering.

"What will you have?"

"Tea and toast," he said, mechanically.

"Very good, sir," said the landlord.

"Tea and toast," he muttered to himself. "I see—slept out all night in company with people he oughtn't—drank more than he ought, and has been tumbled about more than he ought; got more cuffs than ha'pence, and more mud than sits well on a cloak, thought it might do well for the inside of a mud-cart."

"Tea and toast," he said, as he looked over the bar to the mysterious place where the manufacture was going on.

"For one?"

"Yes, for one."

"Fine morning this, Mr. Smith," said a customer in a rough coat to the coffee-shop keeper.

"Very fine indeed, Mr. Jones."

"Been a very bad night."

"An uncommon bad night."

"Streets too dirty to lie in."

"May be, sir, and may be not."

"Eh?"

"Why, some gentlemen may think so, and some may not."

"Indeed!"

"Some of my customers mightn't like to do it, and others might. You understand me, Mr. Jones."

And the landlord threw his huge thumb over his shoulder, and winked

hard at Mr. Jones, as much as to say,
—"Him as is in the next box rather
prefers it."

"I understand," said Jones, with
a grunt. "You don't happen to
know of a living mop as wants a
job?"

"A living mop?"

"Yes."

"No, I don't."

"I am sorry."

"What do you want one for?"

"Only to mop up the mud at our
street-door; it goes on accumulating
in spite of everything."

"Indeed! Can't you get a rag
mop

"No, they wear out so soon;
whereas a living one, if he gets worn
down, why, nature will make good the
damage, and keep him in working condition."

Bertram neither heard nor heeded
these remarks, for he was by far too
deeply buried in his own schemes to
take the least notice of anything that
was going on around him in the
shop.

The tea and toast being now ready,
the landlord walked up to the bar,
took it off, and marched up in proces-
sion to the box where Bertram sat.

"Tea and toast, if you please, sir."

As he spoke, he pushed the little
tray upon the table.

Bertram, who had been leaning his
head upon his hands in deep thought,
now turned round with a fierce glare
and a peculiar expression of the eyes
such as only the insane could exhibit,
and stared at him for nearly a minute.

The landlord staggered back, and

gasped for a second or two in great trepidation. He had never seen anything like it before, and he was taken by surprise.

"Well, I never! What a blood-thirsty fire-eater he looks. Now, I'm morally certain, and I'm never certain but I'm right, that that man would no more mind committing murder, than he would mind bilking me out of the reckoning, or of putting a knife in my waistcoat and ribs afterwards."

This was an uncomfortable state of things, and Mr. Smith's reflections were of a very uncomfortable character.

"Bilked and burked," he thought. "Ah, I see a regular doer. I suppose I mustn't ask for my reckoning."

Bertram was unconscious of the effect he had produced. Again he looked towards the landlord, and, seeing him still standing by him, he thought he wanted money.

"Oh!" he said; "you want to be paid?"

The landlord shrank into a small compass, and said, with a most affable smile upon his countenance—

"It is usual, sir, to prevent mistakes, to pay on delivery. No offence, I hope —all alike."

"None."

"See the notice, sir."

Bertram saw a notice put up, that, to prevent mistakes, it was requested the gentlemen would pay on delivery.

"All alike, sir."

"You shall have it."

As Bertram spoke, he thrust his hand into his pocket; but the landlord got out of the way, for he muttered—

"Now—now, perhaps he'll bring out his knife, and then there will be more cold meat in the larder than will be sold while it's fresh. Merciful Providence!"

These latter words were uttered in consequence of Bertram bringing out a purse, from which he took a sovereign —there being more in it—and threw it on the table saying—

"Take your reckoning out of that."

"Yes, sir—certainly, sir."

The landlord seized the sovereign, and carried it backwards to the bar, for the purpose of weighing it, and getting the silver; but, as he passed Mr. Jones, he whispered in his ear—

"Jones."

"Well—what?"

"He's a swell."

"Eh?"

"He's a swell."

"What——"

Here Mr. Jones jerked his head in the direction of the box in which Bertram was sitting.

"Yes."

"Well, I thought so. He's an uncommon swell when you come to consider what a death-hunter is after a spree."

"He's more than that."

"Ay—ay?"

"Yes."

"What?"

"Regular out-and-out swell."

"You don't mean it?"

"Look here. He has plenty more of the same sort in his purse, I can assure you."

"Indeed."

"Yes, he has."

"He's been in for it last night, sure enough. He's all over mud; what a figure to go home in. My eye, won't the family be in a nice state of convulsions!"

"Ha—ha—ha!"

"He's been at a funeral."

"And got drunk."

"And with the gals."

"Ha—ha—ha!"

The landlord, after a great many winks, with which he finished the conversation, walked up to the bar, and said—

"One tea and toast out of a sov."

The change, after due counting, was handed over, and duly carried by the landlord to Bertram.

*   *   *   *

Bertram sat some time before his food without partaking of it. It was some time before he ate or drank a mouthful; indeed, it was almost believed that he had forgotten it; but he soon after ate and drank what was before him mechanically, as though he took it as purely a necessary, and not a matter of pleasure.

After he had long pondered over the events of the night, he determined that before he undertook any further adventure, or pursued any particular course of action, he would sleep. He was fatigued—much fatigued, and felt rest to be necessary even to him. He turned to the landlord, and said—

"Do you let beds?"

"No, sir, else I should be most happy to accommodate you."

"Never mind," said Bertram; and he arose and left the place, to proceed towards his own lodgings.

"I will sleep," he said; "yes, I will sleep upon it; then—and yet, no time like the present; I will arrange all for quitting the country and travelling abroad."

He sought the packet office, and there engaged the attention of one of the clerks.

"At what time does the Calais packet start?"

"Early in the morning."

"Can I book a place?"

"You may come on board and take your place."

"Very well—about luggage?"

"That goes with the passengers," said the man.

"Oh! I see," said Bertram, as he walked out. "I must get a passport, and then I must go by some other conveyance from London. Ah! a coach—that will be best—coach to Dover; here is the office."

He walked up the steps, and entered the office; the clerks were busy; some calling out names and directions of parcels, and others entering them in large books and flinging them about.

"Do the French packets go from Dover?"

"Yes."

"Do the Dover coaches go from this office?"

"Yes."

"Have you any outside places for to-morrow?"

"Yes—how many?"

"One."

"Money, sir."

Bertram threw down a sovereign.

"What name?"

"Never mind the name. I have paid you a deposit, and shall be here at the hour," said Bertram.

"Very good, sir; if you ain't, coach starts just the same."

"I know it."

"Glad of it, sir, because money's forfeited, if passenger dies, and can't come," said the man at the books.

Bertram heeded not the remark; indeed, it is quite questionable if he heard it, he was so deeply buried in his own thoughts. Indeed, Bertram was now at all times absorbed in deep meditations, when he was not speaking, that he might have been called absent in mind, though present in person; and any one would have deemed him insane who had much cammunication with him; and in doing that they could not have been wrong.

He wandered through the streets an object of great wonder to many people, until he came to his lodgings, into which he at once entered, and then having, according to custom, thrown himself into a chair, he fell into a deep fit of abstraction.

"Yes—yes," he muttered; "she and her paramour—she and her paramour! I am not so blind but I can see that. Who else should it be?—no one—no one so likely. Who else could step between me and her?—no one. Who else would step forward and protect the adultrerous wife from the wrath of the injured husband? No one but he who caused the mischief."

He paused, and with his clenched hand smote the air, as if some imaginary being stood before him—some object of his greatest wrath—some one against whom he had the greatest antipathy, and whose life he would probably have taken, had they happened to be present.

"Yes—yes," he muttered; "they talk finely of my discomfiture—of my bruises and my escape; they both of them think they have well chastised me; but there is a day of retribution, which will come sooner or later—sooner or later. Ay, it must and will come—they shall know it—they shall know it. Yes; poverty will cling to her like a leprosy. She must, and will feel it. I will leave her; she is much reduced; and even if he support her, yet, in the course of time, she will become wretchedly poor, wretchedly diseased, and care and famine-worn. Yes—yes; that is the result of this great sin."

He rose and walked about; and

then, as if weighed down by some supernatural weight, and pressed upon by a sense of fatigue and drowsines, in a few moments, he threw himself upon the bed.

He had scarcely touched the bed, when he fell into a profound sleep. He had suffered much from blows, fatigue, and inclemency of the weather, which had been great and continued.

His sleep for some time was too deep to be troubled ; but yet, when rest had in any part restored the body to some of its functions, then his rest became partial and disturbed.

Such was the case at present ; for while lying and enjoying the benefit of the rest and repose, his thoughts returned to their accustomed wandering, in that strange and dim light of reason, in which float many images, all jumbled together more or less, and more or less distinct.

As Bertram thus lay in this dreamy kind of trance which precedes waking, he was conscious of many things that seemed to float through his mind, and give him notions of the future.

The first was the happy past—the first love—his meeting with Margaret —her beauty—her melancholy.

All, all, came with fresh force and vigour upon his mind—all as fresh as life itself. Oh, how he loved her then ! And yet the thought—perhaps it was an after thought—that she did not love him—she merely passively permitted his addresses—was wormwood infused into his cup of joy, and turned delight into bitterness.

Then again came the courtship—the marriage.

Yes—yes, and then came the denunciation—the death of her whom he had wronged, and of her whose death he had caused—and the mother's curse— all, all, came fresh as life !

Yes, that curse clung to him; he felt it, and acknowledged it, too—a dreadful curse ; and full well he knew he deserved it, too. None could tell so well as he that that curse was well earned.

There could be no doubt of that. He felt it was so ; and yet it made him not the less thirst for vengeance. He felt he deserved all ; and yet he would

do no less than revenge the outrage that had been committed by his wife and by Danton.

Then came the present. Yes, he remembered the cloak. He wore it now. It was his livery, and not more sombre and sad than his own prospects or than his purposes.

He remembered Mrs. Blair too. She was like a spectre in his mind. He could not tell what, but something indistinctly floated about them, that told him she was an enemy. He did not like the woman. She had too intimate a knowledge of some few facts connected with his career, and which would have caused some unhappiness, if known, and would have been a standing reproach against him, and he could never have said in any case,]
" You have done wrong."

Yes ; he knew his own moral guilt; he knew he had been capable of, and had committed acts, which were of far deeper guilt than the one he was now accusing his wife of.

Yes, greater, because her supposed lapse of morality arose through the unexpected return of an old and valued lover, whom she had loved; and, despite her own efforts, whom she did love ; moreover, she did not love the man whom she married, though she honestly endeavoured to do so, but she honoured and obeyed him.

He had planned and succeeded in the ruin of one who had confided in him—who loved him, and who had trusted him—he, who had sworn, as solemnly, ay, more so than if he had taken the oath at the altar, to love and protect her; and yet how had he done so ? he had left her to perish, and she had perished a victim to his heartlessness and perfidy.

Then came the event at the hotel. The suspicions and inuendos of Mrs. Blair, with her accusations, and his journey to the hotel, while all the while attendant spirits of evil hovered about him, and urged him onward to the spot, where he saw the sight that for ever blasted his happiness.

Then there was a lape of time, things seemed strangely jumbled together; there was mystery and gloom through which it was impossible to pierce.

However, there was a dim shadowing

forth of deep passions and fierce denunciations; disgrace and blows had been inflicted upon him; all was dim, dark and obscure.

* * * *

The scene shifted; he thought he was on the banks of a river. A beautiful, swift, deep stream; in the shallows of which grew the long horse-tail weed, whose daisy-like blossoms, for so they appear at a distance, make the moving flood appear like a crystal flower bed.

Then, too, came the water-lily, caudock weed, and its beautiful long yellow blossom looked like a king among the water weeds; the tall sedges, too, and rushes; the river's winding course, the willow trees, all made it a beautiful spot to sit and contemplate the wonderful works of nature.

It was quiet and calm.

Where the stream was shallow there was abundance of weeds, but the stream was here swift; a plank from side to side was stretched from the trunks of two stout trees, supported by cross pieces.

About three yards up the stream was a deep bend, where the water flowed silently and swiftly. Below, at some three or four hundred yards, was an extensive pool, deep, swift, and extensive, as though it were a basin, which overflowed into shallow streams or outlets, round willow beds, and filled with water plants.

A boat was in the middle of the stream.

A man stood up in the boat, and a woman was on her knees in that boat, in the attitude of supplication.

He recognised his own cloak on the shoulders of the wearer. Who could it be? He shuddered when he saw the features of both turned towards the land.

They were those of Margaret and his own.

Then the figure unloosened the rope by which the boat was fixed to the rope that was stretched across from side to side, and committed it to the mercy of the stream.

He then stamped, and caused the boat to sink; and, with a fearful shriek, the unfortunate Margaret was carried down the stream, despite tears and prayers, and then, with a loud, heart-rending shriek, that found an echo for miles, she sank to rise no more.

* * * *

He started from his sleep; and he awoke from his dream. His trance was over. He saw no more of the river or the boat; all had vanished. No sight met his eyes; no sound reached his ears save that which he had been accustomed to.

* * * *

"What is it?" he muttered; "what is it? It is but a dream—but yet a horrible dream; it was a dream, and yet horrible. Did I say horrible? Pshaw! it was the event I most desired. Ah, more of this another time. It will serve for a hint. A dream is it? It may become a reality with but very little trouble. I'll think on it."

* * * *

He now arose from his bed and walked about the room; but the place seemed to be too close and confined.

"I'll walk for a time," he muttered; "and then, when more at ease, will con this matter over in my mind."

He left his room, and then the house, determining that he would walk about until he felt fatigued or better.

The streets were filled with passengers, and the people walked and jostled each other; but young or old, busy or idle, all alike had a passing glance to bestow upon the dark, sombre figure that stalked along the streets —a figure that everybody shrunk from.

He was an object of curiosity; his singular long black cloak made him appear as if some follower at a funeral had been overtaken by some misfortune —drink or madness—and wandered about from the rest of the mourners.

Bertram saw he was noticed, and slunk away into some side streets where he would be less likely to meet with notice than in those in which there were greater numbers of people.

He had scarcely done so, when a man, who seemed to have been watching him, came up and touched him.

Bertram started. He had never met

with any one who had evinced any desire to speak to him.

"You are unfortunate," he said.

Bertram spoke not, but stood as if he expected the stranger to speak on.

"You are unfortunate."

"Well, I may be."

"You are—your looks bespeak it; but whether in mind or world's riches, you can best tell."

Bertram started.

"Take this," he said; and as he spoke, he forced a letter into Bertram's hands, who said—

"This is not for me."

"Wherefore not ?"

"Whom is it for ?" said Bertram.

"For you, Bertram."

"Ah !" exclaimed Bertram, startled and surprised—so much so, that he made a step backwards, then immediately the stranger turned and was out of sight, leaving Bertram with the mysterious-looking packet in his hand, and looking alternately at that and then at the spot where the stranger had stood.

"He's gone," he muttered, when he had recovered from his surprise—"he is gone, and it is useless to follow him, quite useless."

He turned, and placing the letter about his person, he again retraced his steps to his lodging, where he arrived in a short time; but no sooner did he behold the room than the dream he had experienced but a few hours since now recurred to his diseased imagination, and he sat down and pondered over it.

He remained in one attitude for some time, when he suddenly aroused himself, and said, aloud—

"No, no; I will not now. Some other time; but I will not now. My mind is scarce fit for the contemplation, much less the successful planning of any plot."

He turned his eye round the room. There were a few old, well-used books, without covers, for the most part, upon the shelf, thrust up in one corner.

His eye rested here for a moment or two, and then he arose, and walking to the books, he muttered—

"Ay, anything will do—anything will do to distract my attention from its present course, and give me time—ay' time is all I want, so that I may do nothing rashly, and nothing prematurely, else failure will be the consequence. Besides, such revenge as mine keeps."

He took down one of the books—the first that came—it mattered not to him which it was; he sought but to engage his attention for awhile, and then he would think of things that were now crowding fast on his mind.

He opened the book, and read as foilows :—

THE SPECTRAL BRIDEGROOM.

NOT far from Hermansdat, lived Hermione, only child of the Baron Hengreatta. He was the only descendant of a long line of barons, who had traced their origin as far back as the inroads of the Goths and Vandals, when they overran this place, conquered the country, and settled in many parts of it.

However, Hengraetta was a proud man, and was proud of his beautiful and lovely daughter, Hermione.

"Hermione," he would say, "has all the points and beauties of her ancestors; and, since Heaven has denied me a son, and decreed that I should be the last of the line of Hengraetters, why, I could not have a choicer gift to leave behind me to posterity."

"Indeed, he could not have a choicer beauty, or more amiable disposition than Hermione Hengraetter.

And was the beautiful Hermione such a rare beauty, and at the same time not adored by the youth of Hermansdat ?

Oh, no; forbid it Heaven ! that were a disgrace to human nature. There were many suitors; but two in particular made a different progress from all the rest.

Two ! ay, too lovers !

How ominous this sounds ! and how ill it sounds, too, when we say that Hermione had two lovers, who made a different progress from all others ; but we will explain how that came about, because it will look very like coquetry on Hermione's part.

The baron, her father, had designed in his own mind, that she should become the bride of Hoenloe, the young baron of Hestelle, a rich, and not an unamiable young nobleman. This was a suitor favoured by the father of Hermlone, and was received with respect by the daughter.

But there was another lover—one who was less favoured by fortune, but more by nature. This was Hermann Sclaws, a youth about two years older than Hermione—one who—but we will defer, and let the youth speak in his own proper person.

The time was evening; the red sun had sunk beneath the horizon, and all birds were hushed, save the evening song of the nightingale, which on the continent sings earlier than in this country. There was not a breeze—not a zephyr to waft a leaf, or sigh the softest music on the Eolian. The scene was a garden belonging to the baronial residence of Hengaretta. There were long, long walks, beautiful flower-beds, fountains, and trees, and groves, where it was delightful to walk beneath the shades of the tall trees.

Beneath these trees were two figures. They were those of Hermione Hengraetta and Hermann Sclaws.

"Dear Hermione," said the youth, as he passed his hand round her slender waist; "dear Hermione, day after day does that Hoenloe lead you down the dance; he presses your soft hand to his lips, and gives out that he is loved by you."

"And yet it is not so."

"It would be impossible for me to believe otherwise; but yet I cannot tell the misgivings I sometimes feel."

"Have you no confidence, Hermann?"

"I have," said the youth, proudly, "and think it impossible that you, Hermione, should deceive me. I will think or reckon upon nothing else but angel purity from you, my Hermione."

"And nothing else will you find."

"I am sure of it—certain as that I live."

"Then why, Hermann, should you have so many fears and faintings of heart about Hoenloe?"

"It is not as you describe, dear Hermione; I cannot with patience, much less pleasure, see another press your hand and kiss your fingers. I cannot bear they should do this with patience, much less pleasure."

"Oh! now, Hermann, look how selfish you must be. Do you not seek my hand?"

"I do."

"Is it any less than it used to be?"

"Not at all, that I can perceive."

"Then, if it be not less according to your eyes, you must admit it is to you the same as before."

"Yes; well?"

"Only this, the young baron has not despoiled you of any portion of my hand, since it is still as it was."

"I see it; but I would not let him touch the rosy fingers of my Hermione."

"But my father?"

"Yes; there is the hardship of the case. Your father's a rich man—he's a rich man, and I a poor one."

"Not poor."

"Comparatively so. So much so that he would reject me for a son-in-law, were I to propose myself."

"But you know our compact, Hermann—a compact that we have sworn to so solemnly that he or she who breaks it must suffer punishment truly terrible."

"We should. I well remember the terms of that oath."

"And so do I."

"It is," said Hermann, "that whichever of us two should become untrue, should suffer in this life or the next. That, living or dead, we should be true to each other; and as to commit a breach of this oath, by contracting a marriage with any other person, under any stress of circumstances whatever, we have called down the direst vengeance of Heaven to visit the enormity of the sin with a proportionate punishment."

"Such it is," said Hermione, as she crossed herself. "So be it! I hope when I break it, that the dead may rise and bear me away in their arms, and cast me into perdition."

"The same also for me," said Hermann.

"When do you quit these parts?" said Hermione.

"In a few more days, Hermione, and in one year I return, and then, Hermione, you will be mine—ay, mine, despite all the efforts of the baron and young Hoenloe."

"I will, Hermann; I have sworn it."

"I am sure none will ever live to reproach you with infidelity to such a vow, Hermione, and I never can think of aught good, beautiful, and true, but it will recall thine image to my mind."

"And dear Hermann will never be absent."

"Then farewell, Hermione, and when we meet again, we will renew our present happiness."

"Farewell, Hermann, and fortune be with thee."

"If I have thy love, then, indeed, fortune is with me. Thus blessed, I am doubly blessed."

*   *   *   *

The lovers parted. Hermann Sclaws departed upon an errand of fortune—one that would, if successful, render him a comparatively rich man, and give him a higher rank than that in which he then moved. It would remove one, and but one, of the obstacles between him and marriage with Hermione.

However, it would have been impracticable if all the obstacles had been removed, such as related to fortune and rank; because the baron had made an arrangement to marry Hermione to Hoenloe, and, having made a resolution, he felt bound in honour to keep it, though the resolution was confined to his own breast, and had never been uttered to human ears.

The fact was, the baron was one of those men who deemed it necessary to appear to have a character for firmness, which firmness, in his opinion, could only be shown by sticking obstinately to any one point, and following it up through thick and thin.

The baron never would admit the expediency of any proposition of his own; but the more impracticable it appeared, the more sure he was to carry it, the means being exerted far more than adequate to the object proposed to be gained.

Thus it was he was determined that Hermione should marry Hoenloe, and never once thought of the necessity of consulting the inclinations of his daughter; this, indeed, he would have deemed superfluous and quite unnecessary on his part. She had been a very good daughter, and, no doubt, would be so still; and then there was no need of his anticipating her disobedience to his wishes.

It so happened that Hermione, knowing her father's infirmity of disposition, received his intimation in silence, not daring to offer any objection to his choice, especially for one who was, in his eyes, far less eligible than young Hoenloe, his favourite.

But though Hermione succeeded in eluding the vigilance of her father in this matter, yet she could not do the same with the young Hoenloe; he, with all the watchfulness of a lover, saw that his only favour arose from the fact of the father's countenance, and that in private he was coldly received, or rather received in the light of an old acquaintance, or friend of the family, and treated as a privileged person, of whose sayings and doings there was no need to take any notice.

Hoenloe could make no head against this, as all his passionate declarations of love were treated as complimentary common-place, and thus he was at fault.

He saw this could not be without some cause, and that cause must be some favoured lover, a secret one, since it was not known generally, or even to her father, else he would have mentioned there was a difficulty in the way which would have to be overcome by their joint endeavours.

He set to work and determined he would discover, if possible, who this could be; yet would, by these means, defeat all his endeavours to obtain the consent of Hermoine to wed.

Having succeeded in his object, and discovered Hermann Sclaws to be his rival, he saw but one means of extricating himself from the difficulty of making a suit that was not likely to be productive of anything, save disaster and disagreeables, and that was in having his more fortunate rival assassinated.

This he considered safe and expeditious, and caused him to hire a couple of men to watch and dog him wherever he went, and when the oppor-

tunity offered, to stab him and kill him.

This the ruffians undertook to perform to the satisfaction of their employer, who was to reward them liberally for their work.

The deed was done, and Hermann Sclaws had scarce left Hermione, and walked two or three hundred yards, ere he was suddenly stabbed in the back, and he fell dead without a groan.

This done, the ruffians returned to their master, and demanded their reward for their deed of blood.

The young Hoenloe now knowing his rival to be dead, urged on his suit with Hermione, assisted by the baron her father.

Hermione's grief at the death of her lover was great, but she was under the necessity of concealing it, so far as it could be concealed, under the plea of illness.

The baron, her father, urged on the suit of the young Hoenloe, and the youth himself was urgent.

What could be done? her lover was dead, and she was disconsolate, and had now no object to love; but young Hoenloe loved her, and was always in her society, so that by degees she became reconciled to his presence and suit, and finally she lent a favourable ear to his tale of love, and eventually forgot her old lover, whom she had reason to love living or dead, and to whom she swore never to have another lover.

Those vows were forgotten, and now new vows were given and taken, and even the wedding day was fixed. It was then that the old baron felt all the pride of the father and the great man; his longings were fully gratified by such a son-in-law, whom he believed to possess all the qualities that render one of his rank desirable.

* * * *

The wedding day was come, the ceremony was performed amid much splendour and beauty. The guests were numerous, and many were wealthy; but all added to the splendour and gaiety of the scene.

The day wore away, and the evening came. The state halls were lit up, and the whole castle was illuminated with the lights, and the gates were thrown open, for the baron kept open house that day; there were feasting and revelry for all who came. There were no hungry stomachs in the neighbourhood on that day.

As the evening approached, the festivities became more and more gay, and the music and dance became the theme of all; every one drank among the gentlemen, to say nothing of the ladies; while all the latter danced or affected to do so, and all the world knows that was the same.

But, hush; what is going on? It is the baron proposing the health of the bride, his daughter, and the bridegroom, and it is midnight; hark, the chimes of the castle clock!

At that moment a tall figure enters the grand hall, and walks up to the bride; the bridegroom turns, and stares, and staggers; the bride turning, screams and faints. It is the form of Hermann Sclaws, all pale and bloody; his flesh is wasted, and his body indistinct and shadowy; he seizes her by the arm, and he says in tones that cause every soul to shrink back aghast—

"Hermione, thou art mine, and I thine, living or dead; such are our vows, and I claim thee!"

Thunder seemed to shake the fabric to its foundation, all was darkness, and when lights were brought, the young Hoehlce was found dead on the floor, while Hermione was no longer to be seen, nor was she ever again heard of.

CHAPTER LXVII.

THE MYSTERIOUS VISION. — THE DETERMINATION OF BERTRAM TO FOLLOW IT.

BERTRAM looked up from his reading. He certainly did feel to some extent withdrawn from a too close consideration of his own peculiar sorrows, by thus plunging into the realms of fiction.

He thought that now he could surely retire to his couch again, if not to sleep soundly, at all events to enjoy some sort of repose, which would not be haunted by such visions as now had of late too frequently disturbed him.

It was strange that, somehow or another, he had never blamed himself sufficiently to strike at the real root of all his misfortunes; but with a kind of gloomy suicidal philosophy, had considered that he was himself the injured party, without for once dreaming of the possibility of his having all along been very much in the wrong, and most wofully mistaken.

Perhaps, if such a thought did cross his mind, it was too agonising, as well as too humiliating, to be long entertained, and, therefore, he speedily dismissed it.

After so long a period of time, to think that he had been heaping misery upon his own head, as well as upon the head of his innocent wife and unoffending child wrongfully, may well be supposed to be an idea which, when it did present itself, was fraught with positive madness.

And yet, could it be for ever absent? Could it be possible there was no day in the year, no hour in the day, when the fallibility of human nature would appear so fixed a proposition, that he might be led to doubt if all his seeming evidence of his wife's infidelity was but some dreadful delusion after all?

Yes, he—even he—half maddened as he was, had some of those moments of what we ought to call maddening thought.

And although, as we have remarked, that when these ideas came across him, he strove as much as he could to chase them from his consideration, yet they would obtrude themselves; and on this particular night, of all others, they seemed resolved to stay by him with a pertinacity that resisted all his efforts to shake them off.

He lay down and closed his eyes, and then after a time he must have, with his mind full of such impressions as we have mentioned, fallen into a kind of dreamy reverie, which cannot be described as slumber, but yet which so far clouded the reasoning and reflective powers, as to give to the imagination sufficient power to prevent the judgment distinguishing accurately between the real and the unreal.

When the fancy is full of any particular subject, it has a tendency to prevent bodily repose of that calm, deep, refreshing character, which is so beneficial; but when there is much physical weariness combined, as in Bertram's case, with such a state of things, the almost invariable consequence will be the subsidence of the mental powers into that half sort of activity which goes by the name of reverie.

And it was this state, then, into which Bertram fell now, after he had in vain tried completely to wean his mind from what may be truly called the horrors that oppressed it. He fancied, as he lay there in the stillness and the silence of that chamber, that the door was gently opened, and a tall, majestic figure glided into the room.

It was not so much fear as an intense sort of surprise that came over him, as he looked upon the countenance of his unknown visitor; for although that countenance had on it a touch of exquisite sadness, it was nobly and grandly beautiful.

The form, and the whole appearance of this visitant looked not like those of any mortal man, and Bertram, with a silent kind of awe, felt convinced that he was in the presence of a superior intelligence, who had come to promise, to warn, to denounce, or to threaten. There was something fearfully solemn in the silence which reigned in the apartment, and Bertram afterwards distinctly recollected, that at the moment he asked himself if he were awake or sleeping, and continuing the visions of that most disturbed night.

For a few moments, he thought the stranger was profoundly still, and then he lifted from his side a small hand mirror, which he held before the eyes of Bertram. Small as was the hand-mirror, as Bertram looked in it, it seemed to present to his eyes a large field of vision, and he saw represented the interior of a spacious and handsome apartment, furnished with all the costly appliances of taste and luxury that could be well heaped together in one favoured room.

As he continued looking, he saw the exact likeness of himself sitting upon a couch, while partly reposing on a costly ottoman at his feet, and partly resting on his knees, was a young and beautiful child.

It was a girl, and the long glossy ringlets of her raven hair floated in most admired disorder around her neck and shoulders.

About the room there were, engaged in different child-like occupations, several young creatures, all of whom, by some sort of impulse, he felt as if he could have claimed as his own.

The moment he came to this conclusion, he saw as if the door of the handsome apartment represented in the mirror was gently opened, and a female form, arrayed in the most becoming and chaste morning garments, made her appearance. It was his wife. He knew her at once. She wore her old aspect of calm and gentle beauty, tinged with the more matronly air which years of happiness might have brought upon her.

He thought that she went from child to child of that young group that was in the room, and kissed each tenderly. Then he fancied she came to him, and placing her hand gently in his, she looked smilingly in his face, and pointed to the little ones with such an expression that he felt a sudden emotion come over him, too weighty for utterance.

"This is what might have been," said the sage-looking character who held the mirror—"this is what might have been, Bertram; but you cast from you the good which God had given you, and you shall now see what it is."

The small mirror was turned, and Bertram, after a moment, saw that it seemed to be divided, as if down the middle by a wall, into two portions, similar to some scenes at the theatres, when two interiors are to be represented at one and the same time upon the stage.

One of the pictures showed him himself, lying in that wretched room of his, looking as miserable as he indeed really was. It was no exaggerated picture that. Indeed it required none. The other represented a wretched hovel, which looked like an out-building of some farmhouse, which had been completely deserted by the well-housed and well-fed animals of the homestead.

Although, however, this out-house might not be considered good enough for the accommodation of cattle, there was something human in it, and Bertram, after a time, saw the figures of his wife and child.

Margaret was lying upon some straw, in a half reclining position, sleeping apparently, while the child—that child which he had the means of surrounding with all the comforts which those dear little ones ought to have around them—was in a state of squalid wretchedness, slumbering on its mother's breast.

As he looked, the form of his wife moved, he thought, and he could see through the clinks in the walls and the roofing of the wretched hovel as if the daylight was coming.

"Behold!" said the shade who held the mirror—"behold!"

He felt as if compelled to look, and he saw this vision of his wife gently awaken the child. He saw her pass her hand across her eyes, and glance towards the opening in her wretched place of shelter, which proclaimed that another day had come. Then he saw her place the child upon its knees in her lap, and her voice came upon his ear as she said—

"My darling, it is morning, and you must say your prayer."

He heard then his own child repeat the Lord's Prayer; but after it was an addendum, which it took from the lips of its mother, and repeated after her.

God of Heaven! could he hear those words unmoved? They were a blessing on himself—yes, a blessing on his head.

The mother, in all her misery, in all her depths of affliction, and despite all the dreadful injustice that had been done to her by him, Bertram, still did not forget to teach the child to know his name and to lisp its infant supplication to Heaven for him.

"Margaret—Margaret," he said—"Margaret."

Even as he spoke, the form of his supernatural visitor grew dim and indistinct, and the vision in the mirror gradually faded away.

The sound of his own voice awakened Bertram from his reverie, and he sprang to his feet, trembling in every limb, and the dew of fear standing on his brow.

"Is this another dream?" he gasped—"is it a dream or a reality? Heaven direct me now—Heaven direct me now."

There was a knock at his chamber door at this moment, and he sprang as far from it as he could, with a feeling of intense alarm that something was about to happen, which might drive him to positive distraction.

It was morning, too, for light—the cold grey light of the early day—was struggling through the dingy panes of glass in his window. The knock was repeated, and it was then only by a great effort that Bertram could gasp out the words—

"Come in—come in."

He forgot, at the moment, that he had made his door fast, as usual, and that it was out of the power of the person demanding admission to comply with the injunction. He saw the handle of the lock turned, but, of course, the door remained closed.

A strong presentiment of danger to himself came over Bertram, if he were to open the door. He trembled at the idea of doing so, and yet he felt as if impelled by some irresistible impulse to move slowly towards it for that purpose.

As he neared it, he resolved upon questioning the person demanding admission before he granted it; so making a great effort—for it really required one—to command his voice sufficiently to enable him to speak without so much of the evidences of fear as his feelings would have prompted him to throw into it, he said—

"Who knocks? Speak—speak!"

There was no reply to this adjuration, but, with a monotonous perseverance, the knocking for admission continued, as if whoever it was who wished to have the door opened was perfectly voiceless and passionless.

It was very strange, and Bertram trembled with dread.

"Who knocks?" he said again; and this time the voice was fainter than before, and he seemed not near so capable of controlling the strong emotions of fear which shook his frame.

Still there was no answer; and now his hand was upon the small bolt that constituted the only fastening on the inside.

"I cannot help it," he gasped, "I cannot help it. Were death itself on the other side of the door, I must open it."

Even as he spoke, he drew back the bolt, and the door was free. But it would appear as if he, whoever it was, that in so mysterious a manner had wished to come into the room, did not know that the only obstruction to letting himself in had been removed, for the knocking still, as before, continued, and Bertram had time, which he eagerly availed himself of, to retreat to the window which was opposite, he before said, in a voice which had tones of despair and fright in it—

"Come in, come in, be you whom you may. Come in, the bolt is withdrawn."

Slowly the door was opened. Bertram kept his eye, as may be well supposed, fixed with a glance of horrible intensity upon the opening of it, and he saw the figure of a man, enveloped in a cloak, about as sombre and strange looking as his, Bertram's, own black mantle, enter his apartment.

The cloak so completely encompassed the stranger, even to the lower part of his face, that no one who even had known him ever so well could have recognised him. Bertram, however, would have been puzzled to pronounce who he was had he come in more,

openly, and undisguisedly shown his features.

The solemnity of manner with which this man walked into the miserable room reminded him, Bertram, strongly of the sage whom he had seen in his dream or reverie, and such was the state of mental excitement into which he had been thrown, that he would scarcely have been surprised to have had revealed to him, by the removal of the cloak, the form and features of the noble and venerable-looking being with the mirror, which were so fresh in his recollection.

He did not speak, and he who came in thus strangely was equally silent. He closed the room-door after him, and shot the little bolt into its place. Then he advanced to the centre of the apartment, and in a deep-toned voice, which had in it all the melancholy cadences of a broken heart, he said—

"Your name is Bertram?"

"It is—it is!" said Bertram. "But I know you not, although there is something which tells me I ought to know you."

"You should know me—it is necessary that you should know me, Bertram; and, from this day henceforward, you shall know me well, and, I also hope, know yourself better."

"Name yourself, and I shall be the better able to judge of the concealed meaning of your words. Do you come as a friend, or as an enemy? But why do I ask? I have none of the former —I have many of the latter."

"You have one of the latter," said the stranger, "who has achieved your ruin."

"Yes—yes; and his name is—"

"Bertram! Bertram is his name; for, if ever mortal man lived to be his own most bitter and relentless foe, you are that man—yes, you are, indeed, that man; for there is no living being —no, not the exertions of the whole world to injure you could have accomplished one hundreth part of what you have done yourself."

Bertram was awed by the solemnity of manner in which the stranger spoke to him, but he was, on the other hand, much relieved to find, as seemed now clear to his perceptions, that he who addressed him was no supernatural agent, come to terrify him from his reason.

"I should surely know that voice," said Bertram; "somewhere, I think, I must once have heard it."

"You did hear it once, and in a moment of danger to yourself you heard it. It is a wonder that at that time when your hand was uplifted against her whom you had sworn to love, you did not hear it for the last time you were capable of hearing any voice in this world."

Bertram made a step towards the bed, as he exclaimed—

"Speak, speak again. I feel convinced that you are—"

"Go on, why do you pause?"

"I may be mistaken. My brain seems on fire. Why have you sought me here, if you are not, and why have you sought me he, if you are——"

"Theodore Danton."

"Yes, you are he! You have come to triumph over some of the misery that you have made, but it shall be a triumph of short duration—death, death!"

Bertram, from a place of concealment about the bed, snatched a pistol, but before he could make the least use of it, or even put it in a proper state to discharge, Theodore Danton, for it was indeed he, rushed upon him.

There then ensued a short but decisive struggle. Theodore wrested the deadly weapon from his hands and cast it through a window. Then he held him with a grasp that could not be shaken off as he said—

"I have come here to say to you what I will say, Bertram, and what you shall hear. Your opposition is in vain. I am not so mad as I was, but yet there is sufficient, perchance, of the frightful energy lurking in my system to make me dangerous. You shall hear me, I say, and far better for you will it be to hear me calmly."

There was a terrific earnestness in the way these words were uttered that made them sink deep into Bertram's heart.

———

CHAPTER LXVIII.

THE INTERVIEW.—THE ACCESSION OF MADNESS.—THE PROMISE OF BERTRAM.

BERTRAM, when now he felt assured by his own admission that this was indeed Theodore Danton who was with him, and found with what terrific energy he had been at once overpowered and disarmed, began to feel as if his last hour was surely come.

He had, too, a most vivid recollection of him. He had been struck down in the street while he was threatening Margaret, and now he was able to couple that evident act of a furious madman with the name of Theodore Danton, he considered that his life was in his hands, and not worth a moment's purchase.

If he were to cry out for assistance, in all probability he would be but at once expediting a fate which, if it were to be at all avoided, must be done by finesse, rather than by force, or anything that bore an aspect of opposition.

His terror, however, was too plainly depicted on his countenance to be mistaken, or to escape the observation of Theodore, and after holding him tightly by the throat for some moments with a clutch that it was well for Bertram was principally confined to his clothing, he released him, saying—

"Coward, you tremble now! and yet how great and blustrous a bully you were when your only opponents, if such they could be called, were a woman and a child!"

"What do you want with me, Mr. Danton?" said Bertram.

"Oh, indeed!" said Danton, in a voice of terrific scorn; "I am, Mr. Danton now, am I? Why do you not call me a villain? Why do you not twit me with being the seducer of innocence, and the disturber of your peace; for if I am not all that, where is your justification for all the course of conduct you have pursued so long? I say, Bertram, I demand of you, where is its justification? I, plain Mr. Danton. Do you understand me, Bertram?"

"I wish to have no altercation with you," said Bertram.

"Indeed!"

"No, I have only one favour to ask of you, and that is, that you will leave me to myself; a favour I think I ought to receive."

"Undoubtedly a poor one to ask. But how is this? It was only a few minutes since that your indignation was so great you could have taken my life, and perchance you would have done so, or inflicted, at all events, some grievous injury, had I not deprived you of the means to do so. You are silent. It is fear now that induces you to smother your passions, and treat me with a seeming courtesy."

Bertram felt too bitterly the truth of these words to attempt any reply to them. After a pause, Theodore Danton continued—

"Well, I cannot choose with what feelings you are to listen to me. All I could promise to myself was, that listen to me you should; and, therefore, that you do so, through so ignoble a motive as personal fear, I cannot help, although I would much rather it were from a better impulse."

"What can you have to say to me?" said Bertram.

"Much as regards its importance, but little as regards the number of words in which it may be placed."

"Say on, then."

"I will; but let me warn you, Bertram. You have made an attempt here against my life. I will overlook it; but I know the same feelings that induced that attempt still remain, since nothing has occurred to alter or to modify them. So I warn you, I have a sharp and a wary eye,—attempt aught else of such a character, and you are within the minute a dead man."

"I do not intend," said Bertram, with more alarm still. "I do not intend. I give you my word you shall go in safety."

"Your word! A poor reliance, indeed! I will accept of your fears as my guarantee. Those fears which are legibly written on your craven countenance."

"I am not disposed to quarrel; say what you please."

"Yes; I may say now what I please, because you have found that I am physically your superior, and so I will at once proceed to the object of my mission. Bertram, this is the first time you and I have ever met upon such a subject; I hope that it will be the last, so that all I have to say shall be here said."

"I can guess the subject."

"Yes, you may well do so; the guilty may always guess, that any unpalateable discourse is upon the subject of their offences."

"I know not how you make me guilty."

"Do you not? then, that I will tell you. You have been guilty of lying, sir, in the face of Heaven; that is what you have been guilty of."

"You charge me harshly."

"Not at all. You swore to love Margaret; and, although love is a passion of the soul, which, in its rise, its progress, or its continuance, cannot be subjected to the will, so as to be made properly the subject matter of an oath, yet how have you fulfilled even the commonest obligations of a husband towards that being whom you induced to venture all her capital of happiness with you?"

"You can answer the question you propose yourself," said Bertram. "There are obligations on both sides of the matrimonial agreement, which, if broken on either side, form a ground of good cause for the lapse on both."

"Agreed. And so, if Margaret had chosen to forget the vow she made to be yours and yours only, she might, according to your expressed opinion, have done so without censure?"

"Nay."

"Nay! but, sir, I say yea! You would insinuate that it was she who broke the social compact, and so empowered you to do so; but that is false—false as the bad heart that conceived the object of her ruin, and found in you a ready tool for achieving it."

"To what do you allude?"

"I allude to that bold, bad, dreadful woman, Mrs. Blair."

"Mrs. Blair?"

"Yes; you know her well; she had a secret of yours to keep; a secret which concerned your character as a man of honour—ay, as a man of common ordinary humanity, and so you chose to allow that fiend in human shape to assume a position in your own house, which terminated in your own ruin, and in the destruction of one, dearer by far to Heaven than a thousand such as you can be."

"Where have you acquired a knowledge," said Bertram, with surprise, "of my private affairs?"

"It matters not; I have made it my business to know all, and I do know it. Oh, fool, fool! what a treasure have you cast from you! You are as one walking in the glorious light of day, who purposely closes his eyes, that he may tumble in his path, and encounter dangers, which by the merest observation he might have avoided. Fool, fool! but that your conduct had been fraught with fearful consequences to others, far more estimable than yourself, I could stoop perchance to pity you, and so divest myself of some portion of the scorn with which I now regard you."

"I again ask you to leave me. This is a fruitless dialogue."

"I will not leave you, Bertram, nor is the dialogue fruitless; you shall confess the wrongs that you have done, or one of us, or both, perchance, shall give to this place such a frightful reputation, that the curious shall come far and near to look upon it, and fill their greedy ears with the particulars of a tale that shall in its very memory startle the sleeper who at the dead still hours of the night awakens for a moment to its memory."

Bertram felt faint and ill.

"You hint at murder!" he gasped.

"No," cried Theodore Danton, "I hint at retribution. I do believe I am the sole surviving relative of your much injured wife, and it is my sacred duty, therefore, to stand between her and all evil; to protect her even from you."

"This house is full of people," said Bertram; "you do not know your danger. Any noise, or cause for alarm, would soon bring abundance of assistance."

"Danger," said Theodore, "is a word which I have erased from my vocabulary. I only live now to right the oppressed."

"But, would my death right them?"

"Yes, you shall right them living, or you shall die; and, as you have made no will—ah, I see you have not, by that sudden change of countenance—I say, as you have, then, made no will, your much injured wife and child shall inherit, at your death, what you possess, and so be, to some extent, righted. You understand me, now?"

This was a review of the case, as unpleasant as it was novel to Bertram, and he said, faintly—

"I am willing to listen."

"'Tis well," added Theodore, "you should pray while you do listen, that Heaven may grant you grace to believe. You may yet, if you are so minded, repair some of the evil which you have done, and purchase some hope, by repenting of the remainder."

"I have said that I would listen to you."

"You listen by compulsion; and now, Bertram, I tell you that there lives not a more innocent being than your wife."

Bertram made a gesture of impatience.

"I repeat it," said Theodore, with vehemence; "and you shall have a plain unvarnished tale, which will—or which ought—to bring the conviction of her innocence fully to your mind."

Bertram did, as Theodore said, listen by compulsion to what was told him, and hastily as he could, consistent with precision in his details, did Theodore state what had happened. At its conclusion, he said—

"And now, sir, these are the real circumstances out of which you have contrived to make such an abundance of misery. Your wife is innocent; you cannot recompense her in any way for what she has endured. Heaven alone can and will do that, while the sin of it shall lie at your door; but you can prevent a continuance of those evils that afflict her."

Bertram had listened with mingled feelings to the narration of Theodore Danton. At one moment there came over him an irresistible idea that it was the simple truth that he heard; but then, again, when he recollected from

whose lips it came, he would imagine it just possible that this was but a well-contrived artifice to wring from him a provision for one who if she had been guilty, of course deserved none.

When the story was concluded, his countenance expressed a variety of emotions, and he said to Theodore Danton—

"Margaret is the most injured of women, or you——"

"Go on ; I am quite content to hear the alternative. You would say that I was the most arch hypocrite that ever stepped. Be it so. I admit one or the other to be true, and assert the former to be the case. What have you to say ?"

"I know not what to say. You give me no evidence."

"Does not the tale itself, in all its circumstances, bear evidence of its truthfulness ? Does not your heart tell you, that such a woman as that Mrs. Blair was capable of such conduct as that which I attribute to her ?"

"I do not know—I cannot know. Leave me. I will think—I will think."

"I will not leave you yet ; I had a sacred purpose to fulfil, and I have fulfilled it. It was to tell the truth. If you will not believe it when you hear, I have another duty to perform—a duty, perchance, more human than sacred, but still a duty."

"What is that ?"

"The duty of requiring justice against the traducer of one akin to me by blood as well as by feeling ; you are that one's persecutor, and I warn you that I am her defender."

Again there was a strange gleaming sort of light visible in the eyes of

Theodore Danton, which more than once Bertram had observed, as if to indicate to him that the fire of insanity was not extinguised, and he feared it.

As for Danton himself, he could scarcely be considered for a long time past as quite rational; but then his mental characteristic had been a cold, gloomy, misanthropical sort of ferocity, which was subdued before the more wild, daring, and headstrong passions which lent fire and energy to his mental excitement.

How he had contrived to pick up so accurately as he had done all the really authentic particulars which he had of Margaret and Mrs. Blair, will appear in due course, but certain it is, he had the whole of the circumstances in such a manner, that they must have come from some one whose information was most extensive and accurate.

"Decide," he cried, firmly. " Will you do justice to those you have injured, or must I do justice against you as the injurer of them ?"

"I know not what you can require," said Bertram ; "if now I were to cry out aloud, even from here, help ?"

"Hold ! another word of such a nature, so uttered, is your last. Think you I cannot see through the flimsy device by which you would call for assistance, and so spoil my purpose? I tell you, I set my own life as nothing in the matter, compared with the cause in which I am embarked. Through me, most unwittingly and innocently, has Margaret suffered. Through me, then, shall she be righted, and if it require my death to do it, I can cheerfully resign my being for the accomplishment of that object which is now its great end and aim."

"What would you have me do?"

"Find her out. Discover whither she has fled for safety."

"And do you not know where she is ?"

"Alas, no—alas, no !"

"When you attacked me in the street, I left you with her, as you must well remember. That attack you have yourself to-day referred to."

"I have. You did leave me with her, and I protected her as well as I could ; but disease and dejection of the intellect came over me, and I have but a dim recollection that we went from place to place, and that she tended upon me, like some ministering angel. Then we were compelled to part. I got an asylum in the house of a benevolent man, who has recovered me to something of what I once was."

"But how and when did you leave her ?"

"I cannot tell you; that part of my tale must be a blank, and I have come to you that you should, with a conviction of her innocence, take yet some steps to save her, and to save yourself."

"Leave me, and let me think."

"You will promise to do justice

"Hark you," said Bertram, suddenly. "Bring me but one piece of evidence that what you have said is true, and I—I—will then—perhaps—believe."

"I will then give you one piece of evidence."

"What is it ?"

"Once, when I was lying exhausted both in mind and body, and scarcely able to comprehend external objects, a scene occurred which aroused all my dormant energies of life, and which I shall never forget."

"Tell it to me."

"I will ; we were miserably poor, I presume, for I lay upon some straw only, and she was tending me; she thought I slept, and she placed the child—your child whom you have deserted—upon its knees, and, as the morning light faintly streamed into the wretched hovel, she taught the infant a prayer."

Bertram trembled at the close resemblance which this bore to the vision he had seen in the small hand-mirror.

"Go on," he said ; " go on ; what prayer was it ?"

"It was the Lord's Prayer."

"I knew it—I knew it."

"What say you——"

"Nothing—nothing. Go on. Tell me what followed. Tell me all."

"I will. The prayer was over—the common prayer which the child was taught, but the mother had not yet taught it all the supplication she intended it to make to Heaven."

"No—no—she had not, as you say, yet taught it all."

"She made the infant, with its tiny broken form of speech, pray for a blessing on the head of its greatest enemy. That is you."

"Yes; the child prayed for me. It prayed for a blessing upon me; I knew it—I knew it."

"And did you deserve the prayer?"

Bertram was silent, but he covered his face completely with his hands, and he shook with a visible emotion, while Theodore Danton regarded him fixedly and sternly.

"Is the proof sufficient?" he said; "or, must you have more before you can do justice to the injured and innocent, whom you have made so full of wretchedness?"

"I have told you," said Bertram, "that I would think. You have shaken me. You have much shaken me."

"Indeed! have I? Oh, does not your guilty heart tremble now? Do you, in imagination, now quail before those eyes, whose best brightness you have dimmed for ever? The veriest wretch brought out to die upon the scaffold, surely, is a king in thought to you. What may he have done? Made war in the dire calamity of his distresses against some rich man's hoards; some rich man, perchance, as bad a man as thou art, Bertram."

"Forbear!"

"No; I will not forbear. I say, what is such an one to you, who have systematically, and with a devilish ingenuity, contrived to heap a world of unmerited suffering upon the head, deserving only at your hands abundance of happiness. Oh, fool, fool! You won a jewel which you knew not how to wear."

"These reproaches are useless," said Bertram. "They but aggravate where you should endeavour, if all you have said be true, to implant different feelings."

"Aggravate you! Why, what right have you to speak of aggravation? Was the voice even of nature dead within you, when you looked upon your child? Did not one appealing glance from its eyes reach your callous heart?"

"No—no—no more—no more."

"Nay, I am glad I can make you feel at last. I tell you that one look from that child, when you appear with it before the great judgment throne of Heaven, will be more than sufficient to hurl your guilty soul to perdition. You know it will—too well you know it will."

"Curses!" muttered Bertram, springing to his feet, half maddened by these reproaches; "curses on your head. I will hear no more."

"You shall hear more!" cried Theodore Danton, in a voice that not only rang through the room, but reached the ears of every one in the house besides. He forgot all caution for the moment. The violence of Bertram had awakened in his heart a corresponding amount of violence, and hence he spoke on a sudden impulse in the tone he had been so careful to deprecate in Bertram.

The latter now hesitated no longer, but cried aloud for help; and scarcely had the words passed his lips twice, before both he and Theodore were clasping each other by the throat with the most deadly intentions.

Half maddened, as Bertram now was, by the bitter and cutting reproaches which Theodore Danton had heaped upon him, he was nearly a match for his opponent, and the issue of the struggle might indeed have been a fearful one, and such as would have imparted to Theodore's words, in the early part of the excited conversation, a terrific truth, had not the room-door been suddenly burst open, and a number of persons without, rushed in to separate the combatants.

That was no easy matter to do in their terrible state of excitement; but at length it was accomplished by main force, and Theodore was torn from his hold of Bertram, dragging in his hands part of the collar of his coat, which he would not let go his grasp of.

Then, before any one could stop him, or have the least idea of what he was about to do, he darted down the stairs, and made his complete escape from the house, leaving Bertram, who was nearly fainting from exhaustion, to place what construction he chose upon the mysterious and violent piece of business in which he had been engaged.

———

CHAPTER LXIX.

THE SEPARATION OF MARGARET AND THEODORE.—THE RETIRED PHYSICIAN.—THE CONFESSION OF MRS. BLAIR.

THE state of Margaret, when she got back to the cottage, after the night of terrors that she spent in London, was such, that she was little better than Theodore Danton himself. Fatigue and terror had done sad havoc with her, and she could scarcely stand by the time she arrived at the gap in the hedge, the usual entrance to the garden of the deserted cottage.

She paused here, and for some moments she could not stoop; for, if she did, she feared her inability to rise again. However, she did get through, and when on the other side, she felt truly thankful she had no further to go.

Indeed, but for the fact of her staying an hour or two in town to rest and refresh herself, she could not have performed her task at all—she would have sunk. Nature could have done no more.

"Thank God!" she mentally exclaimed, "I can now rest without the fear of any more of those insults and disturbances I have been subject to. How my health and strength stand it, I cannot imagine; but the necessity seems to be met with the ability to endure that I never believed to have existed.

"But poor Danton, what has become of him all this while—perhaps dead from want of food and attention? Poor, helpless being! I could not however have done otherwise than I have done; my conscience is clear, but misfortune seems to dog my steps.'

She seemed animated, and now at once entered the garden, and then the house, and proceeded to the room in which Danton had been left.

He lay on one side, motionless; his eyes were closed, and he looked so pale and emaciated, that she believed him dead, and at once rushed forward, exclaiming in agonising accents—

"Theodore — Theodore! Alas! alas! he's gone!—gone from me, for ever—and thus too. Oh, Heaven, am I never to have anything but misfortune? Is an evil genius always to dog my footsteps, and turn every hope to despair?"

She had hardly uttered these words, when Theodore awakened from a profound sleep into which he had fallen, opened his eyes and gazed upon her face. She started.

"Theodore — Theodore!" were the only words that escaped her lips, as she looked on him, and clasped her hands.

"Margaret," he replied, faintly, "where are we?"

"Do you not know the cottage we took refuge in? We have been here many, many days."

"Oh! now I do remember something of it. I have been very ill, Margaret, have I not?"

"You have, Theodore, you have; and God grant that this may be a signal of your recovery. I have not seen you look or speak like this since I accidentally met you."

"I have been very ill, I know; but I am better, Margaret, I am better. I have slept long, I think; but, oh, how weak I am. Is—is there any food, Margaret?"

The tone in which this was spoken plainly evinced the want, but the fear also of there being none, and it was with inexpressible pleasure that Margaret was able to say there was some. All her pains and sufferings were forgotten as she said,—

"Yes, dear Theodore, yes. I have some food. I will get a fire, and you shall have warmth and food. You have fasted long, I see, for there is the only morsel of food I left, and that is untouched."

Margaret immediately lit a fire, by means of some of the old wood lying about—parts of the wood-work of the house, and shutters and doors, as they might come off, and be useless in other respects.

However there was wood enough, and dry enough, too, to last for some time; there was no slackness of fuel in this respect, and in a short time a good fire was blazing away.

The viands that were procured by Margaret were such as Theodore most required; they were nourishing, and such as Theodore Danton had not had for many weeks; but now, however, Margaret, with all the care of a sister, prepared for him.

It was a great relief to her to find that he who had done so much for her, or, rather, suffered so much through her, was now getting better. There was a probability of recovery, though it might, as before, terminate unfavourably.

"There may be a chance," she muttered to herself; "and Heaven send it may turn out a certainty of his cure. I have seen him suffer till my heart is nearly breaking, and I hope that this apparent recovery may be a real one. It quite revives me to see him. I hardly know that I have been fatigued."

Poor Margaret! What she suffered no one can well imagine, and yet how soon she forgot all in the joy and happiness of seeing him, who thus loved her, recover from what appeared one of the most terrible afflictions man could suffer.

"You have been away long, Margaret," he said; "very long, have you not?" he inquired.

"I have," she replied—"I have, Theodore."

"Something tells me you have. I cannot tell why; but I fancy I can remember waking some time ago and calling for you."

"You call for me, Theodore?"

"Yes, Margaret—yes, I did; but you answered not."

"I was away, Theodore, far away, and could not hear you call," said Margaret, as she gazed upon him.

"No, Margaret, you could not, I know that. Now, I think I can remember that it must have been many hours ago, through all of which I have slept soundly."

"Thank God, you have, Theodore!"

"My disorder has taken a turn—it might have been the crisis, and hence I feel light and easy, but terribly weak, and so very hungry, that I am quite famishing."

"Then here is food for you; but let me implore you to be very careful in what you do. Eat but a little at a time; you are yet weak."

"I am—I am," he said, as he endeavoured to prop himself up, and felt he was unequal to the task, without aid; and then when he was so placed, he found that he could not long sustain himself in a sitting posture.

However, he contrived to sit long enough to partake of what was offered to him by the carefulness of Margaret; and when he had finished his meal, which, by her advice, was a slight one, he lay down scarcely so fatigued as before he began.

"If I can but gain strength," he said, "Margaret, I will find some immediate means of getting a living; and then, in due time, I can from my at present locked up resources. You shall be raised above your present abject state; but I have been placed so that I have been unable to assist you."

"I know it, Theodore—I know it. Say no more, but rest in quiet. Your strength, if you do not over-exert yourself, bodily and mentally, will be improved more rapidly than you may imagine."

"I think I shall recover very quickly, Margaret. I can, even at this moment, feel myself so much the better, that I can scarcely believe myself the same man."

"Rest, Theodore, rest."

"I will, Margaret; and you, too—do you rest. Alas! how much you must require it, beyond anything I can."

"You, Theodore, you are unable at present to do more than rest, and, in truth, I am fatigued myself."

Theodore Danton forbore to speak again, for he could see how poor Margaret needed rest, and therefore he at once relapsed insensibly to sleep, hoping that Margaret herself would partake of the blessing.

In truth she did, but at the same time she fell not asleep as soon as he did, for she lay thinking upon the past, and looking at the bright sun as he coursed his way through the infinite space of the heavens.

She thought how fortunate all had been, and even regretted not the evils, toil, and danger she had gone through, in recovering from her state of wretchedness she before laboured in, for so she deemed the life she had led with Theodore. Now that he was recovering, there was a hope that he would do better, for her life would become easier, at least, even if no very great change were made for the better.

"He will not see me want," she thought; "for the sake of my child I should be glad of a change for the better."

Thinking thus in her own mind, she, too, fell fast asleep, in a long and deep sleep.

*　　*　　*　　*

It was late in the afternoon when they awoke, and Margaret was the first to awake. There was not a sound to be heard, save the birds on the outside, which seemed disposed to roost for the evening.

She arose, and saw that the sun was setting, and that she, after sleeping as she had done, was scarcely any better than before. She was, in fact, overfatigued, and it would take more than a day or two's rest to recover her from fatigue alone.

She arose and re-lighted the fire, which had gone out during her sleep, and in doing this she awoke Theodore, who had slept soundly, but now lightly.

"Margaret," he said, "is that you ?"

"Yes, Theodore."

"Is it morning or evening ? I don't know, my faculties are so much confused, I can't tell."

"It is evening or approaching to that time, Theodore, for we have slept some hours."

"I am glad of it—very glad of it. Are you better, Margaret? Do you feel less fatigued ?"

"I can scarcely say I am, Theodore ; but I shall be, I dare say, better to-morrow. The first rest after a long journey seldom refreshes one so much as a second."

"It does not; but do not fatigue yourself thus in waiting about upon me here. I am strong enough to move about and wait upon myself."

"Oh! no, no ; not yet,"

"I am," said Theodore ; and he, with a slight effort, arose from his recumbent posture, and sat himself up. It was what he could not have done in the morning; indeed, he made the attempt, but he did not succeed without aid.

"Theodore ! Theodore!" said Margaret, "recollect your new-found strength cannot aid you long. It must fail after a little while, and exertion now may bring on a relapse."

"Well, you are right, Margaret, as you always are."

"I wish I was," said Margaret ; "I always wish to be so ; but the fact is farther from the wish."

"The time will come now, Margaret, that will see you placed in a different position to that which you are so lamentably placed in now."

"It may, Theodore ; and yet I think at times I have got in such a train of misfortune that it will only end with my existence."

"Think not so."

"I don't know why I should ; and yet there is but little reason to hope, save in yourself."

"And in myself you have every hope, Margaret. It is only with the hope of saving you—of being of use to you—of lifting you out of this present misery, that I care for life. But for this, I would die and cease to be."

"Oh ! Theodore——"

"Nay, Margaret, I speak only what I mean. What other hope in life have I ?"

"Every one."

"Not one, I repeat, Margaret—not one ; have I not lost you? Who can supply your place in my heart? Who can be to me what you have been to me ? Not one. No ; never, never can I love another."

"Say no more, Theodore."

"Forgive me, dear Margaret ; I meant not to disturb you. Not another word shall escape my lips. Come, Margaret, do not let that gloomy look overspread your countenance. Forget it ! Nay, do what you were about to do before I spoke."

"I will," said Margaret ; and she arose, and by the aid of a few imperfect means they had, Margaret got ready some of that, to them, rare beverage, tea.

This, and the one in the morning, were the only comfortable meals they had had since they had met in the manner described in the streets.

"Margaret, your care will be amply repaid."

"In what way, Theodore?"

"In seeing your patient restored, for now I feel to grow well most rapidly; there seems suddenly to have come a change over me I cannot explain; but life seems to have suddenly become fresh—as new as though a spring had suddenly gushed up, endowing me with new strength and spirits."

"I am more than thankful to hear you say so, Theodore—more than grateful. You have been to me what none other ever can be; but to see you recover, well and strong, will give me more pleasure than aught else I can imagine."

"Thank you, Margaret, and should I recover, I shall now look upon you as my preserver; you have saved my life, and I shall never forget it, or be ungrateful."

"Oh! Theodore, what do I not owe you?"

*   *   *   *

Thus passed the recovering hours of Theodore; the kindly interchange of such spirits was sure to bring consolation and quietude to both, and they felt much relieved.

That evening they passed in comparative happiness; for though their prospects were not further advanced than the health of Theodore was likely to affect them, yet the prospect of a very speedy change in that gave them both so much hope that tranquility seemed suddenly to come over them, and they conversed as they watched the sparks of the wood-fire fly upwards.

Then they slept the long, dull night through a healthy, undisturbed sleep, awakening when the sun's broad rays shone warmly into the apartment.

Margaret arose, and again a wood fire appeared in the room, blazing and crackling away, and before Theodore was awake there was another frugal but wholesome meal ready for him, prepared by the hands of Margaret.

"Theodore," she said, as she saw him open his eyes; "Theodore, are you ready?"

"Ready!" he repeated, rising and gazing around him; "rea dy! What mean you, Margaret?"

"Here is your breakfast."

"Breakfast? Why, have I again slept for hours?"

"Yes, and so have I," said Margaret; "but here is your breakfast, and may it do you as much good as what you took yesterday seemed to do you."

"Thank you—thank you, Margaret; you are ever considerate, careful of all save yourself; you do not seem to think that you have any need to do for yourself what you do for others, and yet it is equally necessary."

"I do not stand in need of it."

"You do, dear Margaret; but I feel so much better, that to-day I must go into the garden."

"You must be careful."

"I will be careful, Margaret; but I must get out, for to-morrow I hope to leave this place altogether."

"You, Theodore?"

"Yes, Margaret; I cannot remain here; I must endeavour to do something; we must not starve; surely I shall get some kind of employment somewhere, surely people want occasional assistance, now and then, and I must meet with something of this sort," he said in a desponding tone.

"Never despair, Theodore; we may yet do well."

"I do not care if we can purchase food by my labour, however poor it may be."

"I hope you may be successful; but you must consider your strength is not at present great."

"True, I do not forget that; but at the same time, if I work as an invalid I get paid as an invalid; but as long as I get some, I do not care what."

"Premature labour may disable you permanently."

"I care not if it were," said Theodore; "I want it but for a time, till I can prove who I am, and obtain possession of what is my own. When I can once lift myself above the sad condition in which I am now placed, I will make my way through the world creditably; and you, Margaret, are the grand object for which I am willing to do all—for one who has done so much for me."

"What have you not suffered for me?"

"Talk not of the past, it cannot be recalled; we look but for the future—in that is our hope and our strength; without it, we might sink and die."

"We might."

"And, moreover, the past is a scene of unhappiness—the future a prospect of good. At least, I hope and believe it will be so. I have, or shall have the means of making us both happy."

"Thank God! if I can—not be happy—but breathe a tranquil hour, and watch the budding of the intellect of my child; to live, and to see him launched out into the world so as to be beyond a mother's care, then, indeed, I shall be too glad to exchange the cares of this life for the quiet of the grave."

"Do not have any such sad thoughts, Margaret; hope yet—we are young."

"But hope has decayed."

"Say not so, Margaret; she will but spring up the stronger, and be more permanent."

"I hope it may be as you say."

That day Theodore Danton found himself quite strong enough to get into the garden, and there to sit in the sunshine.

The air was balmy and serene; it was especially refreshing to Theodore, who sat there; occasionally he walked about, and seemed to gather strength beyond his hopes.

By the evening, he walked a short way down the road and back again.

"Margaret," he said, "I have recovered indeed—most miraculously recovered—I can walk. My strength could not have been so much exhausted, as my energy and power of mind were, for the time, in abeyance, and my body sunk."

"You were very bad," said Margaret, "and certainly did not promise life several times."

"Very possible."

That evening was spent as the last, and then the night came over them, and all was still and dark.

That night was a calm and happy one to both; neither of them were disturbed in the serene and quiet sleep that came over them from the first.

Then came the morning sun, with the dim light in the east, and then the rapid and gradual illumination of the whole heavens, from one extremity to the other; then the red sun rises rapidly through the masses of clouds till he clears them all, and the light of day beams upon the land.

That was the last morning that Margaret Bertram and Theodore Danton awoke in that house; they rose and took a last meal by the wood fire.

"This is another attempt, Margaret, to get out in life, and by one's own exertions to plod through the world for a short space of time."

"I hope it will meet with the success it ought," said Margaret. "Heaven knows it is not to commit any evil we strive, on the contrary, we wish to do our duty, and to refrain from even the semblance of wrong."

"True, Margaret, true," said Theodore; "but let us have our breakfast. You seem to feel melancholy. I hope you are not so in point of fact."

"I have seen some little trouble in this house, and I hope I may never meet with the like, or that I may never undergo such again."

"We often think we cannot go through what we have gone through, and yet, when the time comes, we shall find strength to compass our difficulties."

"I hope it may be so in your case, Danton."

"And yours, also; but, Margaret, we are going on a journey; therefore, take the proper sustenance to enable you to perform your part with less fatigue—you are much in want of strength."

"I have no inclination to eat to-day," said Margaret; "but I feel quite refreshed."

"I am glad of it," said Theodore Danton; "but yet, let me persuade you to eat—you will need it."

After much earnest entreaty, Margaret complied, and eat a little of what she had procured for their breakfast.

When all was done, the remains were carefully wrapped up and secured,

and everything was taken that was worth taking which they had, and Theodore Danton said—

"Well, Margaret. you are now about to leave this place. I shall never forget it; it will live in my remembrance as long as I can remember the perils I have gone through—so long shall I not forget the means by which I was saved."

"Then we leave here, Theodore; where do we now go?" inquired Margaret.

"Heaven above knows," said Theodore; "but I shall travel from place to place, and ask at every place I come to; surely there will be something that I can do."

"I hope so for your sake!"

"And I yours; but come, Margaret, all is ready, and we lose time, and that is precious at present. We leave it, as we entered the cottage—unknowing and unknown."

They left the place in silence, and took their way towards the road, near which the cottage stood, but which they approached in a circuitous manner.

After proceeding some time in silence, Margaret, being employed in watching the tottering walk of Theodore, said—

"You are not so strong as you thought you were, Theodore; your walk betrays you have not become so yet. Do you not think it would be advisable to return to the cottage?"

"No, Margaret, we have left that place never to return; and the difficulty you think I encounter in walking, does not arise from weakness, but in my feet not being used of late to step out, and bear the full weight of my body."

"Very likely,—I hope you'll be able to do so," said Margaret; "you do not calculate upon fatigue."

"Do not attempt to deter me; it would only cause me to be worse, if I were to return to that cottage; for, while I am moving onward, I feel as if I were bustling about doing something, and it raises my spirits, though with false hope, and I have been terribly damped of late. If I can obtain health, I can encounter any difficulty."

"Be it so, Theodore; I am ready to follow you, and go with you where you will."

*   *   *   *

Thus they went on for several hours, and walked up to one or two houses, and pleaded for some employment; but no one seemed to entertain the idea for a moment of giving him anything in the shape of work.

"Work!" said an individual to whom he applied for work.

"Yes," said Theodore.

"And what kind of work can you do?"

"Any sort that you may have to be done," said Theodore; "I am willing to do anything, no matter what."

"Work, eh!" said the old man; "you're more fit for the workhouse than work; I have none for such as you; and let me advise you to get out of this parish as quick as may be, for it strikes me you will run some chance of being caged for vagrants."

Theodore turned away with inexpressible disgust from the man, and silently proceeded on his journey.

He thought within himself this was an unpropitious beginning, and that it would serve but to instil little hope in the breast of poor Margaret, and he, too, thought it ominous; but he was determined not to be outdone under any circumstances.

While he had strength to travel on and on, he would do so; so that he would shrink from nothing that would in any way aid or assist him in procuring means to subsist on.

Again and again, he made the attempt, nothing daunted by each rejection and each rebuff; he tried again and again, but with the like want of success.

"The evening grows apace," said Margaret; "I fear that you will do no good here; indeed, you have done enough for one day, and that day the first you have been out, after a long and severe fit of illness and weakness such as you have suffered."

"Well, I think I must give up for to-day myself," said Theodore. "We will rest here, and then we will proceed onwards for a mile or two, and then we will stop for the night."

As they spoke, he stopped before a small ale-house; the sun was setting and the windows bore a very inflamed appearance; so much so that they were painful to look at.

Danton walked up, and seeing a seat empty outside, opposite to a table, he pointed to the seat, saying—

"Sit down, Margaret; we will eat to-night, though we have none to-morrow; in fact, we have had nothing since morning, and it is as necessary for you as myself."

So saying, he went into the ale-house, and asked the landlord for some food and some ale. Seeing he was pale and emaciated, the landlord said, as he handed him the articles he wanted—

"No, no; I'll take for the ale, that's in the way of business; but, as for the meat, that's only so much broken victuals; I will give you that, you are welcome to them."

"Thank you," said Theodore, "the gift is more welcome than you may imagine."

"You have been ill?" said the landlord.

"I have; long and severely."

"And what are you doing now?"

"Travelling about in search of work," replied Theodore, "which I shall be glad to take at any price or place."

"Ah, well, you won't get any about here; you had better get into a more crowded place, where there are more people, and you may have a better chance; about nine miles on is a larger place, where you may stand a chance;

but, I'm sorry to say, it is only a chance."

"Thank you," said Theodore; "I must do as others have done, I suppose, though I hope my chance of success may come before my strength fails me."

"I hope so, too."

Theodore Danton then came outside with the food, which he placed before Margaret, saying—

"Here, we have this as a gift, except the ale; but drink, it will give you strength to go on the remainder of our journey, for we cannot stay here to-night."

"Very well, Theodore," said Margaret; "I am thankful to see you so well for this gift."

They sat down and gazed upn the setting sun; at the same time they ate their food they silently thought upon the prospect before them, until the approach of twilight, and the disappearance of the sun, reminded them they had some distance to walk yet, for the alehouse was nearly a lone house.

Taking the things once more into the house, and thanking the landlord for his kindness, Theodore and Margaret resumed their journey, much refreshed by what they had eaten, and the rest they had had at the ale house.

"Well, Margaret," said Theodore, "though I haven't succeeded to-day, yet I still feel sanguine and stronger."

"I am glad of it, Theodore; it gives me fresh strength and spirits to see you so much better."

They proceeded onward for a mile or two, and then darkness came on apace. At first there was some moonlight, but the clouds seemed to come up apace, and the wind rose too, sweeping the clouds over the face of the moon, and obscuring the dim light she cast.

"A storm is coming on I fear," said Theodore Danton; "we must take the first shelter we can get to."

"It is coming very fast," replied Margaret: "the wind blows sharp and cold. How sudden it has come upon us; a few minutes ago it was all calm and light."

"It was so, but the face of nature is soon changed by the state of the heavens. When they are obscured and overcast, the whole world seems to borrow the sombre and sad hue of the skies themselves."

"Most likely; in fact, I have noticed it myself; but how strong the contrast between our own troubles and the serene and happy sunlight seems, as it shines over the fields.!"

"It does, Margaret. I have seen it. Our own misfortunes cannot affect the face of nature; but the reverse is true, for the appearance of nature has much influence upon us."

Thus they talked, until they came to a part of the road where a lane branched off, and a few yards up this lane there was something that appeared to be farm-buildings, and, upon closer inspection, it appeared to be a barn.

"This," said Theodore, "must be our resting-place for the night."

"It will be a warmer and better lodging than that which we had at the deserted cottage."

"I think so too," said Theodore, "for here is plenty of straw, and we can sleep secure from draughts, and on a softer bed by far than what we have had for many a day."

"Shall we get into any difficulty if we sleep here, do you think, Danton?" inquired Margaret.

"None; who could make any objection to our sleeping under the shelter of this roof? All we have to do is to leave it an hour or so before the men come in the morning."

"At what hour do they come?"

"About six; we can leave before five.'

So saying, Theodore placed Margaret and himself in as secure a place as possible. The storm now come on with double fury; the wind howled, and tore round the old barn; and the owl in the roof gave out its peculiar too-wit, too-woo, in a doleful and dismal manner.

"Hark," said Theodore, "how the rain pours down like a deluge!"

"It does," said Margaret; "what a sound! we should have been washed away."

"Indeed, we should. Oh, how wet and miserable we must have been; and to lie in such clothes all night, too, we should soon have had another scene of illness and misery."

"It is a narrow escape."

"It is. Hark how the wind roars! It's terrible to lie here and listen to it."

Terrible, indeed, it was to listen to the roar of the wind and the rattling of the rain, which could be heard so plainly there; for the barn was a large building, and there was a great extent of boarding, and against this the rain pelted most piteously.

Then again the wind would come in fearful gusts, as though it would have swept the old barn from the face of the earth, and scatter the contents to the four quarters of the globe.

Listening to this war of the elements, and being both fatigued, they feel asleep, and dreamed not of the morrow; but lay wrapped in profound slumber, till the sun had risen high in the heavens, and men were busy.

*   *   *   *

"Hilloa! hilloa!" shouted a hoarse voice.

"Hilloa, there!" shouted another.

"What the devil's the meaning of all this?" inquired another person, and by far the most important person, as could be gathered from the import of his speech.

Margaret started up from her sleep with a suppressed scream, and it was a moment or two before she knew where she was, or what had happened; and then she saw some men standing by. The barn door was wide open; one of the men had seized and was shaking Theodore Danton.

Theodore opened his eyes, utterly confounded at what was going on, and could not speak—he was staggered.

"Hilloa! here's pretty goings on in my barn. D'ye think I'll convert it into a country residence for paupers? No; d—me, I'd burn it down first."

"I'm sorry to have done anything to offend you," said Theodore, appealing to the man; "but I was wandering about, and the storm came on as I got here. We went in, and fell asleep. I hope we have done no harm—we wanted shelter."

"Well, why not get it at the ale-house?"

"I'm out of work."

"Oh! I see how it is. A pauper—vagrant—wants a settlement, and sleeps in my barn. D—me, if i don't punish him. Here, Jem, go and fetch the constable. He and his brat shall go to the bridewell at once."

Jem immediately hastened for the constable, and Theodore endeavoured to appease the farmer's wrath, by explaining to him that he had done no harm.

That was a position, though ever so true, which could not be made plain to such a comprehension.

Then, seeing that nothing could be done with such an obdurate brute, he turned to Margaret, saying,—

"Well, I have said enough; we will now go on our journey. It will be long before we see another such as he. Come away."

"No, you don't."

"But we shall," said Theodore. "I have done no evil, and no one has a right to detain us."

"We will see that," said the man—"we will see that;" and he placed himself before Danton, who immediately seized him, and threw him on one side by a sudden exertion of strength, and then endeavoured to pass him.

"Here, Bill, you skulking brute! will you see your master used in this way? Seize him."

Bill, an herculean countryman, immediately came to the rescue, and the two seized hold of Danton, who resisted manfully for a time; but, finding his strength failing, he called out to Margaret, saying,—

"Escape, Margaret. Run, and make the best of your way off; don't stay for me."

Impelled by a sudden impulse—she knew not why—Margaret Bertram rushed from the spot, holding her child close to her breast, fearful lest she should be deprived of that; for it would then be dreadful to part mother and child.

In a few minutes more, the constable came, and Theodore was given into his custody as a vagrant, and for having committed an assault upon the farmer, in whose premises he had slept.

Margaret was nowhere to be seen, and Theodore Danton was carried along by the constables, who declared he must be a most desperate vagabond, to resist anybody in that parish.

The house of the nearest justice was not far off, and it would take but a few minutes to get there; so thither they all proceeded in company.

Having arrived at this private asylum for justice, they were all ushered into what was called his worship's office.

There were several chairs, a long table, a desk, a variety of papers, some books, and shelves filled with law books; and behind the desk before mentioned, sat his worship.

"Well," said his worship, "what have we here? Some desperate offender, I dare say. Look at him, doctor; mark his face."

This latter part was addressed to a venerable, but gentlemanly man, of benevolent expression of countenance.

"Ay, your worship, he is a desperate offender; he didn't like coming here at all.

"Offenders against society never do. They meet with condign punishment —that is the reason."

"The man seems very ill," said the doctor. "He'll faint; he is very bad indeed."

"I dare say he is bad, doctor—a bad man altogether; but never fear; he'll not stand longer than he can help it, you may depend upon that, I assure you. I know human nature too well."

The doctor said no more.

"What is the charge?"

"Vagrancy, your worship," replied the constable.

"The particulars?"

"He and a female slept in Mr. Higgins's barn all night, and committed an assault this morning."

"Well, Mr. Higgins—glad to see you, hope you're well—pray state what you know about this man."

"I and my man found him asleep in my barn, all amongst my corn; and when I woke him up he was insolent, and committed an assault upon my man."

"Was he alone?"

"No; he had a woman and child with him. She escaped in the confusion attendant upon securing him."

"Well, fellow, what have you to say?"

"Simply this; we were walking past the barn last night, when the storm came on, and we took shelter in it, and slept there till this man came in."

"Ay, he had a better right than you to be there," said the magistrate, with a cunning grin, and then he added—

"What is your name?"

"Theodore Danton."

"Ha—ha! Theodore; what a fine name for a bridewell!"

"What have I done that you should send me there?" said Theodore. "I have injured no one, and done no wrong that I am aware of, nor have I broken any law."

"You have committed an act of vagrancy, and, as a vagrant, I shall commit you to gaol for six weeks."

"Good Heavens!" exclaimed Theodore; "and can the laws be administered by such hands? But never mind. I am too ill to proceed, so I may as well embrace the opportunity of being confined in prison."

"I don't understand him," said the magistrate.

"He is dreadfully ill," said the physician. "I can see it in half a glance. I tell you what, he'll faint in another minute. He wants assistance and medical treatment rather than punishment. Look at his face; he has the manners and language of a man used to another state of life, and not the one he appears in."

"Well, what can I do with him?" inquired the justice with a perplexed air. "There he goes."

This was uttered by the justice, in consequence of Theodore Danton having fallen down in a fainting fit.

* * * *

The remainder of the scene is lost, for Theodore Danton recollected nothing more; he was insensible.

The first intimation of his returning sensation was in the evening, when the sun's rays came along his bed to his eyes.

He gazed around him, and endeavoured to recollect where he was; but it was impossible. He was on a soft bed, and in a well furnished apartment; his bed had curtains and furniture around it; his room carpeted, and the walls ornamented with black framed engravings, a sampler, and a few profiles.

"Where am I?" at length he muttered, half aloud.

As he spoke, the curtains were drawn on one side, and a gentlemanly-looking man gazed upon him.

"Are you better?" he inquired, touching his wrist lightly.

"I have been very ill, I know—very ill; but how I came to be here I cannot tell, or who you are."

"Very likely; but you must not talk now; you must be content to remain quiet until to-morrow, and then I will explain more to you; at present you are under medical treatment."

* * * *

A few more words, and the physician left the side of Theodore Danton, and his place was supplied by the nurse who attended him. This personage was utterly deaf to all his inquiries, and refused to make any answer to any of them.

He, therefore, gave it up, and waited for the morrow with the best of patience he could muster; and when his kind physician came, he could do no less than utter his gratitude in the most fervent manner.

"Tell me," he said, "what has happened, and how I have come here, for I know nothing; and where is Margaret Bertram?"

"Margaret Bertram?" repeated the physician, thoughtfully.

"Yes," said Danton; "she was with me on the last day I can remember. God knows how long that may be since."

The physician then told him all that had happened from the moment he fainted at the justice's, until this time, saying he had him brought home to his house, as he saw his illness was of a severe character, and the name struck him.

"I thought I heard you name Margaret Bertram."

"I did."

"May I ask your confidence, so far as to disclose to me the nature of your acquaintance with her? I have a particular motive in asking."

"You are entitled to it," said Theodore, and he at once related the whole of his misfortunes, from the first to last.

"My motive is no longer a secret," said the physician; "I have some time since retired from the profession; but I have a young friend who has an appointment as the head surgeon of a workhouse infirmary, who wrote to me to relate a curious occurrence—the death of a woman named Blair—the housekeeper to Mr. Bertram; but you shall see his letter, and that will inform you of all she confessed to, and the interest I took in your name."

"I see," said Theodore Danton, as he returned the letter; "I see the villanous practices against the happiness of poor Margaret; I will devote my energies and time to discover both Bertram and Margaret."

"You are not strong enough yet awhile; you must not stir for a week or two; you know not yet the effect these repeated attacks of disease would have upon you; you must not do so."

"Your kindness overpowers me; may I hope for your aid in the meanwhile, to discover Margaret Bertram?"

"You may. All I can do, I will."

"I have the means of repaying all you have done for me; but not immediately; do not, however, think that while I speak of it, I'm the less grateful for your kindness; for I feel you have, indeed, saved my life."

* * * *

It was some time before Theodore recovered sufficiently to be able to walk; his recovery was this time slow and tedious; but he was at length pronounced to be more perfectly recovered than he had yet been since his departure from the hotel; much of this was owing to judicious treatment and nourishing diet, but at length the time came and he was able to trust to his own powers.

By the kindness of the physician, he was furnished with ample means, and he had now two objects in view, the discovery of Bertram, as well as that of Margaret; and of placing the conduct of Mrs. Blair fairly before the former.

CHAPTER LXX.

THE ARRANGED MEETING BETWEEN BERTRAM AND HIS WIFE.—MORE MADNESS.

THOSE who have thus far watched and reflected upon the career of Bertram, may by this time be well convinced that somewhere lurking in his brain was an incipient kind of insanity, which only wanted a strong provocation to exhibit itself.

That provocation might not, through a long life, have really occurred, for these mental affections, like physical diseases, will sometimes linger in the system an amazing time, ay, even until death itself shall arrive, unless some combination of circumstances shall call them from their dormant state into life and activity.

The tremendous feeling of jealousy was the existing cause, then, that in Bertram fully developed, what we feel justified in calling, the weak or insane point in his character.

Had he been a rational man, notwithstanding all that had occurred, and the full belief in the guilt of his wife, he would not have acted in the extraordinary manner that he had done? but having so acted, he, by the gloomy and desolate condition in which he placed himself, actually fed the disease of which he had become the victim.

But still it was rather the madness of eccentricity, than that mental derangement of a more marked and positive character, which induces a man to make positive mistakes of facts, and to indulge in absolute delusions.

He had something to go upon, but the interview he had had now, a strange and enforced one it as was, with Theodore Danton, certainly staggered him much in his belief of the reality of his wife's guilt.

Each word that was uttered at that interview, although it had awakened such a storm of passion within him, yet could not be forgotten, and hours afterwards he thought it all over, and dreamt of the possibility that he was, after all, mistaken.

This, to such a man as Bertram, was a feeling that was likely to produce a sad convulsion of mind; it made him positively ill; and, perhaps, never had he been in such real and imminent danger of death as now that the thought of Margaret's innocence obtruded itself upon his mind.

With painful and agonized correctness he thought it all over, from the minutest circumstance which had first awakened the fiend jealousy in his breast, to that awful time when Mrs. Blair had taken him to see Margaret enter the hotel, where Theodore lay upon a bed of sickness, and when he had been infuriated to a pitch of almost madness, so as to render himself almost incapable of anything like rational inquiry.

"And can I have been deceived?" he asked himself; "is that possible? Oh, thought of agony—death—death in any shape were better than now to feel, that for years I have been harbouring a resolution so destructive of my peace."

It was just what might be expected, that when once Bertram's mind began to receive as possible the likelihood of his wife's innocence, the idea would grow upon him hour by hour, and a thousand incidents which before had swelled the presumption of her guilt, he found might possibly be received in quite a different aspect. He had but to get over the one idea that Mrs. Blair was the arch hypocrite, the Mephistophiles of his domestic circle, and then the innocence of his wife would stand out surely in bold and startling relief.

And if such were the case, how could he ever look upon the face of that most suffering and injured being? How could he even frame words sufficiently abject, in which to ask her to forgive all the wretchedness he had heaped upon her?

Unhappy Bertram!—unhappy in your suspicions—but more unhappy still, if that be possible, now that you tremble on the verge of having these suspicions proved worthless, and all untrue—what can you expect ¿that the injured Margaret should say to you?—what can you hope for in the after-life of your child; but a feeling of deep horror of you, its father, as being the author of its poor mother's greatest miseries?

"Have I been deceived?" he groaned; "have I been deceived after all? Have I, who considered myself a man of thought and calculation, been, after all, a dupe of such a woman as Mrs. Blair? Oh, God! if such be the case, have you no vengeful lightning with which to smite me, and so at once annihilate my life with my remorse?"

But these fits of deep dejection, as well as of wild excitement, would change almost as rapidly as thought itself, and he would again fall back upon the possibility of Theodore Danton deceiving him, and getting up the specious tale he told for the purpose of acquiring some portion of what was now a hoarded fortune for himself, and from the wife who had stooped from her high estate to become what he, Bertram, had so long thought she was.

Thus torn by conflicting emotions, he passed a wretched time. His pulse became fevered—he almost lost the power to think, until suddenly he bethought him that the curse which had been launched upon his head by the mother of her whom, before his marriage, he had turned aside from the paths of virtue, had clung most strangely and completely to him, and became fulfilled in almost all its intensity.

"Yes, that curse—oh, that dreadful curse!" he exclaimed; "it clings to me like some fell disease; and the black mantle, which was sent to me as a gloomy and horrible present, from the moment that it became mine, has clung around my very heart, hiding all the sunshine of joy from it. Oh, Heaven help me!"

This was the first time the sacred name of Heaven had passed the lips of Bertram for many and many a day except as a mere expletive; but now it was uttered with something like a rational fervour—a fervour of one who really sought aid from that throne of mercy, to the great and good occupant of which not even the most guilty shall call in vain.

He felt a calmness now pervade his mind, and he rose from the wretched couch on which he lay. He staggered across the floor, till he came to a miserable, triangular-looking piece of glass, which was held to the wall by the side of the window of his poor apartment by two nails; and he looked at the reflection of his own face therein long and steadily.

Oh! what ravages had the years of suffering he had compelled himself to endure made in his countenance!

For the first time was it that, with an inquiring eye, he had glanced at himself since he left his own house, in order to gloat over means of vengeance against his wife; but now his face seemed to him like a tablet, on which was written all the sufferings that he had gone through, and every idea of agony that from first to last had haunted his soul.

He looked, at the very least, twenty-five years older than he seemed when he was presented to the reader at the church door, some moment or so before the curse was uttered by the aged woman—that curse, which he now felt had indeed clung to him like some frightful contagion which he could not shake off.

"What a change," he said; "what a dreadful and terrible change! Oh, what am I now, in comparison with what I might have been? Heaven look down with mercy upon me!"

Again, as he uttered this aspiration, he felt that some portion of the agony of his soul was lifted from off him; and before he could think of aught else to do or to say, a low, murmuring voice, in gentle accents, from the apartment which was next to his, came upon his ears.

By some sudden and irresistible curiosity he felt impelled to open his door a little, and to listen. It was a child praying — repeating after its mother a simple and innocent prayer, such as sounds so sweetly from the lips of lisping infancy.

How vividly did that scene bring to his recollection the simple but deeply affecting incident that had been related to him by Theodore Danton, and of his own child being taught by its much injured mother to pray for a blessing on his head.

He tottered back to his own room, for it was upon the landing that he heard the prayer, and in his eagerness he had gone quite to the room door from whence it came, and then he burst into tears.

Yes, he, Bertram, the man who with a fixed and dreadful resolution had defied all goodness, all holiness, and had condemned to the saddest fate the

wife of his bosom and his own child, now wept like a child himself.

"God," he said, "God, I thought that long since the fount of tears was dry."

And still he wept. For nearly an hour he wept, until a sensation of blessed calmness came over him, and he said,—

"I must do reparation for the past, and so have a hope of earning Heaven's forgiveness. Oh! no, no! I cannot earn it. It is in its mercy that I can alone hope for it. No, no, no! But I will try to establish some faint claim upon that mercy. Margaret, Margaret, where are you now? Oh! if I could but this moment look upon you, all might yet be well. Margaret, and you, my child —my little one, from whom I have been so long severed—Heaven help you,

dear, dear objects of what should have been my dearest love. Oh! I have been mad—I have been mad—mad, indeed."

Overcome by these various emotions, he sobbed and groaned; and while self-accusation, with all its torments, oppressed him, and he told himself in frantic accents that he was ready to make all possible atonement, a kind of fiendish voice seemed to whisper to him—

" No, Charles Bertram, no, no! It is too late! it is too late now. You cannot; you may not do it; it is too late. You have done all the evil already that was in your nature to do, and that has been amply sufficient to destroy those innocent beings, who should have been the objects of your love, and likewise quite sufficient to hurl thy soul to perdition."

"No—no!" he said, as if it were an actual voice that had spoken to him, and not the mere whispering of his own conscience. "No—no, it is not, it cannot be too late; it is never too late to do justice."

"Yes," said the voice again to his imagination; "yes, it is too late when the victim is no more. It is too late when the babe and its mother have passed away, and found with God an asylum; which you, who had in your hands, as his delegate on earth, their fate, denied them. It is too late."

"Fiend, fiend!" he cried, "torture me no more."

He fell upon the floor from off the couch, on which he had cast himself, and there, in his agony of spirit, for a time let us leave him to see what became of poor Margaret and her child, after the only one who would protect her was torn from her.

It was the dread of being separated, either in a prison or in a workhouse, from the dear child, that made her fly with such precipitation when Theodore was apprehended on what is the high crime and misdemeanour in this country of being destitute. But whither to fly she knew not, and despair alone lent her strength to travel some miles before she ventured upon seeking any repose.

Then she crossed a stile which was by the road side, and sat down in a corner of one of the most beautiful meadows she had ever seen.

The prospect it commanded was one of many miles, over a vast tract of country, the horizon of which was bounded by hills, the sweet blue colour of which blended beautifully with the azure sky, and was a great relief to the deep green foliage of the mimic forests that clothed their bases with verdure.

A river, too, ran winding through one of the most luxuriant valleys for verdure she had ever seen. It was to the presence of that river that it owed such a luxuriance of vegetation, and so much of its charm as a piece of picturesque scenery.

And full as she was of her own griefs, she could not look unmoved on the many natural beauties of hill and dale, and tree and stream, which met her eyes,—those eyes which filled with tears as she gazed.

She clasped her dear little one closer to her heart as she said,—

"Oh, what a beautiful world has the great God of all given to his creatures, if they would be content to enjoy it, as surely he meant them to do, and not mar all its loveliness by the self-created storms of their own evil passions."

As she made this reflection, and it was made in a saddened and not a cynical spirit, she heard the sounds of the chase coming from a distance, and presently about half a mile from where she was, she observed a field of horsemen, many of whom were clad in scarlet, galloping, with all the ardour which distinguishes those who engage in that exciting amusement, towards the meadow where she was.

A small pack of hounds were a short space in advance; but what they were pursuing she could not tell, as, within a few hundred yards of where she was, the dogs seemed at fault, and commenced rambling about instead of pursuing the steady course which had marked their mode of progression when first she saw them.

Many of the horsemen soon came up, until, with the exception of some stragglers, who were not so well mounted as their companions, the whole had collected in that one meadow.

The confusion was immense. The dogs were yelping, and many persons spoke at once; but what had occurred to produce such a confusion and cessation of the chase, Margaret could not guess, until one galloped up to her, and said in a loud, brutal voice,—

"Did you see the fox?"

To this question, so put, Margaret made no reply, and with a coarse oath it was repeated, accompanied by a personal threat.

The colour came upon Margaret's cheek in such a flush as not for long had visited it, and she rose without answering one word, and approached the horsemen.

"What's all this?" cried another, riding up.

"That man," said Margaret, "has threatened to strike me.'"

"Oh, nonsense. My lord, you did not mean it."

" By God ! I only asked her where the fox was, and she did not so much as answer me. If she did not know, why did she not say so at once ? She's a tramper, of course ; and now, by Jove, that I come to look at her, she's devilish pretty, although rather the worse for poverty."

" Who are you ?" said the other, as he threw a half sovereign to Margaret.

She could not stoop to pick it up, but, bursting into tears, she turned and walked slowly towards the stile which she had crossed to reach the meadow.

" A beggar's pride, by Jove," said the first horseman ; " she want's you to dismount and hand it to her, I suppose."

" Which I shall do," said the other.

" The devil you will. Well, please yourself ; I shall go back and see if any one has news of the fox. I suspect there must be a watercourse somewhere hereabout, into which reynard has got. Whoop ! Tally ho ! ho ! ho !"

Away rode the unfeeling brute, whom we consider not half so respectable, or entitled to consideration, as the poor animal he came out, with all the paraphernalia of dogs and horses, to hunt ; while the other hastily dismounted, and, flinging the bridle of his horse over his arm, he picked up the gold coin he had thrown to Margaret and approached her, saying,—

" If I have inflicted a pang upon you by the mode in which I sought to relieve your evident distress, believe me it was unintentional, and all I can do is to make the *amende honourable*, by handing to you what it hurt your feelings to stoop for."

Margaret turned her face towards him —that face which had now lost all its transient colour, as she replied,—

" Sir, I am unused to any kindness, and, therefore, ought not to have troubled you. But it was the unmanly threat of your companion that brought some of the pride of better days back upon me, and inflicted such a pang upon my heart as I do not often suffer now."

" Forgive me asking you ; but are you quite destitute ?"

" I am."

" Then, for the sake of your child, why do you not seek that protection which the laws of the country provide for you, and towards which, all who have the means are made to subscribe so largely ?"

" I know what you allude to—the workhouse."

" Is it not more honourabe than depending upon private bounty ?"

" It may be ; but is it not full of horrors ? Oh, sir, they would part me from this precious little one, who is my only solace."

" Nay, that is, or should be, discretionary. Take my card, and go to the parish. You see yon white-faced building, there to the left. Say I sent you, and that you are not to be separated from your child ; you understand ? To-morrow some inquiry shall be made concerning you, and we will see what can be done for your permanent benefit. Take heart, now, and live in hopes of happier days."

The gentleman—for a gentleman he was, and most amply and well deserved the title—gave her the card and the half-sovereign he had first cast to her, and then he mounted his horse and rode away.

It was not so much what he had said that reached the heart of poor Margaret ; but it was the tone and manner of real sterling goodness in which he had said it, that assured her he was one of those great and good spirits who never feel so much pleasure as when alleviating the distresses of his fellow creatures. And yet the dread of the workhouse was too much for Margaret.

" No, no," she said. " This sum that he has given me, and which the God of Heaven will repay him a thousand-fold, will yet keep us from such a fate as that, with care, for many days. No, no. Not the workhouse yet—not the workhouse yet."

CHAPTER LXXI.

THE DANGEROUS GIFT, AND THE FEARFUL SITUATION OF MARGARET BERTRAM AND HER CHILD.

It would have been, we do not hesitate to say, much better for poor Margaret had she taken the advice of the gentleman who had given her the half-sovereign and the card, and gone to the poor-house ; for doubtless he, when he heard her tale of woe, would have done something to rescue her from the state of helplessness into which she had fallen.

But such was her dread—and we do not wonder at it—of anything bearing the hateful sound of a parish work-house, that she could not make up her mind to go to it, even under the promise of such extra protection; while to fly from it needed but a natural impulse.

That she looked upon as a very last resource, and not then as a source for herself, but for the child; and she dreaded another winter to come, with all its terrors, while she was in such a state of wretchedness.

Her mind was tortured, too, with thoughts of what had become of Theodore, who, in his present weak and debilitated state, she was sure required the most careful tending.

"God help him!" she said, as she passed into the high-road from the meadow—"God help him, and save him from all evil! He has suffered, and suffered much, too, for loving me, and yet how innocently and sinlessly has he loved."

The day crept on apace, and, as some threatening clouds began to show themselves in the horizon, and then each moment to creep on, obscuring more and more of the brightness of the sky, she became most anxious to find some place of shelter for herself and the child.

After walking about a mile, she observed, a little off the road-side, a small public-house, which, although it by no means presented the most inviting appearance as to cleanliness and comfort, she at once preferred entering to going further and, perhaps, faring worse.

Moreover, she knew that her shabby and poverty-stricken appearance would provoke much remark, if not insult, at a respectable place, and she made the miscalculation of supposing she would avoid that in the little house of entertainment which she now approached.

Scarcely, however, had she gained the threshold, when a man came out, and said, passionately, as if some deadly injury had been done him,—

"Be off—be off! D——n! we will have no trampers here."

Margaret was terrified at the vehemence with which the order was given,

and, in her fright, she hastily showed him the gold she had, saying,—

"I do not come to beg. I can pay for what I have."

"Pay! Oh! that's quite another thing. Walk in then. So you have money, have you? Well, well that's sufficient. Come along; here's good entertainment for man and beast, so surely we can find some for you and a child. Come along."

Poor Margaret was thoroughly foot weary; and, besides, she had carried the little one for some considerable distance, so, although she felt that she would get no courtesy there but what she paid for, she did enter the house.

At her own request, she was permitted to go to the kitchen, where she seated herself by a good fire, the cheering blaze of which, as it crackled and roared up the chimney, made her feel quite a sensation of comfort, to which she had long been a stranger.

The child, too, held up its little hands to the cheering blaze, and laughed in its mother's face; alas! poor Margaret, she tried to return the smile, but tears gushed to her eyes instead. It would be many a day, she thought, if ever she should laugh again, as it had been many a day now since a smile had lit up her countenance.

She ordered some of the simplest and cheapest refreshments she could, and changed the half-sovereign, which was all her treasure, spending only sixpence out of it; and then she was on the point of thinking of asking at what price she could be accommodated with a bed for the night, when a young girl, who had, on various culinary errands, come frequently in and out of the kitchen, suddenly came up to her, and said, in a low tone,—

"You have not got much money, but still quite enough to be a temptation to some here."

"Good God! what do you mean?"

"Be off, as quick as you can, and don't think of sleeping here. Don't you know that this is a notorious thieves' house?"

"And you ——"

"Never you mind what I am; I'm not so bad as some believe me, and a great deal worse than others think me. Take my warning, and be off."

"I thank you from my heart."

The, girl who was about as course and common looking a specimen of female humanity as one might chance to see on a long summer's day, made an impatient gesture, and then went closer to the fire to superintend something that was stewing upon it in a huge iron pot.

At this moment the landlord of the house, with the assumption of an indifferent air, strutted in, and coming up to Margaret he said,—

"It's going to be a rough and stormy evening; you had better make up your mind to remain here till to-morrow. We shan't be exorbitant in our charges to you."

"I thank you," said Margaret; "but—but——"

"She says she's going to the market town, which is only three miles farther on," put in the girl who had given her the friendly warning.

"Who the devil asked you?" he exclaimed, ferociously.

"And who cares," she cried, in a loud screaming voice, "whether you asked me or not? Am I going to be schooled by you? Don't speak to me; you know what I am, and I know what you are. If you say another word that I don't like, you shall have a ladle of this boiling soup in your face. Do you think at this time of day, that you can bully me? I will soon let you know your mistake."

"D—n you, for the greatest vixen ever I came near," said the fellow; "I only wonder why I don't turn you neck and crop out of doors."

"You wonder why you don't?"

"Yes, I do."

"Then you may leave off wondering as soon as you like, for I'll tell you at once why you don't. It's because you are afraid. Yes, afraid. You would have done so long ago, but that you are afraid. Now you know the reason, so don't pretend to wonder about it any more, if you please."

There was such a tone of defiance about the manner of his speech, as well as the matter of it, that Margaret would not have been at all surprised at some desperate act of violence emanating from the man. Indeed, with terror she watched his countenance, in expecta-

tion of seeing some storm of passion depicted upon it, that in a few moments would be followed by the perpetration of some desperate deed of violence.

But Margaret had yet really to learn that rank cowardice is the inherent principle at the bottom of the heart of every bully. The man was subdued. When he found that he was really met with tones of defiance, and there was not the least notion of shrinking before him, he stepped back, saying, in dogged tones,—

"There you go as ususal. Why, what put you out of your way, I wonder? I'm sure you have enough of your own liking."

"And I'll have more."

"Well, d—n it, say what you like. There's no argufying with a woman."

The girl turned her attention again to the huge pot that was on the fire, as if she were now content to repose under the laurels she had gained, for she unquestionably, in the wordy war that had ensued, might be looked upon as a conqueror.

"You won't think of going on?" said the man to Margaret.

"Yes," she said, taking the hint that had been given to her. "I shall go on to the next town, as it is not very far."

"There's bad weather brewing, I can tell you, and it will overtake you before you get half way there."

"I cannot help it—I wish to go on."

"Come, now, I pity the little one. We have several spare beds, here; and, as I was a little rough or so when first you came up to the door, you shall have a bed for nothing. You needn't mind what I say. It's only my way, and sometimes when I mean the best, I speak in my rough sort of manner, that people who doesn't know me, thinks quite different of me."

"I thank you, but I must proceed."

"You won't stay?"

"I have made other arrangements now, and have determined upon proceeding."

He turned aside, and Margaret heard a frightful oath come from his lips, which only the more confirmed her in her wish immediately to depart from a house which now she regarded with dread, and regretted she had ever entered. Such was her state of apprehension of some violence, that she felt half inclined to hand to the man the remainder of her money, with a request that he would let her go in peace, since she had given him all.

Probably, had she been alone completely, this is an expedient that she might have adopted, however unjust it might be for her to be driven to; but when she thought of her little one, and how long it might be before she met with another one equally generous-minded with the gentleman who had bestowed upon her such a, to her, large sum, she shrunk from depriving the child of the ordinary comforts which the money she had would produce.

She rose and walked slowly to the door of the suspicious inn, and she was followed by the landlord, who said, when they were upon the threshold—

"Oh, I see how it is now; that young woman there in the kitchen has been saying something to you, but you need not mind her. I can tell you she is mad, in consequence of family misfortunes."

Margaret made no answer, but walked slowly over the threshold of the house; she was determined that come what might, she would not commit the girl who had given her so friendly a warning.

"Do you hear me," cried the landlord, brutally. "D—n it, ain't it common civility to answer a fellow?"

"I have nothing to say to you," said Margaret, as she tremblingly walked on with her heart full of fear.

The fellow hesitated for a moment, as if he were considering whether he should follow her or not, and then he turned upon his heel and went into the house. Margaret did not dare to look back, but her sense of hearing was exerted to the uttermost, to catch the least sound that should be indicative of pursuit; and it was not until she found that the road was making a turn, which would soon hide the public-house altogether from her view, that she ventured to look round.

All was still. No one was following her, and she felt a great sensation of relief from the conviction that, at all events, now she had left, most probably a great danger behind her.

And now that her mind was relieved from some of the apprehensions that almost entirely engrossed it, she had time to look around her, and observe that the prognostications of the landlord of the public-house, with regard to the weather, were likely to be verified, for the sky was getting blacker and more murky each moment, and a cold, strange sort of wind, was sweeping along the earth, gathering up dried leaves and other matters, and making them dance round and round in wild and eccentric circles.

The low of distant cattle came plaintively upon her ears, and the birds flew in a disordered manner, almost brushing her very face with their wings, as they sought shelter from what they knew well would be a storm of no common character.

These indications of a coming strife of the elements terrified Margaret, for there was no place of immediate shelter near; but not for one moment did she regret leaving the public-house.

"No—no," she said; "the wind and the rain, and even the forked lightning, will be kinder to me than man. They, too, are in the hands of Heaven."

She saw now, down a lane to her right, what appeared to be a porter's lodge of some mansion; and, as a low, indistinct muttering, as of some thunder afar off, met her ears, she hurried down the lane, with the hope of obtaining shelter at the lodge, at least till the fury of the storm had abated. She reached it, and rang a bell, in answer to which a woman appeared.

"I am weary," said Margaret, "and a storm is coming; can you spare me shelter until it has passed away?"

"We don't take in vagrants, here, my good woman," was the reply; "we pay our poor's-rate, and that's quite enough."

Bang went the door in poor Margaret's face. She shuddered, and pressed her babe closer to her heart, as she said—

"Then our trust must be in Heaven alone!"

There was just a faint hope in her breast that the storm might yet hold off for a time, so as to enable her to reach the next town, which, considering the distance she had already walked, could not now be above two miles further on. But, alas! it would take poor Margaret, foot-weary as she was, and burdened with the child, the better part of an hour to accomplish two miles, and she soon saw that far from the storm holding off for any such period of time, that it was likely to have come, and expended all its fury by then.

The prospect now before her was dreary in the extreme, for she came upon the confines of a heath, throughout the whole expanse of which she could observe no indications of a human dwelling.

There were deep excavations here and there in the heath, which apparently had been dug for the purpose of procuring sand and gravel, while rank vegetation, including many varieties of flowering shrubs, grew about in great luxuriance.

Here and there, too, was a clump of fir trees, whose dark foliage contrasted well with the bright green grass that grew near them, but which now scarcely showed themselves against the black clouds that obscured the brightness of the sky.

This heath was, in reality, exactly between Margaret and the town which she was desirous to reach, and which was situated on its opposite margin, but owing to the many undulations of the ground, she could not see the least trace of the town, so that she as stood upon the margin of that desolate tract of country, with her back towards the unfriendly habitation to which she had just been so roughly refused access, she might, without any great stretch of imagination, have fancied herself alone in the world.

A strange feeling of awe and loneliness crept over her, and that was a feeling which a loud and rumbling peal of thunder did not at all tend to diminish, although it added fear to it, —fear for the sake of the little one whom she had with her, and who comprehended in itself the sole link that held her to life. The thunder awakened the softly slumbering child, and it sobbed in terror, as it clung closer to its mother's breast.

"Hush—darling—hush!" she said, "All is well; you are in your mother's arms. Look in my face, dear one! Ah! you have no fear now, and can smile again."

The child was reassured; for Margaret managed to speak to it in a voice of cheerfulness which her heart but ill responded to; and then she thought that, until the storm was over, instead of taking shelter under the trees, which she well knew, in thunder storms, was a dangerous expedient, she would creep down into one of the deep excavations, and there endeavour to find more security. This she did; and, at all-events, she got out of the current of the hurricane of wind that each five minutes had swept across the heath, with a violence almost sufficient to throw her down. There, then, she resolved to wait until the storm had passed away, and soon she had reason to congratulate herself upon having chosen even such a place of shelter as that, for before another quarter of an hour had elapsed, the tempest came on in all its fury.

The forked lightning darted from cloud to cloud, in livid streaks, while the incessant roll of the thunder seemed as if it would never cease. This state of things was succeed by rain, which came down with such a tremendous weight and velocity that the earth was covered by a misty spray, which resembled actual steam. And now, from the higher parts of the heath, numerous rivulets, formed entirely by the rain, came pouring down into those excavations we have mentioned, but they affected not Margaret, for below, considerably, where she sat, crouched up between some furze bushes, with her child, was a great depth of hollow, into which the water went roaring and hissing, until it was converted into a mimic lake, which slowly rose higher and higher, until it came within a very feet feet of where Margaret was.

She began to get apprehensive that she should have to leave her place of tolerable shelter, but the heavy rain sensibly abated now, and altered its character from the positive pelting deluge with which it had fallen, to a heavy, misty sort of vapour, and then suddenly that ceased altogether.

A streak of light showed itself in the horizon, from whence the wind blew, and the storm clouds had passed over.

"Thank heaven!" said Margaret.

Scarcely had she uttered these words, when, from the top of the excavation above her, she heard the sound of voices, and presently these words, distinctly uttered—

"Confound her, she has given us the slip, after all."

"But how, I should like to know?" said another. "She cannot have made such speed in the storm as we did."

"Then she has got shelter somewhere."

"There's nowhere to get shelter. They would not, at Harefield Lodge, shelter a fly, if they could help it; and there ain't a house between here and the town."

"Then she's somewhere on the heath yet, and we may as well have a good hunt for her. Who knows how much money she may have about her, as she changed gold for a sixpence, you know. It's quite providential, as we have had no luck lately."

"Ah! if we catch her; but don't you go reckoning your chickens, old fellow, before they are hatched."

"Not I; but don't you think, now, it's modest of Bill to want half the swag, because she happened to come into his house?"

"Ay, indeed; and when she would have stayed, too, and saved us all this trouble, had it not been for his hang-gallows looks, that, I'll be bound, scared her away. He ain't fit for business. He's too rough and ready, he is."

"Why, yes, he does want a little oiling. But I tell you what, old fellow, if she's anywhere on the heath, it's in one of the hollows, so let's come and have a look."

Terror almost froze up every faculty of poor Margaret as she heard this conversation, which so evidently related to herself; and she gazed upon the little lake of rain water at her feet, as if she almost meditated a plunge into its recesses, to save herself from the horrors that might possibly await her at the hands of those ruthless men.

Oh, what a curse, now, instead of a comfort and a blessing, had that too-generous gift of the huntsman become. How was she to convince them now of her willingness to give up all the money she had, and that that was all, and there was no more which she was concealing from them?

"God help me now!" she murmured. "Oh, God help me now."

She heard the men coming down into the pit, with all the caution which the slippery state of its banks, in consequence of the heavy rain which had fallen, rendered so necessary.

"Mind how you come," said one. "Its more slippery than ice. I have nearly been headlong down half-a-dozen times. Place your foot against some of the roots, and then you'll get a hold."

"By Jove!" said the other, "it's an awkward place, indeed. How the deuce shall we ever get up again out of it?"

"Oh, we must make a scramble for that. Come along steady—steady's the word, or down you go as safe as the bank."

"D—n it!" said the other, "if all banks were no safer than these are, they would be rather slippery affairs to have anything to do with. Here I come."

The fellow slipped at this moment, and would inevitably have upset his companion, and they both would have fallen into the lake below, had he not had the presence of mind to catch hold of a projecting piece of the root of some tree in the vicinity, which had spread its underground growth far and wide.

"What's the row?"

"All's right; but I was as near down as possible."

"Upon my soul, it's like walking on butter."

"It is—it is."

They now reached the ledge upon which Margaret was, and she felt quite certain that she must be seen in another minute. Oh, what worlds of agony were now concentrated in the feelings even of a few moments! There she was, to all intents and purposes, a prisoner, without the power of flying from those who came avowedly to seek her, and on that desolate heath, where

BERTRAM AWAITING

THE ARRIVAL

OF

MARGARET AT THE OLD FERRY

chance might not bring a passenger to take her part for hours.

She was in a state of agony almost bordering upon delirium; and well she might be, as the two men consulted now together for a few moments. They must find her by the merest observation of the most casual character around them; but they were saved that trouble, for the child suddenly spoke and at once betrayed the inefficient hiding-place of the distracted Margaret. The men, in an instant, dashed aside the furze-bush which alone slightly hid her from their view, and then one of them exclaimed—

"Hilloa, my lady-bird! You are here, are you? This is lucky, by Jove! we have hit upon the right place marvellously well."

"Mercy—mercy!" cried Margaret, as she held in her hand the silver she had received as change from her half sovereign. "There is all I have. Take it—take it freely. I give it, and will not call you robbers. It is all I have —take it, and leave me, and I will bless you."

"Indeed," sneered one. "That's very likely. All you have, is it? Oh —oh!"

"It is, as Heaven is my judge!"

"Do you see anything green about us, young woman? Come—come, hand out the blunt. You have had a slice of luck of some sort, and have got money. There can be no mistake about that; and we are gentlemen at present rather in difficulties. We will trouble you for a loan, which we intend to have by fair means or by force; we don't much care which; but as you may, I advise you to out with it at once."

" Oh, spare me!"

" Not a bit of it. The money—the money."

" Is here—all here. I have no more. Half a sovereign was given to me. I have changed it, as well you know, and you cannot have more than I have left. I swear to you by all my hopes here and hereafter, that I have no more."

" Gammon."

" It is here. Oh, why should I seek to deceive you hopelessly? Do you fancy that I would call upon my God to witness to a falsehood for any money's worth? No—no; take all I have and leave me."

" I say, Jem," said one of the men to the other, " this will be a troublesome job, after all, and there will be a little squeaking. We ought not to be both down here, because if we are, we don't know when it's time to be off, in case anyone should come across the heath. Now, I don't care which stays, and which goes. Choose your own share of the matter, and I'll do what you leave to be done."

" Oh, I don't care. It's a good thought. I'll scramble up again while you get the money from her. I know you won't stand any nonsense."

" Not a bit of it. I'll just give her a knock on the head if she makes much of a row over it. Time's precious, and we ought to be off now as quick as we can."

He who had chosen the task of keeping watch upon the heath, with some difficulty made his way to the edge of the excavation again.

" Is all right?" cried the one below.

" Yes; not a soul to be seen except one!"

" One?—the devil!"

" No, it's not; it's a donkey."

" You mean yourself. What a fool you must be, when there's business on hand, to come any of your tricks. Now, ma'am, if you please."

" Take all—take all," cried Margaret. " There is the money."

" That's silver. You have gold."

" No—no—no."

" But I say you have—I'm certain of it. Come, now, put down that brat, will you, or else I'll throw it into the

pond here that the rain has made. Your money we must and will have. I'll find it if you were to scream till the heath echoed again."

" No—no. Touch me not. What have I done to you? Surely—surely you are human. Did you never love any one? If you did, fancy her for a moment in my situation, and let that thought disarm you."

" It's all in vain. Money we must have. Give it up, and I'll be off; but you cannot persuade me that that half sovereign was all you have. I won't, and I don't believe it."

" Then, God of Heaven, my trust is in thee!"

The fellow stumbled as he advanced towards her, for the ground was frightfully troublesome to walk upon since the rain; and then when he was about half way between the edge of the sort of hillocky platform on which she was and the lake behind him, a sudden thought came like a suggestion from Heaven to Margaret.

" I am saved!" she cried—" I am saved!"

" What do you mean?" cried the man starting with alarm—" what do mean?"

" Those horsemen—oh, there are horsemen, on the opposite bank."

" D——n!"

She had, as she spoke, pointed over his head to the other side of the excavation; and he, not at all suspecting the *ruse* that was being played off upon him, instantly turned, when, with a sudden rush forward, Margaret sprang upon him, and with one push, sent him headlong into the lake below, into which he fell with a sudden splash and a loud cry of terror.

" Help—help!" screamed Margaret now, for she doubted not the other fellow would descend the excavation to rescue his companion, when they would both take vengeance upon her for what she had done.

" What is it?" shouted the man above, while the drowning wretch made frantic but vain efforts to scramble up the slippery bank of the water, which only came away in smeary masses of wet clay in his hands. He screamed twice, and then again he sank.

"There's a carriage coming," cried the one who was above; "and it will soon be devil take the hindmost. I'm off."

Margaret now could plainly hear the sound of the wheels of some approaching vehicle which was coming across the heath, and horrified at the dreadful death to which she had consigned the robber, as well as at the perils of her own situation, she still called loudly for help, and in a few moments she was answered by a voice, exclaiming in loud accents—

"Hilloa! below there—what's the matter?"

She glanced up, and saw a person in livery standing close to the brink of the chasm.

"Help! Oh, come down," she cried; "come down directly."

"But I can't," he said.

However, his actions belied his words, for his foot slipped at that instant, and he was down in a moment, falling into the very centre of the furze-bush which was close to Margaret and her child.

CHAPTER LXXII.

MARGARET REACHES HIGHAM-HILL.—THE ATTACK AND THE RESCUE.

THE alarm of the footman, when he found himself in the centre of the furze-bush, was excessive, and yet it partook of a little of the ludicrous. He shouted for help as loudly as if he had been in the hands of half a dozen assassins, each of whom was armed with deadly weapons, and intent upon taking his life.

But when, as he did, after a few moments, find that it was not a trap into which he had fallen, but merely a furze-bush, and that the more he struggled the deeper he got among the entanglements, he left off making any violent effort, but contrived to roll off in some way without receiving much more personal injury, so that he came to the feet of Margaret in a very undignified kind of a heap.

"What's the row?" he said as he scrambled to his feet as well as he could, when the slippery nature of the ground is considered.

"You have saved me," said Margaret, "from death."

"Indeed! Well, then, I don't mind so much having about a hundred and fifty of those confounded prickles in me. Was that the fellow who made off just now across the common?"

"Yes; that was one of them."

"Where's the other? Let me catch him. One of them, you say?"

"The other," said Margaret, with a shudder, "is there."

She pointed to the swollen pond at the bottom of the excavation, as she spoke, with a shudder. At this moment a voice from above called loudly upon the footman, and, by the respectful manner in which he replied to it, Margaret thought that it could be no other than that of his master.

"Yes, sir," he said, "It's all over. Some one was attacking a poor woman, sir, but the fellow has run away, I say," he said to Margaret, "if I were you, I wouldn't trouble myself to say anything about the gentleman in the pond. You'll only have a world of trouble."

"Do you think so?"

'Upon my word I do. Let him be. Come, I'll help you out of this place, and my master, who is not a bad fellow, although rather of the passionate description, now and then, will give you something, I dare say, to help you on the way."

"I want nothing of him."

"Well, that's as you please. Mind how you come; for it's as slippery as ice here. I'll be hanged if I do think I shall get out of this place any more. There I go again—no; not quite, but deuced near, though. Confound this soft clay! when once it gets wet, there's no such thing as keeping a foothold for a moment upon it."

Indeed there was a considerable amount of difficulty in getting out of the excavation; and it is doubtful if Margaret was not to the full as much assistance to the footman, as he was to her.

At length, however, really by dint of uncommon perseverance, and after a great many slips, they did both reach the ordinary level of the heath.

The carriage was still waiting, and a gentleman was looking from the window, with that screwed-up, anxious, irascible-looking face, which always betokens an excitable and nervous disposition, but not a bad heart.

"What is it?" he cried. "Am I to be kept waiting here all day, while people are scrambling out of holes? What the deuce, woman, did you get down there for? Eh—eh?"

"To avoid the storm," said Margaret.

"Yes; but what a bawling you made. If you were being murdered, it was not worth while, surely, to make such a disturbance about it. There—there's a sovereign; come now, don't accuse me of saying anything to you that is not civil. I'm in a hurry."

"Sir," said Margaret, "I ought not to accept your generous bounty."

"And why, pray?"

"Because I am not in immediate need of it."

"Stuff, stuff! you may be for all that. Good day—good day."

Margaret, in obedience to a great number of winks from the footman, rather than from any wish of her own to do so, took the sovereign, and then the eccentric occupant of the carriage drew up the window, and was driven away.

Margaret burst into tears. The imminent danger she had gone through, and the great excitement of the last half-hour, combined with a sad and dreadful memory of the death of the wretched man, who had fallen a victim to his own iniquities, had dreadfully shattered her nerves.

She felt compelled to sit down, even upon the damp earth, for her limbs refused to support her, and it was only the caresses of the child that, after a time, succeeded in restoring her to anything like equanimity.

"Heaven above," she said, "knows, that even in self-defence I am morally guiltless of that man's death, because I did not at all contemplate his coming to such a dreadful end."

The idea of having been in the smallest degree instrumental in taking a human life was so terrific to Margaret, that it required all the reason she was mistress of to prevent it from taking too strong a hold of her imagination. She, however, found that her tears wonderfully relieved her; and, after a time, she was able to proceed with something like a show of outward composure.

And Margaret found herself, comparatively speaking, wonderfully rich. She had not only the change of the half sovereign, the possession of which had nearly cost her her life, but she had likewise the sovereign which had been given to her by the gentleman from the carriage.

"Now," she said, "I may, indeed, when I come to any habitable place, command some more than ordinary comforts for my little one."

She pressed her dear child to her bosom as she spoke, and found, in the wrapt contemplation of her child's countenance, a solace for all ills.

Oh! what joy can be compared to that of a mother looking upon the sweet face of her child, and in her heart of hearts thanking the great God above for bestowing on her so precious a gift!

There can be nothing half so beautiful, half so humanizing as such a sight; and whether the love of one's offspring be an instinct of human nature, as well as of the brute creation, or an acquired feeling in the former, it certainly is one of those feelings which tend to lighten the burthen of human woes more than aught else, and to lift nearer to heaven, than any other earthly sensation could do, the human heart.

The heath was still of considerable extent, stretching as far almost as the eye could reach; but Margaret felt renovated strength, and she walked on more quickly than she had done, inhaling, with a positive feeling of pleasure, the cool, fresh air, which, since the thunderstorm, had seemed to have double its former share of vitality about it.

But what is that she hears? She pauses to listen. Then again what can it be? It sounds like the tramp of a human foot coming at great speed towards her. Why does her heart beat with alarm? She glances around her and trembles. There, at still a considerable distance off, she sees the form of a man approaching her.

A cry of terror comes from her lips. Too well in her memory is the appearance of that man fixed. It is he who, on the sudden approach of the carriage to the edge of the precipice, made his hasty escape. Now again he comes upon her track, no doubt intent as well upon avenging the death of his comrade as upon robbery, and any violence his passion, foiled as he has been, may dictate.

Margaret, for a moment or too, and most precious moments they were, felt as if paralyzed, and unable to proceed a step. It seemed to her as if there she must, by the fiat of some destiny which she could not contend against, await the arrival of her deadliest foe, who was coming so quickly up to her.

But although the time seemed long to her that she remained in that trance-like state, it was, in reality, the agony of a very few moments indeed, and then she sprang forward, ejaculating,—

"Now, Heaven help me !—Heaven have mercy upon me !"

That was a fearful race which now ensued.

The heath lay before poor Margaret, wild and desolate, apparently for miles, and she was encumbered with the weight of the child, who, participating in its mother's fears, now screamed aloud as Margaret flew with the frantic speed of despair onwards.

There was no house visible, and not the least sign or sound of an approaching human being from the direction to which she hastened. She knew not if she were taking the nearest route or not to any human aid; but all she strove for was to increase her speed, and to keep on in as straight a line as possible.

Infuriated at the manner in which she sought to avoid her pursuer, the fellow shouted aloud to her; but his cries only added, as may naturally be supposed, wings to her speed, and she continued to rush onwards at a rate which let him perceive that, as he gained upon her so triflingly, she would be clear of the heath, or probably reach some assistance, before he could run her down.

Infuriated at this, and, perhaps, from a better knowledge of the locality he knew that such might be the case

sooner than Margaret could have any idea of, he shouted,—

"Stop, or, by the living God, I'll shoot you."

In order to utter this shout sufficiently loud for it to reach her ears, he was for a moment compelled to pause. To run at great speed and to shout out at the same time is a feat few can accomplish.

Margaret heard him, but she heeded not the threat.

And now there appeared, about a quarter of a mile in advance of her, a clump of tree, through which a foot-path wound its devious way. Margaret did not know, but her pursuer did, that, once through that clump of vegetation, she was safe, for there were several cottages then close at hand.

Fury took possession of him; he stopped and took a double-barrelled pistol from his pocket, and, without any other word of warning, he took a steady aim at the flying figure of Margaret.

In another instant he fired; she heard the report, and a scream of terror came from her lips.

"Hit her, by Heaven !" cried the fellow.

He was mistaken. It was fear, not a wound, that had caused her to utter that cry. The suddenness of the shock, too, made her slightly stumble, which the further, for the moment, confirmed him in the idea that he had shot her; but it was only for a moment that he exulted in his supposed crime, for she again, with, if possible, more speed than before, rushed forward.

Foiled in this his attempt to murder her, or to inflict upon her some serious injury, he levelled the other barrel of his pistol at her and fired. That, too, missed her, for now she had increased her distance from him.

She reached the wood; a scream of joy burst from her lips, and she fell into the very arms of a small party of four soldiers, who were, with their corporal, marching upon some military expedition.

These most welcome strangers just emerged from the little clump of trees at the moment the villain fired the second barrel of his pistol, so that they all saw the act, and that it was levelled at a woman, too, with a child in her arms.

The fellow was for a moment blinded

by the smoke from his own pistol ; but when a puff of wind cleared that aside, he saw his danger in an instant, and that his purposed victim was saved.

With an oath of the most frightful character, he cast the discharged pistol from him, and, in his turn, turned to fly.

"After him, my lads," cried the corporal—" after him."

It needed no second order to induce the soldiers to commence their pursuit, and, trailing their muskets after them, they set off chasing him who, a short time since, had been the pursuer.

And now the scene became most exciting. The would-be murderer, in the despair to which he was reduced, made the most prodigious efforts to get away. The speed with which he ran was perfectly terrific. It was a wild, headlong pace, that no man in his senses could have kept up with for a moment : and as Margaret watched the chase, she saw that, encumbered as the soldiers were with their marching implements and muskets, they could not hope to catch him, unless he failed from fatigue.

But now the corporal, who had not only directed his men to make chase of the fugitive, but had himself headed it, paused, and called out with a loud, clear voice,—

"Surrender yourself, or I fire !"

The man paid no heed to the summons, but tore on, as if maddened.

Then the corporal knelt on one knee, and raised his musket. He took a steady aim for about a moment,—there was a sharp report, and the villain who had fired at Margaret rolled over and over several times upon the heath, and then lay completely motionless.

"Oh, God ! oh, God !" said Margaret, as she sunk upon her knees, "when is all this dreadful tragedy to end ?"

The soldiers now advanced leisurely to the object of their pursuit, and Margaret, from where she was, could see them grouped around him, and talking, using animated gestures as they did so. Then they raised him from the ground, and, laying him across two of the muskets, they carried him again towards the little road from whence they had emerged.

It was with a shudder of horror that Margaret watched the approach of the party, and, when they got near, she doubted for a moment if she had not better fly at once, rather than face the dreadful sight which awaited her.

"Is he dead ? oh ! tell me, is he dead ?" she cried.

"Not at all," said the corporal; "he's only bit in the leg."

"Thank Heaven !"

"Do you know him ?"

"No ; not further than his being one of two men who, some short time ago, tried to rob me on the heath, but were foiled, and since then he pursued me, as you saw."

"Ay, we saw him fire upon you," said the corporal; "I have only winged him, you see; I didn't want to cheat the hangman."

"Curses on you all !" groaned the fellow.

"Oh ! curse away,—it will do you good. You can't well walk, or you should, so we must carry you back to the inn we have just left."

This was done; and when Margaret, who had followed the soldiers closely, got clear of the wood, which, by-the-bye, she found was of much larger extent than she had at first imagined, she found that there were numerous cottages close at hand, and, about half-a-mile further on, a town of considerable size.

"We will lodge this fellow, my dear," said the corporal, with rough civility, to Margaret, " we will lodge this fellow in the town-gaol, where, no doubt, they will attend to his wound, and you can give such information to the magistrates as will ensure his being prosecuted. We are on military duty, and must go on; but our evidence will be forthcoming when wanted to prove that he fired upon you, and that will be enough to put a hempen cravat round his neck."

"No," said the villain; "it will not; I shall disappoint you there. You cannot prove that there was anything but powder in my pistol."

"Cannot we indeed !" said one of the soldiers; "I wonder, then, where this pistol-bullet came from that lodged in the corner of my knapsack, when you fired at the young woman, you unmanly vagabond ?"

The fellow saw that this quibble would not serve him, and now, what with the pain of his wound, and the anger of his mind, he became absolutely furious, so far as his tongue was concerned, and vented the most horrible oaths.

"Oh! swear away," said the corporal, "if that will do you any good. You are welcome as possible. You'll make another sort of face presently, when, perhaps, some bungling country surgeon, who never saw such a case, has to cut you almost to pieces to extract the musket-bullet from you."

This apprehension at once reduced the fellow to the most abject state of fear, so that, when they arrived at the gaol, which they did escorted by all the idlers of the place, he was quite an object of derision to the multitude, on account of the manner in which he cried and begged for mercy.

The keeper of the prison had some doubts about receiving him without a warrant, but a magistrate was sent for, who at once, upon Margaret and the soldiers' depositions in brief, remanded him for a fortnight, and desired that he should be placed in the prison infirmary.

"At the end of that time you will remember," said the magistrate, "that you will be expected to appear as evidence against him; and, if he be well enough to be brought up before me, I shall, no doubt, commit him for trial."

"I will attend," said Margaret, with a sigh.

"And as your evidence, likewise," added the magistrate, "will be essential, I will write to your commanding officer about it."

"Thank you, sir," said the corporal; "I shall only be too happy to be of any assistance in seeing justice done upon such a scoundrel. To fire upon a woman and a babe in that way, was one of the most savage things ever I heard of."

"It was indeed."

"I had great difficulty, sir, in keeping my men from shooting him dead upon the spot, I can assure you."

"I don't wonder at it. And now, Margaret Bertram, I must bind you over in your recognizances to appear, as well as in sureties, unless you will give me your word of honour that you will not fail."

"I do give you my word, sir."

"Very well; I will take it; and now I need not detain you any longer, unless you have anything else to say to me."

"I have only to say that, although my life is of little worth, yet, as these brave men have saved it, I hope that something will be done which I cannot do, to make them see that, upon principle, they have done a deed worthy of commendation. For my own part, I have nothing but thanks and prayers to offer."

"Make yourself easy about them," said the magistrate; "the public press will do justice to them, as well as their officers, to whom I will write an account of the transaction."

CHAPTER LXXIII.

MARGARET'S HOPES. — THE OLD FRIEND OF THE FAMILY.—THE PILGRIMAGE RENEWED.

AND now Margaret was once more in safety, and she had, moreover, sufficient funds to last her well for the fortnight, during which she had pledged her word to the magistrate she would remain near at hand, in case she was wanted as evidence against the man who lay wounded in the county gaol.

But what, then, was to become of her when that fortnight expired? what was she to do? As she asked herself these questions, a strange and untangible hope arose in her breast, that Bertram might see, by the reports in the public papers, to what danger she was exposed, and that, in consequence, he might relent, and at last, for the dear child's sake, do something to aleviate so much misery, and prevent the likelihood, if not the possibility, of such events again occurring.

Alas! this was but a weak hope, and yet it was one.

To persons situated as poor Margaret was, anything to cling to that had the shape of hopefulness was full of joy, and she would not relinquish this idea, although she felt it would not stand the test of rigid inquiry.

She took an humble lodgings for herself and child in the town, and the idea occurred to her of endeavouring to procure some employment.

This was a thing which, once to be thought of, was likely to be of a nature to make a great and a permanent impression upon her; so, within an hour of the thought coming across her, she made various inquiries.

The result was, that she found there was nothing to do, except she could get work at a factory which was some miles off; but as that involved labour from an early hour in the morning until a late one at night, and a separation from her child, she would not for a moment entertain it.

So troubled was poor Margaret, and so willing was she to do what she could to avoid actual begging, that she applied for a place of domestic servitude, but there she found herself rejected, for the very reason which induced her to attempt such a thing—namely, the child.

Yes, that became, with all the ladies to whom she applied, a ground of refusal. They were so rigidly virtuous, that, as they could not positively know that Margaret was innocent and blameless, they gave her not the benefit of a doubt of guilt, but all the evil consequences of a doubt of innocence.

"No, no," said one. "Really we are religious people, and cannot take you."

"And what is to become of me?" suggested Margaret.

"Oh, you ought to pray to the Lord," was the reply.

She walked away with a heavy heart, and proceeded to another, who did not seem so much inclined to object to Margaret because of the little one, who clung to her for protection, and for whose sake it was that she sought even such employment.

But there was another reason which influenced this lady. She believed in the infallibility of her husband's attractions, and she must have been very modest as regards her own, for, after looking at Margaret for some time, she said,—

"Oh! you wouldn't do for me. Mr. Smith is a gay man, and you are good-looking."

The indignant blood flew to the cheeks of Margaret, as she said,—

"Madam, you are in a position, if you please, to insult misfortune; but I grieve that anything in the shape of a woman should so far forget all that is due to her own sex, as to gratuitously add a sting to misfortune."

"Oh! it's all very well; but we don't have any but ugly servants here."

Reader, this is no caricature. There are thousands of ladies, as they call themselves, who act upon this principle. They will not allow a girl who is good-looking to attempt to earn an honest living by her labour, for fear, forsooth, she should, because she is handsome, be otherwise than virtuous. Surely these ladies, being ordinary themselves, must have a strong impression that, by thus condemning the beautiful, they are retaliating upon Providence in some way for making such a distinction, and placing them in the worst class.

But poor Margaret suffered by all this. First, because she had a little child dependent upon her, she was not allowed a fair chance of getting a livelihood; and, secondly, because nature had on her countenance painted some of the beauties of the mind within, she was pronounced to be dangerous.

But Providence does not behave thus to its children. The really pleasing in expression are, almost invariably, the pleasing in disposition, and there surely can be but one poor, wretched reason why the ordinary are presumed—we say presumed only, because we believe the really contrary to be the case—to be the most virtuous; and that must be from want of temptation.

With a heavy heart, poor Margaret found herself rejected, and turned from the last door she applied to, full of depression.

As she did so, there drove up to the inn door, to which she happened to be, a travelling carriage, and, with a cry of joy, she recognised the arms and liveries of a family which had visited her when she inhabited a handsome house with Bertram.

But the feeling of joy was an impulse. In another moment she remembered that, in all her distresses, these people had never come near her.

And yet she walked to the carriage

THE MURDER

AT

THE OLD FERRY.

window, at which was seated a lady who had called her, while sitting in her, Margaret's, drawing-room, all the loves and dears she could interlard her conversation with, and said,—

"Do you know me, Mrs. Thistleton?"

"Oh! God bless me! Mrs. Ber-—no—no—I don't know you."

"You do."

"No, I don't. Go away, impostor. You are an impostor, and I shall give you to the police if you don't go away from the carriage window directly."

"Can this be possible?" said Margaret.

"Go away, go away; I dare say you have come out of some gaol. Don't be laying your hand on the carriage panels."

"Good God!" Margaret said, with a shudder.

"Here, John! John!" cried Mrs. Thistleton; "send this woman away. I don't know you, woman; go away."

Margaret walked on, and Mrs. Thistleton threw herself back in her carriage, exclaiming,—

"Really, I do wonder at the dreadfully bad taste of paupers, who have once been better off, addressing anybody they knew before. Really, they ought to go into some workhouse, and—and —die."

"Yes, ma," said her daughter, who was being brought up in the way she was to go; "yes, ma; but pa says, of all the obstinate people in the world, paupers are the worst, and that they never will die when they are wanted."

"Which is perfectly true, my dear. You know who that was?"

"Oh, yes, ma! but, of course, I wouldn't speak."

"My dear, you are a love. It's quite flustered me. The idea of being spoken to by anybody so dreadfully reduced! It's my idea there ought to be some public place like a—a—prison, you know, or something of that sort, to put in people who have been once respectable, but got reduced; for, of all the disagreeable things to any one who, like ourselves, continues respectable, and sees the best society, the most disagreeable is to be accosted by any one who has gone down in the world."

"Yes, ma."

"And so, my dear, you will take a lesson by what you have seen to-day, and you'll know what to do if ever you are spoken to by any such persons."

"Oh, yes, ma!"

Mrs. Thistleton was satisfied. What a delightful thing it is for a parent to feel that he or she is doing his or her duty. Margaret was very sad; but, after all, it was no more than what she expected; and her feelings partook more of a regret that she should have for one moment imagined that she had a chance of receiving any other reception than that which she had done.

"It is in vain for me," she said, "to expect aught else; when I am deserted by him who should have protected me, and who swore in the sacred temple of God to do so, what can I expect from others who have imposed upon themselves no such obligations? I ought not to look for it." There Margaret was wrong. She ought to have looked for it; but, certainly, she ought not to have been surprised when she found it not. That was the whole of the proposition.

She had not proceeded far before a man met her, and said—

"Oh! you are Mrs. Bertram, I believe?"

"I am."

"I have been to your lodging in search of you. The magistrate who remanded the man that shot at you wants to see you directly. I am an officer, and have been sent in search of you."

"I will follow you," said Margaret.

She did so; and when they reached the magistrate's house, she was ushered into a room and told to wait a few minutes. She wondered much what all this portended, and at length the magistrate came in, and said—

"Oh! Mrs. Bertram, we can dispense with any further evidence from you against that man I committed on your complaint."

"Can you, sir?"

"Yes; and for the best of all possible reasons—he has gone out of my jurisdiction."

"How so, sir?"

"He is dead."

Margaret looked surprised, and the magistrate added—

"The fact is, that his wound was of the most trivial character; but, in consequence of the dreadful state of heat he had put himself into just previous to receiving it, he inflamed his whole mass of blood, so, as the medical man tells me, that nothing could save him."

"Heaven grant him mercy."

"He is well known to the police as a man of the very worst of characters, and I am happy to say that the whole nest of bad characters residing at, and connected with the public-house—where, if you had staid, you would doubtless have been murdered—has been rooted out, and the house will be taken down."

"I am glad to hear it, sir."

"And now allow me to remark that, from your manner and conversation, it is evident to me you have moved in some very different sphere from that in which you are now."

"Alas! yes."

"If, then, as a magistrate, I can be of any assistance to you, command me freely. I shall listen to anything you may have to tell, only I do not, of course, wish to pry into any of your secrets."

"Sir, I have no secrets."

"Well, then, so much the better. Can I aid you?"

"Alas, I know not. I am married, but separated from my husband."

"Indeed."

"Yes; I know not why I, being innocent, should shrink from stating the cause, or the alleged cause; for Heaven only knows if it be the real one."

"And what was it?"

"He chose to suspect me."

"Oh, I understand. But you have your remedy. You can compel him, you know, to support you; and if the charge he brings against you is unfounded, you will permit me to say, you owe it to your child to force him to the proof."

This was putting the affair in a light which had not occurred to Margaret before. Any argument which affected the welfare of her dear child was sure to have its due weight with her; but she hesitated, much as she disliked and shrank from the idea of going to law with even such a man as Bertram, cruelly as he had used her.

"You hesitate," said the magistrate.

"Yes—yes; I do hesitate."

"Let me beg of you to deal frankly with me; I have made you a candid offer, and I hope a kind one, for I assure you I intend it to be such. Do not deceive me. If there be really anything that can be imputed to you which your husband can urge in his defence, do not involve me in an affair which can result in no good to you; but if, on the contrary, you are really innocent, and your hesitation only results from some romantic feeling of supposed independence of the man who has used you ill, let me tell you that I consider that as nothing more than foolish obstinacy."

There was something so matter-of-fact and reasonable in what the magistrate said, that Margaret was half inclined to coincide with him.

"Sfr," she said, "in reply to your request, I beg to say that I am perfectly innocent, and that my husband can allege nothing that has the shadow of a presumption of guilt about it against me. In the name of Heaven, I declare my innocence."

"I am satisfied."

"But still I do hesitate."

"Ah, from the feeling I have described. But the only way you can rescue that unoffending child from the brand of shame his father's conduct towards you has attached to it, is by commencing proceedings against him."

"Shame—shame, to this dear innocent?"

"Yes, certainly, in the eyes of the world; what else can you expect? It is your sacred duty to vindicate yourself; and, in doing so, you vindicate your child."

This was a cogent argument. Margaret considered for some moments, and then she said in a voice full of agitation—

"Sir, I feel that I owe you abundance of thanks; but give me till to-morrow to consider of it."

"Oh, yes, as long a time as you like."

"Only till to-morrow. Already my mind is more than half made up to follow your advice, which I feel convinced is given to me in all possible sincerity. You have placed the matter before me in a new light."

"It is one you would do well for the future to consider it in."

"I will, sir, I will. At this time to-morrow, if I come here, can I be permitted to see you?"

"Certainly; you will find me disengaged at this hour."

"And then, sir, should I make up my mind to follow the course you propose, I will trespass upon your patience with the particulars of my melancholy history, so that you yourself shall be able to judge of what likelihood of success there may be."

"Do so. That will be an important step. I have friends connected with the law in London, who will take up the case properly. And this husband of yours may find that it is far easier to make charges than to substantiate them."

"He cannot, with truth substantiate, aught against me; but that too well, and too submissively I have kept those vows which he has utterly forgotten; at least, in the spirit, if not in the letter."

Margaret felt somewhat comforted in the midst of her affliction by what the magistrate had said to her; for although it cannot be denied but that she was aware she had a legal remedy against Bertram, she had never dreamt of exercising it, because she had never had it presented to her mind in such a shape before.

"For your sake, dear one," she said,

as she that night lay down beside her child ; "for your sake, I will yet make your cruel father feel and acknowledge his error and the grievous sin he has committed in so long deserting you."

CHAPTER LXXIV.

BERTRAM'S PROGRESS.—THE NEWS-PAPER REPORT.—THE LETTER.

AND not only do we consider that Bertram had committed a grievous sin against his wife and child ; not only is he answerable before God and man for the common injustice of deserting those who were dependant upon him; but what calamities had he brought upon himself?

Is he not an object of pity, as well as of condemnation ? Of what a host of pleasures had he not deprived himself! He had thrown from him the affections of one who would have gilded his days with the sincerity of domestic joy. He had deprived himself of the caresses and the smiles of his own child, than which can aught else of joy the world can offer be more truly delightful ? And all because he chose to be a man who would not stoop to inquire. All because an insane feeling of revenge against others arose in his breast, he chose to inflict upon himself such a world of unhappiness.

Alas! he had not to wait for the retribution which was sure to be attendant upon his faults—his crimes, we may call them ; for he took care himself that that full and entire retribution should come hand in hand with them. There was not a pang that he inflicted upon Margaret that he did not inflict upon himself—an answering one ; and yet, as we see, with a wild obstinacy, he for years had persevered in his desperate and foolish course.

We do not expect to get any good out of Bertram now. He is too far gone. He is too much vitiated by long indulgence in the company of his own evil passions. We are nearly done with him, as far as any hope goes of his ever becoming anything like a rational man again. But still, as he has an important part yet to play as regards the fortunes of those in whom we feel so

largely interested, we must, however we dislike him, revert to him again.

Perhaps Bertram really, now that a suspicion came across him that after all he had played the fool to so serious an extent, suffered more than he had ever yet done. The more he pondered over the interview, strange and violent as it was, which he had had with Theodore Danton, the more fearfully evident did the words which he, Theodore, had uttered appear to be stamped with truth.

"If he were," thought Bertram, "but playing a part on that occasion, such a skilful actor never yet trod the earth. But no, he could not—it is quite impossible; he could not deceive me. There is but one chance, and that lies in the supposition that he is mad."

This idea for a time took possession of Bertram, and if it were true, that certainly would account for much that Theodore Danton had uttered. But still Bertram was ill at ease ; and what we may truly denominate as a dread of the truth came most vividly across him. He would ten times over have preferred, after all that had happened, heaping up proof upon proof of his wife's guilt, in preference to finding that he had so long deceived himself, and wrongfully punished her.

There was something dreadfully humiliating in the thought that he should after all have been wrong; so that, torn by conflicting emotions after the interview with Theodore, there was not a more miserable wretch in existence than Bertram. Then he began to ask himself—

"What can I do? I know not where she is, if I were willing to go to her aid. I am helpless."

He wandered about the streets as usual at nightfall; for there was now about his manner, in consequence of his long isolation from society, a wild and strange look, and he felt as if he were an intruder in the daylight.

Besides, he was conscious that people shunned him. Some would cross over to the other side of a street rather than pass close to him; for there was something strange and dangerous-looking about him. Others again would shrink close to the houses, so as to leave as great a space as possible for him to pass, in order that he should have no excuse for pretending any offence. But these did not trouble him so much as the more curious and thoughtless, who deliberately turned and stared after him till he was out of sight.

There are hundreds of people in London who will do this to any one who in dress or manner presents the least singularity. They will stop all aghast, heedless of any feelings they may outrage, and gaze after the individual who has attracted their attention, as though he had been some strange and new animal such as they had never seen before that time.

These people annoyed Bertram amazingly, and then a grade of persons, if that be possible, lower than they again, would be so angry that he looked peculiar, that they would go after him and abuse him for it.

We will warrant that a person shall not go far through the streets of London showing any peculiarity, whether it be the doing of nature or himself, without meeting with some reproaches of the coarsest character upon the subject from people who ought to know better, certainly, but who, we fear, never will.

Bertram had found out all these amiable traits of character among the lower classes of London, and frequently, as he ground his teeth together, and hatred was swelling at his heart, he would mutter—

"My bitterest curses light upon you all! Can it be a matter of wonder that those who are high and powerful, that those who can do so with impunity, take a pleasure in riding rough-shod over those beneath them? I would do it, and I may do it yet."

But he found that his gloomy philosophy was not sufficient to enable him to endure patiently such insults, and, consequently, he always went out at night instead of in the day-time, during which period he shut himself up, and mused gloomily upon his condition.

A week might have thus elapsed, when he had borrowed, as he was now and then in the habit of doing, a newspaper of a neighbouring publican,

who had had the good sense to treat him civilly upon several occasions, and with that he wiled away a tedious half-hour until he, according to custom, went to bed.

Bertram always read in bed. He would bring close to the bedside two chairs out of the scanty furniture of his miserable apartment, and placing an old piece of board across the backs of both, he had the candle, which he put thereon, of a sufficient height to enable him to read with comfort.

He felt an unusual degree of nervousness as he opened the newspaper; but he did not pay much attention to such a feeling, although it seemed strangely and suddenly to seize hold of him, as if it were a prognostic of some coming event which was calculated to move him much.

Several common-place, uninteresting paragraphs met his eyes, until at last he gave a sharp, faint scream, and half rising up, he read as follows—

"Considerable sensation has been created in the town of Underhill, in consequence of a coroner's inquest having been held upon a man who was shot by a party of military while endeavouring to make his escape across Underhill Heath, after firing no less than two pistol-shots, one of which was seen by the military, at a woman, with a child in her arms, who gave the name of Margaret Bertram."

"God of Heaven!" he said, and the newspaper fell from his hands.

For many minutes such a shivering came over Bertram that he thought his last hour was come, and more than once he was upon the point of calling out aloud for assistance to the people of the house.

By degrees, however, he succeeded in conquering this feeling, and after rising and partaking of some stimulant, which he kept at hand as a remedy when memory would come over him sometimes with all its events of the past, and almost destroy his reason, he felt himself better, and able to resume the reading of the newspaper paragraph.

It contained, which we need not trouble our readers with, an account of the coroner's inquest, that was, of course, held in the gaol, upon the man who had been wounded by the corporal, and there died. The particulars merely consisted of Margaret's evidence to the fact, that he had fired at her, and been pursued and ultimately shot by the military.

The surgeon of the prison stated the cause of death to be erysipelas, arising from the state of the system. But at the end of the paragraph were these words :—

"We understand that considerable mystery is connected with the woman, Margaret Bertram, who, from the style in which she gave her evidence, showed that at one time she must have moved in a very respectable sphere of life, and was, beyond all question, an educated person. Whether Bertram was her real name, or who or what she may really be, remains a mystery upon which we cannot enlighten our readers."

"'Tis she," said Bertram, " yes, 'tis she, and exposed to great danger. The child too, whom I have repudiated. The little one who claims to call me by the name of father, that might have received a double wound at the hands of a murderer, and I not there to close its eyes, or to shed one tear. Tear—tear, what have I to do with tears ? The fount of tears is dry—I shall never shed a tear."

Even as he spoke he rose, although the hour was late, and dressed himself. He was so accustomed now to night wanderings, that, although he knew it to be nearer one o'clock than twelve, he had no hesitation in going at once out into the open air.

Attiring himself, then, in the strange, old, faded apparel which he had taken it into his head to wear recently, he walked to the door of his apartment, and there, for a moment, he paused, saying to himself—

" Shall I take with me that black mantle, which has become so associated with my destiny, or not ?"

For several moments he seemed irresolute, and then suddenly he walked up to a part of the wall of the room on which hung that sombre cloak, and, taking it down, he carefully wrapped it round him, adding—

"Yes, yes ; be it so. Let it witness my humiliation, as well as my revenge —perhaps my death."

Then he walked down the staircase with a hasty step. He opened the street-door, and in another moment stood in the cool air of early morning. He glanced up at the house he had left, and said in a strange tone—

" I wonder if I shall ever be beneath that roof again ? I think not. Something seems to tell me that I shall not. Well—well, be it so ; farewell for ever ! I have no ties to bind me here. And now to the town of Underhill, mentioned in that newspaper, where I must make inquiries for myself."

The name of the town was familiar to him. He knew that it were situated some distance beyond Epping, so he at once proceeded in that direction, and was, in a couple of hours, clear of what may be properly called London.

He was in the suburbs of the gigantic city; those suburbs which stretch so far into the sweet, open country, that the pedestrian, when on leaving London, or on arriving to it, may in vain vex himself to know where the great city begins, and where it really ends. But Bertram was too busy with his own thoughts to pay much heed to surrounding objects. All he looked at, occasionally, was to see if he was on the right road, and then he walked on, making in his mind a thousand strange projects for discovering, without committing himself in any way, if what Theodore Danton had told him was the real truth or not.

He felt no fatigue. The state of his mind thoroughly kept him from thinking of the distance he was walking, and so muttering now and then to himself strange, disjointed sentences, and scarcely meeting a soul, he walked on until afar off, and by the dim light of the early day, he saw Epping Forest before him.

CHAPTER LXXIV.

WHAT BECAME OF THEODORE DANTON. — THE RECOVERY OF HIS PROPERTY, AND THE SURPRISE OF THE LANDLORD OF THE HOTEL.

LEAVING now Bertram, as we hope sincerely, in a more healthy frame of mind than we have found him in for many a day, and knowing that, so far as regards her personal comfort, we need be under no sort of apprehension concerning Margaret, we will follow the footsteps of the half-maddened Theodore Danton after he left Bertram.

Hoping but little from the interview he had had with one now whom he looked upon as but a degree or so removed from actual lunacy, he walked on till he recovered his composure.

"Alas—alas! poor Margaret," he said; "there is little for you now, as regards that man who has so cruelly injured you doing you justice. But I have made the effort. He has rejected the evidence which ought to have brought him to repentance; and now I will, from this moment, persevere in a plan which for some time has occupied a place in my imagination."

This plan was to take Margaret and the child with him away from England, if he could get her consent to such a course, and, in some quiet, happy home in Switzerland—a country which he had visited and knew well—there enable her to pass the remainder of her days with him in happiness.

"I will discover her," he said, "and make such a proposition to her; I will urge her, by all the love which she has for her dear child, to embrace my proposal."

He, now that the experiment which he had brought himself to make upon Bertram had been made, and, to all appearance, had wholly failed, turned his attention entirely to his own affairs, and to finding Margaret, and, in the first place, he made his way to the hotel where he had lain ill so long, and from whence, it will be recollected, he had disappeared so ungentlemanly, so far as the knowledge of the landlord and others connected with the establishment went.

Theodore was, in consequence of the care that had been bestowed upon him by the kind persons into whose hands he had fallen, considerably improved in personal appearance. Something like the hue of health was again upon his cheeks, and he was as different-looking as when he had left the hotel, as anything could be different from another.

Oh! how many bitter and pleasing recollections crossed his mind as he ascended the steps of that establishment. He thought of how he had first come there, elate with the hope of making Margaret his. Then the deep and dreadful disappointment of finding her another's came over him, and he remembered the sensations he had endured when he fairly, at last, felt himself compelled to give way to illness, and had laid down on a bed of sickness from which he had not thought ever to rise again.

But more agonizing than all, there came the recollection of the visit which poor Margaret had made to him—that visit which had caused to her such a world of woe, and from which might be traced nearly the whole of the disastrous consequences which had followed.

It was that visit, actuated as she was by the purest, the holiest, and the best of motives, which had given the arch hypocrite, Mrs. Blair, an opportunity of presenting to the too easily deluded Bertram what looked like evidence of the guilt of that wife, who was only by such conduct the more entitling herself to the admiration of her husband, as well as to his affections. But, alas! villany and the most terrific misrepresentations had triumphed, and he well knew what had ensued.

These recollections of the past crowded on Theodore as he ascended the steps of the hotel to such an extent, that he felt his strength for a moment desert him, and he heaved a deep sigh as he was compelled to lean against one of the columns that supported the doors.

At the moment that he did so, he must have been seen by some one inside, for a waiter came bustling out and addressed him—

"God bless me, sir, not well? Something the matter with the *dury matter,* sir; or is it a *accidento,* as we say in Latin?—ah, hem! Only a sort of *faustibus* sensation; all owing to the *muccy membrane,* sir."

It was our old friend, the learned waiter. He was there still, and as dictatorial as ever; while, from the accounts of coroner's inquests which he had daily read, no doubt, he had wonderfully increased his store of medical language.

"Thank you, I am better now," said Theodore. "Is your master within?"

"Yes, sir; the governor is in, sir. Not very well, sir, he ain't. A sort of affection, sir, of the face, sir, vulgarly called tooth-ache; but we scientific men, we call it a—a conglomeration of the *jawibus.*"

"Do you, indeed?"

"Yes, sir. It is not fit, of course, that everybody should know the out and out scientific way of saying things. Do you know, sir, you remind me very much of a gentleman as was here, sir, a good while ago."

"Do I?"

"Yes, sir. He was ill; the physicians all gave him up. Perhaps I ought not to say it, but I cured him."

"Indeed?"

"Yes, sir. I saw what was the matter with him—something wrong in his *chiterlins,* sir—that's all, and I prescribed for him and cured him."

"What became of him?"

"Went abroad, sir—went abroad."

"Really, you are a wonderful fellow. Now it strikes me forcibly that he left the hotel suddenly, and no one knew where he had gone to; at least, so I heard."

"You heard, sir? Oh, dear, no, he knew better than that, sir. When he went away he took me by the hand, and says he, 'James, you are a scientific man. I know you, so give me leave to say you have saved my life.'"

"Oh, no," said Theodore. "You are wrong. He went away without as much as seeing you. Surely, I ought to know, when I am the same person, now come back to take possession of some things that I left here."

James gave such a start that he nearly went through a plate-glass door that was behind him, and then looking steadily at Theodore, he became assured of his identity.

Oh, genius of impudence, you at that moment assisted James to the full extent that you assist scientific men as usual. He recovered in a wonderfully short space of time, and giving a short cough to clear his throat for the lie that he was about to utter, he advanced his head close to Theodore, and said,—

"Do you think I did not know you, sir? Ha—ha—a good joke, wasn't it? Do you think I did not know you?"

"I am sure you did not, or you would not have ventured upon telling such a number of abominable lies."

"Oh, that was only, sir, to hear what you would say; Lord bless you, sir, I knew you. Do you recollect, sir, the young lady as came to see you?"

"Yes, yes."

"And how she cried, and how ——"

"No more of that—no more of that. Where is your master?"

"In the bar, sir. And don't you recollect how she was afraid you was all for to be about going, sir, to kick the bucket?"

"That will do."

"Ah," thought James, "I can see he don't want to hear about the young lady, so I'll serve him out if he stays here as often as I can about her, just because he took me in so, and would not tell me at first who he was."

Theodore Danton soon made himself known to the landlord, who expressed himself very glad to see him, and congratulated him upon his restoration to health, adding,—

"I have, quite safe, sir, all the articles you left here, although, to tell you the honest truth, I expected never to set eyes on you again."

"I was half maddened," said Theodore, "probably by bodily illness, and probably by mental afflictions, and when I left here I really scarcely knew what I was about; but although I have yet upon my mind much to give me great uneasiness, I shall not again lapse into so serious a state."

"I hope not, sir, for your own sake."

"I shall now be considered, if you please, as again a resident here, for I

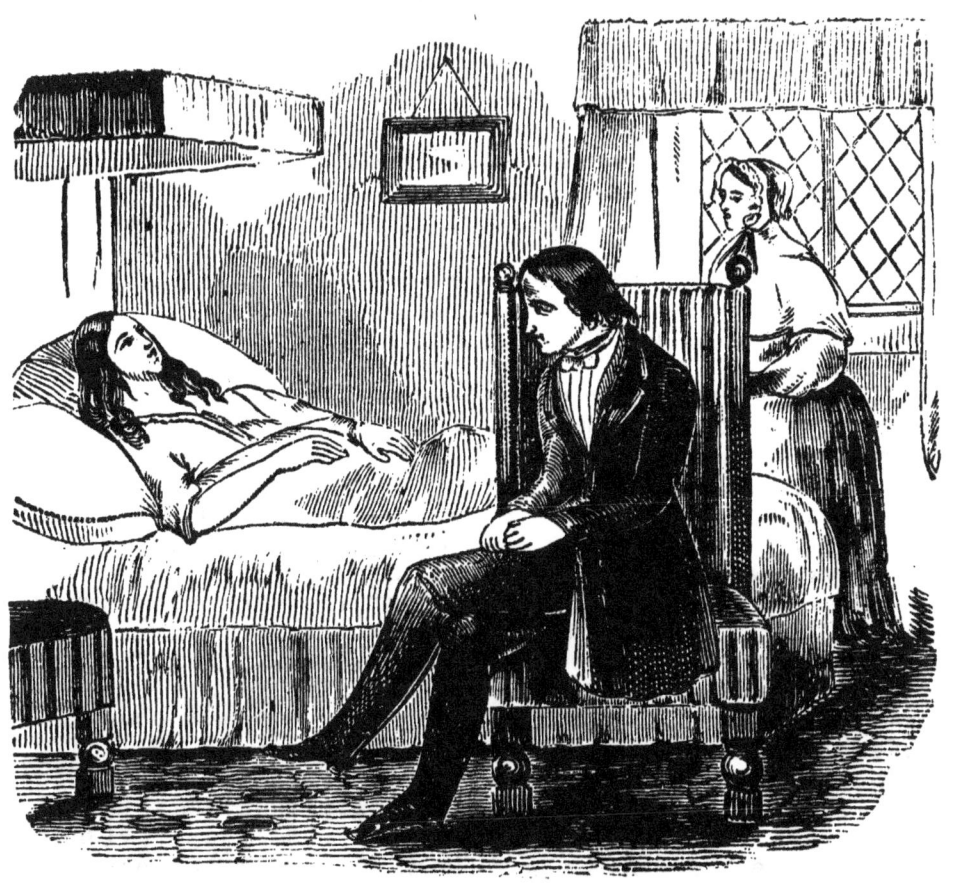

THEODORE AT THE SICK-BED OF MARGARET.

have some affairs to settle, which make it necessary I should have an address in London, although I have occasion to leave it almost immediately, to prosecute a search for one whom I hope soon to find."

"Any accommodation which we can give you, sir, you may depend upon receiving at our hands. I can assure you that your strange disappearance has often been a subject of the most uneasy reflection to me."

"I owed it to you to come back again as soon as I could, and I shall not readily forget the tenderness I have experienced here, notwithstanding the eccentricities of your medical waiter."

"Ah, he is still here—an honest fellow—although really quite a nuisance with his pretended science. I often say he ought to be a professor at the London University, and take his turn as they all do at being dean of the faculty. He would just suit them."

"He would; and now I shall only remain here two hours; but I shall always communicate to you where to send to me if I remain in any one place long enough for a communication to reach me, because I hope that a note in answer to an advertisement which I mean to insert in a number of newspapers may come here, as I shall put this address."

"Very good, sir."

James looked very shy at Theodore Danton; for, although he had, with consummate confidence, got out of the affair, as he thought, by pretending to know him all the while, yet he could well perceive that that part of his story was not taken for gospel, and that Mr. Danton had bowled him out in a most atrocious invention.

He thought, however, that if he continued worrying Theodore Danton about the young woman who called upon him when he was ill, he would somehow get the better of him, and he very imprudently, while Theodore was writing, came into the room; and, while he pretended to be dusting some glasses, he said,—

"Beg pardon, sir, but hope you continue better in your *corpus delicto*, sir, eh, sir? Beg pardon."

"Yes—yes—yes!" said Theodore, rather impatiently.

"Oh, glad to hear it, sir—very glad to hear it! Hope the young lady, sir, who came to see you, when you were ill, sir, is quite well, sir, inside and outside, sir!"

"Take that!" said Theodore.

As he spoke, he flung the inkstand at James's head, against which it came with tolerable force, giving James a contusion on which to exercise his scientific skill, without any one for a moment questioning his right to do so.

"Murder—murder!" cried James. "He's going mad again! Murder—help! I'll have the law of him for this!"

"And if you do," said the landlord, stepping in from another apartment, the door of which was partially open, and from which he had heard all that had taken place—"if you do, I'll come and be evidence against you, that, by your own impertinence, you provoked the chastisement you have received."

"Eh, what?"

"Yes! you may stare, but, unless Mr. Danton choses, which, if I were him, I would not, to say that he will look over your impertinence, you shall leave my service within a couple of hours from this time!"

"The deuce!" said James. "I shall have to set up as a quack doctor, and sell my royal patent anti-everything and cure-body-and-soul pills!"

"Let him be—let him be!" said Theodore. "He is but a fool, and I ought not to have minded what he said."

"Yes, sir," said the landlord; "it's very kind of you to say so, but there was, or there seemed to me to be, some malice at the bottom of his conduct."

"Well, well, I forgive him!"

"Do you, though?" said James. "Then I shall continue to shed an importance upon this establishment, I presume, governor?"

"Get out with you—get out of the room, you rascal!" said the landlord. "I wonder at myself for putting up so long with such a mass of conceit!"

"He did blunder over a subject," said Theodore, "which, I will admit, is one upon which I feel acutely. It is to discover that very young lady who visited me here, and who has suffered much upon my account, that I am going to advertise. So pray take in all communications that may be addressed to 'T. D.'"

This the landlord duly promised to do; and Theodore, after remaining for about a couple of hours at the hotel, and making such preparations as were necessary, sent the advertisement, of which the following is a copy, to the principal newspaper offices; after which he started for the part of the country where last he had seen Margaret, with the hope of being able to trace her footsteps.

"If Margaret B. will write to T. D., informing him where she is to be found, he will throw the protection of a friend around her, of the good faith of whom she is well aware.—Address to T. D., at Aitchison's Hotel, London,"

"Heaven send that this may meet her eye!" he said. "My poor, poor Margaret, what may you not have suffered by this time!"

Theodore hired from a livery-stable keeper, to whom he had been recommended by the landlord of the hotel, a horse, and mounting, about midday, he, at a gentle trot, left London in the direction of that part of the country where the barn was situated in which he had last left Margaret.

CHAPTER LXXV.

MARGARET'S DECISION. — THE INQUIRIES OF BERTRAM, AND MARGARET'S ALARM.

POOR Margaret found it no easy matter to resolve upon the question which had been submitted to her by the magistrate.

Her accurate powers of reflection let

her see, at once, all the bearings of the case, and to what serious animadversions she would lay herself open if she should refuse to carry on legal proceedings against Bertram.

She knew that then the presumption, as a matter of course, would be that she dare not do so, and that there was something in her history which she feared should meet the light of careful investigation.

And yet, while she shrank from laying her character open to so grievous an imputation, she likewise did shrink from any appeal to the laws, but rather felt that she was treating her husband with an amount of contempt which he deserved, by not applying to him even for the means to live.

But the question was not to be taken merely upon its solitary merits, she knew well, as regarded herself. What was to become of the child? What if, by some sudden calamity, her life were to be sacrificed? Who could then stand forward, and take the part of that young and unoffending child?

And had she not narrowly, only, escaped such a catastrophe? What if one of the pistol shots which had been aimed at her by the ruffian who had paid, by a shameful death, the penalty of his crime, had taken effect upon her, and deprived her of life—what then would have become of that little one who was dearer to her than life itself? This was a dreadful consideration, and, when she came to take it in all its bearings, it was one which nearly decided her.

But then, she had an awful dread of Bertram. Had he not already attempted to take her life; and, but for the sudden appearance of Theodore Danton—an appearance which must have been providential—would he not surely have done so, and, perhaps, in his insane rage, he might actually have taken the life of his own child, and so committed one of the most awful crimes of which human nature can be guilty.

This dread, then, of his necessarily discovering, as a consequence of her commencing legal proceedings against him, where she was, made her pause. She resolved to seek the magistrate, and inform him of the extent of her fears in this respect, asking him if that were not a sufficient argument to induce her to pause before she allowed such a wild madman as Bertram to know where he could successfully pounce upon her.

Our readers may well imagine how utterly inefficient such a reason as this will appear to any one acquainted with, and in the habit of having recourse to legal proceedings; so that when Margaret went to the magistrate, and informed him why it was that she hesitated, he smiled as he said,—

"And are persons who are guilty of vengeful acts to be allowed to escape with more or less impunity, according as they are more or less violent against those whom already they have greatly injured?"

"But I fear——"

"Which fear you must be taught now to banish. Why, such a doctrine as that would be at once holding out a complete bonus to evil doing of all sorts. A man has nothing to do but to commit some great social wrong, and then his victim is to be bullied out of appealing to those laws which are expressly made to meet such cases, and to assist the weak against the strong."

"My reason echoes all you say; but——"

"But what?"

"My fears, not for myself, but for this little one, beset me."

"Before I say another word upon this subject, Mrs. Bertram, will you trust me with the particulars of your story?"

"I will, sir; you are entitled to my confidence, from the friendly sympathy you have shown to me. I will tell you all, and you shall judge for yourself."

Margaret, then, as rapidly as the various incidents of her eventful career could be put into language, informed him of everything; and when she had concluded, he said,—

"Good God! and you have suffered all this mysery, not because you are guilty of any wrong, but because the very kindness of your disposition shone out in affectionate acts, which the demon of jealousy turned to your disadvantage."

"I am innocent."

"I am convinced you are so more than ever; likewise am I now convinced that this is a case which calls loudly for interference. He shall see—this mad-brained husband of yours—that the law can and will step in to the assistance of an injured woman ; and he will find himself compelled to maintain you and your child in a manner suited to his fortune."

" Oh! I want nothing of him my-self."

" But you must have your rights. You have suffered enough, Heaven knows, through his infatuation."

" But tell me, sir, of one thing; and it is a question upon which hangs all my happiness, so I implore you to tell me as nearly to the probable truth as you can."

" Go on; I will answer any questions."

" Will, then, those proceedings which you undertake in my favour have by any possibility a result that will deprive me of the only solace and joy I have in the whole world ?"

"'The child ?"

" Yes, the dear little one. If right is to be purchased at such a price as that, let Bertram still repudiate us both, and we will rather beg our bread from door to door, than be beholden to him for a palace, and yet be separated."

"'This is a serious question," said the magistrate.

"'To me, sir, it is life or death."

" I am inclined to think that the Lord Chancellor would give you, upon a proper application to him, embodying all the circumstances, the sole charge of the child. But most certainly the husband might resist such an application."

" And he might succeed in wresting the dear one from me ?"

" I cannot say that it is utterly out of his power to do so. When your child shall have reached the age of seven, he is the legal guardian of it, and can force it from you, unless you can show good cause to the Lord Chancellor to induce him to make an order that it shall remain with you."

" Then we will be, sir, as we are," said Margaret, " and ten times poorer than we are, rather than run the risk of so horrible a catastrophe."

" Nay, now, be not hasty. We will do nothing without due consideration ; and now that I am acquainted with all the facts of the case, I will in the course of a few days get the opinion of a legal friend in London, who can be relied upon. If we find it adverse to us, nothing is easier than for us to forego the contemplated proceeding, and then it shall be my care to do something for you which shall better your condition."

" Sir, I owe to you a world of thanks," said Margaret.

" Not at all—not at all."

Margaret had still some of the money left which had been given her, and, therefore, she declined accepting any bounty from the magistrate, although he, with great kindness, offered to supply her.

" No, sir," she said ; " we have enough for the present, and I do hope that something may arise which will enable me, with ordinary industry, to suppor myself and my child. I would rather do that a hundred times, than be indebted to Bertram for the most costly house he could be compelled to place me in."

" Well, well, I cannot but say that to some extent I admire the spirit which actuates you, only you must not carry that sort of feeling too far. Come to me in a day or two, and I may by then have heard from London, for I shall write off for the opinion I want by this night's post, and may have it even to-morrow if my friend's leisure serves him sufficiently to enable him to attend to the case, which I hope it will."

Mrs. Bertram left, with feelings of the most grateful character, the house of the justice.

She felt, too, as is always the case, much relieved by having told the story of her woes to a sympathising and attentive listner, so that, upon the whole, whether she went to law with Bertram or not, she felt that her circumstances were not so desperate, but that Heaven had raised her up, in the person of this magistrate, a friend who, one way or another, would do something to alleviate the distresses of her condition.

She looked with a face of hopefulness now upon her infant's slumbering beauties, as it reposed in her arms.

" My own, my beautiful," she would say ; " there may yet come a time when you will be told the story of your mother's memory, and feel deep in your heart the care and the affection she had bestowed upon you. But for you I should long ere this have lain down and died by the wayside, for never, never should I have had courage sufficient to bear up against all I have gone through,"

And Margaret was right. There can be no doubt whatever but that it was the thought of the child that had supported her through all her grievous trials, and as she herself truly said, but that her heart was always reassured by that undying affection which a mother feels for her child, she must have sunk under such a load of ills; and ere that time, in all probability, would have gone to the grave with all her fears and all her sorrows.

But this was not to be; if, for a season, such hearts as Margaret's are suffered to know affliction, it is that some sweet result, full of beauty and harmony, should spring out therefrom.

And most especially wrong is it, of course, for people to grumble because they may be picked out by Providence to work out its beneficial ends. They should, on the contrary, feel a pious sort of fever on the occasion, and be quite delighted at all the pain and all the misery they go through, because they ought to feel that it is for some good purpose in the great scheme of creation: and who would not cheerfully suffer for the good of others? who, indeed! There are some captious people who might say, " No, thank you," but we do not appeal to them.

Could Margaret but have known now what had become of Theodore, she would almost have been happy; but whenever she thought of him, there came over her mind a thousand fears, and dreadful misgivings as to his fate.

And she had the agony of feeling and of knowledge that it was for her that he had foregone all that could make life desirable; that for her he had, in a manner of speaking, confined himself, and in the very spring-tide of his existence wasted those energies and feelings which ought to have been garnered up to make the happiness of maturer life.

" Oh," she said, " if I could but know what had befallen him; if I could

but be assured that he lives and is well, I should lie down in peace; but while I am ignorant of his fate I cannot hope to do so."

She had no resource to make inquiry concerning him; and even if she had, that dread of being discovered by Bertram, if she made the least public stir which might point to where she was, would have kept her back.

At one time she thought that she ought to go back to the precise spot where last they had parted, and there endeavour to learn about him; but then when she considered the chances of the inquiry, and that she had to take with her the child, who had already suffered from such repeated changes of location, she gave up the idea with a sigh.

She blamed herself, though, for not begging of the magistrate to make some inquiry for him, and she accused herself of selfishness; she, who knew not what that feeling was, but, on the contrary, had a heart all generosity itself.

And now, while Margaret is congratulating herself that, at all events, not without due caution, would the least chance be given to Bertram, to discover where she was, she little thought of those busy media of intelligence, the newspapers. She never, for one moment, gave it consideration that an account of the whole affair, regarding the attack upon her on the heath, and its results, would be sure to be printed, in order to feed the ear of curiosity, and that then there were many chances which might make her name strike upon the attention of Bertram. Had some one, or her own imagination, suggested this contingency, she would not so quietly have lain down to rest on the evening of her last interview with the magistrate.

And Bertram as he walked into the town, passed actually the house in which she was. He, with the usual dread of the daylight, had put up about a mile and a half from Underhill, at a little road-side public-house, and there he had waited until the shades of night came before he would venture into the streets of the little, but bustling enough place.

At this public-house he made some cautious inquiries, but he soon found out that they knew nothing more of the circumstances than what he had read in the papers.

That is to say, they knew nothing more which was of an interesting character to him, for he wanted to hear of Margaret, and all their gossip related to the man who was shot, who, in the neighbourhood, had borne by far the more important character.

Of him they professed to know a great deal, and Bertram was duly informed who and what he was supposed to be, and what he said, and where he was buried, and how many people attended the funeral.

"But of the woman?" he said.

"Oh! she as was shot at?"

"Yes—yes."

"Why, you see, as she wasn't hurt, nobody cared much; and she was a quiet sort of person, too, and nobody knew her."

"Did she leave the place?"

"Don't know. She was, of course, only some tramper; but, you see, as he didn't hit her, she was of no consequence. Now, if he had shot her and the baby, there would have been a famous story to tell."

"Very," said Bertram with a shudder.

"But now people have nearly forgotten all about it, almost."

"And you cannot tell me what has become of the—the—woman, who was so nearly killed?"

"No; she has gone away, no doubt. We pay our poor-rates here, and don't encourage beggars."

"Indeed. 'Tis well."

Bertram's eyes blazed so fiercely, and he cast such a look upon the person speaking to him, that he drew back in alarm, thinking that surely it was an escaped lunatic with whom he was conversing.

"I hope," he said, "I haven't offended you?"

"No, no," said Bertram, "I know enough of the world not to be now offended at any amount of uncharitableness."

Even as he spoke his conscience smote him, and he thought he might truly have added, that the principal instance of uncharitableness with which he was acquainted had its origin in his own conduct to his innocent wife.

He now relapsed into a strange, gloomy state, so that, when he asked the house of the magistrate, of whom he intended to inquire what had become of Margaret, he was just of that appearance which was likely to beget the most serious suspicions of his intellect. He did not imagine it likely that Margaret had made a confident of any one as regarded her real condition of life, or, probably, he would have shrunk from going to that house, lest there he should find one who might guess who and what he was. He knocked at the door, and inquired of a servant if the magistrate were within, and was answered in the affirmative, and asked his name and his business.

"My name," he said, "is Jenkins, and I have come to make an inquiry which I do not choose to make to any one but to the magistrate himself. If he refuse to see me on that condition, I can go as I came."

It was not likely that any one holding an official appointment connected with the administration of the laws would refuse to see one who professed to have some communication to make; so, in a few minutes, Bertram was admitted to the room where had sat his unhappy wife but so short a time before, and detailed her adventurous career to the friend whom Providence had raised up for her.

"Well, sir," said the magistrate, after he had taken a scrutinizing look of Bertram, which by no means increased his desire for an acquaintance with him, "well, sir, will you be so good as to state what your business is?"

"Yes; I want the address of a person calling herself Margaret Bertram, who has been before you on account of some transaction in which a man was shot by the military."

"Oh! the whole affair is fresh in my memory. Who are you, and for what purpose do you desire the information?"

"My name is Jenkins."

"Which is a mere assumption."

"Sir?"

"I say, which is a mere assumption. I have seen, in my magisterial capacity, too much of human nature to be so easily deceived. If you choose to declare who you really are, and what your real motive is in seeking Mrs. Bertram, I will then consider whether or not I can consistently accommodate you with her address."

Bertram felt that he was foiled, and he suspected that he was known. After a moment's pause, he said—

"Sir, you refuse me the information, I see, except upon terms with which I do not see the necessity of complying; therefore, I bid you good evening."

"Very good."

The magistrate rang a bell, and ordered very coolly that Bertram should be shown out; but, the moment his back was turned, he sent a trusty and confidential servant after him, to watch his footsteps, and then he said to himself—

"If that is not the jealous husband, I never was more deceived in all my life. He answers to just the sort of man which, in my imagination, I had pictured him to be. He must, through the public press, have heard what has occurred; but I must ascertain if his purpose be for good or for evil, before I allow him to encounter his wife. She, too, must be warned, the first thing in the morning, of his proximity, for there may be some desperate and dangerous purpose lurking in his mind."

CHAPTER LXXVIII.

THEODORE DANTON'S PROGRESS ON THE ROAD.—THE DEAD BODY ON THE HEATH, AND THE HANDKERCHIEF.—DREADFUL SUSPICIONS.

THEODORE DANTON'S emotions, as he started upon his pilgrimage in search of Margaret, were of the most painfully conflicting character.

He reckoned in his own mind how much time had elasped since he had last seen her on that memorable occasion when both he and she were denied the poor luxury of a shelter from the fury of the elements in a humble shed.

And, as he calculated that lapse of time, he felt, indeed, that it had been amply sufficient in amount to enable

the worst of evils, and the most perilous of misfortunes, to have fallen upon her whom he would have shielded from the very winds of heaven, had they—

"Visited her cheek too roughly."

He felt that until he found her,—until he could once again look upon that calm, pale, beautiful, but suffering face, he should know not a moment's peace in this world.

"Margaret! Margaret!" he would cry, as at such moments he urged his horse to speed, "may Heaven grant that we may soon meet, and that I may so be able to cast around you the protection of a love which is imperishable. Oh! what a fate has been yours; framed as you were to grace a happy home with every attribute of womanly dignity and loving beauty, you are made an outcast, instead of being cherished, and punished because partial nature made you so full of every charm of mind and feature."

Theodore Danton was thus far correct. Beauty is a most perilous gift indeed,—one of these gifts which are all powerful for good or for evil, and so most precious to the possessor.

It is like giving to some human soul a chance of winning some enermous prize in the lottery of life; but if it lose, terrible is the loss.

Theodore's object, as the reader is aware, was to go down to the same part of the country in which he had, by force of untoward circumstances, left poor Margaret, and then, by dint of diligent inquiry, he hoped to get upon her track, and so ultimately find her.

It was the only rational plan he could pursue; and in its pursuit he had to cross that very heath upon which Margaret had gone through so fearfully perilous an adventure.

She had taken the route to London when she was accosted by the huntsman who gave her that piece of gold which had well nigh proved her death, so that Theodore was likely, unless he deviated from the high-road, which was not probable, to ride through the very town where now Margaret was staying, and enjoying more calmness and peace than she had known for a considerable period of time

The horse which Theodore rode was a good one; that is to say, without being anything extraordinary as a fast horse, it was one that kept up a good, steady pace, so that he actually did, at a very early hour, ride through the town, and pass the very door of the house where Margaret was staying, and there, with her child pillowed upon her breast, slumbering, and dreaming of happier days yet in store for her.

Oh! Theodore, could you but have guessed the proximity of her whom you loved so truly, with what a change of feeling would you have paused in that place through which you now passed, with a melancholy aspect, absorbed in sad thoughts, and only hoping for that blessing which you were at each step leaving farther and farther behind you.

If some beneficient spirit had but whispered in your ear, " Go no further, Theodore Danton, for she whom you seek is close at hand," with what rapture would you have hurried into the town, and looked eagerly around you for a verification of the prophetic greeting!

But no such blessed intimation reached him. A few idlers looked after that solitary horseman, as he rode on, and wondered he did not stop there, as there was no house of road-side entertainment for some miles beyond it, and then they resumed their idleness or their occupation as he rode beyond the power of their vision.

There was a cold and nipping air as Theodore emerged through the wood, which has before been mentioned as that from which the soldiers appeared, only in time to save Margaret from being murdered, and he allowed his horse to walk, as he inhaled with pleasure the fresh, breezy atmosphere that blew across that great extent of open country.

There were several roads across the heath, diverging from one another, and well known to the inhabitants of the locality as leading to different towns and villages some miles further on; but Theodore, although he knew that such a heath lay on his proper route, which he had studied before he had started on his journey, was now rather puzzled to know which of the various roads to take.

After some consideration, he resolved to take the widest-looking, and that which had the appearance of being the most frequented, which, fortunately, was the same that had been traversed by Margaret.

And yet we scarcely ought to say fortunately, because not only was he going from her, but he was preparing for himself a shock such as he would have been spared, had he gone by any other route.

It will be remembered that Margaret had said nothing of the robber who had perished in the muddy pool that was formed by the rain at the bottom of the excavation.

Having at first not mentioned that frightful circumstance, she had shrunk from doing so afterwards,—a natural enough feeling, and yet one which might have produced a considerable amount of mischief, on the broad principle that all concealments of such a nature are bad.

She had reasoned with herself as to whether she ought to make, even late as it was to do so, a declaration of the fact, but she had been advised, as the reader will recollect, to say nothing about it—a foolish piece of advice, but one which she took.

Certainly she did no harm to any one, or to society at large, by keeping that circumstance locked up in the recesses of her own heart; and when she came to consider that there could be no possible good arising from a declaration concerning it, she had decided upon letting it rest where it was.

Much rain had since fallen, but for the last day or two the weather had cleared considerably and been much finer, so that a great amount of evaporation had taken place, and, consequently, what with that, and the soaking up of much of the rain in the ground, that pond which had so completely submerged the robber was now but shallow,

By mere accident, as Theodore Danton rode on, he happened to cast his eyes into the deep excavation, close to which the road, it will be recollected, wound, and there in the shallow, stag-

THE LOVE-CONFESSION OF MARGARET TO THEODORE DANTON.

nant pool, he saw something of a suspicious looking character, which so closely resembled a human body, that he involuntarily paused to look more narrowly at it.

The more he gazed, notwithstanding the distance which he was from the object, the more he became convinced that his first supposition was a correct one, and that it was a dead body that he saw floating in the pool.

Shocked at this discovery, he looked around him for something to which he could tie his horse, while he should himself descend the excavation and take a closer look at what was there.

Upon that heath, however, he could find no such convenience, for although there were firs and other trees growing majestically beautiful on its outskirts, they were too far off for him to avail himself of them.

While he was in this dilemma he saw a country lad coming along the road at some distance.   Theodore immediately hailed him.

He quickened his pace in answer to the summons, and soon reached the spot on which the young and ardent lover of Margaret had halted with his steed.

Doubtless he thought that some opportunity was about to arise of earning a few pence easier than by weeding or ditch mending; and by the fixed manner in which Theodore Danton looked into the excavation any one might partly have imagined that he had dropped something of value down its precipitous bank, and was anxious for some one to descend and recover it for him.   At least that was the impression of the country lad, who with many an awkward congee now reached him.

CHAPTER LXXVIII.

THE DISCOVERY. — THEODORE'S AGONY.—THE NEW PURSUIT.—THE DISAPPOINTMENT AND THE GIPSIES' ENCAMPMENT.

THE impatience of Theodore caused him to believe the time, before the lad could reach him, was an age, and when he did come, with a hasty gesture, he pointed to the object lying in the pool of stagnant water, saying,—

"Do you see that, boy—is it not a body?"

"Yes, sir, it be uncommon like one," and the boy looked very hard at the object, but said nothing further; apparently well satisfied with having made an answer to the question put to him.

"I must see what it is," said Theodore; "it seems to be that of a female. I am in search of some one. Here, hold my horse while I get down to see it."

"I'll go, sir," said the lad; "if you want the body fished out, I'll undertake to do it. I want a job, and I see you be a gentleman and won't mind paying for a poor fellow's trouble. I'll go down, sir, and fish it out."

"No, no," said Theodore, "I must see it myself; I'll pay you. Do you stand here and hold my horse; I shall better satisfy myself than you can, as to whom the body might belong."

"You'll fail, sir, the pits are undermined in many places and there are great holes; if you don't take care you'll be suddenly buried or thrown headlong into the pool at the bottom."

"Than any one walking near the edge of the pits and losing their way, might suddenly get thrown into the water, by the sides of the pit giving way in some places?" said Theodore, as the thought suddenly crossed his mind that, after all, if it were Margaret, she might have been drowned more by accident than design.

"That they might," returned the lad; "but anybody as knows the place as I do can go down without so much danger. You see, sir," he continued, endeavouring to detain Theodore, desiring to obtain the job that promised to pay best—"you see, sir, the soil is gravelly and sandy; these pits are dug for gravel and sand, and whenever a load was to be had better than anywhere else, there, of course they dug it and undermined it; so in consequence down runs whole tons of gravelly earth, and people sometimes get buried in it and never come up any more."

"Never mind, never mind," said Theodore; "I will go down myself, it will suit me better to do so. I should be compelled to come down and see the body, since you could not bring it. Stop here and wait till I return, and hold my horse."

The boy did as he was bidden, as being better than nothing, and consoled himself as well as he could.

"Ah, he'll have a tumble before he goes far, and then he will be sorry he didn't send me. Never mind. I wonder what he'll give me? Something, I suppose; sixpence, perhaps. Well, sixpence earned in master's time is something, that's one consolation, and it's a rest, besides; so never mind. I wish I had gone down and pulled her out; I'd have made a great splash, and should, perhaps, have got half-a-crown. Why, it would be a good week's wages; and I could then have gone to the fair some time or other."

In the meantime Theodore Danton descended the sides of the pit with as much expedition as he could. From the nature of the place, however, he could not go very fast, for he found the sides in some places hard and in others so shifty and loose that he could not stand, but slid along until some impediment stopped him from being precipitated down below.

In some places, too, there were pieces of stunted vegetation, and here he would expect to find a hold; but when he grasped them he found they came away, soil and all.

At length he came to a place where there were some furze bushes growing out of the soil, and some moss-like grass vegetating around.

Here something attracting his attention; it was something white fluttering in the air, having struck upon a furze-bush and become entangled upon it.

"Ah!" he exclaimed; "what can

this be? something that may have belonged to the unfortunate Margaret. It is, at all events, a handkerchief. I will have it."

As he spoke he cautiously strode along until he came to the bushes; but he was compelled to make a circuit round them; for they were impenetrable of themselves, and offered too strong a barrier to be penetrated even by Theodore Danton, ardent as he was in the pursuit he had undertaken, and almost insensible to fatigue and pain.

The object was gained, and Theodore snatched the handkerchief from its position, and thought he could recognize it from its very appearance; however, to satisfy himself and be assured, he hastily looked at the corners of the handkerchief and there saw the words, "Margaret Bertram," written at full length.

He gave a start, and had nearly fallen over; for he stood at the brink of a piece of broken ground.

"God of Heaven," he murmured; "and has she really been here? Alas! poor Margaret! Here, across this desolate waste, in the vicinity of danger, and in distress. What a fate! what misery!"

He was almost forgetful of his position, and stood some moments contemplating the handkerchief he had in his hand, and ceased almost to think, so deep was the reverie in which he was thrown by this sudden occurrence.

However, the boy above having watched him for some time in his descent, for a time lost sight of him, as Theodore wound his way below a projection, and then he lost him entirely for some time, but awaited his appearance below.

However, as Theodore stopped there for some time, the boy became anxious, or, at least, curious, to know what had occurred, and to ascertain if he had been lost, or fallen a victim to his own timerity in attempting the descent.

"Ah, he should have let I gone down," he muttered, "and then I'd have been down at the bottom before now. He knows nothing of going down a gravel pit, any more than I do about going up in a balloon, that's quite another affair, too. What can he be up to, I should like to know?"

Not being satisfied with waiting in the dark, as respected the fate of the proprietor of the animal he held, he made a bit of a detour to get a glimpse under the projection; but he was no better off there; he could see nothing of Theodore.

"Well, I'm dang'd!" he muttered; "but I can't make anything out on 'en; but if he went down he must be down, and I haven't heard any splash in the water, so he can't have got there."

This was a point quite decided in his mind, that Theodore Danton must be somewhere down, dead or alive; but he was desirous of ascertaining which.

"Hilloa—hilloa!" cried the lad, in as loud a voice as he was able; and, certainly, it did his lungs credit; for it rang and echoed from place to place. The sides of the pit gave back every echo; and then he waited to see what answer he would receive.

"I wonder," he muttered, "if I should get anything at all if he was to die? Lord save us! they wouldn't say I pushed him over, would they? How terrible! What would measter say?"

This was a terrific consideration, and he again exerted himself to make Theodore hear him.

Theodore did hear him this time, and was anxious to get up again, to make certain inquiries respecting the owner of the handkerchief. Perhaps the lad could tell him if she had been by. He would return and make the inquiry.

Then, with more speed than was compatible with safety, he began to ascend the sides of the pit; however, he met with no serious obstruction, although he had one or two narrow escapes, from the earth upon which he stood giving way, and slipping from under his feet.

When near the top, the boy said—

"He shouldn't have come this way. Further to the right. You'll slip all the way back if you come up there. I told you so; you will break your neck presently if you don't take care. I see you ain't used to pit climbing."

This was certainly the truth, and if

it had no other merit than that, it deserved so much commendation. Theodore Danton, however, neither heeded nor understood what was said by the boy, and came on, catching at anything that promised to assist his ascent, and in a few moments more stood again upon the road.

"Well, I'm danged! I could never have believed he could have got up there," said the boy. "I thought it would ha' sunk down wi' him."

Theodore paused a moment, and, when he recovered breath enough to speak, turned to the boy, and said—

"Have you seen anybody go by here to-day, boy?"

"Yes, sir."

The boy was no way backward in answering, when he had any idea of what was wanted ; and then the affirmative mode seemed to him to satisfy most, and give a greater probable prospect of a profitable return ; and when Theodore asked him if he had seen any one pass by in the morning, with anything peculiar in her manner, he answered with much coolness—

"What kind of person do you want, sir ?"

"A female with a child in her arms," said Theodore, still looking at the corner of the handkerchief.

"Yes," replied the boy.

"You saw her?" said Theodore anxiously.

"I did."

"Did she seem under distress, and as if she were in great trouble, and poorly clad ?"

"Yes," replied the boy ; "she did seem in a great taking. The child cried very much."

"Ah, poor thing! Oh! Margaret, you were in want, and starvation was the cause of this !"

"Yes, she said she was starving," said the boy.

"And which way did she go, when she went away?" inquired Theodore, horrified at the notion that she was reduced to such extreme distress as to be on the verge of dying of want.

"You see yonder tree—there, that one with the top bent over on one side ?"

"Yes—yes, I do."

"Well, she took that road, and when I last saw her, she was going over that hillock, and when she was on the other side, she was out of my sight."

"I will follow her," said Theodore, throwing himself into the saddle, and then he was about to set spurs to his horse; but the boy kept hold of the bridle.

"Leave go of the bridle, boy ; what do you hold it for ?"

"Please, sir, I held your horse."

"Well, then, leave go," said Theodore, angrily.

"Yes, sir, so I have ; but you promised to give me something for my trouble, and master will deduct my loss of time from my day's wages."

Theodore made no answer ; he had forgotten all about the promise he had made the boy ; but he drew a piece of silver, which he threw him, and galloped off.

"I'm danged !" said the lad, " if he ain't mad ; but he pays well. He had nearly forgotten to pay at all, though ; but I'm glad I didn't go down, now, for I am as well off. I gave him information, and I have got money."

This was a gratifying piece of reflection to him, for he placed the coin in his pocket, and gloated over it as a miser would his treasure, and made the best of his way onward, lest his interrogator should make any attempt to overtake him.

After riding some time, Theodore Danton came to a public house by the road-side. The sign was the Trotting Horse and swung in front of the house. There was no one here, and Theodore pulled up, and called out for some one to come ; but nobody took the trouble, though he hallooed loud enough to have been heard by the seven sleepers.

At length getting tired of this kind of exercise, he looked around for some place where he could place his horse, and found suddenly that there was a gate immediately before him, which stood open; this might in some measure account for the fact that he did not at first see it—however, he now rode in, and saw a lazy-looking ostler, standing with his back against a post, looking at a female milking a cow.

"Halloo !" said Theodore ; " is there

any one alive here? I have hallooed till I am hoarse."

"Was that you who hollered so just now?" inquired the ostler, looking up at the traveller.

"Yes."

"Well, I thought it was somebody as wasn't used to these parts, or he'd ha' come in at once."

"But, thinking it was a stranger, couldn't you have come and told him where to go?"

"It was too much trouble; and where's the use? ain't you come in without it? We never take any unnecessary trouble here at the Trotting Horse," said the ostler.

"Perhaps it is too much trouble to take charge of a horse, and to give him a bait, then?"

"That's our business."

"Well, then, see if you can attend to it. Give this horse a bait, and then rub him down the while. Has any one been seen here this morning—any traveller?"

"Two or three."

"Did a female come with a child in her arms, apparently in great distress?" inquired Danton, in great agitation.

"Yes."

"When did she arrive here?" he inquired.

"Not very long since. She's in the house now; at least, I think so," he replied, taking the bridle of the horse, as Theodore hastily dismounted, and walked to the inn by a door-way that stood before him open.

"Not that way, sir—not that way; blessed if you won't walk into the tank, and it's very deep. You'd be stifled, if you weren't drowned, before we could get you out again. There, go out the same way you came in; 'twas only the other week that a man fell down and was drowned."

Guided by this gentle admonition, Theodore left the yard, and proceeded towards the house, which he found was occupied by some men who were seated before a fire eating and drinking, and laughing in a most unmistakeable manner.

"Well," said one, "I have nothing to fear; I have done my duty and care for nothing."

"Done your duty! ha, ha, ha!—

shooting a man doing your duty! why, you hypocrite, you ought to have eaten him afterwards, you ought, and then you would have done your duty."

"No, that would have been too much of a good thing; you and I should say a little of that goes a great way."

"So I should say; but I can't see the harm a poor fellow does in taking a pheasant or hare; I am sure they belong neither to you nor me, and they take as much from the poor man's field as they do from the rich man."

"That may be all very well, you know; but I say, Jepson, I hear somebody coming in at your front door; hadn't you better see they don't help themselves?"

"Well, they must be dishonest people, if they take what isn't their own," said Jepson.

"I don't know much about that; all I can say is, I should help myself, if I hadn't known the house before now, or I had to wait till you served me."

"Ah, well—well," said the landlord, "business is business, though it's a great plague; I must get up and go to 'um."

"He's been holloring long enough."

"He'll be thirsty," said the landlord, as he arose, and went out of the room which he had been sitting in, and coming towards the door at which Theodore Danton stood.

"Is yours an open house or an empty house?" inquired Danton, whose patience seemed exhausted.

"It's open house, your honour, with plenty of room left for you; will you walk into the parlour?"

As the landlord spoke, he opened the door of a decent room, into which he asked Theodore Danton, and before the latter could speak, he said—

"What shall I have the honour of doing for your honour? tell me, your honour, as I am a man of business, and I see your honour has had waiting enough."

Seeing he was likely to have little attention paid to him at this place without propitiating the presiding genius of the place, he ordered some refreshments. When they were brought by the landlord himself, he thought he would question him.

"Landlord, have you any traveller in the house? I mean a female and child in distress?"

"Yes, sir, there is now."

"Where are they?" inquired Theodore, anxious, if possible, to see who this was before he tasted of the landlord's fare, but mine host was somewhat imperative, and said—

"Can't see her directly, sir, but I'll send her to you immediately, and then you can tell if she be them you mean."

Danton was impatient, but there was no help, and waited until the landlord contrived to execute his promise. In the meantime, he partook of what was placed before him, more for form sake, as he had ridden his horse rather sharply across the heath, till he came to this odd out-of-the-way place of an inn.

In due time the landlord entered the parlour with a sickly-looking labourer's wife, with a child in her arms.

"Here, your honour, here she is; what do you think on her now? Here's a full-length portrait of the sign of life; do you think anybody in London could have done it better? There's a pair on 'em."

"That is not the person I mean," said Theodore, much disgusted with the landlord's manner.

"Oh, it ain't, ain't it?"

"No; the person that I wish to see is not so stout as she is," replied Theodore; "she has a light shawl on, and her dress has been made of good things —for a lady, but they are worn and soiled greatly; sorrow and want are strongly marked upon her features; she is thin, too, and appears hardly strong enough to carry her own child."

"Then, you are not the person," said the landlord, "so you may go now— his honour has done with you."

The woman looked wistfully, as if she would have said something, but feared to do so. Theodore divined her feelings, and sympathising with her distress, he threw a piece of silver down on the table, saying as he did so—

"There, my good woman, I have caused you some inconvenience—it is but right I should pay you for it."

The poor woman took the money, and with a curtsey, thanked Theodore for his bounty.

"There, thank your stars for such a windfall as that. Go on, and don't trouble his honour with any palaver. The worst of these people about here," said the landlord, "is, there is no getting a word in edgeways. I never came near the like of them. They quite put the stunners upon me when I first came down—they beat Irishmen hollow."

"Well, you have a pretty easy flow of talk yourself," said Theodore; "I have been waiting some time, in hopes of getting an opening to say a few words."

"Say on, your honour, I am as attentive as a cat at a mouse-hole—I'll not lose a syllable."

"You were about to speak of some other person whom you had seen pass by here."

"I was."

"Then, just tell me if you have seen any one that will at all answer my description—I wish particularly to discover the party I am in search of."

"Exactly, sir. Well, I saw such a person as you speak of, who passed by here at a very slow pace, some time since. Indeed, she stopped here—that is, at the door. She sat down on the step, and looked very hard at a countryman who was eating his breakfast, chucking pieces at the dog, who caught them, and ate them up. By-the-bye, the man noticed her, and seeing how she was, gave her part of his breakfast, and a drop of beer."

"Poor thing."

"She was thankful enough, I warrant you," continued the landlord, "for she burst into tears, and went on."

"Which way did she go?" inquired Theodore.

"Straight along the road, sir, as far as I could see. She appeared to be journeying onwards without any particular object. She was very tired, very weak, and appeared to be suffering from grief, and almost terror-stricken."

"It must be the same," said Theodore to himself; "I must ride after her and overtake her."

"You'll be sure to do that, sir, if you start an hour hence. She can't walk far without a rest, and that very slowly."

This was an inducement for Theodore to hurry away to overtake her as soon as possible; so he threw the landlord down the reckoning, and speedily quitted the house; but there was a new cause of delay in the yard— the horse was not ready. Angered beyond endurance, Theodore saddled and bridled the horse without assistance, and rode off, leaving the ostler to lament the loss of his gratuity, and the perverseness of human nature, which induced people to do without payment, when they hadn't got value received.

Theodore Danton heeded none of the remarks of the ostler, but rode rapidly out of the yard, and then along the road that had been pointed out to him by the landlord.

It did not take him long before he had travelled over the ground for a few miles. He knew his horse would go till the poor animal dropped, and never required the spur, and he had occasion to try it, as he rode over the rough and uneven road he was now compelled to pass over.

"If poor Margaret," he thought, "had to pass over this road, Heaven help her weary feet! Great as her former lot was in misery, yet, now she is alone, she must be much worse. I wish that I could overtake her, and reward her for the past; she has done much for me, poor, unhappy woman."

Theodore thought how much she had suffered, and how unjustly—how little she deserved the fate that seemed hovering over her—how pure, how spotless she was, and yet how persecuted.

There were many bitter reflections that rose to his mind as he rode along, and he failed not to perceive that much, if not the whole of it, was caused by himself, unknowingly, and without any act, indeed, voluntary or involuntary, on his part.

It made him the more anxious, and the more so as he was in a position to alleviate much of the distress and misery she now felt—such misery and such distress as only one so placed, and so tenderly nurtured as she, could feel.

Each person he met he questioned, lest he should miss the object of his search. The first he met with was a labourer. He stopped, and inquired if he had seen a female with a child in arms, walking along the road.

"What sort of woman, measter?" inquired the man.

"One that seems in great distress, weak and weary, and in the greatest want. Her dress, too, has been made for a different class of life to that in which she now moves."

"May be," said the man, "may be."

"Have you seen such a one as she whom I describe?" inquired Theodore Danton, "either lately or within a few hours?"

Here the man paused a moment, turned his head first one way, and then the other, and finally said in a grave voice,—

"No, I ain't."

He then moved on, leaving Theodore, who would have been angry at any other time; but now he had scarce leisure to be angry, and certainly none that would permit him to stay there and inflict any chastisement upon the boor, for he well knew it would occupy time, and, therefore, he abandoned the half-formed, hasty resolution to allow the fellow to feel the weight of his horse-whip.

He turned away and rode forward until he came to a turnpike-gate, and as he pulled up to pay the toll, he demanded of the man if he had seen such a person pass as the one he desired to meet with, describing the appearance of Margaret Bertram as when he last saw her.

"Yes," said the man. "I did see some one that partook of the appearance you speak of, but I didn't notice. We don't notice much who comes or goes through the gate, you see, only they who pay toll."

"Exactly. I thought as she was much distressed and afflicted she might have attracted your attention."

"That is true," he said; "some one has been by of that description. She seemed as if she had seen better days."

"So she had. And now she is at an extremity of poverty, want, and distress," said Theodore.

"If it's the same I mean," said the

turnpike-man, going into his house, "she has been gone through the gate these three hours."

"It must be the same," said Theodore. "Did she speak at all as she passed?" he inquired.

"No; I barely saw her, and certainly I did not speak, nor she either," and the turnpik-man walked into his wooden abode.

Theodore rode forwards upon the vain pursuit; but he had no doubt but that Margaret Bertram had been through the gate at some time, and certainly over the heath where he had found the handkerchief.

As he thought of the certainty that she must be on the road somewhere, he pushed his horse on in hopes that he might by some piece of good fortune chance to overtake he; he would have gone through any amount of fatigue and anxiety to have secured the unfortunate Margaret from further misery.

After riding for nearly an hour he came to a place where the road branched away from a point in different directions, and Danton was for some moments in doubt which way he should take. Seeing a man breaking stones by the road side in the parish dress, he called to him, saying,—

"My man, have you seen a female with a child in her arms pass this way?"

"Yes," said the man, leaving off his work, to look at the traveller, "I have."

"How long since?"

"Well," said the man, looking up at the sun, "I should say about an hour since, or a little more."

"She seemed much distressed in mind and body?" continued Theodore.

"Yes, yes—she was."

"Which of these roads did she take, that to the right or to the left?"

"Why," said the man, pausing to look first at Theodore, then at the horse, and then finally in the direction in which he thought she did go, he continued, "I'm thinking she must have gone on somewhere a-head, but whether to the left road or to the right I cannot well say; but I rather think she must have gone to the right; that road bends more, and she was sooner out of sight than if she went the other."

"Thank you," said Theodore; and he threw the man a few half-pence, which he gathered up with satisfaction.

Theodore took the right-hand road, and pursued it for some distance, until he came to a wild and desolate spot, where there was an encampment of gipsies.

He did not notice the encampment until he was in the midst of them. It was a wild and dreary spot; and the road had for some distance assumed the appearance of a lane with high double hedges, as well as the earth of heathy character.

Theodore pulled the bridle, and seeing a gipsy woman, he said to her,—

"Have you seen a female pass this way with a child in her arms, not long since?"

"Yes; she's here now."

"Indeed?—how fortunate," said Theodore. "Tell me where they are and I will reward you."

"Here, Jack," said the woman to a boy, "come and hold the gentleman's horse. You must dismount, sir, and I will take you to the place where she is resting."

Without a moment's thought or suspicion, Theodore complied, and immediately dismounted, and followed the woman into a tent, which was at some yards distance.

"Has she been long here?" inquired Theodore, as he followed the woman towards the opening in the tent.

"Not very long," she replied, "not very long—stay here, a moment, while I go in and tell them a stranger is here."

Accordingly Theodore stood still while the woman pushed aside the opening of the tent and went in. Some words were uttered in a low voice, but Theodore, who had been abroad, and had become acquainted with some foreign words the gipsies use, partially comprehended their import; but, though he had his suspicions awakened, yet he would not refuse to enter—he had too important an object in view; and while he thought of Margaret, he would dare any danger.

"Come in," said the woman, appearing again at the opening of the hut, and beckoned Theodore, who immediately entered.

THE NURSE DELIVERS A LETTER TO THEODORE.

" Where is she ?" he exclaimed.

" There," pointed the woman, to a female with a child in her arms; but she was evidently one of their own tribe, and Theodore would go no further than the opening.

" That is not she whom I seek," said Theodore.

" Approach and examine," said one of the men, who had been sitting down, but who now arose and approached the opening.

However, Theodore, who was well satisfied that Margaret Bertram was not one of the number, attempted to withdraw, while, at the same time, the man made an attempt to throw himself upon Theodore, and two more rushed forward to help him.

Chance favoured Danton, who had retained his riding-whip, and he struck the man on the head heavily, and he fell, while the second got entangled with the tent pegs, and fell.

Theodore waited for no more, but springing backward, he made for his horse, which the boy, who had charge of it, had led to the other side of the encampment.

However, the horse being restive, attracted Theodore's attention, and he made direct for the horse, which the boy would have taken away from him, but could not ; seizing the bridle with one hand, and bestowing a hearty cut with his whip across the back of the youngster, who held him, he mounted his horse just as the men reached him, and endeavoured to recapture him, but his heavy riding-whip did them such severe injury, that they permitted him to go on without further interference on their part.

Theodore had escaped, no doubt,

from robbery, and, probably, murder, for he was well calculated to make resistance, and would do so against any odds, rather than suffer detention at that moment, with such an object in view.

Theodore Danton had now made an escape, but he was on the wrong side of the encampment to return the road he came, and yet he had rather done so, for he thought there was little prospect of Margaret's having been through such a place, and yet he thought, to one in her condition, there was little danger from these people, seeing she had so little to lose.

"She might pass and repass with impunity," he said, " while I am liable to excite their cupidity."

As this passed through his mind, he was determined to pursue the road for a few miles further, at all events, and ascertain where it led to.

Acting upon the impulse of the moment, he turned his horse's head and was about to proceed; but, as he did so, he received a heavy blow, which, evidently intended for his head, fell upon his shoulders.

Upon looking whence it came, he saw two men had crept up to him unperceived, and had, no doubt, aimed the blow at his head, but fortunately he turned round his horse's head at the moment, and thus saved himself from the effects of the murderous effort, for he would have been felled to the earth.

In an instant Theodore returned the blow, and struck the man to the earth, while the other having seized the bridle, endeavoured to force the horse upon his haunches, and thus throw over both horse and rider; but Theodore frustrated the attempt by striking the hand that held the rein with the iron handle, and, in an instant, the arm fell useless by his side.

" Curses on you," muttered the man; " may your hopes be blighted and withered, as you have broken my arm."

Theodore paid no attention to this, but, as soon as he found himself at liberty, he made the best of his way off, and it was fortunate he had done so, for the encampment was nearly empty at that moment; but the men were returning to it, and Theodore met several as he galloped away.

He had not, however, gone far, before he found the lane became more and more wild, until it was lost in an open plain of heath ground, and the road ran through the centre of it; this he pursued for some time, congratulating himself upon this escape from the murderous gang of gipsies.

The road was open; no trees on either side; all was bare and desolate; however, after riding a mile or so, he could perceive when the road entered a more cultivated district, and then he hoped he should have some opportunity of making some inquiries that would help him to discover the lost track of the unfortunate Margaret Bertram and her child.

CHAPTER LXXVIII.

MARGARET'S DREAM.—THE HASTY JOURNEY.—THE STORM, AND THE REFUGE AT THE FERRY HOUSE.— THE STRANGER, AND THE NOTE.

IT may appear strange to many of our readers, when we come to consider the great provocation which poor Margaret had received, and the manner in which she had been treated by one who ought to have been the person, above all others, to shield her from harm, that she should have hesitated a moment about the advice which the magistrate had given her.

It is rare, indeed, that any one in the state of society in which we live, has civil rights which they hesitate to exercise : but, then, Margaret's was a mind of a rare order—an intellect so pure —so beautifully unselfish—that she was not of those who are always considering what they can do, but with a holy and remarkable resignation, she rather put up with wrong than went about the means of resenting it.

There was something, to her pure spirit, revolting in the idea of going to law with the husband of her love, and the father of her child.

True, he had done much to alienate himself from her. He had done amply sufficient to justify her in not considering for one moment his feelings or his convenience; but she still hesitated, notwithstanding all that had passed upon the subject.

The magistrate was not a man that was disposed to think harshly of human nature, although, Heaven knows, the specimens of it that were from time to time brought before him, were enough to make him do so; but he understood the feelings of Margaret, and he respected them.

He could well believe how a timid woman shrinks from the first feeling of going to law with one whom she has in the sight of Heaven sworn to love, to honour, and obey, and he felt certain that her consent would be wholly owing to the fact, that she was bound to do justice to the innocent child.

But something was yet to happen that was to give him a shock, as regarded the truth of what Margaret had told to him; and that something was of a nature one would hardly have expected from Margaret, because it had a superstitious origin, and she was certainly not by any means what in the ordinary acceptation of the word would be called a superstitious person.

On the contrary, her mind was perfectly free from all those feelings which hold such sovereign sway over many hundreds of people, whom we should hardly expect, from their rational conduct, as regards the other concerns of life, would be obnoxious to such fancies.

But there will often exist in the human mind a vein of superstitious fancy which no circumstances will call into action for many a year—a species of superstition which is not acted upon by the ordinary stimulants to that feeling, but which is most powerful when the means which are sufficient to call it into action actually do arrive.

This, perchance, was the case with Margaret. Ordinary feelings and ordinary prognostics might have no effect upon her, and yet something might arise that would affect her greatly, when others, again, might be free.

She retired to rest, on the evening after our last notice of her, at an earlier hour than usual. She fancied that she felt a strange somniferous feeling creeping over her, which she could not resist, and she soon dropped into a slumber, which for a time was profound and dreamless.

This was a state, however, which did not last long. Suddenly she thought that she stood at the door of a house in a street which she knew well by sight, as well as by name, as one she had often walked down in London, because it was near to where she had resided before her marriage with Bertram.

In her sleep she took particular notice of this street, and seemed, as it were, to tell herself its name, in order that it might not readily slip her memory when awake; for, strange to say, she had a kind of dim consciousness that she was dreaming.

The door of the house by which she stood she thought was wide open, as if inviting her to enter; and she felt so strange an impulse to do so, that she scarcely, for a moment, resisted it, but walked in, and proceeded up a flight of stairs, which, in consequence of a peculiarity in the papering of the wall, she felt perfectly assured she should know again in a moment.

She did not hesitate. No fear was upon her at all; but, on the contrary, a strange feeling of satisfaction soothed her, and pervaded her heart. When she reached the landing of the staircase she walked right on, and gently pushed open a door, which was only closed sufficiently to leave but a small crevice, through which streamed some light.

Inside the apartment, which was thus, in her dream, disclosed to her observation, she saw her husband. He was kneeling by a chair, and with a deep sigh she heard him say—

"Margaret! Margaret! I am now convinced that you are innocent!"

At that moment she awoke, as if the purpose of the vision that had visited her slumbers had been accomplished. It was with a saddened feeling, however, that poor Margaret reflected upon this dream, and its extreme improbability.

"No, no," she said; "this is but one of those fancies which the disordered mind creates for itself out of nothing. If he thinks me innocent, why does he not seek me? Ay, surely, he has the means if he had the will to find me."

With such reflections as these she dropped again into a slumber; when, strange to say, the selfsame vision of slumber came over her as before. Again she stood in the street which she knew so well; again she saw the house, with the door wide open; and, ascending the staircase, she again caught a view of Bertram, and heard him with despairing accents say— " Margaret! Margaret! I am convinced that you are innocent." And she awoke.

As may be supposed, this repetition of the dream was far more calculated to disturb her than the first, because that might be easily allowed to lapse into forgetfulness, along with the whole host of other such visitations to which all are subject; but when it came to be repeated so exactly, it was a something to reflect upon.

She felt disturbed and uneasy. She asked herself what it meant, and she strove at one moment to think that it was nothing; while at another it assumed to her the aspect of some direct communication from Providence, which was to be the means of indicating some course of action that would procure ample justice for herself and child without having recourse to the harsh measures recommended by the justice.

But, still, the more she thought over the matter, the more she became convinced of the possibility of the second dream being so far contingent upon the first, that the only connection it might have with it might very reasonably consist in the fact of memory, a second time, bringing it to bear upon the imagination.

When she thought of this mode of explaining the matter, she was, to some extent, satisfied that she was not called upon to take any further notice of the vision of her slumbers, and a third time she slept. But what was her surprise, not unmingled with some degree of alarm, when a third time there came across her the same dream, without the smallest amount of variation whatever.

Now she started from her couch, for she began to fancy that, indeed, she saw in the affair a visible interposition of Heaven. She began to think that this was something more than the mere chimeras of a disturbed imagination; and if it meant anything at all, what could it mean but that she was to go to London, and there find it verified?

It was strange, now, how suddenly she resolved to obey the vague impulse of a dream. She wrapped the child carefully in a shawl, and by the first grey tint of early dawn, she was on her route to London, determined not to pause longer than was absolutely necessary for rest and refreshment, until she reached that street which she had dreamt of.

And, as she proceeded, strange to say, her feelings on the subject became more and more precise; and she seemed as if each step that she took was taken with a consciousness that she was at last accomplishing something towards rescuing her child from the precarious situation in which it now really was, and had been, during what ought to have been the sunniest, and the happiest portion of its young existence.

And so powerfully did the impulse of carrying out the suggestion that the dream had given her act upon her mind, that she thought but as a secondary affair of what impression she should leave behind her on the mind of the magistrate who had interested himself so much in her favour.

The morning dawned with great beauty. The birds sang blithely and merrily from every tree and bush, and the early sunlight was beautiful to see upon every object that lay within the sphere of its delightful influence.

But Margaret was by far too busy with her own thoughts to pay that attention to the many beautiful objects that lay around, to enable her to do more than bestow upon them a passing glance of admiration.

She still considered the dream, which thrice had visited her, as some sort of direct communication from Heaven, to tell her which way she should go for the purpose of doing justice to her child.

Probably, under the circumstances in which she was placed, no reasoning in the world would have been sufficient to banish such an idea from her mind; but then it would have remained, exerting an influence which she could not herself have defended, but which, had she not followed it, she would always have regretted.

It is not for us, mortals as we are,

and with our limited perceptions, to question or to scrutinize the ways of that Providence whose interference, direct or indirect, with mundane affairs, never can be otherwise than for good; but we shudder at the possible fate to which poor Margaret was hurrying.

We, who know, what happened eventually before she reached London, would fain that even now she drew back, and rather met the chivalrous, noble-hearted Theodore Danton, than trusted to the frail services of the half-lunatic Bertram. But it was to be. There was no turning aside the arrow which destiny had levelled at her heart. It was to be; and we have, therefore, but to record its effects.

We have said that the dawn was beautiful, and so it was, but, as events proved, it was a doubtful beauty.

It was one of those sweet, mild, balmy, promising days, which are sufficient to seduce people abroad from their dwellings, luring them far away among green fields and pleasant woods, and by the banks of running waters; but treachery was in the sunshine, for about noon it faded away. Huge masses of clouds swept across the sky—rain fell in torrents, sent hither and thither in all directions by the sudden gusts of wind that carried it, and poor Margaret found herself far from any perceivable shelter, and exposed to the mercy of the clouds again, which seemed to take especial pleasure in expending their utmost fury on so innocent a head.

Thus many a promising day has not only an indifferent conclusion, but one which we would shrink from meeting. Such was the probable conclusion of the one now in progress of becoming.

The wind now swept across the open country for miles with undiminished fury, for there was no object to break its force upon—all was level and flat; and though there was beauty enough in the scenery, yet, at such a moment as the one we are describing, the vision becomes gradually limited, until confined within a few yards surrounding the spot where the wayfarer treads, and then its beauty is not seen.

Indeed, there is a desolate spot, with no object near that can relieve the eye from the dismal sight that meets the gaze turn which way you will.

True, there are a few trees—tall, gigantic elms—through whose branches the winds whistle, and with a rushing sound, that chills the heart, and renders hopeless the expectation of ever regaining any shelter from the fury of the blast or the deluging shower.

Poor Margaret walked on—she scarce knew whither—she was lost in wide and almost interminable meadows, the long wet grass of which often entangled her feet, and caused her to stop—besides the effect it had of wetting through every article of wearing apparel that came in contact with it, and which clung round the limbs with a deadening effect.

A more wretched evening could not have been chosen—a more wretched heart could not have been exposed to its inclemencies; and thus it often is, that our bitterest moments are rendered more bitter by adventitious circumstances that heighten the effect, and render it more miserable than it otherwise would have been.

Still, Margaret pushed onward, her weary feet traversed ground that to her seemed never to have any end; it appeared as though she had been walking around some field, and had come back again to the same spot; she had been, she thought, doubling upon the same course, and gone over the same ground.

She thought she must have made some such mistake as the one we have named, and when she came to the corner of a hedge that came close to the gravelly edge of a path that ran by the river side—a towing-path—she became convinced that there was by no means insufficient ground for coming to such a conclusion.

By this spot she had, she felt convinced, passed more than once, if not more than twice, but twice certainly.

"Yes," she muttered, "this point—I cannot mistake it—is a marked place. There are the May bushes, and over the river are the tall poplar trees that roar in the blast, and below there is the mill. I can hear it roaring and crushing, with a dreadful sound."

At that moment, while she stood undecided what she should do, or whither to go, she heard the sound of feet; she turned, and a figure muffled up, passed by her hurriedly; she felt something passed in her hand, she stepped back, and her foot slipping, she slid down the bank a few feet, until she came into the meadow below.

The pathway was a made one where she stood then, and there below rose the meadow, a natural one, the former serving as a barrier between the river and the meadow, and also as a path upon which horses could work to draw barges along the water.

It was a mere slip, but it brought her hands to the ground; the letter, for such it was, fell to the ground; she picked it up and looked around her—she was alone.

From side to side she looked, but could descry no form that was human, and reascending the bank of the path, and going round the corner of the hedge, she gazed for some time in silence, but saw nothing.

Neither could she hear, all was silent, ay, as silent as the grave, for not a sound, save that caused by the elements, reached her ears; she tried to catch the slightest sounds that came along the dreary waste, for such it seemed,

The day was darkening around her, and there she stood with the note in her hand; she had paused like one suddenly striken to stone, while around her fell the torrents of the storm.

The wind, too, whistled through the tall trees; there was a mighty rushing sound, that would have made you believe there was a tornado, so great and fierce was the struggle between the elements and the vegetation of the earth with each other.

There, too, at the distance, was the heavy rushing sound of waters, the waste of the stream, and the heavy, dull, monotonous sound of the water-wheel of the mills.

"Whence comes it?" she said— "whence comes it? my heart misgives me while I hold it—so mysterious and strange, it seems like a vision, a vision that sprang whence I cannot tell, and gone Heaven alone can say; may it preserve me from evil!" She looked at the note. "Heaven!" she exclaimed,

with a start; "it is Bertram's hand; how came he to know I was here?"

With a trembling hand she opened the note, and then by the dim light yet left, she read as follows:—

"Margaret Bertram,

"Meet me this night at Higham Hill.

"BERTRAM."

She read the note two or three times, without any apparent meaning being derived from it, by herself; she turned it over and over in her hand, and read and re-read it, till it was not possible to mistake a letter of the contents.

"Meet him there to-night," she muttered; "ay, meet Bertram; so then, he may, after all the injustice he has committed, now be convinced by some one or other, that I have not deserved the fate he has given me up to, he may yet do me justice; he may yet rescue my child—his child, and save it from the depths of poverty and wretchedness it is likely to become consigned to."

There was something like hope in all this; it infused, for a moment, a new life in her; she appeared to feel there was yet a prospect that she might not yet be abandoned by God and man; and, oh, how sweet is the hope of renewed happiness! nay, how much more for her child's sake did she not cherish the transient gleam of sunshine amidst the hours of adversity, than for her own.

"Yes; its father may yet acknowledge and own his own offspring; it would, indeed, be cruel to refuse to do that justice by the child, which the very beasts of the field would not hesitate to do; they teach their young to care for themselves, and effectually too; surely man ought not to hesitate to do so; may his heart be softened towards us, and justice take possession of his mind, for more I care not for."

Thus spoke Margaret, and she gazed around on the wild scenery by which she was surrounded, and the deep, rapid river in her front seemed to offer a refuge from wretchedness, but she shuddered and turned aside.

"Higham Hill," she repeated to herself; "where shall I find that, and where shall I inquire—of whom can I ask the question? What can be done?"

This was well enough to ask, and things that would naturally suggest themselves; but as it was, the finding of an answer was by no means a thing of such facility, and she was compelled to give up the notion until chance should throw some one in her way, of whom she could make the inquiries she desired to make.

None appeared; and, after some consideration within herself, she determined upon going on, and this time she resolved upon keeping the towing-path, seeing that was a road habitually used, and, therefore, there was every chance of there being some place where she could make inquiries, and where she could rest awhile.

"This is the haunt of men, and, however long, it must lead onwards. I shall not be again brought back upon my own path, to the same point from which I had started." The pathway was rough and shifty, and the loose stones galled her feet, which rendered the exertion of walking more and more fatiguing, and the wind every now and then making a sudden rush, caught her first on one side and then on the other, as the winding course of the path exposed her to its fury.

The night, or evening, was inclement in the extreme, and now added to approaching darkness additional disagreeables, and, in her case, additional miseries; for where the mind is not at ease, every other circumstance partakes of the peculiar colour in which it is cast, and wretchedness is more wretched when the mind is previously diseased, or affected by force of circumstance, for sorrow or vexation is truly a mental disease.

After some walking she came to a bridge, over which she now walked, and there, on the other side, was a small cottage, surrounded by palings, the river in front and on one side. The wind blew, and the rain fell in torrents.

"Here, at length," she exclaimed, "I can make some inquiries. I am now near a human habitation. What manner of place can this be?"

She walked round the cottage, but could not see where the gate or entrance was. She called, but no answer was returned. That might be because the wind blew directly from the house, and prevented her voice from reaching it; and, moreover, the continual barking of a dog, and the fall of water through the lock-gates prevented anything being heard very effectually by any one within doors.

"Surely no one would be out such a night as this," murmured the unfortunate and wearied Margaret; "and no one can dream of travellers in such a storm, and who would come to look for them? it would be to encounter the storm to no purpose."

The wind seemed to have lulled, and the rain fell quiet and gentle; but it came down so close and fine, that it was effective in the extreme, as could be easily felt by any one exposed to its effects.

Margaret paused and looked around her; she gazed down the road she had to go, but could see no light, no prospect of any human habitation besides the one she stood before at that moment, and the dog continued to bark furiously, and the water to splash sullenly through the crevices in the lock-gates, and making an incessant noise that became monotonous from the continuous nature of the sound, the action of falling water.

"No—no," she muttered, "I will not go back there; the road seems too lone, too far away. I will return to the point where I had this letter. The being who gave it to me went that way, and surely there must be more houses in that direction than any other; it comes on nearer to London."

She gave another cry for help before she left; but she could not succeed in obtaining any attention, and there being no light, it was more than probable they were fast locked in the arms of sleep, and perfectly oblivious to all worldly care and troubles.

How Margaret wished that she were so too—that she felt not the evils that oppressed her.

However, she gave over thinking, and with a wearied step, began to retrace her steps towards the very point to which she thought he had more than once returned.

It required some minutes' walking to reach that spot, and, when she came within a certain distance, the sound of the mill gave her an indication that she was approaching it.

"Thank Heaven!" she said; "if I can but see a human being that can but direct me on my way—that can but tell me when I can, or where I can, meet with shelter, I shall be truly grateful."

When she reached the mill there was a lock—a deep and dangerous place, where she had nearly fallen down, for there was no partition, no fence, or rails, or posts.

Having recoiled from the place with horror, she walked to the bridge, and, seeing some houses to the left, she walked towards them, and there being a turnpike beyond, she thought there was a probability of discovering some one who would be willing to direct her on her road.

However, the turnpike was shut up, and nobody seemed near, and she saw no house but a public-house, and that was shut up; but presently she heard a footstep; she turned round and saw a miller approaching her; he seemed wearied and exhausted, and was walking but slowly towards his home.

As the man approached, there was an air of indecision about him. He seemed to regard her in the light of some one who had risen from the dead, for, in the dim light that seemed to pervade nature, the outline alone was visible; but on he came, until within a few paces of Margaret.

"My friend," said Margaret, "can you tell me where I am?"

"Yes, ma'am, you be here."

"What!" exclaimed Margaret, "would you mock me because I asked you a question? Surely you can tell me the name of this place, if you will."

"Yes, ma'am; and I told 'ee; but as to the name of this place, that wasn't what you asked me before."

"Well, what is its name?"

"Clay-street," said the man.

"Clay-street," remarked Margaret; "where is that?"

"That be here, too, ma'am; but it's in the parish of Walthamstow also—that's all I know on."

"Can you direct me to Higham Hill?"

"Yes, ma'am; you must follow the road round until you come to the hill, and then take the path that leads over the hill to the left and down to the water's edge."

"That is the hill I require," said Margaret. "I cannot miss it, I suppose the road is straight?"

"Oh! yes, ma'am, straight a-head; if you go on, you'll come to the end in no time."

"Do you know the distance?"

"Yes; about two miles, or thereabouts. Good night, ma'am, I have got to go to work at six o'clock."

"Thank you—thank you," said Margaret; and she turned from the man, and slowly proceeded up the ominous Clay-street, which looked more like an indifferent road between two ditches and hedge-rows, and an abundance of tall trees.

Owing to the wet weather, the soil, which was indifferently coated with stones, was cloggy and sticky, and the walking was very bad indeed; there was scarce any possibility of walking, save but by wading through moistened mud and clay.

However, time effects wonders, and Margaret found she had got over the worst part of this journey, and came upon a little rising ground of somewhat of the same character, but then it was not so soddened—the rain had run off, and left only a slippery surface.

Up this hill she was forced to plod her way, weary and tired in the extreme; but still, though she shed tears, she went up with something like hope.

"This, then, is Higham Hill," she muttered, as she looked at the tall trees that surrounded her, and, had it been daylight, she would have seen a beautiful prospect of sylvan scenery—of rich meadows and the winding stream, with the dark woods in the distance; but it was night, an hour ere midnight, and she could only listen to the falling rain, and the peculiar noise made in the earth during wet weather. She had now reached the summit, and proceeded to go down its side towards the river.

THEODORE DANTON RIDING BACK TO MARGARET TO TELL HER THAT
BERTRAM LIVES.

CHAPTER LXXIX.

THE MEETING ON THE RIVER
LEE.—THE SUPPOSED MURDER
AT THE OLD FERRY.—REMORSE.

IF the reader will now turn back
to the first number of this veritable
history, he will there find that Margaret, with her child in her arms, kept
the appointment that had been made
with her by that husband, whose conduct upon that occasion went further
to stamp him insane than upon any
other.

It will then be found how all his old
violent and evil passions conspired
against her whom he had already
worked so much evil for; and it will
be seen that instead of listening to the
dictates of prudence—of honour—or of
common good feeling, he, on the
contrary, with some wild and fanciful
ideas of his own, tried an experiment
which, for all he knew—and which,
indeed, to the best of his belief—turned
out to be fatal.

And it was not until this desperate
and fatal result had been achieved that
he really began to feel those pangs of
remorse which should have found a
place much earlier in his breast. No,
it was not until he believed that he was a
murderer that his diseased imagination
appeared to awaken from the delusions
that had taken possession of it; and he
really, while reason was tottering on
its throne, felt how he had not only
made war against himself, but against
the holiest and best of beings.

Then, and not till then, he found the
value of the treasure that he had lost,
and would have given worlds to be able

to retrace his footsteps for the last two years of his existence.

But the reader knows that Margaret and her babe were saved; he knows that by the kind and unremitting exertions of the medical man who attended upon them at the village inn, to which, in a state resembling death, they were conveyed, they were again restored to vitality, among the living.

Probably that Heaven, which knows and can read the hearts of its creatures, was well aware that only through such a means could such a man as Bertram be reached, and, therefore, was it that matters were so arranged as they were now.

And who shall doubt that all was not for the best? True, Margaret had gone through a vast amount of suffering; but who shall say there is not joy to come for her—an amount of joy that shall so successfully compete with a recollection of the misery that has gone past, that ultimately it shall crush it, wholly and entirely, leaving scarcely the most dim remembrance of it in her mind.

It is by contrast with the misery that we have suffered that we find out the full joy of which we are the present recipients; and so shall Margaret be repaid wholly for all that she has endured, and have her just reward both in this world and in that which is to come for all her sufferings.

*   *   *   *

And now, while she is under the kind care of those who will impart to her no pang, let us inquire what is becoming of Theodore Danton, on his pilgrimage of love and goodness in search of the persecuted Margaret.

We left him, after he had escaped from among the gipsies, who, probably, had he remained much longer with them, would not have scrupled about the means they employed to transfer whatever cash and valuables he possessed from his pockets to their own.

When he perceived that he was near to the outskirts of some town or village, he slackened his speed, and looked anxiously about to endeavour if possible to discover what part of the country he was in, and if it was one which he had seen before.

There was, however, nothing that he could perceive in the surrounding scenery that he was at all familiar with, and he resolved upon asking the first person he met the name of the place towards which he gently trotted. In a short time he observed a woman sauntering along, apparently in a pensive manner, and when he had gained sufficiently close upon her to speak, he said aloud—

"Can you tell me where I am, and what town," for now he perceived it was one, "that is now before me?"

"Fairlight, it is called," she said.

"Thank you," said Theodore; "I do not know if I am right or not in offering you money. If you are not poor enough to accept this, give it to the next person whom you think a deserving object."

As he spoke he drew from his coat-skirt pocket his purse, for he had placed it there for convenience, and, taking a shilling, he stooped from his horse and handed it to the young woman, for young she was, whom he had questioned.

"I am starving," she said, "and, therefore, receive with thankfulness your bounty. But you have, in drawing out your purse, dropped your handkerchief."

She picked up the handkerchief, and Theodore seized it with avidity, as he exclaimed—

"I thank you indeed for drawing my attention to this handkerchief; I would not have lost it for the world."

"Indeed!"

"Yes, I set far more store by it than its seeming worth; it is to me a precious relic."

"I am very glad indeed then, sir," continued the young woman, "that I happened to see it, and I do not know but what the information that I have seen it before may, by some possibility, be interesting to you."

"What!" exclaimed Theodore Danton, "you have seen this handkerchief?"

"I have."

"Oh, tell me when, and where, and in whose possession? Speak quickly, I charge you; you know not how my heart pants for an answer. Where, oh, where saw you this handkerchief?"

"I saw it in the possession of a young female."

"Yes, oh, yes, and a child was with her?"

"True, a young child was with her. She was beautiful, although sorrow had clouded some of her charms, and there was no mistaking the fact, that she had suffered much, while from the kind, and good, and patient aspect of her face, one could swear that she had suffered most wrongfully, and that great injustice had been done her."

"You are right, oh, you are right indeed."

"The traces of tears were upon her cheek, not such tears as are ordinarily shed for ordinary sorrows, but such tears as come almost from a broken heart, and never fail to leave the semblance of their presence behind them."

"Your words convince me that you have seen her whom I seek; you have looked upon a face I have travelled many a weary mile with the fond hope that Heaven in its mercy would permit me to look upon it again. And now let me implore you to tell me where you saw her?"

"I will."

"Let me beg of you to omit not even the slightest particular concerning her. You shall find that you will not have wasted time in talking to me of her you saw with this handkerchief in her possession. Come, I will dismount and lead my horse, so that you will be able to talk with me more pleasantly."

He did so, and throwing the bridle of his steed over his arm, he walked on by the side of the young woman, whom probably our readers have already guessed was she who had been so strikingly instrumental in saving Margaret from robbery, and perchance from murder, at the lone public-house from which, and from its iniquitous inhabitants, she had had such immense difficulty in escaping.

With a clearness and precision in her story that one could hardly have expected from a person who had been for so long subjected to the depressing influences of a class of life that was about the very worst that can be imagined, the young woman related to Theodore Danton the whole particulars of how Margaret with her child had come to the public-house and there incurred so much danger.

And Theodore Danton, as he listened, betrayed by his changing countenance how deeply he sympathised in the narration.

At one moment all his fears of some impending catastrophe would be aroused, and the colour would fade upon his cheek, and then again when she told him of how Margaret had finally left the public-house in safety, he ejaculated fervently, "Thank Heaven!"

"Reserve your thanks," said his informant, "you have not yet heard all; the danger which I have related to you as having been successfully passed through by her concerning whom you feel so great an interest, is as nothing to that which she still had to endure."

"Go on! go on!" said Theodore faintly.

The girl then proceeded to relate to him, as she had heard them, all the proceedings on the heath, where Margaret had run such great hazard of her life, and she concluded by relating that the magistrate of the very town to which they were advancing had acted a friendly part towards Margaret, and no doubt could at once tell him where she was.

"Here then," said Theodore, "ends my pilgrimage, and by the luckiest possible chance I have acquired information which I should have flown from as soon as I discovered I had doubled on my track, and was riding again towards London."

"I rejoice," said the girl, "that I have been able to give you such information, sir, and now, with thanks for your bounty, bid you farewell."

"Hold!" said Theodore Danton, as she was about to leave him, "we part not thus; at present I am too much engaged in the pursuit of this suffering creature of whom you have told me such a fearful history, to attend to aught else, but in a short time I hope that it will be in the power of my leisure to seek out every one who has even uttered to her a word of kindness. You must tell me where I can find you, and then you may be assured that the time will not be far distant when you shall hear from me."

"I cannot."

"You cannot? Oh, bethink yourself; surely you can give me some address?"

"Alas, no; I am a wanderer, and know not where I may be on the morrow; but if you will tell me where I can find you, I will, should my necessity induce me, send to you, or call upon you myself."

"Do so," said Theodore, as he wrote the name of the hotel in London upon the back of one of his cards. "There you will either find me, or a communication left there will reach me, and in the meantime take something for your present exigencies."

He forced upon her acceptance three sovereigns, although she was averse to taking them, saying,—

"You can hardly estimate the danger to which you expose one so poor as I by giving me so much money at once."

"Danger!"

"Yes; remember that the possession of a sixth portion of this sum was sufficient to place the very life you seek in jeopardy."

"Oh, but you are favoured by being forewarned, which she was not; so do not scruple, I pray you, to keep the money, and, mind, I shall be very much disappointed if I do not hear something of you very shortly."

Tears crowded to the girl's eyes, and she could not speak, but continued to look after him as he rode away until distance hid him from her view. She then sat down on a grassy hillock by the road side and wept abundantly.

And wherefore did she weep, she, that child of woe, of rude buffets from evil fortune, and much misery? Wherefore did she weep? Simply because she had most unexpectedly met with kindness; that was all; kindness which was so new and strange to her that it awakened all her better feelings, and almost reconciled her to the world.

And let the false, hollow worldling affect to smile at the thought that kindness is so appreciated by those who are unused to it. Let him hug himself in the cold and brutal belief that the lowest of the classes of society are beneath the fostering breath of gentleness. We envy him not such a false philosophy. We know that such is not the fact, but that when a generous and noble heart stoops to listen to the woes of those who are reckoned scarcely of the great family of man, and speaks kindly to them of hope which is to come, he is ever met with an amount of grateful feeling that puts to shame refined emotions.

And now, elated at the prospect of soon discovering his Margaret—he could not help calling her his Margaret—Theodore Danton put his horse to a sharp trot, and soon entered the town from which he had so recently gone.

Alas, what a game at cross-purposes will those who are the most anxious to meet sometimes unwittingly play. Had Margaret been at all aware of how near to her Theodore Danton was, or could some genius have whispered in her ear that by remaining where she was he would soon come to her, not all the visions of slumber in the world would have induced her to leave that place.

But she had not, of course, the remotest idea of seeing him. No, on the contrary, she rather considered that the course she was pursuing, namely, the going to London at once, would give her a better chance of falling in with him again.

And although, as we well know, that was not the real reason that took her so hastily to the metropolis, yet it formed a part of her pleasantest anticipations as she went on her journey, which were doomed to be interrupted in the strange manner that has already been at large related to the reader.

When Theodore reached the town his first visit was upon the magistrate, whom he saw, and who, upon hearing his name, at once informed him of the address of Margaret, for he was as yet ignorant of her having left the place.

It will be remembered that Margaret had unreservedly told this gentleman her whole history, and that she could not do without the name of Theodore Danton being apparent in it, and therefore, when he heard it he felt at once that there was no occasion to keep the address secret.

Theodore then at once went to the lodging of Margaret, but, oh, bitter disappointment! she had gone.

There was a note lying upon the

table, which was open. She had left it for any one apparently to peruse who might feel sufficiently interested in her fate. The contents of the note were as follows :—

" Margaret Bertram, for reasons connected, she fondly hopes, with the well-being of her child, has proceeded to London."

" To London !" exclaimed Theodore, " to London ! Alas, I shall search in vain for her amid the crowded streets of the metropolis. Oh, Margaret—Margaret, why did you not remain here, if it were but a few hours longer, that I might have seen you and assured you of a protector who never more would have left your side ?"

For a time he seemed so inconsolable as to be perfectly irresolute, but then he suddenly rose, and mounting his horse again, he took the road to London.

It was with a heavy heart that Theodore Danton rode on. He feared that some evil influence had been at work, and that poor Margaret had suffered something to actuate her movements that would destroy her. He knew the dreadful and revengeful mind of Bertram, whom he looked upon as quite in a state of insanity, as regarded his jealousy; and consequently capable of contriving anything inimical to the interests of his wife and child—the very beings whom he ought to have protected.

Tortured, therefore, by a hundred doubts and fears, Theodore Danton pursued his way; but in so doing, he forgot that his horse had already travelled much ground, and was in need of repose. In the hurry and excitement of his own thoughts, he was, what probably never before in his life had he been, heedless of the feelings of an animal; and the consequence of this was a misfortune, which delayed him longer than as if he had waited to give his steed some hours of needful repose.

As he was descending a hill at by no means a sharp pace, the jaded horse stumbled, and Theodore, being much absorbed in his own thoughts, by no means had the horse well in hand, so that he could not save him, and, therefore, was thrown, not with violence, but still sufficiently so as to render him insensible.

Luckily the accident happened close to some cottages, into one of which he was at once carried ; and as for the horse, he did not attempt to run away, but really looked as if he were jaded.

When Theodore Danton recovered, he had the satisfaction of finding himself on a little truckle-bed in a cottage, and a respectable-looking man standing by him, who announced himself as the medical practioner of the place.

" You are not hurt, sir," he said to Theodore, " although the fall you have had has stunned you."

At first Theodore felt in such a state of confusion, that he scarcely understood what was said to him, but reason again soon resumed her sway, and the events which placed him in his present position at once came back upon him.

" I hope," he said, as he made an attempt to rise, but found all his limbs dreadfully stiff—" I hope I shall be able to resume my journey."

" To-morrow, I think you may, sir."

" Not till to-morrow ! I feel, I think sufficiently capable."

" Probably you might; but the same cause which produced you one fall, may produce you another, which you may not be so lucky as to escape only with a few common contusions."

" The same cause !" said Theodore with a look of surprise; " what same cause, sir ?"

" Your horse being over-ridden. The creature fell from exhaustion."

" Good God ! yes. I never thought of that. And I, of all persons, too, in the world, who may be said to have a feeling for these creatures, almost amounting to affection. Alas ! alas ! You must pardon me, sir; but my mind is and was so full of affairs near and dear to my heart, that I thought of nothing else. I will now wait patiently."

" By to-morrow," added the medical man, " I have no doubt that you and your horse will be sufficiently recovered to proceed ; and all I can say to you is, that you are really only shaken by your fall, and should take a little exercise on foot, which will do you more good than lying down or imbibing any medicines."

" Sir," said Theodore, as with some difficulty he rose, " I am very much beholden to you for this disinterested advice."

" Oh, not at all," said the medical man, smiling ; " I do not want to make a case of you ; and as far as my own interest is concerned, I daresay that will be quite as well looked to by getting you off again on your journey again quick, as if I succeeded in detaining you here a week."

" To the full," said Theodore.

" I thought as much. I am certain from your manner that you want to be off, and now I advise you, seriously and sincerely as a friend—not dictate to you as a medical man—that you will delay your departure until to-morrow morning."

" I will do so."

" By that time, your horse, which I have ordered proper persons to take good care of, will have recovered completely, and you likewise will be in a better condition to proceed ; and the probability is, that you will not really lose any time, for you will then be able to make good speed."

There was so much reason in this advice, that Theodore Danton felt it would be the height of folly and obstinacy not to follow it ; so he assented and begged that the medical man, who pleased him by his frank and unassuming manner, would dine with him that day.

" Dine with you," said the doctor, with a smile ; " my dear sir, where would you invite me to ?"

" Why, I suppose there is some inn ?"

" Not at all. There is a little, dirty public-house in the village, which, to be sure, offers good entertainment for man and beast ; but a man would need to be as little particular as any beast who could dine there. No, no ; you cannot ask me to dine with you, but as an amendment upon that proposition, I can ask you to dine with me, and I trust you will accept the invitation as frankly as it is given."

There was no denying the awkward circumstances in which he was placed, and, therefore, as he had to wait where he was, and the surgeon's invitation was given with a frankness that showed he really meant it to be accepted, Theodore did so.

" Sir," he said, " I certainly need not say that I had no intention of intruding upon your hospitality, but I will do so with a hope that we may some day meet again, when I shall be able to return it."

" Very good, then," said the doctor ; " come along, then. Pray take my arm, for I have no doubt there is not a joint of your body that is not as stiff as an old door-hinge."

" I think I am," said Theodore, " in some such condition."

Truly, when he began to walk, or rather to make an attempt to walk, he found it was a very lame affair, indeed, but perseverance for a short time got him over a great deal of that, and by the time he reached the surgeon's house he was able to go along without any assistance, as if he had left off crutches.

The surgeon introduced him, after inquiring his name in a whisper, to his family, who were amiable people, so that if Theodore could have shaken off the corroding care which he felt for the situation of Margaret, he could have passed the time he had to stay in the family of the medical man pleasantly enough.

But never, f r five minutes together, did he forget Margaret ; and that evening, when the ladies had retired, and he and the surgeon sat chatting by the fire-side, Theodore told him his whole history.

There was nothing of a nature to prompt secrecy, as regarded the events of his life, whenever he should come across one to whom he chose to be communicative, and Theodore found the surgeon so thorough a gentleman, that, in his case, he did not hesitate for a moment.

" Well," said the surgeon, when Theodore had finished ; " of course, now I do not wonder at your anxiety to be gone. It is natural enough. But really this man, Bertram, has been long enough, in all conscience now, allowed to persevere in his mad career, and, with the proofs that can now be brought forward of his wife's entire innocence, it really amounts to a kind of criminal laxity for you, or any one interested in her fate, to allow the affair to rest without legal interference."

"I have thought of that. Of course, she has legal rights?"

"Most certainly; and which may be easily enforced, without the shadow of a doubt."

"It would be but just."

"Certainly so; and, as regards the child, it becomes a matter of very grave consideration how far that child, when grown up, might not feel justified in blaming his mother and her advisers for not legally asserting her rights."

"Yes," said Theodore; "that is a most serious view of the subject, and one deserving of the most attentive consideration. It is one which you may depend I shall urge upon Margaret, when I shall—which I hope soon will be the ease—be fortunate enough to meet with her."

"I would; and urge it most strenuously, too."

In such like conversation as this the evening passed away, until it was time to retire to rest; and Theodore, if we may except some disturbed dreams during the earlier portion of the night, in which he fancied Margaret under all manner of dangerous circumstances, had seldom enjoyed a better repose than beneath the friendly roof that thus sheltered him, and all his cares and troubles.

In the morning, he felt so much refreshed, that he would gladly have proceeded, had not the groom, to whom the horse had been entrusted, given it his decided opinion that the animal required the whole day's rest.

This was conclusive, and Theodore did not urge the point any further, although it placed him in a painful condition of mind, during which he conjectured all sorts of possibilities concerning Margaret.

At sunset, however, he arranged, by the consent of everybody, that his departure should take place; and, as that hour approached, he longed to be upon the road again, even with the hope that he was approaching nearer and nearer still to Margaret, and that he would be in time to save her from any serious evil that might befal her.

Nothing can by any possibility be so dreadful a misery as suspense, and poor Theodore Danton was now, as regarded her who was the one great anxiety of his existence, just in a situation to feel that most corroding of all feelings to the greatest possible extent. He knew not what had taken her to London, nor when he should reach the metropolis, did he know where even to look for her.

And then his painful state of mind rather increased than diminished as the hour came when he was to bid adieu to that tranquil and pleasant family who had done their very utmost to amuse him.

He told them, over and over again, that he could not sufficiently thank them, but that he must put off even the attempt until happier days had dawned upon him—days in which, perhaps, the great care which at present oppressed his mind would have no existence at all, but be completely submerged in the consciousness that she whom he had loved so well was happy.

And now it wanted but an hour of the time that he, Theodore, ought to have departed, when an arrival took place at the surgeon's house. A friend of his, likewise in the medical profession, called to see him, and was introduced as a Mr. Andrews, by the surgeon, to Theodore Danton.

"I have been expecting you for some days," said the surgeon, "to make me your promised visit."

"Oh!" said Mr. Andrews, "I have been fully occupied by professional business, which must plead my excuse."

"Oh, certainly."

"And there have happened, perversely enough, several cases which were of an interesting character."

"Now, Mr. Andrews," said the surgeon's wife, "I desire that you pause there; I know very well what you call interesting cases, and I don't want to be horrified with a description of them."

"My dear madam," said Mr. Andrews, smiling, "if I said anything you may be sure it would be in medical language."

"Which, of course, you think that no woman knows anything about; but I have not been a surgeon's wife for ten years for nothing. I have picked up a great smattering of medical and surgical knowledge—quite enough to make me feel uncommonly uncomfortable whenever you begin to talk of interesting cases."

"Then I won't talk of them, you may depend."

"Yes; but Sarah is only joking," said the surgeon. "She don't mind hearing of such cases at all. Indeed, I am sure she rather delights in the horrible than otherwise, if one may judge from the books she reads."

"Yes," said the wife; "but it is a very different sort of horrible to surgical horribles, which have no romance whatever about them."

"Well, I certainly admit they have not much romance."

"None at all."

"Then, Mr. Andrews," added the surgeon who was Theodore Danton's host, "you will oblige us by not being at all explicit regarding the interesting cases until the ladies have retired, you understand?"

"Ah!" said Mr. Andrews heaving a deeply ludicrous sigh, "then do I hope that I may never be called upon to be explicit when such a menta action has to be preceded by a deprivation of the sunlight of the ladies' presence."

"Very good, Mr. Andrews," said the surgeon's wife. "We don't intend leaving yet for a considerable time."

"Well, but," added Mr. Andrews, "I have an interesting case that you would all like to hear."

"Indeed?"

"Yes, and it has no surgical details. Not the least taste of the horrible about it, I can assure you, although some of the sympathetic and the sentimental."

"Oh, you are joking."

"Nay, may I be compelled to swallow——"

"Some of your own physic?" said the surgeon's youngest daughter, with such an air of simplicity and *naivete* that a roar of laughter succeeded, at the expense of Mr. Andrews, who in vain protested that that was just what he was going himself to say.

"No—no!" said the surgeon; "we won't believe that; no, no!"

"Well, well," said Mr. Andrews, "as you like. Believe it or not; but tell me, am I to tell the tale of the sentimental individual, that's the question? It won't take above half a dozen or two words in the telling, so prepare for woe. But, seriously speaking, I have been much affected by an affair that my old friend, Dr. Bailey, has told me, and, indeed, he has taken me to see the parties."

By general consent, then, Mr. Andrews was allowed to proceed, which he did as follows:—

"You have all, I have no doubt, heard that if anyone is apparently drowned in the Lea river, some mile hence, to use an Irishism, they are really drowned; for the ordinary means of resuscitation which succeed in other cases will not succeed if the Lea river is the stream in which the unfortunate person has been immersed."

"Yes," said the surgeon, "we have all heard that."

"Well, I have it in my power to dispute the supposed fact, for I know of a case, or rather two cases, to which old Dr. Bailey has directed my attention, where a perfect recovery has taken place, consequent upon his unremitting attentions to restore animation.

"And where was it?" said the surgeon's wife.

"Oh, at the nearest point of the Lea from here—by Higham Hill, in fact."

"And the two people?"

"Were a mother and her child. The presumption is, that they were both attempted to be murdered; but, strange to say, she will accuse no one, and, in her exhausted debilitated state, it is not considered correct to press upon her the subject at all."

"Certainly not. And they have quite recovered so far that there is no danger?"

"Most completely. It appears that, with some difficulty, they were rescued from the stream, and as the child

recovered soon, some hopes, although faint ones, were entertained of the recovery of the mother, which, by perseverance, were crowned with the most complete success."

"Thank Heaven for that," said the surgeon's wife. "But who have they turned out to be, Mr. Andrews?"

"Oh, she seems a most unexceptionably respectable person, and talks evidently as an educated woman. She gave her name to old Dr. Bailey as a Mrs. Margaret Bertram."

Theodore sprang from his seat with a suddenness that alarmed the whole family, with the exception of the surgeon, who, from a knowledge of the story that Theodore Danton had confided to him, at once, of course, recognised in the name the same which belonged to her who was the subject of his anxieties and all his terrors.

The ladies screamed, for they really thought something dreadful was about to happen, and that Theodore himself possibly was taken ill, and was about to make up an interesting case for Mr. Andrews; but when he spoke, he soon dispelled that idea.

"Sir," he said, "speak that name again. Do you really mean to tell me that the—the lady of whom you speak gave the name of Margaret Bertram?"

"Most certainly."

"Thank Heaven—thank Heaven! Then the pilgrimage is over."

The persons present looked at Theodore Danton with surprise, as well they might; and probably some slight suspicion of his sanity might have entered their minds, for they looked at each other in a sort of way that, at all events, seemed suggestive of the question of—

"Is he mad, or not?"

Seeing this, and he could not be off seeing it, Theodore felt that it was, at all events, incumbent upon him to say something, and accordingly, rising, he hus spoke—

"I am well aware that my conduct may appear inexplicable, and that possibly it may be considered scarcely consistent with good breeding; but I am sure you will all excuse me when I tell you that this very lady who has been mentioned by your friend, Mr. Andrews, is one who I am seeking. She is a relation of my own, and one who has already suffered so much, that I am most anxious to spare her more."

"I can well understand what your feelings must be," said the surgeon, "and will not delay or oppose your departure for a moment, Mr. Danton."

"Many thanks, sir; and as there is really no secret in the story of Margaret Bertram's wrongs, which I have already related to you, I trust that your recounting them to your amiable family, which you have my full permission to do, will plead my excuse for this abrupt departure. Ladies, I bid you good day."

Even while uttering these remarks, Theodore's agitation was very great and perceptible, and he was glad to leave the room at once.

He was followed out both by the surgeon, who had been so hospitable to him, and by Mr. Andrews, and the latter hastily wrote in pencil on a blank page of his pocket book the name of the place where Margaret was to be found.

The horse, now completely refreshed by the rest he had had, was brought to the door, and Theodore Danton mounted, full of hope that now he might count the time by minutes only which would elapse ere he again looked upon the face of his much-loved Margaret, whom but a short time before he had sighed for in vain.

"Oh, blessed chance," he cried, "that led me in the way of receiving such intelligence; most blessed chance both for thee and for me, Margaret."

The distance was short, and his wearied steed tramped steadily onwards; so that, obeying the direction he had received, he soon came to a part of the Lee River across which was a rustic sort of bridge, that certainly did not look the most secure thing in the world.

But that was not a time for Theodore Danton to pause, or be critical about the absolute safety of his route, so he crossed it without agitation, notwithstanding it trembled under him, and pursued his way unharmed.

Although he was told that the road he had to take was so easy a one that it would be next to impossible that he should miss his way, he thought it prudent to inquire for the public-house before he went any further.

Addressing, therefore, the first person he met, he had the pleasure of hearing he was quite correct, and that it only lay a mile ahead of him.

This was cheering, and he could not resist putting the horse to a canter, that in a very few minutes would suffice to clear that space. And now he saw the swinging sign of the public-house, and a strange confusion of ideas arose in his breast.

He who would have shrunk at no possible amount of danger, now felt almost as if he could have dropped from his horse, such was the amount of nervousness that came over him at the thought of being so suddenly and unexpectedly near to Margaret.

"I shall see her again," he said, "never more to part with her. Once again I shall look upon that saddened countenance, once so radiant in beauty. Yes, we shall now meet to part no more. My Margaret, I will take you far away from the frightful persecution which you have endured; but not until your innocence shall have been established, and he who has, by his inhuman conduct, inflicted so much misery upon you, met with, at least, some of the consequences of his criminality."

Such were Theodore's reflections as he reached the door of the public-house, close to which, however, he could not get, in consequence of a little pony-chaise occupying the doorway.

He was seen, however, by the landlord, who came hurrying to receive so well-mounted and gentlemanly-looking a guest.

"Want your horse put up, sir, or

only a mouthful of water, and a drop of hay? Dear me, what am I a saying? I declare, ever since that ere drowned young woman and her blessed baby has been here, I'm always putting the horse before—no, the cart behind—I mean before the horse."

"No,—yes," said Theodore, as he dismounted. "What you please—anything."

"Thank you, sir; we always keep that in the house, at any rate. Hilloa! you, Dick, come and look after this gentleman's horse. This way, sir, if you please. This way, sir, if you please. This way, sir. Sorry you could not come right up to the door; all in consequence, sir, of Dr. Bailey's chaise."

"Doctor Bailey," said Theodore, as the name struck upon his ears; "is he here?"

"Yes, sir. But you seem to know him, sir; he's here, sure enough, sir; lor bless you, he's one of the best creatures as ever lived; only he don't approve of brandy-and-water so much as he might; live, and let live, say I; I never finds fault with any of his physic."

"Yes. Oh no."

"What a very odd gentleman," thought the landlord; "he don't seem very well, either. Well, it is a good thing Doctor Bailey is here, after all."

Theodore had sunk into a chair, as he said—

"You will take a gentleman's compliments to Dr. Bailey, landlord, and tell him I shall be glad to see him at his leisure. Do not disturb him if he is with his patient; mind that; I can wait."

"Very good, sir. He is with the drowned young woman, sir, as was picked up out of the Lee, with her baby.",

"Are—are—they both well?"

"As well as can be expected, sir, I believe they are; Dr. Bailey says as there's no danger now, whatsomedever. A wonderfully clever man he is, sir; lawk, if you had but been here, you would have opened your eyes above a bit, sir; he made us all tear about like mad; hot water, hot bricks, hot everything; I've fancied myself in hot water ever since."

"That was when she was recovered?"

"Yes, sir; and then only to think! when the old doctor had recovered 'em both, sir, I seed him, when he didn't think as nobody seed him, a crying like a baby, all on account, you see, sir, of being so pleased, 'cos you know, sir, he'd brought 'em both round again—you know, sir—you understand?"

"Most perfectly. You will be so good as to deliver to him my message."

"Yes, sir; a—hem! what was it you ordered? Bad memory, sir; but I'm quite sure you said something"

"Bring me anything you like; it don't matter; just whatever you please."

"Certainly, sir. Would you like it hot?"

"Yes, or cold."

"Exactly. Hang me if I know what to make of him. He beats me altogether. He don't know what he's saying of. Not he. Lor, no; he hasn't the least idea what he's saying, no more than the blessed man in the moon."

In truth, what with the effort he was obliged to make to overcome his feelings, now that he found himself in the same house with Margaret, Theodore could hardly speak at all; and yet he longed to ask the landlord a thousand questions which hovered upon his tongue, but which he did not utter, lest it should betray the overwhelming interest he had in the invalid who was being at that moment attended to by Dr. Bailey.

And that was the very thing, of all others, which he wished to avoid doing; for, impatient and anxious as he was to look upon Margaret, he would not run the chance of agitating her by a sudden knowledge of his presence until he had seen the medical man, and thoroughly ascertained that with safety he might communicate with her.

It seemed to him an age of time while the landlord was away; but when he came back he amply repaid him for being so long absent, by saying—

"I thought I'd wait, sir, till Dr. Bailey came out of the room, you see, sir, and then he could come to you at once, and here he is, sir."

Dr. Bailey entered the apartment into which Theodore had been conducted, and courteously bowed to him as he said—

"I understand, sir, that you desired to see me?"

"Yes—yes," said Theodore. "You may leave us, landlord."

"Oh, dear, yes, I don't want to hear nothing, God bless me, how very provoking now that is. You may leave us, landlord! I dare say I may. Now, what can he want with old Dr. Bailey, I wonder?"

The landlord left the room, and the moment he was gone, Theodore seized one of the doctor's hands in his, to the no small surprise of the kind-hearted practitioner, and as he shook it with warmth, he said—

"May the Almighty, sir, bless and reward you as he will. Accept, sir, the thanks of one who, but for you, must have passed broken-hearted through the remainder of his existence. I owe more than my life to you."

"My good sir," said Dr. Bailey, "this must be some mistake, for I certainly never in my life, to my knowledge, had the pleasure of seeing you before."

"You are quite right, sir," said Theodore. "We have never met before; but I hope now that we shall meet very often, and I only wish that some mode of adequately testifying my gratitude to you would suggest itself to my mind."

"Gratitude to me, sir!"

"Yes, to you—to you. You have saved the life of one dearer to me than my own existence. She whom you rescued from the mimic death which too soon would have lapsed into the real one, is the person to whom I allude."

"Oh, the lady who was brought here, supposed to be drowned?"

"The same, sir, the same. I am the only relative she has in all the world, and was painfully seeking her to afford to her shelter and succour, when, through a Mr. Andrews, a medical friend of yours, I heard what had happened to her, and of her being here under your care. You can now, sir, fully understand the source of my grateful feelings towards you."

"Oh, my dear sir," said the doctor, "don't think of that. I am, I must confess, not a little pleased that I have been successful in restoring her and her child to life. Of course, I am delighted; but then I don't see that I am entitled, you see, to any credit for that, because I am bound to do so, you understand."

"Oh, sir, say what you will, you can never lessen the debt of gratitude which I owe to you. It is useless to attempt to do so. I have no words in which adequately to thank you."

"Say no more about it, my young friend—say no more about it."

"And now, sir, can I see her?"

"Ay, surely, if she will see you. I do not see any objection to your seeing her. If you will favour me with your name, I will take it to her myself, and prepare her for the visit."

"The shock will be too great for her?"

"Not at all. Agreeable shocks seldom do much harm, I can tell you, so don't think anything of that. Besides, it will not be much of a shock if I tell her beforehand that you are coming."

"My name is Theodore Danton."

"Theodore Danton! Why, it was among the first words she spoke when she recovered the use of her faculties. She was wandering a little in her mind—very slightly delirious, and she spoke of you in the kindest manner."

"Ah, sir! when last we parted it was under such circumstances of doubt, and difficulty, and danger, that it was one hundred chances to one against our ever meeting again. She was one who ought to have known nothing but joy, and yet whose cup of sorrow has been filled to the very brim—ay, even to the overflowing."

"I can perceive that she has suffered. The traces of deep affliction are upon her brow. I could see that from the first moment that my eyes fell upon her face, and when I heard her voice—so sad, so melancholy, and so subdued—I was confirmed in my opinion. But you remain here, and I will prepare her to see you."

The doctor moved towards the door, but before he could open it the landlord rushed in with a tray, on which were too steaming glasses of hot brandy-and-water.

"What is that for?" cried Dr. Bailey.

"I beg your pardon, doctor, but the gentleman told me to bring just what I liked, and if I don't like brandy-and-water, I'm a Dutchman, that's all."

"Get out with you! get out of my way! I'm quite sure the gentleman don't want any of your brandy-and-water."

Dr. Bailey went out of the room, and the landlord, placing the tray upon the table, took up one of the glasses very deliberately, and said—

"After what the doctor has said, sir, perhaps you'll think there's a something the matter with the brandy-and-water here. But does this look like it—or this—or that?"

In successive draughts, the landlord, in honour of his own liquor, drank off the contents of one of the glasses entire, and then giving a kind of half nod to Theodore Danton, as much as to say, "after that you can have no sort of hesitation in drinking the other," he left the apartment.

CHAPTER LXXX.

MUTUAL EXPLANATIONS. — MARGARET'S STORY OF THE MEETING WITH BERTRAM.—THE EXTORTED PROMISE FROM THEODORE DANTON.

IN the course of about ten minutes the doctor returned, and beckoning Theodore Danton to follow him, an invitation that the former was not slow in obeying, he led him up the staircase of the inn to Margaret's door.

"There," he said, "you will find her there, and none the worse for knowing who has come too see her. Walk in, and I will wait below for you, as I want to have some talk with you before I leave."

In such a confusion of happiness at the idea of meeting Margaret again that he scarcely heard the latter part of the worthy doctor's speech, Theodore Danton pushed open the door of the apartment.

The room was darkened, but sitting in an old-fashioned easy chair, by the fireside, he saw, in a moment, his much-loved, nearly lost, Margaret.

We are not writing for prudes or for those who fancy that rules of conventional propriety should govern every action of people's lives, so we have no hesitation in saying at once, that Margaret stretched out her arms to Theodore, and, in another moment, he clasped her to his breast.

For more than a minute neither of them spoke, and then it was almost inarticulately that he said, while he still held her in his fond embrace—

"Dear—dear Margaret, and so at last we meet again after all dangers? Oh, Margaret, my own, my much-loved Margaret, how near was I to losing you for ever!"

"Hush—oh, hush!" she said, faintly, as with a gentle violence she disengaged herself from his embrace; "you forget that tne barrier that has hitherto divided us still exists; I must not hear you talk thus—I dare not."

"My Margaret, I speak but the dictates of a heart that loves you."

"But, do not—oh, do not, Theodore, mar my joy at this meeting by the utterance of one word which the world would say a wife ought not to hear."

"Margaret, I am rebuked. It is enough; I will not speak to you in such a strain; but as your only relative, and, therefore, the nearest, I may say I love you."

"Yes, dear Theodore; and my dearest are you as well as my nearest."

He kissed her fair brow, and she could not find in her heart to chide the action; she turned and pointed to the bed that was close at hand, as she said—

"Do you see, Theodore, who sleeps there?"

"Yes—yes, the dear child."

He went to it, and kissed its soft cheek, as it slept, and then he came back to Margaret, who wore such a sweet smile upon her face as he knew her to have of old, before he had gone abroad, with that romantic dream of his boyhood at his heart, which induced him to believe that he would find her, upon his return, even as he had left her, like some flower of wondrous beauty which was only to be plucked and worn by him.

"You are happy, Margaret?" he said.

"I am happier," she said, "than I have been for many and many a day. Something seems now to assure me that the many troubles and miseries I have endured are all over now, and that this last piece of wretchedness that I have gone through was the end of all ; and yet I know not why I should feel so."

"It is a blessed feeling, Margaret ; hold to it—hail it with delight. It is nothing but the truth. We will never part again—never—never ! I will for the future dedicate my whole life to you, and you shall know no care that the most zealous affection can ward off from you."

"But you forget, Theodore, that he lives still."

"I care not, my poor Margaret. He shall be compelled to do you justice. But you have not yet told me how it was that this dreadful accident happened to you and the dear little one. Let me know all, I pray you."

"On one condition, Theodore, I will."

"Name it."

"It is that you will found no course of conduct upon what I shall tell you, except it be first communicated to me, and fully approved of by me. You must make me such a promise on your sacred word, before I tell you aught."

"Oh ! Margaret, the asking for such a promise as that implies your expectation that the tale you have to tell will create some feelings in my heart I should find it difficult to subdue."

"You are right ; and, therefore, must I have the promise first."

"You have it. I give it to you freely, Margaret ; and the more freely that I have hope that you will listen to reason, after all your grievous trials, and no longer suffer yourself to be made the sport of one who has sacrificed you to his own bad passions."

"Hush !" said Margaret ; "no more of that. Listen to me, Theodore, and control your feelings while you listen. I owe my recent danger to my husband."

Theodore sprang from his seat.

"I dare not—will not tell you more," said Margaret, "unless you promise me that you will be calm."

He sat down with a deep sigh, as he said—

"I will strive to be so. Go on—go on. I have heard the worst, so now I think I may be calm indeed."

She then related to him clearly and distinctly all that is already known to the reader concerning the immersion of herself and child in the river ; and Theodore listened to her with his whole soul, while the eloquent play of his features betrayed the great effect which the narration had upon him, and the great efforts it cost him to keep from, some exclamation of his feelings upon the occasion.

When she had concluded, she added rapidly—

"Now, mark me, Theodore. I cannot say that it was Charles Bertram's real intention to take the life of the little one. You will see that, although goaded to the deed by him, yet that it was essentially my own act and deed, so pause and give the benefit of a doubt."

"Oh, Margaret, little, indeed, does he deserve such consideration at your hands. Had you perished, he would, in the sight of Heaven, as surely been your murderer, as that I am sitting here, with the joy of knowing that you are still living."

"Nay, Theodore, we will not talk of what might have been, but of what is. I am happy now, for I think that after this he will feel the injustice he has done me."

"If such a man can feel."

"Well, if he do not, I will say nothing of the scene that has taken place ; but for the sake of the dear child who has his name, I will demand some justification from him."

"Thank Heaven, Margaret, you have come to such a mind as that."

"Not for my own sake have I come to it, but for my child's will I assume now the defensive. I will not think that in after life it should have to blame the supineness of its mother, who would not make an effort to rescue it and herself from most unmerited opprobrium."

spoken; and even had I you a promise that ties my hands, anything could have prevented me from personally insisting upon satisfaction for your wrongs at the hands of Charles Bertram, what you have now said would have that effect."

"And now, Theodore, what I want you to do," said Margaret, "is, to find me out some quiet, suitable abode in London, with people who will protect me, and tell them who and what I am, and my object, namely, to sue my husband for justice, so that eventually they will be paid for that which I require of them."

"Margaret, my resources are yours. But we will not take up our precious moments by talking of such a subject. You look fatigued."

"I am, Theodore. You must think that I am but weak yet, and little accustomed to what I may call my new existence. Leave me now."

He rose and left her after some few words more of affection had been spoken; and it was not until a note was placed in his hands from Dr. Bailey, that he remembered that that gentleman said he would wait for him. The note merely stated that he, the doctor, could not wait any longer, nor would he disturb Theodore, but enclosed his address, and expressed a hope that he would favour him with a call.

CHAPTER LXXXI.

THEODORE CALLS ON DR. BAILEY. —WHAT BECAME OF CHARLES BERTRAM IN LONDON.

ALTHOUGH Theodore Danton felt certain that such a man as Doctor Bailey would readily excuse his, Theodore's, apparent rudeness, in keeping him so long waiting, as to prevent him from saying to him what he wished; yet he felt, at all events, that there was a great necessity for calling upon the worthy doctor, if it were but to renew to him those expressions of grateful feeling which he had before attempted to give utterance to.

"But for him," thought Theodore, "how absolutely desolate by now would my heart have been, and how truly stale, flat, and unprofitable would have appeared all the uses of this world. But for him my heart would have been for ever widowed, and I could never again have known what joy was."

The relation, too, that Margaret had given him of the kind manner in which the doctor had behaved to her, was more than sufficient to produce in the mind of the generous and noble-minded young man the warmest sentiments of esteem and gratitude.

He went at once now to call upon Dr. Bailey, whom he felt that he should now for ever regard as one of his best and dearest friends. He found the old gentleman at home, rather anxiously, to tell the truth, waiting for the appearance of Theodore Danton; for he had, from a conviction of the honesty of her character, and the appearance of deep suffering which she evidently exhibited, taken an interest in the fate of Margaret that made him extremely anxious to hear more of her history than he liked to ask her himself.

"My dear sir," he said to Theodore, after they had been seated together for some time, "you will, I am sure, acquit me of being actuated by any feelings of mere idle curiosity, when I tell you I much wish to know more of the history of her whom I have been fortunat enough to find some efficacious means of rescuing from death."

"Sir," said Theodore, "you, of all men, are the most justified in asking for particulars."

"I thank you for saying so; and now I may as well tell you at once that I strongly suspect and believe that some one ought to be punished for the danger into which Mrs. Bertram was thrown."

"You are right."

"Ay, and that same one is, I think I may truly say, an individual she wants to screen."

"You are right again, sir. Her kindly and noble, generous nature will not permit her to do as she, in my opinion, ought to do—namely, assert her right to prosecute him against whom she has so heavy a cause of just complaint. But I will tell you all, sir, and you shall yourself judge of the circumstances, and I then hope that you will join with me in consideration of what is the best to be done in the matter which I shall fully and unreservedly bring before you."

"With pleasure, my young friend, with pleasure. I don't know if it arises from the fact of having, thank God! taken a world of pains to recover her from apparent death, that has given me such an interest in her as I have, or her own excellences; but I have such an interest, I can assure you, and will do whatever lies within the compass of my power and means to make her happy."

"Of that I am assured, and so is she."

Theodore then gave it as his decided opinion to the doctor, for it had really upon reflection, became such, that Bertram had attempted the life of his wife and child, and consequently deserved all the punishment and all the reprehension that could be cast upon his head for so foul a deed.

"It would really seem so," said Dr. Bailey. "What an unhappy wretch that man must be!"

"Unhappy, indeed, if he ever really awakens to a sense of that which he has done. One would think one pang of that remorse which he ought to feel would be sufficient to drive him to madness."

"And, of course, you have no idea of what has become of him?"

"None in the least."

"Think you, sir, he would linger about the neighbourhood, or do you incline to an opinion that he would attempt an escape, after seeing what he must have seen—for the fate of the poor beings whom he plunged into the stream, or, at all events, saw plunged in, must have been evident to him?"

"He has no doubt fled," said Theodore. "But as regards the measure of his guilt, it is to my mind much the same whether he goaded poor Margaret, by threatening the life of her child, into plunging into the river, or actually threw her in, and, had she died, would equally have been the cause of her death, there can be no doubt, and equally ought he, and shall he, if I can accomplish so much, bear the burthen of the consequences of such an offence."

The old doctor was silent for some moments, and then he said—

"The great truth—and I care not whether people call it a scriptural one or not—that out of seeming evil springeth great good—is one that I think this is a case that may exemplify greatly."

"Indeed, sir! As how?"

"Thus. I think that if this man, Bertram, can be found, something could be done to awaken him now to a sense of the deep injustice with which he had acted."

"Do you really think, doctor, that such a heart could be acted upon by any kindly feelings or emotions?"

"On my word, I do so."

"But how? In what way do you fancy such a consummation, so devoutly to be wished, could be brought about with such a man?"

"Why, I would attempt it thus:—I would stir all my energies to find him out, and then I would reproach him with the supposed fact of the success of his dreadful work; and I would surround him with all the proofs of his wife's innocence; and then, when he could not but give way to such a mass of evidence in her favour as you can produce, I would for a time leave him to the pang of thinking himself virtually, if not actually, a murderer."

"He deserves, indeed, to have his heart so wrung."

"Yes; and I think that then such a lesson would have been taught to him, that he might safely be trusted with the fact of his wife and child's existence, and he would surely do that amount of justice to them, which he has for so long a period denied to them."

"It ought to be so. It is a plan which may be tried."

"You are, I know—I can see, at least, that you are doubtful of its success, and probably knowing better the character and personal habits and feelings of this husband than I do, you are all the better able, of course, to come to a conclusion respecting him. But try it; no harm can result from such a course, if no good does; and, at least, you will have the satisfaction of

feeling that you have made an attempt to do an act of kindness to all parties before you sought, by a more vigorous course, for justice to some."

" I have no disinclination to adopt your advice, sir ; but I have not the least notion of where to find Bertram. True, I did know where he lived once, but I do not know now, for it is extremely unlikely that he would go back to that place, with the consciousness that he must be amenable to the laws for what he has recently done."

" Well, now, I think I can give you a clue."

" You, sir ! you give me a clue to the retreat of Bertram ?"

" Yes ; look at this short statement in this evening paper, and tell me if you think it affords any chance of your identification of the man we wish to find in it. Read it out."

The doctor handed to Theodore a capy of an evening London newspaper, and pointed out to him a paragraph, to the side of which he had placed a black mark. The paragraph was as follows :—

"A MYSTERY.—Yesterday, about two o'clock in the morning, a man was picked up, in a state of utter insensibility, from a coal-barge, moored close to the Palace Stairs at Westminster. His appearance was respectable enough, and a considerable sum of money was found concealed about him. He had all the appearance of being immersed in the river ; but if so, how he came to be lying on the barge in a state of insensibility is beyond all calculation. The dead body—for so it at first was presumed to be—was removed to the nearest hospital, where, by unremitting attention, he has recovered. He appears plunged in grief, and will give no account of himself, but now and then utters the name of Margaret. It is hoped that publicity through the press may be a means of throwing some light on so mysterious an affair."

"What think you of that?" said Dr. Bailey.

"It must be Bertram—it must be he; I will go to London at once, and find him out. I will confront him once again, and tell him what he has done. Oh! if he have not a heart of positive marble, he will most surely feel acutely the pangs that I shall bring home to him."

"Go, my young friend, I strongly advise you to do so; but do not carry the matter too far with him, for you should always recollect that the future advantage of the innocent Margaret and her child, is of more advantage and a higher object than the punishment even of such a man as Bertram."

"I will remember that, you may be assured. The higher object shall not be forgotten, at the same time I hope to pursue the lower one to a climax. I wish you would come with me, and then I should have the advantage of your cooler reason to guide me. But I suppose I cannot even hope for such an addition of strength to my cause."

"No," said Dr. Bailey, "I cannot. A medical man, you know, dare not move. As for taking, perhaps, a whole day or two in London, to the neglect of my patients about here, I cannot think of such a thing; why, for all I know, some of them might get well, you know."

The old doctor laughed as he spoke, and Theodore rose, saying—

"I did not expect, my dear sir, that you could spare time from your professional labours. I shall say nothing of my intention to Margaret, but proceed to London, and see if I can find, in the man of whom this paper speaks, Bertram, who has inflicted far more injury than he can ever repair upon those who should, above all others, have been the especial objects of his protection and fostering care."

"Too true; but it is upon such that men of bad passions generally do inflict the worst of injuries you will always find. Others will not give way suffi-

ciently to them to be injured by them; so they take a mean and unfair advantage of the forbearance of the very persons who, as you say, should be always the especial objects of their care."

Theodore Danton did not stay much longer with Dr. Bailey, but he made what haste he could to get to London. Before he left, however, he wrote a brief note to Margaret, telling her that some hours, perhaps a whole day would elapse before he saw her again; and then, on horseback, he proceeded to the metropolis.

He had in his pocket the newspaper which Dr. Bailey had given to him, and the more he reflected upon the whole, of the circumstances, the more he became convinced that in the person who had been mentioned so mysteriouly, he should find Charles Bertram, the great enemy of him, Theodore—the great enemy of the persecuted Margaret—but by far the greater enemy to himself; for the happiness he had deprived himself of could scarcely, if reflection should come to him, bear thinking of without such an agony of regret as would be nearly sufficient to overturn the reason.

*   *   *   *

On the night of the attempted suicide by Bertram, as three river pirates were industriously plying their vocation near Westminster Bridge, a black mass was seen by the half-obscured moon to be floating towards where their craft was moored. With a boat-hook it was stopped in its progress, and drawn alongside the craft by one of the pirates, while the others lifted it out of the water. Not many minutes elapsed ere they discovered it to be the body of a man in ordinary attire, but who had on his person sufficient valuables to induce them to nearly tear all the clothes off the supposed corpse, to become possessed of them. As soon as they had accomplished their purpose, they threw the body on the deck of a barge that was near and went with the tide towards London Bridge. The body was eventually found by a waterman, who gave an alarm, which brought assistance, and it was immediately removed to the hospital.

The unremitting exertions of the house-surgeon and his assistants succeeded in restoring the suspended animation, and he was put in a warm bed to leave nature to effect his perfect recovery, as art could do no more.

It was on the following morning that Theodore Danton called on the house-surgeon, and after an hour's consultation, during which time Danton gave the surgeon a brief recital of Bertram's life, the surgeon gave orders that the patient should be removed from the general ward to one that was quite private, to enable Mr. Danton to converse with the guilty man freely and without interruption.

Shortly before Bertram was removed, his imagination pictured every one he saw as an officer of justice, who only waited his return to convalescence to pounce upon him and bring him to an ignominious death; and when he was being removed he seemed to be confirmed in this idea, thinking that they were placing him there for better security. He, however, had not the power to rise, and there was no fear of his making an attempt to escape. He lay racking his mind with the bitter thought that he had murdered his wife and child; and he saw things with a clearer vision now he thought it was too late, than when he was hurried on and blinded by a mad passion. He could now picture to himself his innocent wife, and wonder how he could ever believe her to be otherwise than innocent. He accused himself a thousand times of want of discernment and folly in being deceived and imposed upon by persons of such mean intellects as Mrs. Blair and her unprincipled sister, Mrs. Primrose. He took a retrospective view of his past conduct; and bitterly did he reproach himself for thrusting domestic happiness and contentment of mind from him when he had so many opportunities of grasping it, and being a blessing and protection to those who were so near, and who ought to have been dear to him. He pictured to himself what he might have been if he had allowed himself to have been guided or advised by his better spirit. In this frame of mind he continued to silently cogitate, when the door was slowly opened, and the fine athletic figure of Theodore Danton made its appearance, with a countenance overspread with a tinge of melancholy.

Neither spoke for some moments, but continued to look steadfastly at each other, as though the one would read the other's thoughts.

"Bertram," at last said Theodore, "I have not come here to taunt you with the crime of murdering your wife and child—with murdering the only relative I have on earth, for the law which you have offended will look to you for reparation, as far as possible, for that; your conscience has long told you, I know, that Margaret was a faithful, obedient, and innocent wife; besides, I have undisputed testimony to the fact. My object in coming here is to see if you have one spark of honourable feeling left—to see if I can prevail upon you to do one act of justice to her memory now she is no more, which you would not do while she was alive."

"Name what it is that you desire of me, and I will do it. Oh! that I had seen things as clearly before as I do now, I would not have sacrificed her gentle spirit to my indomitable temper, which was so worked upon by designing fiends in the shape of human beings. Oh, Danton! that I could recall the past, or that I could make ample recompense to you for the evil that I have inflicted on you, and the ungrounded and unjust suspicions I entertained towards you, I should die more at ease now that my time is so short on earth."

"You are ill, Mr. Bertram; but not seriously. You will soon be convalescent again."

"Never," said Bertram; "by this time to-morrow my earthly career will close. But let me hear what you were about to propose."

"I want you, as I said, to do a piece of justice to the memory of your poor dead wife. Will you sign a declaration of her innocence if I draw one up?"

"I will sign anything that will at all tend to freeing her memory from a stain. Be with me early to-morrow; I am fatigued now, and require rest. Don't be late, as my time is so short."

Theodore Danton left the repentant man again to his own though and descended to the offices of the house-surgeon, to whom he communicated all that had transpired. He also asked him if there were any symptoms of danger, to which he replied in the negative, at the same time saying that he had known instances of individuals prognosticating their own death, and actually dying at the stated time, although the usual symtoms had been wanting. He urged Danton to lose no time in carrying out his intentions, lest death should intervene and prevent him making the reparation he was willing and desirous of making.

Theodore hastened with the tidings to Margaret and Dr. Bailey, who were anxiously awaiting his return, and counting the passing minutes as though they had been hours. In due time Theodore arrived and gave them the desired information. Margaret could scarcely be persuaded to take any repose; but wanted to hasten to the side of Bertram's sick couch and assure him of her forgiveness for all his past faults. It was only by the almost fatherly authority of Dr. Bailey, and the earnest entreaties of Theodore Danton, that she was prevailed on to remain till morning.

Early on the morrow, however, the three friends arrived in London, and they were not long in reaching the hospital which contained Bertram, for whom Margaret entertained feelings which most people would have thought obliterated long ago. "He is my husband," she would remark repeatedly, "and I am bound to love him in spite of all his cruelties and injustice to me and my little one. The ties between husband and wife are so indissoluble that no ordinary nor extraordinary occurrence should sever them."

Theodore prevailed on Margaret to remain with Dr. Bailey in the surgeon's room while he got Bertram to sign the declaration of her innocence, and while he prepared him for the reception of the intelligence that his wife and child lived. The doctor stated that it would be necessary for him, Danton, to be very careful on breaking the subject to him, or the consequences would be fatal. He promised to observe every care, and at once proceeded to the chamber allotted to the sick man's use.

Bertram was in a very weak state; an age seemed to have passed over his head since Theodore last saw him, so emaciated and death-stricken did he look. He welcomed Danton in a feeble voice, and asked him if he was prepared with the document he spoke of on the preceding day; Danton answered in the affirmative, and produced it. He called for writing materials, which were brought to him, and at the sick man's request assisted him to rise to a sitting posture, to enable him to sign it. No sooner was this done than Danton commenced his task of informing Bertram of the existence of his wife and child. He used as much circumlocution as was required to excite the attention of Bertram, and to arrest his wandering thoughts, and no more. Bertram listened with eagerness; and as Danton drew towards a climax he burst into tears, and begged that Danton would not aggravate his misery by such recitals. His mind was in the course of half an hour more prepared for the interview with his wife, and at a signal from Theodore, Margaret threw open the door, and entered the room; in another instant her arms were round the neck of Bertram, lavishing on him all the tenderness in woman's nature, as though he had been one of the best and most affectionate of husbands.

The constancy of her affection was too much for him—he fainted in her arms, and to all appearance lay as if dead. Dr. Bailey was summoned, and he administered a revivifying draught, which brought in action again the overpowered faculties. He asked for his child, which he fondly embraced, and asked Theodore Danton to be a father to it, when he was no more, as he then had but half an hour to live.

The surgeon and Doctor Bailey had a whispered consultation, and they came to the conclusion that as symtoms had arisen over which they had but little control, it was likely that the sufferer would not be long among the living.

In silent sadness they stood round

the bed of the sufferer, watching for a return of consciousness, for during the past few minutes his failing senses had been so wavering, that one moment he would be alive to all around, the next his powers were obscured.

To the astonishment of all he suddenly rose to a sitting posture, and said that in five minutes he should be a corpse. He asked Margaret for her hand, and as he took the hand of Theodore in his, and joining them together, he said—

"May Heaven prosper you both, and may you avoid all the shoals upon which I have struck, and be to each other true and faithful companions during the remainder of your lives. God bless you both, and you, my dear neglected little one."

He gently sunk on the pillow. His spirit had flown to the great giver of all things, to render an account of its earthly sojourn.

* * * *

He was buried in accordance with his rank and station, without that usual pomposity that attends the funerals of the wealthy, in his family vault. Doctor Bailey threw the Black Mantle, the type of his misfortunes, into the vault with his coffin. It had been an earnest request of Bertram's that he should do so.

Twelve months after the funeral cortege had carried Bertram to his last home, two carriages were seen driving in the direction of the little village church of Beane, each containing two ladies and two gentlemen. This was the marriage party of Theodore Danton and Margaret Bertram.

CHAPTER LXXXII.

THE DYING WOMAN.—THE CONFESSION.—THE CURSE REMOVED.

DANTON and Margaret passed the first few days of their marriage in that calm, quiet happiness, which is, after all, more like true bliss than any other emotion that can be exhibited. They used often to spend a few hours a-day in riding about from place to place, thus enjoying to the full the leisure hours that they possessed, in a manner more conducive to health than the crowded assemblies and balls which their position in society would enable them to figure in.

One day they were returning towards their house, when an occurrence took place that it may be as well to record, as it disposes of one of the *dramatis personæ* who figured in the early part of our tale. They were coming towards town, when, tempted by the beauty of the evening they resolved to get out and walk for a space, and send the carriage slowly forward, and they could overtake it at a certain point, and, if they chose, re-enter when tired.

After walking some little distance, they could not but admire the beauty of the evening, and the apparent happiness of all around them, when Margaret said—

"And yet, notwithstanding our happiness, Theodore, and notwithstanding the apparent happiness of all around, there are many who are in the utmost state of wretchedness, misery, and crime."

"That is very true, Margaret; but we, alas! cannot help that; and the consideration of all the ill that humanity is heir to will only embitter the joys we have for our share."

"But have we not earned them?"

"We have, Margaret, we have; but I grudge not now the price I have paid for my present felicity, for I deem it cheap at any price."

"Then I need not, I am sure; and I am equally sure I do not. I would, I was about to say, go through the same to arrive at the same end."

"I have been noticing these cottages," said Theodore; "they are very old and tumble-down in appearance."

"They are. I should be terrified to sleep in one; and yet they do so year after year; but hark, there is something like a groan coming from one of them, I think. Did you not hear the sound, Theodore? I heard it."

"Yes; I thought it was so myself."

"Shall we go and see? We may be the means of saving some poor creature by doing so."

"You shall do as you please, Margaret; and, as you have proposed it, so I will be your attendant."

"My almoner."

"Yes, certainly," he replied, laughing; "we will go in, and hear what it is that disturbs the pleasure of the scene; some old crone troubled with the rheumatics, I dare say."

They now came to the cottage-door, and entering it, Margaret said to an old woman who stood by—

"Is any one ill here? I thought I heard some one groan, as if in great pain."

"Yes, ma'am," said the woman; "there is a mortal creature a dying up in the corner there. She says as how she can't die till she has confessed."

"Is she a Catholic?"

"Can't say, ma'am; but I thinks as how she's got something on her mind—very little on her stomach—but that's no matter now, as she's going."

Theodore and Margaret looked in at the cottage, the upper half of the door of which was open.

There was a fire-place at one end, with the smallest possible amount of fire; a truck bedstead, before which was hung a piece of patchwork quilt, which hid the occupant from the view of any one who might look in at the door.

There were one or two cupboards, and some few odd domestic utens is the whole bespeaking poverty and want in the owners or occupiers of the place.

"Good Heavens!" said Danton; "you do not mean to say that you have a woman dying yonder?"

"Yes I do," said the woman.

"Can we see her? she may want some assistance or consolation in her last moments."

"Well, I reckon she does; though it's all about her soul or mind. I don't know much about it, but you can ax her, an' you please."

So saying, the woman opened the door, and Danton and Margaret entered the hut. As they approached the bed, they heard a terrible groan, and a smothered voice say—

"Mercy — mercy! Oh, God! I cursed him—yes, I cursed him. I am guilty of all, and he is innocent; and whatever he did through me, I am chargeable with."

"My good woman," said Margaret, as she pushed aside the curtain, "what ails you?"

The woman turned her head slowly from the wall, at which she had fixed her eyes, and said, as she did so—

"Death ails me; but he will not claim his own. My spirit will not quit this earthly tenement; I——"

"Have you anything on your mind you would like to speak of before you quit this world?"

"I have—I have."

"Be assured respect shall be had to your dying words. I would have aided you living, if I could."

"You cannot. Oh, I see—I see! 'Tis she—'tis she—'tis she! Oh, this is a judgment—a judgment!"

"What is a judgment, my good woman?"

"You don't know me?" said the woman, looking earnestly at her, as she spoke.

"No, indeed I do not."

"But I know you—you are Margaret Bertram."

Margaret started as the woman spoke, but replied—

"How is it you know me? Where and when did you ever see me? I cannot remember you."

"No—no, you cannot, unless you can remember the day of your marriage with Bertram; and remember that as he and you came out of the church, I cursed him. Yes—yes; it was I who cursed him, and was the cause of all that has followed. May God forgive me for all the misery that curse has occasioned."

"My good woman, I do recollect something of what you then said; but it was attributed to madness, or something else. However, I know you not."

"No—no; he would not let you. But Bertram seduced my daughter, and was the cause of her ruin and her death. I was maddened when I saw all that."

"Your troubles have been heavy."

"They have—they have. But I cursed him—I cursed him on his wedding day."

"You were, no doubt, hurrid on to say what you did by the recollection of your injury and daughter's death."

"I was—I was."

"But Bertram now is no more. He has gone to render up to Heaven an account of his good and evil deeds. Turn your thoughts from the contemplation of earthly matters, and seek to make your peace with Heaven."

"It is too late, I fear. I have been the cause of all his misery, all his misfortunes and his death. Forgive me, Heaven, if, when misfortunes were heavy upon me, I drew down thy curse upon him whose hand had caused that affliction! But," she added, turning to Margaret, "you know not all—you know not all."

"Indeed!" said Margaret. "What do you mean?"

"This: when I saw him married—when my daughter was dead, I sent him a mourning cloak—a black mantle, and all complete, as mourning for my daughter. I cursed him, and wrote—what I can scarcely recollect now—but I have no earthly doubt but he felt at heart the pang I intended to cause him. But—but my race is run—my time is come. I fail in breath; but, with the last breath I have, I say, may God forgive him and me, and may the curse no longer be on him!"

"My good woman, your frame of mind is just. We are all liable to err; none of us are without our troubles. You repent at last, and may Heaven forgive you, is all I can say, and all I can pray for."

"And do you pray for me?"

"I do sincerely."

"God bless you, and may Heaven have the keeping of your happiness, for you deserve better than you have experienced. It is the last prayer of one who has suffered much in this veil of tears. I am dying."

Margaret could not look upon the scene with a dry eye; she could not think of the misery she had endured without a shudder—the misery of the poor woman was very great, and her end was as wretched as her life.

"Ah!" said the old woman, who had let them in; "she's a-going now, poor soul; there's an end to her miseries; she won't feel them much longer."

The rattles, indeed, were in her throat, and she turned her eyes towards Margaret, but she could not speak; she tried, but the words died on her lips;—her eyes closed, a slight shiver passed through the body, and all was still.

"She is quite dead," said the old woman; "oh, yes, quite dead. Well, it's a good thing it is over. Dying ain't pleasant, and I daresay it's best done at once."

Margaret heeded little what the woman had said, but gave her some money, with orders to have the body decently interred, and she would bear the expense.

"Just as you please, ma'am," said the old woman; "but the money would do the living more good than the dead, and the parish would pay for the burial, and it would be no expense to nobody."

There was no reply made to the old woman's speech, but Margaret and Danton left the cottage together. There was a shadow of melancholy thrown over the halo of happiness which surrounded them but a short half hour since—and which was not extinct—but a momentary shadow passed over it.

"Such is the last scene of this drama, I hope," said Danton; "it is painful, Margaret; but cheer up, you have done your part, and do not let melancholy settle upon your brow. But here is the carriage; we may as well ride the rest of the way."

So saying, they both entered the carriage, which drove rapidly from the spot.

CHAPTER LXXXIII.

THE CONCLUSION.

IT is scarcely necessary to say that after this Margaret, although the scene she had gone through was not one calculated to give her pleasure, yet she felt more relief that it had occurred, than as if she had remained in ignorance concerning the person who had bestowed upon Bertram the black mantle.

Without giving way to any superstition, she could not but feel and perceive that with the gift of that sombre article of apparel had become associated a vast amount of misery, and notwithstanding she had certainly acquired from the confession of Mrs. Blair, and the confirmation of that confession by Mrs. Primrose, some information on the subject, still much of it was involved in conjecture, until the vindictive woman, whose death-bed scene she had witnessed, spoke so fully.

She had more than once suspected, even before these occurrences were brought to her memory, and before she had commenced those series of misfortunes which had banished her from home, and for so long a period made her the prey and sport of circumstances, that Mrs. Blair must have had some means of exercising an undue influence over Bertram.

But now the whole affair was transparent, and she fully understood how, shrinking for his own offences coming to light, Bertram had placed himself in a position to listen to the atrocious falsehoods circulated concerning her.

"I little thought," she said to Theodore, "when that woman, whose death we have witnessed, accosted Bertram at the church door, after our marriage, that she was anything but the maniac she really seemed."

"There can be no doubt, Margaret," replied Theodore, "that a sense of her wrongs had driven her distracted. No one possessed of their ordinary senses would have thought of so singular a mode of revenge as she adopted, although, perhaps, from no calculation on her part, it turned out to be so well adapted to act upon the individual whom she wished to affect."

"It was well adapted, indeed," said Margaret; "for from the first moment the effect upon Bertram was prodigious, and I cannot but believe that his mind at once gave way, to a greater extent perhaps than he was himself aware of, beneath the shock of that curse which had been hurled at his head."

"And yet how strange it is, Margaret, that Bertram, knowing himself to have been guilty of conduct which laid himself open to such animadversions, should be so desperately uncharitable to others."

"I think it is ever so," said Margaret. "It is a knowledge of guilt which breeds suspicion. The innocent are full of merciful consideration, because they know little of iniquity."

"It must be so," said Theodore; "and I presume it is upon the same principle that those who have been slaves themselves, and know the bitterness of subjection, are always the hardest taskmasters."

"It is invariably so, Theodore; and if I knew but the spot of earth which contains the remains of the poor creature's daughter, whom Bertram must have affected to love, I would raise some simple monument to her memory, if it were but to repudiate the assertion that one woman never can forgive another."

Hour by hour, Theodore became more and more impressed with the conviction of the treasure he had gained in uniting himself to her; although no one could be but a few minutes in her society without appreciating to a considerable extent her many excellences. Yet she required to be well known, and intimately associated with, for any one to acquire a perfect knowledge of the glorious characteristics of her disposition.

It was a great happiness to them both to find that the child had not suffered from the hard life it had for a time, along with its deeply-injured mother, been compelled to lead.

It grew in health and beauty, and Theodore loved it not the less that occasionally, in an expression of its features, or a tone of its voice, he was reminded of its father.

The tour which he and Margaret, accompanied by that little one, made through all the different scenes of the dreary pilgrimage which she had taken, alone and friendless, was productive at once of the pleasantest results.

Dr. Bailey, who accompanied them a considerable distance, was most especially delighted, and to the great neglect of all his patients, some portion of whom, as he facetiously remarked afterwards in a letter to Theodore, got well in spite of him while he was away. He accompanied them a considerable distance on their tour.

Indeed, such was the affection which the old man entertained for Margaret and the child, that it was a great inducement to him to break up his esta-

blishment out of town eventually, and come and live in the metropolis.

The fact of his having recovered Margaret and the child from apparent death, after they had been taken from the river Lea, appeared to have given him a sort of vested interest in their continued existence.

Had he been Margaret's own father, he could not have taken a greater interest in her welfare; and, on one occasion, when a guest at their house, from seeing the affectionate terms upon which the old man was with them, made the mistake of actually supposing such was the case, he declared that he considered it was the greatest compliment that could be paid him.

There were other parties, however, in the tour which both Theodore and Margaret were most anxious to see, and most particularly the case was that with regard to the magistrate who had behaved so kindly to Margaret in her distresses.

We need not say how delighted was that gentleman at the change in her fortunes.

As they were returning, they crossed the heath where Margaret had met with the fearful adventure in the old gravel-pit; and as their equipage consisted of an extremely handsome travelling-carriage, it created no little sensation among the rustics of the neighbourhood.

Theodore ordered the postilion to stop while they surveyed the scene, and Margaret pointed out to him exactly where she had hidden during the thunderstorm, previous to the attack which had been made upon her by the two ruffians, who, for the possession of the mere change from a half-sovereign, which it will be recollected she received at the lonely public-house, would have taken her life.

"That circumstance," said Theodore, "although not the greatest misery, I look upon as the greatest peril you endured."

"No, Theodore," she said; "I think I was in more danger than that when you rescued me from Bertram, at a time when I am certain insanity had taken possession of him, and he would have murdered me."

"He might have done so; and yet, I cannot but think he must at the last moment have shrunk from the perpetration of so dreadful a deed."

"I would fain hope so; but let us leave this spot, for now that the first feeling of curiosity connected with visiting it has passed away, it awakens in my mind some of the most painful sensations."

"Hark," said Theodore, "do you hear that horn? There is a hunt somewhere in the neighbourhood; I see there is a field of horsemen and dogs."

"They come this way."

"They do. I detest hunting myself, and yet I can easily fancy what an exhilarating amusement it must be to many."

The huntsmen rapidly approached across the heath, and, from the wandering manner in which the dogs ran too and fro, they all seemed to be at fault.

Margaret suddenly laid her hand upon Theodore's arm, as she whispered—

"Theodore, Theodore, in the recital of my adventures, I told you how in a meadow once I paused to rest with my child, and that just such a field of huntsmen as we now see before us came sweeping onward. From one I got unmeasured abuse and obloquy, because I was supposed to be in the way of the sport; from another, I got kind words and sympathy."

"Yes, Margaret, I recollect; but why do you look so earnestly on that advancing sportsman?"

"Because that is the man who considered that worse language than he need use to his dogs would suffice for a fellow-creature who was poor and destitute enough to sit down for shelter by the way-side."

Indignation flashed from Theodore's eyes.

"He shall soon perceive,' he cried, "that there is in this world a retributive justice."

"He shall, Theodore, but not in the way I know you are thinking of. You have promised that you will be guided by me in these matters, and, therefore, I speak to you freely, pointing out to you that sportsman as the man who so addressed me."

"He approaches the carriage. Can it be possible he knows you again?"

"There is no likelihood in that."

The scarlet-coated man, who no doubt considered that in hunting a hare to death—one of the most harmless and timid creatures Heaven ever created—he was doing something specially great, merely cantered his horse up to the carriage, and lifting his hat as he came sufficiently near to it to speak, he said, in an affected, drawling tone—

"I beg sincerely to apologise if you have been in the slightest degree alarmed by the dogs. The fact is, madam, we had a hare, but we have lost her; but if you have been alarmed that will be a source of much deeper regret."

"Sir," said Margaret, "if but a small portion of this courtesy had been exercised towards me when we last met, I should have seen you now again with more pleasure."

"When last we met, madam? Had I the honour of seeing you at the Countess of Rattledale's entertainment last week?"

"No, sir; the last time we met, I was a poor beggar woman, and this child whom you now see in costly apparel, and surrounded with every luxury, was in my arms attired in rags. Your crawling adulation on this occasion is nearly as disgusting as your heartless insolence on that."

"And," said Theodore, "if I had not promised this lady to allow you to escape, I would take that riding-whip from you, and lay it across your shoulders."

"Oh, mad people—mad people," said the fellow; "I see, being taken to some lunatic asylum. Good day— good day."

He rode away quickly; but his face pale with passion, sufficiently betrayed the effect which Margaret's words had upon him.

This was the only disagreeable incident which they encountered, and they reached town without meeting with a cross accident.

There was one person, however, whom both Theodore and Margaret were anxious to discover, and that was the young girl who, at the public house near the heath, had warned Margaret of her danger, and prevented her from staying there for the night.

There was great difficulty in finding her, and from the fact of her not having sought for him, as he, Theodore, had requested her to do, he and Margaret feared some unfortunate accident must have befallen her. But money will produce wonders, and by judicious inquiry, aided by unlimited means, she was at last discovered, and Margaret had the happiness of completely rescuing her from the dreadful life she had been leading, and making her a useful as well as a happy member of society.

After residing for some time in London, Theodore and Margaret, whose tastes and pursuits by no means accorded with the dissipations of the metropolis, looked out for some country abode, which, while it should not be so far off as to prevent them from enjoying some of the more refined pleasures which a large city affords, was yet sufficiently distant to enable them to enjoy the delights of the country.

After some trouble, they found a place suited to their minds. It was a small freehold estate, pleasantly situated, and possessing abundance of old majestic trees, such as can only be found on estates that have been in cultivation for many years.

The mansion was one of those ancient Elizabethan structures which have so picturesque an appearance when embosomed in such a mass of beautiful foliage as that which surrounded this house.

There was a sweet stream of water, too, meandering through the grounds, and along the banks of which, on many a calm summer evening, when the slant rays of the setting sun shed a lustre on every object, Theodore and Margaret would take a pleasant walk.

Sometimes they would converse of the past, contrasting it with the present; at others, they would lose themselves in pleasant anticipations of the future.

And as, in the course of time, their children frolicked on before them, making the pleasant shades beneath the old trees ring again with happy laughter, Margaret would turn her eyes, beaming with serenity and pleasure, from them to Theodore, with a look of happiness which words would be too weak to express—a happiness which reflected in his eyes, and which induced them both to think that the troubles and afflictions they had known, after all, made up by contrast much of their felicity.

THE END.